THE END TIMES
FALL OF EMPIRES

WARHAMMER®
CHRONICLES

WARHAMMER®
CHRONICLES

Other great stories from Warhammer Age of Sigmar

WARHAMMER®
CHRONICLES

THE END TIMES
FALL OF EMPIRES

PHIL KELLY • JOSH REYNOLDS • CHRIS WRAIGHT
GRAHAM McNEILL • DAVID GUYMER

BLACK LIBRARY

A BLACK LIBRARY PUBLICATION

Sigmar's Blood first published in 2013.
The Return of Nagash and *The Fall of Altdorf* first published in 2014.
'The Bone Cage' first published digitally in 2014.
'With Ice and Sword' and 'Marienburg's Stand' first published digitally in 2015.
This edition published in Great Britain in 2023 by
Black Library, Games Workshop Ltd., Willow Road,
Nottingham, NG7 2WS, UK.

Represented by: Games Workshop Limited – Irish branch,
Unit 3, Lower Liffey Street, Dublin 1,
D01 K199, Ireland.

10 9 8 7 6 5 4 3 2 1

Produced by Games Workshop in Nottingham.
Cover illustration by Paul Dainton.
Maps by John Michelbach.

A CIP record for this book is available from the British Library.

ISBN 13: 978-1-80407-538-8

See Black Library on the internet at

blacklibrary.com

Find out more about Games Workshop
and the worlds of Warhammer at

games-workshop.com

Printed and bound in the UK.

The world is dying, but it has been so since
the coming of the Chaos Gods.

For years beyond reckoning, the Ruinous Powers
have coveted the mortal realm. They have made many
attempts to seize it, their anointed champions leading
vast hordes into the lands of men, elves and dwarfs.
Each time, they have been defeated.

Until now.

In the north, Archaon, a former templar of the
warrior-god Sigmar, has been crowned the Everchosen
of Chaos.

He stands poised to march south and bring ruin
to the lands he once fought to protect. Behind him
amass all the forces of the Dark Gods, mortal and
daemonic, and they will bring with them a storm such
as has never been seen. Already, the lands of men are
falling into ruin. Archaon's vanguard run riot across
Kislev, the once-proud country of Bretonnia has
fallen into anarchy and the southern lands have been
consumed by a tide of verminous ratmen.

The men of the Empire, the elves of Ulthuan and the
dwarfs of the Worlds Edge Mountains fortify their
cities and prepare for the inevitable onslaught. They
will fight bravely and to the last. But in their hearts, all
know that their efforts will be futile. The victory of
Chaos is inevitable.

These are the End Times.

CONTENTS

SIGMAR'S BLOOD

Phil Kelly

Tower of Melkhior

Heath Cairn

Crippletown

Former site of
Mordheim

Sage's
Ruin

Vale of Dead
Trees

Fool's
Rest

Hunger Wood

Cairn Circle

Sylvania

Helsee

Grim
Moor

Castle
Templehof

The Ruins of
Vanhaldenschlosse

Uflheim

Red Cairn

Falls of Despair

Vale of
Darkness

Fort Oberstyre

Templehof

Grim Wood

Konigstein
Tower

Deihstein

The Broken Spine

Vargravia

Unterwold

Castle Sternieste

Vale of
Vain Hope

Arfeit

Naubonum

Lichehure

Vosca

Mons Hault

Swartzhafen

Drakenhof

Nulheim

Spider Haunts

Araknos

Castle Drakenhof

Haunted Hills

Crowtop

The Wailing Way

The
Unclean
Wood

Ghoul Wood

N

Aver Reach

Derelict
Temple

Vassel

Vladis

Kleiberstorf

Corpse Run

Forsaken Forest

Oakenhammer

Averland

CHAPTER ONE

TEMPLEHOF CRAG

Sigmarzeit, 2522

Today, the sun had not risen at all.

Standing high up on the crag, a bald figure robed in yellow stared hard at the horizon. His focus was such that it looked as if he was trying to bring the sunlight through willpower alone. The robed man had been there for hours, yet all that the day had to show for itself was a gradual thinning of the darkness. An insult to the dawn, the figure thought. An insult to the name Sunscryer, come to that.

It had started less than a week ago, the great darkness that had been drawn like a shroud across the province of Sylvania. No one truly knew why, not even Sunscryer himself. Most of the theories had to do with supernatural creatures. More specifically, most of them had to do with vampires.

Already vegetation was beginning to wither and die. The animals would be next, starving for lack of sustenance. Before too long, the men and the women would follow them. And the children.

Something had to be done.

CHAPTER TWO

THE CONCLAVE OF STATE

Imperial Palace of Altdorf, 2522

With a tremendous crash, a rain-sodden corpse burst through the stained glass dome of the Grand Atrium. It slammed onto the banqueting table, bouncing a foot into the air and shocking the assembled elector counts seated around it before landing sprawled across the enormous map in their midst.

The dignitaries barely had time to shout in alarm before daggers of leaded glass sliced down. Though the Emperor himself was unhurt, Wolfram Hertwig had looked upwards reflexively at the crash and lost an eye to a splinter depicting Sigmar's Triumphs. Helmut Feuerbach's yellow Talabecland silk turned red as coloured shards sank into his flesh. Boris Todbringer earned yet another facial scar. Gausser of Nordland stared in shock at the wedge of stained glass pinning his hand to the polished mahogany of the table, and a shattered image of the Empire's warrior god stared back. At the glassy icon's feet was a depiction of Nagash Defeated. The Great Necromancer's orb-like eyes glinted in the misty rain that drifted from the broken dome above.

The aides and servants ranged around the electors fared even worse. Elder Kattarin's hunched back had been sliced to the spine by a pane the size of a stable door. Rudiger had been neatly decapitated in the act of picking up claimant-scrolls that Count Ludenhof had scattered in a fit of pique a few moments before. Shouts, cries, and challenges filled the octagonal hall, its famous acoustics magnifying the din into sheer bedlam.

'Order!' bellowed Grand Theogonist Volkmar. 'Order, for Sigmar's sake!' He gestured sharply for his arch lectors to tend the wounded. 'Stop squawking and just *listen*!'

The old warrior priest's frustration had been simmering for a while. Five hours of watching the electors bicker over geopolitical boundaries had been close to torture for him, and now his ire had boiled over. Whether at sermon or in battle, Volkmar could out-bellow a minotaur, yet even he was struggling to make himself heard.

Emperor Karl Franz picked up the massive Book of State from the mahogany table and slammed it back down with a cannonshot boom. The confusion of voices instantly ceased. All eyes went to the head of the table. The only sounds were the whimpers of the wounded and the slither of blades sliding from their scabbards.

'Less panic, more thought, please,' said Karl Franz, coolly. 'This corpse – intended as a message, no doubt. But from whom?'

The Grand Theogonist leaned over the body in their midst. Rainwater drizzled down gently upon it, pattering from the warrior priest's shaven head as he stooped to investigate. Volkmar had given a shout of alarm as soon as he had seen a winged shadow disturb the moonlight illuminating the vellum map, but his warning had come too late. Now the highborn blood of several elector counts had been spilt, and several servants had met a sudden and messy end. Yet despite the body's impact, the rainwater pooling around the cadaver was completely clear.

Reaching over, Volkmar moved the corpse's arm from its pallid face. He shook his head slowly. This man had clearly died in a great deal of pain. A roll of thin leather had been jammed deep into his gullet, forcing his mouth open in a permanent scream. Volkmar yanked the scroll out and tucked it behind his arm in one smooth motion, turning to face Karl Franz with a curt bow.

'As you say, my lord, a macabre message,' said Volkmar, his voice cold. 'Your eminence will remember my petition to follow up the disappearance of one Gunther Stahlberg, a witch hunter I despatched to investigate the rumours about Drakenhof Castle two years ago?' The Grand Theogonist closed the corpse's staring eyes and made the sign of the comet upon his chest. 'By the looks of it, his body has been drained of blood for a long time.'

'Careful, dolt!' interrupted Count Gausser, spitting in indignation at the nervous aide attending to his injured hand. 'Drained of blood, eh?' he said, turning to Volkmar with a face as sour as lime. 'You can tell that without cutting him open, can you? I see no wounds. No doubt you think that *vampires* are to blame?'

'A single vampire, to be precise,' replied Volkmar. 'Mannfred von Carstein.'

Several of the more flamboyant electors scoffed in disbelief. It was widely known that Mannfred, the last of Vlad von Carstein's evil brood, had been slain at Hel Fenn over four hundred years before. The Sylvanian aristocrat had been cut down by an alliance of dwarfs and men, finally bringing about the end of the Vampire Wars.

To their credit, most of the electors from the east of the Empire remained silent. Graf Haupt-Anderssen of Stirland made the sign of Morr, his features solemn. 'As I have said many times now, my Emperor, darkness is rising in Sylvania.'

'And further afield, it would seem,' replied Karl Franz. He motioned Volkmar to continue.

'The rainwater around his body shows not even a trace of discoloura-tion, my Emperor. In my experience only a vampire can drain a body of blood so completely,' said Volkmar. 'He was... delivered to us by a winged creature, one strong enough to bear a corpse and yet stealthy enough to evade discovery. The hellbats of Sylvania have long been under the curse of undeath. Those creatures are large enough to bear a horse, and even the living ones have a hunting strategy based upon surprise. Lastly, the corpse is sprawled across the part of the map that depicts Sylvania. I doubt that is coincidence.'

'Really?' sneered Gausser. 'And are these monsters of yours also known for their impeccable aim? I see you've deftly leapt to the conclusion that this poor fellow's arrival is not your own mistake coming back to haunt you, nor is it an unfortunate side effect of our beloved Emperor's menagerie, but instead a message from a minstrel's villain who even now flees Altdorf on the back of a giant bat.'

'Yes,' said Volkmar, holding up a tightly rolled tube of leather. 'And I've come to that conclusion because it is Mannfred von Carstein's seal upon the scroll I just removed from the corpse's throat.'

Emperor Karl Franz ordered the scroll broken open and read immediately. Though the missive was still slick with rainwater, its thin leather held the words in crisp detail. Volkmar's scalp had prickled with an odd sensation when he realised that the scroll was made from human skin. The words had been not so much inscribed as tattooed. As the Grand Theogonist scanned the elegant, but archaic, calligraphy, he felt his blood rise. The message had a formal tone, but it was a challenge through and through.

'Fellow counts,' read the Grand Theogonist, his teeth gritted in disgust at having to give voice to the words of the undead.

'I hereby make eternal claim to that which is mine. Sylvania thus secedes from thy petty Empire, as do all who dwell within her borders. Mortal or grave-bound, they are mine by feudal law, and let none dispute it. Look to the east and thou shalt find I have drawn a shroud of night across my rightful realm. In this way I demark it from thine own lands, where sun-light and hope are still welcome guests.

'If this fact displeases thee, think long upon this. As the last great count of Stirland, my claim to the throne of the Empire is as true as thine own. My lineage runs deep and red, undiluted by the blood of fools and whores. Only one amongst thee can claim the same. Yet despite his great and noble ancestry, thy priest is old and spent.'

Volkmar swallowed a hard knot of rage. He looked long at Karl Franz, eyes locked in silent communiqué, before reading the rest of the letter.

'Perhaps I will attend thy yearly feast of words someday, and feast upon thee in turn. Worthless and brief as you are, it would be a mercy. I predict little nourishment, and little challenge. For how can the great leaders of the

Empire protect its borders, when they are barely aware of what is taking place under their noses?

Yours eternal,

Count Mannfred von Carstein,

The True and Lawful Lord of Sylvania'

Volkmar let the letter fall away onto the banqueting table, his heart pounding at its implications. Under their noses – an odd turn of phrase. Perhaps that meant...

'The vaults!' shouted Volkmar, instinctively reaching for the blessed warhammer hanging at his waist. 'We have to get down there, right now!'

Karl Franz's eyes widened. 'By Sigmar, you don't think that...' He looked to his right for a moment, and swore under his breath. 'Zintler, take as many Reiksguard as you can find and accompany Arch Lector Kaslain down to the Temple Vaults with all haste. If you find Schwartzhelm on the way, send him up here at once. Go!'

The moustachioed Reikscaptain saluted smartly and strode out of the octagonal hall alongside Arch Lector Kaslain, their armour chinking as they broke into a run. At Zintler's command, the Reiksguard detachment that had stood vigil outside the Grand Atrium since the last change of guard broke position and joined them. Soon the wide, vaulted corridors resounded to the clangour of metal, the sound diminishing as they pounded down the hall.

Back in the Grand Atrium, Volkmar read over the vampire's missive once more before slamming his fists onto the banqueting table so hard the corpse at its centre jumped a full inch into the air.

Reikscaptain Zintler strode down the wide flagstone stairs that led from the Imperial Palace to the undervaults of the Great Temple, a dozen-strong detachment of Reiksguard behind him. Flanked by the authoritarian figures of Arch Lectors Kaslain and Aglim, the officer met only the most perfunctory of challenges from the warrior priests guarding the entrance to the sacred vaults below.

'Any trouble down there, may I ask, gentlemen?' inquired Zintler.

'None that I know of, sir,' said the eldest warrior priest, making the sign of the comet. 'Sigmar Exalt.'

'Sigmar Exalt.'

Behind Zintler's back, Arch Lector Kaslain exchanged a baleful look with his opposite number, Aglim, but they kept their peace.

As the detachment entered the first circle of crypts, the torches that lined the underground passageways illuminated monolithic stone gargoyles carved in the likeness of beasts. Each was a depiction of a legendary creature Sigmar had slain over his lifetime. The cobwebbed statues did little to lighten the mood.

Scanning the dusty reaches of each vault as they passed through, the Reiksguard made the symbols of Sigmar and Morr against their chests.

'Keep together, please,' said Zintler, smoothing his waxed facial hair. 'Maintain two paces, nothing more. I want eyes on every corner.'

His men murmured their acknowledgements, none wishing to disturb the silence any more than necessary. Down here were the bones of every Grand Theogonist to have taken office, their souls united in an eternal vigil over the Cache Malefact at the heart of the vaults. Faint ghostlights flickered on the edge of vision above each sarcophagus. Technically it was blasphemy even to speak in the presence of these strange guardian spirits.

The grandiose tombs of Volkmar's predecessors fanned out in maze-like circles that the investigators passed through on their way towards the cache. There the Sigmarite cult kept every magical relic it had recovered over two thousand years of war against the dark powers.

The Reiksguard probed further into the murk, and the air became charged with indefinable energies. Soon it was difficult to draw more than a shallow breath. Arch Lector Kaslain hefted the Reikhammer, his symbol of office and chosen weapon both. The hulking warrior priest cast a grim glance at his fellow arch lector as they passed the obsidian statues guarding the inner circles.

'That smell...' whispered Aglim, his brow furrowed.

Kaslain nodded in assent. The cold, musty tang of limestone hid a definite undertone of decay.

As the investigators passed the threshold, the intermittent light cast by their torches illuminated splintered wood and broken stone scattered across the flagstones. Thrice-locked chests had been smashed to pieces and suspended glass orbs dripped luminous fluids onto the consecrated ground beneath.

Amongst the debris were severed arms, legs and heads that drooled congealing blood. Kaslain nearly tripped over a torso with only one leg still attached, its livery that of the Templar Inner Guard. He curled his lip in distaste, nudging the human remains out of their way with his foot.

'A proper benediction will be held for these men,' he whispered, 'but it can wait.'

Judging by the disembodied limbs scattered around the chamber, the intruders must have been creatures of unnatural strength. Yet there was no sign of the force that had wrought this destruction. Bright shimmers of gold, pearls and even the sickly glimmer of wyrdstone punctuated the debris. Whatever had done this was evidently not interested in wealth.

A funnel-shaped hole gaped in the middle of the floor. As Kaslain looked down into it an oily, rotten odour wafted up to assault his nostrils. Something foul had burrowed up through the limestone at speed, a feat no man could have achieved without suffocating.

'Weapons please, gentlemen,' said Zintler, his civility incongruous in the charged atmosphere of the deep vault. Almost as soon as he had spoken, a low gurgling growl came from the alcove at the back of the cache.

Whatever had done this was still in there with them.

* * *

There was a sudden flash of corpse-flesh as two pallid monstrosities swung down from their hiding places in the vaulted ceiling. Though they stooped low, when standing straight each one would have dwarfed a dockyard ogre. From their backs jutted great crests of overgrown vertebrae. Their hairless heads were those of degenerate old men forced into a life of cannibalism. Hanging from the talons of the rearmost beast was an ornate crown that looked too large even for its own massive skull.

The ghostlights of the sanctum's Sigmarite guardians swam around the creatures, attempting to banish them back to the hells from whence they came. The creatures swatted at them absently. Suddenly the vile apparitions gave a deafening screech and loped towards the Reiksguard, accelerating with simian speed. Even Kaslain took a step backwards at the sight.

The first of the monsters barrelled into the Reiksguard with such force it smashed eight of them to the ground, impaling itself upon half a dozen swords and losing one of its hands in the process. It thrashed and flailed, snapping its stinking jaws. Aglim was pressed up against a pillar by the ghoulish thing's flank. A mass of white flesh sweated unclean fluids onto his formerly spotless tabard.

The beast reared up, its gangly arms raised. To Kaslain's amazement the red wounds the Reiksguard had opened in its torso were already healing closed. A raw stump had sprouted from its severed wrist, the suggestion of fingers pushing out. It swept its forearms across the Reiksguard ranks like a champion swimmer, bowling over yet more of the knights and forcing Kaslain to take another step back. Something was wrong about this fight. Their attacker was making itself a target for as many warriors as possible. In the cramped confines of the Cache Malefact, it was huge enough to bar their advance completely.

Kaslain touched the head of the heavy Reikhammer on the flagstones behind him for a brief moment before bringing it over his head in a glimmering arc. It smashed into the creature's clammy pate with such force that its head burst clean apart. Foulness sprayed over everyone nearby as the decapitated body toppled backwards, arms splayed wide.

'Grow *that* back, you bastard,' said Kaslain, spitting on its twitching corpse. 'Anyone hurt?'

The fine plate of the Reiksguard knights had been dented and stained, and two of their number lay dead and broken against the pillars around the edge of the cache. The rest of the escort was more or less intact. They mumbled and picked themselves up as Kaslain and Aglim searched around the chamber and looked up in the ribbed vaults, weapons raised.

Of the second of the two monstrosities, there was no sign.

'Shit,' said Kaslain, grimly. 'That's not good.'

'Excuse me, sir?' said Zintler. 'We drove the damned things off, didn't we?'

'That second one,' replied Kaslain, peering down into the darkness of the narrowing hole in the middle of the vault. 'It had the crown.'

'But the Emperor has the crown. We just saw him at state.'

'Not the Imperial tiara, you bloody moustache on legs!' said Kaslain, his voice trembling. 'The bloody Crown of Sorcery! The Crown of Nagash.'

As the forbidden name echoed around the silence of the crypts, the torches of the Reiksguard flickered green for a second and went out.

Zintler's detachment had returned in shocked silence to report to the Emperor, but now the Grand Atrium was getting another chance to show off its acoustics. Volkmar's rage was always impressive, no matter how many times Kaslain saw it. Today, it was incandescent.

The elector counts had the good sense not to interrupt whilst Volkmar filled the air with thunderclouds of invective. He paced up and down in front of the returned delegation, systematically stripping Reikscaptain Zintler of every ounce of his dignity. Even Kaslain, the closest thing Volkmar had to a friend, had already been pinned beneath Volkmar's towering wrath for close to five minutes. It had not been a happy feeling.

The Grand Theogonist had every reason to be furious. Technically speaking, the artefacts in the Cache Malefact were under the sole protection of the Sigmarite cult. The blame for the disappearance of the Crown of Sorcery would be laid squarely at Volkmar's door, and everyone knew it. Since his return from the wars in the north, the old man had more than enough detractors ready to tear him down. The loss of such a potent relic would be the last nail in his political coffin. If it was not recovered within a matter of days, it could see him banished from office forever.

The stolen artefact had been found ten years ago after the breaking of Waaagh! Azhag, a greenskin invasion of such scale and ambition it had collapsed a swathe of the northern Empire. Altdorfer spies had claimed that whenever Azhag the Slaughterer had worn the crown he had talked to himself almost constantly, often replying to himself in sepulchral tones. The hulking orc had begun to show displays of uncanny military genius as well as the ability to wield the energies of death itself. At the Battle of Osterwald, however, he had fallen to the charge of the knightly orders nonetheless.

Since that day the relic had rested in the depths of the great temple, theoretically as safe as sacred Ghal Maraz itself. In practice, the vault's wards and guardians had been unable to banish the fleshy horrors that had burrowed into it like worms in the darkness. The chances of the Sigmarite cult recapturing the crown from one as cunning as Mannfred were vanishingly small.

'It's obvious what happened, you fool!' roared Volkmar, his red-veined face a finger's breadth from Zintler's nose. 'The vampire wanted his master's crown, so he ensured he had our attention long enough to snatch it. Stahlberg here,' he said, motioning towards the fallen body as it was carried away by liveried servants, 'was a decoy. The true attack was taking place beneath our feet! And we fell for it! *You* fell for it!'

Zintler apologised for the twentieth time, eyes down, but Volkmar was in full flow. Only the interruption of the Emperor spared the Reikscaptain from death by spittle.

'Volkmar!' shouted Karl Franz, exasperated to the point of intervention. 'We need more than strong words to fix this.'

The Grand Theogonist turned to face the Emperor, shoulders slumping in despair. Behind him, Zintler surreptitiously dabbed his face with a handkerchief.

'I cannot allow rebellion in my Empire to go unpunished,' said the Emperor. 'Let alone an uprising led by a vampiric dynasty we presumed long gone.'

'No, my lord,' replied Volkmar.

'We have been hearing for weeks that the situation in Sylvania is dire,' continued Karl Franz. 'And today, it has been made painfully clear that these claims of a magical darkness haunting the province are based in fact. This bizarre act of secession needs putting down, immediately and finally.'

'Yes, your eminence,' replied Volkmar with a bow. 'You speak wisely.'

'Dissent amongst allies is not the solution. And neither is mustering the Altdorf army, before you suggest it,' said Karl Franz, casting a warning glance towards the assembled elector counts. 'We have our hands full in the north. Besides, we want to ensure the extinction of that slippery bastard's line once and for all. We cannot afford to announce our intentions until we have him trapped. A grand show of force will merely drive him back into hiding.'

Karl Franz turned his attention to the gathered electors, meeting their gazes one by one.

'Our foe in Sylvania is functionally immortal. He has all the time in the world to play hide and seek. We, however, do not. So, I put the question to you all. What do you intend to do about it?'

'I will attend to this crisis personally, my Emperor,' said Volkmar. 'I... I will lead my own army of the faithful into Sylvania.'

The old man seemed to straighten as he spoke the words, his rounded shoulders setting firm.

'I will lead a crusade of light against the darkness,' he continued. 'A crusade of the righteous and the vengeful, united in faith. I swear to you now, with the great and the good to bear witness. I will hunt down and destroy the fiend Mannfred von Carstein and reclaim the Crown of Sorcery from his ashes, or I will die in the attempt.'

Meaningful glances passed between several of the elector counts, but no one spoke a word.

'Fine words, old friend,' said Karl Franz softly. 'Though, I am not sure that they are wise ones.'

'I *must* go, my lord,' replied Volkmar. 'I have no choice. I am Sigmar's appointed representative in the Old World, and therefore I must act in his name, regardless of the danger.'

'Very well,' said the Emperor, his tone resigned. 'You have a better chance than most. Faith is a powerful weapon against the powers of darkness. Though, you will need help. Help that my armies cannot give.' Karl Franz paused for a second and scribbled something down on a nearby parchment before passing it to a uniformed aide.

'Go, then, and prepare the muster of the faithful,' said the Emperor, laying down his quill. 'Take Kaslain with you. Arch Lector Aglim can tend the flock in your absence.'

'Thank you, your eminence,' said Volkmar softly, meeting Karl Franz's level gaze for the briefest moment. The look that passed between the two dignitaries was as close to a fond goodbye as circumstances would permit.

'Don't be so quick to thank me. I only hope you make it back alive. The darkness gathers thick these days.'

Volkmar bowed his head for a moment before starting towards the door.

'May I ask how you intend to find your quarry?' said Karl Franz.

'Ah,' said Volkmar. 'Well… there is… There is one of my witch hunters still active in Sylvania, my Emperor. A man who knows that benighted realm like his own reflection. You will not like it, but he truly is our best chance at finding the vampire.'

The Emperor sighed. 'Let me guess. Alberich von Korden?'

'Indeed, my lord,' said Volkmar, taking a deep breath. 'Alberich von Korden.'

CHAPTER THREE

THE CROW AND HAMMER

Konigstein, 2522

The witch hunter reloaded his silver-chased pistols at the top of the stairs of Konig's Coaching Inn, pouring in gunpowder before priming the flints. He calmly slotted his powder horn back into his bandolier, taking his longboot from the neck of the troglodytic ghoul that had sought him out. The inhuman beast had stopped twitching a while back, but it was always better to be cautious when it came to the living dead and their kin.

One down, three to go.

Cutting through the ghoul's neck with a sharp blow from his sabre, the hunter kicked its body down the stairs and hung its disembodied head on a butcher's hook at his waist. He laughed softly to himself, fingering the still-smoking hole in the beast's forehead. A brace of ghouls' heads was always useful for keeping the roadwardens quiet.

He had the upper floor of the inn to himself, by the look of it. The sound of flintlock shots and the blood splashed up the walls would keep the inn's patrons cowering in their beds, at least until the rest of the pack showed up.

Sure enough, another ghoul skittered around the corner of the upper corridor. The foul thing cried out in a strange gurgling yelp that the hunter recognised as a pack-call. He glanced backwards and shot the creature silently creeping up behind him without so much as a blink of surprise. His consecrated bullet passed into the thing's open mouth and blasted out of its back in an explosion of brown blood.

The witch hunter turned back to confront the ghoul loping down the corridor just as it sprang for his throat. He shot it in the chest mid-leap. Deftly stepping to one side, he let its flailing body smash into the ghoul bleeding out behind him. A sweeping heel kick sent them both tumbling down to join their headless friend at the bottom of the stairs.

Three down, one left.

The last ghoul was always the largest of the pack, a mark of cowardice in a species too devolved to care. He could hear it scrabbling around on the

layered straw of the roof above him. He ducked to avoid a taloned arm that
shot through the thatch and swiped at his face. 'Stupid cannibal bastards,'
the hunter said. 'Never get your timing right.'

Dropping the spent pistols, the hunter grabbed the flailing arm and
pulled hard. A muscular ghoul tumbled down into the corridor, dust and
straw filling the air. It leapt to its feet with surprising agility for a creature
that looked like it belonged at the bottom of a swamp. No time to regain
the pistols and reload. No time to use the white ring, either, come to that.

The foul thing leapt forward, talons swiping out. It was fast, hellishly so.
One of its dirt-encrusted claws went for the witch hunter's eyes, knocking
off his feathered hat and opening his lip instead. The hunter growled as
he tasted his own blood.

Pink spit-flecks formed at the corners of the hunter's mouth as he jabbed
a witch-pin into the side of the beast's neck. A kick to the chest shoved it
backwards, buying a second of precious time. The ghoul recovered quickly,
pouncing forward once more, but the hunter had recovered too. The beast
leapt straight into a brawler's forearm jab. The hardwood stake strapped to
the hunter's wrist punctured its breastbone with a sharp crack. The witch
hunter pushed the beast backwards all the way to the end of the corridor,
impaling it against the crude wooden panels of the inn's rearmost wall. The
ghoul writhed there like an insect pinned to a cork board.

The hunter nailed the squealing creature's arms to the wooden planks
with a carpenter's precision, driving his witch-pins home with a small rep-
lica of Sigmar's own warhammer. He drew his butcher's knife and sliced
the beast's hamstrings before unhurriedly reloading his pistols in case
any more of the foul things turned up. Once the flintlocks were primed
and checked, the hunter put his jutting chin within biting distance of his
captive's needle-toothed maw. It was in too much pain to notice, its beady
red eyes swimming with tears.

'Yes, you feel that, don't you?' said the hunter, grinning. 'Vampire, ghoul
or common man, a length of wood stuck into the heart always hurts like
hell. I left it nice and splintery, just for you and yours.'

The witch hunter stowed his butcher's knife and drew out a pair of sharp
filleting blades, running the edges along each other with a slight musical
chime. His cold smile widened, blood staining his teeth.

'Boss?' came a timid voice from behind him.

'*What?*' shouted the hunter as he wheeled around. His face would have
scared a daemon.

'Message for you, boss,' said the hunter's lieutenant, Unholdt. The
mercenary was cowering like a beaten dog, despite the fact he practically filled the corridor. 'From the lads up at the watch. They says it's from
the Old Man himself.'

Turning back to the wall for a second, the witch hunter sucked in his
breath before putting one of his pistols under the beast's chin and pulling

the trigger, blowing the top of its head off in a spray of gore. He shoved his way past Unholdt, snatching his hat from the floor as bits of the ghoul's brain pattered down from the ceiling.

'This,' hissed Alberich von Korden, 'had better be big.'

CHAPTER FOUR

KONIGSTEIN WATCH

The Vale of Darkness, 2522

The witch hunter strode through Konigstein's rural outskirts, Unholdt trailing in his wake. Together they made their way through the gloom towards the ramshackle watchtower they had taken as a base. Jutting from the foothills at the base of the town's peak, the tower was a forbidding sight. Jawless skulls kept a vigil from each of its eight walls, and the giant metal skeleton that crested its battlements stared down impassively at their approach.

Brass sentinels, the effigies were called. Cleverly designed by the Colleges of Magic as a way to impart information over large distances, each construct's arms could be positioned like the hands of a clock with the turning of a few cranks. When used correctly, specific signals and even individual words could be passed from hilltop to hilltop. Even a message from as far afield as the Imperial Palace could be relayed across the Empire in less than a day.

Von Korden's fellow hunter Stahlberg had told him that the alloys used in each brass sentinel's construction were brewed by the alchemist-mages of the Gold College. Those observers with the second sight could perceive signals sent days or even weeks before – the traces made by the skeletal hands lingered in the air for those with the wit to read them. *Sounds like witch's work*, von Korden had said at the time. *Give me quill and parchment any day.* Stahlberg had laughed and cocked his head knowingly in response, an odd habit of his that always made von Korden's trigger finger itch.

'Why do they have to look like skellingtons?' moaned Unholdt, picking up on von Korden's thoughts about the brass sentinel. The big man could be unusually perceptive, sometimes suspiciously so. He cast a baleful glance around the scattered tombs and ivy-covered walls that dotted the lands around the watchtower. 'Don't make sense to make the place look even more nasty, if you ask me,' Unholdt continued. 'Enough skulls and bones in the vale already, eh boss?'

'I didn't ask you, you fat oaf,' said von Korden irritably. The brass effigy's form made perfect sense to the witch hunter, but then he was something of an expert in inspiring fear.

'Huh. That's sturdy and handsome oaf, to you,' Unholdt muttered under his breath.

As the two hunters approached the watch, a figure looked over the battlements for a second. Its helmeted silhouette was barely visible against the darkness of the Sylvanian sky. Despite their walk from the inn taking them just past noon, the afternoon sky already looked more like dusk.

Since the great darkness had fallen three weeks ago the colour had slowly been leached out of the province. Even the tough, wiry bloodweed that usually thrived in the vale was slowly dying through lack of sunlight, and most of the peasants had sought refuge in neighbouring provinces. Von Korden scowled. Give it a week and his men would most likely be the only living things left.

'Open it now!' commanded von Korden as he approached the heavy wooden door of the watchtower. A series of clunks and thuds came from the other side in response. The door opened half a foot, exposing the scarred snout of a large and ugly pig. It sniffed the air for a moment before its porcine owner licked its lips and grunted the all clear. It looked up expectantly at its witch hunter master with its beady black eyes.

'Hello Gremlynne, you fat old sow,' said von Korden, pushing open the door and tousling the pig's tattered ears. He held out a pair of ghoul's ears on his upraised palm, and they were snaffled up greedily, leaving the witch hunter with a handful of stringy spit. Only a pig could dine on ghoulflesh and get away with it, and the old beast had developed quite a taste for it in her years as a witch-sniffer. Von Korden wiped the pig slobber on Unholdt's greatcoat and absently made the sign of the comet as he crossed the threshold.

'Any attacks, Steig?' said the hunter, looking sidelong at the tall guard waiting beside the door.

'Nah,' said the lanky Stirlander, fiddling with his ruined teeth. 'They might try for a kill when your back's turned, but not even a corpse-eater's stupid enough to attack us here.'

'Don't bet on it, or that line of thought will get you killed,' said von Korden. He cleaned the soles of his boots with the pitted bronze sword the garrison used as a boot-scraper, flicking the mud into a grave-pit outside the door. 'This is Mannfred's lot we're talking about, after all. I found Heinroth Carnavein chewed up in his bed this morning. That makes me the only one of the order left in the province.'

'Bloody bells,' said Steig, shaking his head sadly. 'That's a damn shame, that is.'

Unholdt looked over at his comrade, a puzzled frown on his broad face.

'Bastard owed me for cards,' said Steig by way of explanation.

Unholdt rolled his eyes and moved over to the fire, poking it with the head of his long-handled mace. 'Just tell 'im the bloody news, Sticks,' he said, staring into the flames. Behind him, Gremlynne lay back down on her dirty rug and began to snore gently.

'You can tell me in a moment,' said von Korden. 'I've a feeling I'm not going to like it.' The hunter hung his battered hat on the bat-like skull of the Templehof vargheist, its wide brim covering the bullet hole under the gruesome trophy's eye socket. He sank into an old leather armchair that puffed out all the dust it had accumulated since his last visit, and swung his longboots up onto the lip of the crumbling well at the watchtower's centre. Settled in, he lit a bone-handled pipe and raised his eyebrows at Steig. A fug of blue smoke curled around his greasy grey-blond hair.

'Well?'

'Well, you got a message from the old Volcano himself, boss,' said Steig, scratching his armpit like a flea-bitten dog. 'You're needed back in Altdorf, quick and double-sharp. Freidricksen reckons them clueless ponces at the conclave decided the sun going out was important after all.'

'Ha! So they want me back at court, do they? Short memories.'

'Looks that way,' said Steig. 'All's forgiven when the lights go out, as my pa used to say.'

'Hmph. Reikland idiots. They're all as corrupt as each other. Right,' said von Korden, tapping out his pipe and rising to take his hat from the vargheist skull on the wall, 'I'm off to the Stir, then to try and buy passage back west. Unholdt, try to keep this lot alive until I get back, or at least give them a proper burial when you balls it up.'

By the fire, Unholdt looked at his captain preparing to leave and shook his head in wonder. Less than a minute of rest and von Korden was already heading off on another near-suicidal journey.

'And if you do see our charming friends, the brothers Ghorst,' continued von Korden, 'for Sigmar's sake stay the hell out of their way. No one wants a berth on that godforsaken cart. Steig – is there anything else I should know before I leave?'

'Nah,' replied Steig. 'The high-and-mighties just want information, by the sound of it.'

'Oh, they'll get it,' said von Korden darkly, snatching his parchment case and a pot of ink from the mantle on his way out the door. 'Finally. They'll get it.'

—⟨ CHAPTER FIVE ⟩—

THE OLD WEST ROAD

The Vale of Darkness, 2522

The slow toll of an ancient bell rang out through the mist shrouding the Sylvanian country roads. Its peals were like the plaintive cries of a trapped child who knew no one could hear it.

The foul carriage the bell was mounted upon shivered and slid through the muddy ruts. Though the cart would perhaps pass as a peasant's wagon from a distance, the creatures that pulled it were not mules, and its cargo was unusual even for Sylvania.

Lurching at the carriage's front were two pairs of rotting corpses, the cross-spars of the cart's yoke protruding from their ravaged chests. Gruesome fluids seeped from their punctured lungs and opened hearts as they strained to pull the contraption along. Maggots spilled from their sides with every bump in the uneven road. Their bare feet squished through the mud at a plodding but relentless pace, their broken ankles and missing toes no hindrance.

Behind them, the cart's chassis was fashioned much like a giant upturned ribcage. Heaped amongst the bony spars were dozens of corpses in various states of decay. Those at the bottom were black with putrefaction, their organs dribbling yellowish fluids into the puddles of the road behind. Blind, hungry rats nipped at baggy stomachs and distended guts, scurrying back and forth in their quest for edible meat.

Atop the heaped corpses sat a hunched figure, cross-legged and robed in the manner of a mendicant. He crooned a lilting song over and over, a farrier's loop he had written long ago to enliven the making of horseshoes. He had sung it for his brothers in life. The least he could do was to sing it for them in death, too.

The cart hit a rut in the ground and lurched sideways, causing one of the cadavers piled atop it to slide into the mud in a jumble of floppy limbs. The hooded figure tutted and the cart ground to a halt. The corpses at its fore slumped in their harnesses as if exhausted.

'Come on, lads,' said the robed figure. 'We've been over this.' His reed-thin voice had a forced jollity to it, like an exasperated teacher with a difficult pupil. 'If you hit the ruts at an angle, we usually lose someone, and then we have to stop the cart again.'

His brothers moaned and drooled mindlessly, gnashing their broken jaws and lolling their skinless heads. The figure sighed. They used to be so strong, so reliable. Before the Plague of Blue Roses came, of course. Then everything changed.

If only he had been able to court the plague's kiss too, he would at least have some measure of peace. But for some reason the spores had left his flesh without their signature rosettes, and he had been unable to catch it.

'Not for lack of trying, mind,' the figure whispered to himself.

That was when he had first used the spell. The spell of... life. It was a spell of life, no matter what the voices said.

Blinking to clear away the unwelcome thoughts, the figure called to mind the words his new friend's book had taught him. He was so lucky he had fled into forbidden Vargravia after the incident in the village. Such wonders he had seen since that day.

As the robed figure began to chant, the cadaver that had slid into the mud slowly untangled its limbs as if rearranged by an invisible hand. All of a sudden it jerked upright like a puppet. The bell on the back of the carriage tolled of its own accord as dark powers welled around the cart.

As the fallen cadaver approached the ribs at the cart's side, hands writhed and twitched in the heap, reaching out and helping the corpse back up into their midst.

'I just knew you were going to be trouble, Master Carnavein,' muttered the necromancer, looking disappointedly at the half-eaten corpse as it climbed aboard and collapsed backwards onto the pile. The cadaver's mouth was open in a wordless scream. As the figure looked down, a rat wriggled inside its open jaws. 'That's better,' said the figure. 'Wedge yourself in tight. We're all friends here.'

Helman Ghorst raised his eyes up to the dark skies rumbling above. Night was almost upon them. His friend Count Mannfred would be very upset if they were late.

'Honestly,' he whispered to himself. 'At this rate we'll never get to Konigstein Watch.'

CHAPTER SIX

SYLVANIAN BORDER, THE RIVER STIR

Five days later

The *Luitpold III* chugged through the night at a deceptive pace, smoke billowing into the trees that lined the river. The forests on either side of the Stir were so ancient their canopies entwined above the watercourse, their twisted branches linked together like the fingers of suicidal lovers. Strange howls echoed in the depths, and the occasional flurry of movement caught the eye of the guards ranged along the giant barge's length.

Ten handgunners from the Stir River Patrol had been stationed port and starboard, but nobody seriously expected any trouble. The bestial tribes and forest goblins that haunted the riverbanks were savage, but they were not stupid. The armoured steam barge was a leviathan almost a hundred metres in length, a river-going fortress that boasted nautical-grade cannons and handgun nests along both sides. Unlike its predecessors, the *Luitpold III* was built to last.

Volkmar stood on the barge's upper deck in the morning air, breath frosting in the cold as he straightened out his aching back. Mighty as it was, the armoured barge was no *Heldenhammer*. He felt a pang of loss at the grand old warship's theft earlier that year, taken by stealth mere hours after he had refused to aid the pirate lord Jaego Roth in his quest to slay the vampire Count Noctilus. Now another priceless relic in the care of the Sigmarite cult had been stolen from under him.

Instead of his four-poster bed in the galleon's Grand Templus, the Grand Theogonist had to make do with a cramped cot stained by the sweat of a dozen former occupants. He had left his dubious berth to get some fresh air, sick of the fug below decks and unable to sleep with his imminent disgrace hanging over his thoughts. Killing something that was already dead would make him feel better, no doubt. He was almost looking forward to plunging into lightless depths of Sylvania, far from the accusing eyes of the Altdorf court.

Standing upon the prow of the barge was von Korden, booted foot on the rail and eyes fixed on the river ahead. As far as the Grand Theogonist knew, he had been standing up there all night. He was quite a piece of work, that one, and as driven as any man he had ever met.

Years back, Volkmar had tasked the witch hunter with rooting out Chaos worship from the nation's capital. The covert operation had backfired spectacularly. The witch hunter had been mercilessly effective, stirring up a hornet's nest of corruption that stretched all the way from Marienburg to Kislev. The latter stages of the debacle had seen von Korden burn an entire cult of Chaos-worshipping nobles at the stake. That was all well and good as far as Volkmar was concerned; the realm could use a few less traitors to the crown. The problem was that the witch hunter had also burned dozens of 'accomplices', family members and servants who had committed no crime other than being linked to the guilty parties by blood or even solely by profession.

That had been just the beginning. Before the year was out von Korden had a reputation for executing as many of the innocent as he did the guilty. Pressure was applied from the guilds to have the hunter disposed of, and events had spun even further out of control. Karl Franz himself intervened by having von Korden reassigned to Sylvania, where his pitiless attentions could be directed towards the restless dead instead of the living.

The Emperor's course of action had proved wise. Despite the persecution of his order by the forces that haunted the Vale of Darkness, von Korden had thrived there. He had three vampire kills to his name already, and the fanged skulls to prove it. Earlier that day he had boasted to Volkmar that he fully expected Mannfred to be the fourth.

The forces of undeath were fighting back, though. According to the extensive journals the witch hunter had handed Volkmar in the Grand Temple, von Korden had been the only one of his order left alive in the entire province. The rest had been hunted down and killed in their beds.

Volkmar suppressed a surge of rising temper at the thought. Merciless killers or not, the witch hunters were operatives of the Sigmarite cult, and he could ill afford to lose them. To fight the monsters of the world, one must sometimes become a monster, or a madman at the very least.

His thoughts strayed to the brotherhood that called themselves the Tattersouls, busily whipping themselves bloody below decks as part of their morning prayers. Not madmen as such, just... fanatically zealous. Especially in the presence of a blessed relic like the war altar of Sigmar, or – say – the head of the Sigmarite cult. The Grand Theogonist blew a long, frosting plume of breath out of his cheeks. Perhaps that was another reason why he loved prayer time so much. It was about the only time the bloody maniacs left him alone.

'Your holiness?' came a respectful voice. 'We're approaching it now.' Captain Vance of the *Luitpold III*, a heavily tattooed veteran of the River

Patrol, moved up beside Volkmar and motioned him forward. Volkmar picked up the hem of his robes and stepped over the rope-stops until he got to the front of the barge, deliberately keeping a few paces between himself and von Korden. Whatever the witch hunter had in that pipe stank to high heaven.

The river wound on with majestic slowness, the forest eaves silent to either side. Volkmar was on the verge of asking Captain Vance what he was talking about when they turned a bend in the river and the scale of the curse affecting Sylvania became horribly clear.

A curtain of almost tangible darkness had been drawn across the horizon, or what they could see of it. The wall of grey-black gloom obscured everything on the other side – Volkmar could just about make out the waters of the Stir, but little else. He shook his head slowly. Von Korden had not been exaggerating after all.

'It's worse than it was,' said the witch hunter, dolefully. 'Even since I left, it's got noticeably worse.'

'Shadow magic, you think?' asked Volkmar.

'A corrupted version, perhaps,' replied von Korden. 'This has to be something far stronger, though. It's killing the whole province from the bottom up. First the plants die, then the creatures that eat the plants die, and then, when the food runs out altogether...'

'The people start to eat each other,' finished Volkmar.

'It happens,' said von Korden darkly, his sidelong glance meeting the Grand Theogonist's eye for a moment. 'It happens more often than you'd think.' The witch hunter's face twisted into a mask of rage for a second, startling Volkmar with its intensity.

The hunter took a long draw from his pipe, masking his features with his hand before continuing. 'The von Carsteins,' he said. 'They've always brought the night with them, especially when going to war. Swarms of bats, thunderclouds even. It's something to do with their curse. They can't stand direct sunlight. But this... this is something else.'

The two men stared out into the Sylvanian darkness, each lost in their own thoughts. Behind them, the barge's crewmen were surfacing from below decks, a handful of the Talabheimers that Volkmar had requested as reinforcements from Leitzigerford in their wake. There were muttered comments and a few gasps as more and more men emerged onto the deck.

'My apologies, your honour,' said Captain Vance. 'I've spoken to the lads. We respect what you're doing and all, but we're not much for this cursed murk. We'll take you as far as Helsee, but that's us done. The river widens enough even for the *Luitpold* to come about, down there. The idea is to be heading back before night falls. Well, proper night, if you take my meaning.'

Volkmar looked at von Korden for a second, his eyebrow raised.

'Helsee'll do fine,' said the witch hunter quietly, his eyes still straining into the darkness.

'Understood,' replied Volkmar. 'Captain, you've more than done your duty getting us this far this quickly. See us safe to Helsee and you can return to Altdorf with my blessing. The temple will reimburse you for your time, and for the coal.'

'My thanks, your holiness,' said the captain, sketching a bow and heading back to the steamhouse at the barge's stern.

The curtain of darkness came closer with every passing minute. As the barge neared within a stone's throw, the Grand Theogonist felt a powerful urge to head below decks so the unnatural darkness could not touch his skin. For a moment he even considered cancelling the whole crusade and heading back to the safety of the light. He fought the feelings off with ease, but they disturbed him nonetheless.

'Felt that, did you?' said von Korden, his humourless smile widening as they passed into the shroud of darkness.

'I did indeed. Someone wants to be left alone.'

'That someone,' said von Korden, 'is in for a surprise.'

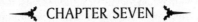

CHAPTER SEVEN

HELSEE

The Vale of Darkness, 2522

Helsee, the vast body of water that fed into the Stir from the heart of Sylvania, was poorly named. It might well have seemed like a sea to the peasants that first discovered it, for it was larger than any other lake in the Empire, but according to Captain Vance it could theoretically be crossed with less than a day's sail. Volkmar gazed out across the thin mist that covered the waters. The peasants had got the first part of the name right, at least. Woe betide the fool who plied it in anything less than a waterborne fortress.

The lake's waters were black with some nameless curse. Grasping little waves clawed at beaches whose sands were little more than powdered bone. Scattered amongst the osseous dunes were the bleached remains of strange and indefinable monsters that prowled Helsee's depths. Their skulls reminded Volkmar of the dragon bones he had gawped at as a boy in the Altdorfer Mausoleum; he had spent the rest of the day slaying invisible dragons with the wooden Ghal Maraz his father had carved him. Precious times, far too long in the past.

On the shores of the lake the crusaders were debarking from the *Luitpold III* with commendable efficiency. With the help of the barge's crew and the strongest of the crusade's warriors, even the war altar's mighty carriage had made it to the shore without getting wet. Atop the barge's foremost turret stood Captain Vance, shouting orders in a voice used to command. He had clearly performed similar operations a hundred times before. The upper parts of the fortified barge's flanks had been splayed and pivoted to become great ramps that looked like they could support a steam tank. Nearby, Volkmar's troops were filing out and forming up without complaint.

Volkmar surveyed the men on the bone-white beach, his pride at the efficiency of their disembarkation marred by the fact there was so damn few of them. Less than a hundred, all told, even with the reinforcements that Karl Franz had arranged to meet them at Leitzigerford. Still, what they lacked in numbers they more than made up for in faith. Volkmar and Karl Franz had made sure of it. Even the Talabheimers had been individually selected for the strength of their religious beliefs. In the war against the evils of the world, true faith was worth a dozen swords. In battle against the horrors of undeath, it was priceless.

By the shore were Sigmar's Sons, a regiment of devout and reliable swordsmen that Volkmar had fought alongside against the Chaos worshippers of the north. They were helping to debark an Imperial great cannon that had begun its military career at the Gorstanford witch trial many years ago. At the foot of the ramp von Korden was briefing the champion of the swordsmen, Eben Swaft, along with Bennec Sootson's artillerymen and the dark-skinned leader of the Knights of the Blazing Sun, Lupio Blaze. The Estalian officer's knights wore polished black plate adorned with suns of solid gold, and the warhorses they led down the barge-ramps wore scalloped barding lacquered with stylised solar flares.

The Estalians worshipped the warrior goddess Myrmidia over Sigmar, but their faith was strong nonetheless. Preceptor Blaze had practically begged Volkmar to let his men join the crusade, and though the Grand Theogonist had initially refused them on grounds of divergent religions, he had eventually come round to the idea. A unit of heavy cavalry could be very useful indeed.

Down on the bone beach the Tattersouls were chanting devotional hymns as they carried the war altar up to the path. Once on firm ground the giant wheeled conveyance could be properly constructed, lashed to its warhorses, and its giant griffon statue restored to pride of place. Vance's bargemen had already got a system of pulleys rigged up, but their calm methodical approach was lost on the wild-haired zealots that insisted on helping them. The ragged figures pushed and pulled with more enthusiasm than skill, warbling and bellowing praise to the Empire's warrior god. Volkmar watched in horror as a pulley slipped the rope, sending the griffon swinging down to crush one of the doomsayers under its colossal weight.

'O Sigmar, I come to thee!' cried the dying flagellant, eyes wet with rapture and pain. 'The end, the end!'

'Don't just stand there like eunuchs at an orgy!' shouted Curser Bredt, marksman-sergeant of the Silver Bullets. 'Give the clumsy bastards a hand!'

Four of Bredt's men kissed the bullet talismans that hung around their necks and rushed forward, bodily wrestling the statue back up into place. It was too late for the unlucky zealot, though; his ribcage and right arm had been crushed into a bloody mass. Somehow he was still smiling gummily, his watery eyes fixed on some faraway paradise. Volkmar shook his head as Kaslain gave the final blessing to the dying man. The war altar was a source of great faith and determination, but by Sigmar, the damn thing was heavy.

The hubbub of the muster was pierced by a shout from one of the Tattersouls. Nothing special in itself, but there was a note of warning in its tone that made Volkmar spin round. Something was moving in the shallows. The Grand Theogonist took a few steps forward, brow furrowed. Sure enough, the skulls and bones on the bed of the lake were moving. Femurs shivered, claws twitched, and vertebrae rolled as if pulled by hidden threads. Piece by piece the skeletons were coalescing, coming together once more into the predatory beasts that once haunted the waters.

'Form up!' boomed Volkmar at the top of his voice as he strode down to the water's edge. 'We're under attack!'

His men rushed towards their banners, some still tightening their bootstraps or hurriedly strapping on armour. The monstrous skeletons in the shallows were piecing themselves together faster and faster, spines clacking into place and arm bones reattaching to shoulder sockets like a dissection in reverse.

A three-eyed skull rose out of the shallows on a thick bony neck. Unclean water poured from crocodilian jaws as the skeletal titan rose up to its full height. Behind it the remains of a monstrous limbed fish lurched onto all fours with a splash, a weird crackling coming from its grinning skull. Behind it, five more misshapen skulls breached the surface. Along the waterline a dozen sets of bubbles began to boil.

The Silver Bullets were the first to act, sending a volley towards the largest of the skeletal creatures. A few of the shots hit home, but most went whistling straight through. Vance's barge was next to fire, a cannon-ball blasting between two of the foremost creatures and taking out a third in a spray of shattered bone.

Volkmar pulled his warhammer from his back and splashed out into the shallows until the water lapped around his knees. Setting his feet in the shale, he bared his teeth and willed the beasts to come closer. Von Korden appeared at his side, silvered pistols drawn. To either side of them armed crusaders splashed into the water, shouting defiance as they formed a wall of blades.

Three of the undead beasts crashed into the Talabheimers at the shore-line, fleshless jaws snapping and tearing. Swords stabbed and slashed in response, but even the most determined attack did little but nick their algae-slicked bones. A three-eyed monstrosity loped towards Volkmar, jaws open as it reared back to strike. Von Korden blasted a pair of holes in its skull with such force and accuracy that it toppled backwards in a jumble of bone. Volkmar scanned the waterline during the second's reprieve the hunter had bought them. The blades of his men were having little effect.

The Grand Theogonist took a deep breath as the fish-headed quadruped splashed towards him. He alone could break the magics at work here, and even then it would take a miracle. Yet he had little choice. Plunging his sacred warhammer into the cursed lake with both hands, he channelled all his hatred and revulsion into a blast of spiritual energy.

'Die in the name of the Heldenhammer!' he boomed, bloodshot eyes bulging. 'Die, I command you!'

Golden light suffused through the waters like the spilt blood of some celestial being. Tendrils of pure energy spread outward from Volkmar's gauntlets, touching the bony legs of the guardian beasts. One by one, the monsters collapsed back into the water, the binding magics that had animated them undone.

Volkmar straightened and thrust his arms into the air with a roar of triumph. Golden droplets sprayed out in all directions from his still-glowing fists.

'Look upon this act, men of Sigmar, and find hope!' he bellowed. 'The evils of this realm, undone by strength of will and by the force of the one true faith!'

Standing in the shallows a few feet away, von Korden pulled a sour face, eyebrows knitted as he protectively dried his pistols with a lambskin cloth.

'If you got any of that water inside these barrels, old man,' he whispered, 'I'll kill you myself.'

◄ CHAPTER EIGHT ►

KONIGSTEIN ROAD

The Vale of Darkness, 2522

Von Korden trudged along the roadways of Sylvania at the head of a small column of troops, the occasional crunch of shattered bone punctuating the squishing of thick black mud. The place had become even more dismal since he had left for Altdorf. Thin rain pattered down from the charcoal skies above, and the howls of the wind had taken on a very unsettling tone.

A rivulet of rainwater dribbled off the broad brim of the witch hunter's hat, spattering his knees. The image of an armchair, a pig and a pipe by the fireplace swam to the surface of the hunter's mind. He crushed it out with practiced ease. Not long now, a few more miles at most. And if he was fortunate enough to meet Ghorst and his brothers on the road, well, he had more men than ever to ensure they were cut down and burned to ash. He would warm his hands over the flames and be done with it.

The crusade's victory over the monsters on the Helsee shores had raised the spirits of the men for a time. With von Korden leading the way, they had made good speed past the nearby cairn circle whilst its guardians were still dormant in their tombs, and avoided the quagmires of Grim Moor in the process. When they had finally reached the palisade walls of Uflheim that evening, the soldiery's victory celebrations had drained every last barrel in the town. Most of the Talabheimers had to be kicked out of their beds the next morning. Von Korden ground his teeth at the recollection. Idiots all. It was premature indulgence at best, and a fatal mistake at worst.

Now the crusade was back to marching through the thick of the Sylvanian gloom. The unnatural darkness had a way of getting to the common man, but the witch hunter found it strangely relaxing. Behind him, nearly thirty state troops marched as best they could along the road, Blaze's warhorses taking shifts to pull the great cannon in their wake. It was slow going, and morale was sinking with every passing hour. Many of the men were already complaining about the grim conditions of the march. Von

Korden snorted in disdain. If a bit of mud and twilight was such a problem, then Sigmar help them when night fell.

Eben Swaft, the sergeant of the Sons, walked up level with the witch hunter. His gaze was fixed on the road ahead.

'So tell me again the reasons we've split our forces up?' the sergeant asked casually, flexing the blade of his rapier with a gloved finger. The witch hunter sized him up with a sidelong look. Swaft was a large man, and his body was tattooed so thoroughly with Sigmar's Triumphs it would impress a Marienburg stevedore. Yet despite his muscular build, even when walking through thick mud the swordsman showed the poise and balance of a born duellist.

'It's as simple as you are, Swaft,' the witch hunter growled. 'Volkmar wanted to investigate Fort Oberstyre, whereas I thought that was a foolish waste of time and manpower. I'm going to Konigstein and that's that. You rabble are coming with me.'

'But... he's the Grand Theogonist. The spiritual descendent of Sigmar himself, and all that.'

'And?'

'And surely what he says goes? Especially for one of you witch-botherers, right?'

Von Korden wheeled around to face Swaft, grabbing the man's rapier by its razored blade and stepping inside its reach so the soldier could smell his breath. Blood dripped from between the fingers of the witch hunter's gloved hand as the sword cut deep. In the mud below, leech-worms writhed.

'Listen to me, you self-satisfied little shit,' hissed von Korden, 'Ober-styre is riddled with ghosts, and not the kind you learned about at your grandmother's teat. The last garrison of state troops that spent the night in its allegedly deserted chambers got ripped to pieces. Since our friend Count Mannfred has a twisted sense of humour, their tortured spirits are now bound into its walls alongside their killers. Perhaps you want to join them, eh?'

The swordsman recoiled a little, but to his credit he stood his ground.

'With respect, sir, I never thought of you as a yellowgut.'

Von Korden swelled visibly, eyes staring death and nostrils flaring. The witch hunter bent the duellist's sword close to breaking point, droplets of blood running fast down the blade. His other hand whipped upward, the point of a filleting knife less than a finger's width from Swaft's eye.

'Konigstein is within the prowling grounds of Helman Ghorst, Mannfred's accomplice,' he said coldly. 'If I get the necromancer under my blades, I'll have the path right to von Carstein's coffin within the hour.'

The witch hunter breathed out, lowered his knife and pushed the swords-man's rapier away. He nodded towards its blooded blade. 'Swords?' he sneered. 'Lances? Useful tools against Ghorst and his corpse-puppets.

Bugger all use against ghosts. I found that out the hard way, boy. Faith's the only weapon they fear. And Volkmar and his maniacs have plenty.'

'Right,' said Swaft, slowly and carefully. 'Well, that does make some sense, I suppose...'

Von Korden turned on his heel and splashed off along the muddy path, shoving his pistol back into its holster and closing the hold-clip. The duellist returned to his men, his finger making circular motions next to his forehead.

The witch hunter pulled his hat low, grimacing in pain as soon as he was around a bend in the road. He was cold, he was wet, and his hand stung like hell. As soon as he had left the altercation with Swaft he had shoved a piece of lambskin into his glove to soak up the blood, but it still hurt to flex it.

The Talabheimer had a right to ask, truth be told. To a soldier, it made no real sense to split up their already pitifully small army. Yet judging by the thickening darkness, time was running short. They had to pick up Mannfred's trail somehow.

To von Korden's mind they had dallied far too long at Helsee, burying the fools who had rushed into battle. To make matters worse, some of the Talabheimers had thought that simply boiling the lake's black waters would make them safe to drink. Idiots all. They had deserved to die in pain, clutching their bellies and gasping like beached fish. The Silver Bullets had insisted the corpses were buried face down. They had pressed pennies for Morr into the eyes of the dead, placed wild garlic and hawthorn in the mouth; the whole damn lot.

The witch hunter knew a quicker way to ensure against the dead coming back to life – cut their bloody heads off and throw them in the fire. Yet the suggestion had not gone down well. They had tarried so long that they had no choice but to spend the night at Uflheim, and even though they had set off early, the dim half-light of their second day on the road was already fading fast.

As the forlorn procession crested the crags that led to Konigstein, the town's tumbledown temple of Morr came into view by the side of the road. Von Korden felt his spirits rise a little at the familiar sight. His hand strayed to the pocket that contained his pipe.

Around the temple's graves the sprawling garden of black roses was turning brown, starved from lack of sunlight. Von Korden peered inside as he walked past. The font was dry and the cracked altar was dotted with fox droppings. Pale patches on the plaster showed where the temple's holy symbol had once hung. Despite the potential value of the silver plating, no Sylvanian peasant or bandit would have been sacrilegious enough to steal it, especially not from the god of the restful dead.

To hear the gossips tell it, the icons of every last temple across the realm had been taken over the last few years. The work of Mannfred's Strigany agents; von Korden was sure of it. Most likely the artefacts had already been melted down or buried somewhere where living men fear to tread. Sylvania had been without priests since the days of Mannfred's blood-father, Vlad von Carstein, so no one had been too concerned about their holy symbols. Now the abandoned temples were the only evidence that the gods of the Empire had ever had a home in Sylvania.

Down in the shallow valley von Korden could see the scattered build-ings of Konigstein, but not a single light glimmered from their windows. Six hours since leaving Uflheim and they still had not seen a living soul. Even the hunter's watchtower was a cold black silhouette bereft of any sign of life. The brass sentinel's bony arms still jutted out in the same position as when the witch hunter had left it over a week ago.

A low moan echoed across the vale, making von Korden's hackles rise. It was a noise he had learned to hate. He listened hard for the toll of a bell, but there was only silence.

'Form up on approach!' von Korden shouted down the trail, gesturing for his small army to spread out. 'Battle line in less than three minutes!'

The state troops behind him fanned out over the other side of the crag, relieved to have some room to manoeuvre. As the last of the Knights of the Blazing Sun moved past with the great cannon in tow, Bennec Soot-son waved the Estalian cavalrymen over to a crested ridge. His men began unshackling the artillery piece from the last of the warhorses with quick, practiced efficiency.

Lupio Blaze left his men and trotted over to von Korden on his massive war stallion, raising his helmet's visor as he came close. It clicked neatly into place against a crest fashioned in the shape of a burnished metal sun, revealing a handsomely tanned face beneath. The triple plume of feathers that fanned out from the helmet was magnificent and bolt-upright despite the pattering rain. If anything, the rainwater made the knight's burnished armour look even more lustrous than usual.

Von Korden decided he did not like him one bit.

'You are expecting trouble?' the knight asked, his lilting accent irritating to von Korden's ears.

'Yes,' said von Korden dismissively.

'The dead, they do not sleep well here,' said Blaze in a mournful tone. 'It is said by many.'

'Many are right. Watch the ground as well as the road.'

The knight pursed his lips and nodded thoughtfully before continuing. 'We say "Myrmidia shine upon our blades," to give favour.' He smiled widely as he shaped the rays of the rising sun with his fingers. 'She is needed here, no?'

Von Korden snorted and made the sign of the comet against his chest instead. Myrmidia indeed. Soft southern gods, all face and no fight.

The knight took the witch hunter's silence as a hint and wheeled his horse around, cantering back to rejoin his men.

'There are wolves,' Blaze called over his shoulder as he left. 'The horses feel them.'

'At least the nags are useful, then,' muttered von Korden.

Von Korden watched the state troops taking their positions, and found himself quietly impressed. The Silver Bullets took up a staggered two-line formation on the left flank, just below the low ridge where Sootson had set up the Hammer of the Witches. Von Korden recalled the first time he saw the great cannon fired, during the burning of the twisted witch that Sootson's fellow villagers called the Grey Hag. The witch hunter's execution had gone badly wrong when the old woman had taken control of von Korden's flames, rather than the other way round. Sootson, the town's blacksmith at the time, had primed the newly-repaired cannon, shoved a bucketful of horseshoes into it, and finished the job by blasting the she-devil across the square. Quick thinking, but not quick enough to stop Gorstanford going up in flames.

Taking the front line on the right flank were Sigmar's Sons, moving forward in ranks four deep with the Bullets covering their advance. Lupio Blaze kept his cavalry behind the leftmost ridge, patiently waiting for the cannon fire that was their signal to charge in.

Von Korden himself was leading from the front, as was his custom, the regiment of swordsmen a few paces behind him. The witch hunter peered through the thin mist of rain that shrouded the tomb-strewn wilderness around Konigstein Watch. The tower's shuttered windows had been broken apart and the graves around the place gaped open to the night sky.

'The spoor of necromancy,' said von Korden to the swordsmen behind. 'There are undead here, sure as those graves are empty.'

Suddenly there was a dull wooden crack and a cry of alarm from up on the ridge. The hunter scanned the area, but he could see nothing moving in the mists ahead. Looking back up to the Silver Bullets, he saw the handgunners' musician, Lutiger Swift, standing lopsided. His left leg was knee-deep in the splintered coffin exposed by his one-man mudslide, and his free hand reflexively clutched the talisman around his neck.

'Bloody balls,' exhaled Swift, his city-born Talabheim accent unnaturally loud. 'I knew I'd end up in a casket eventually, but this is a bit sudden!' His comrades laughed and jeered as their comrade extricated himself from the wooden ruin of the grave. 'Sorry, gents. One of the local girls was a bit lonely,' the musician joked, shaking his leg to dislodge a shattered ribcage that clung to his foot. 'Very hospitable, this lass.'

'Didn't know you liked 'em *that* skinny, Lute!' said Ulf Weissman, propping the standard of the Sigmar's Sons in the crook of his neck in order to make an obscene gesture in Swift's direction.

Von Korden stormed back up the ridge, his face twisted into a wild-eyed snarl and his hand palming a filleting knife. Discipline would be restored, one way or another.

The hunter stopped suddenly, sniffing the air. Something foul lingered under the peaty smell of wet earth. A moment later the dull moaning that von Korden had heard minutes earlier drifted through the mist, coming from the tumbled walls just beyond the tower. The witch hunter listened carefully.

This time, he distinctly heard the low toll of an ancient bell.

Waving his arm behind him in signal, von Korden darted back to the front line and crouched down behind a shattered tombstone. Sure enough, there were ghostlights in the gloom. Strange figures began to coalesce in the misting rain, skeletal shapes that moved in jerky synchronicity. One by one, a clutch of dead things scraped and staggered their way towards the trespassers. They stalked with painstaking slowness around the yawning graves and jutting hillocks, forming up in front of a tumbledown wall. Their ranks were a mockery of a proper military unit. Slack jaws dangled from fleshless skulls and rusted armour clanked gently on ice-cold bone.

'Sigmar's sack, just look at 'em all,' exhaled Swift.

'Shut your damn mouth, Swift, you've embarrassed yourself enough already,' growled Curser Bredt, taking a bead on the skeletal warriors with his rifle. 'Concentrate. As soon as I give the order, make every one of those bullets count.'

Hastening back to the vanguard, von Korden gestured forward and right. In response Sigmar's Sons double-timed as best they could towards the abandoned watch. It did not bode well that Unholdt and the rest of his men had not yet emerged onto the roof. Still, they needed to secure the tower, whatever horrors lurked inside.

The mist ahead thinned for a second. It revealed hunchbacked shadows that moved like long-limbed toads across the grass, leap-stop-leaping towards the swordsmen. Von Korden almost called out a warning, but bit his tongue. Ghorst would be close by, and the necromancer would flee if he knew his old persecutor was on the field. The hunter was relieved when Bredt spoke out a second later.

'Change target, new marks below!' shouted the gunner-sergeant. 'Mind the Sons!'

The Silver Bullets swivelled as one, taking a bead on the ghouls in the mist below them as the Sons broke into a hunched run. The handgunners fired a sharp fusillade, hurling one creature backwards and taking another in the throat so hard it left its head dangling on its back. The ghoul kept going for a second before collapsing into a grave-pit. Von Korden met Sootson's eye up on the ridge, and a few seconds later two more ghoul-things were blasted apart by the Hammer of the Witches. Two of the pallid creatures were ahead of the rest, leaping on the rearmost swordsman and tearing great strips of flesh from his back. The rest of the unit formed up, turning as one at a barked order from Eben Swift.

The swordsmen fought hard to lock their shields, stabbing at sore-pocked faces and necks as the ghouls groped and slashed with their long, dirt-encrusted fingers. Arterial blood spurted in the mist, the hot red of the state troops splashing uniforms alongside the brackish brown of ghoul gore. Von Korden wished he was in the thick of it with them, but he had other matters to attend to.

Horses snorted and tack jangled to the witch hunter's left as the Knights of the Blazing Sun galloped down into the fight. He waved them on, gesturing with a pistol in the direction of the skeletal warriors that were stalking towards the Silver Bullets. With the skeletons engaged against the knights on the left and the ghouls fighting tooth and nail against Sigmar's Sons on the right, von Korden was free to pursue his own agenda.

Heldenhammer be praised. There he was.

Lurching through the mist ahead came Helman Ghorst, stooped atop his charnel cart. Four grotesque corpse-things pulled it forward in fits and spurts. The putrid stench of the cart's rat-infested cargo was like a living thing in its own right. The witch hunter broke cover for a second and ran in a crouch from gravestone to tomb, a feral grin stretching his features. He gestured back to Sootson's cannon, an open hand that meant 'hold fire'. He needed Ghorst alive if they were to find Mannfred before the realm of Sylvania was lost altogether.

Ahead, Ghorst was scanning around, mumbling something that von Korden strained to hear. Suddenly the arcane words grew deafeningly loud. The necromancer stood up to his full height, eyes blazing with purple-black energy. Twin bolts of raw death shot out from his sunken sockets, narrowly missing Lupio Blaze and burning into the charging knights behind him. Two finely-armoured Estalians convulsed and writhed, falling from their saddles in explosions of ash. A pair of empty suits of armour clattered into the muddy grass.

The charge of the Myrmidian knights hit home nonetheless, slamming into the ranks of the skeletal warriors with tremendous force. Their lowered lances took skulls from necks and punctured rusted breastplates with ease, and the sheer weight of the armoured stallions and their plate-clad riders proved a powerful weapon in itself. Over a dozen of Ghorst's skeletal warriors were smashed apart by the momentum of the charge. Blaze's cries to Myrmidia rang out as fleshless limbs and scraps of armour were hurled in all directions. The back ranks of the undead regiment snapped into action as if waking from a dream, setting their shields and bracing just in time to stop their unit's utter destruction.

Von Korden was within a stone's throw of his quarry when he saw the slinking, malevolent shadows of giant wolves dart out of the scattered trees on the left flank. An unearthly howl keened through the mist, and the hunter caught a glimpse of rotten sinews and yellowed bone that gleamed under ragged patches of half-sewn skin. The undead pack would be falling upon the rear of the knights in no time at all, and they were too far away for von Korden's pistols to count.

The witch hunter swore under his breath, taking off his gauntlet and pulling out the ivory ring he kept on a thin chain around his wrist. The artefact had been given to him by the white wizards of Templehof as a reward for slaying the vargheist that was preying on their town, and he had always intended to use its powers against Ghorst. Yet he could not afford to lose the knights, not yet.

'Be banished!' shouted von Korden, standing up from his tombstone cover and pressing the ring flat against his bare palm. A serpent of pure light streaked out from its centre into the midst of the undead wolves just as they were about to pounce upon Blaze's knights. The luminous apparition wrapped around three of the canine creatures and squeezed them into nothingness. A moment later Curser Bredt's voice rang out, and a volley of shot blasted the rest of the pack into chunks of maggoty meat.

Von Korden barely had time to smile before a tangle of pale limbs grabbed at him. Unclean fingers snatched his collar and dug painfully into his cheek. A moment later Ghorst's foul carriage was upon him, bell clanging wildly. Rotten teeth bit hard into his shoulder a heartbeat before the cart's wooden yoke knocked him into the dirt. The hunter tried to rise, but a clammy and twisted foot pressed the side of his face into the mud. Out of his other eye he could see a jagged wheel coming right for his neck.

There was a sharp Estalian war cry and Ghorst's carriage veered suddenly to the right. Its wheel came on, ripping out a great hank of the witch hunter's hair and nearly scalping him in the process. Through a haze of confusion and pain he could just make out the glinting armour of Blaze's knights wheeling around through the damp grass. The mist thickened for a moment, and the toll of Ghorst's bell faded away to be replaced by the thunder of hooves.

As the horses passed by von Korden stumbled back to his feet. Badly winded, bleeding profusely and spitting out a mouthful of grave-dirt, he still grasped a mud-covered pistol tightly in his good hand. Nearby, the Knights of the Blazing Sun had broken formation. Their warhorses were stamping down hard on the disembodied skeletal arms that had burst from the ground to claw ineffectually at their legs. Over by the watchtower, Sigmar's Sons were chasing down the last of the ghoul-things, hacking at unarmoured backs and cutting heads from necks.

Ghorst's macabre carriage was nowhere to be seen.

Von Korden swore a blue streak as he marched up towards the watchtower, smearing the worst of the grave-mud from his face and checking that his holstered pistol was still sound. His head rang with pain and one of his eyes was swelling shut, but the rage boiling inside him kept his mind sharp. Once his message was sent from the watch he could allow himself to tend his wounds, but not before.

'Get the hell out of my way,' he spat at the Sigmarite swordsmen still hacking the heads from the ghoul corpses outside the watchtower. They moved aside immediately, sensing that they were in more danger from von Korden than from any of the walking dead. 'Swaft, Weissman, you're with me.'

The two Sons exchanged a meaningful glance as the witch hunter strode between them. 'Well, Volkmar did say,' murmured Weissman, handing the regiment's banner to a nearby comrade before following von Korden to the heavy wooden door of the watchtower. Swaft came reluctantly after him, wiping gobbets of thick brown blood from his blade.

The hunter pushed the door with an open palm, and it swung open on its hinges. There was no sound, no motion inside. The entire lower floor of the building was in total disarray. The writing desk was upturned, its inks spilled like black blood across the flagstones to pool around the shattered skull of the Templehof vargheist.

Suddenly Unholdt's corpse lurched out from behind the door, bowling into von Korden with such force it knocked them both flailing onto the floor. Weissman pushed inside the doorway just as the thing that had once been Steig clambered out of the disused well, blood-covered tongue flapping. The Sigmarite soldier edged around the well, blade ready for a killing thrust, only to find another undead guard barrelling out from behind the tower's grandfather clock to grab him in a biting, tearing bear hug. Swaft moved in, blade readied as he looked for his moment to strike.

Wrestling Unholdt to one side, von Korden discharged his pistol into his old comrade's dead bulk. The corpse jerked upward for a second before falling back down again, teeth gnashing a few millimetres from the witch hunter's eye. The grotesque thing's rotten breath invaded von Korden's nostrils, and strings of blood laced drool draped across his cheek.

Setting his teeth and bracing his knee on the wall, the witch hunter jerked sideways. He rolled the corpse of his former lieutenant off him and pushed against it with one hand as he fumbled to draw his cutting sabre with the other. The scabbard was empty. The corpse pushed back, its weight tremendous. Von Korden's muscles began to shake, then to give. Unholdt's chomping, stinking mouth came closer, inch by tortuous inch.

A high-pitched squeal rang out, ear-piercing in the confines of the watchtower. A moment later a hairy mass of hogflesh burst out from behind the stairwell curtain and barged into Unholdt, knocking him bodily from von Korden. The corpse rolled with the impact, some vestige of its brawler past coming to the surface as it scrabbled to its knees. Its hands flew down to Gremlynne's neck, sinking into the pig's dense throat as von Korden regained his feet. With a roar, the witch hunter grabbed a splintered chair leg from the floor and slammed the sharp end right through his dead lieutenant's back. The corpse shuddered for a moment and lay still.

Von Korden spun round to the Sons, but they had already despatched the animated cadavers that had once been Steig and Freidricksen. The whole altercation had taken less than half a minute.

'You two, check upstairs,' said von Korden, clutching his bruised arm. The Sons nodded in assent, moving past him and as they climbed up into the stairwell. Once they were gone, the witch hunter moved over to Unholdt and, with a great effort, rolled his body to one side. Gremlynne looked up at him with one watery eye, her front legs broken and her breath hissing in ragged gasps through the bloody ruin of her throat.

'Oh no,' said von Korden, anguish flooding his soul. 'No, Gremlynne!' He cradled the dying pig in his arms, stroking her ears as she wheezed bubbles of blood from her snout. 'Not you as well,' he said, trying to stem the red rivulets that poured from her neck. 'Hang on, old girl, I'll... I'll get some bandages or something,' he said, the words catching in his throat. He laid her down gently, frantically scanning for something to use as a tourniquet. A low rattle came from behind him, and with an effort of will he turned back.

He was too late. The pig had breathed her last.

'You bastards!' cried von Korden, kicking the stonework of the well so hard a part of it crumbled down into the darkness. He threw the shattered table leg across the room, and it clattered in the corner. 'You'll pay for what you did to us!' he shouted, tears stinging in his eyes. He slumped into what remained of his armchair, hand questing for the cameo portrait that hung next to his heart. With his wife's pig gone, the necklace was all that was left of the old days. It was the last remnant of the farm they had loved so much. Even Alberich von Korden – the man he had been – had died a long time ago.

'Lynn, my dear,' he gasped as he pried open the jewelled image, 'Oh, Lynn, I'm sorry... I'm sorry I was too late to save the girls.' Alberich shut his eyes hard, fighting to stay in control as a decade of suppressed emotion roiled inside. 'I'm so sorry I never told you that I needed you, my love.'

His shoulders shook, but no sound would come.

'I'll make them pay, Lynn,' said Alberich to the female portrait lying in his bloodstained hand. 'I promise you.'

There came a cascade of footfalls from the stairway, and Weissman pushed his way in through the curtain.

'Trouble?' he asked.

Von Korden was standing in the middle of the room, facing away from the stairwell as he fussed with his pistols. He did not turn around.

'No,' he said, with a sigh. 'Just... I just thought I saw one of them twitch, that's all.'

'Right,' said Weissman, 'Well, glad we got the bastards before they got us. Nothing much on either floor, up there. Bit o' grub in the cupboards. You want to send the message whilst the going's good?'

'Yes. Get some lamp oil on the signal cogs, goose fat, whatever you can find. I'll be up in a minute.'

'Right you are,' said Weissman, heading back upstairs.

Von Korden took a long and ragged breath, as deep as he could. He held it for a long time before heading upstairs to the battlements.

CHAPTER NINE

THE COLLEGIUM OF LIGHT

Templehof, east of the Vale of Darkness, 2522

There it was again. A glimmer of witch-light, tiny but distinct, emanating from the peaks on the other side of the vale.

Jovi Sunscryer of the Light Order squinted into the gloom, his heart quickening at the prospect that someone might be using Konigstein's brass sentinel to communicate. He ran a hand across the brown leather of his pate and down over his eyes, gently humming the Seventh Rumination of Shem to help him focus. There was a message there, he was certain of it.

He leaned over the banister of the spiral staircase that led down into the Collegium's library and tinkled the small bell that hung from the brass serpent at their top.

'Fetch the scrying lenses, please, Khalep,' he called.

There was no response.

He tried again, leaning over a little further. 'Khalep, be a good fellow and fetch the scrying lenses.'

One... Two... Three... Still nothing.

'*Khalep!*' the old man bellowed, the wattle of skin on his scrawny neck wobbling. There was a scuffle, a creak and a thump from the floor below. A few moments later a blinking young man blinked up from the bottom of the stairs, hastily rearranging his ceremonial robes.

'Yes, m-m-magister?' stuttered the youth.

Jovi glowered up at the overcast skies. They glowered right back.

'Khalep, I was wondering if you would be so kind as to fetch me the scrying lenses before I turn you into a legless toad.'

'Certainly, m-m-magister, right away.'

The acolyte scurried off. There was some serious work ahead for that boy.

The elderly scholar turned his attention back to the glimmering lights on the horizon. They had changed, but the sigils of the previous communiqué hung behind them in time, a message that only one trained in the magical arts could read.

Less than a minute later the young apprentice staggered up the spiral staircase laden with a contraption made of brass rods and calibrators. Held suspended in their metallic web was a set of softly glowing lenses shielded by cups of beaten copper. Neftep, the second of Jovi's two acolytes and arguably the least incompetent, was close behind, a blazing lantern in his hand.

'Neftep,' said Jovi, patiently. 'This gloom,' he gestured vaguely above his head, 'hangs heavy in my soul, just as it does in yours, I am sure. I would dearly love to lift it from the skies. But when we are trying to perceive a distant light, a light close at hand is worse than useless.'

Neftep nodded once. 'Yes, magister,' he replied sagely.

'So be a good fellow and toddle off back downstairs, before you ruin my night vision entirely and I am forced to hurl you from the balcony with a great shout of angst.'

'Of course, oh master,' replied Neftep, making his way back down the stairs.

Jovi Sunscryer blew out his cheeks, gathering his focus once more. Khalep, to his credit, had already assembled the scrying lenses and was busy focusing them on the light in the distance.

'Ah, good show,' said Sunscryer. 'Might I perhaps be permitted to fine-tune the device, Khalep? Or would you prefer me to sit here and quietly die of old age?'

'N-n-no, ma-magister,' said Khalep. He stepped backwards, allowing his tutor to lean down to the eyepiece of the scrying device.

The flickering light was indeed a message, and a long one, too, by the looks of it. The magister recognised the personal sigil of von Korden at the message's end, a circle of fire that symbolised the judicial pyres of the witch hunter. Jovi licked the end of his vulture feather quill and inked it, writing down the message as he deciphered it.

> *MANNFRED CONFIRMED ACTIVE. CRUSADE ALREADY IN*
> *VALE. SEEKING END DARKNESS. FEW MEN. CRUSADE AND*
> *THEOGONIST LIKELY DOOMED.*
>
> *REQUEST REINFORCEMENTS. ALTDORF. TEMPLEHOF.*
> *ANYWHERE.*
>
> *SEND HELP. VON KORDEN*

Sunscryer stared off to the peaks on the other side of the vale for a long minute before gathering his things and heading downstairs to the stables.

The wind moaned like a dying man as the wizards escorted the Collegium's Luminark to the top of Templehof Crag. A pair of barded Stirland Punchers was yoked to the forebeams, slowly but surely pulling the wheeled war machine up the winding path.

Even without the Collegium's warhorses lashed to its carriage the Lumi-nark was massive. Half chariot, half enormous lens array, the thing dwarfed even the coaches of the Sylvanian aristocracy. The carriage's central cabin was capped with a candle-strewn roof, atop which was a circular metal dais that held up a long and ornate construction of cast iron. Eight hoops of finely wrought silver were attached at regular intervals along its length, jutting up from the baroque framework in a manner reminiscent of a tele-scope. Each hoop held a convex disc of shimmering glass that sparkled greenish-yellow in the low light of Khalep's lantern. Attuned correctly, the wyrdglass lenses could harness the invisible winds of magic and focus their aethyric energies into a searing lance of light that could burn a town to ash.

Once the Luminark had been hauled to the top of the winding path that girdled Templehof Crag, the acolytes pulled off the last of the dustsheets and busied themselves with adjusting screws and resetting glass lenses. Sunscryer hummed tunelessly to himself as he took measurements with his aethyric resonators and slide glasses, motioning for Khalep to revolve the contrap-tion's dais wheel a degree clockwise, then half a degree counterclockwise. There was precious little natural light left, but with the right incantations, even the fickle Wind of Hysh could be channelled from a wafting zephyr into a powerful beam. Neftep balanced precariously on an outcrop of rock in order to polish the last of the wyrdglass lenses with a lambskin cloth.

Deeming the alignments to be to his satisfaction, Sunscryer climbed the rungs that led to the cabin's upper platforms and flexed the control levers with a sigh of appreciation.

A lone bat flitted through the twilight, its path seemingly random as it wound around the crag. Sunscryer's expression soured. He called out an ancient phrase in Nehekharan, pitching the crescendo just as he gave the control levers a sudden twist. The machine thrummed for a moment before a beam of magical light shot out from the Luminark's lenses. A moment later the remnants of a scorched wing spiraled down to rest at Khalep's feet.

'G-g-good shot, m-magister,' said the young acolyte, eyebrows raised.

'Why thank you, Master Sulenheim,' replied Jovi, brushing a mote of dust from the cast iron of the Luminark's frame. 'Horrid little spies, those things. Though before this is over, I fear the bats we will be facing might be somewhat larger.'

Midnight was approaching, and the wizard's coded message still flick-ered into the night. Each pulse would look much like distant lightning to a common man, but could be read as clear as day by one skilled in the arts.

Though the Luminark had been built as an engine of war, Jovi had long ago worked out the exact settings that would end in an instantaneous light-message to the Orbulus of his fellows in the Altdorf Colleges of Magic. From there, the message would be transferred to the offices of Balthasar Gelt himself. Though Gelt and Sunscryer had never seen eye to eye – it had been the Supreme Patriarch who had 'suggested' Sunscryer set up the collegium in Templehof in the first place – Gelt's mastery over the alchemical arts was so great it might be able to help them in distant Sylvania. Whatever aid they could garner from their fellow wizards would be gratefully received. Better yet, Gelt had the ear of Karl Franz himself, and if anyone had influence enough to help them fight back against the darkness it was the Emperor.

Over the last few hours Jovi had adjusted every lens and screw to within a minute degree of accuracy, and his acolytes had joined him in a three-fold chant designed to sharpen and increase intermittent pulses of magical energy.

Jovi pulled out a leather-bound telescope and focused it on the flickering beam that probed into the distance before making adjustments with his other hand: on, off-on, off-on-off. Over the last few hours, the stuttering pulses reached out across to the other side of the vale, but no further. It seemed to Sunscryer that the unnatural gloom itself was smothering the light-message like a witch suffocating a newborn.

Sunscryer had a nasty feeling that impression was disturbingly close to the truth.

'M-m-magister,' stammered Khalep, breaking the chant. 'I think I n-n-need water, magister.'

The elderly wizard tutted and made a chopping motion, indicating that Neftep should stop. 'No stamina, you lot,' he croaked, testily. In truth he was glad of the reprieve; his own throat was getting raw too. He stared balefully at the thickening darkness on the horizon. 'Very well. There's a carafe in the cabin, bring it up when you're done.'

Khalep slunk below, handing up a snake-handled jug and some wafers to his fellow wizards.

'Dammit,' said Jovi, rubbing his eyes and taking a sip of water. 'There's definitely something acting against us. This darkness was summoned by a ritual of some kind, I feel sure – and a powerful one at that. I've a book down in the library that tells of a similar event plaguing the rule of the Priest King Alcadizaar – a 'great darkness' that was unquestionably the work of the Great Necromancer himself.'

Neftep blanched and made the sign of the rising sun over his chest, fingers splayed.

'For a spell of this magnitude to last this long, and continue to get worse with each passing day,' continued Jovi seriously, 'would require a power source of godly proportions.'

'Is there any other way we can get the message out, master?' said Neftep.

'Well, the Deathknell Watches might work over time, though by the look of it our friend von Korden already has that side of things covered. And time is a commodity we do not have. Part of the Luminark's genius is that its light-message is functionally instantaneous.'

'So can we bolster it somehow, overcome the curse through sheer force?'

'Theoretically speaking, yes,' said Jovi. 'If we could get the Luminark up higher still, and channel even more of the Wind of Hysh into it, we could potentially overcome even this unnatural darkness. I do recall seeing a lens that would do the job, in my youth. The end piece of a scrying scope. Impressive piece, though not as finely wrought as one of my own creations.'

'We could fetch it for you, master,' volunteered Neftep. Khalep looked over his master's shoulder at his companion, his eyes wide and his head shaking from side to side.

'Hmm? Ah, well, I think perhaps we should all go, Neftep,' said Sunscryer, nervously. 'It's in Vargravia, you see. The hidden necropolis.'

—◀ CHAPTER TEN ▶—

THE GREAT WESTERN ROAD

The Vale of Darkness, 2522

Robed worshippers chanted their adulation as Volkmar rose above the stone circle, dark energies crackling around him. He was immense, and powerful beyond measure. Bound spirits whirled around him, shrieking his name. He would have his revenge upon his enemies and bind them to his will for the rest of time. His hand burned fiercely, but the pain merely invigorated him, making his hatred all the more potent. He breathed out a billowing cloud of death, and the mortal fools gathered in worship below him withered away to nothing.

The Grand Theogonist awoke with a start, jerking upward from the lectern of the war altar at the rear of the crusading host. The disturbing dream still clutched at him. His left hand throbbed with a strange mixture of numbness and pain, but his right flew to the sacred warhammer at his side, and the strange sensations quickly faded away.

Somehow, he had allowed himself to fall asleep. Volkmar chided himself, pinching the skin on his wrist so hard he left a red-black blister behind. To sleep at the lectern of the war altar was an unforgivable lapse, heresy even, especially after the events at Fort Oberstyre. Yet none of his men had noticed, thank Sigmar. Even Kaslain was intent on the road ahead.

A lucky escape, then. With the stakes as high as they were, Volkmar could not afford to show weakness, not even to his own men. He was expecting the same from them, after all.

The grand exorcism of Oberstyre had been mentally and spiritually draining. Those of the Tattersouls whose faith in Sigmar had not proven sufficient had died in terror, the cold claws of the fortress's ghosts closing around their hearts. Many more had met grisly ends in the lightless maze of cellars beneath Oberstyre, fighting blind against the troglodytes that infested the underground tunnels.

They had not given their lives in vain. Not a single evil soul had dwelt there by the break of dawn. The spirit-bound guardians of that haunted keep had been obliterated forever, burned out of the walls by the sheer golden light of the Sigmarite faith. Those stone-gheists that had proved powerful enough to linger had instead met their demise at the end of Volkmar's blessed hammer. Mannfred's dark work had been undone, even if the vampire's trail had long gone cold.

The remains of the Tattersouls continued their procession through the mud, wailing, muttering, even dancing wildly as they accompanied the war altar along the Great Western Road. Arch Lector Kaslain strode at the front of the procession, stoically ignoring the screeching and gnashing of the zealots behind him as he ploughed on through the muck towards Deihstein.

Coming from the other direction along the wide road was another procession of sorts, looking if anything even more desolate than Volkmar's own tattered crusaders. Malnourished oxen drew carts full of pockmarked, disfigured children along the muddy ruts, the peasantry on the riding plates hunched under threadbare blankets. Those not berthed on a cart dragged mud-sleds along the road, their meagre possessions lashed to wooded slats. Pregnant women rode sidesaddle on cows and mules whilst slow-witted adolescents picked their noses and ate the dubious treasures they had unearthed.

It took some time for the presence of the war altar to register in the oncoming throng. When it did, whispers spread through them like wind through a blighted crop. Carts were wheeled over into ditches, young children and old crones alike spilling out with cries of protest. Goats were shoved bleating into dry brown hedgerows, and mules were led into fields of rotten crops in order to let the war altar pass. Many of the peasants went down on their knees in the mud, eyes downcast.

'An omen! Sigmar is here to save us from the darkness!' screeched a wizened old grandmother.

'Bring back the sun!' shouted a tiny girl child. 'There's no plants for Gurden!'

A group of the peasants surged forwards towards the war altar, arms outstretched and eyes alight with hunger. Their advance was met by the Tattersouls, the flagellants flowing forward in a line of unwashed bodies that blocked the road. The peasants pulled up short, cowed by the madness in the eyes of the men barring their path.

'The End!' screeched Gerhardt the Worm into the face of the nearest peasant. 'The End is here! All shall die!'

'Nothing new,' replied the lowlander, his badly cleft lip blurring his words. 'We grew up here, mate.'

'Sigmar!' shouted the zealot. 'Sigmar shall deliver us if we fling ourselves bodily into the next life!'

'We're flinging ourselves bodily into Ostermark,' said the peasant, drily. 'Nothing here for us now but graves.'

'And them wot used to lie in 'em,' muttered a tangle-haired matron by his side.

The peasant looked up at Arch Lector Kaslain, ignoring Gerhardt as best he could. 'Is that bald bloke s'posed to be the Lord Theogonite or something? Sigmarzeit festival's cancelled, I reckon.'

'It *is* the Grand Theogonist, simpleton. And you'd do well to keep your tongue civil in his presence,' rumbled Kaslain.

'Well swap me blind,' said the peasant, making the sign of the hammer. 'Temple's hollow, holy symbols gone, but Shallya's smalls, here comes the old Volcano himself. Using our road, no less. And scant hours after we see a bunch of humourless bastards all dressed up in uniform.' He turned to the woman, touching the dried hound's foot at his throat. 'Something's up, right enough.'

'Uniform?' said Kaslain. 'Was it Talabheim, red and white?'

'Aye, that's them,' slurred the spokesman, motioning his wife and fellows back. 'City types, they were. Reckon you'll catch 'em up if you hurry. Watch the roads, though, and the fields. Bad types about.'

The peasant brushed his way past the Tattersouls, casting a remark over his shoulder as he went.

'And if you lot find what you're lookin' for? Sigmar help you all.'

CHAPTER ELEVEN

SOUTH OF TEMPLEHOF

The Vale of Darkness, 2522

Since leaving Templehof Crag for Vargravia the Light wizards had made slow but steady progress along the country roads. The light was fading to pitch black, and their spirits had faded with it. Neftep had grown sick of humouring his master's attempts to keep up morale, and had pulled a greased leather over his head to keep off the drizzling rain. Khalep took a turn at keeping the old man occupied instead.

'So w-w-w...'

'The location we're headed to, since you asked, Khalep, is the abandoned manse of an astromancer, built on the highest point of the Vargravian mountains. Riddled with ghosts, though, the whole place. They say the celestialist buried himself alive to escape them.'

'W-wonderful,' said Khalep.

'We won't be tarrying, never fear,' said the elderly wizard, his tone dark. 'I strayed in there once, when I was younger even than yourselves. The scythe-gheists that guard the place scared me half to death, quite literally. My hair turned white and fell out in clumps. No wonder the Sylvanians avoid the place like the plague. Still, at least it wasn't Whispering Nell playing host.'

Silence stretched out before Khalep gave in.

'W-w-w...'

'Who's Whispering Nell, you say, Khalep? Ah, but she's a nasty one. Countess Emmanuelle von Templehof, to give the old bitch her due. Once the cousin of Konrad the Bloody. A femme fatale in life and even deadlier in death.'

'How so?' asked Neftep, fearing the answer.

'Ah, well. They say that if she whispers your true name within earshot, your body dies and your soul is hers for all eternity. Horrid fate, she's not the looker she once was. Too many maggots.' Sunscryer took out his telescope and peered into the distance before continuing. 'I'd be much obliged if neither of you referred to me by name when we're within Vargravia's borders. I'll do the same for you, of course. Sound good?'

The acolytes shared a look. Shaking his head in despair, Neftep made to get off the Luminark, but Khalep grabbed him by the robes and pointed to the darkness that choked the skies above. Slump-shouldered, his comrade sat back down with a sigh.

The warhorses under the Luminark's yoke ploughed on through the mud. The trio of wizards rounded a corner, and the loose hedgerow opened to reveal a large black building with shattered windows that bled gold in the night.

'Is that...'

'It is indeed! The Drunken Goat, arguably the most robust of Sylvania's roadside taverns. Excellent pork. And it looks like old Bors left the lanterns on before he took to his heels.'

The three wizards approached the dripping eaves of the inn together, the sleeves of their robes held overhead to keep off the worst of the rain. The door was stout oak, though claw marks had gouged furrows into it. A piece of broken fingernail was still embedded in the jamb. Sunscryer reached out with his serpent-tipped staff and rapped hard on the studded planks of the front door.

There was no answer. He pushed, but the door was barred fast.

The elderly wizard held up a cautionary finger towards his acolytes before pulling a lodestone from his robes and moving the magnetic lump across the door. There was a solid, metallic thunk from the other side.

'Ha! Gelt's not the only master of magnetism in the colleges,' said Sunscryer, pushing the heavy oak open with a creak.

A crossbow bolt thrummed through the air and embedded itself in the doorjamb less than an inch from the old wizard's head. A dozen blades were thrust in his direction, including spears, farming implements and even the sharpened handle of a long skillet. Behind Jovi, Neftep began Shem's Chant of Blinding, the Nehekharan syllables sounding raw and strange in the silence.

'Oh, do put a sock in it, Neftep,' said Sunscryer to his acolyte. 'Is Bors about, gentlemen?'

A great cry of relief came from the huddled patrons of the inn. The wizards were roughly pulled inside and roundly slapped on the back, so much so that Khalep stumbled face first into the stained and wobbling chest of Big Delf the cook. Bors Ratsnatcher came out from behind the grandfather clock, cudgel in hand, and motioned for Long Cobb to pour each of the wizards a drink. Before a minute had passed the trio was seated at one of the oaken tables, foaming tankards of Troll Brew in their scrawny hands.

'We thought you lot'd be long gone by now,' said a brawny hard drinker with a smile only a tooth doctor could love.

'Bernhardt!' said Jovi, draining the last of his tankard. 'I don't think I've ever seen the Goat quite so busy.'

'You say that,' replied Bernhardt, 'but this is it. This is everyone.'

'Whatever do you mean?'

'Pretty much everyone else in Sylvania has legged it, as far as we can make out. Headed for Ostermark, the Moot, even the mountains. It's this bloody darkness. Everythin's dyin' off.'

'And you fellows intend to make the difference, do you? Fight back?'

'Not exactly,' said Bernhardt darkly, pressing another tankard of ale into Sunscryer's hands. 'We intend to get drunk.'

CHAPTER TWELVE

DEIHSTEIN RIDGE

The Vale of Darkness, 2522

The wind rustled through the dying oaks of Deihstein Ridge, casting another handful of leaves onto the canopy of the canvas-covered wagon below.

'Well? What do you wait for?' asked Exei von Deihst, his thick Strigany urgent and low as he pointed at the witch hunter in the distance. 'That him, Voytek. I tell you. Take shot.'

The sharpshooter scratched the underside of his stubbly jaw before belly-ing forward for a better angle. Below their hidden caravan at the side of the road, brightly-uniformed Talabheimers were fighting hard against the von Vassel clan. Eager as ever to prove themselves, the von Vassels had sprung the ambush too early. Still, the outlanders were too preoccupied fending off the ambush to pursue the corpse-laden cart escaping into the distance, let alone pay attention to the von Deihsts.

'Hush, Exei. I like part where life and death hang in balance,' grinned Voytek, his hunting rifle's barrel poking out of the painted canvas of the wagon. 'Savour it. Second best part of having long gun.'

'Take shot, Voytek,' said Alexei, a warning tone in his voice. 'Pale count will not be happy if Ghorst caught. Feed you to wing-devil.'

'Be still, little grandmother,' mocked Voytek. 'You shake so much you spoil aim.'

'Voytek. Take shot.'

'Just...give...second...' said Voytek as a distinctive witch hunter hat bobbed in his sights. 'There. Got him.'

The Strigany sharpshooter pulled the trigger.

There was a tremendous crash as the war altar thundered over the crest of the Deihstein Ridge and ploughed into the Strigany caravans hidden by the side of the road. Its colossal weight bundled over two of the hooded wagons just as the crack of a hunting rifle rang out. Two gangly men spilled out of the rear of the larger of the two wagons, screaming in shock as the iron wheels of the war altar ground through one's midsection and crushed the other's legs.

Volkmar sounded the Horn of Sigismund as his surprise attack hit home, the brazen roar of the war horn ringing out across the fields. It struck fear into the faithless – like the scum scattering below – and let the Talabheimers know help was on its way.

Heartened by the sound and the sight of the war altar, the Talabheimer state troops attacked with renewed purpose, slashing and stabbing at the dusky horsemen in their midst. Several of the nomads' horses had bolted at the sound of Volkmar's war horn, but many more of the Strigany had danced out of reach and taken a position by the side of the wooded ridge, puffs of smoke coming from their rifles.

A great maniacal shriek came from the wooded rise above the road and the Tattersouls spilled into view, hurling themselves from the lip of the ridge like cultists united in a mass suicide pact. Several of the crusaders smacked bodily into the horse nomads, bearing them to the ground before strangling them with their flails, ropes, even dirt-encrusted hands. Many more of the zealots missed their targets and thumped down hard into the muck, writhing as they cried out in an ecstasy of pain.

The remaining Strigany broke and galloped off, leaving their wounded and dying behind them in the dirt. On the road ahead, von Korden's Talabheimers recovered themselves and saw to their own fallen, binding wounds and giving Morr's grace to those who had died.

As he surveyed the situation from atop his pulpit, Volkmar saw a wounded nomad in the shattered remains of a covered wagon behind the altar. The Strigany pulled a knife from the stock of his long rifle and cried out in his strange language before taking the blade in both hands, turning it round, and plunging it deep into his own throat.

Placing his hand firmly on the chassis of the war altar, the Grand Theogonist leapt over the balustrade at the front of the pulpit. He landed deftly in the mud below, ceremonial robes billowing around him. Hastening over to the dying man, he kicked the thug's knife into a ditch and knelt down, placing his hand over the pulsing wound. A golden light spilled from between his fingers. When he took his hand away, the gash had healed over, though it was still slick with arterial blood.

'Not so easy, I'm afraid, young man,' said Volkmar to the Strigany gasping for air beneath him. 'I know someone who wants a few words with you.'

CHAPTER THIRTEEN

THE VARGRAVIAN MOUNTAINS

The Vale of Darkness, 2522

'Oh for Shem's sake, Khalep,' said Sunscryer, testily. 'I swear, you've got the bladder of a pregnant shrew.'

Robes hitched, Khalep was relieving himself against a boulder at the side of the winding road that led up to the borders of Vargravia. Behind him the Luminark creaked in the winds that whipped around the high peak road, wyrdglass lenses tinkling. At its rear, a few dozen of the Goat's finest were taking advantage of the break to tap the barrels of wine they had hoisted into the rear cabin of the war engine. Sunscryer had not approved one bit, but a heavier load was well worth the thirty or so brawlers that they had convinced to fight at their side over the course of the night. Stirland's Revenge, they called themselves, the last dregs of a province that had all but given up the fight. It was a rather grand name for such a scruffy collection of drunkards. The elderly wizard only hoped they could live up to it.

Even Jovi felt like perhaps a little Marienburg courage might not be such a bad idea, but he quickly quashed the thought. When involved in the business of spellcasting, a single mistake could lead to a painful death – or worse, a daemon-breach. As his acolyte Vorac had learned many years ago, a tipsy wizard could be more dangerous than an entire army of normal men. The Collegium's rear wall was still missing to this day.

Ahead of them, Sunscryer could just about perceive the ironbone fence-work that had been erected by some nameless mason to keep the peasants out – or more likely to keep the dead in. Behind the rotten borders were timeworn peaks, each dotted with tombs so ancient they had been eroded smooth and covered in clinging moss. The occasional statue rose bravely out of the slinking mists that haunted the sprawling necropolis, and in the distance, the silhouette of an astromancer's dome was just visible against the glowering skies.

A ghastly howl wound out of the mists, getting louder and louder before stopping abruptly. Some of the peasants from the Goat made the signs of

Sigmar and Morr. Others, including Khalep and Neftep, looked longingly at the barrels of wine at the Luminark's rear.

'Ready then?' called out Jovi from the lens deck as his men milled about below. 'Make your peace if you have to. Oh, and remember, no names. Names have power, and I'd rather not risk our souls as well as our lives.'

Mumbling sullenly, the ragtag expedition made their way through the tombs and sepulchres that dotted the outlying peaks of Vargravia. Ghost-lights gathered in the holes and recesses that honeycombed the eroded limestone, glowing a sickly green wherever one of the trespassers got close. Sunscryer thought he saw the flicker of a haggard female face in a few of the holes, but he said nothing.

'Ho!' called Bernhardt, pointing at the gravel-strewn muck that formed a crossroads with the path they were following. Neftep halted the Luminark, the men milling around it. 'Them's recent tracks,' continued Bernhardt, pointing to the faint shapes of horseshoes in the scree. The path led deeper into the maze of tombs, its edges delineated by the parallel grooves of a heavier carriage, a cart or similar construction that had passed that way not too long ago. A muddle of bare footprints cropped up in between the dusty ruts, some of which were clearly missing toes.

'Reckon them's dead men's feet,' said Bernhardt.

No one contradicted him.

'Well then,' said Sunscryer. 'That's where we're headed.'

The expedition changed direction, hauling the Luminark around and fol-lowing the tracks that Bernhardt had spotted as they wound further into Vargravia's grave-dotted wastes. A scattered rearguard loitered at the back, absently testing the swords and cudgels they had acquired over the last few weeks. Tombstones and mausoleums broke the rolling mounds at irregular intervals, some of which yawned open to the sky as if waiting to be filled.

'Look at that one, Ferd,' said Long Cobb, pointing at a gravestone. 'That's one with your name on it there.'

'Sigmar's guts, you're right enough – Ferdinand Lessner. That's today's date an' all.'

Nearby, a starveling raven perched on the statue of a sightless angel, cawing softly. Its beady eyes gleamed green in the twilight as it followed the trespassers' progress. Worms writhed in the rot at their passage.

'Come to think of it, Breck, that's yer actual proper name on that one, isn't it? Johann Breckner?'

Breckner made the sign of Morr over his heart. 'Not funny, Ferdy.'

Big Delf took a swig from his wineskin and stared back at the men behind him, his eyes narrowed. 'Oi, Cobb. You heard what the old man said back there. Shut your bleeding traps.'

'You shut yours, Delf Cook, or I'll shut it for you.'

'Hey!' shouted Bernhardt, leaning around a scattering of twisted trees to look back at the rearguard making their way through the graves. 'You lot at the back. Don't think I can't hear you natterin' away.'

'Yeah yeah,' called out Delf, giving Bernhardt a two-fingered salute. 'Here,' he whispered, pointing a chubby finger at a statue-crested mausoleum to the east. 'Look at that one, the big one there with the torch. 'Here lies Jovi Sunscryer.' Ain't that the name of his holiness himself?'

'Damned if I know,' said Lessner.

'Bloody hammer,' swore the fat man. 'I'm having second thoughts about all this. I keep expecting to see a stone with 'Delf' on it and my first wife lurkin' at the bottom, all rotted up.'

'Shut yer gabbin', Cook. Bernhardt's already pissed off at us,' said Long Cobb. 'And for Sigmar's sake, stop sayin' out names.'

Bernhardt led the expedition forwards as it made its way further into the peaks, climbing higher and higher by the hour. A thick mist had begun to coalesce around the tombstones and shattered statuary, white as a shroud and cold to the touch. Through a combination of leading by example and occasional accusations of cowardice Bernhardt was just about keeping discipline amongst his men, though it was just as much through their fear of turning back alone as it was through drunken bravado.

Up ahead, the wizard Sunscryer was fiddling with the lenses of his wagon's glass contraption, turning screws and tweaking iron rods. His assistants were chanting quietly, eyes rolled back in their heads. Must be the way wizards prepare for trouble, Bernhardt mused. He could practically taste the tension in the air.

'Weapons up, I think, lads,' said the big man, coming to a halt. He took a swig from his wineskin and rolled his shoulders. The soft but insistent tang of Estalian brandy filled his mouth, making him glad he had brought something stronger than wine. The militiaman tested the edges of his swords against one after another before adjusting the tension on his crossbow and sighting down its length on a fanged skull half-buried in the dirt.

When Bernhardt looked back up the mist ahead was winding upwards, twisting and writhing as if alive. As he watched, it coalesced into a series of man-sized shapes, beggar-thin and clad in wisps of smoke.

'All right lads, blades up!' he shouted, dropping his wineskin and drawing his swords. 'Look lively and hit 'em hard!'

There was a thin shriek and a dozen gheists came forward, ectoplasm trailing like the clothes of drowning men. Bernhardt raised his crossbow and shot one in the face. It passed straight through the apparition's misty skull as if there was nothing there at all.

A gurgling scream came from Bernhardt's left as a robed spectre rose up from an open trench and plunged its blackened claws into Bruger Steick's chest. Blood bubbled from Steick's mouth as he toppled sidelong into the yawning grave that bore his name on its tombstone. Derrick Vance thrust

a spear through the creature's torso as it passed. The crow's foot strapped
to its shaft tore away a scrap of ectoplasm, but the blow achieved little else.

Bernhardt took a step forward and thrust his lucky blade through the neck
of the creature drifting after Richter Swartz. It tore away the gheist's head,
but the body kept on going, wrapping its long arms around Swartz's neck
like a cloak and bearing him into a half-open tomb with a chilling screech.

All around the militiamen swords slashed into misted limbs and skull-thin
faces. The weapons wielded by the Stirlanders passed right through, their
wildly swinging blades unbalancing their wielders as they flailed ineffectually at the spectres attacking them.

Bernhardt risked a glance behind him, on the verge of making a break
for it. More of the scrawny things were emerging from the graves to their
rear, cutting off any chance of escape. The closest one floated towards the
big man's chest, rictus jaws agape.

'Drop!' came a cry from atop the Luminark.

To their credit every one of the surviving Stirlanders remembered to fall
the ground, eyes covered. There was a sudden flare of light that curved
around in a blistering circle, the heat of its passage burning away the mist
and the gheists with it. Bernhardt could feel it crackle overhead, a wash
of heat and light that reverberated inside him. He risked a glance upward.
Every time the burning flare touched a gheist the damned thing would
crackle and disappear with a whiff of brimstone.

A shocked silence descended as the Luminark completed its circuit.

One by one the surviving militiamen rose to their feet, eyes blinking and
mouths open. There was no sign of any gheists, no living mists, nothing
apart from the Luminark still humming and plinking gently on the path
ahead. Sunscryer's young assistants were applauding politely, the bald
old buzzard himself taking a bow at the rear of the Luminark's lens array.

'Well swap me for a three-eyed fish,' muttered Bernhardt. 'That works
pretty good, then.'

'She is indeed most efficacious,' replied Jovi Sunscryer with a grin. 'But
then I did design her specifically for adaptive banishment in battlefield
conditions.'

'You what?' said Long Cobb, marching up from the rear with his sword
hilt clenched tight. 'Why d'ya wait for four of us to die before you used
the bloody thing?'

'Ah yes, my apologies. Had to harness as much of Hysh's energies as
possible.'

'That wizard talk don't mean nothin' to me,' said Cobb, pointing an accusatory finger. 'Just that you let my mates die. How are we supposed to fight
these bloody things?'

'Aye,' shouted Janosch Velman, stepping up behind Cobb. 'How?'

'With faith,' said Neftep, pointing at the twin-tailed comet symbol emblazoned on Velman's stained surcoat.

'Oh, bloody wonderful,' said Cobb, throwing his sword point-first into the rocky ground.

The unlikely procession wound onwards into the peaks, Bernhardt cursing himself for volunteering to take the lead. Still, it had been the only way to keep the peace after the battle with the gheists. Cobb and his lot were still sullen at the death of their drinking cronies, and Sunscryer seemed intent on making matters worse. Bloody wizards. So fond of their fancy ways.

Something on the path ahead was bothering Bernhardt, nagging at him even more than the atmosphere of chill sinking into his bones. That was it; there was something wrong with the shadows that pooled around each crypt and stone. They were... well, wriggling. That was the best way he could put it. Moving around. The ground underfoot was becoming stranger, too. Up this high in the peaks there should not really be any mud, nor earth to speak of. Yet the ground was soft and yielding, a bit like... well, a bit like meat. Rotten brown meat.

Bernhardt was jolted from his unsettling thoughts by a call of warning from atop the Luminark. He raised his blades, squinting into the mist. A swarm of glowing orbs were up ahead, like the ghostlights they had seen earlier, but moving in pairs, like eyes. They moved with a strange, flowing motion, up and down, back and forth.

The big man stifled a yawn. He decided to sit down on a nearby grave-stone so he could better take stock of the lights dancing up ahead. He puffed out his cheeks as he sat, loosening his belt a bit so it did not bite into his stomach quite so much. These endless paths, they just stretched upwards forever and ever. The lads obviously felt the same, and had taken a break as well. Some of them were already lying down.

Even the old boy and his apprentices were slumped over on their wagon. Everyone needs a rest now and then, thought Bernhardt. Even a big lad like me. In fact, he deserved to have a little bit of a nap. Just to rest his eyes for a moment. No one would blame him making himself a bit more comfort-able. The gravestone had his name on it, after all.

◄ CHAPTER FOURTEEN ►

DEIHSTEIN RIDGE

The Vale of Darkness, 2522

The cries of injured men and the dying Strigany horse nomads punctured the silence as the crusaders gathered for the advance once more. Volkmar stood at the head of the gathered Tattersouls, glowering down the hill as von Korden made his way up the path to the top of Deihstein Ridge. The death toll had been low, comparatively, but tending to the wounded had cost them valuable time.

'And so Ghorst escapes again,' spat von Korden as he approached, his face twisted in barely suppressed anger.

'Even a necromancer has allies,' replied Volkmar, emerging from the lee of the war altar. 'We cannot afford any more delays. We need to stay on track, find the von Carstein. Your friend Ghorst's carriage-ruts will likely lead us straight to him.'

'Unlikely,' scoffed the witch hunter. 'The necromancer may be slow but he's not a fool. Plus a few dozen peasants have taken their wagons along this road since he passed. Tracking Ghorst's cart won't be so easy.'

'In that case, there's someone you should meet. Come.'

Volkmar turned and walked back to the leeward side of the war altar, von Korden behind him. In the shadow of the towering carriage, Gerhardt the Worm was keeping guard over a slumped form covered head to toe in mud.

The Strigany sharpshooter was bound hand and foot, a hessian rag stuffed in his mouth. His matted hair stuck out in all directions, and his leg was bloody where a spar of bone poked through. He glared fiercely at Volkmar as the old man approached, shouting muffled curses into the cloth.

'Gerhardt the Worm's underclothes,' explained Gerhardt the Worm, grinning wildly.

'Charming,' said Volkmar. 'Right. Von Korden, you like this sort of thing. Get some answers out of our guest here – who he works for, where his master is. Kaslain, keep your eyes open. I'm going to get the crusade up and ready to move as soon as you've procured the answers we need.'

'Of course, my lord,' said Kaslain, bowing his head as Volkmar departed.

Von Korden squatted down in the muck, pulling the Strigany up by the throat and pushing him against the wheel of the war wagon. Kaslain stood next to them as still as a statue, his face impassive. The witch hunter grinned with all the mirth of a corpse, ripping out the dirty cloth between his captive's teeth and squishing his bloodied cheeks together with a pinch of his gauntleted hand.

'We both know you're going to talk, so I'll let you keep your lips,' he said. 'For now.'

The Strigany let fly a complex curse, his bloody spittle pattering into von Korden's face. Without taking his gaze from the nomad's, the witch hunter grabbed hold of the bone sticking out of his captive's leg and twisted it, eliciting a howl of pain.

'I'm going to gouge your eye out with your own shinbone,' hissed von Korden over the nomad's screams. 'What do you think of that?'

'No!' shouted the Strigany. He looked up at Kaslain, eyes wide. 'Get maniac away! I talk!'

'Back off, von Korden,' said the Arch Lector, solemnly.

The witch hunter moved away, his face as dark as sin.

'Right,' said Kaslain, arms folded. 'Where is he?'

'Who?'

'You know who.'

'Pale count? He... He in Konigstein...'

'Von Korden, the knives this time, please,' said Kaslain, turning away. Von Korden stepped forward, sharpening his filleting knives against each other with a metallic chime.

'No! No, the count... He is with wing-devils.'

'Wing-devils?' repeated von Korden, sharply. 'The Devils of Swartzhafen?'

'No, Empire man,' croaked the Strigany, teeth bared in a bloody smile. 'Konigstein.'

'Swartzhafen. His eyes tell it,' said the witch hunter, drawing a pistol from his surcoat and shooting the Strigany in the forehead in one smooth motion. Getting to his feet, he broke into a loping run down the ridge towards his Talabheimer escort.

'Up! We march to Swartzhafen, right now!'

Kaslain shook his head in sadness. Touching his chest with the Reikhammer's head, he knelt down in the mud, intoning a prayer to Sigmar as he closed what was left of the nomad's eyes.

CHAPTER FIFTEEN

THE HIDDEN NECROPOLIS

Vargravia, 2522

A strangled cry came from behind, startling Bernhardt from his daze. One of them young wizard idiots, he thought. Probably worth a look.

The big man blinked away the clouds in his mind, and turned his head in the direction of the lens wagon. A white giant was looming out of the mist, ragged and corpse-like. It was so large the weird machine barely came up to its waist. It swung a fist the size of a barrel at the slumped-over wizard on the back plate. That will kill the old buzzard right enough, Bernhardt thought idly.

There was a sudden blaze of light, and something blurred around the bald wizard's neck. Bernhardt watched as a glowing yellow shape floated out and caught the giant's fist. The old man's ghost, he thought, or something like it. Fighting with that giant.

'Looks like it's winning, an' all,' he murmured to himself.

'Huh?' said Cobb, sitting up next to him and picking gravel out of his cheek.

'That glowy thing. Is' tearin' bits off that giant. Look.'

Sure enough, the golden figure that had emerged from Sunscryer's robes was ripping great chunks of dead flesh and rotten bone from the giant's frame. A second later the white monstrosity just fell apart, and the golden figure had vanished. The old man Sunscryer was up, now, pointing past Bernhardt and shouting some of his complicated wizard words.

There was a sudden flash of light, and as one, the militiamen spasmed from their trance. Bernhardt jumped up with a roar, shaking off the bony arms that had reached through the cold earth below him to grasp at his shoulders. He ran over to his men and yanked them to their feet, Cobb at his side. Together they kicked away the skeletal limbs and leering skulls that had been grasping and gnawing at their fallen comrades. One by one, the men regained their feet, stamping the bones back into the dust.

'What the bloody hell just happened?' said Delf, his jowls shivering.

'S-s-site spell,' said Khalep.

'Indeed,' added Sunscryer, straightening his robes. 'Somewhat embarrassing, really. If it weren't for my little helper I think we might all be dead as hobnails.'

'What helper?' asked Bernhardt, struggling to comprehend what had just happened. 'That glowing thing? I thought that was your soul or something.'

'Dear me, no! What you saw was a light-djinn, a kind of elemental.'

'You're a kind of mental,' grumbled Cobb, brushing grave dirt from his jerkin. Bernhardt shot him a look as Jovi continued on. 'It was bequeathed to me by a gifted but impractically rotund magus I befriended during my studies in El Khabbath,' said the wizard. 'We have mutual enemies in the von Carstein dynasty. But never mind all that. Shall we press on?'

'Let's,' said Bernhardt sourly.

The Templehof expedition wound through the hidden necropolis of Vargravia. Still the hoofprints and cart ruts guided them, though the darkness was thickening. Bernhardt turned to face the rest of the Goat's finest, trudging through the scree like condemned men heading towards a gallows. The taint of something foul hung in the air, a vile aftertaste on the back of each breath that promised evils yet to come.

Something writhed beneath Bernhardt's boot. It was a thick, serpentine mass buried in the meaty earth, like a root, or a vein. Numbness spread up his leg, making his hands shake. Behind him, Derrick Vance went down with a cry, his habitually bare feet turned shocking crimson by a writhing mass of root-veins. Vance's comrades rushed to help him, attempting to pull him free, but it was too late. Blood pooled in the hollow where his feet had been burrowed into by the vampiric roots. The rest of his lifeless body was white and pale.

'To hell with this. We should go,' said Bernhardt. 'Get out of here fast, before any more of us get killed.'

'I think you might be right, at that,' said Sunscryer, biting his thumbnail and looking back the way they had come.

'M-m-master!' gummed Khalep, pointing at a break in the mist. 'Isn't that the m-m-manse?'

Sure enough, the domed top of a ruined manse was silhouetted against the rough glow of Morrslieb. It poked through the mist, its scrying scope glinting like a cyclopean eye. Its rough bricks were limned with a greenish tinge that emanated from behind the ramshackle building.

The expedition had reached the heart of Vargravia.

Gritting his teeth, Bernhardt boosted himself up onto the plinth of a nearby monument and peered into the mists. The manse was less than thirty yards away from him. Behind it he could just about make out something glowing a sickly green in the fog.

As he squinted, the thing seemed to resolve itself in greater detail. It looked like an ornate construction of black ironwork gates welded closely together, or perhaps a set of fused bones melded to look like a cage. It was glowing from within. Mounted on a series of carved stone slabs, the dark cage contained a shackled casket that positively thrummed with power. It hurt Bernhardt's mind even to look at it.

The militiaman closed his eyes tight, but the after-image was still there, dancing behind his eyelids – the negative image of casket, its purplish glow encasing a hand of purest black.

At the fore of the strange construction was a lectern made from a human corpse that held a giant grimoire upon its back. The tome's pages crackled with tendrils of purest darkness as they flapped back and forth. As Bernhardt watched, a gaunt figure rose up from the stonework and loomed over the book, his hissing syllables cutting through the mist. Low moans came from all around the expedition. The Stirlanders formed up tight, blades held ready.

'That's... no, it can't be...' said Sunscryer softly, peering into the mist. 'That's an unholy reliquary, it has to be!'

'Whatever it is, there's a black hand inside the middle of it,' said Bernhardt, grinding his fists into his eyes. 'I can't stop seeing it.'

'There is!' Jovi hissed in triumph. 'The book, the hand... I was right, Neftep! That cage holds the reliquary of the Great Necromancer himself!'

'Surely that disappeared centuries ago, master?' whispered Neftep.

'Yet clearly Mannfred has found it! That tome on the front – it's one of the Nine Books of Nagash, my boy. It's where the darkness is coming from!' he crowed. 'It's all powered by the thing inside that reliquary, a casket containing the disembodied claw of Nagash, cut from his wrist at the fall of Nagashizzar! That's what's behind all of this!'

As their necromantic master's name was spoken out loud, the grave-things around the manse rose up as one. A milling swarm bore the reliquary aloft, shrieking loud enough to wake the dead.

'Oh dear,' said Jovi Sunscryer, his hand flying up to his mouth.

Khalep cracked the reins and sent the warhorses surging forward, the war machine juddering in their wake. Something white flashed on the other side of the machine, a brief flurry of lace and long hair that flitted from one grave to the next.

'*Delf Cook*,' came a ragged female voice. '*Lie with me forever.*'

By Bernhardt's side, the fat militiaman clutched at his throat, gasping for air. Something vaporous slid out of his mouth into the mist, and he toppled over, stone dead.

'*Johan Breckner*,' it said. '*Ferdinand Lessner. I claim your souls.*'

Two of the Goat's finest fell to their knees amidst the ranks of their fellows and slumped over, disappearing into holes in the ground that closed over the top of them like mouths.

Barely a few feet away a worm-eaten visage surrounded by a mass of floating black locks pushed out from the side of a slab of stone. The apparition stared straight at the knot of militiamen, cold malice bleeding from its empty sockets. The nearest Stirlanders cried out and lurched backwards, features twisted in shock.

'Jonas Cobb. Rest with me in eternity.'

The tall halberdier's eyes rolled up into his head before he fell over in a heap, his polearm clattering to the ground.

'Bloody well do something!' shouted Bernhardt up to the wizards. 'That's Nell! She's killing us!'

He fired a crossbow bolt straight at the ghastly spectre's head. It pinged off the rock behind, spinning off into the mist.

'What, sorry?' shouted the figure on the lens deck of the receding Luminark, cupping his ear.

At the sound of his voice, the ghost of Emmanuelle von Templehof turned to face the old wizard, arms outstretched.

'Jovi Sunscryer,' it said, tendrils of darkness pouring out from its mouth. *'Die.'*

CHAPTER SIXTEEN

ARFEIT/SWARTZHAFEN BORDER

Vale of Vain Hope, 2522

The crusade had made good time across the fordable point of Unterwald River and pressed on with its forced march, von Korden striding determinedly at their head. The witch hunter had not spoken a word nor slowed in the slightest since the battle against the Strigany at Deihstein Ridge. Every iota of his deadly conviction was focused on finding his quarry, and anyone who hailed him was met only with stony silence.

Volkmar, by contrast, was blinking away exhaustion. Flashes of memory from Fort Oberstyre assailed him whenever he closed his eyes, and the war altar was juddering along at such a pace it was impossible to get any kind of rest. The Tattersouls, having picked up on the urgency in the air, were chanting and lashing themselves with even more zeal than usual, some of them even breaking into short runs when their fervour overflowed.

The Grand Theogonist looked back through the thinning light at his unsteady flock. He did not know whether to be reassured or disturbed by their manic energy. He was sure they had grown in number since the crusaders had passed the refugee train. For a second, he thought he could make out the peasant with the cleft lip they had talked to, trailing at the back with his wife. They gabbled strange syllables and tore at their hair, eyes rolling.

'Sigmar! Sigmar through the Great Fires!' shouted Gerhardt the Worm, grinning up at Volkmar. 'Plunge through the Great Fires and transcend to the world of glory!'

The Grand Theogonist muttered a prayer to the Heldenhammer and turned back to the road. Keeping this pace was madness. He wanted to sleep for a week, a year, maybe even to just lie down forever. But the trail was still warm, and Sylvania needed him still.

An hour of hard slog later, the steepled roofs of Arfeit hove into view. There were still a few windows with light in them, and the promise of decent beds. The town's protective border of stakes bore many a corpse, each in a different stage of decomposition. Ravens picking at strings of decaying flesh stopped their feast to look up at the vanguard's approach, cawing in disapproval. Arfeit was a defensible position without a doubt, and potentially a vital night's sleep for the soldiery.

'No time!' shouted von Korden from the front of the marching column.

Volkmar's shoulders sank down. 'He's right,' he said in answer to Kaslain's questioning stare. 'We press on.'

Dawn should have arrived by now, even by the shallow standards of the last few days. Volkmar could taste the morning dew in the air, mouldy and chill. Yet the skyline remained as grey as a month-old corpse.

Up ahead the vanguard had spotted the von Swartzhafen mansion, its ruined and slouching walls a patch of pitch black on the horizon. Already the war altar had passed statuary and shattered stonework, and the decaying vegetation that had been lining the road had thinned out to sparse brown twigs. As the ground opened out Volkmar could see something else up ahead, barring their path. At this distance it appeared no more than a thin white line in the mist.

Volkmar looked up, his eye caught by motion from the mansion's tower. Morrslieb's wan glow broke through the clouds for a moment, and bat-winged things were illuminated in silhouette.

'Fan out and form up,' called Volkmar, his voice strained. Several of the Talabheimer men turned questioning looks in his direction. 'Just do it!' he shouted. 'Now!'

The ragged crusade spread out, taking advantage of the open ground in front of Swartzhafen's gates. A low cry cut through the air, a sound that a living man could not have made. Blades were drawn, but kept low.

In the distance, a bell tolled.

Von Korden span around to look straight at Volkmar, an expression of wild bloodlust in his eyes. Turning back, he signalled his Talabheimer escort to move forward, waving Bennec Sootson's cannon crew up the field on the right. The state troops obeyed with surprising speed, hustling forwards towards the distant gates.

'You faithful,' said Volkmar, motioning to the Tattersouls below. 'Forward, and fast.'

CHAPTER SEVENTEEN

THE HIDDEN NECROPOLIS

Vargravia, 2522

'I can't hear you, I'm afraid, lads!' bellowed Sunscryer as he trundled away from the shouting Stirlanders. 'Candle wax in the ears! Just in case Whispering Nell makes an appearance!'

Dropping his swords and roaring in desperation, Bernhardt snatched something from his coat pocket and flung himself straight at the female gheist that was drifting around them. A small knot of his men charged after him. Militiamen thrust their spears and blades into the midsection of the gaunt horror, but they passed straight through. Bernhardt's brawler instincts took over, his left jab passing straight through the gheist's maggot-chewed face. Quick as a daemon his right hook came around in a haymaker punch that connected hard, tearing the hideous thing's skull into a scrap of diffusing ectoplasm. There was a dwindling screech as the apparition sunk into the ground, mist roiling in her wake.

'How in Sigmar's name?' said Janosch Velman, coming up to Bernhardt's side.

'Not Sigmar,' said Bernhardt, unfurling his fist to expose a pair of smoking pfennigs. 'Morr.'

Up ahead, the horses pulling the wizards' contraption into the lee of the tumbledown manse struggled to make it the last few yards to the highest point of the peak. Bernhardt led his men in a loose run towards it, heedless of the ghastly faces roiling in the mist. High up at the manse's dome, a glowing figure was wrestling free the scrying lens at the end of the astromancer's telescope, bearing it down and angling it above the Luminark so that it glowed in sympathy with the glass discs ranged along the machine's length. As Sunscryer shouted an arcane phrase of staccato syllables, a stuttering light shone out across the peaks – weak at first, then with increasing stridency – until the necropolis was lit with the strobing of the Luminark's distress call.

The Stirlanders had reached spitting distance of the glowing Luminark when the air was split by a hideous screech. A group of hooded, flaming wraiths rode out from the wall of the ancient manse, their skeletal steeds passing straight through the rear carriage of the arcane war machine and heading down the scree towards the militiamen. The wraiths held their burning scythes high as they drove through the Stirlanders' ranks, sweeping their blades low to cut into the men that flailed ineffectually at the flanks of the undead horses. The strange hooked scythes of the apparitions did not cut the flesh of their targets, instead passing straight through them. The wraiths galloped on, and five militiamen fell lifeless to the ground as if every tendon in their bodies had been severed at once. The rider-gheists wheeled around for another pass, screeching wildly as the unnatural green flames around them burned bright with stolen energy.

'The Wind of Hysh repels you!' shouted Jovi Sunscryer, standing on the riding plate of the Luminark and gesturing fiercely at the strange apparitions. The skies flashed white, and two of the wraiths were obliterated by lances of energy that darted from the gloom.

A second later a latticed net of light flickered into existence in front of the remaining wraiths. They galloped right into it and were held fast in the air, the strange magical trap curling around them as it threw dancing shadows everywhere. The fell creatures screamed curses in a language that Bernhardt did not understand, though the wizards were shouting louder and louder in a repetitive chant that sounded suspiciously similar.

There was a chime of glass as Khalep swung the apparatus around, releasing a searing blast that burned straight into the trapped wraiths. When Bernhardt blinked away his shock, the figures were no longer there, and the echoes of their dismayed shrieks were fading away to nothing.

Bernhardt breathed a shallow sigh of relief until he realised that the men guarding the far side of the Luminark were crying out in pain. Two of them staggered back in horror as a robed grave-gheist rose out of a nearby tomb and cut them open to the spine with its long, hooked scythe. The big man darted through the gravestones towards them, only to see a contorted knot of militiamen sinking in on themselves, their flesh darkening like fruit succumbing to a season's rot in the space of a few heartbeats.

Drifting towards the dying men was the ironbone reliquary that Bernhardt had seen rise into the air upon their arrival. Ghostly forms whipped around it, bearing it forward at a slow but inevitable pace. The ropes of black energy that crackled around the casket at its heart reached out, extending like the tentacles of some undersea nightmare. At their caress, Stirlanders blackened to skeletal ash and blew away, scattered by ethereal winds that caressed Bernhardt's sweating forehead with the chill of the grave.

'Run! Get out of here!' he shouted. 'It's hopeless! We're all dead! We're all dead!'

He sank to his knees, gibbering in misery and gouging at his eyes in an effort to remove the stain that the black claw inside the casket had seared into his sight. It was no use. It was still there, and getting bigger and more oppressive by the moment.

'Run...' he said, weakly, but everyone else had already fled.

The howling of gheists grew louder and louder as the cadaverous guardians of the claw rode slowly towards Bernhardt, their glowing blades raised for the kill. The militiaman's head was torn upwards by an invisible grip, and was slowly turned around so he could fully appreciate the majesty of his oncoming doom.

Just as the reliquary filled his whole world, a blinding bolt of energy speared out from the lee of the manse, blasting into the stone carriage of the palanquin. A deafening, mind-numbing shriek of anguish rose up into the night as the magic binding the reliquary was shredded. The sound was like a thousand tortured souls all screaming themselves hoarse at once. It looked to Bernhardt's addled perception as if the hellish thing was dissolving, shimmering into a river of greenish mist that wound away into the darkness like a serpent's ghost.

The last thing he saw before he fell unconscious was the Luminark shuddering after it in pursuit, a trio of haggard wizards hanging grimly onto its wrought-iron chassis.

CHAPTER EIGHTEEN

SWARTZHAFEN

Foothills of the Broken Spine Mountains, 2522

The crusade's men, gathered into as tight a battle line as the outskirts of Swartzhafen would allow, padded through the darkness towards the settlement's wrought-iron gates. Once a rich town jealously guarded by the reclusive nobleman that lived in its mansion, Swartzhafen had fallen into decay. Much of its defensive perimeter had been torn down by nameless assailants. As the mist thinned, Volkmar saw that another line of defence had been raised up, one far more dangerous than a mere gate.

Dozens of dead peasant bodies were packed tight in each of the gaps in Swartzhafen's walls, some still clothed in flesh and rags, some no more than mouldering bone. They were caught in mid stumble as if they had been abandoned by time itself. Dead wolves dotted the fore of the corpse army, frozen still as they prowled. Stretching into the mist by their side was a pack of ghouls, held fast in mid-lope as they had attempted to flank the approaching forces. Behind the gates leered the necromancer, Ghorst, atop his macabre cart. Even he was immobile. The entire tableau was disturbingly still.

With one exception.

At the head of the wall of undeath was a heavily built figure, mounted on the back of a giant stallion-corpse. It was clad in ornate armour, its plates fashioned as an overlapping series of bat wings, and in its gauntleted hands were long, bladed weapons that glowed dully in the gloom. A cloak of blurring shadow-spirits billowed around the figure's shoulders, their tiny skeletal mouths open in silent screams.

The figure's face was hideous, a mask of cruelty rendered in dead, dew-slicked flesh. Its hairless grey head tipped backwards as it bared its fangs slowly, cocking a hooked claw and motioning Volkmar to come close.

'He looks like a von Carstein all right, in all that armoured finery,' said Kaslain. 'Wants to parley, by the look of things.'

'Oh, there will be a parley, all right,' spat the Grand Theogonist. 'A parley of blades, and of fire.'

'Old man!' called an ancient, cultured voice through the mist. 'Volkmar of the Hammer, who is called The Grim! Thou hast come to mine gate at last!'

Volkmar ground his teeth. 'That's him. Mannfred,' he growled, the name a bitter curse.

'I wish to discuss matters that thy... common folk need not hear,' said the vampire, motioning dismissively at the state troops taking position opposite him. 'Fools, kindly leave thy master and I to our grandsire's talk.'

Several of the Talabheimers jerked as if they had been burned and made to flee, but their comrades held them fast, slapping them back to their senses and pushing them into the ranks once more.

'Ha! So many true believers,' said Mannfred, his tones appreciative. 'So many thoughtful gifts thou hast brought me, my tired friend. Myrmidians, Sigmarites I see, even Morr's playthings... and a new golden ornament for my halls.' The vampire motioned towards the war altar as if it were no more than a trinket to be easily dismissed. 'I cannot wait to gorge on the blood of the faithful – it has such a distinctive tang. Thine most of all, I am wagering, old man.'

'We come to burn you in the name of Sigmar, fiend, and nothing more,' said Volkmar. 'Your sorcery has no hold over us.'

The von Carstein laughed incredulously, the sound surprisingly human from one so monstrous. 'Thine years have been far from pleasant, old man,' he said, wiping away a tear of blood as his smile faded into a mask of derision. 'Thou art spent. As is thy rabble. The smell of defeat is upon thee. Let me release the strength that flows in thine veins. It is a rare vintage indeed, and I alone know the power it can bring.'

'Fire!' shouted von Korden from the Talabheimer flank.

The vampire snarled a strange syllable in response. A split second later the Hammer of the Witches boomed and a black cannonball streaked straight towards the von Carstein. The vampire exploded in black shadow, coalescing in the cannonball's wake before flying towards the war altar at terrible speed.

'Charge!' shouted Volkmar as the motionless wall of undead suddenly unfroze and poured towards them. 'In the name of all that's holy, charge!

The Silver Bullets opened fire, and a heartbeat later a clutch of frozen ghouls were bowled backwards into the mist. Bounding through the remainder of the troglodytes came eyeless wolves with skin flapping from their jaws. Von Korden could see Ghorst on the far side, his cart's cursed bell tolling loud. The witch hunter growled in disgust as the necromancer chanted his thrice-damned resurrection rite, summoning the dead ghouls back to their feet.

Well, if gunpowder was not enough to keep the undead scum down, he had other ways of dealing with them. The witch hunter peeled back his glove and placed the ivory ring that the wizards had given him against his bare palm. 'Be banished!' he shouted. A triple-headed serpent of light streaked out towards Ghorst's cart like a sinuous thunderbolt.

The necromancer ducked down into his morass of corpses as the spell struck home, blasting apart the infernal bell and setting fire to the carriage's rear. Von Korden gave a short cry of triumph, gesturing for the swordsmen behind to move forward as his attack drew the undead canines in close. When they were only a few feet away, the witch hunter calmly stepped back into the ranks of Sigmar's Sons, their sharpened swords coming together in his wake.

The ghastly wolves leapt forwards just as von Korden had planned, skewering themselves on the Sons' blades in their haste to snap and bite. Two sets of slavering jaws closed down hard, tearing Sigmarite heads from necks as they bore the front rankers down with their rotten weight. One was hacked into pieces as it sprawled amongst them, whilst the other was blasted free by one of von Korden's pistols. The decapitated remains of the wolves' prey fell slowly backwards, spurting blood over the red and white cloth of their comrades' uniforms.

At the insistent tattoo of Redd Jaeger's drum, Sigmar's Sons shouted in unison and stepped forwards, pushing back with shields and stabbing through the gaps into the dead flesh of their assailants. Their frenzy spent, the undead beasts fell apart in a sloughing mass of worm-eaten meat. The Sons stumbled forward, leather shoes and bare feet alike squishing on the remains of their foes.

Cantering out of the darkness of the wooded right flank, the Knights of the Blazing Sun accelerated into a gallop, ploughing straight into the mass of pallid ghoul-flesh that was bearing down on the Silver Bullets. Lances speared sunken chests, and several of the ghouls were pinioned to the peaty earth, never to rise again. Frog-like, several of the hunchbacked things leapt up at the cavalrymen as they rode past. Their filthy claws and needle teeth scratched ineffectually at lacquered black steel before they were shoved roughly away with lance shafts or, in Lupio Blaze's case, dislodged by a visored head-butt.

Von Korden called out a warning as three massive, winged figures fell out of the misted skies and screeched towards the Myrmidian riders. The fiends were huge, their leathery pinions expansive enough to cover a horse nomad's wagon. Vargheists, the Sylvanians called them – lesser von Carsteins who had been altered to a form more pleasing to their elders' desires.

The monsters threw their clawed legs forward as they landed, grabbing at the knights like swooping raptors seizing up vermin. Two of the armoured warriors were plucked from their saddles and borne screaming up into the air. The witch hunter fired a long-range pistol shot, blasting a chunk of hip from the largest of the beasts. The Silver Bullets followed suit, their volley of shot tearing the wing of one of the vargheists and slamming into the torso of another. The wheeling creatures screamed and released their prey, letting their captives drop into the battle below.

One of the falling knights ploughed into the ranks of the Tattersouls, bowling several of them over just as they charged into the corpses shuffling out of the town's broken gates. The momentum of the charging zealots faltered as confusion broke out in their ranks. Some looked in rapturous awe at freshly broken bones, others looked skywards to see if Sigmar himself was throwing down reinforcements.

Scant yards away the corpse-horde lunged from the gates as if propelled by some unseen force, lopsided jaws gnashing and broken hands outstretched. The Tattersouls roared in delight, crying out about the mortification of flesh and the end of days. A handful of their number threw themselves bodily into the mass of corpses with a shout, bearing several of the cadavers to the floor. Their bellies and backs were pulled open by the claws of those undead milling behind, the martyrs dying in bloody agony. Taking advantage of the distraction, the front rank of the Tattersouls whirled their flails skyward and brought them down with crushing force, splitting open heads and tearing arms from bodies.

Still the dead things came on, crowding in. Yellowed teeth sank into tattooed flesh, farm implements jabbed spasmodically, and faithful blood spurted.

'I am Sigmar's Holy Worm!' shouted Gerhardt, his eyes alight with madness. 'Burrow into the grave and out the other side!' He lashed out with his elbows and knees as he looped his bare foot around a fallen flail and flicked it up into a corpse's face. 'Burrow, damn you!' he shouted, pushing his thumbs through the milky white eyes of another gnashing corpse and pulling its head free in a curving spray of grave-fluids. He used the disembodied head to smash another corpse-puppet's head clean from its neck. 'Burrow like a worm!'

Calmly reloading his pistols on the right flank, von Korden took stock of the mayhem unfolding around him. To the left he could see a mass of stalking bone emerging from the mists and charging into the Hammer of the Witches, rusted blades raised. The war machine's crew valiantly defended their cannon for a moment before stumbling back into the woods, unintentionally exposing the flank of the Sons. The swordsmen he had left in order to close with Ghorst were too preoccupied to notice, fighting hard against the mismatched wolves that had somehow pieced themselves back together and attacked with renewed vigour.

Up above, the vargheist servants of the vampire were falling once more upon the sun-worshipping Myrmidians in a strange vertical battle that the knights were ill suited to fight. Through the tumbled gates of the town's border, yet more corpses were staggering towards them through the mist. All around the battle hung in the balance, but it was the scene at the war altar that made bile lurch up into von Korden's throat.

The Sigmarite war machine had ploughed forward so far into the ranks of the corpse-horde that it had become swamped, its wheels jammed with tangled limbs and dead flesh. Worse still, the vampire von Carstein had left his incorporeal steed and had leapt onto the pulpit of the great chariot. He was hunched over in a duellist's crouch less than a few feet away from Volkmar. Von Korden watched in incredulity as the fiend become a blur of motion, his glowing sword looping in a figure of eight to send the old man's sacred warhammer sailing from his grip. The vampire stood up tall, seeming to swell with dark power as wings of shadow blossomed behind him. Von Korden touched his pistols to the Sigmarite symbol hanging around his neck and took careful aim.

Volkmar's fists flared white as he roared forward, staggering the beast with a blast of pure faith as he roared the First Catechism of Banishment. Mannfred fell back, weapons tumbling from his twitching hands. The count's cloak of screaming souls whipped out at the Grand Theogonist's face, driving him back in turn. Von Korden took his chance, hot silver flashing out as he fired with both pistols at once. Blurring downward, the vampire dodged behind the war altar's lectern, claws clacking onto its topmost ledge. Yet the shot had bought Volkmar time. As the undead count hoisted himself upward to attack once more, Volkmar grabbed a solid-gold skull from the pulpit's lectern shelf and brought it crashing down onto Mannfred's bald pate.

Screeching, the vampire fell backwards from the war altar only to catch the balustrade and channel his momentum into a swinging leap. He vaulted over the pulpit and kneed Volkmar back against the war altar's Golden Gryphon in one lightning-fast lunge. Weaponless, the von Carstein wrenched a length of ironwork frame from the timber of the war altar's pulpit with a single claw, lifting it high to strike the Grand Theogonist down.

Suddenly a hundred screams filtered through the air from the east of the vale, chilling in their intensity despite being on the very cusp of hearing. Mannfred looked at the Vargavian Mountains on the horizon with an expression of utter shock before launching backwards off the pulpit. He landed with impossible grace, crouched like a Strigany horseman upon the saddle of his deathless mount.

The undead beast reared, hooves flailing, before thundering off eastwards at a pace no mortal steed could hope to match. In the murky mists above the battlefield, the vargheists abandoned their bloody persecution of Blaze's knights and winged off into the night after their master.

'Forge onwards!' coughed Volkmar desperately, regaining his feet. 'Don't let them escape!'

His men gave a great roar and plunged into battle with renewed vigour, cutting down the slumping bodies of their suddenly listless foes. Within less than a minute, there was nothing left of the undead army that was not covered by ankle-deep mist.

Yet it had all been for nothing. Mannfred was gone.

CHAPTER NINETEEN

THE STERNIESTE ROAD

South of the Vale of Darkness, 2522

The Sigmarite crusade staggered along the peaty road that led to Castle Sternieste, its limps, groans, and a general blood-splattered appearance giving it an uncomfortable resemblance to the undead army it had narrowly overcome at Swartzhafen. The war altar rolled along at its head, Volkmar standing braced against the lectern as he murmured the words of one of the carriage's holy tomes. A few yards in front of him was von Korden, hunched almost double as he tracked a set of distinct hoofprints pressed at great intervals into the earth. Mannfred had headed east at great speed, though none of them knew quite why.

Arch Lector Kaslain was in the midst of the throng, spurring the men on with fiery imprecations and speeches to the glory of Sigmar. Volkmar had meant to attend to morale himself, but at the moment he just didn't have the fire to be convincing. He had busied himself with cleansing the altar of the vampire's touch instead. It was likely futile, said a despairing voice in Volkmar's soul. Exhausted and with many of their number badly wounded, they likely marched to their deaths. The men knew it, and in his heart, so did he.

Yet there was no choice.

'Your honour? A word?' came a deep but respectful voice from below.

Volkmar looked down to see Eben Swaft, the duellist leader of the Talabheimer swordsmen he had fought beside in the north, walking alongside the war altar with sword drawn.

'Swaft, well met,' said Volkmar. 'One moment.'

The Grand Theogonist made the sign of the hammer over the *Tome Unberogen* on his lectern, concluding the reconsecration ritual before making his way down the carriage and dropping down next to Swaft on the road. His knees spiked with pain, but he tucked it away with the rest of his burdens at the back of his mind.

'We can't keep on at this pace, your honour, if at all. We've got limbs falling off back there.'

'I realise that, Eben,' sighed Volkmar. 'We can't rest, though. Not when we are so close. One well-placed cannonball and this will all be over.'

'With respect, your honour, the bastard could be miles away by now,' said Swaft, fingering the tip of his blade. 'Our men are dying. We need to stop.'

'Kaslain has it in hand,' said Volkmar crossly, screwing shut his eyes to shut out the pleas coming from the rear of the column.

'Aye, the arch lector's worked miracles back there, true enough. Temporary ones, though. We need sleep. More than that, we need hope.'

'No sleep. We press on.'

A moment's silence passed between the two men before Swaft spoke again.

'You and the witch hunter ain't so different after all, are you, your honour?'

Volkmar spun round in the mud, eyes aflame. His fists were raised in front of his heaving chest and his chin jutted out under his quivering moustache, giving him a distinct resemblance to a dockyard prizefighter from the Time of the Three Emperors.

'That's more like it, old man,' said Swaft with a nasty grin, sheathing his blade and rolling up his sleeves.

'You will address me with the proper respect,' snorted Volkmar, 'or I shall teach you some, here and now.'

'Fine, then,' replied Swaft. 'I can punch some fire back into you if that's the way it has to be.'

A cry of surprise and joy came from the rear of the procession, startling Volkmar and Swaft into a stalemate. Their altercation forgotten, they both rushed to the rear of the war altar, scanning the road behind. Over the crest of the hill a pair of banners fluttered in the wan light, proud and clean against the sky. One of them bore the red cruciform of the Reiksguard, the other royal colours of Karl Franz's court.

Volkmar watched in stunned silence as two brigades of Altdorf's finest cavalry crested the hill. All around him, the crusaders broke formation and rushed to new vantage points, filled with new energy at the prospect of good news. The wounded and their minders stayed behind, taking advantage of the interruption to tend dressings and re-bind broken bones.

First to ride up to the crusade were eight of the Reiksguard, Karl Franz's personal elite. Their red-feathered crests bobbed bright above burnished silver plate that had been engraved with scenes of the Emperor's greatest triumphs. From the vanguard of the crusade, Lupio Blaze called out in greeting, his lance raised high. At the head of the Reiksguard, Hans Zintler took off his helmet and saluted a response, his men raising their own lances in parade ground unison.

The only regiment that could claim equal status with the Reiksguard was the Royal Altdorf Gryphites, and they were not far behind. Three muscular veterans resplendent in shining steel tilted their cavalry halberds in salute to Volkmar as they approached. They were mounted on demigryphs, towering Drakwald monsters that were half eagle, half lion. They too were armoured, their powerful wingless haunches and barrel chests protected by finest Altdorf steel. One of the demigryphs barked a few bursts of aggressive avian noise before lowering its vicious beak and plucking at a roadside corpse.

'Lord Volkmar!' said Hans Zintler as the Reiksguard approached. 'Karl Franz sends his best wishes, and eight of his finest swords. Also Richter Weissmund, no less,' fiddling with his moustache as he nodded at his opposite number in the Gryphites.

Weissmund thrust the butt of his cavalry halberd into the mud and made the sign of Sigmar, bowing his head.

'Grand Theogonist.'

'Captain Weissmund. You and your noble beasts are a sight for sore eyes.' said Volkmar.

'That's no way to talk about the Gryphites, sir,' said Zintler, a wry gleam in his eye.

'We lost nine good men to the Drakwald tribes in the last week, Zintler,' said Captain Weissmund, grimly. 'You would do well not to joke of men that act as beasts.'

Zintler inclined his head in half-hearted apology.

'We answered your summons, your honour,' Weissmund continued. 'Where is the enemy?'

'My summons?' said Volkmar.

'The message from the brass sentinels, your holiness,' replied Zintler. 'The Emperor got a message several days back, sent from Konigstein Watch. Well, we're the reinforcements you asked for, sir. We damn near killed our horses getting here, but there's fight in them yet.'

Weissmund gave a derisory snort. His demigryph started at the noise, a growl in its feathered throat as it looked around for something inhuman to kill.

'I have no idea what you're talking about, Zintler, but I'll be honest – I'm thrilled to see you here. My thanks to Karl Franz,' said Volkmar. 'You two realise who we're hunting?'

'Aye,' said Weissmund, gruffly. 'The von Carstein. So what are we waiting for?'

'Hold on a moment, captain, if you please,' said Zintler. 'Your holiness, may I present to you the Sunmaker.'

The leading Reiksguard opened their ranks with dressage precision to reveal the last two riders amongst their number. Each of their warhorses was yoked to a contraption of tubular rockets and ironwork structures built on top of a wheeled artillery carriage that faced backwards down the road. Its Talabheimer crew stepped off their perches on the carriage and saluted smartly.

'A Helstorm rocket battery, if I'm not mistaken,' said Volkmar. 'Unreliable.'

'Not this one, Grand Theogonist,' said the largest of the crewmen, smugly patting the top of his machine. 'This here's the last work of Jurgen Bugelstrauss. The Sunmaker's not just any Helstorm, your lordship. She'll see you right.'

'Fine, good,' said Volkmar. 'Any help is welcome. But we're wasting time.' He looked down the road to the vanguard, raising his hammer. 'Von Korden!' he bellowed.

'What?' said von Korden, stepping out from behind a twisted oak less than ten yards away.

'Ah, there you are. A message from Konigstein Watch, eh? Good work. I'll excommunicate you for going against my orders when we get back. Get a marching order together fast so we can make the most of our new arrivals. And sound the hunt.'

CHAPTER TWENTY

STERNIESTE

The Vale of Darkness, 2522

Mannfred von Carstein sped along the dirt road on the back of his death-less steed. Dark clouds grumbled above, but no living thing would make a sound. Even chirruping grave beetles fell silent at his approach.

As he cantered the last furlong towards Castle Sternieste, the vampire count bared his fangs in a lipless snarl. Closer to Vargravia than Swartzhafen by far, the castle was a welcome sight. He could feel the reliquary growing closer, and he had plenty of time to marshal his forces before the Child of the Heldenhammer and his fools came knocking. That they would come was beyond a doubt. This phase of the Great Work was almost complete.

Since his cousin Nyklaus von Carstein had met his end in the seas of the Galleon's Graveyard, the shadowy energies drained by his cursed mael-strom had whipped loose across the world. Nyklaus, or Count Noctilus as the traitorous fool had liked to call himself, was never deserving of such power. Since his final demise Mannfred's mastery of the aethyric winds had become more powerful than ever. Simply by clutching a family heir-loom once treasured by his sea-loving kinsman, the count could transform himself and his steed into beings no more substantial than darkness itself.

Yet for Mannfred to leave no sign of his passage would defeat the pur-pose of his flight. Instead he'd pounded every ounce of his stallion's weight into the road that led east to Castle Sternieste, leaving hoofprints that even a blind man could track.

The rolling hillocks that typified the Sternieste countryside punctuated the road in greater and greater number. Each one was a cairn from a bygone age. Mannfred could feel the dull but powerful throb of the dark magic that flowed like a stream into each mound. The lintels above each shadowed doorway had been gouged so badly the original runes were illegible, and the tomb doors lay cracked and mossy on the ground. His Strigany agents had done their work well.

Arms crossed over his ridged breastplate, Mannfred steered his steed through the hillocks with flickers of thought. Slowly, deliberately, it brought him to the burial grounds of the Reavers.

The soaring walls of Castle Sternieste loomed only a stone's throw away. The crumbling citadel was impressive, almost as magnificent a sight as Fort Oberstyre. Though its lightning-blasted towers reached high, the ancient castle had no natural defences like the fortress in the west of Sylvania; no high plateau or deep moat to protect it. No, mused the count, tapping a long fingernail on the armoured collar of his steed. Sternieste's defences were anything but natural.

Mannfred dismounted next to the largest of the cairns, his cruel features set in concentration as he set his glimmering blade on the wilting grass. When he spoke, the syllables crawled out of his mouth as if he were spitting out insects.

'*Nacafareh, Aschigar, vos maloth Nagashizzar...*'

Red eyes glinting, the vampire raised his blade upward, one hand on either end, raising it parallel to the ground until he held it high. His chant was repeated three times, growing to a crescendo that echoed from the walls of the castle.

A few seconds later muffled, grinding sounds emanated from the tombs around him, the chink of metal cutting over the noise of shuffling bone and the rustle of ancient syllables.

One by one the skeletal, heavily armoured forms of the Sternsmen jerked themselves from their rest and stood up straight. Mildewed sockets gaped and scaled armour glinted, flashes of mouldering bone catching rare glimmers of light as Morrslieb peered down approvingly. Half a dozen warriors stood there, then a dozen, then two dozen, then more. Each faced towards Mannfred with its jaws open as if in silent joy.

The largest of the ancient warriors had come from the largest cairn, as was ever the way with the pre-Sigmarite tribes. It wore a high crown of bronze and a tattered cloak of holed green leather that fluttered and snapped in a breeze no mortal man could feel.

A rustling voice rattled in the von Carstein's head as the ancient king turned its empty eyes towards him.

What is thy command, o lord?

'Tarry a little longer, King Verek,' said the von Carstein, 'until the living ones approach. Then cut, and stab, and kill.'

For Sternieste, it shall be done.

The skeletal monarch brought its blade up in jerky salute. Mannfred shook the voice out of his head, breaking his mental bond to the ancient warrior with a snap of thought.

'For Nagash, in fact,' he muttered to the staring wights that stretched into the darkness, 'and, more importantly, for me.'

Von Korden scanned the horizon as Volkmar's crusade heaved the war altar up over the cusp of Licheburg Hill. The Reiksguard and Altdorf Gryphites formed an honour guard on either side – welcome reinforcements at a vital hour. In the distance, Castle Sternieste loomed on the other side of the valley. Its triple towers stuck up like a taloned hand ready to pluck Mannslieb from the dusky night, leaving only its sickly twin to haunt the skies.

Searching the countryside for movement, von Korden silenced the soldiers muttering around him with a sharp word and listened hard for the moans of the waking dead. He thought he saw a flash of light in the hills, but it was gone before he could place it. Only the chink of metal sounded in the distance, impossible to trace with the thin mist distorting the sounds in the valley.

A raindrop plipped onto the brim of von Korden's hat, then another. The witch hunter grimaced. He thought he could see heavy clouds mustering on the horizon, though the darkness made it hard to tell. There was so little light left.

There it was again.

Something was illuminating the thin mist in the valley below, pulsing like a mischievous will-o'-the-wisp. On, off. On-off-on.

Like a signal.

Von Korden grinned wolfishly. This time, the smile reached his eyes.

The crusaders gathered at the base of the cairn-dotted hill, Castle Sternieste a black and forbidding presence up ahead. They could hear the chattering of travellers in the mist ahead, and the jangle of tack. Whatever form these newcomers took, they were alive. No undead creature made that much racket.

'Volkmar!' hissed von Korden, gesturing for the old man to join him on the top of a large and empty cairn. The Grand Theogonist puffed out his cheeks and strode up the hillock, his sacred warhammer held loosely at his side.

Lurching towards them through the misting rain was a flickering machine that very much resembled the Altdorf Luminark, though its lens cannon was longer and more elaborate. It was quite a splendid sight, rivalling the war altar itself in grandeur. Von Korden remembered the first time he saw one being unveiled. Balthasar Gelt had had some choice words to say about the things, at the time. It seemed to the witch hunter that a light-engine would be next to useless in the near-permanent darkness of Sylvania, but the arrival of a battle wizard was not to be turned away, and the Luminark's heavy carriage could ride down a corpse or three if it came to it.

'Ho there!' called out the robed and leathery wizard standing up on the contraption's lens deck. Ranged on the road below him were small knots of dangerous-looking men holding everything from farm implements to crossbows. Amongst them were primitive banners made from tavern signs nailed to timber posts, one bearing the sign of a stylised goat, another a pair of crossed keys, and yet another one a wagon and horses.

'Ho there, friends!' cried the old man.

'A good day for us, it would seem,' muttered Volkmar, turning to von Korden with eyebrows raised. 'The Templehof collegiate. No doubt their presence is the result of that message of yours.'

'Possibly,' said the witch hunter, his expression inscrutable.

'Alberich?' hooted the elderly mage. 'Alberich von Korden? Is that your hat I see gracing that hillock, you horrible old bloodhound?'

Von Korden could just make out two robed apprentices shrinking in embarrassment on the driving plate below. Their master carried on oblivious.

'We're hunting the claw, Alberich! The claw of you-know-who! Mannfred had it hidden in Vargravia!'

'Keep it down, Sunscryer, you'll wake the dead,' said von Korden, scowling.

Behind Volkmar, the crusade was buzzing with rumours and questions. Von Korden listened to the hope build in the tones of the crusade's voices as news of yet more reinforcements spread. He nodded softly despite himself. They might have a chance yet.

At the base of the hillock, the trio of robed wizards dismounted and made their way up towards the Grand Theogonist. A mob of heavily-muscled men came at their back, many of whom von Korden recognised. Militia gathered from villages all over the vale, by the look of it. As the newcomers approached, Volkmar stepped up to von Korden and put his hands on his shoulders, meeting the witch hunter's gaze levelly.

'Forget the excommunication, von Korden,' he said under his breath. 'If this lot make the difference and we take down Mannfred, I'll beatify you instead.'

The crusaders fanned out across the barrows and cairns of Sternieste, its cavalry wing held back in reserve. Volkmar felt determination flare inside him as he watched the riders peel off from the vantage point of his pulpit. Three of the Empire's finest knightly orders at his command, as well as two artillery pieces and a trio of wizards backed up by a core of veteran infantry. Thank Sigmar for human solidarity. With the horsemen, the Light Order and the Stirland militia factored in, the crusade numbered almost a hundred good and faithful men. Plus von Korden, Volkmar added to himself.

The rain that pattered out of the charcoal grey skies was clearly the prelude to something far more severe. The horizon was clustered with menacing black clouds, hanging low in the darkness. Green light flickered in their depths, and every few seconds a threatening rumble rolled across the downs.

Less than a hundred yards away from the crusade movement could be seen in the shadow of the great castle, an indistinct mass of bodies shifting in and out of pitch darkness. Bait, no doubt, thought Volkmar. Well, with a reserve as powerful as his, he intended to plunge right in after it. No better way to get Mannfred to show his hand, and in the process leave himself open to the cavalry reserve's killing strike.

Something dark and huge emerged from the shadow of the castle walls. An armoured rider, his barded skeleton of a steed pawing the mossy ground. When the figure passed into a wan pool of light shed from Morrslieb above, the rider stopped his steed and smiled, rain pattering from his hairless, ridged pate. At this distance, its mouthful of bloodied teeth was a red slash in a white mask.

It was unquestionably Mannfred von Carstein.

'Unberogen!' bellowed Volkmar, sounding the Horn of Sigismund and whipping his altar's warhorses forward. 'Sigmar Unberogen!'

The war cry was echoed by the faithful throng that surged forward across the hilly field. The Tattersouls shrieked and clawed themselves in eagerness to die as the Talabheimer state troops marched forward, faces set in grim masks. Out on the left flank the Luminark clanked onto a low hillock, where its view of the battlefield had been judged optimal by the Light wizards chanting in unison upon its frame.

The clouds overhead rumbled deep, and the Hammer of Witches added its voice to the thunder as rain poured down. Its cannonball shot into the darkness, slamming into the base of the castle and sending a shower of masonry cascading into the milling figures below.

A mass of lurching corpses was lumbering downhill towards the state troops, mouths spilling maggots and twisted fingers clawing the air. To their right, rain-slicked skeletons stop-started their way across the field in sloppy synchronisation.

In the centre of the undead battle line, Mannfred drew something in the air with a long fingernail as a female gheist floated down from the towers above to join him. The vampire pointed at the Tattersouls, mouthing something evil. In the shadow of the war altar's balustrade, the zealots aged decades in the space of seconds. Some of them cried out weakly as they shrivelled, turned grey, and fell away like ash in the rain.

'Sigmar protects!' bellowed Volkmar, slamming his warhammer's head against the metallic frame of the pulpit. The rain turned golden around the Tattersouls for a second, and the curse was lifted, though many survivors were already bent double under the sudden weight of years.

The undead battle line was less than fifty feet away now. The moans of the undead that stalked through the dissipating mist could be heard even above the thunder. Now was the time, thought Volkmar. They could wait no longer.

Volkmar sounded the Horn of Sigismund once more. Behind him, a brace of rockets huffed into the air, fuses crackling. With a tremendous triple bang the artillery volley detonated high above the battlefield, the burning light of its explosions strobing against the slick black brickwork of Castle Sternieste. Their illumination remained as bright as the first detonation as the phosphoric rockets drifted downwards on wide canopies of silk. The luminescence was so bright that it lit the battlefield as clear as a summer day.

'Sigmar!' shouted Volkmar, cracking the war altar's reins as hard as he could and sending the carriage surging forward. Answering his war cry, the entire line of crusaders charged headlong into the wall of undeath coming towards them. The war altar crashed bodily through a mass of skeletal swordsmen, crushing half a dozen to splinters in a second. Volkmar lashed out at skulls and bony wrists below him as the unliving warriors jabbed upward at him ineffectually. To his left the Tattersouls flung themselves into the fray, shattering yet more skeletons with their swinging flails. With the battlefield bright and the fires of righteous ire in their veins, the Sigmarites were cutting down corpses with every strike.

On the right flank, the cavalry thundered around the edge of a cluster of large hillocks to come out at full gallop. They slammed hard into the mass of bodies that boiled out of the lee of the castle, corpse-puppets sent to keep the horsemen from his main battle line. A dozen lances struck home into mouldering torsos, warhorses stamping their hard iron hooves into any that evaded them. Demigryphs screeched as they clawed and slashed and bit, flinging dead meat in all directions. Atop the eagle-headed beasts, Weissmund's Altdorf Gryphites swung their cavalry halberds in great arcs, bisecting cadavers in twos and threes.

Too soon, thought Volkmar hopelessly. The fools had been stalled too soon.

Captain Weissmund's body was ripped into two flailing halves as Mannfred burst out of the shadows and rode past, shearing his sword and his hooked blade through the Gryphite's abdomen in a spray of blood. The Reiksguard knight riding next to him drew his sword and turned with a shout, but the vampire's deathless warhorse swung its heavy skull sidelong into the rider with a clang, unseating him. Mannfred's blade took another Gryphite's head from his neck, the strike so powerful it sheared through without slowing and plunged deep into the throat of its steed. The vampire screeched in ecstasy as hot blood pumped out in great sprays, his ridged black armour stained as crimson as his maw. Lupio Blaze charged at full gallop towards him, lance lowered and a prayer to Myrmidia on his lips. His weapon's tip hit only shadow as Mannfred dissolved into nothingness with a dark and mocking laugh.

Thunder boomed and a streak of green lightning shot out of the clouds, grounding on the highest of Castle Sternieste's open towers. The crackling green bolt did not vanish away, but instead spread into eight smaller fingers; a distorted claw of energy with one fingertip dancing on each of the tower's circle of pillars.

Out from the clouds above came the most terrifying thing Volkmar had ever seen.

Borne upon a palanquin of spectres was an artefact of such eldritch evil it assaulted the mind. Its open lead casket presented the terror of the relic inside to the world. The souls of ancient queens whirled around it, their screams forming a jarring discord that sawed on every nerve at once. The choking stink of mass graves assaulted the nostrils of the Empire line, forcing even Volkmar to gag painfully in disgust. But it was the vision blazing within the reliquary's ironbone cage that offended the senses most of all.

At the heart of the reliquary was a giant taloned hand of purest black, the evil sight clutching at the eyeballs of every living creature that witnessed it. Something about the hand beckoned to Volkmar, making his soul feel filthy and used. A prayer spilled reflexively from the Sigmarite's lips, and the feeling ebbed away.

The militiamen below the reliquary were not so fortunate. As the spectres that bore the palanquin brought their charge lower and lower, the claw's fell energies stripped away the skin, then the muscles, then the tendons of the men underneath it until nothing was left but blood-slicked bone. The gory skeletons shivered and danced before plunging their bony claws into those of their panicked comrades that milled around them or curled into foetal balls.

Up on the hillock, the wizards of the Light Order were screaming their chanted magicks against the storm. Steam smoked from the Luminark's lenses as lances of energy stabbed out again and again at the fleshless horrors stalking towards it. As the reliquary hovered low above the battlefield, the ironwork frame of the Luminark's lens cannon juddered slowly round to point at it instead, the old man at the helm barking ancient syllables and pointing at the casket within.

A flash of white caught Volkmar's eye through the storm as a hideous female gheist appeared next to the Luminark's chanting acolytes. It cupped its hands to the youngest wizard's ears for a second. The apprentice blanched and toppled forwards, dead as a rock. With his demise the wizards' tripartite chant faltered and tumbled to a halt.

Sunscryer cried out in agony as the failed ritual backfired. A moment later he burst into a pillar of white flame so tall it nearly reached the clouds above. Every glass lens in the Luminark shattered at once, its jagged shards raining down onto the screaming acolyte clutching the dead body of his friend on the riding plate below. The human torch that had been Jovi Sunscryer fell burning from the lens deck into the mud with a searing hiss.

Above him, the ghostly palanquin hovered in close, its tortured gheists shrieking in dark joy as they pointed at the reeling figure sizzling in the muck. A cannonball ploughed through their midst, tearing away a few scraps of ectoplasm but slowing them not in the least. The surviving acolyte huddled on the riding plate of the Luminark cried out wordlessly in fear, his skin aging rapidly as the hellish engine grew closer.

Suddenly a bright flare of light burst out from Sunscryer's blackened robes, coalescing to form the upper body of a glowing guardian angel. The giant figure flew upwards towards the reliquary, seizing its ironbone gates and wrestling it backwards whilst the palanquin's ghostly forms shrieked and clawed at its insubstantial flesh.

Volkmar tore his gaze away and shoved a crawling skeleton away from his lectern with the end of his warhammer. Though half a dozen of the ghastly warriors were clambering up the war altar's carriage towards him now, his attention was irresistibly drawn back to the spectacle unfolding atop the hillock. Whilst the luminescent figure was being torn apart by the palanquin's gheists, a trio of ragged zealots had clambered up the chassis of the shattered Luminark. Picking out daggers of wyrdglass with bloodied hands and clasping them between their teeth, the Tattersouls leapt up to grab onto the reliquary's plinth as it hovered above its prey.

Two of the flagellants missed and went flailing down into the skeletons advancing towards them, but Gerhardt the Worm managed to catch an ironbone strut and swing himself up onto the stonework. Gheists plunged through him again and again, wreathing him with unnatural green flame, but the zealot was too deep in his mania to care. He laughed as his flesh crackled and burned, stabbing his wyrdglass shard into the gaunt guardian that hunched protectively over the evil book. The smell of burned meat filled the air as Gerhardt flung his arms around the cowering corpsemaster, the zealot's triumphant scream echoing over the rumble of the storm as emerald fires turned them both to ash.

Though Volkmar and his men were slaughtering the clumsy corpse-puppets wherever they appeared, the unclean things always staggered back to their feet and continued the fight a few moments later. Exertion burned in the Grand Theogonist's arms as he swung his hammer again and again into the clacking skeletons below him. His men were crying out with effort instead of anger now, hacking their heavy blades again and again into dead flesh until their shoulders slumped and their voices gave out. Yet somehow the battle line held.

A cry came from the rear ranks of the Sigmar's Sons, and Volkmar chanced a glance behind their lines. His eyes widened as he beheld dozens of ancient, armoured figures stalk out of the cairn hillocks with rusted bronze blades held high. Behind them mouldering horsemen were emerging through the mist, galloping eastwards at some unspoken command. The ancient tribe formed up on the skeletal king at their centre with uncanny speed and charged, ploughing into the rear of the Talabheimers and their Stirland allies with blades raised.

Eben Swaft bullied his way through the Talabheimer ranks to the rear of his shouting troops, elbowing and stabbing his way past the front rank of armoured skeletons to plunge his blade right into the ancient king's ribcage. Once, twice, three times he jabbed with a fencer's grace. The wight merely stared dolefully at him with its empty eyes before bringing its pitted blade down in a glowing arc. Thunder boomed above them as it cut straight through Swaft's deft parry and sheared off the duellist's head and right arm in a single blow.

The snap of wings sounded, and Volkmar whipped his head around once more to see three bat-like figures drop from their roost underneath a shattered tower. The Devils of Swartzhafen, screeching as they glided low towards him. A skeletal claw clutched at his ankle from the skeletons milling below, and he stamped down hard. By the time he looked back up, the winged vargheists were upon him, kicking him to the floor with their taloned feet. They were huge, filling his vision with their drooling, pointed faces and membranous wings. One of them reached out towards his sacred warhammer and wrenched it out of his grip before dropping it as if it were on fire.

Kaslain fell upon the wing-devils from above, leaping down from his perch atop the Golden Griffon to bring the Reikhammer down in a two-handed strike. The ancient warhammer hit one of the hulking, bat-like creatures right in the nape of the neck, shattering every bone in its torso and pulping it against the altar's iron balustrade. Volkmar kicked its remains away into the skeletons below. At the same time its pack-mate lunged, biting into Kaslain's face with a sickening crunch. Bellowing the Prayer Exalt, Volkmar summoned all of his rage into a white-hot ball and blasted the beast backwards, burning the beast's flesh with the flames of his faith. It screeched and released the arch lector, Kaslain toppling backwards like a felled oak as the wing-devil lurched away on smouldering wings.

Suddenly Volkmar felt something sink into the back of his head, and everything went dark.

In the shadow of an empty cairn, Ghorst stood up to his full height atop his grisly carriage. Two points of burning black energy appeared in his eyes.

'One last time, then, Alberich von Korden,' croaked the necromancer.

Von Korden grabbed a Stirlander militiaman's corpse and hefted it in front of him as twin bolts of darkness crackled out from the necromancer's eyes, blasting the impromptu shield into black wisps of smoke. With his pistols already spent and with no time to reload, the witch hunter picked up a disembodied arm from the ground and sent it spiralling towards the necromancer's head. Taking advantage of the momentary distraction, von Korden darted to the right as the cadaverous cart lurched towards him, swinging himself up into the morass of decomposing bodies held in the upturned ribcage of its chassis. Dead hands clutched at his legs, drawing blood with their bony grip, but nothing could shake the hunter's focus.

Ghorst spat black sparks as he began another spell, but von Korden was on top of him before he could finish it. He grabbed the necromancer's lank hair with both hands and pulled his head down sharply to meet his knee on the way up, crunching teeth and shattering his jaw in a spray of brown blood.

'No more spells for you, Helman,' gloated von Korden. Behind him, several of the cart's passengers clambered up and sank their rotting teeth into his thighs, but the hunter blocked out the pain with an effort of will, pulling out his ivory ring and placing it against his palm. He thrust both hands downward and clamped them over the necromancer's mouth. 'My turn, bastard. Be banished!'

Searing light burst out from Ghorst's eyes, mouth, ears and nose as the energies of the white ring burned him from the inside out. The necromancer spasmed violently, but von Korden held on with grim strength until white cracks appeared across Ghorst's skin and the magical light burned him away completely.

Underneath von Korden's feet the cart sloughed away into a compost heap of rotting flesh and bone. Extricating himself, the witch hunter kissed the cameo hanging around his neck, ignoring the grave-filth that covered his gauntlets.

'That's for you, Lynn,' he murmured.

All around von Korden the battle raged on in the lashing rain. On the hillock behind, the Silver Bullets were firing frantically at a hooded gheist that was drifting towards them with its scythe raised. The handgunners' pinpoint volleys blasted straight through it without effect. Curser Bredt barked a command and the men ripped off the silvered talismans they wore around their necks, reloading and shooting at point-blank range just as the wraith's hooked blade cut down the first of their number. The gheist wailed and came apart as the blessed bullets burst through it. A heartbeat later a pack of incorporeal horsemen rode through the handgunners' ranks from behind, their scythes flickering as they claimed soul after soul.

Ahead, the rest of the state troops were struggling hard against the dead rising up from the ground below them as Mannfred incanted his spells. Not only were half-rotten cadavers and corpses standing back up to clutch at the survivors of the grinding melee, but also the bloody-uniformed Talabheimer dead they had called comrades moments before. A sense of desperation seethed in the air, an imminence that drove men to acts of heroism and cowardice in equal measure.

The big man that had led the wizards' rabble took up a fallen banner-sign from a mound of twitching dead and swung it hard at the vampire count from behind, breaking the goat-emblazoned sign across the back of his bald head. Blood puffed out, but the vampire merely snarled, catching the brawny Stirlander by the scruff of his neck and flinging him onto the lance of the Reiksguard knight that was charging him from the right.

In the lee of the corpse-heap left in Ghorst's wake, von Korden reloaded his pistol with the last of his silvered shot. The vampire had them outnumbered now – at least three to one, by the look of it. Legs were buckling and sword arms flagging as darkness drew in once more, the Sunmaker's flare-rockets dampened and then extinguished by the driving rain. With the cavalry committed, the battle of attrition was sliding dramatically in favour of the dead. Green lightning flashed overhead as the screams of pain and the cries of dying men punctuated the rolling thunder. Worse still, Mannfred was at the height of his power.

The witch hunter was readying himself for one last charge when a lambent flood of light rolled out across the battlefield from the west. It spread like running quicksilver, draining into the earth in seemingly random locations. A moment later the earth shook like the fur of a wounded beast.

Suddenly, miraculously, the earth burst open in a hundred different places. This time it was not the dead that emerged, but the buried symbols of the faithful. Stolen sigil-hammers, steel wolf totems of Ulric, Morrite pennies, even brass suns of Myrmidia burst out of their earthy graves to hang at head height across the field, each glowing with raw magical power.

Von Korden gave a shout of triumph. Mannfred's agents had buried the stolen symbols deep, but not deep enough. His message had been intended for Karl Franz, in truth, but Sunscryer's plan to convey it to the Colleges of Magic had borne fruit at the critical hour. Clearly, Balthasar Gelt, Supreme Patriarch and master of metalshifting, had heard of their plight and offered his own contribution just in time.

A roar of fierce elation was torn out of the surviving crusaders at the sight of their sacred symbols lifted high. All across the battlefield Mannfred's incorporeal gheists were blasted into nothingness by the wave of raw faith that poured out across the field. Even the reliquary drew back into the storm clouds, its guardians crying out in unearthly pain.

A surge of vitality bloomed through the crusaders' ranks at the sign of so much hope made manifest. Swords and axes were raised high once more, tired limbs were reinvigorated and battle-cries found new voice. United in rebellion against the pall of undeath that had threatened to bury them, the crusaders cut down the rotting host one after another until nothing was left but strewn chunks of meat and the stench of death.

Von Korden scanned the battlefield as the surviving crusaders gave thanks to their gods amidst the torn remains of their foes. Slowly his spirits sank, despair filling his heart once more. In the chaos, the vampire Mannfred had made his retreat. Worse yet, the war altar lay on its side, abandoned.

Volkmar was nowhere to be seen.

◀ EPILOGUE ▶

As the battle ground to a sudden halt outside Castle Sternieste, the light in the great open chamber atop its southern tower flickered fitfully. Inside, tree-trunk candles made from human fat spluttered and spat as if disgusted by the robed priest that had been flung into their midst.

A pair of bloodied vargheists paced hungrily around their prize, chattering to each other in their clicking tongue. Even in their dim animalistic minds, they had enough sense not to tread upon the gilded grooves that formed a rough outline of Sylvania upon the chamber's floor.

As his dazed senses returned to him, Volkmar could feel magical power thrumming through the flagstones he was lying on. He raised his head and struggled blearily to focus. Blood pulsed out of the hole in his bald pate where one of the vargheists had bitten down hard. He dared not touch it, fearing he might feel something soft and spongy beneath his fingertips.

The walls around the priest were ranged with shackled figures, dazed by lack of blood or beaten to the point of unconsciousness. Amongst their number were a white-robed healer of Shallya, a bearded brute bearing the mark of Ulric upon his forehead, and a pallid devotee of Morr so badly whipped that he stood knock-kneed in sticky pools of his own blood. The Myrmidian Lupio Blaze was shackled opposite an elf maiden so regal that she was stunning even under a mask of blood and dust. A broken tiara hung from her tangled tresses, the symbol of the Phoenix Court emblazoned upon it. He recognised the symbol of the Everqueen next to it, something the elven envoys to Karl Franz's court had always been proud to display.

Between each of the nine captives were lecterns wrought in the shape of daemons' claws. Giant grimoires were bound in chains to several of the lecterns, their pages rustling as if by their own accord. At the heart of the chamber, the stolen Crown of Sorcery sat on a cushion of human skin, its priceless jewels winking in the candlelight. A flame of defiance burned in the Grand Theogonist. If he could only seize it and escape the chamber, maybe even return it to Altdorf, he could restore his reputation and start the crusade anew...

Volkmar's aching mind struggled to make sense of his surroundings. Suspicions stalked him like thieves in an alley. To amass such an assemblage of dignitaries and artefacts from across the world was the work of months – years even. But to what purpose?

For a second, all the candles in the chamber guttered at once. A moment later, a tall armoured figure loomed over Volkmar. Swollen with arcane power and clad in bat-winged plate of purest black, the newcomer was a figure of ancient legend come to life. Mannfred von Carstein, Gravelord of Sylvania and scourge of the Sigmarite Cult, placed his metal boot on the Grand Theogonist's back and pressed down hard.

'Look at thee, wriggling on the ground,' said Mannfred von Carstein, his voice cultured under its sneering tone. 'The great Volkmar, high priest of the Heldenhammer. They say that the blood of Sigmar runs in thy veins, my friend. And perhaps they are right.'

Above Volkmar, the vampire count gestured to his vargheist minions. They fell upon the unconscious figures ranged around the wall of the chamber, ripping open their wrists with pointed teeth. Blood pattered onto the flagstones, pooling in the candlelight until it found its way into the gilded grooves that ran scant inches from each captive.

Volkmar cleared his mind of pain and thought only of the warrior god Sigmar, he who had banished the Great Necromancer when the Empire was young. The priest felt his bones knit and heal as a golden light flowed through him. He shucked his powerful shoulders, dislodging the armoured boot that held him prone.

Suddenly, an explosion of pain blossomed behind his eyes as the vampire count dug his claws into Volkmar's gaping head wound and used the inside of his skull to pull him to his feet. A pallid, leering face swam in the Grand Theogonist's blurring vision. Volkmar balled his fist and punched Mannfred hard in the mouth. He felt fangs break under his knuckles, even through the screaming black pain that was burning into his mind.

'Now, now,' said Mannfred, spitting a tooth onto the floor and smiling crimson in the candlelight. 'It's too late for such primitive nonsense, I'm afraid. Too late for you, and too late for the Empire.'

A fell wind raced through the arrow-slits of the chamber, snuffing out the candle flames. An instant later, the chamber became deathly cold, and a diffuse green light turned the blood that trickled around the flagstones jet black. Volkmar felt his tendons freeze and his mind grow numb. As the elements raged above, the night sky filling the chamber's open roof was eclipsed by a howling tempest of ghosts that bore a cage of ironbone towards them. The vargheists raised their voices in supplication, howling in worshipful glee.

'The blood of Sigmar,' the von Carstein said, licking his fingers as Volkmar gazed up in horror. 'The last ingredient I need to claim the realm that is rightfully mine.'

The vampire stalked around the stunned priest, talons flexing. 'Great things can be accomplished with the life essence of true believers.' A black and pointed tongue slithered along his lips, smearing traces of stolen blood. 'Sylvania will soon become a realm where faith has no power, and your precious holy symbols are little more than trinkets. All because the blood of the faithful has been turned against them.'

At an unspoken signal from their master, the vargheists darted forwards and held Volkmar's arms fast. With a single swipe of his claw, Mannfred slit open Volkmar's wrist, and blood pulsed out.

Eyes glinting, the vampire squeezed the priest's arm above the cut in his weapon arm, forcing the wound to open like a wet mouth. Ever more blood drizzled down the old priest's hand, swiftly finding the grooves in the floor. It mingled with that of the holy men and women flowing around the chamber until the gold of the cartograph laid into the flagstones ran scarlet throughout.

Grinning vilely, Mannfred grabbed Volkmar by the neck and lifted him from his feet. He carried the struggling priest to the edge of the chamber without effort and slammed him bodily against one of the arches that formed the tower's windows. In the far distance around the mountains that ringed the vale, the old man saw an unhealthy crimson light spread, its passage echoing the blood-filled borders cut into the flagstones below. Beneath the light were explosive eruptions of movement. A fortress wall of bone was bursting up from the ground wherever the crimson light touched the ground.

Volkmar burned with anger as Sylvania became completely drained of what little life was left to it. The old priest struggled for breath, a muffled roar of desperation and despair bursting unbidden from his lips. He pushed at the vampire with a surge of strength, channelling the raw power of his faith in Sigmar into one last great blast of defiance.

Nothing happened.

'Too late,' said Mannfred once more, his voice cold as death's own claws as he slowly stalked closer. 'No mortal can defy my will.'

The vampire count bared his fangs and lunged for Volkmar's throat.

THE RETURN OF
NAGASH

Josh Reynolds

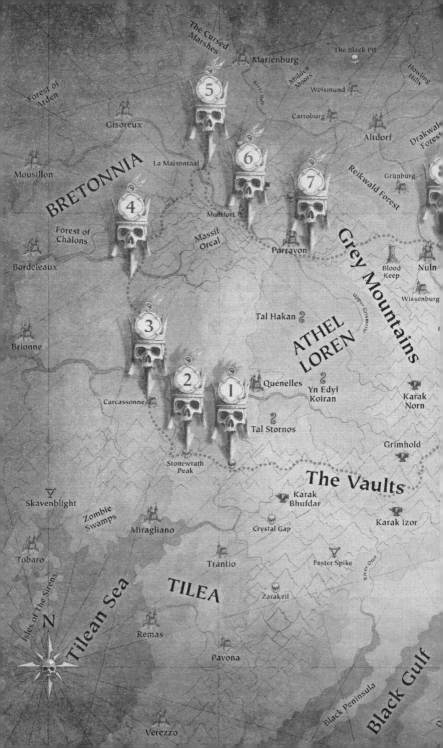

1. A CONCLAVE OF THE DEAD ••••
Arkhan reunites with the Lichemaster Heinrich Kemmler and Krell – his vassals during Mallobaude's abortive campaign.

2. THE VENGEFUL DEAD ARISE ••••
Arkhan and Kemmler raise the wights of Stonewrath Peak to form the core of the army they will lead into Bretonnia.

3. THE RAZING OF CARCASSONNE ••••
Arkhan's army advances across the plague-ridden southern counties of Bretonnia. Scores of villages and towns are overcome by his legions, which grow larger with every victory.

4. DUKE TANCRED'S FALL ••••
Duke Tancred II, recognising the work of his father's old foe, the Lichemaster, musters the survivors of ruined Quenelles to face him in battle. Tancred succeeds in dealing Kemmler a vicious wound, but is hacked down by Krell in return for his temerity. Tancred's army is routed soon after, and the duke raised as a zombie so that Kemmler might slay him again and again.

5. THE TWELFTH BATTLE OF LA MAISONTAAL••
Arkhan's forces breach the sanctified walls of La Maisontaal Abbey to reclaim Alakanash.

6. BARON CASGILLE RIDES OUT ••••
Baron Casgille receives word of a dark presence making its way across his lands. Summoning the knights of neighbouring

villages, he rides out to challenge it. Casgille and all who follow him are slain when Arkhan raises a horde of plague-ridden dead to pull the horrified knights from their saddles.

7. ORION'S WRATH ••••
Athel Loren's Wild Hunt falls upon Arkhan's army as it crosses Parravon. Realising his minions are outmatched by the wood elves' fury, Arkhan escapes into the mountains whilst Krell's forces hold the Wild Hunt at bay.

8. BETRAYAL AT BEECHERVAST ••••
Anark von Carstein, commander of the Drakenhof Templars, attempts to destroy Arkhan and claim Alakanash (and Mannfred's favour). Arkhan defeats the would-be assassin, and leaves him manacled to the gatepost of Beechervast's Sigmarite Temple.

9. THE FALL OF HELDENHAME ••••
United once more, Arkhan and Mannfred lay siege to Heldenhame, and slaughter the Knights of Sigmar's Blood.

10. DEATH AT THE NINE DAEMONS
Eltharion the Grim leads an army of high elves in a desperate effort to stop Arkhan from resurrecting Nagash and rescue the Everchild. As Mannfred's undead host holds the elves at bay, the ritual begins…

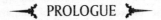 PROLOGUE

Late summer 2522

The world was dead.

It simply didn't know it yet.

That was the bare truth of it, and it pleased the one who considered it to no little end. Oh, there were things to be done yet, debts to be paid and webs to be spun or broken, but the weight of the inevitable had settled across the way and weft of the world. Time was running out, and the beast was all but bled white.

Long fingers – scholar's fingers – stroked the murky surface of the blood that filled the ancient bronze bowl before him. The bowl was covered in the harsh, jagged script of a long-dead empire. It had once belonged to another scholar, who had come from a still older empire even than the one that had produced the bowl. That scholar was dust now, like both of the empires in question: all three erased from the tapestry of history by hubris and treachery in equal measure. There were lessons there, for the man who had the wit to attend them, a voice that may or may not have been his own murmured in the back of his head. He shrugged the voice off, the way a horse might shrug off a stinging fly.

The scryer considered himself susceptible to neither arrogance nor foolishness. Were it any other moment, he might have admitted that it was the height of both to think oneself beyond either. As it was, he had other concerns. He ignored the soft susurrus of what might have been laughter that slithered beneath his thoughts with a surety that was the result of long experience, and bent over the bowl, murmuring the required words with the necessary intonation. The empire of Strigos might be dead, and Mourkain with it, but its language lived on in certain rituals and sorcerous rites.

The blood in the bowl stirred at the touch of the scryer's fingertips, its surface undulating like the back of a cat seeking affection. Its opacity faded, and an image began to form, as though it were a shadow flickering across a stretched canvas. The images were of every time and no time, of things that had been, things that would be and of things that never were. The scryer desired to know of the calamitous events that afflicted the world, events whose reverberations were felt even in his tiny corner of the world. The world was dead, but with a voyeur's eagerness, he wanted to see the killing blows.

The first image to be drawn from the depths of the bowl was of a twin-tailed comet, which blazed across the crawling canopy of the heavens, fracturing the weak barrier between the world of man and that which waited outside as it streaked along its pre-destined course. In its wake – madness.

A storm of Chaos swept across the world, spreading outwards from the poles to roll across the lands of men and other than men one by one. Daemons were born and died in moments, or tore their way through the membrane of the world to sow terror for days or weeks on end. There was no rhyme or reason to any of what followed; it was merely the crazed whims of the Dark Gods at work. The scryer watched it all with a cool, calculating eye, like a gamesman sizing up the opening move of an oft-played opponent.

In the cold, dark reaches of Naggaroth, the sound of drums set the ice shelves to shivering and caused avalanches in the lower valleys. A horde of northmen poured across the Ironfrost Glacier, and in their vanguard swooped down the elegant, crimson shape of Khorne's best beloved. They smashed aside the great watchtowers, and the mighty hosts sent against them only stoked the fires of their fury. As Valkia exhorted her followers towards the obsidian walls of Naggarond itself, the scryer stirred the bowl's contents, eager to see more.

The image shifted, and then expanded into great walls of pale stone, which thrust up from the green nest of the jungles of distant Lustria; here, scaly shapes warred with nightmares made flesh in the heart of the ruins of Xahutec. Elsewhere, the jungle was afire, and once great temple cities had been cast into ruin, as a continent heaved and burned.

Lustria's death pyre flared up so brightly that the scryer winced and looked away. When he looked back at the bowl, the scene had changed. Red lightning lit the sky and strange mists spread down the slopes of the Annulii Mountains, bringing with them the raw power of Chaos unfettered. The land and its inhabitants became warped into new and terrible forms, all save the elves. The walls of reality wore thin and tore, and daemons flooded into Ulthuan. The forests of Chrace burned as the rivers of Cothique and Ellyrion became thick with virulent noxiousness, while in the heartland of the elven realms, the great cities of Tor Dynal and Elisia fell to the assaults of Chaos, rampaging daemons overwhelming their embattled defenders. As daemons scrambled in a capering, cackling riot towards a battle line of Sapherian Sword Masters, and elven magi drew upon every iota of power at their command to throw back their enemy, the image shattered like a reflection in a droplet of water, reforming into another scene of warfare.

Across the glades and valleys of Bretonnia, disgraced knights and covetous nobles flocked to the serpent banners of Mallobaude, illegitimate son
of Louen Leoncouer, and would-be king of that divided land. The scryer
watched as the nation over the mountains descended into fiery civil war,
and his eyes widened in surprise as he saw Mallobaude throw down his
father at Quenelles with the aid of a skeletal figure clad in robes of crimson
and black. A skull blazing with malignant power, with teeth as black as the
night sky, tipped back and uttered a cackle of victory as Leoncouer was
smashed to the ground, seemingly dead at his offspring's hand. Arkhan
the Black was in Bretonnia, and that fact alone tempted the scryer to try to
see more. But the image was already dissolving and he let the temptation
pass. There would be time later for such investigations.

A new picture rippled into view. In the deep, ice-cut valleys and towering
heights of the mountain range known as the Vaults, the dwarf hold known
to the scryer as Copper Mountain tottered beneath the assault of a tempest
of blood-starved daemons. The legion that assailed the stunted inhabitants
of the hold was so vast that the hold's defences were all but useless. But as
the dwarfs prepared to sell their lives in the name of defiance, if not victory, the daemonic storm dissipated as suddenly as it had gathered, leaving
only blue skies and a battered shieldwall of astonished dwarfs in its wake.
As the dwarfs began to collect their dead, the scene dissolved and a new
one took its place at the scryer's barest gesture.

The scryer chuckled mirthlessly as the next image wavered into being.
Another mountain hold, but not one that belonged to the dwarfs. Not any
more, at least. In the deep halls and opulently decorated black chambers
of the Silver Pinnacle, the self-proclaimed queen of the world, Neferata,
mother and mistress of the Lahmian bloodline, led her warriors, both
dead and undead, in defence of her citadel. A horde of daemons, backed
by hell-forged artillery, attacked from above and below, laying siege to the
main gates of Neferata's chosen eyrie, as well as surging up from its lower
depths. But these daemons vanished as abruptly as those who had attacked
Copper Mountain. The scryer frowned in annoyance. It would have been
far better for his own designs for the mistress of the Silver Pinnacle to have
fallen to the daemon-storm. He gestured again, almost petulantly.

What came next returned the smile to his face. The great city on the
mount, Middenheim, reeled beneath the tender ministrations of the
Maggot King and the Festival of Disease. Pox-scarred victims staggered
through the streets, begging for mercy from Shallya and Ulric. The open
sores that afflicted them wept a noisome pus and their bodies were thrown
on the pyres that marked every square, still crying out uselessly to the
gods. How Jerek would have cringed to see that, the scryer thought, as he
laughed softly. The image wavered and changed.

His laughter continued as beneath the shadowed branches in the depths
of Athel Loren, the great edifices known as the Vaults of Winter shattered,

and a horde of cackling, daemonic filth was vomited forth into the sacred glades of Summerstrand. Ancient trees, including the Oak of Ages, cracked and split, expelling floods of maggots and flies, and the forest floor became coated in the stuff of decay. Desolate glades became rallying points for monstrous herds of beastmen, who poured into the depths of the forest, braying and squealing. Amused, the scryer waved a hand, dispelling the image.

His amusement faded as the blood rippled, revealing a scarred face, topped by a massive red crest of grease-stiffened hair. An axe flashed and a beastman reeled back, goatish features twisted in fear and agony. It fell, and the axe followed it, separating its malformed head from its thick neck. The wielder of the axe, a dwarf, kicked the head aside as he trudged on through the fire-blackened streets of a northern city, fallen to madness and ruin. The dwarf, one-eyed and mad, was familiar to the scryer from a past encounter of dubious memory. Snow swirled about the dwarf as he battled through the city, his rune axe encrusted with gore drawn from the bodies of beastmen, trolls, northern marauders and renegades, all of whom lay in heaps and piles in his wake. The scryer saw no sign of the doom-seeker's human companion, and wondered idly if the man had died. The thought pleased him to no end.

The image billowed and spread as the dwarf trudged on, and the scryer was rewarded by the sight of the River Aver becoming as blood, a scarlet host of howling daemons bursting from its tainted waters en masse to sweep across Averland, burning and butchering every living thing in their path. As with the other daemonic incursions, the bloody host evaporated moments before they reached the walls of Averheim.

Averheim grew faint and bled into the dark bowers of the Drakwald. Trees were uprooted and hurled aside as a veritable fang of stone, taller than the tallest structure ever conceived by man, tore through the corrupted soil and speared towards the sky. The crown of the newborn monolith was wreathed in eldritch lightning. Similar malformed extrusions rose above the tree line of Arden Forest and the glacial fields of far Naggaroth, as well as in the Great Forest and the embattled glades of Athel Loren. Some wept flame, others sweated foulness, but all pulsed with a darkling energy. Beastmen gathered about them to conduct raucous rites, the worst of which caused even a man as hardened to cruelty as the scryer to grimace in repulsion. With a hiss of disgust, he dashed his fingers into the blood, banishing the activities of the beasts from sight and eliciting another image.

Nuln erupted into violence as crowds of baying fanatics and self-flagellating doomsayers filled the streets. The mansions of the wealthy were ransacked and unlucky nobles were hung or torn apart by the screaming crowd. Even the Countess von Liebwitz was dragged from her boudoir, amidst a storm of accusations ranging from adultery to sorcery. The scryer stabbed the swirling blood, dissolving the Countess's screeching visage and replacing it with the snowy hinterlands of Kislev.

As with Naggaroth, Kislev shuddered beneath the tread of masses of northmen, all moving south. All lands west of Bolgasgrad were awash with daemons and barbarians. Along the River Lynik, the Ice Queen led her remaining warriors in a series of running battles with the invaders. As the Tsarina led her Ungol horsemen against the howling hordes, the scryer stirred the bowl, trying to ignore the murmur of the voice that pressed insistently against his awareness, demanding to be heard.

He was in Bretonnia again, as a figure clad in green armour hurled aside his helm, revealing the features of Gilles Le Breton, lost founder and king of that realm, now found and ready to reclaim his throne. The scryer laughed and wondered what Mallobaude and Arkhan would have to say about that.

He focused on the rippling blood, banishing images of the reborn king, and saw the armies of Ostermark, Talabecland and Hochland clash with a ragged host marching under the banner of the sorcerous monstrosity known as Vilitch the Curseling in the fields and siege ditches before the battlements of Castle von Rauken. Aldebrand Ludenhof, Elector Count of Hochland, mounted the ramparts of the besieged castle and put a long rifle bullet into one of the Curseling's skulls, forcing the creature to retreat and scattering its host.

The scryer waved a hand. The images were coming faster now, some of them appearing and vanishing before he could properly observe them. His skull ached with the frequency and intensity of the scenes playing out in the bowl.

The hordes of the Northern Wastes did not merely assault the south and west. They went east as well, hurling themselves at the Great Bastion in their thousands. Khazags, Kul and Kurgan mustered daemon engines, and dozens of warlords and chieftains led their warriors against the defences of the Bastion. The smoke of the resulting destruction could be seen as far south as the Border Princes. The image wavered and faded before the scryer could see whether the Bastion had fallen.

In the desiccated deserts of the south, the unbound dead of a long-gone empire readied themselves for invasion, and the chariots of the tomb kings rolled westward, towards the caliphates of Araby. The dwarfs sealed their holds or mobilised for war as the foundations of the world shuddered and long-dormant volcanoes rumbled, belching smoke. In the Badlands, the numberless hordes of greenskins gathered and surged towards the civilised lands as one, as if in response to some unspoken signal. The ogre tribes too were on the march, bulbous bellies rumbling. In the roots of the world, the clans of the skaven scurried upwards, attacking the unprepared nations of Estalia and Tilea in such unprecedented numbers that even the scryer was slightly dumbfounded. City after city fell, and the tattered clan banners of the Under-Empire rose over the lands that had once belonged to men.

Perturbed, he swept out a hand, stirring the blood without touching it. A familiar sight, this one, and his lips peeled back from his teeth in a triumphant snarl. An old man, clad in the robes and armour of the Grand Theogonist of the Empire, wrestled against a dark shape, cloaked in shadow. The shape twisted, becoming first a man – aquiline, noble and yet feral, with eyes like crimson pits and a mouthful of fangs – then swelling to a giant, clad in armour such as no man had ever worn, wreathed in eerie green flame. The giant's features were fleshless, and its head was a skull bound in black iron and bronze. Skeletal jaws opened wide, bone stretching and billowing impossibly as the giant thrust the struggling shape of the old man between its jaws and swallowed him whole.

The scryer dismissed the image quickly, before the eyes of that giant could turn towards him. Something chuckled and spoke, just out of earshot. He ignored it, and concentrated on the next image as it began to form in the swirling blood. The bowl began to shake slightly, as if it were being rocked by the weight of the pictures rising up out of it.

The scryer hissed in recognition as the world's northern pole, where the membrane between worlds was nonexistent, came into view. Daemons beyond measure were assembled there, divided into four mighty hosts of damnation such as had once sought to envelop the world in aeons past. The scryer cursed loudly and virulently, his composure momentarily shaken. What he was seeing was the merest spear-point of an invasion force, a host of such magnitude that only the raw unreality of the Chaos Wastes could contain the sheer number of daemons gathered. From amid the numberless hordes came four exalted daemons – those creatures highest in the esteem of the Dark Gods.

One by one, each of the four sank down to one knee before a figure that was tiny by comparison. The latter was clad in heavy armour, and cloaked in thick furs, its features hidden beneath a horned helm. The helm turned, and eyes that blazed with a radiance at once malignant and divine met those of the scryer, across the vast stretch of time and space that separated them. The blood in the bowl began to bubble and smoke. A will more than equal to his own beat down suddenly against the scryer like a hammer-blow. A voice like seven thunders reverberated through his skull and said, '*Rejoice, for the hour of my glory fast approaches.*'

The bowl shattered. What was left of the blood slopped across the scryer's hands and splattered on the stone floor. Snuffling, grey-skinned, hairless shapes, wearing the filthy remnants of what had once been fine clothing, crawled across the floor, splotched tongues licking at the spilled blood with eager whimpers. The degenerate creatures were all that remained of the once proud family that had, in better times, called Castle Sternieste its home. Now, they wore the miscellany of ancestral finery, smeared with grime and foulness, as they capered and gibbered in debased mockeries of courtly dances for their master's amusement, or raided the tombs of their ancestors for sustenance.

Mannfred von Carstein sucked the blood from his fingers as he considered the remains of the bowl speculatively. He glanced up at the body whose blood he'd carefully drained to fill it; the corpse was clad in the robes of an acolyte of one of the great Colleges of Magic – the Light College, Mannfred knew, by their colour. He'd opened the boy's throat with his own fingers and strung him up by his feet from one of the ancient timbers above, so that the dregs of his life would drain into the bowl. There were few ingredients more effective for such sorceries than the blood of a magic user. The ghouls looked up at him expectantly, whining with eagerness. He gestured and, as one, they gave a ribald howl and began leaping and tearing at the body, like hounds at the feet of a man on the gallows. With a sniff, Mannfred pulled his cloak tight about himself and left the chamber, and its contents, to his ghoulish courtiers.

Well, wasn't that informative? The world writhes, caught in a storm partially of your making, and where are you? The voice he'd heard as he watched the images in the bowl, the voice he'd heard for more centuries than he cared to contemplate, spoke with mild disdain. Mannfred shook his head, trying to ignore it. A shadow passed across his vision, and something that might have been a face, or perhaps a skull, swam to the surface of his mind and then vanished before he could focus on it. *Where are you, then? You should be out there, taking advantage of the situation. But you can't, can you?*

'Shut up,' Mannfred growled.

Konrad talked to himself as well. As his habits went, that was probably the least objectionable, but still... We know how he ended up, don't we?

Mannfred didn't reply this time. The voice was right, of course. It was always right, curse it. Laughter echoed through his head and he bit back a snarl. He wasn't going mad. He knew this, because madness was for the foolish or the weak of mind, and he was anything but either. After all, could a madman have accomplished what he had, and in so short a time?

For centuries he had yearned to free Sylvania, which was his by both right of blood and conquest, from the yoke of the Empire. And, after the work of many lifetimes, he had accomplished just that. The air now reeked of dark enchantments and an unholy miasma had settled over everything within the province's borders. He strode out onto the parapet and looked out towards the border with Stirland, where a massive escarpment of bone now towered over Sylvania's boundaries. The wall encircled his domain, making it over into a sprawling fortress-state. The wall that would protect his land from the doom that waited to envelop the world was the result of generations of preparation. It had required the blood of nine very special individuals – individuals who even now enjoyed his hospitality – to create, and getting them all in one place had been an undertaking of decades. He'd done it, however, and once he'd had them, Sylvania was his and his alone.

So speaks the tiger in his cage, the voice whispered, mockingly. Again, it was correct. His wall, mighty as it was, was not the only one ringing his fiefdom. 'Gelt,' he muttered. The name of the Arch-Alchemist and current Supreme Patriarch of the Colleges of Magic had become one of Mannfred's favoured curses in the months since the caging of Sylvania. While Mann-fred had battled an invasion force led by Volkmar the Grim, the Grand Theogonist, and enacted his own stratagem, Gelt had been working furi-ously to enact a ritual the equal of Mannfred's own. Or so Mannfred's spies had assured him.

Mannfred frowned. Even from here, he could feel the spiritual weight of the holy objects that caged his land. In the months preceding his notice of secession from the broken corpse that was Karl Franz's empire, he'd sent the teeming ghoul-packs that congregated about Castle Sternieste to strip every Sylvanian temple, shrine and burial ground of what holy symbols yet remained in the province. He'd ordered the symbols buried deep in unhallowed graves and cursed ground, so that their pestiferous sanctity would not trouble his newborn paradise.

Or such had been his intent. Instead, Gelt had somehow managed to turn those buried symbols into a wall of pure faith. Any undead, be they vampire, ghost or lowly zombie, that tried to cross it was instantly oblit-erated, as several of his vampire servants had discovered to their cost. Mannfred was forced to admit that the resulting explosions had been quite impressive. He couldn't help but admire the raw power of Gelt's wall. It was a devious thing, too, and only worked in one direction. The undead could enter Sylvania, but they could not leave. It was the perfect trap. Mannfred fully intended to congratulate Gelt on his cunning, just before he killed him.

In the months since he'd destroyed Volkmar's army, Mannfred had pored over every book, tome, grimoire and papyrus scroll in his posses-sion, seeking some way of countering Gelt's working. Nothing he'd tried had worked. The wall of faith was somehow more subtle and far stronger than he'd expected a human mind to conceive of, and his continued failure gnawed at him. He had wanted to isolate Sylvania, true – but on his own terms. To be penned like a wild beast was an affront that could not be borne.

But Gelt's sorcerous cage wasn't the only problem. Dark portals had opened in certain, long-hidden places within Sylvania, vomiting forth daemons by the score, and the distraction of putting paid to these incur-sions had eaten into his studies. After the last such invasion, Mannfred had resolved to find out what was going on in the rest of the world. The young acolyte of the Light College whom he'd used to fill his scrying bowl had been taken prisoner, along with a dozen others, including militiamen, knights and a few wayward priests, during Volkmar's attempt to purge Sylvania.

Finding out that Sylvania wasn't the only place afflicted by sudden daemonic sorties hadn't quelled his growing misgivings. In fact, it had only heightened the pressure he felt to shatter Gelt's wall and free Sylvania.

The world was tottering on the lip of the grave and, amusing as it was to watch, Mannfred didn't intend to go over with it. There were still things that needed doing. There were tools that he still required, and he had to be able to cross his own borders to get them.

Tools for what, boy? the voice asked. No, not 'the voice'. It was pointless to deny it. It was Vlad's voice. Mannfred leaned over the parapet, bracing himself on the stone, his eyes closed. Even now, even centuries after the fact, the shadow of the great and terrible Vlad von Carstein hung over Mannfred and all of his works. Vlad's name was still whispered in the dark places and burying grounds, by the living and the dead alike. He had etched his name into the flesh of the world, and the scar remained livid even after all this time. It galled Mannfred to no end, and even the joy he'd once taken from his part in his primogenitor's downfall had faded, lost to the gnawing anger he felt still.

He'd hated Vlad, and loved him; respected him and been contemptuous of him. And he'd tried to save him, though he'd engineered his obliteration. Now, for his sins, he was haunted by Vlad's voice. It had started the moment he had begun his great work, as if Vlad were watching over his shoulder, and only grown stronger in the months that followed. He'd been able to ignore it at first, to dismiss the shadows that crept at the corner of his eye and the constant murmur of a voice just out of earshot. But now, when he least needed the distraction, there it was. There *he* was.

Do you still think that the design of the web you weave is yours, my son? Vlad hissed. Mannfred could see his sire's face on the periphery of his vision, so much like his own. *Can you feel it, boy? The weight of destiny sits on you but not yours.* As if to lend weight to the thought, Mannfred caught sight of his shadow; only it wasn't his – it was something larger, and a thousand times more terrible than any vampire, lord of Sylvania or otherwise. Something that flickered with witch-fire and seemed to stretch out a long arm towards him, seeking to devour him. *You speak of tools, but what are you, eh?* Vlad purred. *Who is that who rides you through the gates of the world?*

'Quiet,' Mannfred snarled. The stone of the parapet crumbled in his grip. 'Go back to whatever privy hole your remains were thrown in, old man.' Without waiting for the inevitable reply, Mannfred drew his cloak about him and turned to go, not quite fleeing the voices and shadows that taunted him, but moving swiftly all the same.

He made his way through the half-ruined corridors to the great open chamber that crouched at the top of the southernmost tower of the castle. Once, it had been a meeting room for the Order of Drakenhof, a brotherhood of Templars devoted to eradicating the evil that they believed had corrupted Sylvania. Vlad had taken great pleasure in hunting them over the course of long centuries, Mannfred recalled. Every few hundred years, the knights of the order stirred in their graves, reforming and returning to their old haunts. The definition of insanity, Mannfred had heard, was doing the same thing over and over again and expecting a different result. If that was the case, then the Drakenhof Templars had been quite mad.

While Vlad had been content to play with them, as a cat plays with mice, Mannfred had little patience for such drawn-out displays of cruelty. They served no purpose, and to have such a thorn work its way into his side every few decades was an annoyance he felt no need to suffer through. When he had returned to Sylvania in the wake of Konrad's disastrous reign, he had immediately sought out every hold, fortress and komturei of the order and wiped them out root and branch. He had wiped out entire families, butchering the oldest members to the youngest, and leaving their bodies dangling from gibbets about the border of Sylvania as a warning to others. He had made a point – unlike Vlad or Konrad, Mannfred would not tolerate dissent. He would not tolerate enemies on his soil, worthy or otherwise. After the last knight had gasped out his final breath in a muddy ditch south of Kleiberstorf, he had reformed the order and turned it over to those of his creatures that found pleasure in parodying the traditions of knighthood.

Where once men had met to discuss the cleansing of Sylvania, Mannfred now stored the tools of his eventual, inevitable triumph, both living and otherwise. A ghoul clad in the remains of a militiaman's armour and livery crouched near the entrance to the chamber, leaning against a gisarme that had seen better years. The ghoul jerked in fright as Mannfred approached and yowled as he gestured sharply. It scrambled towards the heavy wooden door to open it for him. As it heaved upon it and turned, something hurtled out of the chamber beyond and caught the ghoul in the back of the head with a sickening crunch.

The ghoul flopped down, its rusty armour rattling as it hit the floor. The chunk of stone had been thrown hard enough to shatter the cannibal's skull and Mannfred flipped a bit of brain matter off the toe of his boot, his mouth twisting in a moue of annoyance. 'Are you finished?' he asked loudly. 'I can come back later, if you'd prefer.'

There was only silence from within the chamber. Mannfred sighed and stepped through the aperture. The room beyond was circular and large. It stank of rain, fire, blood and ghouls, as most of the castle did these days. But unlike the rest of the castle, the stones of this chamber thrummed with a heady power that was just this side of intoxicating for Mannfred. It was the one place that he was free from Vlad's voice and the lurking shadows that dogged his steps.

The room was lit by a profusion of candles, made from human fat and thrust into the nooks and crannies of the walls and floor. The latter was intercut by gilded grooves, which formed a rough outline of Sylvania, and a semicircle of heavy stone lecterns, each carved in the shape of a daemon's claw, lined the northernmost border of the province. Giant grimoires,

THE RETURN OF NAGASH

bound in chains, sat on several of the lecterns, their pages rustling with a sound like the whispers of ghosts.

At the heart of the chamber sat a plinth, upon which was a cushion of human skin and hair. And resting on the cushion was the iron shape of the Crown of Sorcery. To Mannfred's eyes, it pulsed like a dark beacon, and he felt the old, familiar urge to place it on his head stir within the swamps of his soul like some great saurian. The crown radiated a malevolent pressure upon him, even now, and even as quiescent as it was. There was an air of contentment about it at the moment, and for that he was grateful. He knew well what monstrous intelligence waited within the crown's oddly angled shape, and he had no desire to pit his will against that hideous sentience. Not now, not until he'd taken the proper precautions. He'd worn it, briefly, on his return from Vargravia, and that had been enough to assure him that it was more dangerous than it looked.

He was so caught up in his study of the crown that he didn't turn as another rock surged towards his head. He caught the missile without looking and crushed it. He held up his hand and let the crumbled remains dribble through his fingers. 'Stop it,' he said. He looked at the walls behind the barrier of lecterns, where his nine prisoners hung shackled. Except that there were only seven of them. Two were missing.

Mannfred heard a scrape of metal on stone and whirled. A man clad in once-golden but now grime-caked and dented armour, decorated with proud reliefs of the war goddess Myrmidia, lunged for him, whirling a chain. Snarling Tilean oaths, the Templar of the Order of the Blazing Sun swung his makeshift weapon at Mannfred's face. The vampire jerked back instinctively, and was almost smashed from his feet by the descending weight of a heavy stone lectern in the shape of a daemon's claw, wielded by a brute clad in furs and a battered breastplate bearing a rampant wolf – the sigil of Ulric.

Mannfred backhanded the Ulrican off his feet with one hand and snagged the loop of the Myrmidian's chain with the other. He jerked the knight towards him and wrapped the links of the chain about his neck. He kicked the knight's legs out from under him and then planted his foot between the man's shoulder blades. Wrapping the chains about his wrist, he hauled upwards, strangling the man.

The Ulrican gave a bellicose roar and staggered towards him. Burly arms snapped tight around Mannfred's chest. He threw his head back and was rewarded by a crunch of bone, and a howl of pain. Mannfred drove his foot into the back of the knight's head, driving him face-first into the stone floor and rendering him unconscious. Then he turned to deal with the Ulrican.

The big man staggered forwards, blood streaming from his shattered nose. His eyes blazed with a berserk rage and he roared as he hurled himself at Mannfred. Mannfred caught him by the throat and hoisted him into the air. The man pounded uselessly on the vampire's arm, as Mannfred slowly choked him comatose. He let the limp body fall to the floor and turned to face the other seven inhabitants of the chamber. 'Well, that was fun. Anyone else?'

Seven pairs of eyes glared at him. If looks could kill, Mannfred knew that he would have been only so much ash on the wind. He met their gazes, until all but one had looked away. Satisfied, he smirked and looked up at the shattered dome of the tower above, where fire-blackened support timbers crossed over one another like the threads of a spider's web. He could see the dark sky and stars above, through the gaps in the roof. He whistled piercingly, and massive, hunched forms began to clamber into view from among the nest of wood and stone.

There were two of the beasts, and both were hideous amalgamations of ape, wolf and bat. Mannfred had heard it said that the vargheist was the true face of the vampire, shorn of all pretence of humanity. These two were collectively known as the Swartzhafen Devils, which was as good a name as such beasts deserved. One of the creatures clutched something red and wet in its talons and gnawed on it idly as it watched him. He had given the beasts orders not to interfere with any escape attempts on the part of the captives.

Mannfred claimed the body of the ghoul and dragged it into the room by an ankle. The vargheists were suddenly alert, their eyes glittering with hunger. He rolled the body into the centre of the outline of Sylvania and stepped back. The vargheists fell upon the dead cannibal with ravenous cries. The captives looked away in disgust or fear. Mannfred smiled and set about rebinding the two men. That they'd escaped at all was impressive, but it wasn't the first time they'd tried it, and it wouldn't be the last. He wanted them to try and fail, and try again, until their courage and will had been worn down to a despairing nub.

Then, and only then, would they be fit for his purpose.

His eyes flickered to the lone nonhuman among his captives. The elven princess did not meet his gaze, though he did not think it was out of fear, but rather disdain. A flicker of annoyance swept through him, but he restrained the urge to discipline her. Instead, he moved towards the prize of the lot, at least in his eyes.

'Bad dreams, old man?' Mannfred said, looking down at Volkmar, Grand Theogonist of the Empire. He sank down to his haunches beside the old man. 'You should thank me, you know. All of you,' he said, looking about the cell. 'The world as you knew it is giving way to something new. And something wholly unpleasant. Outside of Sylvania's borders, madness and entropy reign. Only here does order prevail. But don't worry, soon enough, with your help, I shall sweep the world clean, and all will be as it was. I shall make it a paradise.'

'A paradise,' Volkmar rasped. The old man met Mannfred's red gaze without hesitation. Battered and beaten as he was, he was not yet broken,

Mannfred knew. 'Is that what you call it?' Volkmar shifted his weight, causing his manacles to rattle. The old man looked as if he wanted nothing more than to lunge barehanded at his captor. A wound on his head, a gift from one of the vargheists, was leaking blood and pus, and the old man's face was stained with both. Mannfred could smell the sickness creeping into the Grand Theogonist, weakening him even further, despite the holy power that was keeping him on his feet.

'I didn't say for whom it would be such, now, did I?' Mannfred said. He rose smoothly and pulled his cloak about him. He looked down at Volkmar with a cruel smile. 'Don't worry, old man... When I consummate my new world, neither you nor your friends will be here to see it.'

PART ONE

Alliance

Autumn 2522–Spring 2523

PART ONE

CHAPTER ONE

Stirland-Sylvania border

The world was dying.

It had been dying for a very long time, according to some. But Erikan Crowfiend, in his long trek from the battlefield of Couronne, had come to the conclusion that it was finally on its last legs. There was smoke from a million funeral pyres on the wind, not just in Bretonnia but in the Empire as well, and the stink of poison and rot was laid over everything. In the villages and wayplaces, men and women whispered stories of two-headed calves that mewled like infants, of birds that sang strange dirges as they circled in the air, and of things creeping through the dark streets that had once kept to the forests and hills.

Beasts and greenskins ran riot, carving red trails through the outskirts of civilisation as nightmare shapes swam down from the idiot stars to raven and roar through the heart of man's world. Great cities reeled from these sudden, unpredictable assaults, and the great gates of Altdorf, Middenheim and Nuln were barred and bolstered, almost as if it were intended that they never be opened again.

Erikan had seen it all, albeit at a remove. He had been forced to fight more than once since crossing the Grey Mountains, and not just with beasts or orcs. Men as well, and worse than men. Then, Erikan wasn't exactly a man himself. He hadn't been for some time.

Erikan Crowfiend's heart had stopped beating almost a century ago to the day, and he had not once missed its rhythm. He moved only by night, for the sun blistered him worse than any fire. His breath reeked of the butcher's block and he could hear a woman's pulse from leagues away. He could shatter stone and bone as easily as a child might tear apart a dried leaf. He never grew tired, suffered from illness or felt fear. And under different circumstances, he would have been happy to indulge his baser instincts as the land drowned in madness. He was a monster after all, and it was a season for monsters, from what little he'd seen.

But he was no longer the captain of his own destiny, and hadn't been since the night a pale woman had taken him in her arms and made him something both greater and lesser than the necromancer's apprentice he had been. So he moved ever eastwards, following a darkling pull that urged him on, across beast-held mountains and over burning fields, and through forests where the trees whimpered like beaten dogs and clawed at him with twisted branches.

Above him, a swarm of bats crossed the surface of the moon, heading the gods alone knew where. Erikan suspected that they were going the same place he was. The thought provided no comfort. The call had come, and he, like the bats, had no choice but to obey.

'Erikan?' a wheezing, slurred voice asked, interrupting his reverie.

'Yes, Obald,' Erikan said, with a sigh.

'It could just be the alcohol talking, or it could be the constant seepage from these inexpertly, if affectionately, placed poultices of yours making me light-headed, but I do believe that I'm dying,' said Obald Bone, the Bone-Father of Brionne. He took another swig from the mostly empty bottle of wine he held in one bandaged claw. The necromancer was a wizened thing, all leather and bone, wrapped in mouldering furs and travel leathers that, to Erikan's knowledge, had never been washed. Obald lay in a travois made from the stretched hide and bones of dead men, constructed by equal parts sorcery and brute strength. He blinked and forced himself up onto one elbow. 'Where are we?'

'Just about to cross the border into Sylvania, Obald,' Erikan said. He was hauling the travois behind him on foot, its straps of dried flesh and stiffened gut lashed about his battered and grime-encrusted cuirass. Their horse had come down with a bad case of being digested by something large and hungry that even Erikan had been hard-pressed to see off. He didn't know what it was, but he hadn't felt like sticking around to find out. Monsters once confined to the edges of the map were now wandering freely, and setting upon any who came within reach, edible or not. 'And you're not dying.'

'I hate to be contrary, but I am a master of the necromantic arts, and I think I know a little something about death, imminent, personal or otherwise,' Obald slurred. His travois was cushioned with empty bottles, and he reeked of gangrene and alcohol. He'd been getting steadily worse since Erikan had extracted the arrow that had taken him in the belly in the last moments of the battle for Couronne, just before the Green Knight had struck off Mallobaude's head.

For the first few weeks, Obald had seemed fine, if in pain, but the wound wasn't healing, and they weren't the sort whom the priestesses of Shallya normally welcomed. Obald had survived worse in his time, but it was as if he, like the world, were winding down.

Obald sank back down onto the travois, dislodging several bottles. 'Did I ever tell you that I'm from Brionne, Erikan? Good pig country that.'

'Yes,' Erikan said.

'I was a pig farmer, like my father and his father before him. Pigs, Erikan – you can't go wrong with a pig farm.' Obald reached out and swatted weakly at the sword sheathed on Erikan's hip. 'Blasted Templar blade. Why do you still carry that thing?'

'I'm a Templar. Templars carry Templar blades, Obald,' Erikan said.

'You're not a Templar, you're my apprentice. It's not even a proper sword. Hasn't even got a curse on it,' Obald grumbled.

'But it's sharp and long, and good at cutting things,' Erikan replied. He hadn't been Obald's apprentice since he'd been given the blood-kiss and inducted into the aristocracy of the night. He smiled at the thought. In truth, there was very little aristocratic about hiding in unmarked graves and devouring unlucky peasants.

'Where's my barrow-blade? I want you to have my barrow-blade,' Obald said muzzily.

'Your barrow-blade is still in the body of that fellow whose horse we stole,' Erikan said. The flight from Couronne had been as bloody as the battle itself. When the Serpent had fallen, his forces, both the living and the dead, had collapsed in an utter rout. Obald had had an arrow in the belly by then, and Erikan had been forced to hack them a path to freedom as the dead crumbled around them.

'Ha! Yes,' Obald cackled wetly. 'The look on his poxy, inbred face was priceless – thought that armour would save him, didn't he? Oh no, my lad. A dead man's sword will cut anything, even fancy armour.' He rocked back and forth in the travois, until his laughter became strangled coughing.

'So you taught me,' Erikan said.

'I did, didn't I?' Obald hiccupped. 'You were my best student, Erikan. It's a shame that you had to go and get mauled by that von Carstein witch.'

'She's not a witch, Obald.'

'Trollop then,' Obald snapped. 'She's a tart, Erikan.' He belched. 'I could do with a tart about now. One of those fancy ones from Nuln.'

'Are we still talking about women?' Erikan asked.

'They put jam – real jam – right in the pastry. Not sawdust and beef dripping, like the ones in Altdorf,' Obald said, gesticulating for emphasis.

'Right, yes,' Erikan said. He shook his head. 'I'm sure we can find you a tart in Sylvania, Obald.'

'No no, just leave me here to die, Erikan. I'll be fine,' Obald said. 'For a man who wears as many bones as I do, I am oddly comfortable with notions of mortality.' He upended the bottle he held, splashing much of its contents on his face and ratty beard. 'Bones, bone, Bone-Father. I can't believe you let me call myself that. Bone-Father... What does that even mean? The other necromancers were probably laughing at me.'

He was silent for a moment, and Erikan half hoped he'd fallen asleep. Then, Obald grunted and said, 'We showed them what for though, didn't we, Erikan? Those blasted nobles and their treacherous Lady.' Obald and a handful of other necromancers had flocked to Mallobaude's serpent banner after the dukes of Carcassonne, Lyonesse and Artois had declared for King Louen's bastard offspring, and they'd raised legions of the dead to march beside the Serpent's army of disgraced knights. But Obald and his fellows had been a sideshow compared to the real power behind Mallobaude's illegitimate throne – the ancient liche known as Arkhan the Black.

Why Arkhan had chosen to aid Mallobaude, Erikan couldn't say. He had his reasons, just as Obald and Erikan did, the latter supposed. And with the liche on their side, Bretonnia was brought to its knees. At the Battle of Quenelles, Erikan had had the pleasure of seeing the Serpent cast his father's broken body into the mud. The southern provinces had fallen one by one after King Louen's death, until the Serpent had cast his gaze north, to Couronne.

It had all gone wrong then. Mallobaude had lost his head, Arkhan had vanished, and...

'We lost,' Erikan said.

Obald gave a raspy chuckle. 'We always lose, Erikan. That's the way of it. There are no winners, save for death and the Dark Gods. I taught you that too.'

Erikan hissed in annoyance. 'You taught me a lot, old man. And you'll live to teach me more, if you stop straining yourself.'

'No, I don't think so,' Obald coughed. 'You can smell it on me. I know you can, boy. I'm done for. A longbow is a great equaliser on the battlefield. I've only survived this long out of nastiness. But I'm tired now, and I'm all out of spite.' He coughed again, and Erikan caught the whiff of fresh blood. Obald doubled over in the travois, hacking and choking. Erikan stopped and tore himself loose from the travois. He sank down beside his old mentor and laid a hand on his quivering back.

Obald had always looked old, but now he looked weak and decrepit. Erikan knew that the old man was right. The arrow that had felled him had done too much damage to his insides. That he had survived the journey over the Grey Mountains and into the provinces of the Empire was due more to stubbornness than anything else. By the time they'd reached Stirland, he'd been unable to ride, and barely able to sit upright. He was dying, and there was nothing Erikan could do.

No, that wasn't true. There was one thing. He lifted his wrist to his lips. He opened his mouth, exposing long, curved fangs and readied himself to plunge them into his wrist.

He paused when he saw that Obald was watching him. Blood and spittle clung like pearlescent webs to the old man's beard. He smiled, revealing a mouthful of rotting teeth. Obald patted him on the cheek. 'No need to bloody yourself, Erikan. My old carcass wouldn't survive it, anyway.'

Erikan lowered his arm. Obald lay back on the travois. 'You were a good friend, Erikan. For a ravenous, untrustworthy nocturnal fiend, I mean,' the necromancer wheezed. 'But as the rain enters the soil, and the river enters the sea, so do all things come to their final end.'

'Strigany proverbs,' Erikan muttered. 'Now I know that you're dying.' He sat back on his heels and watched the last link to his mortal life struggle for breath. 'You don't have to, you know. You're just being stubborn and spiteful.'

'I've been stubborn and spiteful my whole sorry life, boy,' Obald croaked. 'I've fought and raged and run for more years than you. I saw Kemmler's rise and fall, I saw Mousillon in all of its pox-ridden glory and I visited the secret ruins of Morgheim, where the Strigoi dance and howl.' The old man's eyes went vacant. 'I fought and fought and fought, and now I think maybe I am done fighting.' His trembling, wrinkled fingers found Erikan's wrist. 'That's the smart choice, I think, given what's coming.' His glazed eyes sought out Erikan's face. 'Always get out before the rush, that's my advice.' His voice was barely a whisper. Erikan leaned close.

'I miss my pigs,' Obald said. Then, with a soft grunt, his face went slack, and whatever dark force had inhabited him fled into the crawling sky above. Erikan stared down at him. He'd been hoping that the old man would make it to Sylvania. After leaving Couronne, they'd learned that the other survivors were going there, drawn by some bleak impetus to travel across the mountains. There were stories of walls of bone and an independent state of the dead, ruled by the aristocracy of the night. They'd even heard a rumour that Arkhan's forces were heading that way.

It was the beginning of something, Erikan thought. Obald had mocked the idea, in between coughing fits, but Erikan could feel it in the black, sour hollow of his bones. There was smoke on the air and blood in the water, and the wind carried the promise of death. It was everything he'd dreamed of, since his parents had gone screaming to the flames, the taste of corpses still on their tongues. He'd seen a spark of it when Obald had rescued him then, flaying his captors with dark magics. In those black flames, which had stripped meat from bone as easily as a butcher's knife, Erikan had seen the ruination of all things. The end of all pain and hunger and strife.

And now, that dream was coming true: the world was dying, and Erikan Crowfiend intended to be in at the end. But, he'd been hoping that Obald would be by his side. Didn't the old man deserve that much, at least? Instead, he was just another corpse.

At least he was free, while Erikan was still a captive of the world.

Erikan carelessly pried the old man's fingers off his wrist and stood. He dropped his hand to the pommel of his blade and said, casually, 'He's dead.'

'I know,' a woman's voice replied. 'He should have died years ago. He would have, if you hadn't been wasting your time keeping his wrinkled old cadaver from getting the chop.'

'He raised me. He took me in, when anyone else would have burned me with the rest of my kin, for the crime of survival,' Erikan said. His hand tightened on the hilt of his blade and he drew it smoothly as he whirled to face the newcomer. 'He helped me become the man I am today.'

In the sickly light of the moon, her pale flesh seemed to glow with an eerie radiance. She wore baroque black armour edged in gold over red silk. The hue of the silk matched her fiery tresses, which had been piled atop her head in a style three centuries out of fashion. Eyes like agates met his own as she reached out and gently pushed aside his sword. 'I rather thought that I had some part in that as well, Erikan.'

He lowered his sword. 'Why are you here, Elize?'

'For the same reason as you, I imagine.'

Erikan stabbed his blade down into the loamy earth and set his palms on the crosspiece. 'Sylvania,' he said, simply.

Elize von Carstein inclined her head. A crimson tress slipped free of the mass atop her head and dangled in her face, until she blew it aside. He felt a rush of desire but forced it down. Those days were done and buried. 'I felt the summons.' She looked up at the moon. 'The black bell of Sternieste is tolling and the Templars of the Order of Drakenhof are called to war.'

Erikan looked down at the pommel of his blade, and the red bat, rampant, that was carved there. It was the symbol of the von Carsteins, and of the Drakenhof Templars. He covered it with his hand. 'And who are we going to war with?'

Elize smiled sadly and said, 'Everyone. Come, I have an extra horse.'

'Did you bring it for me?'

Elize didn't answer. Erikan followed her. He left Obald's body where it lay, to whatever fate awaited it. The old man's cankerous spirit was gone. His body was just so much cooling meat now, and Erikan had long since lost his taste for such rancid leavings.

'Are we all gathering, then?' Erikan asked, as he followed her through the trees, towards a quiet copse where two black horses waited, red-eyed and impatiently pawing at the earth. Deathless, breathless and remorseless, the horses from the stables of Castle Drakenhof were unmatched by any steed in the known world, save possibly for the stallions of far Ulthuan. He took the bridle of the one she indicated and stroked it, murmuring wordlessly. He'd always had a way with beasts, even after he'd been reborn. He'd kept company with the great shaggy wolves that Obald had pulled from their forest graves, leading them on moonlit hunts. The day Obald had taught him how to call up the beasts himself was the closest he had ever come to true happiness, he thought.

'All who still persist, and keep to their oath,' Elize said. 'I arrived with several of the others. We decided to journey together.'

'Why?' Erikan asked.

'Why wouldn't we?' Elize asked, after a moment, as she climbed into her saddle. 'Is it not meet that the inner circle do so? I saw your trail, and decided to see if you were interested in joining us. You are one of us, after all.'

'I don't recall you asking me whether I wished to be,' he said, softly. Elize kicked her horse into motion and galloped away. Erikan hesitated, and then climbed up into his own saddle and set off after her. As he rode, he couldn't help but muse that it had always been thus. Elize called and he came. He watched her ride, her slim form bent low over her mount's neck, her armour glinting dully in the moonlight. She was beautiful and terrible and inexorable, like death given a woman's shape. There were worse ways to spend eternity, he supposed.

She led him into the high barrows and scrub trees that populated the hills and valleys west of the border with Stirland. Ruins of all sorts dotted the area, the legacy of centuries of warfare. Shattered windmills and slumping manses towered over the gutted remains of border forts and isolated farmsteads. Some were more recent than others, but all had suffered the same fate. This was the no-man's-land between the provinces of the living and the dead, and nothing of the former survived here for long.

As they left the trees and the fog that had clung to them, he hauled back on the reins of his horse, startled by the sight of the distant edifice of bone, which rose high up into the sky, towering over the area. It was far larger than the rumours he'd heard had intimated. It was less fortress rampart than newborn mountain range. Only the largest of giants would have had a chance of clambering over it. 'Nagash's *teeth*,' he hissed. 'I'd heard he'd done it, but I never expected it to be true.' The sense of finality he'd had before, of endings and final days, came back stronger than ever. Sylvania had always seemed unchanging. A gangrenous wound that never healed, but never grew any worse. But now, now it was finally ready to kill. He wanted to laugh and howl at the same time, but he restrained himself.

'Yes,' Elize said, over her shoulder. 'Mannfred has seceded from the Empire. Our time for hiding in the shadows is done.' The way she said it made him wonder if she were entirely happy about it. Most of their kind were conservative by nature. Immortality brought with it a fear of change, and a need to force the world to remain in place. Erikan had never felt that way. When you were born in squalor and raised amid corpses, a bit of change was not unwelcome.

Erikan urged his horse on. 'No wonder the bells have been sounded. If he's done all of this, he's going to need as many of us as he can get.' The thought wasn't a comforting one. Vampires could, by and large, get along, if there was a reason. But the inevitable infighting and challenges for status that would result were going to be tedious, if not downright lethal.

Elize didn't reply. They rode on through the night, galloping hard, the endurance of their steeds never faltering. More than once, Erikan saw distant campfires and smelt the blood of men. The armies of the Empire were on the move, but he could not tell in which direction they were going. Were they laying siege to Sylvania? Or were the rumours of another invasion from the north true? Was that why Mannfred had chosen now of all times to make such a bold statement of intent?

All of these thoughts rattled in his head as Elize led him towards one of the ruins close to the bone bastion. It was far from any of the campfires that dotted the darkness and had been a watch tower once, he thought. Now it was just crumbled stone, blackened by fire and covered in weeds and moss. He saw that three men waited inside, as he climbed down from his horse and led it to join the others where they were tied to a gibbet. Elize led Erikan into the ruin, and he nodded politely to the others as he ducked through the shattered archway. There was no light, save that of the moon, for they needed none.

'What is *he* doing here?' one of the men growled, one hand on the hilt of the heavy sword belted to his waist. Erikan kept his own hands well away from his blade.

'The same as you, Anark,' Erikan said, as Elize went to the other vampire's side, and put her hand over his, as if to keep him from drawing his blade. Anark von Carstein was a big man, bigger than Erikan, built for war and clad in dark armour composed of serrated plates and swooping, sharp curves. The armour had seen its share of battle, to judge by the dents and scratches that marked it. Anark had been fighting in the Border Princes, the last Erikan had heard, leading an army of the dead on behalf of one petty warlord or another.

Elize leaned into Anark and whispered into his ear. He calmed visibly. She had always had a way with the other vampire, Erikan recalled. Then, much like Erikan himself, Anark was a protégé of the Doyenne of the Red Abbey, and had even been allowed to take the name of von Carstein, something Erikan would likely never achieve. Nor, in truth, did he wish to. He had his own name, and he was content with it. That, he thought, was why she had cooled to him, in the end. She had offered him her name, and he had refused. And so she had found another blood-son, lover and champion. And Erikan had left.

He looked away from them, and met the red gaze of the other von Carstein present. 'Markos,' Erikan said, nodding. Markos was hawk-faced and his hair had been greased back, making him resemble nothing so much as a stoat. Where Anark was a simple enough brute, Markos was more cunning. He had a gift for sorcery that few could match, and a tongue like an adder's bite.

'Crowfiend, I never thought to see you again,' Markos said. 'You know Count Nyktolos, I trust?' He gestured to the other vampire, who, like Anark and Markos, was clad in a heavy suit of armour. Nyktolos wore a monocle, after the fashion of the Altdorf aristocracy, and his grin stretched from ear to ear, in an unpleasant fashion. Unlike Anark and Markos, his flesh was the colour of a bruised plum, flush with a recent feeding, or perhaps simply mottled by grave-rot. It happened to some of them, if the blood-kiss wasn't delivered properly.

'Count,' Erikan said, bowing shallowly. He'd heard of the other vampire. He'd been a count of Vargravia once, before Konrad had stormed through, in the bad old days. Nyktolos smiled, revealing a mouthful of needle fangs, more than any self-respecting vampire needed, in Erikan's opinion. If he was Konrad's get, that and his odd hue were probably the least of his problems.

'He's polite. I like him already,' Nyktolos croaked.

'Don't get too attached,' Anark said. 'He won't be staying long. Erikan doesn't have the stomach for war. A real war, I mean. Not one of those little skirmishes they have west of the Grey Mountains.'

Erikan met Anark's flat, red gaze calmly. The other vampire was trying to bait him, as he always did. Just why Anark hated him so much, Erikan couldn't really fathom. He was no threat to Anark. He tried to meet Elize's eyes, but her attentions remained on her paramour. No, he thought, no matter how much he might wish otherwise, he posed no danger to Anark, in any regard. 'I hope you weren't waiting for me,' he said to Markos, ignoring Anark.

'No, we were waiting for– Ah! Speak of the devil, and he shall appear,' Markos said, looking up. The air was filled with the rush of great wings, and a noisome odour flooded the ruin as something heavy struck its top. Rocks tumbled down, dislodged by the new arrival as he crawled down to join them, clinging to the ancient stones like a lizard. 'You're late, Alberacht,' Markos called out.

The hairy body of the newcomer remained splayed across the stones above them for a moment, and then dropped down. Erikan stepped back as Alberacht Nictus rose to his full height. The creature, known in some quarters as the Reaper of Drakenhof, extended a hooked claw and caught Erikan gently by the back of his head. He didn't resist as the monstrous vampire pulled him close. 'Hello, boy,' Alberacht rumbled. His face was human enough, if horribly stretched over a bumpy, malformed skull, but his bloated body was a hideous amalgamation of bat, ape and wolf. He wore little armour, and carried no weapon. Having seen him at work, Erikan knew he needed none. His long claws and powerful muscles made him as dangerous as any charging knight.

'Master Nictus,' Erikan said, not meeting the vampire's bestial gaze. Alberacht was unpredictable, even for a vampire. He looked less human every time Erikan saw him. Sometimes he wondered if that was the fate that awaited him, down the long corridor of centuries. Some vampires remained as they were, frozen forever in their last moment. But others became drunk on slaughter and lost their hold on what little humanity remained to them.

'Master, he says,' Alberacht growled. His face twisted into a parody of a smile. 'Such respect for this old warrior. You see how he respects me?' The smile faded. 'Why do the rest of you fail to follow suit?' He turned his baleful gaze on the others. Bloody spittle oozed from his jowls as he champed his long fangs. 'Am I not Grand Master of our order? Must I break you on discipline's altar?' The others backed off as Alberacht released Erikan and turned towards them. He half spread his leathery wings and his eyes glowed with a manic light. He stank of violence and madness, and Erikan drew well away. Alberacht was fully capable of killing any of them in his rage.

'Not for centuries, old one,' Elize said smoothly. 'You remember, don't you? You gave up your post and your burdens to Tomas.' She reached out and stroked Alberacht's hairy hide, the way one might seek to calm an agitated stallion. Erikan tensed. If Alberacht made to harm her, he would have to be quick. He saw Anark gripping his own blade, and the other vampire nodded tersely when he caught Erikan's eye. Neither of them wanted to see Elize come to harm, however much they disliked one another.

'Tomas?' Alberacht grunted. He folded his wings. 'Yes, Tomas. A good boy, for a von Carstein.' He shook himself, like a sleeper awakening from a nightmare, and stroked Elize's head, as a weary grandfather might stroke his grandchild. 'I heard the bells.'

'We all did, old beast,' Markos said. 'We are being called to Sternieste.'

'Then why do we stand here?' Alberacht asked. 'The border is just there, mere steps from where we stand.'

'Well, the giant bloody wall of bone for one,' Count Nyktolos said, shifting his weight. 'We'll have to leave the horses.'

'No, we won't,' Elize said. She looked at Markos and asked, 'Cousin?'

'Oh, it's up to me, is it? Since when did you take charge?' Markos asked. The flat gazes of Anark and Alberacht met his and he threw up his hands in a gesture of surrender. 'Right, yes, fine. I'll get us in the old-fashioned way. Subtlety, thy name is Elize. Form an orderly queue, gentles all, and Erikan as well, of course. Let's go home.'

◄ CHAPTER TWO ►

Stirland-Sylvania border

Dawn was cresting the tops of the hills by the time they reached the foot of the bastion. As the red, watery light washed across the ridges of pale bone, Erikan sought some sign of an entrance, but he saw none as they galloped along its base. 'How are we getting in there? There's no gate,' he shouted to Markos. The other vampire glanced at him over his shoulder and grinned.

'Who needs a gate?' Markos laughed. He jerked his reins, causing his horse to rear, and flung out a hand. Dark fire coruscated about his spread fingers for a moment as he roared out a few harsh syllables. A bolt of energy erupted from his palm and slammed into the bone bastion, cracking and splintering it. 'Master Nictus, if you please!'

There was a shriek from above as Alberacht hurtled down, swooping towards the point of impact. The gigantic vampire slammed into the wall and tore through it with a thunderous crash. Markos kicked his horse into motion before the dust had cleared, and Erikan and the others rode hard after him. The wall began to repair itself with a horrible rustling sound as they rode through the gap. And there was something else – a weirdling light that spread about them as they rode, and Erikan felt as if something had opened a burning hole in his belly. He heard Elize gasp and Count Nyktolos curse out loud, and saw that they were all lit by witch-fire, but only for a moment. Then they were clear of the wall, and the feeling faded.

The first thing he noticed was that the sky was dark. The second thing he noticed was the dull, rhythmic pealing of distant bells. 'The bells of Stern-ieste,' Alberacht crooned, swiping shards of bone from his shoulders. 'I thought never to hear their lovely song again.'

'Nor I,' Markos muttered. Erikan saw that he was looking at the wall.

'What is it?' he asked. Thunder rumbled somewhere amongst the thick charcoal-coloured clouds that choked the dark sky. There was lightning over the distant hills. Erikan felt invigorated and captivated, all at the same time.

'Did you feel something? As we passed over the border?' Markos asked.

135

'I did. You?'

'Aye,' Markos grunted. His eyes narrowed to slits for a moment. Then, with a growl, he shook himself. 'We should go. If the bells are sounding, then Mannfred will be at Sternieste. And so will Tomas and the others.'

They rode on, more slowly now. Sylvania was much as Erikan remembered it, from his last, brief visit. He had been at Elize's side then, learning the ways of their kind, and she had brought him to Sternieste for a gathering of the Drakenhof Order. Elize had spoken for him, and Alberacht had welcomed him into the order with terrifying heartiness. The old monster had been a good Grand Master, as far as it went. Erikan glanced up at Nictus as he swooped overhead, and felt a pang of what might have been sadness.

They made their way to the castle by the old paths, known to their kind. They passed isolated villages and outposts that sought to throw back the omnipresent darkness with torches mounted on posts and lanterns chained to the walls. There was still life of sorts in Sylvania, though how long that would be the case Erikan didn't care to guess. Most vampires needed little in the way of nourishment, but then, most had the self-control of a fox in a chicken coop. Many of those little villages would not last out the week, he knew.

They rode through the camps of Strigany nomads and sent ghoul-packs scrambling from their path as their deathless steeds sped along the dark track. Loping wolves and shrieking bats kept pace with them from time to time, as did other, worse things. Erikan had heard that when Mannfred had returned to the damned province and first set about the taming of Sylvania, he had thrown open the vaults of Castle Drakenhof and let loose every foul thing that Vlad had ever interred. All were heading east, towards Castle Sternieste. It was as if every dark soul were being drawn to that distant manse, like metal splinters to a lodestone.

It looked like a grasping talon, its trio of crooked towers jutting ferociously towards the moon above. Even from a distance, the crumbling citadel was magnificent. It was a feat of engineering that had, in its day, claimed a third of the lives employed in its construction, and their tattered souls still clung to the rain-slick stones. It crouched in the open, seemingly in defiance of those who might march against it, and Erikan could guess why Mannfred had chosen it – Sternieste was impressive, as citadels went, but it was also situated perfectly along the main artery of Sylvania. Any invaders who took the traditional routes would have to take Sternieste, before they could do anything else. Sternieste, more so than Fort Oberstyre or Castle Drakenhof, was the keystone of the province.

There was also the fact that Castle Sternieste rose high over a field of rolling hillocks. Each of the latter was a cairn of stupendous size and depth, from a bygone age. It might contain a hundred corpses or merely one, but whatever the number of its inhabitants, each dome of soil and withered, yellow grass pulsed with dark energy. And each and every one of them had been broken into. As they rode through the sea of graves, Erikan could feel the ancient dead stirring, disturbed by the passing presence of the vampires.

They passed the burgeoning earthworks being erected by an army of the recently dead. Zombie knights in shattered armour laboured beside equally dead handgunners and militiamen in the mud and dirt, raising bulwarks and setting heavy stakes. Sternieste's master was readying his lands for siege.

Anark had taken the lead, and he led them towards the gaping main gate of the castle. The portcullis had been raised and the gates unbarred and flung open. There were no visible guards, but then, did a citadel of the dead really need them?

As they clattered into the wide, open courtyard, a flock of crows hurtled skywards, disturbed from feasting on the bodies inside the gibbet cages that decorated the inner walls. Heaps of rotting bodies lay everywhere in the courtyard, strewn about like discarded weapons and covered in shrouds of more squabbling carrion birds.

'Lovely,' Markos said, as he slipped out of his saddle. 'It's like paradise, except not.'

'Quiet,' Elize murmured. She tapped the side of her head. 'Can't you feel it, cousin? Can't you feel him? He's watching us.'

'Who?' Erikan asked, though he knew the answer as well as any of them. He could feel the presence of another mind scrabbling in the shadow of his own, prying at his thoughts and probing his feelings.

'Who else? Welcome to Sylvania, my brethren,' a voice called out as the doors of the outer keep opened with a squeal of long-rusted hinges. The heavy, bloated bodies of two gigantic ghouls, each the size of three of its lesser brethren, burdened with chains and rusty cow bells, moved into view as they shoved the doors open. Each of the creatures was shackled to a door, and they squalled and bellowed as a group of armoured figures stepped between them and moved to meet the newcomers.

'Well, look what the dire wolf dragged in, finally. Elize, Markos and... some others. Wonderful, and you're all late, by the way. I expected you days ago,' Tomas von Carstein said as he drew close. The current Grand Master of the Drakenhof Templars looked much the same as he had when Erikan had last seen him. He'd been handsome enough as a living man, but centuries of undeath had crafted him over into a thing of cold, perfect beauty. The warriors who accompanied him were cut from much the same stripe – blood knights, Templars of the Drakenhof Order, who'd fought on thousands of battlefields. Each of them was a capable warrior, more than a match for any living man or beast. Erikan knew one or two of them, and these he nodded to politely. They returned the gesture warily – as Elize's get, he'd been inducted into the inner circle of the order almost immediately, and Tomas was among those who'd been somewhat incensed by what he saw as her profligate ways.

'Welcome to Castle Sternieste, where the seeds of our damnation have been sown,' Tomas continued, extending his arms in a mocking gesture of welcome.

'Very poetic, cousin. But I, for one, have been damned for a very long time,' Markos said. Tomas laughed harshly.

'This is a different sort of damnation, I'm afraid.' He frowned. 'We're trapped.'

'What do you mean? Explain yourself,' Anark demanded. Tomas made a face.

'Must I? You felt it, didn't you? That grotesque frisson as you crossed the border?' He looked at Anark. 'We are trapped here, in Sylvania. We cannot cross the borders, thanks to the sorceries of our enemies – rather, say, Mannfred's enemies.'

'Lord Mannfred, you mean,' Elize corrected.

'Yes, yes,' Tomas said, waving a hand dismissively. 'Lord Mannfred, in his infinite wisdom, decided to openly secede our fair homeland from the Empire. They responded in kind.' He laughed. 'They locked the door behind us after we left, it seems.' His laughter grew, becoming a harsh cackle. He shook his head and looked at them. 'Still, I am glad to see you. At least I'll be in good company for the next millennia.'

'Are we the only ones to arrive?' Alberacht rumbled. 'Where are the others? Where is the rest of the inner circle? Where is my old friend Vyktros von Krieger? Where are the Brothers Howl and the Warden of Corpse Run?'

'Maybe some of us were smart enough to run the other way,' Markos muttered.

Tomas laughed harshly. 'Vyktros is dead, killed trying to breach the damnable sorceries that have us trapped. As for the others, I don't know. What I do know is that Mannfred wished to see us – you – as soon as you arrived. And he's been getting impatient.' He smiled. 'It is to be as it was in the old days, it seems, with us at his right hand. Exactly what it is that we'll be doing, seeing as we are confined to this charming garden of earthly pleasures, is entirely up for debate. Come,' Tomas said. He turned and stalked across the bridge. Erikan and the others shared a look, and then followed their Grand Master through the dark gates of Castle Sternieste.

The castle was a hornet's nest of activity. Skeletons clad in the armour and colours of the Drakenhof Guard marched to and fro, in a mockery of the drills they'd performed in life. Bats of various sizes clung to the ceilings and walls, filling the air with their soft chittering. Ghouls loped across the desiccated grounds, the leaders of the various packs fighting to assert dominance. The dead of ten centuries had been wakened and readied for war, and they stood, waiting silently for the order to march.

There were vampires in evidence as well, more of them than Erikan had ever seen in one place. Von Carsteins as well as others – Lahmians, in courtly finery, and red-armoured Blood Dragons, as well as gargoyle-like

Strigoi. For the first time in centuries, Castle Sternieste rang with the sound of voices and skulduggery. They clustered in the knaves and open chambers, sipping blood from delicate goblets, or fed on the unlucky men and women rounded up at Mannfred's orders from what few nearby villages had not been abandoned and dragged to Sternieste to serve as a larder for the growing mob of predators. They spoke quietly in small groups or pointedly ignored one another. They duelled in the gardens and plotted in the antechambers.

None of them attempted to hinder Tomas and his companions. Everyone knew who the Drakenhof Templars were, and gave them room – even the scions of Blood Keep, who eyed them the way a wolf might eye a rival from another pack. No one was tempted to try their luck at gainsaying him just yet. It wouldn't be long, though. Erikan could smell resentment on the air. Vampires, by their very nature, seethed with the urge to dominate and they chafed at being under another's dominion.

Tomas led them through the castle, up curling stone stairwells and through damp corridors where cold air, and things worse than air, slipped in through broken walls. Ghostly knights galloped silently through the corridors, and wailing hags swept upwards, all drawn in the same direction as the vampiric Templars. It was there, in the bell tower of Sternieste, that the great black bells tolled, calling the dead to their master's side. The sound of the bells was as the creak of a coffin lid and the thud of a mausoleum door; it was the crunch of bone and the wet slap of torn flesh; it was the sound all dead things knew, deep in the marrow of their bones.

Tomas's warriors peeled off as they approached the narrow stairwell that led up to the bell tower. The meeting was obviously only for the inner circle. Erikan felt a twinge of doubt as they ascended, and the others seemed to share his concern, save for Anark and Elize, who chatted gaily to Tomas as they went. Markos caught Erikan's eye and made a face. Something was going on. Erikan wondered if Mannfred had truly summoned them, or this was some ploy on Tomas's part. *Or Elize's,* a small, treacherous voice murmured in the depths of his mind. Those who took the von Carstein name tended towards ambition. To assume the name was a symbol of your devotion to the ideals of Vlad von Carstein, of a vampire-state, of an empire of the dead, ruled by the masters of the night. Only the ambitious or the insane announced their intentions so openly.

When they climbed out into the bell tower, the air throbbed with the graveyard churn of the bells, and the soft cacophony of the gathered spectral hosts that surrounded the top of the tower. Hundreds, if not thousands of spirits floated above the tower, pulled to and chained by the dull clangour. The bell-ringers were ghouls, and they gave vent to bone-rattling howls and shrieks as they hauled on the ropes.

And beyond them, his back to the newcomers, his eyes fixed on the innumerable spirits dancing on the night wind, stood Mannfred von Carstein.

He had one foot set on the parapet, and he leaned on his raised knee as he gazed upwards. He did not turn as they arrived, and only glanced at them when Tomas drew his sword partially from its sheath and slammed it down.

'Count Mannfred, you have called and we, your most loyal servants, have come. The inner circle of the Drakenhof Order is ready to ride forth at your command and at your discretion,' Tomas said.

'I'm sure you are,' Mannfred said. His eyes flickered over each of them in turn, and Erikan couldn't help but feel nervous. He'd only ever served the creature before him at a remove. To see him in the flesh was something else again. Mannfred was tall, taller even than Anark, taller than any normal man, if not gigantic. He seemed swollen with power, and his gilt-edged, black armour was of the finest quality, despite its archaic appearance. A heavy cloak made from the hairy pelt of a gigantic wolf hung down from his shoulders, and a long-bladed sword with an ornate basket hilt was sheathed on his hip. His scalp had been shorn clean of hair, and his face was aquiline and aristocratic, with a fine-boned grace to his features. 'While I am glad that you have come, I expected more of you, cousins and gentles all.'

'These are the greatest warriors of the order, my lord,' Tomas said. 'The blood of the von Carsteins runs thick in the veins of the inner circle. Will you do us the honour of explaining your purpose in summoning us?'

'I should think it would be obvious, cousin,' Mannfred said. He reached out a hand as the ghost of a wailing child drifted close, as if to comfort the spectre. Instead, he crooked his fingers and swept them through its features, causing the ghost to momentarily stretch and distort. 'I am readying myself for the war to come. To wage war, I require warriors. Hence, your presence. Or must I explain further?'

'No, no, most wise and fierce lord,' Tomas said, looking at the others meaningfully. 'But one must wonder why we have been summoned into a land that we cannot then leave.'

Mannfred gave no sign that Tomas's words had struck a nerve, but somehow Erikan knew that they had. The lord of Sylvania examined Tomas for a moment. Erikan saw his eyes slide towards those of Elize, who inclined her head slightly. His hand found the hilt of his blade. Something was definitely going on. He was sure of it now. There was an undercurrent here he didn't like. 'What are you implying, cousin?' Mannfred asked.

Tomas cocked his head. 'Surely you can feel it, my lord. It is the talk of your court, and of the guests who shelter beneath the bowers of your generosity. The borders are protected against our kind. We can enter, but not leave. And as mighty as your walls are, and as great as your army might be, we find ourselves wondering why you gave us no warning?' He looked around him, at Erikan and the others, seeking support. Anark began to nod dully, but Elize's hand on his arm stopped him. Erikan traded glances with Markos. The latter smiled thinly and gave a slight shake of his head.

'If I had, dear cousin, would you have come?' Mannfred asked, turning away.

Tomas tapped the pommel of his blade with a finger, and gave Mannfred a speculative look. 'So what you're saying is that you've knowingly trapped us here, in this reeking sty you call a fiefdom. Wonderful, truly. Vlad's cunning was as nothing compared to your own ineffable wisdom.' He turned to look at the others again. 'Yes, your brilliance is as bright as the light of the Witch Moon in full glow, my Lord Mannfred. I, and the rest of the inner circle of the Drakenhof Templars, stand in awe of your puissance and forethought in calling us all back and trapping us here, in this overlarge tomb of yours.' Tomas clapped politely. 'Well done, sirrah. What will be your next trick, pray tell? Perhaps you'd like to juggle a few blessed relics, or maybe go for a stroll in the noonday sun?'

'Are you finished?' Mannfred asked.

'No,' Tomas said, all trace of jocularity gone from his voice. 'Not even a little bit. I – we – came in good faith, and at your request, Lord Mannfred. And you have betrayed even that shred of consideration and for what – so that we might share your captivity?'

'So that you might help me break the chains that bind Sylvania, dear cousin,' Mannfred purred. 'And you did not do me a favour, Tomas. You owe me your allegiance. I am the true and lawful lord of Sylvania, and your order is pledged to my service, wherever and whenever I so require.'

'Not quite.' Tomas smiled thinly. 'We do serve the Count of Sylvania, but that doesn't necessarily mean you, *cousin*.'

Erikan blinked. Even for a vampire, Tomas was fast. The gap between thought and deed for him was but the barest of moments. His blade was in his hand and arcing towards Mannfred's shaved pate as he finished speaking, and the other had started to turn.

Mannfred was not so quick. But then, he didn't have to be. Tomas's blade smashed down into Mannfred's waiting palm, halted mere inches from the crown of his head. Mannfred examined the blade for a moment, and then tore it from Tomas's grip with a casual twitch of his wrist. Still holding the sword by the blade, he looked at Tomas. 'In a way, Tomas, you are correct. However, in another, altogether more important way, you are decidedly incorrect.' Without a flicker of warning, Mannfred caught Tomas a ringing blow across the side of his head with the hilt of his sword.

Tomas was sent flying by the force of the blow. Mannfred tossed the now-broken sword over the parapet and strode towards the fallen Grand Master. Erikan and the others drew back. Tomas had made his play without consulting them, and the consequences would be on his head alone. He'd likely hoped they'd join him, when they learned of the trap. Then, he had never been very smart, Erikan reflected as Mannfred reached down and grabbed a handful of Tomas's hair. Mannfred hauled the other vampire to his feet effortlessly. 'This, Tomas, is why I called you back. This weakness, this bravado, this mistaken impression that you, that *any of you,* are my equal.' He pulled Tomas close. 'I have no equal, cousin. I am Mannfred von Carstein, first, last and only. And I cannot abide weakness.' He flung Tomas against the wall hard enough to rattle the latter's armour. 'I have begun something. And I would have my servants at my disposal, rather than traipsing off, pursuing their own petty goals when they should be pursuing mine.'

Tomas clawed at the wall and dragged himself upright. He glared at Mannfred. 'The only weak one here is you. I remember you, Mannfred, cousin, scrabbling at Vlad's heels, hiding from Konrad – you were a rat then, and you're a rat now, cowering in your nest.'

Mannfred was silent for a moment. His face betrayed no expression. Then, he made a single, sharp gesture. The air and shadows around Tomas seemed to congeal, becoming sharp and solid. For a moment, Erikan was reminded of the jaws of a wolf closing about a field mouse. The darkness obscured Tomas, and there came a strange squeal as though metal were scraping against metal, and then a horrid grinding sound that made Erikan's fangs ache in his gums.

Tomas began to scream. Blood spattered the stones, and torn and bent bits of armour clattered to the ground. To Erikan, it sounded as if the Grand Master were being flayed alive. Whatever was happening, Mannfred watched it with glittering eyes and with a slight, savage smile creasing his aquiline features.

When it was done, there was little left of Tomas – just something red and raw that lay in the detritus of its former glory, mewling shrilly. Mannfred looked down at the squirming ruin and said, 'Anark, see to your predecessor. I have other, more important matters to attend.'

Anark started. His nostrils flared, but he gave no other sign that his sudden rise to prominence had surprised him. His lips peeled back from his fangs as he drew his sword and advanced on the remains of his former comrade.

Mannfred stepped back and turned to Elize. He stroked her cheek in such a way that Erikan thought it lucky for one of them that Anark was occupied with his butchery. Mannfred leaned towards her and murmured, 'And so I have kept my promise, cousin.' Erikan glanced at the others surreptitiously, but he seemed to have been the only one to hear the exchange. Mannfred drew his cloak about him and left them on the parapet. Erikan waited for the sound of his boots to fade and then said, 'Well, that was unexpected.'

'But not unwelcome,' Elize said. She drifted towards Anark, and rubbed a spot of blood from his cheek. 'Tomas was a fool, and we all know it. His end has been a century in coming, and I, for one, am glad that we do not have to put up with him longer than was absolutely necessary. If we are trapped here, then Mannfred is our best chance of escape. And besides, Tomas had no concept of honour or loyalty. Anark will make a better Grand Master, I think.'

Anark grinned and ran his hand along his blade, stripping Tomas's blood from it. 'Unless someone objects?' He looked at Erikan as he spoke. 'Well, Crowfiend?'

Erikan didn't rise to the bait. 'I wasn't under the assumption that we had been given a vote.' He inclined his head. 'Long live the new Grand Master.' The others followed suit, murmuring their congratulations.

Alberacht even looked as if he meant it.

CHAPTER THREE

Castle Sternieste, Sylvania

Mannfred strode through the damp, cool corridors of Sternieste, trying to rein in the anger that had threatened to overwhelm him for days now. The hunched shapes of his servants scurried out of his path as he walked, but he gave them little notice.

Gelt's barrier of faith still resisted every attempt to shatter it. He had wrung his library dry of magics, and had made not the slightest bit of difference. Soon enough, once the northern invasion had been thrown back, as they always, inevitably were, Karl Franz would turn his attentions back to the festering boil on the backside of his pitiful empire and lance it once and for all. There was nowhere to run, nowhere to go. It might take centuries, or millions of lives, but Mannfred had studied the Emperor for a decade, and he knew that there was no more ruthless a man in the world, save himself. Karl Franz would happily sacrifice Ostland and Stirland, if it meant scouring Sylvania from the map.

Mannfred wanted to scream, to rant and rave, to succumb to the red thirst and rampage through some village somewhere. Everything he had worked for, everything he had conquered death for, was coming apart in his hands before he'd even begun, leaving him still in Vlad's shadow. Tomas had scored a palpable hit with that painful truth, before Mannfred had dealt with him. That the blow was not physical made it no less painful, nor any less lingering. Most of his followers knew better than to question him, either out of fear or because they lacked the wit to see the trap for what it was. In a way, the preponderance of the latter was his own fault. He had eliminated most, if not all, of his rivals amongst the aristocracy of the night. Vlad had bestowed the gift of immortality as a reward, without much thought as to the consequences, and Konrad had been even more profligate, turning dockside doxies, common mercenaries and, in one unfortunate incident that was best forgotten, a resident of the Moot.

Mannfred had dealt with all of them, hunting them down one by one

over the centuries since his resurrection from the swamps of Hel Fenn. Any
vampire of the von Carstein bloodline who would not serve him, or was
of no use to him, he destroyed, even as he had destroyed Tomas. Most of
Vlad's get had been swept off the board at the outset. Tomas and the other
members of the inner circle of the Drakenhof Templars were among the
last of them, and with Tomas's death, Mannfred thought that they were
sufficiently cowed. Elize was more pragmatic than the others, and could
be counted on to keep them under control. At least in so far as monsters
like Nictus, or weasels like Markos, could be controlled.

He reached up and ran both hands over his shorn scalp. He wondered if,
when all was said and done, he would finally be free of Vlad's ghost. When
he had finally broken the world's spine and supped on its life's blood, would
that nagging, mocking shade depart.

No. No, I think not, Vlad's voice whispered. Mannfred neither paused, nor
responded. The voice was only in his head. It was only a trick of long, wasted
centuries, some self-defeating urge that he could ignore. *Am I though? Or
am I really here with you still, my best beloved son?* the voice murmured.
Mannfred ground his teeth.

'No, you are not,' he hissed.

The voice faded, leaving only the echo of a ghostly chuckle to mark its
passing. Mannfred hated that chuckle. It had always been Vlad's signal
that he was missing something that the latter thought obvious. And perhaps he was. But he had weighty matters on his mind at the moment. Most
notably that his demesnes were already subject to invasion, albeit not a
large one, and not one initiated by the Empire. But it was still enough to
give Mannfred pause. His nascent realm had already suffered attack once,
by a horde of daemons. Those had been easy enough to see off, but this
new threat was proving to be more persistent. He'd sent out wolves and
bats to shadow the intruder's approach, but every time the beasts came
closer to the newcomer, Mannfred's control over them had slipped away.
That could only mean that the invader was another master of the Corpse
Geometries, and one unlike the other wretched creatures that had thus far
made it across the border.

Whoever it was had made no attempt to either openly challenge or offer
fealty to the lord of Sylvania. Mannfred had at first suspected that it was
the self-styled Lichemaster, Heinrich Kemmler, who'd been his ally for an
all-too-brief moment, before he'd chafed beneath the goad and taken his
leave of Mannfred's court, his hulking undead bodyguard Krell following
behind him. Mannfred had kept tabs on the necromancer, and the last he'd
heard the lunatic sorcerer had raised an army of the dead to lay siege to
Castle Reikguard, for reasons fathomable only to him.

But the intruder's aura, the taste of his power, was different from
Kemmler's. It was older, for one thing, with its roots sunk deep in disciplines that had existed for millennia. And it was greater, possibly even a

match for Mannfred's own. There were few creatures who could wield such power so negligently – that wretched creature Zacharias the Ever-Living for one, or that perfumed dolt Dietrich von Dohl, the so-called Crimson Lord of Sylvania. And this newcomer was neither.

Which left only one possibility.

Mannfred forced down the anger as it threatened to surge again. If the intruder was who he suspected, he would need all of his faculties to deal with him in the manner he deserved. But before he marshalled his energies for such a conflict, he would need to be certain. Time was at a premium, and he could not afford to waste his carefully husbanded strength battling shadows. That said, the thought of such a conflict did not displease Mannfred. Indeed, after the weeks of frustration he had endured, such a confrontation was an almost welcome diversion. To be free at last to strive and destroy would be a great relief to him.

The loud, raucous communal croak of a number of carrion birds let him know he'd reached his destination, and he quickly assumed a mask of genteel calm. It wouldn't do to show any weakness, emotional or otherwise, to a creature like the Crowfiend. He'd asked Elize's creature to meet him in the castle's high garden. There were things Mannfred needed to ask him, to lend weight to or dismiss those theories now burgeoning in his mind.

A brace of skeletons, clad in bronze cuirasses and holding bronze-headed, long-hafted axes, guarded the entrance to the open-air, walled garden. He stepped past them, and as he entered the garden, a flock of black-feathered birds leapt skywards, screaming in indignation. He watched them swoop and wheel for a moment. Vlad had always felt a ghastly affection for the beasts. Mannfred had never understood how a creature as powerful as Vlad could waste his attentions feeding sweetmeats to such vermin, when there were more important matters to be attended to.

The Crowfiend sat on one of the cracked, discoloured marble benches that encircled the garden's single, crooked tree. The fat-trunked monstrosity was long dead, but somehow it still grew, drawing gods alone knew what sort of nourishment from the castle into whose mortar it had sunk its roots. Erikan stood as Mannfred approached. Mannfred gestured for him to sit. He gazed at the other vampire for a moment.

The Crowfiend had a face that radiated feral placidity. There was no obvious guile in him. Cunning, yes, and cleverness, but no guile. He was not a subtle creature, but neither was he stupid. There was something familiar there as well – a raw need that Mannfred recognised in himself. A hunger that was greater than any bloodthirst or flesh-greed. Mannfred drew close to the other vampire and caught his chin in an iron grip. He pulled Erikan's face up. 'I can see the ghoul-taint in your face, boy. Elize tells me that your kin were corpse-eaters, though not so debased as those that prowl these halls.'

'They were, my lord,' Erikan said.

'They were burned, I am given to understand.'

'Yes,' Erikan said, and he displayed no more emotion than if he'd been speaking of a rat he'd killed. Mannfred wondered if such lack of feeling was a mask. Vampires, contrary to folk belief and superstition, did not lose the ability to feel emotion. Indeed, undeath often enhanced such things. Sometimes every emotion was redoubled and magnified, stretched almost into caricature. Love became lust, passion became obsession, and hatred... Ah, hatred became something so venomous as to make even daemons flinch. And sometimes, they became as dust, only a fading memory of emotion, a brief, dull flicker of fires burned low.

'If I were to say to you that the world is soon to die, what would you say?'

'I'd say that I'd like to see that, my lord,' Erikan said.

Mannfred blinked. He meant it, too. He let him go. 'Is existence so burdensome to you?'

Erikan shrugged. 'No. I merely meant that if the world is to burn, I might as well help stoke the fires,' he said.

'You believe it is time for a change, then?'

Erikan looked away. 'Change doesn't frighten me, my lord.'

'No, perhaps it doesn't, at that. Perhaps that is why Elize chose you – she has always had a streak of perversity in her, my lovely cousin. She was a sister of Shallya once, you know. She was at Isabella's side, when she passed over from the wasting illness, and Vlad wrenched her back from Morr's clutches. Poor, gentle Elize was Isabella's first meal upon awakening. And she served as the countess's handmaiden until her untimely end.'

Erikan said nothing. Mannfred smiled thinly. 'Very loyal is Elize. Loyal, trustworthy, her ambition kept on the tightest of leashes. Why did she toss you aside, I wonder?' The other vampire cocked his head, but did not reply. For a moment, Mannfred was reminded of a carrion bird. He gestured airily. 'I don't suppose it matters. She brought you over, and that is more a gift than most get in this fallen world.' He turned away and strode to the tree. 'You came from Couronne, I'm given to understand,' Mannfred said. He gazed up at the tree. Idly he jabbed a talon into the spongy surface of the trunk. Black ichors oozed out of the cut. He glanced back at Erikan and sucked the sour sap off his finger.

Erikan nodded slowly. 'I did.'

'The Serpent fell, then,' Mannfred said.

Erikan nodded again. 'We were defeated.'

'And what of Arkhan the Black?'

Erikan jolted, as if struck. 'What about him, my lord?'

'What happened to him in the aftermath?'

'I don't know, my lord,' Erikan said. 'I and– I was with Mallobaude's bodyguard.' His face twisted slightly. He shook himself. 'Some say Arkhan was never there at Couronne to begin with. That he had used Mallobaude

as a diversion for some other scheme. Others say that the Green Knight
struck off his head as he had Mallobaude's.'

Mannfred grunted. 'No such luck,' he muttered. He looked back at Erikan.
'But he was there – in Bretonnia – of this you're certain?'

'I saw him, though only at a distance, my lord. It was him. He rode in a
chariot of bone, which bore banners of crackling witch-fire and was pulled
by skeletal steeds surmounted by the skulls of men, which screamed out
in agony as they galloped.'

Mannfred nodded. 'That sounds just ostentatious enough to be truthful,'
he murmured. The liche had long since lost any subtlety he had possessed
in life. Arkhan had none of a vampire's inbuilt sense of discretion. He was
almost... theatrical.

What had the liche been after, he wondered? He was about to inquire further as to Arkhan's activities when movement drew his eye, and he glanced
up. A pale face stared down at him from among the crooked, arthritic
branches of the tree, its features twisted in a mocking smile as flickering
shadows gathered at the corner of his vision. Was it Vlad's face? Or someone
else's... The features were at once Vlad's and those of a youth from some
other land, handsome and terrible and noble and bestial all at once. The
thin-lipped mouth moved, but no sound came out. Nonetheless, Mannfred
heard it as clear as if it had whispered in his ear. 'La Maisontaal Abbey,' he
muttered. He blinked and shook himself. The face was gone, as were the
shadows, leaving behind only a dark echo of a man's sonorous chuckle.
He felt like a child being guided towards a treat. Irritated, he gouged the
trunk of the tree again, leaving five suppurating wounds in its soft bark.

Of course it was La Maisontaal. Of course! Why else would the liche have
bothered with a backwater like Bretonnia? Mannfred stared at the sap seeping from the tree. But why come here, now? Unless... He grunted. Arkhan's
goals were as unsubtle as the liche himself. He had ever been Nagash's tool.
He had no more free will than the dead who served him.

He was coming for those items that Mannfred now possessed, and had
spent no little effort in acquiring. His lips peeled back from his fangs as
he contemplated the audacity of the creature – to come here, to Sylvania,
to take what was Mannfred's by right of blood and conquest? No, no, that
would not do.

'Once a thief, always a thief,' he snarled. He turned, his cloak flaring
about him like the stretched wing of a gigantic bat. Erikan started, and tried
to stand as Mannfred swooped upon him. He grabbed the other vampire
gently by the throat with both hands, forcing him to remain still. 'Thank
you, boy, for your candour. It is much appreciated,' Mannfred purred. 'Tell
your mistress and her oaf of a progeny Anark to ready the defences of this
citadel. I expect the Drakenhof Templars to defend what is mine with their
lives, if it comes to it.'

He released Erikan and strode towards the doorway, cloak swirling.

Erikan rose to his feet and asked, 'And what of you, Lord Mannfred? What should I say you are doing?'

'I, dear boy, am going to confront the invader in person. I would take measure of my enemy before crushing his skull to powder beneath my boot-heel.'

Vargravia, Sylvania

If he had been capable of it, Arkhan the Black would have been in a foul mood. As it was, he merely felt a low throb of dissatisfaction as he led his rotting, stumbling forces through the blighted foothills of Vargravia. It had been a matter of mere moments to use his magics to rip a hole in the immense bone wall that carved off Sylvania from the rest of the world, but the blackened and shattered bone had repaired itself with an impressive speed. More than half of his army had been left on the other side of the gap, but there was nothing for it. He could always raise more to replace them. If there was one thing that Sylvania didn't lack, it was corpses.

And it would be easier now, as well. There was something in the air, here; or, rather, there was something missing. He looked up, scanning the dark sky overhead. It had been daylight when he'd crossed the border, only moments before. But the skies of Sylvania were as black as pitch, and charnel winds caused the trees to rustle in a way that, had he still possessed hackles, would have caused them to bristle. He could taste death on the wind the way another might smell the smoke of not-so-distant fire.

But despite all of that, they were going too slowly. It had taken him longer than he'd hoped to reach Sylvania. The power of Chaos was growing, and Arkhan could feel the world quiver, like a man afflicted with ague. The winds of magic blew erratically, and things from outside the walls of reality were clambering over the threshold in ever-increasing numbers. More than once, he'd been forced to defend himself from cackling nightmares from the outer void, drawn to the scent of sorcery that permeated him. Beasts gathered in the hills and forests, making them traps for the unwary, and the land heaved with conflict in a way it never had before. It was as if the world were tearing itself apart in a frenzy.

Perhaps that was why his master had begun to speak to him once more. Ever since he had been resurrected from his first death by Nagash's magics, an echo of the latter's voice had occupied his head. A comforting murmur that had never truly faded or weakened, even when Nagash himself had ceased to be. For years he had refused to acknowledge it for what it was, and had lied to himself, boasting of autonomy to the soulless husks that did his bidding. An easy thing to do when the voice grew dim, retreating to a barely heard buzz of mental static. But, over the course of recent decades, it had begun to grow in volume again. It had whispered to him in his black tower, compelling him to rise and strive once more, though there seemed to be no reason to do so.

His first inkling that it was not merely a stirring in the dregs of his imagination was when the armies of Mannfred von Carstein had marched on the ruins of Lahmia. Such arrogance was well within the remit of every vampire he'd ever met, but the sheer scale of the undertaking was a thing unmatched in his experience. Von Carstein had wanted something from the ruins of Lahmia. Whether he'd found it or not, Arkhan did not know. Von Carstein had fled before the might of Lybaras and its High Queen. But something had compelled the vampire to strike at Lahmia, and then later, Nagashizzar.

When Queen Khalida had made to return the favour a few centuries later, Arkhan had travelled with her to Sylvania, in pursuit of one of Mannfred's get. Mannfred himself was long dead by that point, sunk into the mire of Hel Fenn, but the dark spirit that had compelled him to attack the Lands of the Dead was obviously present in those creatures of his creation. They came again and again, looking for something. In this case, it had been one of Nagash's lesser staves of power – not Alakanash, the Great Staff, but a weaker version of it.

And like all tools forged by the Great Necromancer, it had had a whisper of his consciousness in it. Nagash had ever imparted something of himself, something of his vast and terrible soul, in everything of his making. Arkhan had taken the staff for his own, and though he'd held it aloft, the voice he'd long thought banished from his mind returned. It had howled in his mind, the chains of an ancient subjugation had rattled and he had begun his quest.

Upon Nagash's destruction by the brute hillman now venerated by the people of the Empire, those artefacts of his design had been scattered to the four winds by plot and chance. The will that pressed upon Arkhan's own had whispered to him his new task – to find these missing treasures. He was to seek out and gather the nine Books of Nagash, the mighty Crown of Sorcery, the Black Armour of Morikhane and the Great Staff, Alakanash, all of which had vanished into the weft and way of history. And there was the Fellblade of foul memory, and certain other things that must be brought together. Lastly, he required the withered Claw of Nagash, struck from the Great Necromancer's arm by the edge of the Fellblade, and lost for millennia.

Once all of these had been gathered, Arkhan could begin the last great working. Then, and only then, could the Great Necromancer return to the world, which was his by right of birth and fate. And it was Arkhan's task to help Nagash do so, even if it meant his obliteration in the doing of it. Such thoughts had rebounded against the walls of his skull for centuries, growing stronger and stronger, until it had reached a crescendo of such power that Arkhan was hard pressed to tell his thoughts from those of his master.

Two of the Books of Nagash were in his possession even now, strapped to the backs of his servants. And he knew where Alakanash and the Black

Armour were. But someone had beaten him to the other items, or so the voice in his skull whispered again and again. And that someone, he had been assured, was Mannfred von Carstein, resurrected from the grave even as Arkhan himself had been.

That the information had come from the sore-encrusted lips of one as untrustworthy as Heinrich Kemmler, the self-proclaimed Lichemaster, did not make Arkhan doubt its veracity overmuch. Kemmler had returned to the Grey Mountains after some time in the Empire, retreating to lick his wounds after nearly losing his head to the bite of a dwarf axe at Castle Reikguard. Mallobaude had sought him out, despite Arkhan's objections. The Lichemaster could not be trusted in such matters. His mind was disordered and he chafed at subordination.

Nonetheless, he had been intrigued to learn of Kemmler's brief alliance with von Carstein, as well as the vampire's acquisition of an elven princess of some standing. Kemmler had seen several of the items in question during this affair, and he, being no fool whatever his other proclivities, knew that there was some black plan brewing in the vampire's crooked brain.

What that plan was, Kemmler hadn't been able to say, and Arkhan felt disinclined to guess. The Books of Nagash were tomes of great power, and the Crown was a relic beyond all others. Any one of them would have served Mannfred adequately in whatever petty dreams fed his ambition. But to gather them all? That was a mystery indeed.

From somewhere far behind him, there was a great crackle of blossoming bone. He turned to watch as the yellowing shell of the wall repaired itself at last. A number of his slower followers were caught and pulverised, their rotting carcasses disintegrating as spears and branches of bone tore through them. Arkhan leaned on his staff, one fleshless palm resting on the pommel of the great tomb-blade that sat in its once-ornate and now much-reduced sheath on his hip.

'Well, that's interesting,' Arkhan rasped. It had required great magic to create that wall, and maintain it. Mannfred had been busy. He reached up and scratched the maggoty chin of the zombie cat laying across his shoulders. He'd found the animal in Quenelles and, on some dark, unexplainable whim, resurrected it. In life, it had been a scar-faced tomcat, big and lanky and foul-tempered. Now, it was still as big and even worse-tempered, albeit sloughing off its hair and skin at an alarming rate, even for a zombie. Arkhan suspected that the animal was doing it to be contrary. The cat gurgled in a parody of pleasure and Arkhan clicked his teeth at it. 'Isn't that interesting?'

Mannfred had sealed off Sylvania efficiently enough, but Arkhan did not think he was responsible for the sour ring of faith that now enclosed the province as effectively as a dungeon door locked and barred by a gaoler. No, that particular working stank of Chamon, the yellow wind of magic – dense and metallic. That meant the involvement of men, for only they employed such basic sorceries for such complex tasks. Arkhan had little familiarity with the barbaric lands of the Empire, though he'd warred on them more than once. That they had sorcerers capable of such a wreaking was moderately surprising. That Mannfred had aggravated them into doing so, was not.

'I still can't believe that you brought that cat with you.' Arkhan turned at the harsh croak, and examined the angular, patchwork face of the man who stomped towards him. Ogiers was – or had been – a nobleman of Bretonnia. Now he was a horseless vagabond, whose once-minor interest in necromancy had suddenly become his only means of protection, in the wake of Mallobaude's failed rebellion. He was also a giant of a man, who towered over the bodies of his former men-at-arms.

'*And I can't believe that something so inconsequential weighs so heavily on your mind,*' Arkhan said. '*And you do have a mind, Ogiers. That's why I pulled you from under the hooves of your kinsmen's horses. What of the others? Did we leave anyone on the other side?*'

'Some. No one consequential. That jackanapes Malfleur and that giggling maniac from Ostland. Fidduci made it through, as did Kruk,' Ogiers said with a shrug. Arkhan stroked his cat and considered the man before him. Ogiers's beard, once so finely groomed, had become a rat's nest, and his face was splotched with barely healed cuts and bruises. Big as he was, he slumped with exhaustion. He'd discarded most of his armour during the retreat over the Grey Mountains, but he'd kept what he could – more, Arkhan suspected, for sentimental reasons than anything else. The other necromancers likely looked just as tired. He'd pressed them hard since they'd reached the borderlands, keeping them moving without stopping. He forgot sometimes, how heavy flesh could be. It was like an anchor around you, bone and spirit.

He considered leaving them, while he forged ahead, but knew that would only be inviting trouble. They were frightened of him, but fear only went so far. He needed to keep them where he could see them.

Mallobaude's rebellion had stirred a hornet's nest of necromantic potential. In the months before his first, tentative missives had reached Arkhan in his desert exile, Mallobaude had sought to gather a colloquium of sorcerers and hedge-wizards to counter the witches of the lake and wood who bolstered the tottering throne of his homeland. Dozens of necromancers and dark sorcerers had responded, trickling over the Grey Mountains in ones and twos, seeking the Serpent's favour. When Arkhan had arrived at last, he'd been forced to initiate a cull of the gathered magic-users. Most were merely fraudsters or crooked creatures with only a bit of lore and a cantrip or two – hardly useful in a war. These he butchered and added to the swelling ranks of dead, where they'd be more useful.

Others he'd sent off to the fringes of the uprising, to distract and demoralise the enemy. The rest he'd gathered about him as his aides. He'd rescued the best of these in the final hours of the rebellion, gathering them to him and whisking them away from harm. Many hands made quick work, and he had much to do. The angles of the Corpse Geometries were bunching and skewing as the world shuddered beneath the weight of some new-born doom. The world had teetered on the edge of oblivion for centuries and it appeared that something had, at last, decided to simply tip it over.

The thought was neither particularly pleasant nor especially unpleasant to Arkhan, who had long ago shed such mortal worries. Death was rest, and life a burden. He had experienced both often enough to prefer the former, but the latter could never entirely be shed, thanks to the grip Nagash held on his soul. '*We will keep moving. Let the dead fall. This land is full of corpses, and we no longer have need of these. They merely serve to slow us down.*' He swept out a hand, and the shambling legions at their back twitched and collapsed as one with a collective sigh, all save the two enormous corpses that bore the heavy, iron-bound Books of Nagash in their arms. The two zombies had, in life, been ogre mercenaries from across the Mountains of Mourn. They and a mob of their kin had been drawn to Bretonnia by the war, and slain in the final battle at Couronne. Arkhan had seen no sense in wasting such brawny potential, and had resurrected them to serve as his pack-bearers.

'This is the first time we've stopped in days. We are not all liches, lord,' Ogiers said, looking about him at his fallen warriors. Arkhan had dispatched them with the rest. If Ogiers disapproved, he was wise enough to say nothing. 'Some of us still require food, sleep... A moment of rest.'

Arkhan said nothing. Behind Ogiers, Fidduci and Kruk made their way towards them over the field of fallen corpses. Franco Fidduci was a black-toothed Tilean scholar with a penchant for the grotesque, and Kruk was a twisted midget who rode upon the broad back of the risen husk of his cousin, clinging to the wight like a jongleur's pet ape.

'What happened? All my sweet ones fell over,' Kruk piped.

'Our master has seen fit to dispense with their services,' Ogiers said.

'But my pretty ones,' Kruk whined.

'If you're referring to those Strigany dancing girls of yours, they were getting a bit mouldy,' Fidduci said. 'Best to find some new ones, eh?' He looked at Arkhan. 'Which we will, yes? This is not a land for four innocent travellers, oh most godly and grisly of lords,' he said cautiously.

'*Frightened, are you?*' Arkhan rasped.

'Not all of us have escaped death's clutches as often as you,' Ogiers said. He looked around. 'Maybe we should take our leave of you. We will only slow you down, lord, and you disposed of our army, thus rendering our contribution as your generals moot.'

The cat examined the gathered necromancers with milky eyes. Its tail twitched and its yellowed and cracked fangs were visible through its mangled jowls. Arkhan stroked it idly, and said, '*No, you will not leave my side. Without me, you would be dead. Actually dead, as opposed to the more pleasing and familiar variety. We all serve someone, Ogiers. It is your good fortune to serve me.'*

'And who do you serve, oh most puissant and intimidating Arkhan?' Fidduci asked, fiddling with his spectacles.

'*Pray to whatever gods will have you that you never meet him, Franco,*' Arkhan rasped. '*Now come, we are a day from... What was it called, Kruk?*'

'Valsborg Bridge, my lovely master,' Kruk said. The diminutive necromancer hunched forward in his harness and pounded on his mount's shoulders. 'Come, come!' The wight turned and began to lope in a northerly direction.

Arkhan gestured with his staff. '*You heard him. Come, come,*' he intoned. Fidduci and Ogiers shared a look and then began to trudge after Kruk. Arkhan followed them sedately. As he walked, he considered his reasons for coming to Sylvania.

Bretonnia had been, if examined honestly, an unmitigated disaster. He had intended to use the civil war as a distraction in order to crack open the abbey at La Maisontaal and secure the ancient artefact ensconced within its stone walls, but Mallobaude had failed him. He'd been forced to retreat, gathering what resources he could. He intended to return, but he required more power to tip the balance in his favour. And time was growing short. The Long Night fast approached, and the world was crumbling at the edges.

There was no easy way to tell how long it took them to reach the bridge, even if Arkhan had cared about marking the passage of time. More than once, he and the others were required to fend off roving bands of ghouls or slobbering undead monstrosities. Bats swooped from the sky and wolves lunged from the hardscrabble trees, and Arkhan was forced to usurp their master's control to protect his followers. Ghosts haunted every crossroads and barrow-hill, and banshees wailed amidst the bent trees and extinct villages that they passed on the road to Valsborg Bridge. It was Mannfred's hand and will behind these obstacles, Arkhan knew. The vampire was trying to slow him down, to occupy his attentions while he mustered his meagre defences.

The bridge was nothing special. A simple span of stone across a narrow cleft, constructed in the days of Otto von Drak, before the Vampire Wars. A thin sludge of water gurgled below it. Arkhan suspected that it had been a raging river in its day, but the arteries of running water that crossed Sylvania were fast drying up thanks to Mannfred's sorcery. Storm clouds choked the skies above, and thunder rumbled in the distance.

His companions had collapsed by the roadside, exhausted by the gruelling pace. Even Kruk hung limp in his harness, stunted limbs dangling. Arkhan looked up at the churning sky, and then back at the bridge. Then he turned to his pack-bearers and motioned for them to drop to their haunches. They sank down, jaws sagging, blind, opaque eyes rolling in their sockets. They would not move, unless he commanded it, and they would not let anyone take the books they carried without a fight. He hefted his staff and stroked the cat, which made a sound that might have been a growl.

Someone – something – was coming. He could feel it, like a black wave rolling towards the shoreline, gathering strength as it came. Arkhan glanced down at his followers. '*Wait here,*' he said. '*Do not interfere.*'

'Interfere with what?' Ogiers demanded as he clambered to his feet. 'Where are you going?'

'*To parley with the master of this sad realm,*' Arkhan said as he strode towards the bridge. '*If you value your insignificant lives, I'd draw as little attention to yourself as possible.*' He walked across the bridge, ignoring Ogiers's shouts, and stopped at the halfway point. Then he set his staff, and waited. He did not have to wait long. The sound of hooves gouging the ground reached him several minutes later, and then a steed of bone and black magic, bearing a rider clad in flamboyant armour, burst into view, trailing smoke and cold flame. At the sight of it, the cat curled about his shoulders went stiff, and it hissed.

The rider hauled on his reins, causing the skeleton horse to rear. Its hooves slammed down on the stone of the bridge, and it went as still as death. Its rider rose high in his saddle and said, 'It has been some time since I last saw you, liche.'

'*I have counted the years, vampire.*' Arkhan scratched his cat's chin. '*Have you come to surrender?*'

Mannfred von Carstein threw his head back and unleashed a snarl of laughter. Overhead, the sky trembled in sympathy. 'Surrender? To a flesh-less vagabond? It is you who should prostrate yourself before me.'

'*I have not come to bend knee, but to reclaim that which is mine by right.*' Mannfred's sneer faded into a scowl. 'And what might that be?'

Arkhan held up his hand, fingers extended. As he spoke, he bent his fingers one by one. '*A crown, a severed hand, and seven books of blood-inked flesh.*' He cocked his head. '*You know of what I speak.*'

Mannfred grimaced. 'And why should I yield these artefacts to you?'

'*Nagash must rise,*' Arkhan said, simply.

'And so he shall. The matter is in good hands, I assure you,' Mannfred said. 'Go back to the desert, liche. I will call for you, if I should require your help.'

'*I am here now,*' Arkhan intoned, spreading his arms. '*And you seem to be in need of help. Or have you discovered a way of freeing your land from the chains that bind it and trap you?*'

'That is no business of yours,' Mannfred snarled.

'*That is up for discussion, I think,*' Arkhan said. He held out a hand. '*Nagash must rise, leech. Nagash will rise, even if I must destroy this blighted land to accomplish it. That is my curse and my pleasure. But he has always held some affection for your kind. If you serve him, perhaps he will let you keep your little castle.'* Arkhan cocked his head. *'It is a very pretty castle, I am given to understand.'*

Mannfred was silent, but Arkhan could feel the winds of death stirring as the vampire gathered his will. The air seemed to congeal and then fracture as Mannfred flung out his hand. A bolt of writhing shadow erupted from his palm and speared towards Arkhan. The liche made no attempt to move aside. Instead, he waited. A freezing, tearing darkness erupted around him in a squirming cloud as the bolt struck home. If he had still possessed flesh, it would have been flayed from his bones. As it was, it merely tore his cloak and cowl. The cat on his shoulder yowled, and Arkhan gestured negligently, dispersing the cold tendrils of shadow.

Arkhan laughed hollowly. *'Is that it?'*

'Not even remotely,' Mannfred snarled.

More spells followed the first, and Arkhan deflected them all and returned them with interest. Incantations he had not uttered in centuries passed through his fleshless jaws as he pitted his sorceries against those of the lord of Sylvania... and found them wanting. Arkhan felt a flicker of surprise. Mannfred was more powerful than he'd thought. In his skull, his master's chuckle echoed. Was this a test then, to separate the wheat from the chaff?

Dark sorceries and eldritch flames met above the bridge between them for long hours, crashing together like the duelling waves of a storm-tossed sea. Cold fire bit at writhing shadows, and black lightning struck bastions of hardened air, as the muddy turf of the riverbanks began to heave and rupture, releasing the tormented dead. Bodies long buried staggered and slumped into the guttering river, splashing towards one another. More skeletons, clad in roots and mud, crawled onto the bridge and groped for Arkhan as he batted aside Mannfred's spells. The cat warbled and leapt from his shoulder to crash into a skeleton, knocking it backwards.

He ignored the others as they clawed at him. There were few forces that could move him once he had set himself. The biting, clawing dead were no more a threat to him than leaves cast in his face by a strong breeze. Nonetheless, they were a distraction; likely that was Mannfred's intent. It was certainly Arkhan's, as he directed his corpse-puppets to attack Mannfred.

The vampire smashed the dead aside with careless blows and hurled spells faster than Arkhan could follow, hammering him with sorcerous blows that would have obliterated a lesser opponent. The stone beneath his feet bubbled and cracked. It had survived a weathering of centuries, and now it was crumbling beneath the onslaught. Arkhan was beginning to wonder if he was going to suffer the same fate. He could feel his defences beginning to buckle beneath the unyielding onslaught. Mannfred's power seemed inexhaustible; vampires were reservoirs of dark magic, but even they had their limits – limits that Mannfred seemed to have shed. Where was he drawing his power from? Some artefact or... Arkhan laughed, suddenly. Of course.

Mannfred had sealed off Sylvania, blocking the sun and the rivers and the borders. Such a working would require some source of mystical power. Mannfred was drawing on those same magics now, and it gave him a distinct advantage. But, such a resource, while advantageous, was not infinite.

Certain now that he had his foeman's measure, Arkhan redoubled his efforts. If he could force Mannfred's hand, he might be able to simply outlast him. Sorcerous talons and bone-stripping winds lashed at him, but he held firm, his hands clasped around his staff. Overhead, the clouds swirled and contracted. Fire washed over him, and a thousand, thudding fists, which struck at him from every side. Wailing ghosts and serpentine shadows sought to drag him down, but Arkhan refused to fall. He sent no more spells hurtling towards his foe, instead bolstering the dead who fought at his behest.

Mannfred was howling with laughter, and Arkhan could feel the weight of the mighty magics that thrummed around the vampire, waiting to be unleashed. As Mannfred gathered them to him, the words to a powerful incantation dropping from his writhing lips, Arkhan readied himself.

Nevertheless, the first shaft of sunlight was as much a surprise to him as it was to Mannfred. It burst from the clouds high above and struck the bridge between them. The latter's skeleton mount reared and hurled him from his saddle. Arkhan staggered as the pressure of his enemy's magic faded. The expression on Mannfred's face as he clambered to his feet was almost comical. The vampire looked up, eyes wide and hastily released the murderous energies he had been preparing to hurl at Arkhan back into the aether. The clouds roiled and the sunlight was once more choked off by the darkness.

'*Well, that was an amusing diversion,*' Arkhan rasped. He started across the bridge. '*Are you prepared to listen to reason now?*'

Mannfred shrieked like a beast of prey, and drew his blade. Without pause, the vampire leapt at him. Arkhan drew his tomb-blade and blocked Mannfred's diving blow in a single movement. The two blades, each infused with the darkest of magics, gave out a communal cry of steel on steel as they connected, and cold fire blazed at the juncture of their meeting. Mannfred dropped to the bridge in a crouch before springing instantly to his feet. He sprinted towards Arkhan, his sword looping out. This too Arkhan parried, and they weaved back and forth over the bridge, the screams of their swords echoing for miles in either direction. Overhead, the sky growled in agitation, and the noisome wind swept down with a howl.

Below them, in the mud and stagnant water, the dead fought on, straining against one another in a parody of the duel their masters fought above them. Arkhan could feel Mannfred's will pressing against his own. He'd foregone magic, save that little bit required to control the dead. Their battle was as much for mastery of the warring corpses below as it was against each other. The vampire came at him again, teeth bared in a silent, feral snarl. His form flickered and wavered as he moved, like a scrap of gossamer caught in a wind storm. A living man would have found it impossible to follow the vampire's movements, but Arkhan had long since traded in his mortal eyes for something greater.

He matched Mannfred blow for blow. It felt... good, to engage in sword-play once more. It had been centuries since his blade had been drawn for anything other than emphasis or as an implement of ritual. The ancient tomb-blade shivered in his hand as it connected again with Mannfred's. The embers of old skills flared to life in the depths of Arkhan's mind, and he recalled those first few desperate battles, where a gambler's skill in back-alley brawls was put to the test by warriors whose names still lingered in legend. It was good to be reminded of that time, of when he had still been a man, rather than a tool forged by the will of another.

Arkhan wondered if Mannfred knew what that was like. He thought so. The vampire's magics had that taste, and his voice was like the echo of another's, though he knew it not. Arkhan could almost see a familiar shape superimposed over his opponent, a vast, black, brooding shadow that seemed to roil with amusement as they fought.

I see you, Arkhan thought. This was a test and a pleasure for the thing that held the chains of their souls. Arkhan's master had ever been a sadist and prone to cruel whimsy. This battle had been a farce, a shadow-play from the beginning. There was a power in that knowledge. A power in knowing exactly how little of it you yourself possessed. It allowed you to focus, to look past the ephemeral, and to marshal within yourself what little will your master allowed.

Arkhan the Black was a slave, but a slave who knew every link of the chain that bound him by heart. Mannfred had yet to realise that he had even been beaten. Their blades clashed again and again until, at last, Arkhan beat the vampire's sword aside and swiftly stepped back, his now-sodden and torn robes slapping wetly against his bare bones.

'*We are finished here, vampire.*'

Mannfred's eyes burned with rage, and for a moment, Arkhan thought he might continue the fight. Then, with a hiss, Mannfred inclined his head and sheathed his sword with a grandiose flourish. 'We are, liche. A truce?'

Arkhan would have smiled, had he still had lips. '*Of course. A truce.*'

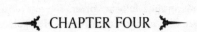

CHAPTER FOUR

Heldenhame Keep, Talabecland

'The problem isn't getting in. It's just a wall, and walls can be breached, scaled and blown down,' Hans Leitdorf, Grand Master of the Knights of Sigmar's Blood said, glaring at the distant edifice, which towered along the border of Sylvania. That it was visible from such a distance was as much due to its sheer enormity as to the height of the parapet he and his guests stood atop. 'It's what's waiting on the other side. They've had months to erect defences, set traps and build an army out of every scrap of bone and sinew in Sylvania. And that's not even taking into account the things slipping over the border every night to bolster the cursed von Carstein's ranks. Strigany nomads, strange horsemen, beasts and renegades of every dark stripe.' He knocked back a slug from the goblet he held in one hand. Leitdorf was old but, like some old men, had only grown harder and tougher with age. He was broad and sturdily built, with a barrel chest and a face that had seen the wrong end of a club more than once. He wore a heavy fur coat of the sort Ungol horsemen were fond of, and had his sword belt cinched around his narrow waist. 'We've tried to stop them, but we're too few. I don't have enough men to do more than put up a token effort. And when I ask for more men from the elector and Karl Franz, I get, well, you.' He looked at his guest.

Captain Wendel Volker gave no sign that Leitdorf's insult had struck home. The fourth son of a largely undistinguished Talabecland family tree, he hadn't expected a man like Leitdorf to be happy with his arrival. His uniform was still coated in trail-grime, and he shivered beneath his thin officer's cloak. It was cold up on the parapet, and it had been a wet trip. Volker was young, with a duellist's build and a boy's enthusiasm. The latter was swiftly being sapped by the circumstances of his current posting, but, as his father had said on multiple occasions, one mustn't complain.

'Oh he's not so bad, is our young Wendel. He guarded me ably enough on the road from Talabheim,' the third man on the parapet rumbled, as he stroked his spade-shaped red beard with thick, beringed fingers. He was a big man, like Leitdorf, though his size had more to do with ample food supply than anything else, Volker thought. There was muscle there, too, but it was well padded. Despite that, he was the most dangerous of the three men on the parapet. Or, possibly, in the entire keep. 'Able, aristocratic, attentive, slightly alcoholic... All virtues as far as I'm concerned,' the third man went on, winking cheerfully at Volker.

'You hardly needed an escort,' Leitdorf said. 'The Patriarch of the Bright College is an army unto himself. There are few who would challenge Thyrus Gormann.'

'I know of one,' Gormann grunted, tugging on his beard. He waved a hand and, for a moment, a trail of flickering flame marked the motion of his fingers. 'Still, neither here nor there, all in the past, all friends now, hey?' He scratched his nose and peered at the distant wall of bone that separated Sylvania from Imperial justice. 'That is one fine, big wall the little flea has erected for himself, I must admit.'

'The little flea,' Volker knew, was Mannfred von Carstein. Even thinking the name caused him to shudder. Still, on the whole, it was better than going north with the rest of the lads. He'd take the dead over daemons any day. Nonetheless, he couldn't repress a second shudder when he looked at the distant wall. He caught Leitdorf looking at him and stiffened his spine. As terrifying as Mannfred von Carstein was, he was over there, and Leitdorf, unfortunately, was right here. Leitdorf snorted and turned back to Gormann.

'Volkmar isn't coming back,' he said.

'Did you think he would?' Gormann asked. 'No, he'd have torn those walls down if he'd been able. It was a fool's errand, and he knew it.'

'He had to try,' Leitdorf said softly.

'No, he bloody didn't.' Gormann shook his shaggy head. 'He let his anger blind him, and now we have to muddle through without him. Stubborn old fool.'

'Friend pot, have you met cousin kettle?' Leitdorf asked.

Gormann looked at the knight and frowned, but only for a moment. He guffawed and shook his head. 'I always forget that you have a sense of humour buried under that scowl, Hans.'

Volker watched as the two men – two of the most powerful, if not influential, in the Empire – continued to discuss the unpleasantness just across the border and decided, for the fifth time in as many minutes, to keep his opinions to himself, just as his mother had counselled. 'Keep quiet, head down, ears perked, nose to the trail,' she'd said. A hunting metaphor, of course. Big one for hunting was mumsy, big one for the blood sports and the trophies and such.

Blood had always made Volker queasy. He licked his lips and looked longingly at the jug of mulled wine that Leitdorf clutched loosely in one hand. Occasionally, the Grand Master would refill his goblet, or Gormann's.

Volker had not been offered so much as a taste. Another snub, of course. A sign of his new commander's displeasure. Mustn't complain, he thought.

As the wizard and the warrior conversed, Volker kept himself occupied by examining his new post from the view the parapet afforded. He'd heard stories of Heldenhame as a boy, but to see it in the flesh, as it were, was something else again.

At its inception, Heldenhame had been little more than a modest bastion, composed of a stone tower and a wooden palisade. Now, however, a century later, Heldenhame Keep was the grandest fortress in Talabecland. The old stone tower had been torn down and replaced by a castle that was many times larger, and the wooden palisade had been discarded in favour of heavy stone walls. Within the walls and spreading outwards from the castle was a bustling city, filled with noise and commerce. It was a grand sight, for all that it still bore the marks of the greenskin tide that had sought to overwhelm it the year previous.

The western wall was still under repair from that incident. Volker watched the distant dots of workmen reinforcing and repairing the still-crippled span. It was the only weak point in the fortress's defences, but such repairs couldn't be rushed. Volker knew that much from his studies. As he examined the wall, he saw what looked to be a tavern near it. His thirst returned and he licked his lips. 'Worried about the western span, captain?' Leitdorf asked, suddenly. Volker, shaken from his reverie, looked around guiltily.

'Ah, no, sir, Grand Master,' he said hastily, trying to recall what sort of salute one gave the commander of a knightly order. Leitdorf gazed at him disdainfully.

'You should be,' he grunted. 'You'll be stationed there. You're dismissed, Volker. I trust you can find your quarters and introduce yourself to the garrison without me holding your hand?'

'Ah, yes, I believe so, sir. Grand Master,' Volker said. Leitdorf turned, and Volker, relieved and dying for a drink, scurried away.

Karak Kadrin, Worlds Edge Mountains

Ungrim Ironfist, king of Karak Kadrin, ran his thick, scarred fingers across the map of beaten bronze and gilded edges that lay before him on the stone table. The map was a thing of painstaking artifice and careful craftsmanship, and it was as lovely in its way as any silken tapestry or a portrait done by a master's hand.

Ironfist, in contrast, was a thing of slabs and edges and could, in no way, shape or form be called lovely. Even for a dwarf, the Slayer King was built on the heavy side, his thick bones weighed down by layers of hard-earned muscle, and his face like a granite shelf carved sharply and suddenly by an avalanche. His beard and hair were dyed a startling red and, as ever, he wore a heavy cloak of dragon-scale over his broad shoulders.

His craggy features settled into a taciturn expression as he stared at the map. It wasn't alone on the table. There were others stacked in a neat pile near to hand, and opposite them a number of metal tubes, containing statements and reports culled from every watch-post and lookout tower for a hundred miles in every direction. Ironfist had read them all and more than once. So often, in fact, that he knew what each one said by heart.

More reports were added by the day, as rangers and merchants brought word to the Slayer Keep from the furthest edges of the dwarf empire. These too Ironfist committed to memory. None of what he learned was comforting.

There was a strange murk upon the dust-winds that rolled west from the Dark Lands over the eastern mountains, and the sky over that foul land was rent by sickly trails of green, as if the moon were weeping poisonous tears upon the blighted sores that covered the skin of the world. Plagues such as the world had not seen in a thousand years were loose in the lands of men, and worse things than plagues, too. Devils and beasts ran riot in the Empire, and traders returning from Tilea, Estalia and Araby brought word that it was just as bad in those lands. The vile rat-things had burst from their tunnels in unprecedented numbers, and subsumed whole city-states and provinces in the same way they had the holds of his people so long ago.

The Badlands were full to bursting of greenskins; the clangour of the battles fought between the orc tribes carried for miles in all directions, and as soon as one ended, another began. Soon, as was inevitable, they would flood into the mountains and the lands beyond, hunting for new enemies. But this time they would do so in unprecedented numbers: in their millions, rather than their thousands.

However, that was as nothing compared to word from the north, where strange lights writhed across the horizon and arcane storms raged across the lands. Daemon packs hunted the high places and barbarians gathered in the valleys as long-dormant volcanoes belched smoke and the earth shook as if beneath the tread of phantom armies.

Ironfist had, in all his centuries, never witnessed such a multitude of troubles, all occurring at once. Bad times came and went, like storms. They washed across the mountains and faded away with the seasons. But this was like several storms, rising and boiling together all at once, as if to wipe away the world. He shook his head, trying to clear his thoughts of the miasma of foreboding that clung to them.

Ironfist tapped a point on the map. 'What word from the Sylvanian border? Are the rumours true?' he asked the dwarf sitting across from him. Snorri Thungrimsson had served at his king's right hand for more years than could be easily counted. He was old now, and the fat braids of beard that were tucked into the wide leather belt about his midsection were as white as the morning frost on the high mountain peaks. But he still served as his king's hearthwarden and senior advisor. It was Thungrimsson who collected and organised the diverse streams of information that came into the hold from messengers, scouts and spies, and readied it for Iron-fist's study.

'You mean about the, ah, bones?' Thungrimsson asked, gesturing. He grimaced in distaste as he asked it.

'No, I mean about this year's turnip festival in Talabheim. Yes, the bones,' Ironfist said.

'They're true enough. The whole land is surrounded by battlements of bone. It's sealed off tighter than King Thorgrim's vaults.' Thungrimsson traced the border of Sylvania on the map. 'The rangers can't find a way through, not that they tried very hard.'

Ironfist sat back in his chair with a sigh. He tugged on his beard and let his gaze drift across the high alcoves of the library, where the watery light of hooded lanterns illuminated stone shelves and pigeonholes, each one stuffed with books, tomes, scrolls and papyri. The library was one of his great pleasures, when all was said and done. It had been built carefully and over centuries, much like the rest of Karak Kadrin. 'Well, what are you thinking, hearthwarden?' he asked finally, looking back at Thungrimsson.

'It is a shame about the turnip festival,' Thungrimsson said. Ironfist growled wordlessly and the other dwarf raised his hands in a placating gesture. 'I'm thinking that Sylvania has been a boil on our hindquarters for more centuries than I care to contemplate. Whatever is going on in there bears keeping an eye on, if nothing else. And we should send word to the other holds, especially Zhufbar. The blood-drinkers have attacked them before.'

Ironfist gnawed on a thumbnail. Every instinct he possessed screamed at him to muster a throng and smash his way into that blighted land, axe in hand. There was something on the air, something that pricked at him, like a warning only half heard. There were other threats to be weighed and measured, but Sylvania was right on his hearthstone. He had been patient for centuries, waiting for the humans to see to their own mess. But the time for patience had long since passed. If the *zanguzaz* – the blood-drinkers – were up to some mischief, Ironfist was inclined to put a stop to it soonest.

His eye caught a golden seal on one of the more recently arrived mes-sage tubes. He recognised the royal rune of Karaz-a-Karak, the Pinnacle of the Mountains, the Most Enduring. He flicked the tube open and extracted the scroll within. He frowned as he read it. When he was done, he tossed it to Thungrimsson. 'We'll have to settle for keeping watch. At least for now. The Grudgebearer has called together the Council of Kings.'

Thungrimsson's eyes widened in surprise as he read the scroll. 'Such a council hasn't been convened in centuries,' he said slowly. His eyes flick-ered to the scrolls and maps. He met Ironfist's grim gaze. 'It's worse than we thought, isn't it?'

Ironfist pushed himself slowly to his feet. He tapped the map again. 'It seems I'll be able to alert my brother-kings as to the goings-on in Sylvania in person,' he said softly.

Lothern, Ulthuan

Tyrion's palms struck the doors of the meeting chamber of the Phoenix Council like battering rams, sending them swinging inwards with a thunderous crash. Eltharion of Yvresse winced and made to hurry after his prince.

The latter's haste was understandable, if not strictly advisable. Then, the Warden of Tor Yvresse had never been fond of haste. Haste led to the mistakes and mistakes to defeat. A slim hand fastened on his arm. 'Give him a moment. He's making an entrance.'

'That's what I'm afraid of, Eldyra,' Eltharion grated, brushing the hand from his arm. He turned to glare at the woman who followed him. Eldyra of Tiranoc had once been Tyrion's squire; now she was a warrior in her own right, albeit an impetuous one. She was a vision of loveliness wrapped in lethality. She had learned the art of death from the foremost warrior of their race, and her skill with blade, bow and spear was equal to, or greater than, Eltharion's own, though they had never put that to the test.

'No, you're afraid he's going to kill someone.'

'And you're not?'

'Better to ask whether I care,' she said pointedly. 'The idea of our prince taking off the head of that pompous nitwit Imrik fills me with a warm and cheerful glow.'

Eltharion shook his head and followed Tyrion into the council chamber. Tyrion had interrupted the aforementioned Imrik, Dragon Prince of Cale-dor, in mid-speech. The Phoenix Council had been discussing the same thing they'd been discussing for months – namely Imrik's assertion that Finubar had ceded his right to the Phoenix Crown.

The Phoenix Council had been paralysed for months by disagreement among its members and disillusionment with the current wearer of the crown. Finubar had sealed himself in the Heavenlight Tower in order to divine the cause of the recent disasters that had beset Ulthuan, at a time when his people most needed his guidance. Eltharion could not help but wonder what was going through his king's mind; the longer Finubar sat isolated in his tower, the more that discontent spread through the halls and meeting chambers of the elven nobility. As Chrace and Cothique were overrun by daemon-spawn, and their peoples scattered or exterminated, Finubar had yet to reappear, and had, so far, allowed only one to impinge upon his solitude – Tyrion's brother Teclis. Teclis had come out of that meeting certain that Tyrion must take command of Ulthuan's armies.

Tyrion, however, had taken some convincing. Not that Eltharion blamed him for being preoccupied. He and his companions had only just returned from the citadel of abomination known as Nagashizzar, where they'd failed to rescue Aliathra, firstborn daughter of the Everqueen, from her captor, Mannfred von Carstein. Aliathra had been captured earlier in the year by the vampire while she had been on a diplomatic mission to the High King of the dwarfs at Karaz-a-Karak. Dwarfs and elves both had been slaughtered by Mannfred in pursuit of Aliathra, and when word reached Ulthuan of her fate, Tyrion had been driven into as wild a rage as Eltharion had ever seen.

The reason for the sheer force of that rage was known to only two others, besides Eltharion himself. Eldyra was one and Teclis the other. The three of them shared the weight of Tyrion's shameful secret, and when he'd made it known that he intended to rescue Aliathra, Eltharion, Eldyra and Teclis had accompanied him. But the expedition to Nagashizzar had been a failure. Mannfred had escaped again, and taken the Everchild with him.

Teclis's spies, both living and elemental, had confirmed that the vampire had taken Aliathra into the lands of men, and Belannaer, Loremaster of Hoeth, had sworn that he could hear the Everchild's voice upon the wind, calling from somewhere within the foul demesne known as Sylvania. Failure ate at Tyrion like an acid, making it impossible for him to focus on anything else. He had been planning for a second expedition when Teclis had forced him to see sense. Now his rage at Aliathra's fate had been refocused, and for the better, Eltharion hoped.

'Our lands are in turmoil, and you sit here arguing over who has the right to lead, rather than doing anything productive. No wonder the Phoenix King hides himself away – I would as well, had my advisors and servants shamed me as you now shame him,' Tyrion said as he stalked into the chamber, the stones echoing with the crash of the doors. Clad in full armour, armed and flanked by the armoured forms of Eltharion and Eldyra, the heir of Aenarion was an intimidating sight. At least if you had any sense.

'Ulthuan needs leadership. Finubar is not fit to be king. Not now, not when we are on the precipice of the long night,' Imrik growled. He glared at Tyrion as fiercely as one of the dragons his homeland was famous for. 'Speaking of which, where were you? First Finubar locks himself away in his tower, and then the Everqueen vanishes to gods alone know where. The Ten Kingdoms heave with the plague of ages and you, our greatest champion, were half a world away!'

'I am here now,' Tyrion said. He drew his sword, Sunfang, from its sheath and swept it through the air. The ancient sword, forged to draw the blood of the daemons of Chaos, burned with the captured fires of the sun. Runes glowed white-hot along its length and the closest members of the council turned away or shaded their eyes against the sword's stinging promise. Only Imrik continued to glare, undaunted.

Tyrion looked at the council, his eyes blazing with a heat equal to that which marked the runes on his sword. 'You will cease your nattering. You will take up blade and bow as befitting lords of Ulthuan, and marshal your forces to defend the Ten Kingdoms. Any who wish to quarrel further can take up their argument with the edge of my sword and see what it profits you.'

Imrik shot to his feet and slammed his fist down on the table. 'How dare you?' the Dragon Prince roared. 'What gives you the right to speak to this august council in such a disrespectful manner? We are your betters, whelp! Who are you to demand anything of us?'

Tyrion smiled humourlessly. 'Who am I? I am the Herald of Asuryan, and of the Phoenix King, in whose names I would dare anything. That is all the right I require.' He pointed Sunfang at Imrik and asked, 'Unless you disagree?'

Imrik's pale features tightened and his lean body quivered with barely restrained rage. 'I do,' he hissed. He circled the table and strode past Tyrion. 'Strike me down if you dare, boy, but I'll not stay here and be barked at by you.'

Tyrion did not turn as Imrik stalked past him. 'If you leave, prince of Caledor, then do not expect to be included in our councils of war. Caledor will stand alone,' he said harshly.

Imrik stopped. Eltharion saw his eyes close, as if he were in pain. Then, his voice ragged, he said, 'Then Caledor stands alone.' Imrik left the chamber without another word. No one tried to stop him. The remaining council-members whispered quietly amongst themselves. Eltharion looked at them and frowned. Already, they were plotting. Imrik's star had been in the ascendancy, and now it had plummeted to earth. Those who had supported him were revising their positions as those who had been arrayed against him moved to shore up their influence. None of them seemed to grasp the full extent of the situation. He saw Tyrion looking at him. The latter crooked a finger and Eltharion and Eldyra moved to join him.

'Thank you for watching my back,' Tyrion said quietly. 'But now that the council has been tamed, I need you two to do as you promised. Make ready, gather what you need for the expedition, and set sail as soon as possible.' His composure evaporated as he spoke, and his words became ragged. Eltharion could see just how much it was costing his friend to stay in Ulthuan. There was pain in his eyes and in his voice such as Eltharion had never seen.

'You have my oath as Warden of Tor Yvresse,' Eltharion said softly. He hesitated, and then placed a hand on his friend's shoulder. He looked at Eldyra, who nodded fiercely. 'We shall rescue Aliathra, or we will die trying.'

La Maisontaal Abbey, Bretonnia

The three men descended down the dank, circular stone steps, following the woman. She held a crackling torch in one hand, and its light cast weird shadows on the stone walls of the catacombs. 'The abbey was built to contain that which I am about to show you,' the woman said, her voice carrying easily, despite the softness with which she spoke. 'Rites and rituals went into the placement of every stone and every slather of mortar to make this place a fitting cage for what is imprisoned here. And so it has remained, for hundreds of years.'

'But now?' one of the men asked. They reached the bottom of the stairs and came to a vaulted chamber, which was empty save for a wide, squat stone sarcophagus the likes of which none of the men had ever seen. It had been marked with mystical signs, and great iron chains crossed it, as if to keep whatever was within it trapped. The woman lifted her torch and let its light play across the sarcophagus.

'Now, I fear, we are coming to the end of its captivity. Something is loose in the world, a red wind that carries with it the promise of a slaughter undreamt of by even the most monstrous of creatures that infest our poor, tired land. Or those of its greatest heroes, Tancred of Quenelles.'

'This is what he was after,' Tancred, Duke of Quenelles, said staring at the stone sarcophagus. His breath plumed in the damp, chill air. Part of him yearned to touch the sarcophagus, while a greater part surged in revulsion at the thought. The thing that lay inside seemed to draw everything towards it, as though it weighed more than the world around it. Tancred felt the weight of his years settle more heavily than ever before on his broad shoulders. 'This is what Arkhan the Black was after, then, my Lady Elynesse?'

'Perhaps,' Lady Elynesse, Dowager of Charnorte, said. Her voice was soft, but not hesitant. She was older than even Tancred, whose hair and beard had long since lost the lustre of youth, though her face was unlined and unmarred by time. 'Such a creature weaves schemes within schemes, and concocts plots with every day it yet remains unburied.' She held her torch higher and circled the sarcophagus. 'This could be but one goal amongst many.'

'What is it?' one of the others asked. His hands were clamped tightly around the hilt of his blade. Tancred wondered whether the other knight felt the same pull towards the sarcophagus as he did. Though Fastric Ghoulslayer was a native of Bordeleaux, he had shed blood beside Tancred and the third knight, Anthelme of Austray, in defence of Quenelles in the civil war. The Ghoulslayer was a warrior of renown and commanded a skylance of Pegasus knights, and there were few whom Tancred trusted more.

'Whatever it is, I'd just as soon it stays in there,' Anthelme said nervously.

'And so it shall, if we have anything to say about it,' Tancred said, looking at his cousin. Anthelme, like Fastric, was a trusted companion, even beyond the bounds of blood. There were none better with a lance or blade in Tancred's opinion. 'Our kingdom lies broken and bleeding, and the one who struck that blow will return to capitalise on our weakness. The Dowager has seen as much. Arkhan the Black wanted this sarcophagus and its contents, even as the Lichemaster did in decades past. But we shall see to it that La Maisontaal's burden remains here, in these tombs, even if we must die to do so.'

'But surely whatever is in here is no danger to us? The true king has returned. Gilles le Breton sits once more upon the throne of Bretonnia, and the civil war is over. We have passed through the darkest of times and come out the other side,' Anthelme said. Those sentiments were shared by many, Tancred knew. When Louen Leoncouer had been felled at the Battle of Quenelles by his treacherous bastard son, many, including Tancred, had thought that the kingdom's time was done.

Then had come Couronne, and Mallobaude's last challenge. The Serpent had challenged the greatest knights in the land on Quenelles, Gisoreux, Adelaix and a hundred more battlefields, and had emerged victorious every time. But at Couronne, it was no mortal who answered his challenge; instead, the legendary Green Knight had ridden out of the ranks, appearing as if from nowhere, and had met Mallobaude on the field between the armies of the living and the dead. In the aftermath, when the surviving dukes and lords inevitably began to turn their thoughts to the vacant throne, the Green Knight had torn his emerald helm from his head and revealed himself to be none other than Gilles le Breton, the founder of the realm, come back to lead his people in their darkest hour. The problem was, as far as Tancred could tell, the darkest hour hadn't yet passed. In fact, it appeared that Mallobaude's rebellion had only been the beginning of Bretonnia's ruination, the return of the once and future king or not.

'And so? Daemons still stalk our lands, and monsters burn the vineyards and villages. Mallobaude might have lost his head, but he wasn't the only traitor. Quenelles is in ruins, as are half of the other provinces, and home to two-legged beasts. Bordeleaux is gone, replaced by a daemonic keep of brass and bone that even now blights the surrounding lands. No, we are in the eye of the storm, cousin. The false calm, before its fury strikes again, redoubled and renewed. I fear that things will get much, much worse before it passes,' Tancred said firmly. He looked around. 'Come, I would leave this place.'

He led them back up the stairs and out of the abbey, ignoring the huddled masses of peasants, who genuflected and murmured respectful greetings. More and more of them came every day, seeking the dubious sanctuary of the abbey's walls as the forests seethed with beasts and the restless dead, and the sky blazed with blue fire or was split by the fiery passage of warpstone meteors.

As they got outside, Tancred gulped the fresh, cold air. It was a relief, after the damp unpleasantness of the catacombs, and the close air of the abbey, redolent with the odour of the lower classes. He looked about him. His father, the first to bear the name of Tancred, had funded the fortifying of the abbey in the wake of the Lichemaster's infamous assault some thirty years earlier. The Eleventh Battle of La Maisontaal Abbey had been a pivotal moment in both the history of his family and Bretonnia as a whole.

The fortifications weren't as grand as Tancred's father had dreamed, but they were serviceable enough. There were garrison quarters, housing hundreds of archers and men-at-arms, as well as scores of knights, drawn from every corner of Bretonnia. The abbey sat in the centre of an army.

Somehow, he doubted that would be enough.

He turned as he heard a loud voice bellow a greeting. The broad, burly form of Duke Theoderic of Brionne ambled towards him, his battle-axe resting on his shoulder. 'Ho, Tancred! They told me you were slinking about. Come to inspect the troops, eh?' Theoderic had a voice that could stun one of the great bats that haunted the Vaults at twenty paces. He was also the commander of the muster of La Maisontaal. He'd come to the abbey seeking penance for a life of lechery, drunkenness and other assorted unchivalric behaviours, and had, according to most, more than made up for his past as a sozzle-wit.

They clasped forearms, and Tancred winced as Theoderic drew him into a bear hug. 'I see that the Lady Elynesse is here as well,' he murmured as he released Tancred. He jerked his chin towards the Dowager, who swept past them towards her waiting carriage. She had come to show them what was hidden. Now, having done so, she was leaving as quickly as possible. Tancred couldn't blame her. Lacking even the tiniest inclination to sorcery, he could still feel the spiritual grime of the thing that lurked in the depths of the abbey. He could only imagine what it must be like for a true servant of the Lady. 'Has she foreseen trouble for us?'

'Arkhan the Black,' Tancred said.

'I thought we sent him packing, didn't we?' Theoderic grunted.

'Do such creatures ever stay gone for as long as we might wish?'

'Ha! You have me there. Never fear, though – if he comes, we'll be ready for him,' Theoderic said, cradling his axe in the crook of his arm. 'Some of the greatest heroes of our fair kingdom are here. Gioffre of Anglaron, the slayer of the dragon Scaramor, Taurin the Wanderer, dozens of others. Knights of the realm, one and all. A truer gathering of heroes has never been seen in these lands, save at the court of the king himself!'

Tancred looked at Theoderic's beaming features and gave a half-hearted nod. 'Let's pray to the Lady that will be enough,' he said.

Somewhere south of Quenelles, Bretonnia

The voices of the Dark Gods thundered in his ears and Malagor brayed in pleasure as his muscles swelled with strength. He snapped the gor chieftain's neck with a single, vicious jerk, and snorted as he sent the body thudding to the loamy earth. He spread his arms and his great, black pinioned wings snapped out to their full length. Then, he looked about him at the gathered chieftains. 'Split-Hoof challenged. Split-Hoof died. Who else challenges the Crowfather?' he bellowed. 'Who else challenges the word of the gods?'

None of the remaining chieftains stepped forward. In truth, Split-Hoof hadn't so much challenged him as he had voiced a concern, but Malagor saw little difference between dissension and discomfort. Neither was acceptable. The gods had commanded, and their children would obey, whether they were inclined to do so or not. He snarled and pawed the ground with a hoof, glaring about him to ram the point home. Only when the chieftains looked sufficiently cowed did he allow them to look away from him. They wouldn't stay cowed for long, he knew. The children of Chaos did not have it in them to be docile, even when it served the gods' purpose. In their veins was the blood of the gods and it was ever angry and ambitious. Soon, another chieftain would voice dissent, and he would have to fight again.

His goatish lips peeled back from yellowed fangs. Malagor looked forward to such challenges. Without them, there was no joy in life. Taking the life of an enemy with the sorceries that hummed in his bones was satisfying, in its way, but there was no substitute for feeling bone crack and splinter in his grip, or tasting the flesh and blood of an opponent.

Malagor folded his wings and looked about him as he idly stroked the symbols of blasphemy that hung from his matted mane and leather harness. Icons plucked from the bodies of human priests dangled beside twists of paper torn from their holy books, all of them stained and soiled and consecrated to the gods, who even now whispered endearments to him as he pondered his next move.

The forest clearing around him echoed with the raucous rumble of savage anarchy. Beastmen yelped and howled as they danced to the sound of drums and fought about the great witch-fires, which burned throughout the clearing. All of this beneath the glistening gaze of the titanic monolith that had sprouted from the churned earth months earlier. The strange black stone was shot through by jagged veins of sickly, softly glimmering green, and it pulsed in time to the thudding of the drums.

Ever since the dark moon had waxed full in the sky, and the great herdstones had risen from their slumber beneath the ground, so too had the voices of the gods hummed in his mind, stronger than ever before. And they had had much to say to their favoured child. They had demanded that he join the beast-tribes south of the Grey Mountains, and lead them into war with a man of bone and black sorcery. But his fractious kin had been preoccupied with battling their hated enemies, the wood elves.

It had taken Malagor months to browbeat, bully and brutalise a number of tribes and herds into following him into the war-ravaged provinces of Bretonnia, only to find that his prey had already slipped over the mountains and into the north. But all was not lost. The gods had murmured that Arkhan would return. And that he would fall in Bretonnia. That was their command and their promise. The skeins of fate were pulled taut about the dead man, and there would be no escape for him again.

'The Bone-Man must die,' Malagor bellowed. 'The gods command it! Death to the dead! Gnaw their bones and suck the marrow!'

'Gnaw his bones,' a chieftain roared, shaking his crude blade over his horned head. Others took up the chant, one by one, and soon every beast in the clearing had added its voice to the cacophony.

Malagor's muscles bunched and he thrust himself into the air. His black wings flapped, catching the wind, causing the witch-fires to flicker, and bowling over the smaller beastmen. He screamed at the sky as he rose, adding his howls to those of his kin.

The liche would die, even if Malagor had to sacrifice every beastman on this side of the Grey Mountains to accomplish it. The Dark Gods demanded it, and Malagor was their word made flesh. He was the black edge of their blade, the tip of their tongue and their will made into harsh reality. He flapped his wings and rose high over the trees. Overhead the sky wept green tears and crawled with hideous shapes, and Malagor felt the blessings of his gods fill him with divine purpose. He roared again, this time in triumph.

Arkhan the Black would die.

Near the King's Glade, Athel Loren

The gor squealed and staggered back, grasping at its sliced belly with blood-slick paws. Araloth, Lord of Talsyn, darted forward to deliver the deathblow before the beast recovered. The ravaged glade rang with the sound of blade on blade, and the death-cries of elves and beasts. Blood, both pure and foul, turned the churned soil beneath his feet to mud.

A shadow fell over him, while his sword sent the beastman's brutish head spinning from its thick neck. Araloth glanced up and saw a minotaur raising its axe over him, its bestial jaws dripping with bloody froth as it gnashed its fangs. Its eyes bulged from their sockets, and it whined and lowed in mindless greed. The minotaur stumped forward, reaching for him with its free hand. He tensed, ready to leap aside, a prayer to Lileath on his lips.

Then a second, equally massive shape slammed into the bull-headed giant from the side, bearing it to the ground. The two enormous figures ploughed through the fray that swirled about them, scattering elves and beasts alike as they smashed through the trees of the blood-soaked glade. Araloth could only watch in awe as Orion, the King in the Woods, rose over the fallen minotaur, a hand gripping one of its horns.

Orion dragged the dazed beast to its feet and locked his arm about its throat. He grabbed its horns and threw his weight to the side. The glade echoed with the crack of crude, Chaos-twisted bone, and then Orion threw down his opponent and let out a roar of victory that caused the trees to shiver where they stood.

The beastmen began to retreat, streaming back the way they had come, first in ones and twos, and then in a mad panic, bellowing and braying in fear. Orion put his horn to his lips and sounded a long, wailing note. Glade Riders galloped off in pursuit of their fleeing enemies. Orion met Araloth's gaze for only a moment, before turning away and loping after his huntsmen. Araloth shivered and sheathed his blade.

There had been nothing but rage in his king's eyes. Even sorrow had been burned away, and reason with it. Only the battle-madness remained.

Despite his fear, Araloth could find no fault in that. Ariel was dying, and the forest with her, and there was nothing Orion or anyone could do. He understood the king's rage better than most, for was he not the queen's champion? 'Much good I did her,' he murmured, looking about him. Every muscle in his body ached, and his hands trembled with fatigue. He had been fighting for days on end, trying to drive back this latest assault on the deep glades of the forest.

The source of the sickness that afflicted the Mage Queen was not readily apparent, but in its wake came a rot on the boughs of the Oak of Ages, and then a sickness that spread through the forest, twisting and tainting everything. Glades that had gone unaffected by the shifting seasons since the first turning of the world now withered, the trees cracking and splitting, their roots blistering and turning black as the forest floor heaved with decay. Madness swept through the ranks of the dryads and treemen, making dangerous, unpredictable enemies of ancient allies as the children of Chaos poured into these now-desolate glades in their thousands.

These were not the usual herds who perennially spent their blood beneath the forest canopy, but bray-spawn and mutant filth from hundreds of leagues away, migrating from every direction, as if drawn to the weakened forest by some unvoiced signal.

Araloth looked about him, at the piles of twisted bodies that littered the ground, and the pale, slim shapes that lay amongst them. No matter how many they killed, no matter how many times they repulsed them, the creatures continued to pour into the forest. He leaned forward on his blade, suddenly feeling more tired than he had in centuries. He wanted to sleep for a season, but there was no time for rest, let alone slumber.

He opened his eyes and began to clean his sword. There would be another attack. The king and his Wild Hunt might have driven off this one, but there were more herds in the vicinity, and all of them were moving towards the King's Glade. Eventually, they would get through. And when that happened…

He turned as he heard the thud of hooves, dismissing the dark thoughts. A rider burst into the glade, and headed for Araloth. The wood elf swung down out of her saddle and thrust the reins into Araloth's hands. He blinked in surprise. 'What–' he began.

'The council requires your presence, champion,' the rider gasped, breathing heavily, though whether in excitement or fear he couldn't say. 'The Eldest of the Ancients has awoken, and he speaks words of portent. You must go!'

Without further hesitation, Araloth swung up into the horse's saddle and dug his heels into its lathered flanks. The horse reared and pawed the air with its hooves before turning and galloping back the way it had come, carrying Araloth into the depths of the forest.

As he rode, he wondered why Durthu had chosen now to awaken, and whether it had anything to do with their visitor. Several months after Ariel had fallen ill, an intruder had somehow navigated the worldroots and penetrated the King's Glade. The newcomer had allowed the startled sentries, including Araloth himself, to take her into custody and asked only that they grant her an audience with the Council of Athel Loren. Araloth, bemused, had agreed, if only because it wasn't every day that Alarielle, Everqueen of Ulthuan, visited Athel Loren.

His bemusement had faded when he had learned of her reasons for braving the dangers of the worldroots. The forest was dying, and it seemed that the world was dying with it. The balance of the Weave was shifting, and all that his folk had fought so long to prevent was at last coming to pass. The doom of all things was upon them, and no one could figure out a way to stop it. Araloth bent low over the horse's neck and urged it to greater speed.

But if Durthu had at last risen from his slumber, if the Eldest of the Ancients had decided to address the council, as he had done so infrequently in recent decades, then perhaps that doom could still be averted.

And perhaps the Mage Queen could still be saved.

Hvargir Forest, the Border Princes

'Die-die, filthy man-thing!' Snikrat, hero of Clan Mordkin, shrieked as he fell out of the tree onto the panting messenger. The man – a youth, really – died as soon as the skaven struck him, the weight of the rat-thing landing on his neck and the bite of the cruel, saw-toothed blade the latter clutched, serving to tumble him into Morr's welcoming arms before he knew what was happening. Snikrat bounded to his feet, tail lashing, and whirled about excitedly, hunting for more foes.

Relief warred with disappointment when he saw nothing save the hurrying shapes of his Bonehides scrambling over the thick roots and between the close-set trees of Hvargir Forest. The clawband of black-furred stormvermin swarmed towards him, chittering in obsequious congratulations. Snikrat tore his blade free of the messenger's body and gesticulated at his warriors. 'What good are you if you cannot catch-quick one man-thing?' he snapped. 'It is a lucky thing that I was here, in this place where you see me, to dispose of the creature whose body I now stand on with this blade I hold in my paw.'

Beady black eyes slid away from his own bulging, red-veined ones, and the stink of nervous musk filled the immediate air as his warriors bunched together and the front ranks shuffled back. Snikrat knew that he cut an imposing figure. He was bigger than any two of his Bonehides put together, and clad in the finest armour warpstone could purchase. His blade had belonged to a dwarf thane, once upon a time, and though it had changed hands and owners several times since, it was still a deadly looking weapon, covered in dolorous runes and smeared with several foul-smelling unguents, which, to Snikrat's knowledge, did nothing – but better safe than sorry.

He spat and looked down at the messenger. 'Search the man-thing there on the ground and the clothes that he wears for anything of value, by which I mean things of gold and or conspicuous shininess, and then give them to me, your leader, Snikrat the Magnificent, yes-yes.' He kicked the body towards his followers, the closest of whom immediately fell upon it in a frenzy of looting. A squealing squabble broke out. Snikrat turned away as the first punch was thrown.

He scrambled back up the tree he'd been hunched in before the messenger had disturbed his well-deserved meditation. From its uppermost branches, he could take in most of the forest, as well as the distant stone towers and wooden palisades that dotted the region. The lands the man-things called the Border Princes was cramped with duchies and fiefdoms, most no bigger than a common clanrat's burrow. The messenger had likely been heading for one of them, sent out to bring aid to the keep the rest of Clan Mordkin was, at the moment, busily sacking.

Snikrat hissed softly as he thought of the slaughter he was missing. War-lord Feskit had led the assault personally, from the rear, and he had wanted Snikrat around while he did it. Snikrat grunted in grudging admiration – no one had ever accused Feskit of being stupid. Indeed, the leader of Clan Mordkin was anything but, and under his beneficent rule, the clan had recovered much of the wealth and prestige it had lost over the centuries since its ousting from Cripple Peak. Though he was growing older and less impressive with every year, he had managed to avoid every serious challenge and assassination attempt made on him.

Perched on a branch, anchored by his hairless tail, Snikrat hauled a flap of tanned and inked flesh out from within his cuirass and carefully unfolded it. The map wasn't much, but it served its purpose. Carefully, his pink tongue pinched between his fangs, he used a stub of charcoal to draw an 'x' over the keep they'd just come from. There were still six more between them and Mad Dog Pass, which meant plenty of chances for him to add to his own meagre pile of campaign spoils. Idly, he reached up and plucked an egg from the bird's nest that sat in the branches above. He'd eaten the mother earlier, and it seemed a shame to let the eggs go to waste. As he crunched on the deli-cate shell, and eyed the map, he considered his fortunes, such as they were.

It was a time of great happenings and glories, from the perspective of an ambitious chieftain, such as he, himself, Snikrat the Magnificent. The sky wept green meteors and the ground vomited up volcanoes as unnat-ural storms swept the land. It was as if the great Horned Rat himself had opened the door to the world and whispered to his children, 'Go forth and take it, with my compliments.'

Granted, that was easier said than done. True, the man-thing kingdoms of Tilea and Estalia, as factitious in their own way as the skaven themselves, had fallen quickly enough to the numberless hordes that had surged upwards from the network of subterranean tunnels. Every city between Magritta and Sartosa was now a blasted ruin, over which the ragged banner of one clan or another flew. But there were other victories that proved more elusive.

Snikrat scratched at the barely healed mark on his throat. A gift from Feskit, and a sign of his mercy. Snikrat hunched forward and ate another egg. It had been his own fault, and he, Snikrat, was pragmatic enough to admit that, in private, in his own head. He had thought that the omens were a sign that he, Snikrat, should attempt to tear out Feskit's wattle throat. Instead, it was he who felt his rival's teeth on his neck.

Still, there was plenty of time. The world was the skaven's for the taking, even as Clan Mordkin was for his, Snikrat's. And then, the greatest treasures of the clan would be his... Including the Weapon – that oh-so-beautiful sword of glistening black warpstone that Feskit kept hidden behind lock and chain. Even he, Snikrat, had heard of the Fellblade, the slayer of kings and worse than kings, on whose edge the fortunes of Clan Mordkin had been honed. With a weapon like that in hand, there would be no stopping him, and he, Snikrat, would be a power to be reckoned with in the Under-Empire.

Snikrat chattered happily to himself and ate another egg.

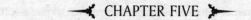

CHAPTER FIVE

Castle Sternieste, Sylvania

The woman who knelt before Mannfred von Carstein was pale and beautiful, and deceit oozed out of her every pampered pore. She claimed to speak for the Queen of the Silver Pinnacle, but so too did half a dozen other similar women, all of whom were mingling with his guests in a manner he found somewhat amusing. He accepted the scroll and waved a hand. She rose gracefully and retreated, leaving the garden behind. As she left, the guards crossed their blades, blocking any further entry.

Mannfred tapped the scroll against his lips. His eyes slid to his cousin, Markos, as the latter refilled his goblet from a jug of magically warmed blood. 'Where is the liche? He practically demanded that I include him in these meetings. I find myself slightly disappointed that he chose not to show up.'

Markos hesitated. His eyes went unfocused for a moment, and then snapped back to their usual keenness. He finished filling his goblet. 'He's in the old library in the west wing, poring over those books and scrolls you lent him.'

Mannfred frowned. It had been weeks since the battle at Valsborg Bridge and its inconclusive climax. He had played the part of the dutiful aristocratic host, inviting his new... ally back to Castle Sternieste. Arkhan had accepted the offer with grating sincerity, and had been as good as his word. He had made no attempt at treachery, asking only that he be allowed to see those relics he had come for, and that he be included in any councils of war, as befitted an ally. Mannfred had yet to grant the former request, both out of suspicion and a perverse urge to see how far he could push the liche's magnanimity.

The line between ally and enemy was often only the thickness of ambition's edge, and could be crossed as a consequence of the smallest act of disrespect or discourtesy. Thus far, Arkhan had given no obvious notice to the passing of time, or Mannfred's attempts to evade his request. He wondered if the liche's absence was a subtle thrust of his own. 'And his creatures?' he said, studying the scroll of papyrus the Lahmian had given him. Arkhan's coterie of necromancers were as untrustworthy as their master, but they had enough raw power between them to be useful. 'What of them?'

'They've settled in nicely. Several of their fellows reached us weeks ago.' Markos tapped his chin. 'We have quite the little colloquium of necromancers now. Enough to raise a host or six, I should think.'

'You shouldn't, cousin,' Mannfred said. He hefted the scroll and it curled and blackened in his hand, reduced to ashes.

'Shouldn't what?' Markos asked.

'Think,' Mannfred said. He ignored Markos's glare and looked at Elize. He gestured to the ash that swirled through the air. 'What of the handmaidens of the mistress of the Silver Pinnacle? Can they be trusted, or will they seek to sabotage my efforts for lack of anything else to do, if they haven't already?'

Elize blew an errant crimson lock out of her face and said, 'They're cunning, but cautious. Overly so, in my opinion. Without word from their queen, they seem content to watch and nothing more.' She frowned. 'If the barrier of faith falters, even for a moment, they'll make for the mountains as quickly as possible. We may want to inhume them somewhere out of the way, if for no other reason than to deny the Queen of Mysteries what they know.'

Mannfred paused, considering. It was a pleasant thought. But that was for the future. He shook his head. 'No. As amusing as that thought is, the Queen of Mysteries is too dangerous an opponent to antagonise needlessly.'

'Besides which, for every one of her creatures you see, there are at least two you don't,' Erikan said. He sat in the tree, whittling on a length of femur with a knife. Mannfred glanced up at him.

'You are correct,' Mannfred said. 'And they're not the only maggots hidden in the meat.' He looked at Nyktolos. 'What of Gashnag's representatives? Will the Black Prince of Morgheim throw in with us, or will I be forced to bring him to heel like the brute he truly is? And can we trust those creatures of his, who currently enjoy my hospitality?'

'Those who hold true to the banners of mouldy Strigos are, for the moment, with us.' Nyktolos hesitated, and then amended, 'That is to say, with you, Lord Mannfred.' Nyktolos took off his monocle and rubbed it on his sleeve. 'And the beasts you brought from Mousillon are as content as such creatures can be. Nonetheless, it is my informed opinion that we cannot trust them, being as they are snake-brained, weasel-spined, marrow-lickers, fit only to be staked out for the sun.'

'Well said,' Alberacht grunted from where he perched on the high wall, wings drooping over the stones like two leathery curtains. His lamp-like eyes sought out Mannfred. 'We cannot trust the spawn of Ushoran, Count von Carstein. They are animals, and unpredictable ones at that,' he growled, with no hint of irony.

Markos nearly choked on a swallow of blood. Mannfred glanced at his cousin disapprovingly. While mockery was a game he enjoyed, Nictus was deserving of more respect. He was a monster, and addle-brained, but loyal. And, in his own way, the Reaper of Drakenhof was as much a power in Sylvania as any von Carstein. Nictus had been of the old order, a cousin to Isabella and a nephew of Otto von Drak. Von Drak had ordered Nictus chained in an oubliette for some unspecified transgression, and only Isabella's pleas had moved Vlad to bother digging him out. Nictus had served Vlad faithfully in life and then in undeath, with a dogged, unswerving loyalty that Mannfred had, at the time, found amusing. Now, centuries after his own betrayal of Vlad, he found Nictus's continued, unquestioning, loyalty almost comforting.

He heard a sibilant chuckle inside his head and felt a flash of anger. He pressed his fingers to his head and waited for it to pass. Pushing his thoughts of Vlad and loyalty aside, he asked, 'What of the others? The so-called Shadowlord of Marienburg? Cicatrix of Wolf Crag? Have they sent representatives or missives?'

'No, my lord. Then, Mundvard was never one to be accused of knowing his place. When Vlad died, he went his own way, as so many of us did,' Alberacht said. He shook his head. 'Marienburg is his place now, and he'll not leave it or invite us in, if he can help it.'

'And Wolf Crag, even ensconced as it is within our borders, has not responded. If Cicatrix still lives, she may well have decided to throw in her lot with von Dohl, given their past history. She was ever fond of that perfumed lout,' Anark said.

Mannfred sighed. Not all vampires in the world congregated in Sylvania, but Mannfred saw no reason that they shouldn't be made aware of what he had wrought. And if they chose to come and venerate him as the natural lord of their kind for it, why, who was he to turn them away? Granted, he tempered such musings with a certain cynicism. He had travelled among his farther flung kin, journeying through the stinking jungles of the Southlands and the high hills of Cathay, and knew that, whatever their land of origin, vampires were all the same. Uniformly deceitful, treacherous and arrogant.

They could be allies – but subordinates? He smiled to himself at the thought. There was little humour in the expression. Soon, however, he thought, they would have no choice. He felt the weight of destiny on his shoulders such as he never had before, even during those heady months when he had first taken control of Sylvania. The time was fast coming when all of the descendants of the bloody courtiers of long-vanished Lahmia, whether they lurked in jade temples, insect-filled jungles or mouldering manses, would have to bend knee to the new master of death.

And are you so sure that master is you, my boy? Vlad's voice murmured. Mannfred closed his eyes, banishing the voice. For all of the old ghost's

THE RETURN OF NAGASH

attempts to undermine his surety, Mannfred felt all the more certain of his path. The world would be broken to the designs laid out by the Corpse Geometries, and made a thing of unflinching, unfailing order, ruled over by one will – his.

'Did you hear me, my lord?' Anark asked, startling him. The big vampire had grown into his role as the Grand Master of the Drakenhof Order, bullying and, in one case, beheading, any who might challenge him. In the weeks since Tomas's charred head had been relegated to a stake on the battlement for the amusement of the crows, Anark had weeded out the favour-curriers and courtiers, leaving only a hardened cadre of blood knights equal to any produced by the drill field of Blood Keep. Mannfred looked forward to employing them on the battlefield.

'What?' Mannfred blinked. He shuddered slightly. He felt as if he'd been lost in a dream, and was slightly ill from the sweetness of it. He felt the eyes of the inner circle on him, and he cursed himself for showing even the briefest of weaknesses. It wouldn't take much to incite a cur like Markos, or even lovely Elize, to start sharpening their fangs, and he could ill afford to have them start scheming against him now.

'I said that we have reports that the Crimson Lord has returned to Sylvania, and is claiming dominion over the citadel of Waldenhof,' Anark said.

Mannfred waved a hand. 'And so? What is that to me? Let that dolt von Dohl pontificate and prance about in that draughty pile if he wishes. He knows better than to challenge me openly, and if he chooses to do so… Well, we could use a bit of fun, no?' He clapped his hands together. 'See to our strategies for the coming year. Everything must go perfectly, or our fragile weave is undone. I must speak with our guest.'

He left them there in the garden, staring after him, and was gone out the door before they could so much as protest. He knew what they would say, even if they hadn't been saying it every day for weeks. The incessant scheming, strategising and drilling was wearing on them, even Anark, who lived for the tourney field. Vampires were not, by nature, creatures of hard graft. They were predators, and each had a predator's laziness. They exerted themselves only when the goal was in reach, and had not the foresight to see why that path led only to a hawthorn stake or a slow expiration under the sun's merciless gaze.

All save me and thee and one or two others, eh, boy? Vlad murmured encouragingly. *I taught you to see the edges of the canvas, where one portrait ends and another begins, didn't I?*

'You taught me nothing save how to die,' Mannfred hissed. He quickly looked around, but only the dead were within earshot. The truly dead these, rather than the thirsty dead, wrenched from silent tombs and set to guarding the corridors of his castle. He paused for a moment, eyes closed, ignoring the shadows that closed in on him. It was no use; he could feel them, winnowing into his thoughts, clouding his perceptions.

Vlad had indeed taught him much, his words aside. The creature who had given him his name had been as good a teacher as any Mannfred had had up until that point in his sorry life. He had learned from Vlad that the only true path was the one you forged for yourself.

In their centuries together, Vlad had taught him to change his face, and the scent of his magics, so as to hide his origins from prying forces who would seek to use the secrets of his turning against him. Vlad had taught him to trust only his instincts, and to be true to his ambitions, wherever they led, to use his desires like a blade and buckler. And, in the end, Vlad had taught him the greatest lesson of all – that power alone did not shield you from weakness. It crept in, like a thief in the night, where you least suspected it, and it slit your throat as surely as any enemy blade – Nagash, Neferata, Ushoran and, in the end, Vlad himself had all been humbled by their weaknesses. And so too had Mannfred.

But unlike them, he had risen from the ashes, remade and all the stronger for his failure. And he would not fall prey to his weaknesses again. 'I learned my lessons well, old man,' he murmured as he opened his eyes. 'I will be beholden to no man or ghost, and ambition is my tool, not my master.'

Something that might have been laughter floated on the dank air like particles of dust. Mannfred ignored it and continued on through the halls, his mind turning from the past to the future and what part his newfound ally would play in assuring that it came about.

He found the liche in the library, as Markos had said. Arkhan sat at one of the great tables, his fleshless fingers tracing across the page of one of the large grimoires that Mannfred had collected over the course of his life. His pet sat curled over his shoulder, its milky orbs slitted and its ragged tail twitching. He peered over Arkhan's shoulder, and saw the complicated pictographic script of lost Nehekhara. 'Dehbat's *Book of Tongues,*' he said. The cat hissed at him and he replied in kind.

Arkhan didn't turn as he reached up to scratch the cat under the chin. '*I knew Dehbat. He was one of W'soran's pets, in better days,*' he said, as he carefully turned the page. The book was old, older even than Mannfred, and was a copy of a copy of a copy.

'He was wise, in his way, if unimaginative,' Mannfred said, circling the table and heading for the great windows that marked the opposite wall. It was dark outside, as ever, but the sky was alive with a hazy aurora of witch-light. The light was not of his doing, and he knew that it was bleeding through his protective magics from the world outside. Time was running short. Eventually, Sylvania would be shorn of its protection, but still trapped by the wall of faith.

'*W'soran did not choose his apprentices for their creativity,*' Arkhan said. He closed the book. '*I cannot say why he chose them at all, frankly. They were all disreputable, undisciplined overly ambitious vermin, without fail.*'

'So speaks Arkhan the Black, gambler, murderer, thief, sorcerer, and secret animal-lover,' Mannfred said. 'I know of your history, liche. You are hardly one to speak of disrepute and discipline.' He looked at Arkhan, and the latter's jaws sagged open in a wheezing laugh that caused Mannfred's teeth to itch in his gums. 'Did I say something funny? Why are you laughing?'

'*I am laughing, von Carstein, because your misapprehension amuses me,*' Arkhan said. He hefted the book and tossed it to Mannfred, as if it were nothing more than a penny dreadful from a street vendor's stall.

'Enlighten me,' Mannfred said. He caught the book easily and set it back gently on the table. His fingers curled in the fraying hairs that hung lank and loose on the cover. The scalp had belonged to some night-souled shaman from one of the tribes in the Vaults, who had copied the book into its current form, and then been gutted and scalped at his own command by the savages whom he'd ruled. It was a lesson in the fine line between dedication and obsession.

'*You assume that I am Arkhan the Black,*' Arkhan said.

Mannfred froze. Then, slowly, he turned. He said nothing, merely waited for Arkhan to continue. Arkhan watched him, as if gauging his reaction. The liche's skeletal grin never wavered.

'*Arkhan the Black died, vampire,*' Arkhan rasped. He touched one of the other tomes. His skeletal fingers clicked as they touched the ancient bronze clasp that held it shut.

'And was reborn, as I was,' Mannfred said, trying to read something, anything, in the flicker of the liche's eye sockets.

'*Was I? Sometimes, I wonder. Am I the same man I was then, the man who drank of Nagash's potions, who chewed a drug-root until his teeth turned black, who loved a queen – and lost her? Am I him, or am I simply Nagash's memory of him?*' He tapped the side of his head. '*Are my thoughts my own, or his? Am I a servant – or a mask?*'

Mannfred said nothing. There was nothing he could say, even if he had wanted to. He had never had such thoughts himself. They smacked of philosophical equivocation, something he had no patience for. He saw a flash of something out of the corner of his eye, heard Vlad's dry chuckle, and bit down on a snarl. 'Does it matter?' he snapped.

Arkhan cocked his head. '*No,*' he said. '*But you asked what I found so amusing. And I have told you. You are missing several key pieces, are you not?*' He rubbed the cat's spine, stroking the bare bone and causing the foul beast to arch its back in a parody of feline pleasure.

'I am aware of the gaps in my collection, yes, thank you,' Mannfred said acidly. He threw up his hands. 'And were I not trapped here, I would have those items in my hand even now.'

'*The staff, the blade, the armour,*' Arkhan said.

'And two of the Nine Books,' Mannfred said slyly. 'Or are you offering those to me, as a gesture of our newfound friendship?'

'*You said that with a straight face. Your control is admirable,*' Arkhan said. Mannfred grunted, but said nothing. Arkhan inclined his head. '*And I am, yes.*'

Mannfred's head came up sharply, and his eyes narrowed. 'What?'

'*The books are yours, should you wish,*' Arkhan said. He stood and drifted towards the window, hands clasped behind his back. '*This place is as safe as any, for the time being, and we both desire the same end, do we not?*'

Mannfred stepped back and looked at the liche. 'Nagash,' he said. Shadows tickled the edges of his vision, and he heard what might have been the rustle of loose pages as a draught curled through the library.

'*Nagash must rise. As you promised the sorcerer-wraiths of Nagashizzar, the black cults of Araby, and the ghoul-cabals of Cathay, when you sought their aid in gathering your collection, as you call it.*' Arkhan pressed a bony digit to the window, and frost spread around the point it touched the glass in a crystalline halo. He looked at Mannfred. '*For you, he is a means to an end. For me, he is the end unto itself. Yet we move along the same path, vampire. We tread the same trail, and follow the same light. Why not do it together?*'

'We are,' Mannfred said. 'Have I not opened my castle to you? Have I not given shelter to your creatures?' Though he meant the necromancers, he gestured to the cat, which glared at him with dull ferocity.

'*Yes, but you have still denied my request to gaze upon those items that are necessary to our shared goal. You have denied me my request to see those prisoners whose blood is the base of the sorceries that protect Sylvania – and trap you here.*'

Mannfred tensed, as he always did when the wall of faith that caged the laughable cess-pit he called a realm was mentioned. Arkhan scraped his finger along the window, cracking the glass. He had allowed Mannfred to play the genial host for long enough. It was past time for action. The world was cracking beneath the weight of warring destinies.

Arkhan had felt it, as he crossed the mountains and journeyed to Sylvania, though it had taken him the quiet weeks since to process those ephemeral stirrings into something approaching a conclusion. They were approaching a pivotal moment, and they were not doing so unobserved. Eyes were upon them, even here, in this place. Arkhan could feel the spirits of Chaos whispering in the spider-webbed corridors and rumbling far below the earth, and he had cast the bones and understood the signs. There were powers gathering in the dark places, old powers, no longer content to simply watch.

Time was their enemy now. And he could not allow Mannfred to cede any more ground, not if their shared goal was to be accomplished. '*They are part of it, you see. The magics used to bind you here, like a cur in a kennel, are your own, twisted back upon you.*' He decided to sweeten his bitter draft with a bit of flattery. '*Why else did you think it was so powerful, vampire?*'

The living have no capacity for such magics, not on their own. You have made your own trap and you can break it, if you so desire.'

Mannfred twitched. His eyes narrowed and he asked, simply, 'How?'

'There is a ritual,' Arkhan said.

'What sort of ritual?'

'I doubt that you would agree to it.'

'Let me be the judge of that,' Mannfred hissed. 'Tell me!'

Arkhan said nothing. He scratched the cat's chin. Mannfred's upper lip curled back from his teeth and he glared at Arkhan furiously. Arkhan met the glare patiently. He could not force Mannfred into what needed doing, not without fear of provoking the vampire. No, the easiest way of getting a vampire to do something was to tell them not to do it. Mannfred snarled and struck the stone sill of the window with his fist, cracking it. 'What sort of ritual, damn you? We do not have the time to play these puerile games of yours, liche.'

'A sacrifice,' Arkhan said. He removed the cat from his shoulder and deposited it on the table. *'You possess nine prisoners, do you not? That is the number required for the blood ritual you enacted to seal Sylvania against threats divine and worldly, if my memory serves.'*

Mannfred started visibly. 'You know it?' he asked.

'I know more than you can conceive, von Carstein. All such sorceries derive from a single source, like the rivers of the Great Land. And I am most intimately acquainted with that source, if you'll recall.' Arkhan gave a negligent wave of his hand. *'Sacrifice one of the ones whose blood you've used to anchor your rite, any one of them, and it will create a momentary breach in the wall of faith that encircles your land.'*

'Sacrifice?' Mannfred asked. He shook his head. 'Madness. No. No, I'll not cripple the very protections I worked so hard to create.'

'Then, we'd best get used to one another's company,' Arkhan said. *'Because we're going to be here for a very long time. Out of curiosity, how long can one of your kind last without blood? A few decades, I expect. After that, you'll be too withered and shrunken to do much more than gnash your fangs fetchingly.'* He cocked his head. *'By my calculations, your servants will have drunk this province dry within a month, at least. They glut themselves without consideration for the future, and you let them, to keep them distracted and under control.'*

'How I control my servants is my business,' Mannfred growled.

'Correct,' Arkhan said, *'I cannot force salvation upon you, von Carstein. I merely offer my aid. It is up to you to accept it, or to gnaw your liver in continued frustration. But you are correct. Time grows short. What happens in a month, or a week, when your prisoners are the only living things left in this place? How long will your control last then? How long before you face revolt from your servants, and from your own unseemly thirst? Is it not better to sacrifice one now, so that you might be free to utilise the others as you wish, unimpeded?'*

Mannfred turned away. 'Which one?' he asked.

'*I will need to see them to answer that. I have ways of determining which of them is the least necessary for your pattern.*'

'And now we come to it,' Mannfred snapped. 'All your offers of aid and books are nothing more than your attempt to burrow your way into my vaults, are they not? You could not defeat me in open battle, and now you seek to trick me. You came to Sylvania to claim those items I won by my guile and strength, and to demand that I swear fealty to the broken, black soul whose cloak hem you still cling to. Well, you'll get neither!' Mannfred whirled and caught up the table, wrenching it up over his head in a display of monstrous strength, spilling books and the yowling corpse-cat to the floor. His lean frame swelled with inhuman muscle as his face contorted, becoming as gargoyle-hideous as that of any of his more bestial servants. 'Nagash is not my god, liche. He does not command me!'

Arkhan looked up at the table, and then at the face of he who held it. He could see, though just barely, an enormous, ghostly shape superimposed over Mannfred's own, and heard a rustle of sound in the depths of his own tattered spirit that might have been laughter. Mannfred's face twisted, and Arkhan knew that the vampire heard it as well. The tableau held for a moment, two, three... And then Mannfred set the table down with more gentleness than Arkhan had expected. He seemed to deflate. The library was as cold as a crypt, and frost clung thick on the windows, as if something had sucked all of the heat from the room all at once.

'*Which are you, I wonder – servant or mask?*' Arkhan asked.

'I am my own man,' Mannfred grated, from between clenched fangs. He closed his eyes. 'Nagash holds no power over me. I am merely in a foul humour and my temper is short. Forgive me.' The excuse sounded weak to Arkhan. The defiance of a mouse, caught in the claws of a well-fed cat. Mannfred was bowing beneath the weight of another's will, no matter how much he denied it, and he knew it too. The thing that held his soul in its talons had done so for far longer than Mannfred likely suspected, Arkhan thought. It battened upon him, like a leech, and only now had it grown strong enough to be felt.

Memories of his own life, in service to Nagash, before things went wrong, spattered across the surface of his mind, brief bursts of colour and sound that pulsed brightly and faded quickly. It had taken him years to understand the plague that was Nagash. How he infected his tools, both living and inanimate, with himself, with his mind and thoughts. He hollowed you out and took your place in your own skull, pulling the red rags of your psyche over himself like a cloak, emerging only when necessary. Mannfred had never had a chance... Vampires were the blood of Nagash. It was his essence that had transformed Neferata into the creature she now was, and from her had sprung fecund legions, whose veins ran with the black blood of the Great Necromancer. While creatures like Mannfred persisted, Nagash would never truly be gone.

Arkhan felt a pang of something that might have been sympathy for the creature before him. For all of them – puppets on the end of his master's strings, though they knew it not. Some were more wilful than others, with longer strings, but they were still puppets, still slaves to the song of blood and the Corpse Geometries that hemmed them in.

Mannfred's head came up sharply, and his nostrils flared. 'Ha!' he barked. He looked at Arkhan. 'You wanted to see the prisoners, liche? Well let us go visit them.'

'*What changed your mind?*' Arkhan asked.

Mannfred chuckled and swept for the door. 'They're trying to escape.'

'*You don't sound concerned,*' Arkhan said, as he hurried after Mannfred, his robes rustling. The liche's hand fell to the pommel of his blade, as he examined Mannfred's broad back. It would be no effort at all to simply slide the blade in. Well, perhaps some effort. Mannfred was no guileless peasant, after all. Destroying him now might spare grief later. Vampires were unpredictable at the best of times, and this was most assuredly not the best of times. Right now, Mannfred thought he was in control. Eventually, however, he would try to openly resist Nagash's return, especially once he realised what fate awaited him, should they be successful.

Nonetheless, he still required the vampire's aid. Many hands made for quick work. Arkhan let his hand slide away from the blade. No, the time to dispose of Mannfred had not yet come.

'I'm not. I want them to try,' Mannfred said. I want them to try again and again, and grow more desperate with every failure. Their spirits must be broken. There can be no resistance, come the day. Nothing must stymie us.'

'*I couldn't agree more,*' Arkhan said.

⟨ CHAPTER SIX ⟩

Castle Sternieste, Sylvania

Volkmar stood knee-deep in ash and dust. Harsh smoke caressed his aching lungs and stung his weary eyes. Every limb felt heavy, and his heart struggled to keep its rhythm. He was bitterly cold and terribly hot, all at once. His hammer hung almost forgotten in his hand, its ornate head broken, and its haft soaked in blood and sweat. His breath fogged and swirled before his eyes, and he could see faces in it. Men and women, some he knew, others whom he found familiar though he could not say why or how.

There was blood on his face and hands, and his gilded armour was stained with tarry excretions and reeking ichors. The smoke that entombed him stank of funeral pyres, and he could hear the roar of distant battle. Weapons crashed against shields and bit into cringing meat. The air swelled and cracked with a riot of voices, echoing from unseen places. Screams of agony mingled with pleading voices and howling cries of pure animal terror. The air was choked by the smoke that curled about him; he could see strange witch-lights pulsing within its depths, and horrible, ill-defined shapes moving around him, either too slowly or too quickly. He could not say where they were going, or why. Something crackled beneath his foot.

The smoke swirled clear for a moment, and he saw that he stood on a carpet of bones, picked clean by the ages. Old bones and new bones, brown and white and yellow, clad in the shapeless remnants of clothing and armour from a span of centuries that boggled Volkmar's already addled mind. He saw weapons and tools the likes of which he had only seen in the most ancient of barrows, and those that seemed far more advanced than the ones he was familiar with. It was as if someone had emptied out all of the graveyards of history.

Volkmar did not know where he was, or how he had come there. He only knew that he was frightened, and tired, but not yet ready. Ready for what, he did not know, but the thought of it caused him to shudder in horror.

He raised his hammer wearily, preparing himself for what he somehow knew came next.

All about him, the plain of bones began to tremble and clatter. Sparks of weird light grew in the empty sockets of every skull and a eye-searing green fire crackled along the length of every bone. The bones surged up with a cacophonous rattle, and something began to take shape – something immense and powerful, Volkmar knew, though he had never seen it before. A single voice suddenly drowned out all others, silencing them. It spoke in a language that Volkmar had only ever seen written down, and the words were carved into the chill air like sword strokes.

As the thing – *the daemon,* his mind screamed – grew and formed and spoke, the smoke above him cleared. He looked up at the cold, black stars that pulsed in the dead void above. A thought quavered in his head, like the tinny tone of a child's bell. Everything was dead, here. Nothing lived, save him. Nothing moved, or breathed, or laughed or loved, without the whim of the monstrous intelligence that guided the climbing, shifting pillar of bones rising up before him. It had conquered and covered and was the world about him. His world, for he could see the ruin of the great temple of Sigmar, there, rising from the sea of death, and the Imperial palace and a hundred other landmarks, barely visible through the smoke.

His heart sank. He saw the blackened skeletons of the Vagr Breughel Memorial Playhouse and the Geheimnihsstrasse Theatre, the broken ruin of Temple Street, and shattered remnant of the Konigsplatz. Altdorf, he was in Altdorf, and it, like everything else in this world, was dead and buried. The gods were gone, and only this cold, malignity remained.

The thought incited him, freeing him from his terrified paralysis. A hoarse roar slipped from his blistered lips, and he swung the hammer up, catching it in both hands as he forced himself forwards through the clawing tide of dead matter that swirled about him. A light, weak at first, and then growing stronger, suffused him. A corona of heat swirled into being about the shattered head of the hammer as he swung it.

The hammer smacked into a giant's palm. The sliding, slithering bones that made up the titan's claw gave slightly at the force of the blow. Then the massive claws curled down, enclosing the hammer completely, and, like a parent taking a toy from a child, snatched the weapon from Volkmar's grip. The arm was impossibly long, and attached to an equally out-of-proportion shoulder. The constant motion of the bones made it hard to discern the truth of the shape before him, but he saw enough to want to look away – *to run,* a voice screamed.

Volkmar turned and ran. It was not the first time he had done so, and he knew that it wasn't the first time he had faced this enemy either. He had fled from it before, and fought ineffectually against it and been buried by it again and again. He ran, and his hammer was somehow in his hand again, still broken, its weight slowing him down. The thing followed him, ploughing through the smoke and charnel leavings like a shark through shallow waters, absorbing and expelling the bones it rolled over. Sometimes it was beside him, and other times it loomed over him, its shadow enveloping him in a cloak of numbing cold. It outpaced him at times or fell far behind. He had the sense that it was in no hurry. That it was enjoying itself. But he did not stop, he could not stop. To face it, he knew, was to fall. Only in flight was there life, and Volkmar dearly wanted to live.

The courage that had sustained him throughout his long life, that had kept him on his feet through fire and ruin, that had seen him match his hammer against all manner of foes, had failed him. All of his training, all of his rhetoric, all of his faith, had fled him, leaving only the raw atavistic impulse to survive at all costs. So he ran.

He ran in pursuit of the wind. He heard a woman's voice, in the hissing sibilance of the breeze that stirred the smoke. He always heard it, as he ran. Sometimes he thought it was his mother, or an old lover, or the daughter he'd never had, but other times, he knew it was none of those. It was not a human voice. It was a voice that spoke to the wind, and to eagles, and it lent him strength, and propelled him on, easing the weight of his hurts and sweeping aside the dead shapes that lunged for him out of the smoke.

Run, she murmured.

Run, she whispered.

Run, she screamed.

Volkmar ran, and the dead world pursued him. And as his limbs failed, and his blood pounded in his ears, and the rattle of bones grew thunderous in his ears, he grasped at her words, her voice, grabbing for any shred of salvation, of hope, and, as all of the dead of Altdorf heaved beneath him, the Grand Theogonist woke up.

Volkmar's eyes sprang open, and he sucked in a lungful of stale, damp air. He shuddered and twitched, unable to control his limbs. His heels drummed on the stone floor, and his palms flapped uselessly against his battered cuirass. He moaned and tried to roll over, but the manacles about his wrists prevented it. He was forced to squirm about and haul himself up into a sitting position. His body ached, much as it had in his dream. He coughed, trying to clear his throat, and looked around blearily.

'Still alive, my friend?' someone asked. Volkmar peered through the gloom, and caught sight of golden armour gleaming still beneath a layer of filth. He struggled to recall the Tilean's name, through the mugginess of his aborted sleep.

'If you can call it living,' Volkmar coughed. His throat was parched and drier than the deserts of Araby. He squinted at the knight. 'You've looked better, Blaze.'

Lupio Blaze, Templar of the Order of the Blazing Sun, laughed shallowly. 'As have we all,' he said, rattling his chains. His once-handsome features had been bludgeoned into a shapeless mass of dried blood and bruises, but his eyes were still bright, and his torn lips still quirked in a smile. 'Still, it could be worse. It could be raining.'

Overhead, thunder rumbled. The soft plop of water was replaced by the steady downbeat of falling rain. Blaze laughed again, and craned himself backwards, so that his head and torso was caught in the downpour. 'You see, Olf? I say that the gods still watch over us, eh?' Blaze called out, gulping at the rainwater. He made a cup of his hands, and caught a handful of the rain. Then he kicked the legs of the figure chained next to him. 'Up, Olf, have a drink, on me,' he said, pouring the handful of water into the cupped hands of the burly Ulrican priest who was chained to the lectern next to his.

Olf Doggert eagerly slurped the water, and then grudgingly passed the next handful of water to the next prisoner in line, the pinch-faced young priest of Morr, Mordecaul Cadavion. Cadavion drank his share and passed along the next handful, emptying his cupped hands into those of the wan-faced matron named Elspeth Farrier, a priestess of Shallya. Volkmar turned his attention to the figure of the man chained beside her. Wild haired and raggedly dressed even before their captivity, Russett, blessed of Taal looked like a living corpse now. He hadn't eaten in days, and he'd barely drunk anything. His flesh was mottled with bruises where he'd thrown himself at the walls, and bloody marks chafed his wrists where he continually yanked on his chains. One of his ankles had been gnawed to the bone, not by any of Mannfred's beasts, but by the man himself in an attempt to get free of an earlier set of chains.

The nature priest had suffered more physically in captivity than any of them, save Volkmar and Sindst, the sour-faced priest of Ranald, who'd lost a hand and several chunks of his flesh on their journey across Vargravia in Mannfred's bone cage. Russett crouched, wrapped in chains and silently rocking back and forth. Like an animal that had been caged too long, he had gone quietly mad. Now he stared at the cockroaches and rats that shared their prison, as if trying to communicate with them. But whatever esoteric abilities Taal had granted him were not in evidence, not in Sylvania. The voices of the gods, ever faint, might as well have been the only fevered imaginings of a flagellant, for all that they reached their servants here, Volkmar reflected.

He watched Elspeth help Sindst drink. He slurped greedily at the water in her hands, and nodded weary thanks when he'd finished. Volkmar looked around. After Mannfred's last visit, they had been moved from the walls to the lecterns, and had their chains shortened. The reason hadn't been shared, but Volkmar suspected that it was another of Mannfred's demented games. He knew that the vampire enjoyed their futile escape attempts, just as he knew that they couldn't stop trying. Wounded, exhausted and filthy as they were, none of them were yet ready to give up, save perhaps for poor Russett and the Bretonnian, Morgiana, whose mind and soul had been taken by Mannfred long before they had met her. She belonged

to von Carstein now. She murmured to herself in the far corner of the
room, unchained, but unmoving. She lay on her side on the cold stone,
and stroked the floor as if it were a beloved pet, whispering constantly to
it. He caught a flash of a delicate fang as she muttered, and looked away,
sickened by what she had become.

Volkmar caught Elspeth's eye, and the Shallyan priestess shook her head
slightly. Volkmar sighed and winced, as the wound on his head split and
began to leak blood and pus. He reached for it, but Elspeth hissed, 'Don't
touch it. It's having enough trouble healing without you picking at it.'

'I don't think it's ever going to heal, sister,' Volkmar said. 'Mannfred won't
give us that time.' He looked around. 'You can all feel it, can't you? That
heaviness in the air? We're in the eye of a storm, and one that Mannfred
wants to unleash on the rest of the world. He needs us for that.'

'Otherwise why keep us alive, right?' Sindst muttered, hugging his wrist-
stump to his chest. 'We know all of this, old man. That's why we keep trying
to escape. Badly, I might add,' he spat, glaring at Blaze and Olf.

'Keep talking, sneak-thief,' Olf growled. 'Seems to me, if Mannfred needs
you alive, I'd be doing us all a favour by wringing your scrawny neck.'

'Do as you will, brute,' Sindst said, tonelessly. 'We're not getting out of
here upright, none of us. We're all dead, even the pointy-eared witch over
there.' He motioned with his stump to the elf maiden.

Volkmar looked at the elf. He pushed himself to his feet and moved as
close as he could to the lectern where she was chained. Her eyes were
closed, as they had been for the entirety of their brief, inhospitable association. Volkmar gathered water from Elspeth, and got as close to the elf
woman as he could. 'Drink, my lady,' he croaked. 'You must drink.'

Her eyes flickered open. Volkmar realised that she was blind, and felt
his heart twist in his chest. 'Aliathra,' she murmured. Volkmar blinked. He
recognised her voice instantly as the same one he'd heard in his dream,
urging him to run. A weak smile flickered across her face and was gone.
She leaned forward, and he held his hands out. She reached up and took
his hands in hers and bent her face. She drank deeply, and sat back, frowning. 'Tainted water from tainted skies,' she said. 'It tastes of his sorcery.'

'Funny, I thought it tasted of smoke, maybe with a hint of a Sartosan
red?' Sindst said.

'Quiet,' Elspeth said sharply. 'That's quite enough out of you, servant of
Ranald. If you can't be of use–'

Sindst's manacle clattered to the floor. He stretched his good arm and
Volkmar saw a twist of metal sticking from the raw stump of his other wrist,
poking through the filthy bandages. He grinned in a sickly fashion and
said, 'It took a while. I had to hide it where the flesh-eaters wouldn't sniff
it out. And wait for the flying fang-brothers to go wherever such creatures
go when they're not watching us,' he added, referring to the two vargheists that Mannfred had left to guard them.

He heaved himself up and began to free the others. 'This is useless, you know,' he said, as he worked on Volkmar's manacles. 'We're all dying by inches – no food, no water, no weapons, sick, hurt and bled dry thanks to Mannfred and his cursed spell. We won't get far.'

'Then why bother?' Volkmar asked, looking up at him.

Sindst chuckled. 'Ranald is the god of luck, among other things. And you don't get lucky if you don't roll the knucklebones, Sigmarite.'

'I hope we have a better plan than last time,' Mordecaul said, as he was freed.

'Run faster,' Elspeth said.

'That's not a plan,' Mordecaul said.

'Die well,' Olf said, heaving himself to his feet.

'What part of the word "plan" don't you understand?' Mordecaul demanded.

Sindst chuckled. 'For the servant of the god of death, you're not very eager to make his acquaintance, are you, boy?'

Mordecaul hugged himself. 'I wouldn't be in his bower for very long, would I? Death is not the end here.' He looked up, his pale face pinched with grief. 'I can't feel him. Morr, I mean. I can't feel him here.'

'None of us can feel our gods,' Blaze said, kicking aside his chains as Sindst freed him. 'That does not mean they are not there, hey?' He went to the younger man and clapped him on the shoulders. 'I knew a man, he was from Talabheim. His name was Goetz, and he was a brother-knight to me. He grew deaf to the words of Myrmidia, but he fought on, deaf and blind to her light. He still served. And when the time came, when he was at the end, suddenly – there she was!' Blaze made a flamboyant gesture. 'She had been there all the time, and he had been like a blind man standing in the sun, hey? That is what we are, newly blind. We must find the sun.' Blaze patted Mordecaul on the cheek. 'Find the sun,' he said again.

Volkmar watched the exchange silently. Blaze's overt display of faith made him feel ashamed, in some small way. His own faith had not so much been shaken as it had been uprooted. One did not become the Grand Theogonist on the strength of faith alone. Such a position was built on a bedrock of compromise. He had felt the power of Sigmar in his veins, but he had never spoken with his god, or gazed upon his face. He had never felt the need to do so. Sigmar provided him with purpose and the strength to carry out that purpose, and that was enough.

Or it had been. Now he wasn't so sure. He felt eyes on him, and looked around to see Aliathra gazing at him, her face like something carved from marble. In her eyes was something he could not define – sadness, perhaps. Or pity. Volkmar felt a flush of anger and shook off the cloud of doubt that had settled on him. Mannfred had called him 'Sigmar's blood'. Well, he'd show the vampire the truth of those words, when he pulled out the leech's unbeating heart and crushed it before his eyes.

Sindst had gone to the chamber door. 'I can't get it open,' he said.

'Then step back,' Olf growled. He flexed his long arms. 'Still a bit of strength left in this old wolf, I think. What about you, Blaze? What's that you Myrmidians always say?'

'We go where we are needed,' Blaze intoned. 'We do what must be done.' He grinned. 'See, I teach you something yet, yes?'

'Shut up and put your shoulder into it, you poncy pasta-eater,' Olf growled. Blaze chuckled and both men struck the door with their shoulders. Volkmar longed to help them, or to see to Morgiana with a sharp length of wood, but it was all he could do to stand. Instead, he kept an eye on the corner where Morgiana still lay, unheeding of their actions, as well as on the open roof above, just in case the vargheists decided to return. There was no way they could fight the creatures in their current state. It would be a miracle if they made the castle gates. But better a quick death in battle than whatever Mannfred had planned. He rubbed his blistered wrists and glanced down at the blood that flowed through the runnels that cut across the floor.

Then, his eyes were drawn to the gleaming iron crown, where it sat on its cushion of human skin. It seemed to glitter with a strange internal light, at once ugly and beauteous, attractive and repulsive in the same instant. He thought he could hear a soft voice calling to him, pleading with him, and he longed to pick it up.

I should, he thought. It was his duty, was it not? The Crown of Sorcery belonged in the vaults of the temple of Sigmar, in the Cache Malefact with the other dangerous objects. It should never have been brought into the light. How Mannfred had breached the vaults was still a mystery, but Volkmar's fingers itched to snatch up the crown and – *place it on my head* – carry it away from this fell place.

He froze, startled at the thought that had intruded on his own. It had not been his, and he knew it. His eyes narrowed and he mustered the moisture to spit on the crown, which seemed to flicker angrily in response.

'You can hear it, can't you?' the elf maiden murmured, from behind him.

Volkmar licked his lips. 'I can,' he hissed hoarsely. He looked away. 'But it says nothing worth listening to. It is nothing more than a trap for the unwary.'

'I saw Mannfred wearing it,' Mordecaul said. He looked at the crown and shuddered. 'It fit him perfectly.'

'It fits any head that dares wear it,' Volkmar grated. 'And it hollows out the soul and strips the spirit to make room for that which inhabits it.' He grinned mirthlessly. 'Let the von Carstein wear it, and bad cess to him. Let it drain him dry, one parasite on another. A better fate for him, I cannot imagine.'

'That is not his fate,' Aliathra said. Her blind eyes sought Volkmar's. 'He will burn in the end. As will we all.'

'I see the stories of the good cheer of the folk of Ulthuan were just that,'

Sindst said. He hefted a broken length of bone in his good hand. 'If we're going, let's go.'

'The door is giving,' Olf said. The door shuddered on its hinges as the Ulrican and the knight struck it again. Even half starved and beaten bloody, both men were still strong, as befitted the servants of war gods.

Volkmar was about to reply, when a cloud of char and splinters cascaded down from above. He looked up and then turned, caught up Aliathra and Mordecaul and hurled them aside as the vargheist landed with a shriek and a crash. It reared up over Volkmar, wings filling the confined space of the chamber. It screamed again, jaws distending as it lunged for him. Then it jerked back as something soft struck Volkmar's shoulder and hurled itself into the creature's face. A second rat leapt from Volkmar's other shoulder, and then a third leapt from the floor, and a fourth, a fifth – ten, twenty, until it seemed as if every rat and cockroach that had shared the chamber with the prisoners was crawling over the vargheist, biting and clawing. The monster staggered back, crashing into the lecterns with a wail as the tide of vermin knocked it sprawling.

Volkmar turned and saw Russett watching him blankly. The nature priest was surrounded by rats, and his lips moved silently as he sent his furry army into hopeless battle with the vargheist.

'Come on,' Olf roared as he grabbed Volkmar and propelled him into the corridor. 'Leave him and let's go!'

Erikan swept the femur out, and the holes he'd cut into it caught the breeze, making an eerie sound. He leaned back on his branch and placed the femur to his lips. The tune he piped out was an old one; he didn't know what it was called, only the melody.

'Very lovely,' Markos said. 'But weren't you supposed to be helping us see to these strategies, Crowfiend?'

'I am,' Erikan said, not looking down. 'I'll take my hounds of night and silence the watch-posts along the Stir, as soon as we are able to leave. If we strike quickly enough, no one will have any idea that we are out and about.' He whirled the femur again, enjoying the sound it made.

'And by "hounds of night", you mean those mouldering wolves and chattering ghouls that you seem content to spend your time with? What sort of warrior are you?' Anark sneered, glaring up at him, his fists on his hips.

'An effective one, Anark, and a reliable one – Elize, keep your trained ape muzzled, please,' Markos said, poring over the map unrolled across the bench.

'Ape, am I? I am your Grand Master, Markos, and you had best not forget it!' Anark said, reaching for his sword. Elize caught his wrist and prevented him from drawing it. Which was wise, in Erikan's estimation. Markos was just looking for an excuse to humble Anark. Then, so was everyone else. Anark was fine in small doses, but they'd been cooped up with him for weeks, and he was champing at the bit to bully someone into a fight. Mostly he seemed to want to fight Erikan, but anyone would do, by this point. Erikan looked down at Anark and smirked, then he brought the femur up and recommenced playing his tune.

'Oh believe me, I have not,' Markos purred, without turning around. 'You deserve your new position as surely as poor, late Tomas did.'

Alberacht cackled where he crouched, gargoyle-like, on the wall. Anark glared at him, but the monstrous vampire didn't even deign to return it. Instead, he dropped from the wall and ambled towards Markos. He tapped the map with one of his claws. 'Heldenhame, that's where our trouble will come from, you mark me, children.'

'The Knights of Sigmar's Blood,' Nyktolos said. He was running a whet-stone along the length of his sword as he leaned against the garden wall. 'Master Nictus is correct. I have encountered them before. They are dreadful creatures, pious and murderous in equal measure.' He looked up and frowned. 'And Heldenhame is a tough nut indeed. High, thick walls and an armed populace do not for an easy siege make, should we get that far.'

'But it has its weak points. Everything has a weak point,' Elize said. Hands behind her back, she paced back and forth. 'We simply need to find it.'

'And hit it,' Anark added. Elize smiled and stroked his cheek. Erikan, still in his branch, rolled his eyes. He played an annoying little tune, causing her to look up at him. Her expression was unreadable.

'Are you ever sorry that you taught him how to speak, cousin?' Markos asked. Anark's face flushed purple and he made a half-hearted lunge for the other vampire, only to be stopped by Elize and Alberacht.

Erikan made to play accompaniment to the farce below, but lowered his femur as the sound of bells shook the air. He tossed aside the bone and dropped from his perch. 'The bells,' he said.

'Yes, thank you, Erikan. Any other blindingly obvious statement you'd care to make?' Markos snarled as he swept aside his maps and shot to his feet. 'It's why the bloody bells are ringing that I'm interested in.'

A pack of yowling, slavering ghouls surged past the garden entrance, accompanied by slower-moving skeleton guards, clad in rusty armour and brown rags. 'The prisoners are making another escape attempt,' Elize said. She spun and pointed at Alberacht and Nyktolos. 'Get to the courtyard. That's the quickest way out of the castle.' She turned to Markos. 'Rally the rest of the order. We'll need to search the castle, if it's anything like last time.'

'And who put you in charge, cousin?' Markos purred.

'I did,' Anark growled, drawing his blade. 'You will obey her as you would me, *cousin.*'

'She's right, Markos,' Erikan said, striding past the three of them. 'And we have no time for arguments regardless. The prisoners are too valuable to risk either their escape or their deaths at the hands of Lord Mannfred's other guests.' Markos made a face, but fell silent. In the last few weeks, more than one attempt had been made on Mannfred's inner sanctums by various vampires and necromancers enjoying his hospitality. If it wasn't the Lahmians, it was the Charnel Circle, or one of the lesser von Carsteins, seeking, as ever, to supplant their betters.

And while no one liked to mention it, food had been getting scarce. While Strigany caravans were still trundling along the old Vargravian road, bringing wagons full of kidnapped men and women to Castle Sternieste, pickings in Sylvania itself were growing distinctly thin. Only the Strigany or other human servants could pass through the barrier of faith, and fewer of them returned every day. Some likely fell to the Imperial patrols that guarded the hinterlands of the neighbouring provinces, but others had, perhaps, simply decided not to come back.

Erikan was out of the garden a moment later, the others trailing in his wake or splitting off to do as Elize had commanded. Soon it was just himself and Elize and Anark, hurrying in pursuit of the ghoul pack they had seen earlier. The dead that stood sentry in every corridor and stairwell were all moving in the same direction, directed by their master's will.

Volkmar and the others had tried to escape before, with predictable results. Once, they had even made it as far as the stables. But as more and more vampires had flocked to Sternieste, so too had the likelihood grown that another such attempt would lead to more than a beating for Mannfred's amusement. Hungry vampires had all the self-control of stoats in a hen house. Regardless, there were only so many ways that the prisoners could go. Erikan thought that it was likely that they would simply try to bull their way out this time. Subtlety had got them nowhere, after all.

His conclusion was borne out by the trail of shattered bones and the twisted bodies of fallen ghouls that littered the stairs leading down to the lower levels of the keep. Erikan felt a grim admiration for the prisoners. That admiration only grew stronger when they found one of their own, a Drakenhof Templar, with his skull caved in and a jagged length of wood torn from a postern shoved through a gap in the side of his cuirass and into his heart. Anark cursed. Elize shook her head. 'They know us of old, these mortals.'

'Well, you know what they say... Familiarity breeds contempt,' Erikan murmured. He didn't recognise the vampire. Then, there were many in the order he didn't know. Elize had kept him by her side at all times. That was one of the many reasons he'd left, and sought out Obald again.

They heard the clash of arms and followed the screams of dying ghouls. Volkmar and the others had made it through Sternieste to the inner courtyard that separated the main keep from the outer. It wasn't hard to figure out how they'd made it that far – though the castle's population had increased, it was night, and almost all of its inhabitants were out hunting. Those who were left were likely trying to either avoid getting involved, or were waiting to see how far the escapees got. You had to make your own entertainment, in times like these. But it wouldn't be long before certain vampires got it in their heads to try to get in on the fun.

Erikan sprang out into the rain-swept courtyard and took in the fight roiling about him. Only seven of the prisoners had made it this far, but they were giving a good account of themselves. Most of that was down to Mannfred's command that they not be harmed. A matronly woman swung a brazier about her with determined ferocity, sending ghouls tumbling and scrambling to get out of her way. A one-handed man guarded her back, a polearm held awkwardly in his good hand.

Volkmar himself led the way, watching over the elf maiden, who sagged against the shoulder of the young priest of Morr. And the Ulrican and the Myrmidian kept the group's flanks protected. The Myrmidian had found a sword from somewhere, and laid about him with enthusiasm and skill, crying out to his goddess all the while. The Ulrican had a spear, and as Erikan watched, he impaled a skeleton guard, hoisted it, and sent it flying towards the courtyard wall. Volkmar was leading the group towards the portcullis that separated the inner and outer keeps, where Count Nyktolos waited, leaning on his blade, his monocle glinting in the torchlight.

Above them all, shapes, lean and a-thirst, ran along the walls, keeping pace but not interfering, not yet. Erikan recognised a number of Mannfred's more recent hangers-on in that group, their eyes glazed with hunger and ambition as they looked down on the Grand Theogonist. Erikan understood that look, though he didn't feel it himself. Volkmar was the living embodiment of the church that had made the scouring of Sylvania and the destruction of its bloodthirsty aristocracy a central tenet of its dogma. To see him like this, running frightened, dying on his feet, must be like a gift from the gods that Mannfred had barred from his kingdom.

They wouldn't be able to resist the chance to see the old man scream, command from Mannfred or no. He glanced at Elize, and he saw by her expression that she was thinking the same thing. She nodded sharply and sprang for the wall. Anark made to follow her, but Erikan stopped him. 'No, we need to recapture them,' he said. Anark snarled, but didn't disagree.

They split up, each approaching the prisoners from a side. Erikan hurtled the rolling body of a disembowelled ghoul and drew his sword. He arrowed towards the knight, reckoning him more dangerous than the Ulrican, so long as he had a sword in his hand. Even as their blades connected, Erikan saw Nyktolos lunge forward, his sword chopping into the haft of the spear the Ulrican wielded.

The Myrmidian whirled his blade and stamped forward, moving lightly despite his wounds. He still wore the tattered remnants of his armour, and Erikan could smell the pus dripping from the sores beneath the metal, and the blood that had crusted on its edges. Their blades slammed together again. The man was smart – he didn't intend to pit his strength against Erikan's. He was simply trying to drive him back. Erikan allowed him to do so, trying to draw him away from his comrades. If he could get him alone, the ghouls could swarm him under through sheer numbers.

A wild cry caused him to glance up. Mannfred's pet vargheists circled the courtyard, screeching fit to wake whatever dead things had managed to ignore their master's summons. Alberacht swooped between them, looking almost as bestial. He had obviously gone to rouse the beasts into helping with the hunt.

Volkmar cried out as one of the vargheists plummeted down and plucked the elf from the ground. She screamed and struck out at the beast that held her, but it merely screeched again and carried her upwards. Volkmar cursed loudly and turned. Erikan saw Anark rush towards him with his sword raised. He cursed the other vampire for an idiot, albeit silently. The old man ducked aside and looped the length of chain he carried around the vampire's throat. Anark snarled as Volkmar hauled forwards with all of his weight, pulling him off his feet. He fell with a clatter, and his sword flew from his grip. 'Get the blade!' Volkmar roared.

The Ulrican snatched the sword up and spun on his heel, gutting a leaping ghoul. Erikan lunged to meet him, as Nyktolos blocked a blow from the Myrmidian meant to split Erikan's spine. He forced the Ulrican back with a slash. The burly warrior priest swept his stolen blade out in a wild, looping blow. Erikan weaved back with serpentine grace, not even bothering to block the attack. He heard Nyktolos laugh and saw the other vampire back away from his opponent as a mob of ghouls surged forward.

The knight, freed of Nyktolos, came at him from the side, hoping to flank him, even as the ghouls chased after him. Erikan pivoted, and avoided the knight's lunge. He flipped backwards, evading the Ulrican's blade a second time. The ghoul that had been pressing forward behind him wasn't so lucky. It fell, choking on its own blood. More of the cannibals rushed into the fray, trampling their dying comrade in their haste to reach the enemy.

Erikan sprang to the wall and dropped back behind the ghoul pack. Nyktolos had the right idea. There was no sense in risking himself. The two men fought hard, with desperate abandon. Bodies and blood slopped the floor. He saw that Volkmar had managed to get atop Anark and was hauling back on the chains, trying to snap his enemy's neck. The vampire's mouth was wide, and a serpentine tongue jutted from between his fangs as he writhed beneath the Grand Theogonist. Erikan hesitated. It was the perfect moment to be rid of Anark. He might not get another one. He heard Elize cry out and, almost against his will, began to move.

Then, the second vargheist had Volkmar in its claws, and it hauled him upwards to join its fellow. Erikan lowered his sword. 'He who hesitates is lost,' he murmured as he rushed to help Anark to his feet in an obsequious show of concern.

Above, Volkmar cursed and tore at the vargheist holding him, to no avail. The beast had him, and there was no escape. Erikan watched as his struggles became weaker and weaker, until at last he ceased entirely, and hung in its grasp like a corpse. The vargheist dropped him onto a parapet, and sank down on him, like a cat crouching atop its kill.

The sound of applause swept across the courtyard, cutting through the sound of the rain and the whimpers of dying ghouls. Mannfred von Carstein stood on the parapet above the portcullis, Arkhan behind him. 'Well,' he said. 'Look how far you got. I am quite impressed, as I'm sure my comrade is.' He gestured to Arkhan. 'Aren't you impressed?' he asked, over his shoulder.

Mannfred didn't give Arkhan a chance to reply. Instead, he leapt down from the parapet and dropped lightly into the courtyard, drawing his blade as he rose. The torches that flickered, hissed and spat in the rain seemed to dim slightly, as if Mannfred's presence were draining the heat and light from them. 'I'm impressed,' he said again, looking up at the gathered vampires who crouched or slunk about above the courtyard. 'And yet, something puzzles me. Where did you think you were going to go? This castle is mine. This land is mine. I rule everything from horizon to horizon, every mountain, every bower, every ruin and river. All mine,' Mannfred went on. He waved aside the ghouls, who retreated from him with undignified speed. 'Where were you going to go?'

'Back into the eyes of our gods,' the knight said. His voice sounded thin and weak to Erikan's ears. 'Back to the light.'

'There is no light, unless I will it,' Mannfred said, extending his blade. He looked at the Ulrican and the Myrmidian. They were the only two left, save for the priest of Morr, who crouched nearby. The woman and the one-handed man had been knocked sprawling and pinned to the wet ground by Alberacht in the confusion. 'There are no gods, save me.' Mannfred smiled, and Erikan felt a cold wind sweep through the hollows of his soul. Mannfred turned his blade slightly, so that the light caught the edge. 'If you bow, I will not hurt you too much. If you crawl to me, I will not take your legs. If you beg me to spare you, I will not take your hands.'

The stone, when it came, was a surprise, even to Mannfred, Erikan thought. The young priest had torn it from the ground and hurled it with such force that it drew blood when it caromed off Mannfred's skull. He whirled with a cry that put his vargheists to shame and his blade nearly took the young priest's head off. The young man fell back, face twisted in fear and defiance. Mannfred stormed towards him, but before he could reach him, a swirling storm of spirits erupted from the ground and walls of the courtyard and surrounded the man. Mannfred spun, and glared up at Arkhan, who lowered his staff silently, but did not call off the ghosts he had summoned.

Mannfred turned back in time to block the Ulrican's attack. The big man came at him in a rush, silent and determined. His sword drew fat sparks as it screeched off Mannfred's cuirass. Mannfred stepped back and his fist hammered into the man's chest. Erikan heard bones crack, and the Ulrican slumped, coughing redness. Mannfred caught the back of his head and hurled him to the ground hard enough to add to the tally of broken bones.

The Myrmidian hacked at him, and Mannfred caught the blow on the length of his blade and surged forward, driving the knight back against the hall. He pinned him in place. 'We need to sacrifice one, eh?' Mannfred asked, glancing at Arkhan. The liche nodded slowly. Mannfred looked back at the knight, as the latter strained against his strength, trying to free himself. 'This one, then. He's been more trouble than he's worth.' He tore his blade away from the wall, and the Templar staggered forward, off balance. He recovered quickly, and lunged. The blade skidded off Mannfred's side, staggering him. But before the knight could capitalise, Mannfred batted his guard aside and sent him flying backwards to bounce off the wall and topple to the ground, unconscious.

Mannfred looked down and then up, letting the rain wash the blood from his face. And for a moment, just a moment, between the shadows and the rain, Erikan thought he saw something terrible looming over Mannfred, shaking in silent glee.

◄ CHAPTER SEVEN ►

Heldenhame Keep, Talabecland

The empty bottle shattered as it struck the wall. Wendel Volker scrambled to his feet and darted out of the commandant's grimy office. Otto Kross stormed after him, as quickly as a man on the wrong end of a three-day drunk could manage. Kross was bald, with a thick beard and sideburns, which hid his heavy jowls, and a neck that was more an unsightly outgrowth of shoulder than anything else.

'I told you that I'd have you, popinjay, if you countermanded me again. Those men deserved a lashing! Their hides were mine,' Kross bellowed as he lunged, red-faced, after Volker, fists windmilling.

'I didn't countermand anything,' Volker yelped, scooting across the courtyard on his backside, trying to get enough room between himself and his commandant so that he could get to his feet without receiving a faceful of Kross's scarred knuckles. 'I simply placed them on punishment detail. How was I to know you meant they needed a flogging?'

That was a lie, of course. He had known, and hadn't approved. Punishment was all well and good when the men in question had committed an actual infraction or crime. But flogging was a step too far, especially when their only real crime had been to be in the wrong place at the wrong time. He'd placed them on night soil duty, reckoning that would keep them out of Kross's sight until he'd sobered up and forgotten why he wanted them punished in the first place. Unfortunately, someone had spilled the beans. The next thing Volker knew, he was dodging bottles and Kross's fists.

'I'll stop your squawking, popinjay,' Kross snarled. He lurched drunkenly for Volker, tripped over his own foot, and fell face-first to the ground. Volker took the opportunity to get to his feet and made to flee, until he noted the gathering crowd of men. It looked as if every trooper assigned to the Heldenhame garrison was piling into the wide, long courtyard that linked the Rostmeyer and Sigmundas bastions.

It wasn't surprising. The past few weeks had seen a steady increase in tensions among the men. There was something growing in Sylvania, behind those blasted walls; they could all feel it. Not to mention the reports coming from the north. For every ten men who'd marched for the Kislev border, only seven reached their destination, thanks to beastmen, green-skins and plague. The fighting along the border had spilled into Ostermark and Talabecland, and the armies of those provinces were hard-pressed to hold the tide back.

Many men wanted to travel north, to fight the enemy. Others wanted to stay put, out of the way, safe behind Heldenhame's walls. Luckily for the latter, Leitdorf was obsessed with keeping his eyes firmly fixed on Sylvania. Or, as some lackwits whispered, he just wanted to stay good and close to the centre of the Empire, in order to take advantage of what many were coming to see as the inevitable conclusion of recent events.

Sometimes, Volker thought that was why Thyrus Gormann had come. It would be difficult for Leitdorf to get up to any mischief with the Patriarch of the Bright College looking over his shoulder.

Volker heard a voice growl, 'Two bits on the commandant.' He looked over and saw the scowling features of Captain Deinroth. Kross's second-in-command had never warmed to Volker. He shared his commandant's opinion, and indeed that of most of the other captains, that Volker was a man who had bought his rank with gold, rather than blood, and was thus no sort of man at all. Which was a bit unfair, Volker thought; it had been his father's gold after all, not his.

Deinroth, he thought, was the likely instigator of the current situation. In his years as Kross's second-in-command, Deinroth had learned well the art of winding his belligerent superior up and setting him loose like a demigryph in a glassblower's shop. He'd been poking and prodding at Kross to lay in to Volker for weeks now, and it looked as if he'd finally got his wish.

'Three on the popinjay,' a second voice cut through the rising tumult like the peal of a hammer on an anvil. Men fell silent as a robed figure strode to the front of the growing crowd. Stern-featured and grizzled by decades of service on the Sylvanian frontier, Father Janos Odkrier was a welcome enough face. Odkrier wasn't quite a friend, but he was as close as Volker had in Heldenhame.

Odkrier winked at Volker. Around him, money changed hands and men shouted out bets. Kross staggered to his feet, face flushed, teeth bared. He swayed slightly, but didn't fall. He raised his fists. 'I'll wipe that smirk off your chinless face, Volker,' he spat.

'There's no need for this, commandant,' Volker said hurriedly. A brawl wasn't quite as bad as a duel, but the knights frowned on it regardless. Especially in times like these, with northmen howling south in ever-increasing numbers, green comets raining down out of the sky, and a great bloody wall of bone towering over Sylvania's borders. The whole world was coming undone around them. 'If Leitdorf finds out, we'll both get our necks stretched,' he said.

He cut a glance towards Deinroth, who was smirking in his usual unpleasant fashion, and wondered if that was what Kross's right hand man wanted. 'You know how he feels about his officers brawling in front of the rank and file.'

Kross smiled maliciously. 'Leitdorf isn't here, popinjay.' He shuffled forward and threw a blow that would have broken Volker's jaw, had it connected. Volker slid aside, the way his swordmaster had taught him, and drove his fist into Kross's side. The big man spun, quicker than Volker had expected, and caught him a stinging blow on the cheek. Volker fell back onto his rear, and only just managed to bob aside as Kross's iron-shod boot slammed down where he'd been sitting.

Volker's hand flew to his sword. As much as the thought turned his stomach, he knew that he could draw it and have it through Kross's fat gut in a wink and a nod. He was a better swordsman than any of those present. Indeed, he fancied he could even match one of Leitdorf's armoured thugs in a fair bout. But killing a superior officer was even worse than getting into a round of fisticuffs with one. Leitdorf already despised him; Volker had spent the months since his arrival avoiding the Grand Master of the Knights of Sigmar's Blood at every opportunity. Sigmar alone knew what Leitdorf would do to him if he pinked Kross even slightly. He pulled his hand away as Kross gave a bull bellow and charged towards him.

He caught Volker and swept him up in a bear hug. Volker groaned as he felt his ribs flex. Fat as he was, Kross was still strong enough to knock a dray horse off its hooves with a punch. The commandant's alcoholic breath washed over his face, and Volker was suddenly reminded that he had been headed to the tavern, before Kross had called him in. The crowd was cheering and catcalling in equal measure, their faces a blur as Kross spun him about. Volker slithered an arm free and poked Kross in the eye with his thumb. Kross roared and released him. The commandant stumbled back, clawing at his face. He belched curses and snatched his dagger from his belt. Volker backed away, hands raised. Kross staggered after him, blade raised.

Then came the sharp, savage sound of a cane striking something metal and all the cheering ceased. Both Volker and Kross turned as a lean, broad-shouldered figure stumped through the crowd. The newcomer leaned on a cane, and was dressed in the heavy furs and coarse jerkin that all of the members of the Knights of Sigmar's Blood wore when not in armour. His face bore the sort of scars that came from getting pulled off a horse and into a knot of orcs and summarily trodden on. His name was Rudolph Weskar, and he was the closest thing to the word of Sigmar made flesh this side of Leitdorf in Heldenhame.

All of the fire went out of Kross, and he hastily put away his blade. Volker swallowed as the limping man approached them. Deinroth and the other captains were already melting away with the crowd. 'Brawling without prior permission is a pillory offence, gentlemen,' Weskar said, leaning on his cane. His hard, dull eyes pinned Kross. 'Commandant Kross, I can smell the reek of alcohol on you from here. Do not make me regret recommending you to the Grand Master for promotion, Otto. Go sober up, and keep that potato peeler you call a knife in its sheath from now on.'

Kross hesitated. He glared at Volker one last time, then nodded tersely and slunk away. Volker didn't watch him go. He kept his eyes on Weskar. He licked his lips, suddenly dying for a drink. Weskar stumped towards him. 'Wendel, Wendel, Wendel. You disappoint me, Wendel. When I heard what was going on, I was hoping you might finally spit that hog, and thus deliver yourself to the hangman, freeing me to promote a more congenial pair to your positions. Instead, here we are.' He came close to Volker, and the latter tensed. A discreet cough caused Weskar to glance around. Father Odkrier alone had remained where he was, when Weskar's arrival had caused everyone else to scatter. The old Sigmarite wasn't afraid of anyone or anything.

Weskar turned back to Volker. 'Why?' he asked simply.

Volker swallowed. He knew what Weskar was asking. 'Kross was drunk, and bullying an innkeeper. When the man refused him further service, he tried to gut him. The lads intervened. Kross was still drunk when he ordered that they be flogged for laying hands on a superior officer. I thought if I could keep them out of sight until he sobered up...' He trailed off. Weskar grunted.

'That he might regret it, and not punish them further,' he said. 'You know a little something about the regrets overindulgence brings, I think, eh, Wendel?' He leaned forwards again, like a hound on the scent. 'You're dying for a drink now, I'd wager.' Volker didn't answer. Weskar twitched a hand. 'Go,' he said.

Volker hurried past him, his hands trembling. Odkrier caught him around the shoulders and shoved a flask into his hands as they left Weskar standing there, staring after them. 'Drink up, my boy. I'd say you've earned it.'

Karaz-a-Karak, Worlds Edge Mountains

Ungrim Ironfist sat on his stone bench and listened to the basso rumble of dwarf disagreement as the Kingsmeet entered its fifth hour. King Kazador of Karak Azul pounded upon the stone table with a heavy fist, and King Alrik of Karak Hirn crossed his brawny arms and scowled at his fellow monarch. Belegar of Karak Eight Peaks sat hunched and silent in his seat, looking at no one, his face sagging with the weight of constant worry. And glaring at them all, from the far end of the table, sat the High King, Thorgrim Grudgebearer.

As Kingsmeets went, this one wasn't as bad as Ungrim had begun to fear, on his journey to Karaz-a-Karak. He'd learned that the occurrences in Sylvania were already well known, at least by Thorgrim, and that the von Carstein was one of the problems under discussion. One of many problems, in fact. The reports he'd received had only been the tip of the proverbial anvil, and the world seemed to be intent on coming apart at the seams, all at once.

Ungrim didn't find that as distressing as the others. Indeed, it filled him with a bitter enthusiasm. He had long been torn between two fates – that of king, and that of a Slayer. To prioritise the one over the other was impossible, and as the centuries progressed, he had begun to feel as if he, like his father before him, would die still cloaked in dishonour, and that his son, Garagrim, would be forced to tread the same line. Ungrim closed his eyes for a moment, as the old pain resurfaced. Every time he thought it buried and gone, it clawed its way back to the forefront of his mind. Garagrim was dead now, and free of the shame that still held Ungrim. He had died as a warrior, and as a Slayer, though he'd had no dishonour of his own to expunge. He'd thought his blood could buy his father's freedom, but such things were not proper.

Garagrim had meant well, but he had been a foolish boy, with a beardling's bravado and his mother's stubbornness. At the thought of the latter, he felt a pang. He missed his wife's quiet counsel. His queen had a mind second to none, and a clarity of thought that cut through even the most rancorous preconceptions. It was she who should be sitting here. He had no mind for politics, and no patience for querulous oldbeards like Kazador.

Ungrim contented himself with examining the table. It had been carved long before the Time of Woes, and a map of the ancient dwarf empire at its height sprawled across its surface. Holds that had not existed for untold centuries were still marked there, as if to deny their destruction, as if to shout, 'What has been still is and will always be' into the void. Then, that was the way of his people. Like mountains in the stream of time, they sat immoveable and intractable, but worn down bit by bit, over the span of aeons.

He sighed and looked about the chamber, scanning the gathered faces that watched from the ascending rows of benches that surrounded the table and its occupants. Courtiers, thanes, advisors, second cousins twice removed of the aforementioned thanes, and anyone who could get past the chamber wardens was watching. Politics was a spectator sport among the *dawi*. Like as not, someone was collecting bets on when the first punch would be thrown, or the first head-butt delivered.

'The Underway swarms with ratkin and *grobi*,' Kazador said, drawing Ungrim's attention as he cut the air with his hand. 'But they do not attack. Something is afoot. Something is growing in the deep darkness, something foul, that threatens to drown us all when it finally surges to the surface.'

'Or maybe they're simply warring with one another as they are wont to do,' Alrik said. He looked at Thorgrim. 'Their numbers swell and their filthy warrens abut one another in most places. They seek the same holes, and like the vermin they are, they fight over them. If they have gone quiet, it is because they are busy doing our work for us!'

'Then explain the new access tunnels my miners have found,' Kazador snarled, slapping the table. 'Explain the skaven-sign splashed on the walls of the lower levels. Explain the sounds echoing up from the far depths – not of battle, but of *industry*.'

Alrik settled back in his seat, silent and frowning. For several moments, no one said anything. Then, Thorgrim spoke. 'I too have heard these reports, and more besides. I have seen the glowering skies and heard the growl of the stones. Beasts stir in mountain caves, and our northern kin, in their strongholds in the mountains of Norsca, send word of daemons scouring the lands, and of the mobilisation of the barbarians who worship the Dark Gods.' He looked around. 'But these are not new tidings. These are merely old tidings on a new day. Our people are still strong. Our enemies still break themselves on our walls and are swept away by our throngs. Did not the Ironfist shatter such a horde in years past? Did he not take the head and pelt of the Gorewolf?'

Ungrim grimaced. In truth, he hadn't taken the Chaos warlord's head. The Gorewolf had been killed by the renegade Gotrek Gurnisson. In doing so, Gurnisson had saved Ungrim's life, which only added to the Slayer King's already weighty grudge against the other Slayer. Years later, when Gurnisson had returned to Karak Kadrin on the trail of a dragon, Ungrim had considered clapping him and his pet poet in irons and dumping them somewhere unpleasant, to repay the indignity. He had restrained himself then, as before. Gurnisson wore chains of destiny that not even a king could shatter, more was the pity.

'Horde after horde has poured into these mountains and we have shattered them all, be they northmen, orcs or ogres,' Thorgrim went on. 'To seal our gates is to admit defeat before we have even seen the enemy.' He sat back on his seat and looked around. 'I see by your faces that some of you agree, and others do not. Belegar, speak...' He motioned to the king of the Eight Peaks, who looked up, startled. Ungrim realised that he'd been lost in his own gloomy thoughts. He cleared his throat.

'I have little to add, High King,' he said. 'Siege is not new for those of us who make our home in the Eight Peaks. We war with grobi and ratkin both, and they war with one another when we retreat to lick our wounds and entomb our dead. In truth, these tidings mean little to me. I know my enemies, and I fight them daily. I fight them in the tunnels and on the peaks, and what does it matter if the sky above is blue, red or green, when a skaven is looking to gut you with a rusty blade? What does it matter if the earth shakes, when your halls are swarmed by goblins? What do the affairs of the far northern holds matter, when your own is swamped by enemies?'

He held up his hands. 'I have only two hands, brother-kings. I have only a third of a hold – aye, a great hold, and greater still when I have wiped it clean of the remaining filth that infests it, but still... only a third.' He looked squarely at Thorgrim. 'For my part, I am here because I owe you a debt, High King. You helped to defend my meagre holdings against the orcs, when the beast known as Gorfang came knocking at my gates. For your part, I suspect that I am here out of courtesy only, though you would shave your beard before you admitted it, I wager. I am here, because you are worried – all of you.' He turned, taking in the whole of the table. 'We are small for a grand council. Where are the others? Where are the kings of Zhufbar and Karak Izor? Where is the king of Kraka Drak or the lord of Barak Varr?' He sat back and shook his head. 'They did not – or could not come. They are worried. More worried than ever before. The sky weeps and the world heaves, and our enemies have gone silent. They are right to be worried.'

'Well said, brother,' Kazador grunted. He looked at Thorgrim. 'Alrik might be blind, but you are not, Grudgebearer. And if you will not heed me, you might heed another.' He gestured. From out of the throng of watching advisors and hangers-on stepped a thick-set figure who all immediately recognised. A rush of whispers and mutters swept about the chamber as Thorek Ironbrow, Runelord of Karak Azul, stepped forward, one hand resting on the anvil-shaped head of his rune hammer, Klad Brakak, which was thrust through his belt.

'Karag Haraz, Karag Dron and Karag Orrud all belch smoke into the sky, High King,' Ironbrow said portentously. He gestured in a southerly direction with one gnarled hand. The runelord's hide looked like leather, and was puckered by burns and pale scars.

Even by Ungrim's standards, Thorek Ironbrow was a conservative. He was a dwarf who held fast to the oldest of ways, and his words were heavy with the weight of uncounted centuries. He had ruled over the weapon shops of Karak Azul for as long as Ungrim had been alive, and even the sons of kings dared not enter his domains without his prior approval – almost all of the kings in the council chamber had felt the lash of Ironbrow's tongue or the hard, calloused palm of his hand on the backs of their heads as beardlings. That was why he could get away with lecturing them now. The runelord looked about him as he went on, his hard gaze resting on each king in turn, as if they were a group of particularly dull-witted apprentices. 'Mountains that have not erupted in millennia now vomit forth fire and smoke and death. The world shudders beneath a horrible tread, my kings, and unless we are prepared, we will be ground underfoot.'

Ungrim had heard that argument before. Every time a horde swept south, out of the Wastes, or west out of the Dark Lands, Ironbrow made some variation of it. He knocked on the table with his knuckles, interrupting the runelord's rehearsed speech. He grinned as Ironbrow glared at him for his temerity, and asked, 'And by prepared, you mean close the gates?'

Ironbrow hesitated. Then, solemnly, he nodded. 'We must put our faith in strong walls and shields, rather than squandering our strength upon wayward allies.' Another murmur arose at that. Everyone with half a brain knew what the runelord was referring to by that comment.

Thorgrim had earlier spoken of the kidnapping of the Ulthuani Ever-child out from under the noses of the warriors of Karaz-a-Karak, and the subsequent battle at Nagashizzar: a battle that had failed to free her from Mannfred von Carstein's clutches, despite the aid the High King had rendered to the *elgi*. Ungrim glanced at Thorgrim, to see if he'd noticed the dig. It was hard to tell, given the High King's ever present sour expression.

Ironbrow was still talking. He gestured to King Kazador. 'My king has already heeded my council and sealed the main gates of Karak Azul. Will you not do the same, *Slayer* King?'

Ungrim sucked on his teeth, stung by Ironbrow's tone. 'No,' he said bluntly. He cut his eyes towards Thorgrim. 'Not unless so commanded by the High King, I won't.' He swivelled his gaze back towards Ironbrow. 'Karak Kadrin has ever been the edge of the axe, as Karaz-a-Karak is the shield. Let the world shake, and rats gnaw at our roots. We shall reap and slay and strike out as many grudges as Grimnir allows in what time we have.'

'You would doom your people, your hold, and for what? Has your inhe-rited dishonour driven you that mad?' Kazador asked, heaving himself to his feet. 'Our people stand on the precipice of destruction, and all you see is an opportunity for war.'

'And so?' Ungrim asked hotly. He rose to his feet and slammed his knuckles down on the table, causing it to shiver. 'My people know war. And that is what is coming. Not some indecipherable doom, or irresistible event. No, it is war. And every warrior will be needed, every axe sharpened, every shield raised, for our enemies are coming, and our walls alone have never stopped them, as my brother-king knows to his cost.'

There was a communal intake of breath from the crowd above them as the words left Ungrim's lips. Kazador's eyes bulged from their sockets, and his teeth showed through his beard. Ungrim thought for a moment that the old king would launch himself across the table and seek to throttle him.

'Enough,' Thorgrim rumbled. 'That grudge has been settled, and by my hand. Every king here must do as he considers best for his hold and people. But there are other grudges to be settled and the Dammaz Kron sits open and impatient. I have vowed to strike out every entry in the Great Book of Grudges, and it seems that time to do so is running thin. If the throng of Karaz-a-Karak is mustered, I must know who will muster with me. Who stands with the Pinnacle of the Mountains?' He looked at Ungrim first.

Ungrim grinned. 'Do you even need to ask, High King?'

Thorgrim inclined his head slightly, and looked at the others in turn. Alrik stood and nodded belligerently. Belegar too stood and said, 'Aye, the Eight Peaks will march, to our enemies' ruin or our own.'

Thorgrim sat back. The High King seemed tired. Ungrim did not envy him the weight of responsibility he bore. Heavy sat the crown of the High

King, and it was very likely that he was now watching the sun at last set on the empire of the dwarfs. Ungrim smiled humourlessly. Even so, if they were to die, then it was best done properly.

That was the only way dwarfs did anything, after all.

Adrift on the Great Ocean, sailing due east

The great beak snapped shut inches from Eltharion's nose, and a rumbling hiss filled the hold. The horses in the nearby stalls shifted nervously as the griffon hunched forward, its claws sinking into the wood of the deck. Eltharion reached up as the beast's chin dropped heavily onto his shoulder and stroked the ruffled feathers that cascaded down its neck. 'Shhh, easy, Stormwing,' he murmured. He felt one of his mount's heavy forepaws pat clumsily at his back, and heard its inarticulate grunt of contentment.

Around them, the ship made the usual noises of travel. Not even the graceful vessels of Lothern were free of those, though elvish craftsmanship was the finest in the world, and their ships second to none. If he listened, he could hear the waters of the Great Ocean caressing the hull, and beneath that, the melodic hum of the whales that occupied the sea. Their song was one of beauty and peace, but tinged with fear. Even the most isolated of animals could sense that the world was sick.

As he stroked the griffon's neck and head, he looked about him. The horses who shared Stormwing's hold belonged to the Knights of Dusk, a noble family of Tor Ethel. More accurately, the only family, noble or other-wise, of Tor Ethel, which was all but abandoned these days. It sat on the western coast of Tiranoc, and each year coastal erosion took more of that once shining city into the sea, claiming gardens, sanctuaries and palaces alike. The Knights of Dusk hailed from the ever-shrinking group of the city's remaining inhabitants. They were valiant warriors, as were the others who had accompanied him and Eldyra on this journey.

Besides the Silver Helms of Tor Ethel, there were the Sentinels of Astaril, mistwalkers of Yvresse, in whose company he had honed his archery skills as a youth, and the Faithbearers of Athel Tamarha, a company of spear-men who had fought at his side in every campaign but one. A small enough host, but tested, and experienced. They would need to be, to survive what was coming. They were entering unknown territory. The last time he'd set foot in the lands of men, they still hadn't quite grasped the concept that hygiene wasn't a mortal offence. He doubted much had changed in the intervening centuries.

He didn't hate them. He simply didn't see a reason for their existence. They caused more problems than they solved, for all that they were barely more than chattering apes. It had been men, after all, who had allowed the goblin, Grom, to pass through their lands in order to reach Ulthuan. Teclis doted on them, in his acerbic way, something that had always puzzled

Eltharion. Men were the cause of the problems facing them now. Men fed Chaos a constant stream of souls, whether they knew it or not. And if they weren't doing that, they were turning themselves into abominations like Mannfred von Carstein. Men couldn't leave well enough alone. Some small part of Eltharion hoped that whatever was going on would swallow mankind whole before it ended, and that the Dark Gods would choke on their grubby little souls.

As if sensing the direction his thoughts were taking, the griffon grumbled into his ear, its hot, foul breath washing over him. He pushed the thoughts aside and concentrated on calming the animal. Once, when Stormwing was no more than a squalling cub, he'd have taken the beast in his arms like an infant, and carried it about until it was soothed to sleep by the rhythm of his heartbeat. Now the griffon was bigger than the largest of the horses who occupied the remainder of the hold, and a good deal more skittish about the confined space it found itself in.

'I see Stormwing is no more fond of the sea than his master,' a voice said. Eltharion didn't turn. He dug his fingers into the strange spot where feathers met fur on Stormwing's body and gave it a good scratch. One of the griffon's rear paws thumped the deck, and its spotted tail lashed in pleasure.

'Come to check on your own mount, then, Eldyra?' he asked. 'He misses you. I can tell.'

'I doubt that. He's asleep, the lazy brute,' Eldyra said, crossing to the stall where her stallion, Maladhros, stood dozing. The big, silver dappled animal was the only one who showed no concern at Stormwing's presence, though whether that was because they had been stabled together before, or because Maladhros had fewer wits than a thick brick, Eltharion couldn't say. The stallion was strong and fierce, and Eldyra swore that it was a canny beast as well, but Eltharion thought she vastly overestimated its problem-solving capabilities. When he'd come down into the hold, it had been eating an empty bucket.

She clucked and rubbed the stallion's nose, stirring it to wakefulness. Eltharion watched as she fed it an apple, and it crunched contentedly. 'He's taking the trip well,' he said.

'He knows it's important,' she said. She stroked the horse's mane.

'Does he now?' Eltharion smiled.

Eldyra looked at him. 'As a matter of fact, yes, he does. How is Stormwing?' she asked. She stepped across the hold towards him, light on her feet despite the pitch of the deck. She was the perfect blend of grace and lethality, much as Tyrion was, Eltharion reflected. He wondered if the latter was aware of just how much he'd shaped the princess of Tiranoc in his image, and whether he'd find that worrisome. Probably not; in Eltharion's opinion, Tyrion didn't worry as much as he should, at least not about the right things.

'Nervous. He doesn't like confined spaces. He prefers to fly,' he said.

The griffon grumbled and eyed Eldyra balefully. Stormwing didn't care for anyone other than Eltharion getting too close. He had a tendency to snap.

'Why not let him?'

'There's no guarantee he'd remember to come back, rather than fly home,' Eltharion said, rubbing his palm over the curve of Stormwing's beak. The creature butted his chest and made a sound halfway between a purr and a chirp. 'He's not very bright.' He hesitated. 'Then, perhaps he's smarter than both of us.'

'Do you truly hold so little hope?' she asked, quietly.

He smiled thinly. 'I am not known as "the Grim" for nothing,' he said.

'That's not an answer.'

'No, it is not.' He looked at her. 'There is no hope. She is as good as dead, or worse. We are not heroes... We are avengers.'

'Tyrion doesn't think so,' she said.

'Tyrion lies to himself,' he said softly. 'Just as he lied to himself that there would be no consequences for his indiscretion. Those lies are the source of optimism, and his downfall.'

'You think that, and yet here you are,' Eldyra said. She said it as if it were an accusation. And perhaps it was, he thought. He nodded agreeably.

'I am, yes.'

'Why?'

'Why are you here?' he asked.

'My lord Tyrion ordered it,' she said stiffly.

'I was under the impression that he was your friend,' he said. 'Just as he is my friend.' He tasted the word as he said it. It wasn't one he used often, or, indeed, at all. But it seemed fitting, in reference to Tyrion. Tyrion was his friend, and that meant that there was nothing Eltharion wouldn't do to help him. 'And I, like you, am smart enough to know that if we were not here, he would be, and Ulthuan would suffer for it.'

'Or at least worse than it already has,' Eldyra said. 'Do you think...?'

'I do not think. I do not worry. I trust. We have our mission. Tyrion and Teclis will drive the daemonic hosts from our shores, as they did before. And we will find Aliathra, for good or ill, whether she is alive or...' He trailed off.

'She is alive. Of that much, I am certain, Warden of Yvresse,' a new voice cut in. A blue-robed shape descended the steps down into the hold. Pale eyes looked about from beneath a diadem of emeralds, and a thin mouth quirked in disgust. 'Why you two insist on spending so much time in this makeshift stable, I'll never understand. It smells awful.'

'It'd smell worse if someone didn't see to the animals occasionally,' Eltharion said, turning to face the newcomer. He cocked his elbow up on Stormwing's flat skull. 'And you could have waited until we came back up on deck.'

'Probably, yes, but then I wouldn't have been able to interject my opinions so smoothly, now would I?' Belannaer groused. He tapped the side of his head. 'It's all about the seizing the moment.'

'What is?' Eldyra asked, smiling crookedly. She enjoyed teasing the Loremaster of Hoeth, and Eltharion couldn't find it in his heart to blame her. Belannaer had once been the High Loremaster of Ulthuan, before ceding the title and its responsibilities to Teclis. Many, including Eltharion, thought Belannaer had been only too happy to do so, making him a rarity among the Ulthuani. In the years since, he'd found contentment amongst the tomes of yesteryear, forgoing the crudity of politics and war, for a life devoted to study and contemplation. But he'd set such prosaic workings aside when he'd learned of the Everchild's capture. Belannaer knew, better perhaps than anyone else save Teclis, what such an event meant to the fate of Ulthuan. But though he'd shed his reclusive ways and taken up his sword once more, he was still a scholar, with a scholar's stuffiness and a pedant's obliviousness.

'Everything,' Belannaer said. He gestured airily. 'History is made of moments and the people who seized them.' He looked at Eltharion. 'Aliathra has seized hers. I can hear her voice on the wind, stronger now than before, for all that she's growing weaker. Time is running short.'

'We can only sail as fast as the wind takes us, loremaster,' Eltharion said. He knew what Belannaer was feeling, for he'd felt it himself. The growing impatience, the anxiety of uncertainty. There were still hundreds of miles of overland travel between them and Sylvania. They would make up time by keeping to the river, but even then, there was no telling what might arise to stymie them.

'I know, which is why I stoked the winds with my sorcery, so that we might move faster,' Belannaer said. Eldyra looked at Eltharion.

'I wondered why the ship was creaking so,' she murmured. Eltharion shushed her with a quick look and said, 'Something is different, isn't it?'

'Aliathra has shown me... flashes of what awaits us,' Belannaer said. 'There are dark forces on the move, and this is but the smallest shred of their plan. We will need allies.' He said the last hesitantly.

Eltharion tensed. 'Allies,' he repeated. 'You mean men.'

'And the dwarfs, if they can be convinced,' Belannaer said.

'No,' Eltharion said. 'No, the dwarfs are the reason that Aliathra was captured in the first place. I'll not surrender her fate to their hands again.' He felt a surge of anger at the thought of it. 'Neither will I entrust it to men.' He shook his head. 'They are worse even than dwarfs. They cannot be counted on.'

'And yet we must, if we are to have any hope of rescuing the Everchild,' Belannaer said. 'I've ordered the fleet to sail due east, for the Empire of Sigmar. They know Teclis of old, and will be open to our entreaties. We gave them aid, once upon a time, and they owe Ulthuan a debt.'

'You ordered?' Eltharion shook his head, astounded at Belannaer's arrogance. 'I lead this expedition, loremaster, not you,' he said softly.

'You do,' Belannaer said. 'And I am sure you will come to the right decision eventually.'

Eltharion glanced at Eldyra. 'Did you know about this?'

'No, but he's right,' she said.

Eltharion's eyes narrowed. Eldyra spoke quickly, 'Think about it, cousin... Our army is small and we will have to cross lands held by men sooner or later. Better to do it with permission, and perhaps even with allies, than to fight our way through.' She held up a hand as he made to protest. 'We could do it. Our army, small as it is, is better than anything they can muster. But elves will die in the doing of it. And for what – pride? Better to sacrifice pride than warriors, especially where we're going.'

Eltharion listened silently. Some of Teclis had rubbed off on her as well, he thought. Then, given how closely the twins' fates had been linked these last few centuries, that wasn't surprising. Eldyra had learned the art of battle as Tyrion's squire. But she had learned something else entirely by watching Teclis's crooked mind at work.

Regardless, she wasn't wrong, save about his pride. It wasn't pride that motivated him, but caution. What profit could be gleaned from faithless allies or worse, useless ones? They would hamper the clean, quick strike, and slow them down. He was certain their host could cross quickly into Sylvania, before the men could mobilise to question them. But could they then get out again, once victory had been achieved? It would be unfortunate if they succeeded in rescuing Aliathra from one savage, only to fall prey to another.

Finally, Eltharion nodded. 'You are right, cousin, loremaster,' he said. 'Better we ally ourselves with willing primitives than stand alone in defeat.'

'Then the fleet will continue east?' Belannaer asked.

Eltharion nodded. 'East – it is time to see if the Empire of Sigmar remembers its debts.'

The King's Glade, Athel Loren

Durthu, Eldest of Ancients, spoke in a voice like the rustling of branches and the cracking of bark. It filled the King's Glade, travelling through the branches of every tree and slipped from every leaf, until the air throbbed with the sound of his voice. '*The cycle of the world begins anew, and just as the forest once aided the folk of Ulthuan in days now slid from mortal memory, it shall do so again.*' Durthu shifted his immense weight as he spoke, and the air was rent by the squeal of twisting branches and the dull, wet crunch of popping roots. The treeman was the oldest of his kind, and his mind was like the forest itself: vast, wild and unpredictable.

Araloth watched as a ripple of murmurs spread through the assembled ranks of the Council of Athel Loren where they sat. It was rare that Durthu spoke, and rarer still that he spoke so lucidly. More and more often these days, his mind was awash in the forest's rage, and he spoke words of war and madness. But here was the calm Durthu of old, the wise spirit who had so often guided his folk in ages past. Araloth felt a twinge of sadness as he watched the ancient tree-spirit speak. The forest was dying, glade by glade, rotting from within and falling to the madness that had poured forth from the Vaults of Winter. Soon enough, if it was not halted, Durthu would join many of his kin in either decay or madness. And that would be a terrible moment indeed.

Araloth pushed the thought aside and concentrated on Durthu's words. '*But as in those days, there will be a price for the forest's aid, Everqueen of Ulthuan,*' Durthu said, his ageless eyes fixed on the proud figure of Alarielle. She stood before the council, bound in chains of leaves and vines, as was customary.

The Everqueen lifted her chin and said, 'I know nothing of these events, revered ancient, but whatever your price, know that I will pay it willingly and in full.' Her voice possessed a liquid musicality to it that, in other circumstances would have seemed the epitome of beauty to Araloth. But now, he could hear the sadness that tainted its harmonies, and the desperation that had driven its owner to this point.

At her words, the trees of the glade seemed to sigh, though whether in sadness or triumph, Araloth couldn't say. Nor did he wish to guess. The forest had a mind of its own, one that no elf could attempt to fathom, not if they wished to remain sane.

Durthu receded back into his place. Having said his piece, the Eldest of Ancients had fallen silent. The bargain had been struck, and there was nothing more to be said. The Council was quick to act. One of them stood and met Araloth's gaze. 'You heard?' he asked.

'I did,' Araloth said. He knew what was coming next, for it was the only reason that he would have been summoned to witness what had just occurred.

'You, Lord of Talsyn, and champion of the Mage Queen, will assemble a host to pierce black Sylvania, and lend our cousins aid in their rescue attempt.'

'I will,' Araloth said, simply. Nothing more needed to be said. His mind was already hard at work on the logistics of such an undertaking. Axe Bite Pass would be the quickest route. They would head north, through Parravon. There would be dangers aplenty, but he had little doubt that it could be done. He would request volunteers. He would not order any to follow him into such a place.

The chains of vines and leaves fell from the Everqueen as the audience ended. Two of the Mage Queen's handmaidens, Naestra and Arahan, waited to take Alarielle to the place of reckoning, where her part of the bargain, whatever it was, would be fulfilled. Araloth did not envy her the task to come. She glanced at the handmaidens, and then strode towards him. 'My daughter,' she said.

'I will do all that it is in my power to do for her,' he said quietly.

'As will I,' she said, looking into his eyes. She took his hand and squeezed it. He felt a shock as something passed between them. When she released his hand, he saw that she had pressed a locket into his palm. He looked at her questioningly.

'It will lead you to my daughter,' she said. 'Let us hope, for the sakes of those we love, that you reach her in time.'

CHAPTER EIGHT

Castle Sternieste, Sylvania

Mannfred felt a hum of satisfaction ripple through him as he watched Arkhan take in the room, and its treasures. There, the lecterns that held the damned tomes of Nagash. Nine, now, rather than the seven they had been, thanks to Arkhan.

And amidst them sat the Crown of Sorcery, pulsing softly with its weird light. Arkhan stood before the crown, and reached out a hand. Mannfred was possessed by a sudden urge to rip him away from it, but he wrestled the feeling down. It would not do to start a fight. Not now.

From above, the vargheists growled warningly. They hissed and snarled as the liche ran his fingers over the crown, but fell silent at Mannfred's gesture. Arkhan traced the wicked iron points that topped Nagash's crown, and then let his hand drop. He did not look at Mannfred when he said, '*You have the Claw as well.*' It wasn't a question.

Mannfred crossed his arms and smirked. 'Indeed.'

'*Where?*'

'Not here,' Mannfred said.

Arkhan turned. '*Even now, you do not trust me.*' The liche cocked his head. '*You are wise, in your generation.*' He turned towards the prisoners. '*I thought you enjoyed their escape attempts. Why torture them?*'

The prisoners hung in their chains, broken and beaten. They stank of death now, as much as anything else in the castle. Their flesh had been gouged and burned and flayed, and all remaining armour had been stripped from those who wore it. They had been crippled and hobbled, and hovered on the brink of death. Only Mannfred's sorcerous artifice kept them from tipping over entirely into the void. Mannfred strode past Arkhan and wrenched up Volkmar's head. Of the nine, only the old man and Aliathra were still conscious. The vampire looked at the elf woman. Her eyes were closed, but her lips moved silently. He wondered whether she, like the nature priest, had slipped at last into madness. Or worse, into damnation like Morgiana.

Volkmar glared defiantly up at him with exhausted, pain-clouded eyes. Mannfred leaned close, drinking in his captive's pain and helplessness. 'Because the time for games is done. If you can do as you claimed, then it is time to put away childish things and get to work,' he said, staring at Volkmar. He leaned close to the old man. 'Don't you agree, Volkmar? Aren't you tired of this never-ending game of ours? Don't you want to see it end, finally, once and for all?'

Volkmar hawked a gobbet of bloody spittle into Mannfred's face. Mannfred released the old man's head and stepped back. He wiped the spittle from his face and smiled. He felt no anger at the gesture. It was nothing more than the defiance of a peasant on the block. He looked at Arkhan and gestured. 'Well – I allowed you in here for a reason, liche. Tell me... Which one?'

Arkhan picked his way carefully across the blood-stained floor, and he gazed at each of the nine in turn. His hell-spark eyes lingered on the elf woman for a moment, and Mannfred felt himself tense, though he could not say why. Arkhan motioned to the unconscious form of the Myrmidian knight, Blaze. *'You were correct, earlier. This one. His blood is powerful, but not as much as that of the others. It is diluted, and thus perfect for our purposes.'*

Mannfred nodded slightly. 'As I suspected.'

'You have already assembled much of what is required. But we still lack three things.' Arkhan turned. *'Three items tied to the Great Necromancer's death. All lie within reach of Sylvania, and all require but the proper application of force to acquire. Neither guile nor cunning will be necessary. Luckily for you,'* Arkhan said.

Mannfred twitched. He closed his eyes and fought to control his temper. Arkhan was baiting him, but he would not give the liche the satisfaction. 'I know all of this, you black-toothed hank of gristle. What I do not know is how you intend to help me acquire them.'

'I told you – the secret is in the blood,' Arkhan said, motioning to the floor. *'The true question is, how are we to divide the work to come?'*

Mannfred ran his hands over his bare head. 'Ah, well, there I think is my contribution. Before your – ah – *timely* arrival, I was already concocting stratagems for that very purpose. Heldenhame is too obvious a target, and too close. If we strike there first, our enemies will surely know that we have escaped the cage they made for me. For us,' Mannfred said. 'I suggest we divide our forces. You came close to acquiring Nagash's staff, Alakanash, from La Maisontaal Abbey once... Best you succeed this time.'

Arkhan didn't react to his dig. *'And the Fellblade?'*

'Not far from here, as you said. My spies have brought word that it is in the possession of the skaven somewhere in Mad Dog Pass, as you yourself are likely already aware.'

Arkhan inclined his head. *'And you will acquire it?'*

'I will.' Mannfred gestured down at the map. 'We will depart via the western border, I think. It will give you the quickest path into Bretonnia, and me the quickest into the Border Princes. Speed is of the essence, but it will still take us most of the year. I suggest that we save Heldenhame for our coming out party, as it were.'

Arkhan looked down at the map. He looked up. 'Agreed. *It will take me some time to prepare. A few days, no more than that.*'

'Excellent. It will take me that long to see to raising a proper host, to carry us in style to our respective destinations.' Mannfred spread his hands. And to ensure that you return on your shield, rather than behind it, ally-mine, he thought. 'If you were capable of drinking, I'd raise a toast to you, oh mighty Arkhan.'

'*And if I had any interest in drinking with you, Mannfred, I would accept. Go, you may leave me here. I must attune myself to your sorceries and find the right strands to pull and those to cut.*' Mannfred hesitated, and Arkhan gave a rasping laugh. '*Fear not, vampire. Leave your dogs to guard me, if you wish. Summon ghouls or assign your pantomime Templars to stand sentinel over me, to ensure that I do not steal your treasures. I care not.*'

Mannfred bowed shallowly. 'You cannot fault me for being overcautious, Lord Arkhan. Allies, in my experience, are as the shifting sands – untrustworthy as a matter of course. But you shame me with your generosity of spirit, and courtly manner. I leave you, sir, to do as you must. And I go to do as I must.' Mannfred swept his cloak up about him and turned and left.

As he stalked through the corridors of Castle Sternieste, Mannfred forced aside the worries that gnawed at him. He didn't trust Arkhan, but he had little choice at this juncture. As old and as learned as he was in the arts of sorcery, Arkhan was older still. The liche had likely forgotten more about magic than Mannfred would ever be able to learn. He had been present at the birth of necromancy, and he was as good as Nagash's will given form.

But that wouldn't save him, once he'd outlived his usefulness.

Something yowled, and he paused. He looked up and saw Arkhan's detestable cat slinking through the ancient support timbers above. It glared down at him with milky-eyed malevolence, fleshless tail twitching. Mannfred's eyes narrowed. Was it watching him – spying for its master? He raised his hand, ready to blast it from existence, when something stopped him. He caught a glimpse of a massive, gaunt shape, twitching and flickering with witch-fire, out of the corner of his eye, like a giant squatting to fill the corridor behind him, and he whirled with a snarl. But there was nothing there. No giant and no shadow, save his own.

When he looked back up, the cat had vanished.

Mannfred looked around once more, and then continued on his way. He soon arrived at the high garden that he had made his war chamber for the coming campaign. He could not say why he had done so; he had rarely visited the high garden in all the months he had made Sternieste his home.

And do you remember why you avoided coming to Sternieste? Vlad purred softly. *This was my garden, wasn't it? Where I held my councils of war, in that golden age between conquest and damnation, while Sylvania was still to be won. I am honoured that you have chosen to honour my memory in such a way, my most attentive student.*

Mannfred stopped. He ran his hands over the crown of his head. He had had hair once, a luxuriant mane of hair, the hue of a raven's wing. He had been beautiful, and proud of that beauty. But after rising from the sump of Hel Fenn, he had shaved his head. His return was a rebirth. In death, he had been purged of old failings and faults, and vanity was discarded with the rest. Or so he'd thought.

Really, though, it had been to mark himself as different to Vlad. Vlad, with his icy mane and aristocratic mien; Vlad who held to the noble traditions of a long-gone empire – including the superstition that councils of war should be held in the open air, beneath the eyes of the gods so as to gain their favour.

Mannfred felt a chill course through him. Was that why he had been drawn to Sternieste, to the garden? Was he unconsciously imitating Vlad?

How many of Nagash's detestable tomes did I gather again? One or two, surely. Your initiative in that regard is impressive, I must say. Then, you never did know how to quit while you were ahead, did you? Vlad laughed.

No, no, he had chosen Sternieste for the strategic advantage it provided. And the garden... Well, few others even knew it existed, which made it the ideal spot to confer with his subordinates without danger of eavesdroppers.

Am I so poor an example, then? Vlad whispered.

'You're dead. You tell me,' Mannfred muttered. Vlad's laughter accompanied him into the garden, where the inner circle of the Drakenhof Templars sat or stood, arguing loudly amongst themselves. Well, Anark and Markos were arguing, which had become an annoyingly regular occurrence. The two vampires snarled and cursed at one another, and Mannfred thought they might come to blows. He paused, waiting, amused now, his previous uncertainties forgotten.

'Oh very good,' he said, after the spectre of violence had passed on, thwarted. 'I do so enjoy a spirited debate. I hope it was about something important.'

'He refuses to acquiesce to my authority,' Anark growled. Elize had one hand on his shoulder and her other pressed flat to Markos's chest.

'When you show me a reason to respect the puerile demands that flutter from your flapping lips, perhaps I will,' Markos snapped.

Mannfred sighed and strode between them. Elize retreated as Mannfred's hands snapped out and his fingers fastened on the throat of either vampire. Unliving muscle swelled as Mannfred hauled them both up and off their feet and into the air. 'This debate, while amusing, is most assuredly moot, my friends. The only authority here to which you must acquiesce is mine own.' Point made, he dropped them both. Anark, with a beast's wisdom, scrambled away. Markos sat and glared, rubbing his throat. Mannfred ignored him.

'The liche thinks that he can shatter the mystic cage that holds us,' he said, pushing aside the flicker of anger that accompanied those words. 'Out, all of you. Rouse the barrow-legions and draw the souls of the cursed dead from the stones where they sleep. The muster of Sternieste marches to war, and I would have every muck-encrusted bone and ragged shroud ready. Go, fly, rouse my army,' Mannfred said, sweeping out a hand.

Markos and the others filed out of the garden. But before Elize could follow them, Mannfred stopped her. As he did so, he noticed that her pets hesitated. Brute and shadow, Anark and the Crowfiend. Anark hesitated more obviously, waiting like a loyal hound. The Crowfiend lurked outside the entrance to the garden, as if he were only stopping to admire the mouldy tapestries that dangled from the walls there. Mannfred looked at Elize and she motioned delicately to Anark. He turned and left, visibly reluctant. The Crowfiend drifted away a moment later, silent and seemingly unconcerned.

'The loyalty you inspire in your get awes me, Elize,' Mannfred said. He clasped his hands behind his back and strode towards the tree. 'Do I inspire the same devotion in any creature?'

'I am your loyal servant, my lord,' Elize said softly.

'So you have shown again and again, sweet cousin.' Mannfred glanced at her. 'You are one of the rocks upon which my foundations stand.' He looked away. 'We are sallying forth from this besieged province, cousin, and I would have the Drakenhof Templars in the vanguard.'

'We have ever stood at the narrowest point, my lord,' Elize said.

'That point, I'm afraid, is going to become narrower still.' He lifted a hand, and spoke a single, shuddering syllable. The air thickened and the light dimmed, as if a fog had settled over the garden. 'There,' Mannfred said. 'Now we can speak freely with one another, without curious ears eavesdropping. Anark will accompany Arkhan into Bretonnia.'

'Bretonnia,' Elize repeated. She hesitated, and then nodded. Mannfred had not told his inner circle just what he was after, but he had no doubt that the brighter sparks among them had already guessed. 'Are you certain now is the time, my lord?'

'Was that a question, or a suggestion?' Mannfred asked. 'Arkhan's usefulness is finite. Can your pet be trusted to do this thing for me, sweet cousin?' Mannfred asked, looking up at the tree. It seemed to be flourishing anew, its limbs growing gnarled and strong, as if it were feeding on the mortal energies of the dead things gathered at Sternieste. He traced the jagged contours of its crumbling bark with a finger.

'He can, my lord,' Elize said.

'You sound confident.'

'In Anark's strength and willingness? Yes, cousin, I am. I chose him for those qualities.'

Mannfred smiled. 'Ah, cousin, my cousin, you were ever the darling of dear, sweet, mad Isabella's eye, in those glorious times now gone to dust and memory. She relied much on you, in those final days, while Vlad was occupied with the war.'

Elize said nothing, but silence was as good an answer as anything she might have chosen to say, to Mannfred's way of thinking. He glanced over his shoulder at Elize, studying her. 'You were alone among her handmaidens in your practicality and – dare I say it? – your sanity. A mind second only to my own, I have often said.'

'Have you, my lord? I have never heard you say such about anyone,' Elize said mildly. Mannfred raised his brow in surprise. Elize was normally quite circumspect. He expected such comments from Markos, but Elize...

'You are worried, then,' he said, turning to face her. 'Should I send another of your creatures? The Crowfiend, perhaps? Erikan of Mousillon,' he continued, and his smile turned feral as a brief look of consternation crossed her perfectly composed features. 'Oh yes, I smelt the stink of that particular demesne on him, the poor boy. He is the last surviving pup of the Cannibal Knight of Mousillon, of infamous memory, isn't he? The Bretonnians burned that lot in their sewer palaces. The Cannibal Knight, his princess of Bel-Aliad, and their squalling retainers. Royalty, that one, at least insofar as the Bretonni judge these things. He has no idea, of course, and I shall not tell him.' He crossed the space between them and caught her chin. 'That shall be my gift to you, hmm? From one loving cousin to another.' He lifted her chin, so that her eyes met his. 'Shall I send him instead of Anark, perhaps? Or both together?'

'As you wish, my lord,' Elize said.

Mannfred released her and stepped back. He chuckled. 'What game are you playing, sweet cousin, that you will not share your moves with me?'

'It is but a small one, to amuse myself,' she said.

'I've often wondered... How did you woo him? Or did he woo you, the necromancer's apprentice trailing after the beautiful lady without mercy?' Mannfred turned away. 'He angered you, though, your cannibal prince. I know that much. He left to follow his own path, without a word of thanks for all your efforts to groom him into something greater. What was your plan then? Was he to be a stepping stone to influence elsewhere?'

'As I said, my lord, it was but a small amusement,' Elize said.

She was lying. Mannfred nodded nonetheless, as if he believed her. 'Then you will not mind if I send both. If one of your creatures fails, then the other will not.'

Elize's face might as well have been a marble mask. 'As you will, my lord. Who, dear cousin, will accompany you? And who will be castellan here?'

'The latter is easy enough – you,' he said.

She blinked. Then, she inclined her head. 'You honour me, cousin.'

'I know. See that you do not disappoint me. I'd hate to accomplish my goals, only to return to a burned-out ruin, and a scattered army.' He ran his palms over his head and said, 'As for who shall accompany me... Markos and our good Vargravian count, Nyktolos. Both have warred in the Border Princes before, and their experience is required. Master Nictus will stay with you, to act as your good right hand.'

Elize hesitated. Then, 'Are you certain you wish to take Markos?'

Mannfred looked at her. 'Concerned for my wellbeing, sweet cousin?'

'If I were not, would I have warned you of Tomas's intentions, all those months ago, before this affair even began? Would I have warned you that he'd made an agreement with von Dohl, that he was promised command of the armies of Waldenhof, if he took your head?'

'As I recall, you warned me so that I might allow you to choose the next Grand Master of the Drakenhof Order. A straight bargain, Elize.' Mannfred laughed. 'And even if I hadn't known, Tomas would have failed. He was a maggot, nothing more, just like von Dohl, and the cursed Shadowlord and all the others who defy my blood-right.'

'Like Markos?'

Mannfred paused. 'Markos has never been... comfortable in a subordinate role. Vlad spoiled him. He had a peculiar fondness for acerbity in his servants.'

And you would know, wouldn't you, boy? Vlad's voice murmured. Mannfred ignored it and continued, 'It is a fondness that I do not, on the whole, share.' *Of course not. You never could stand to be questioned could you, young prince?* Vlad needled him. Mannfred felt his cheek twitch as he sought to restrain a snarl of frustration. 'I am giving Markos a chance. He will serve, or he will make his move,' he said. 'Either way, I am too close to victory to allow him to remain undecided. We are coming to the sharp end of all things, sweet cousin. The time when sides must be chosen, and banners unfurled for the last time. All games save mine must be put aside, for the good of all who bear the von Carstein name.' He looked at her. 'Including yours, my sweet Elize.'

'Do you dream, old man?' Arkhan asked. He examined Volkmar from a distance, head cocked. He had stood in the same place since Mannfred had left, soaking up the miasma of the place, drinking in the concentrated essence of his master's earthly remains. All that had been Nagash, save for certain pieces, was here, and he could feel the Great Necromancer's presence beating down upon his brain like a terrible black sun. *'I think you do. You can hear his footsteps in the hollows of your heart, and his voice in the sour places of your memory, even as I can.'*

Volkmar said nothing. He glared at Arkhan as silently as he had Mannfred. Arkhan leaned against his staff. He was not weary, but sometimes he felt what might be the ghost of such a feeling, deep in his bones. '*I see the skull beneath your skin, old man. It's no use denying it. He has chosen you.*'

'He *is* chosen, and by Lord Mannfred,' Morgiana hissed. She rose from where she'd been crouching in the corner and sauntered towards Arkhan, as far as her chains would allow. Unlike the others, she hadn't been beaten to within an inch of her life. She no longer had a life to lose. She glowed with the cold fire of undeath to Arkhan's eyes, and he did not wonder why she was still chained. She had been threat enough in life. In death she was even more dangerous. Or she would be, once she learned the new limits of her power.

Arkhan examined her curiously. She was kept with the others both because she made for a cruelly amusing gaoler, and because even Mannfred wasn't so foolish as to let a creature like Morgiana Le Fay wander loose. Her blood still pulsed with the raw stuff of life, as did her magics. It was only her presence that kept the other captives from slipping over the precipice into death's domain. Mannfred had truly wrought something abominable when he'd turned her. Still, there was yet a sliver of the woman she had been within the beast he'd made of her.

'*How did he acquire you, I wonder?*' he murmured, drawing close to her. She hissed and retreated, her eyes narrowing with pain. Arkhan stopped. Some vampires, those with an unusual sensitivity to the winds of death, felt pain in his presence. He was little more than the power of necromancy given form, and for some vampires, that was the difference between being warmed by flames and burned by them.

Morgiana's beautiful features twisted into an expression of bestial malice. 'Drycha,' she spat. Arkhan nodded. The branchwraith of Athel Loren had ever been a changeable and unpredictable factor. It did not surprise him that she had brought Morgiana to Mannfred. That sort of malevolent caprice was what Drycha was best at.

'Free me, liche, and I shall aid you in whatever way you wish,' Morgiana said, the mask of humanity slipping back over her face. She rattled her chains for emphasis. 'I shall abet you and comfort you. My magics – all that I am – will be at your disposal.'

Arkhan let a raspy laugh slip between his fleshless jaws. '*I doubt that, woman. Mannfred keeps you chained for good reason. You are more dangerous now than you were in your enchanted Bretonnian bower.*'

Morgiana snarled and sprang for him. Arkhan didn't move. He had stopped just out of the reach of her chains, and she tumbled heavily to the floor, where she rolled about, writhing and shrieking like a she-wolf in a trap. She spat bloody froth at him, and where it struck the floor, green patches of moss flourished, before swiftly withering and dying.

He turned away from her display, focusing his attentions on the Ever-child, where she hung in her chains, eyes closed, lips moving in a silent song. And it was a song, for Arkhan could hear it, even if Mannfred could not. It was a hymn, a sorcerous prayer, subtle yet powerful enough to pierce the bindings Mannfred had placed about Sylvania. It was a thing of intricate beauty to his eyes and sorcerous sense, a crystalline web that stretched upwards from Aliathra, growing in strength and size, as she powered the spell with her own life essence.

'*I wonder if they have heard you yet, child?*' he asked as he approached her. '*I think they have. I can feel the burden of gathering destinies. Your song calls your kin to your side. Perhaps you have wondered why I have not stopped you?*'

The elf did not reply. Her eyes remained shut, and her lips continued to move. Arkhan brushed a strand of her hair from her face, and he felt her clammy skin quiver at his touch. '*It serves the ends of the one whom I serve, you see. I tell you this so that you understand that we are both pawns, and that there is no malice in my actions.*'

Her eyes flashed open. Arkhan lowered his hand. There was fire there, and rage. It crashed against the coldness of him, and he almost flinched back. As much power as inundated his cracked and ancient bones, the fury that lurked in the elf maiden's blood was greater by far. It was power enough to shatter continents and crack the world's core.

For a moment, Arkhan felt fire and pain. Then it passed, and he was himself again. He found that his cat had returned, its maggoty body pressed tight to his shoulders. Its weight had come upon him unnoticed, and it hissed at the elf maiden with feline disdain. He reached up and stroked the animal's decaying throat. Aliathra's eyes were closed. Arkhan turned away, disturbed.

That disturbance did not lessen in the coming days, as he prepared for the ritual that would allow for escape from the caged province. He saw Ogiers and the others but little over the following days. The trio of necromancers he'd scavenged from the ruins of Mallobaude's army had scattered the moment they arrived, slipping his reins to find newer, more pliable partners or masters. It would have been a matter of moments to summon them back to his side, but for the moment he left them free to pursue their whims. Morgiana, despite her madness and untrustworthy nature, still had an able mind, and she proved an able replacement, in between pleas for release and demands for blood. It was fitting that she was such, for she was, herself, one of the cornerstones of the very ritual that formed the root of their current predicament.

He had faced Morgiana only briefly on the field of Couronne during Mallobaude's revolt, but that confrontation had shown him the nature of the power that lurked beneath Bretonnia's barbaric facade. That Morgiana was still somehow connected to it, despite her current state only confirmed his suspicions. Necromancy, at its base, had been born in elven minds, or so Nagash swore. He had altered it, and forced it into a shape more to his liking, but its seed had been planted in the wisdom of Aliathra's dark kin, even as Morgiana's own had its roots in the secret glades of Athel Loren.

The collegial magics that had been used to create the wall of faith were similar, albeit watered down, and altered still further to account for the frailty of the human frame. Luckily, that was something Arkhan no longer had to worry about.

As the weeks progressed, he eventually ordered Morgiana unchained, to better aid him in preparing his form for the rite to come. His bones had to be carved with the proper sigils and runes, and the ritual knife he would use had to be soaked in the blood of each of the nine captives for a certain amount of time. The proper bindings had to be prepared, as well as the unguents and powders that would be used to mark the circle and feed the braziers. Many hands made for light work, and Morgiana had proved to be pliable enough, once freed.

Time passed strangely for the dead. It moved in fits and starts, as slow as tar and as fast as quicksilver. Arkhan could only keep track of the days by the puddles of melted candle fat, so engrossed was he in studying the Books of Nagash, as well as the other grimoires he ordered brought to him by the whining ghoul pack Mannfred had given him to act as his dogs-bodies. He read and studied and read still more, and as they always did in such times, the unoccupied portions of his mind drifted into the depths of memory, and were reluctant to return. He had once spent a decade brooding on his throne in his black tower in the desert, lost in the grip of his memories. They were all that he had of himself that was not of Nagash's crafting. Or so part of him hoped.

On the last day, when the last mark was added to his scrimshawed bones and the last powder mixed and all preparations made, Arkhan stood in the centre of the chamber, admiring his handiwork. Over the centuries, he had carved and shaped his own bones more than once. Unlike his long-abandoned flesh, his bones always healed, and his work faded eventually. They would not have long before the marks he and Morgiana had so painstakingly made would vanish, necessitating that they start the whole purification rite over again. He sent the ghouls scrambling to alert Mannfred and turned to Morgiana. '*It is time, enchantress. I thank you for your service.*' He paused, and then asked, '*Would you see your land again, one last time? As payment, for services rendered.*' Even as he spoke he wondered when such a thing had occurred to him.

Morgiana looked at him and then away. 'I do not think so. I know what you intend, and I know that I cannot stop you, but I would not see it.'

'*Very well.*' Arkhan looked at her.

'You are going to kill me, aren't you?' Morgiana asked, suddenly.

Arkhan hesitated. '*You are already dead,*' he said.

'No, I am not. If I were, this would not work,' she said, gesturing to the runnels of blood that cut across the floor. 'If I were, I would not feel the way I do.' She ran her hands through the ratty tangles of her once luxurious hair. 'How can anything dead be so hungry?' Her eyes, fever-bright with barely restrained madness, turned towards her fellow captives. All but Aliathra were unconscious, even Volkmar. Morgiana had been feeding on all of them, save those two, to keep them docile while Arkhan completed his preparations. It was the first taste of blood she'd had in a long while, and it was that which had shocked her back to something approaching lucidity. 'It's always with me,' she said. 'I can hear the Lady's voice, but only faintly, as if I am on the opposite shore of a vast, red lake. Sometimes her words are entirely drowned out by the crash of the crimson waves on the white rocks.' She looked at him. 'Can you even understand, dead thing that you are?'

'*I... can,*' he said. He crossed to her as faint echoes of memory were stirred from the sludge of ages and rose unencumbered to the surface of his mind. Of another woman, of another time, of another ritual, marred by poison and betrayal. Unthinkingly, he brushed a strand of hair from her face. '*My spirit will never know peace. I must play my part until the end of time.*'

'I thought I would as well, but the world had other plans,' she whispered, not looking at him. 'My path changed. And I cannot bear to see where it is taking me.'

'*I... knew a woman like you, once,*' he croaked, wondering as he spoke why he was bothering to do so. What matter to him the travails of a madwoman? Then, perhaps his unlife had simply given him perspective. Even as a man, he had never been given to torture. '*She too was afraid, and had lost the voice of her goddess.*' He fell silent.

She looked at him, and for a moment he saw the face of another superimposed over hers. A pale face, framed by hair the colour of night, with eyes like molten pools and lips that could change from kind to cruel with the merest twitch. Even now, when his mind was not otherwise occupied, he could see her face. Her hands reached up to stroke his jawbone. 'What happened to her?' she murmured.

'*She persevered,*' he said. '*She was a queen, and queens do not know fear for long.*'

Morgiana closed her eyes. 'I do not think I will have that opportunity. You will kill me, won't you?' she asked again.

'*I will,*' Arkhan said. '*In the end, nine are required for the final ritual, though eight will suffice. But no less than that.*' He stroked her cheek. Some part of him snarled in warning, but he ignored it. The chamber had been replaced by another in his mind's eye, of cool marble and sandstone. He could smell the ocean, and hear the rustle of silk curtains. '*There will be no pain... That I swear.*'

'Good,' she said. 'That is what I needed to know.' Her hand dropped. A moment later, his knife was jerked from its sheath and Morgiana had its tip pressed to the flesh over her heart. The flesh of her hand sizzled as the malign enchantments wrought into the blade resisted her touch. Marble and silk again became mouldy stone and the stink of abused flesh.

Arkhan lunged forward, hand outstretched. '*Neferata,*' he rasped, momentarily uncertain what was memory and what was reality. She shoved him back, her vampiric strength taking him by surprise. He staggered. '*No, please...*' he said, still caught in the tangled strands of memory. He saw Neferata writhing on her bed, caught in the throes of an agonising death. He felt Abhorash's blade, as it cut him down. The full weight of the last, worst moment of a life badly spent crashed down on him for the first time in centuries, and he could not bear it. '*Please don't!*' The words were ripped from him before he even realised that he'd said them.

Morgiana smiled in triumph. 'My path was changed. But I can change it back.' She wrapped both hands around the hilt, and thrust it into her own heart. Black smoke boiled from the wound, and blood gushed as she toppled forward into Arkhan's arms.

The liche screamed. The sound was one of frustration, rage and despair. As her blood coated his arms and chest, he knew what she had done. It had taken her weeks, but she had ensnared him in her glamour, making him see... and feel. Rage burned through him, and then guttered out. He cradled her close as the last wisps of the glamour faded and he was himself again. No longer Arkhan the gambler, Arkhan the dread lord, now only Arkhan the Black.

He tore the knife from her chest and hurled it aside. He hesitated. Her face was peaceful, in death. But some part of her yet remained. Vampires could not truly die. He could bring her back with but a touch, to stir the black sorceries that flowed through her tainted blood. But still, he hesitated.

From behind him came a yowl. He turned and saw his cat crouched atop Nagash's crown. Its starved, crumbling frame was draped over the iron points, tail lashing. Its empty eyes met his own and he nodded slowly. He looked back down at Morgiana and said, '*No, my lady. Escape is not so easy as all that, I fear.*'

He placed a hand against the wound, and dark lightning crackled briefly from his fingers to course through Morgiana. Her body twitched and her eyes opened wide. Her lips spread and a scream escaped them. It was a sound empty of all hope. She clawed uselessly at him, and he jerked her to her feet. In moments, she was chained once more. She crouched against the wall, sobbing. Arkhan watched her for a moment, before turning away.

He felt eyes on him, and looked around to meet Aliathra's gaze. '*Were you amused, Everchild? I have heard that your folk drink deep of the cup of mortal suffering, finding it to be exquisite.*'

'No,' she spoke, her voice soft. 'I was simply surprised that it worked. I thought dead things could not be ensnared thus. Then, you are not truly dead, are you?' Arkhan said nothing. The elf smiled sadly. 'For that to have worked, there must be some kernel yet of the man you once were, trapped in the husk of you, Arkhan the Black. Some small touch of mercy.'

The cat shrieked, and Arkhan turned away. '*No. There is not,*' he said, finally. He picked up his staff and slammed it down. The chamber echoed with the sound, and he heard the howl of the vargheists who lurked in the shadows above drift down in reply. The cat leapt onto his shoulder. The vargheists dropped down heavily, snarling and snapping at one another. Arkhan pointed his staff at the unconscious form of Lupio Blaze. '*Unchain him, and bring him. I grow weary of Sylvania. It is time to leave.*'

Sylvania, the western border

'We are still agreed, then?' Mannfred asked, hands crossed on his saddle's pommel as he leaned over his mount's neck. The horse-thing was all bone and eldritch fire, and it stank of charnel pits and mouldering ashes. 'West for you and east for me.'

'*As we agreed,*' Arkhan said. He stood at the centre of his carefully pre-pared ritual circle. At his feet, pinned to the ground by crudely forged bronze spikes, was the pain-contorted shape of Lupio Blaze. Black candles, with tallow rendered from human flesh, surrounded the circle, as did a number of smoking iron braziers.

And in the distance, the only obstacle between them and the return of the Undying King. Gelt's wall of faith rode dips and curves of the border; the symbols of Morr, Sigmar, Ulric and a dozen other gods, some real, some not, hung suspended in the air, glowing with a terrible, painful light. The western border was one of the few places where the cursed barrier was visible to the naked eye, and thus the perfect spot to ensure that the spell had actually worked.

Behind Mannfred, the army of Sylvania waited. Arkhan would take only a small bodyguard of Drakenhof Templars and his dissolute cadre of necro-mancers into Bretonnia, while Mannfred would lead the vast bulk of the waiting army into the Border Princes. Above the silent army, the Draken-hof banner fluttered like a dying snake.

'Excellent,' Mannfred said. He leaned back in his saddle and slapped his thigh. 'Well... on with it, liche. I have a world to conquer and no time to dally.' He jerked on his mount's reins and galloped off to rejoin his wait-ing blood knights.

Arkhan watched him go and then looked down at the knight. '*Any last words, warrior?*' Arkhan asked softly. Blaze glared up at him defiantly, and spat something virulent in Tilean. Arkhan nodded respectfully. '*As it should be. A brave man's final words ought to be unrepeatable,*' he said.

Arkhan began to chant, slowly at first, and then faster, the words bursting from him like a cascade of rocks down a cliff-face. He spoke in the tongue of Nehekhara, and it came as easily to him as the memory of his first death. He spat the words into the teeth of the growing wind, and the vast faces, bloated and loathsome that leered down at him through the tattered veils of reality. The words were as much promise as invocation, and the world squirmed about him as his voice tore great wounds in the air. Thunder rumbled overhead. Black lightning, blacker than the dark sky, split the air, creating jagged cracks in the firmament full of squamous, daemonic shapes, which writhed and fought.

Ghostly shapes, half formed and inhuman, spiralled madly about Arkhan and his captive, and wolves, both dead and alive, began to howl. The bitter air grew thick and poisonous, as the weight of the forces Arkhan was invoking settled on the world. He drew the bone dagger from the jewelled sheath on his belt with his free hand and dropped down to crouch over the knight. The same dagger that had almost taken Morgiana's life would now spill the blood of her fellow captive. *'Rest assured that your sacrifice will help to save the world, warrior. Take that thought with you into the embrace of your goddess, for however long it lasts.'*

Then, with two swift movements, he slit the knight's wrist and thigh, releasing twin sprays of red blood to splash onto the thirsty ground. Blaze's struggles grew weaker, and his curses quieter, as his life emptied itself into the soil of Sylvania. Arkhan stood, and raised his hand. His fingers snapped closed and the candles tumbled over, setting the pooling blood alight. The fire raced about the circle, spiralling upwards with a loud roar, consuming everything within, save for Arkhan, who stood untouched by the greedy flames. His robes whipped about him as he raised his hand, and the flames tore at the heavens in reply. The fire whirled about him in a flickering typhoon of destruction, and in the coruscating surface of the flames he could see the faces of his enemies, gnashing their teeth and cursing him silently. Arkhan let the flames spill upwards into the sky.

And then he snuffed them with a snap of his bony fingers. The fire went out, leaving him in a circle of char and ash. He stood for a time, as the magics he had raised coursed through him. He had taken the power that had hidden in the knight's blood into himself, and he could feel it roil in his nonexistent veins. Its fury had momentarily silenced the voice of his master within him, and he felt as if an indescribable weight had been lifted from his old bones. He looked at his hand, considering the power he now held. It would be so easy to use it for himself, to do as he wished, for once. He could dispatch his rivals here, take Mannfred's acquisitions for himself and remake this blighted land into something that would ride out the coming storm better than the eternal abattoir the vampire imagined. A land of order and perfect, beautiful silence, where no daemon or dark power, save himself, held sway.

He looked up and met Mannfred's cool, calculating glare. A giant shadow hung over the vampire, looming above him, its black gaze on Arkhan. He knew that he was the only one who could see it, who could feel the impatient malevolence that boiled off it like steam. Who was it looking out of the vampire's eyes right now? What black brain drove Mannfred in his efforts?

Arkhan knew the answer well enough. He had seen it before, on the Valsborg Bridge, and in Castle Sternieste. The world buckled beneath the weight of a dark fate, and one that he knew better than to try and avoid. '*Nagash must rise,*' Arkhan murmured. He motioned slowly, and the ashes at his feet stirred, rising as if caught in a hot wind. They played about his fingers as he gestured with his knife and called out, '*Bring your standard forward, vampire.*'

Mannfred gestured. A blood knight rode towards Arkhan, carrying the Drakenhof banner. Arkhan anointed the ancestral banner of the Sylvanian aristocracy with a handful of ashes. '*Carry the banner to the wall.*'

The standard-bearer glanced at Mannfred, who motioned towards the partition. The blood knight grimaced visibly, and then kicked his coal-black steed into motion towards the wall of faith. As the armoured vampire extended the standard towards the hovering holy symbols, there was a flash, and one by one, the sigils and symbols tumbled from the air to land heavily on the ground. Mannfred stood up in his saddle and waved his hand. 'Forward!' he shouted. 'For Sylvania, and for the world to come!'

PART TWO

Gathering

Spring 2523–Spring 2524

CHAPTER NINE

Hvargir Forest, the Border Princes

Mannfred lifted the pale arm from his lap and sent it and the bloodless body it was attached to thudding to the ground with a negligent gesture. The body had belonged to a young woman: a peasant from one of the villages they had taken the night before, he thought. Now it belonged to the worms, until he decided to add her pitiful carcass to his legions. He brushed his thumb across his lips and said, 'Bring Duke Forzini forward, if you please. I would speak with our host.'

Count Nyktolos nodded shallowly and stepped out of the tent that Mannfred had claimed for his own. The Vargravian's features were a distorted parody of a man's – too wide and flat by far, his flesh the colour of a bruise. A shark-like mouth stretched from pointed ear to pointed ear, and his eyes bulged unpleasantly. He resembled a puppet, with his monocle and his hair greased flat against his stoat-like skull. Looks aside, he was deadly with a blade and had a keen mind, two things Mannfred appreciated. Even better, his ambitions were just petty enough to be amusing, rather than annoying.

'Since when do you palaver with food, cousin?' Markos asked, from where he stood, examining the hide map stretched across a wooden frame in the corner of the tent.

'Speak of the annoyingly ambitious,' Mannfred murmured. He looked around the tent, taking in the rough decor. It had all the pomp and panoply he expected of the frontier nobleman he had borrowed it from two nights before. Tapestries and animal furs hung from the support poles of the tent, and a quadrupedal, low-slung iron brazier, filled with coals which had long-since gone cold, occupied the centre beneath the smoke hole cut into the top of the tent. A rack of spears – boar, wolf and other more esoteric varieties – stood behind the crudely carved wooden stool he now occupied. He looked down at the staff laid across his lap, and the withered, iron-wrapped thing that had been lashed to the top in ages past: the Claw of Nagash. The thing was a hand – or, more accurately, a claw. It was larger than a man's, and it seemed to ooze a sorcerous miasma. As he looked at it, the long, skeletal fingers seemed to twitch, as if they yearned to grasp his throat. And perhaps they did. Something of Nagash's spiteful spirit was trapped in this claw, just as it was in his crown and his books.

He'd brought the Claw so that it might lead him to the object of his search – the skaven-forged Fellblade – the very weapon that had severed Nagash's hand from his wrist and ended his Great Work the first time. There was a sympathetic vibration between the two, and with a bit of coaxing, the one pointed the way to the other. The Claw whispered to him, and he listened and set his legion marching towards Mad Dog Pass.

It had taken him centuries to discover Kadon of Mourkain's staff and the Claw, hidden as it had been, in the vaults of that lost city. Ushoran, fearing its power, had sealed it away in the deepest, blackest pit he could find, though he'd taken the Crown for himself. Then, perhaps the ancient vampire had thought that he could master one artefact of Nagash's but not two, more fool him. Ushoran's will had not proved equal to the task, though he'd come closer than any save Mannfred himself. Mannfred stroked the staff, and the Claw curled and twitched like an appreciative cat. 'Poor Ushoran. If only you had listened to me,' he murmured. 'I told you that she couldn't be trusted.'

'What?' Markos asked. He sounded annoyed.

Mannfred glanced at him lazily. 'Nothing, brave cousin. Merely talking to myself.'

'An old family trait,' Markos muttered.

'What was that?' Mannfred asked, even though he'd heard Markos quite clearly. 'You have something to say, Markos?'

'I said that this map is out of date,' Markos replied smoothly.

'It's Tilean. What did you expect? Cartography is one of the few arts that they do not claim to have invented,' Mannfred said. 'And in answer to your impertinent query, cousin... This is no mere hunting party, whatever our host claims. Why else bring a troop of armoured horsemen and spearmen?'

'Spears are used in hunting,' Markos said. Mannfred could tell from the glint in his eye that he was being deliberately obtuse. Markos's mood had been positively acidic since they entered the Black Mountains, and hadn't abated with battle. They'd encountered the small force as they descended the mountains and entered the Hvargir Forest. Mannfred had obscured the movements of his forces through sorcerous means as they travelled through the mountains, but Markos and the others had been growing restive when the unfortunate Duke Forzini had crossed their path with his simple 'hunting party'. Forzini was one of a multitude of minor, self-proclaimed counts and dukes who ruled the petty fiefdoms of the Border Princes.

'True,' Mannfred said. 'But what hunting expedition requires a hundred such, as well as cuirassiers, fully armoured knights, and what I believe is called a – ah – "galloper gun", hmm? What were they hunting *for*, cousin?'

Markos opened his mouth to retort, but Nyktolos returned, and shoved a bedraggled figure through the tent flap. The man, bound in chains, and stinking of blood and fear, fell onto the ground at Mannfred's feet. Mannfred clapped his hands. 'Ah, and here he is now! The man of the hour, Duke Farnio Forzini, of the demesne of Alfori. They make a fine millet in Alfori, I'm told. Of course, the prime export, as with so many of these tiny mountain realms is violence.' Mannfred smiled. 'Something I myself am well acquainted with.' He stood and hauled his prisoner to his feet. 'Up, sirrah, up – on your feet. I am a count, and you a duke, and neither of us should kneel.'

Forzini flinched away from Mannfred's grin. The Tilean was a big man, with the muscle of a trained knight. He had fought hard, even after he realised what it was he faced. It had taken two days to beat a sense of fear into him. Forzini saw the dead body of the maid and his face went pale. Mannfred followed his gaze and asked, 'Oh, was she one of your peons? My apologies. I was peckish, you understand. I so rarely allow myself to indulge, but, well, you put up quite a fight and I built up a hellish appetite.'

He looked at the beaten man. He had to reach Mad Dog Pass before the first snows of the season, and that meant moving quickly through the Border Princes. He had no time to indulge in unnecessary battle. If the petty aristocracy of these lands had learned of his approach, and were mobilising to meet him in battle, he needed to know, and sooner rather than later. 'Where were you marching to?' Mannfred hissed. 'Tell me, and I won't gut you and feed you to my horses.'

'S-skaven,' Forzini mumbled, his eyes tightly closed.

Mannfred grunted. 'How many?'

'Thousands – more maybe,' Forzini said. He looked at Mannfred. 'We were riding to aid my neighbour, Count Tulvik, at Southern Reach. His fortress had come under siege.'

'Then you were going in the wrong direction,' Nyktolos said mildly, cleaning his monocle on his sleeve. 'I was once a... guest of old Tulvik.' He blinked. 'Well, his grandfather, actually.'

Mannfred growled. He caught Forzini by the throat. 'I don't care for lies, Forzini.'

'W-we were! I swear!' Forzini choked out. 'But then, a runner brought word that my own hold was under siege. So I turned back – my wife and children, my people!' The last exploded out and Forzini broke free of Mannfred with a convulsive surge of strength. Mannfred let him go. Forzini lunged for the hilt of Mannfred's sword. 'I have to save them!'

Mannfred casually dropped his fist onto the back of Forzini's skull and knocked him sprawling to the ground. He pinned the cursing duke in place with his foot and looked at Markos. The other vampire nodded grudgingly. 'That would explain what we've seen, wouldn't it? This isn't an isolated raid we're talking about, cousin. It's an invasion.'

When they'd descended into the foothills of the Black Mountains, the plains and fenland and forest should have been dotted with proud, if small, cities and fortified outposts as it always had been. What they had seen instead was a land in ruins. Castles were scorched piles, and towns were reduced to smouldering embers. And everywhere, the signs of plague – bodies choked the ditches and mass graves lay full, yet uncovered.

At first, Mannfred thought it was simply the aftermath of one of the interminable border wars, which occasionally flared up and then died away. But the devastation was too extensive. Memories of the portents of doom that he had witnessed in his scrying so many months ago had come rushing back, of the fates of Tilea and Estalia, and he knew that the end that he had witnessed was drawing closer. The weft and weave of the world was realigning and time was running out. That was the only thing that could draw the skaven from their twilight burrows in such numbers as Forzini and his own scrying had described.

He had faith enough in Elize's ability to maintain control of Sylvania in his absence, but he knew that no other could defend his realm better than he could. If the skaven were truly massing in such numbers in the Border Princes, he couldn't count on his sorceries seeing him unmolested to his goal. Better then not to even try, now that he had passed beyond the borders of the Empire.

'How many prisoners did we take?' he asked, after a moment.

'Ah, one, two, three... Fifty or sixty,' Nyktolos said, ticking off his fingers. 'Mostly the duke's household guard. They fought hard for a band of jumped-up bandit-knights.'

'Due to my friend Forzini here, I have no doubt,' Mannfred said. He caught hold of the chains binding Forzini and pulled him close. 'I am not ordinarily in the habit of giving choices, Forzini. It sets a bad precedent, you see, for royalty to allow the dregs to think that they get a say in their own fates. But, if there are thousands of skaven slumping and sneaking through these lands, I'll need every sword I can get, dead or... otherwise.' Mannfred licked his lips. Though the girl's blood had quenched his thirst, he could still detect the erratic thump of Forzini's pulse. Mannfred tightened his grip on the chains. 'Swear fealty to me, Duke Forzini, and I shall save your lands for you. Indeed, you can be the hero who saves the entirety of the Border Princes, if that is your wish. Or die here, and ride at my side regardless as a nameless and mindless thing. Serve me in life, or in death. But you shall serve me. Name your preference.'

He heard Vlad's sibilant chuckle as he gazed down into the flushed, sweating features of the duke. *Those are familiar words. You honour me, my son,* Vlad murmured. Mannfred could almost see him out of the corner of his eye. He blinked, and Vlad vanished. 'Well?' he snarled, hauling Forzini close. 'Make your choice.'

'Y-you will save my people?' Forzini asked.

'I will save everyone,' Mannfred said.

Forzini closed his eyes and nodded jerkily. Mannfred gave a satisfied growl and sank his fangs into the Duke's throat. As he drank, his eyes met Nyktolos's and the ugly vampire nodded sharply and left the tent. When he had finished, he let the duke's body slump to the ground. Crouching over him, Mannfred used a thumbnail to slit his palm, and then squeezed several drops of blood into the ragged wounds he had made in Forzini's throat.

As he rose, his hand was already healing. 'Is this wise, cousin?' Markos asked, looking down at the not-quite-dead man. 'Also, I hope you aren't expecting us to turn his servants. Such a thing is below even my slight dignity.'

Mannfred smiled. Screams echoed from outside. 'The Vargravian is already handling it. By the time we reach our destination, I shall have a bodyguard worthy of an emperor of the dead, cousin.'

Markos was about to reply, when the air was suddenly split by the howl of a wolf. The sound ratcheted through the tent, drowning out even the scream's of Forzini's men. Markos drew his blade and rushed to the tent opening. 'The alarm,' he barked.

Mannfred followed more sedately, wiping his lips with his fingers. It seemed he wasn't going to have to go looking for the skaven – they had come to him.

Brionne, Bretonnia

The castle on the crag had once been one of the great bulwarks upon which the might of Brionne had been built, guarding the province's border against all enemies. Now, it was a fire-blackened ruin, long since picked over by scavengers of all varieties, human or otherwise.

Heinrich Kemmler, the Lichemaster, lifted his staff and thumped the end of it on the ground, calling the dead of the ruined keep to attention. The crackle of bones pushing through the ash and the wreckage of their own flesh filled the air, and Kemmler closed his eyes and moved his hand and staff like the orchestral conductor at the Imperial opera. The dead rose at his cajoling, reaching towards him like penitents in a temple, and a harsh, croaking laugh slipped from Kemmler's lips.

Arkhan watched the Lichemaster draw the dead from their too-brief slumber, and felt no little surprise at the obvious power the elderly necromancer now seemed to wield. When he had last seen Kemmler, in the waning months of the Bretonnian civil war, the Lichemaster had been a mumbling, muttering wretch, barely cognisant of the world around him. Now, Kemmler resembled the Lichemaster of old, full of cold, dark reservoirs of power.

Those reservoirs had barely been tapped in the Vaults, Arkhan knew, when he and Kemmler had cracked open the web-strewn, elf-sealed tombs that lined the high reaches of those mountains months earlier. Kemmler had swept aside the antediluvian magics that chained the wild, selfish spirits that clustered in those mausoleums as if they had been nothing more than cobwebs. Arkhan had done the same, but he knew the origins of his own strength. He knew what lay at the bottom of the inner wells from which he drew his power. Kemmler's newfound strength, on the other hand, was a puzzle and a concern. His wrinkled frame swelled with the winds of death and dark magic, and the dead responded to his smallest gesture. Kemmler's glittering gaze met Arkhan's, and the old man smiled widely, exposing a crooked cemetery of brown and black tombstone teeth.

Arkhan gave no sign that he had noticed the smile. Instead, he let his gaze slide past the puppet to the puppetmaster. Krell the Undying. Krell of the Great Axe, who Arkhan knew of old, and who had served as Nagash's right hand, as Arkhan was his left. The ancient wight, clad in his ornate armour, which was stained a rusty hue by the oceans of gore that he had waded through over the centuries, loomed over Kemmler, his terrible axe hanging from his hand. Krell met Arkhan's gaze, and his great horned helm twitched slightly. Had that been a nod of greeting, a gesture of respect, or simply an idle shudder of the wretched berserker spirit that fuelled the wight, Arkhan wondered. There was no way to tell. Krell's mind was a roiling storm of battle-lust and blood-greed at the best of times.

If Kemmler was a worry, then Krell was a fixed point: the unassailable rampart upon which the future could be erected. Nagash had wrested Krell's mighty soul from the clutches of the Dark Gods, and bound it to him as inextricably as he had Arkhan's. They were his hands, his sword and shield, and his will made flesh.

But was that all they were? He thought again of the Everchild's taunt – had it been a taunt? – that he was, in some way, still the man he had been. He leaned against his staff, gnawing over her words. The effects of Morgiana's glamour had long since faded, but he could still feel the wounds it had wrought in his psyche. It had stirred the embers of a fire he'd thought long since extinguished. And if those embers still existed within him, what of Krell?

He gazed at the armoured bulk of the enormous wight. If there was some part of Krell as he had been left in that powerful husk, what might it do if it awakened? Would even Nagash be able to control such an entity, if its ire was aroused?

And what if it already had been? Krell met his gaze, and the two dead things stared at one another across the courtyard. Whose puppet are you? Arkhan thought. Kemmler laughed, and Arkhan turned towards him. The Lichemaster was directing two of the newly risen dead to fit a scavenged bridle and saddle onto the resurrected body of the lord of the keep. Then, if Krell broke his leash, he suspected he knew where the Great Axe would fall first. The thought was almost amusing. If anyone deserved to be savaged in that way, it was Kemmler.

'What is he doing?' Ogiers asked. 'Is he mad?' Arkhan looked back at his coterie of servants. The necromancers stood nearby in a nervous cluster, watching as Kemmler worked his sorceries. Even amongst the desecrators of the dead, the Lichemaster was in a league of his own. None of them had wanted to come, and Arkhan could tell that even the normally phlegmatic Fidduci was bothered by the company he now found himself in.

'You have eyes. What do you think?' the latter asked. The Tilean was furiously cleaning his spectacles, something he did when he was nervous. 'Of course he's mad. He's always been mad.'

'But useful, yes?' Kruk tittered, stroking his wispy beard. He hunched forward over his cousin's rotting shoulder and stroked the dead man's mouldering features affectionately. 'And it is no strange thing. A horse is a horse, of course – two legs or four, yes?' The crippled midget bounced in his harness and laughed at his own words.

Across the courtyard, Kemmler forced the dead lord to fall onto all fours. Kemmler laughed again, and raised his staff. Dark energy crackled along its length and bodies shuffled towards the kneeling lord. They knelt, linking arms and legs, and his intended mount climbed atop them. The whole twitching mass resembled nothing so much as an awkward pyramid for a moment. Then Kemmler swept his staff out and barked a guttural phrase, and the dead men began to sink and slide into one another with a variety of unpleasant sounds. Bones burst through sloughing meat and crashed into one another, splintering and reforming as flesh melted into flesh, and organs were discarded in splashes of blood and fluid.

A moment later, a conglomerate horror that reminded Arkhan of a spider, if a spider were made of writhing human bodies, pushed itself up on its multitude of hands and feet. Kemmler climbed into the saddle and hauled on the reins, forcing the thing to rear. He laughed again as it dropped down, and leered at Arkhan. 'Well, liche? What do you think of my new pet?'

'*Very pretty, Kemmler. You're welcome, by the way. A less genial master might not have allowed you to indulge your appetites for flesh-craft,*' Arkhan said. He was rewarded by a scowl from the necromancer. While Krell's loyalty was certain, Kemmler had a distaste for servitude that bordered on mania.

'Allow? We are partners, Nehekharan,' Kemmler said. 'You need me.' He grinned at Ogiers and the others. 'My power far outstrips that of your cat paws. Between them, they might just manage to summon a small horde, but you'll never take La Maisontaal Abbey without me.' He spat the name of their destination like a curse. Then, for Kemmler, perhaps it was. He had tried to assault the abbey more than once in his sordid career, and failed every time. Arkhan wondered if Kemmler could feel the call of the artefact hidden in the abbey's vaults even as he himself could. He suspected that Nagash whispered in the Lichemaster's ear, whether Kemmler knew it or not. Else how could he have controlled Krell – if he truly did.

'*Whatever you need to tell yourself, so long as you do as I say,*' Arkhan rasped. Kemmler made a face. He was different. Arkhan could not say why, or how, but it was as if something had been awakened in the necromancer. And Arkhan did not like it. He did not like Kemmler's newfound lucidity, or the threads of power that ran through him. '*We are both servants of a higher power. All of us here serve that power, lest anyone has forgotten.*'

He turned, taking in the other necromancers, and the lazing vampires, who met his gaze with glittering red glares. '*Do not think that you can stray. Time runs slow for the dead, but it runs all the same,*' he said, his voice carrying to every corner and ear capable of hearing and comprehending. He raised his staff and gestured to the sky, which boiled like a storm-tossed sea of green and black overhead. Sickly coronas rippled across the shroud of the night, and green scars carved through the black, streaking down towards distant mountains. It reminded Arkhan of the pearlescent flesh of a corpse succumbing to decay.

The world was rotting inside and out. It was dying. But it would linger on its deathbed for millennia, if the thrones and dominations that stood arrayed in his path had their way. The gods of men and daemons fought to own a world that had one foot in its grave. Only in death would it be redeemed. Only by the will of the Undying King.

The cat, in its usual place on his shoulder, stretched, bones and ligaments popping audibly as it dug its claws into his robes. He felt a surge of purpose in him as he continued to speak, though he wondered, deep in the secret places of his mind, whether those words were his, or those of Nagash. '*We all serve the will and whim of the Undying King, and it is his hand that guides us on this road. It is by his will that we all exist. Vampires were born from his black blood as surely as you walkers of the deathly way follow his wisdom and hearken to his teachings, as certainly as it was by his will that I persist in my task. We owe him our service, our loyalty, for without him, we would be dust and forgotten. Instead, we stand at the threshold of the world's heart and knock. We were the meek, and now we are the mighty. We serve the King of the World.*' He looked at Kemmler. '*All of us. Remember that.*'

Kemmler snarled and opened his mouth to reply, when a black horse galloped into the courtyard, hurtling through the shattered portcullis with preternatural grace. Its rider slid from the saddle as the horse came to a stop near Arkhan. The vampire gestured over his shoulder and barked, 'Company!' The vampire was one of a number Mannfred had insisted he take as an honour-guard. This one was called Crowfiend, he thought, though he resembled neither a crow nor a fiend as far as Arkhan could tell. Nonetheless, Arkhan preferred his company to that of Anark, the brutish commander of the armoured blood knights. That one stank of ambition and impatience, two things that Arkhan no longer understood or tolerated.

Arkhan cocked his head. '*Beastmen?*' His scouts had reported that a sizeable herd of the Chaos creatures were nearby, laying waste to a village in the valley below. Whether they desired battle, or merely wanted to scavenge in Arkhan's wake, he couldn't say.

'Bretonnians,' Erikan Crowfiend said. 'They're flying the flag of Quenelles.'

Arkhan felt a twinge of surprise. His forces had skirted Quenelles's southern border despite the fact that their goal lay in the strand of the Grey Mountains that marked the eastern edge of that province. Instead, Arkhan had led his followers further south, coming down out of the mountains into Carcassonne, rather than risking the wrath of Athel Loren.

The southernmost provinces had been the most heavily devastated in the civil war, stripped of foodstuffs and able-bodied men. He'd done so intentionally, hoping to leave himself a clear path to reach the abbey when he wished. But evidently, the province had not been as devastated as he thought.

'Tancred,' Kemmler snarled. There was an eagerness in that sound that disquieted Arkhan. He recalled suddenly that it had been a previous Duke of Quenelles who had defeated the Lichemaster during one of his periodic attempts to take La Maisontaal Abbey. It was the same duke, or perhaps his son, who had harried the Lichemaster out of Bretonnia and into the Grey Mountains.

'Possibly, or it could be any one of a hundred other displaced aristocrats from that province,' Arkhan said, gesturing sharply. 'It matters little. They are in our way. We will smash them, and continue on. Nagash must rise, and none will stand in our way.'

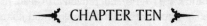

CHAPTER TEN

Hvargir Forest, the Border Princes

When Snikrat saw the tents, arrayed so temptingly on the blighted plains that hugged the edge of the forest, he immediately began to salivate. It looked like yet another of the petty man-thing princelings was attempting to flee. It was the perfect target – big enough to give a fight, small enough that the fight wouldn't last very long, thus presenting him, Snikrat the Magnificent, with the perfect opportunity to cement his heroism in the minds of his followers, without actually risking himself too much.

'Forward, brave warriors,' he chittered, flourishing his blade. 'Forward for the swift-glory of Clan Mordkin! Forward, at the command of me, Snikrat the Magnificent.' Clanrats stampeded past him, most of them already intent on looting the collection of tents and supply wagons, the latter seemingly unprotected. His stormvermin bodyguard, the aptly named Bonehides, knew better than to leave his side. Partially it was because it was their job to see that he survived, and partially because the wiser among the black-furred skaven knew Snikrat's reputation for sniffing out the best loot. Snikrat grinned and gestured towards the supply wagons. 'There! We must flank them, in their side, there, so that none escape, by which I mean flee and thus possibly evade us,' he hissed out loud, just in case any of Feskit's spies were listening. 'Come, my Bonehides – double-fast-move-move!'

Feskit had returned to the clan's lair with the bulk of their army, and the bulk of the loot a few days before, leaving Snikrat to pilfer the scraps and escort the slowest of the hundreds of filthy human slaves Clan Mordkin had taken in their ravaging of the Border Princes. Feskit likely thought he was being generous. Snikrat would show him true generosity soon enough – Feskit would have all the sharp steel he could stomach. The thought of vengeance, ill-defined and unlikely as it was, filled Snikrat with a surge of confidence. First he would kill any humans who tried to flee, as they inevitably did, being inveterate cowards, then he would loot the wagons – and then, yes, then, at some point, inevitably, after a suitable period of time, he would kill Feskit and wrest control of Clan Mordkin from his unworthy paws.

Granted, there were probably some steps in there he was missing, but he'd work those out when he came to them.

He led his stormvermin towards the wagons, looking forward to the screams of the man-things. But instead of screams, all he found was... Quiet. He stopped, and his warriors clattered to a halt around him. Snikrat's hackles itched, and he sniffed the air. It stank of blood and rot, which weren't the usual odours one associated with humans.

Snikrat heard the sounds of his warriors attacking the camp. To his finely attuned ears, it did not sound like a slaughter. At least, not the good kind. His musk-gland tightened and he fought down a sudden surge of irrational fear. What was there to be afraid of? Was he not Snikrat the Magnificent, heir to Feskit, whether the latter admitted it or not?

'Come-come, let us take the wagons, by which I mean these wheeled conveyances here, for the greater glory of skavenkind,' he said. His next words died in his furry throat as the air quivered with a low, harsh growl. That growl was joined by several more. Black, lean shapes moved across the top of the wagons or behind them, and Snikrat looked about, suddenly aware that the wagons weren't as undefended as he'd assumed.

Wolves crouched on the wagons or slunk from beneath them. Each bore numerous wounds, any one of which should have laid such beasts low, Snikrat saw as he extended his blade warily, his stormvermin clustering about him. Yet they didn't seem bothered by the broken shafts of arrows and spears that poked from their sagging hides. 'Dead-dead things,' a stormvermin squealed.

'Nonsense,' Snikrat blustered. 'Spears!'

His warriors levelled their cruelly barbed spears and locked shields, forming a rough hedgehog. He'd learned the tactic from a Tilean slave when he was but a pup. Sometimes he regretted eating the old man as quickly as he had. Nothing alive could break a Bonehides square, especially not a pack of quarrelsome curs.

Something laughed.

There was a promise implicit in that sound. Snikrat recognised it, for he himself had often laughed such a laugh while advancing on wounded or unwary prey. It was the laugh of a wolf-rat on the hunt, and his fur bristled with barely restrained terror as his eyes rotated. There, on the top of the wagons, something purple-faced and dead crouched, eyeing him through the lens of a monocle. The thing grinned, displaying row upon row of serrated, sharp teeth. Snikrat swallowed.

'Oh happy day. A-one, a-two, a-three... So many little rats for me,' the vampire snarled. Then, faster even than Snikrat the Magnificent could follow, it sprang upon them, its sword whistling down like the stroke of doom.

* * *

Brionne, Bretonnia

The spear thrust out at Malagor from the depths of the hay loft. He swatted the rusty head aside with his staff and thrust one long arm into the hay, seizing the spear-wielder and dragging him screaming into the firelight.

The village had already been burned once, but that hadn't stopped the beastmen from trying to burn it again. Malagor drew the wailing man towards him and calmly silenced him by slamming his head into a nearby post. Then, with a flap of his wings, he flew up and out of the barn, carrying his prize.

He caught an updraught, and rode the hot wind above the burning village. It had been prosperous, as such places went, before the war that had recently rocked this land. Malagor's lips peeled back from his fangs in a parody of a smile as he looked down and saw his warriors pursuing frightened peasants. There was little enough sport in this land, and he was glad enough to provide his followers with some small bit, before they went into battle.

The herds he led had been growing restless for lack of entertainment or battle. They chafed beneath his will, and he had been forced to meet more than one challenge in the days preceding the slaughter below. The village had been a gift from the Dark Gods; he'd been running low on chieftains, forced as he was to kill any who brayed a challenge.

But the gods were watching over their favoured child, and he felt their hands lift him up and their breath fill him, as they lent him strength and clarity. Their whispers had only grown stronger as he led the herds away from Athel Loren and into the human lands of Carcassonne, burning and pillaging the pitiful remnants of a once proud province along way. At their whim, he had held fast to the reins of the herd, and not unleashed them against Arkhan's forces when the bone-man and his followers had crossed the Vaults and into Carcassonne. Instead, he had followed them, keeping pace but never allowing the forces under his command to attack the dead legions marching across the landscape. He had been confused at first, but he now saw the truth of the gods' plan, and found it good.

His captive squirmed and Malagor tightened his grip. The man was screaming still, and pleading with him in the incoherent babble of the man-tongue. Malagor ignored it. He hadn't brought the creature up into the sky for a conversation. He had brought it to send a message.

Malagor growled in pleasure as his wings carried him out over the village and away. He saw the serpentine length of the River Brienne and the slumped ruin of the fortress that occupied the crags above the village. A column of smoke extended above the latter, blacker than the night sky it rose to meet. The screams of the dying carried on the wind, sped along by his sorceries. After all, what use a beacon if no one noticed?

And the village *was* a beacon. A signpost for the army that even now

advanced towards it, riding west from Quenelles. Malagor could hear the
horns of the Bretonnian host, and knew that they were close. His wings
flapped, carrying him to meet them. The gods whispered to him, telling
him what he must do, and he did it, happily. He swooped upwards, wings
beating, and tore open the belly of his captive. Its screams were like music,
and he howled in accompaniment as he gutted the squirming, hairless
thing.

The bone-man and his creatures were close by, in the castle on the high
hill overlooking the village and the river. They had been there for some time,
and to Malagor's eyes, the ruin glowed with the faint phosphorescence
of necromantic sorceries. He could feel the dead stirring, and something
else as well – something that drew the attentions of the gods. Whatever it
was, it was powerful, and the gods approved of that power. A surge of envy
washed through him as he went about his task, and he bit and tore at the
now limp body with more ferocity than was necessary. Blood splattered
his muzzle and chest, and gore matted his hair.

Butchery complete, he plunged down, wings folded, cutting through the
air like a missile fired from a ballista, his burden dangling behind him, its
slick intestines looped about his gnarled, hairy fist. At the last possible
moment, he banked, hurtling upwards again even as he released the mutilated corpse, and let it tumble gracelessly to the ground before the front
ranks of the approaching army. Then Malagor was streaking upwards,
across the face of the moon and back towards the village. His warriors
would need to be on the move when the Bretonnians arrived, or they would
become bogged down in battle.

They would lead the humans on a merry chase, and right into the bone-
man's army. The will of the gods caressed his thoughts, soothing his envy
and anger, as if to say, *See? See what we do for you, oh best beloved child?
See how we spare your lives? See how we deliver victory unto you? And all
we ask is that you claim it, as we command.*

The bone-man's army would be weakened by battle, like a stag after
it has fought off a rival, if it was not destroyed outright. Malagor could
smell the stink of strange magics on the human army. But if the bone-man
triumphed, then, like wolves, Malagor and his followers would harry them
as they marched on. The gods whispered of living men amongst the dead,
whose will kept the legions marching. They would be Malagor's prey.
Without them, Arkhan would be forced to use more and more of his power
to keep the dead moving, and less of it to protect himself.

And then, when he was stretched to his utmost, Malagor would strike.
The bone-man would die again... And this time, he would stay dead.

Tancred spurred his horse forwards, his heart hammering in his chest.
He felt weighed down by fear and excitement, by glorious purpose. He let
his lance dip and it rolled in his grip as he angled it towards the massive,

red-armoured shape of Krell of the Great Axe, one of a pair of curses that had haunted the ducal line of Quenelles for centuries. The lance struck like a thunderbolt and exploded in a cloud of splinters. The remnants of it were ripped from his hand and he let it go as his destrier galloped past the reeling wight. Krell roared like a wounded lion and made a flailing grasp for his horse's tail.

Tancred and his men had left La Maisontaal Abbey weeks earlier, in an effort both to conserve what supplies the abbey-garrison had, and to hunt down a particularly pernicious band of beastmen, which had been haunting the border country since the end of the civil war. The survivors of their attacks spoke of one with wings, which had interested Tancred. Such a beast was bound to be important in some fashion, for obvious reasons.

He put little stock in the whispers of the peasantry, who murmured the name of Malagor, for that creature was nothing more than a fairy tale. While the beastmen did have their war-leaders and shamans, they were brute things, no more dangerous than the orcish equivalent. To think that there was one whom all such dark and loathsome creatures would bow to was laughable.

Tancred had brought Anthelme with him on the hunt, leaving the defence of the abbey in the hands of Theoderic and the others. He had had his misgivings at first, but he knew that such a hunt might help ease the chafing boredom of garrison duty his restive knights were already complaining of. Now it was beginning to look as if he were being guided by the Lady herself. When they'd sighted the motley horde of braying beastmen, the creatures had broken and fled rather than giving honest battle, and in pursuing them, Tancred and his warriors had crashed right into the mustering forces of the very enemy he had been preparing the abbey's defences against.

Arkhan the Black had returned to Bretonnia, as Lady Elynesse, Dowager of Charnorte, had foretold, and he'd brought with him an army of the dead: an army that was Tancred's duty, and honour to destroy here and now, before it reached the abbey. He had ordered his men to charge before the undead could organise their battle line, and, like a lance of purest blue and silver, the knightly host of Quenelles had done so, driving home into the sea of rotting flesh and brown bone. He had lost sight of Anthelme in that first, glorious charge, but he could spare no thought for his cousin, not when the cause of so much of his family's anguish stood before him.

Tancred bent and snatched up his morning star from where it dangled from his saddle. It had been his father's, who had wielded it in battle against Krell and his cackling master decades ago. Now it was the son's turn to do the same. 'Father, guide my hand,' Tancred growled as he jerked on his warhorse's reins, causing the animal to rear and turn. He spotted Krell immediately. The wight was already charging towards him, bulling aside the living and the dead alike in his eagerness to get to grips with Tancred. The black axe flashed as Tancred rode past. He slashed at the beast with his morning star.

Krell roared again, a wheezing wail that nearly froze Tancred's blood in his veins. The dreadful axe came around again, braining Tancred's mount even as the animal lashed out at the dead man with its hooves. Krell staggered. The destrier fell, and Tancred was forced to hurl himself away from it and avoid being caught under the dying beast. He landed hard, his armour digging into him. He clambered to his feet as Krell lunged over the body of his horse.

Tancred stumbled aside, narrowly avoiding Krell's blow. The axe hammered into the ground. Tancred whirled back and sent the head of the morning star singing out to strike Krell's wrist. The wight let go of his axe and grabbed for the mace. He seized the spiked ball and jerked it from Tancred's grip. He hurled it aside as he grabbed for Tancred with his free hand. Armoured fingers dug into Tancred's helmet, causing the metal to buckle with an ear-splitting whine. Tancred clawed for the sword at his waist as Krell forced him back, his heels slipping in the mud. The wight was impossibly strong, and when he fastened his other hand on Tancred's helmet, Tancred knew he had to break the creature's grip before his skull burst like a grape. He drew his sword and slashed out at Krell's belly in one motion. Blessed steel, bathed in holy waters by the handmaidens of the Lady herself, carved a gouge in the blood-stained armour.

Krell shrieked and stepped back, releasing Tancred. The latter tore his ruined helm from his head as Krell turned to retrieve his axe. 'No, monster! You've escaped justice once too often,' Tancred bellowed. He cut at the wight's hands, forcing Krell to jerk back. Tancred knew that if the undead warrior got his hands on his axe, there would be little chance of stopping him. He slashed at him again, driving the monster back a step. He felt the strength of purpose flood him, washing away his earlier doubts and spurring him on. His father had gone to his grave, cursing the names of Krell and Kemmler. They had been a weight on his soul that had never been dislodged, and it had dragged him down into sour death at the Battle of Montfort Bridge. But now, Tancred could avenge his father, and Quenelles as well.

He hammered at Krell, and witch-fire crawled up his blade with every blow. He heard the singing of the handmaidens of the Lady, and felt their hands upon his shoulders, guiding him. Every blow he struck was with her blessing, and Krell staggered and reeled as strange fires crawled across his grisly armour and ichors dripped from the sharp, jagged plates like blood. His fleshless jaws gaped in a bellicose snarl and he swatted at Tancred, like a bear clawing at leaping hounds. Men joined Tancred. He still saw no sign of Anthelme, but he had no time to worry. All that mattered was Krell. Spears stabbed at the beast from every side, digging at the wounds Tancred had already made.

The wight flailed about like a blind man, splintering spears and driving back his attackers, but more pressed forward. Tancred growled in satisfaction and looked around. Kemmler would be close by. If he could find the madman, and put an end to him, then Krell would be easier to dispatch once and for all.

'Tancred!' a voice shrieked. Tancred spun, and only just interposed his sword as a stream of crackling, sour-hued fire swept towards him. The flames parted around the blade. A wizened, crooked figure strode through the press of battle as if it were no more important than the squabbling of vermin. 'Duke of Quenelles, I thought you gone to the worms at Montfort Bridge,' Heinrich Kemmler snarled. He swept out his staff and his blade. The skull atop the former chattered like a berserk ape as Kemmler drew close.

'My father, necromancer,' Tancred said. He felt strangely calm. It was as if every moment of his life had led to this point. As if this single moment of confrontation were his reason for being. He felt a weight upon him that he had never felt before, save the first day he had taken up the burden of his ducal duties and privileges. 'I am the son, and it falls to me to see that you at last pay your debt to the world.'

Kemmler cackled and weird shadows wreathed him, obscuring him from sight as Tancred attacked. Tancred struck out at him, but his blade bit nothing but air again and again. 'What's the matter, Tancred? Too long off the tourney field?' Kemmler hissed, as though he were right beside him. A blow caught Tancred in the back and he lurched forward. He turned, but the flickering shadow-shape was gone before he could so much as thrust. More blows came at him. One of his pauldrons was torn from his shoulder, and rags of chainmail were ripped from his torso. His surcoat was in tatters and his pulse hammered in his head painfully. He couldn't breathe, could barely see for the sweat, and his muscles trembled with fatigue.

'I've been waiting for this for centuries,' the necromancer said, circling him, his form rippling like a rag caught in a wind. 'Your father and grand-father – your whole stinking line – has harried me from the day I first had the misfortune to set foot in this pig's wallow of a country. Again and again I have been forced to flee from you, but no more. Today your line ends screaming...'

Out of the corner of his eye, Tancred saw the old man's shape waver into solidity. The necromancer raised his sword for a killing blow, his face twisted in a leer of satisfaction. Tancred spun and his blade pierced the old man's side, tearing through his flickering cloak. Kemmler screeched like a dying cat and he flailed at his enemy with his blade. Tancred avoided the wild blows and moved in for the kill. He could hear Krell roaring behind him, but he concentrated on the hateful, wrinkled, fear-taut features of the necromancer before him. He drove his shoulder into the old man's chest and knocked him sprawling. 'No, old devil, this is the end of you,' Tancred said. He stood over Kemmler, and raised his blade in both hands. 'For my father, and in the name of all those whom you have slain and defiled, you will die.'

Before he could strike, however, he felt a sudden ripping pain, and then everything was numb. The world spun crazily. He struck the muddy ground, but felt nothing. He couldn't feel his legs or his arms. He saw a headless body – *whose body was that?* – totter, drop its sword, and fall nearby. Everything felt cold now, and he couldn't breathe. He saw Krell, axe dripping with gore, kick the headless body aside, and drag Kemmler to his feet. *Whose body?* he thought again, as darkness closed in at the edges of his vision. *Whose body is that?*

Then, he thought nothing at all.

Heinrich Kemmler watched as Tancred's head rolled through the mud. He tried to smile, but all he could muster was a grimace of pain. He levered himself awkwardly to his feet with his staff, its skulls, hung from it with copper chains long ago gone green with verdigris, dangling grotesquely. It was a potent artefact, his staff, and he drew strength from it as he gazed down at the wound Tancred had left him as a parting farewell. Blood seeped through his coat and dripped down into the dirt. The wound hurt, but he'd suffered worse in his lifetime. He scrubbed a boot through the dirt. 'That's the last taste you'll have of me,' he hissed. He looked up as a shadow fell over him.

Krell, coming to check on him, like a faithful hound. Or perhaps a houndmaster, checking on his pet. As he gazed up at the scarred and pitted skull of the wight, Kemmler wondered, and not for the first time, if he was fully in control of his own fate. He thought of the shape he sometimes saw, that seemed to lurk in Krell's shadow – a phantom presence of malevolent weight and titanic malice. He thought that it was the same shape that padded through his fitful dreams on those rare occasions when sleep came. It whispered to him, indeed had been whispering to him all of his life, even as a young man, after he'd first stumbled upon those badly translated copies of the Books of Nagash in his father's haphazard ancestral library.

Those books had started him on his journey, the first steps that had seen him defy death in all of its forms, benign or sinister. He had fought rivals and enemies alike, striving to stand alone. The Council of Nine and the Charnel Congress – rival consortiums of necromancers – had faded before his might, their petty grave-magics swept aside by his fierce and singular will. He had pillaged the library of Lady Khemalla of Lahmia in Miragliano and driven the vampiress from her den and the city, and in the crypts beneath Castle Vermisace he had bound the liches of the Black Circle to his service, earning him the sobriquet 'Lichemaster'.

He had counselled counts, princes and petty kings. He had gathered a library of necromantic lore second only to the fabled libraries of forsaken Nagashizzar. He had waged a cruel, secret war on men, dwarfs and elves, prying their secret knowledge from them, and with every death rattle and dying sigh the voice in his head, the pressing *thing* that had encouraged him and driven him, had purred with delight. Until one day, it had gone silent.

It had abandoned him to a life of scurrying through the hills, a broken, half-mad beggar, his only companion a silent, brooding engine of destruction, whose loyalties were unfathomable. He had thought, once, that Krell was his. Now he knew better. Now he knew that they had been at best, partners, and at worst, slaves of some other mind.

Kemmler's eyes found the tall, thin shape of Arkhan the Black, as the liche oversaw the rout of the remaining Bretonnian forces. With Tancred's death, they'd lost heart. In some ways, the living and the dead were remarkably similar. He glared at the liche and then stooped to retrieve his sword. He grunted with pain, but hefted the blade thoughtfully.

Arkhan heard the same voice he had, Kemmler knew. Krell as well; both liche and wight were slaves to it. And that was the fate it intended for Kemmler. Just another puppet. He could hear it again, though only faintly. But it was growing louder, becoming a demanding drumbeat in his fevered brain. It was inevitable that he would surrender.

Kemmler looked at Krell. He spat at the wight's feet and sheathed his sword. 'Inevitability is for lesser men.'

◄ CHAPTER ELEVEN ►

Skull River, the Border Princes

Mannfred brought his blade down on the rat ogre's broad skull, cleaving it from ears to molars. The beast slid away, releasing its grip on Mannfred's mount, as he jerked his blade free in a welter of blood and brains. Two more of the oversized vermin lumbered towards him, growling and giving high-pitched bellows. He spurred his mount towards them, his teeth bared in a snarl. As his skeleton steed slipped between the two creatures, he swept his sword out in a single scythe-like motion, sending the heads of both monsters flying.

'A heady blow, cousin,' Markos crowed, from nearby. The other vampire's armour was drenched in skaven blood, and his blade was black with it from tip to the elbow of his sword arm. Markos, like the other Drakenhof Templars, had been at the centre of every recent battle.

'Shut up and see to our flanks, Markos,' Mannfred snapped, shaking the blood from his sword. 'I tire of this.' He stood up in his saddle and looked around. When his scouts had brought him stories of the lands ahead literally swarming with the rat-things, he had thought they were exaggerating. But in the past weeks, he had seen that, if anything, his spies had been conservative in their estimates of the number of skaven running roughshod over the Border Princes. This was the fifth – and largest of them all by far – horde in as many weeks to bar his path, and he was growing frustrated.

It was as if some unseen power were seeking to block him from getting to Mad Dog Pass. He'd thought it was the skaven, at first, but the hordes he faced were more intent on pillage and loot than on stopping him. They inevitably attempted to retreat when they saw the true nature of the forces at his disposal, as had the first such band they'd encountered.

He had taken the time to question the spirits of the deceased ratmen, and had found the dead ones no less deceitful than the living vermin. In his frustration, he had torn apart more skaven souls than he had slain living ones. But in the end, his suspicions had been confirmed – the Under-Empire

251

had risen, and the skaven were at last united. They had eradicated Tilea and Estalia, and Araby was even now under siege from above and below.

No, it wasn't the skaven; it was something in the air itself. Arkhan was right. Forces were moving in opposition to them, and not merely those from the expected quarters. Mannfred was playing dice with the Dark Gods themselves. The thought did not frighten him. Rather, it invigorated him. If the Chaos gods were taking a hand in affairs so directly, then he was on the right path. He had faced the servants of Chaos before, and emerged triumphant. This time would be no different.

He looked up at the dark sky, where strange green coronas still swirled and crawled, like flies on the flesh of a corpse, and laughed. 'Come then,' he said. 'Come and set yourselves against me, oh powers and principalities of madness. Let the heavens themselves crumble in, and the earth turn to mud beneath my feet, and I will still triumph. Send your daemons and proxies, if you would, and I will show you that in this fallen world there is one, at least, who does not fear you. I have beaten gods and men before, and you will be no different. The veil of perfect night shall fall on this world, and order and perfection shall reign, according to my will and no other.'

The air seemed to thicken about him for a moment, and he thought he saw cosmic faces stretched across the sky above, glaring down at him in tenebrous fascination. He felt the weight of their gaze on his soul and mind, and he swept his sword out in a gesture of challenge.

A screech alerted him to the skaven retreat, and he looked down. The ratkin were fleeing with all the orderly precision of their four-legged cousins. He fancied that more of the pestilential vermin died in the retreat than in the battle itself. Then, considering the sheer size of the horde in question, perhaps that wasn't all that surprising.

'They flee, my lord,' Duke Forzini said as his horse trotted past. His armour, like Markos's, was dripping with blood, and his sword dangled loosely in his grip. 'If we press forward, we might catch them.' The duke had taken to vampirism with admirable rapidity, and his mouth and beard were matted with gore. Forzini had personally inducted most of his household knights into a state of undeath, binding them to him with blood where before they had been loyal only to his gold.

'No need,' Mannfred said. He sheathed his blade. 'They are going in the same direction we are, and the fear they carry with them will infect those who stand between us and our goal.' He looked about him, and smiled cruelly. Then, with a gesture, he drew the corpses of the two rat ogres he'd slain to their feet. 'Besides, we have a wealth of new recruits to add to our ranks.' More skaven followed the rat ogres' example, their torn and mutilated bodies sliding and shuffling upright.

Despite his bravado, and despite the sheer number of skaven corpses that were even now being washed away down the roaring waters of the Skull River, the battle had been a close one – this swarm had been the largest his forces had yet faced. An ocean of squealing bodies and ramshackle war engines that had momentarily blanketed the horizon. Mannfred had been forced to rouse the dead of three ravaged fortress towns to throw at the horde.

Speed and subtlety alone was no longer going to serve, he thought. The closer they drew to Mad Dog Pass, the greater the likelihood that he would find himself facing similarly sized hordes of skaven. He needed every corpse he could find to throw at them.

He felt a tremor, and glanced up at the Claw of Nagash, where it sat atop the staff strapped to his back. The fingers twitched and stretched, as though gesturing towards the mountains rising in the distance. It seemed that its movements were becoming more agitated the closer they came to Mad Dog Pass, almost as if it were impatient to be reunited with the blade that had severed it from Nagash's wrist, once upon a time. Mannfred could almost feel the dark magics radiating from the Fellblade. His palms itched to hold it, and he could sense the hum of its deadly energies. His hand clenched.

You don't have it yet, boy. You still have a million ratmen between you and that dark blade, and you'd best not forget it, Vlad said. Mannfred opened his hands and looked resolutely away from the shifting shadow-shape that scratched at the edges of his attention. Vlad's voice had only become stronger as they came closer to the Fellblade. When he fought, there was Vlad, watching him as though he were still a boy on the proving ground, fumbling with his blade. Vlad had always watched him that way.

'Nothing I did was ever up to your standards, was it, old man? I never measured up to you or your blasted queen, or the bloody champion. And you wonder why I stole that cursed bauble...' he muttered, running his hands over his scalp. 'Yet here I sit, on the cusp of victory. And where are you? Ash on the wind.'

Better ash than a body rotting in a bog, Vlad said. *Did you enjoy it? Sunk in the mire, a hole in your heart, unable to move or scream. I wonder, did something of that tainted place creep into your veins? Is that why you changed? You were always so vain, and now, you are as foul and as bestial as any of those treacherous animals I locked away in the vaults below Castle Draken-hof. Why, you'll take to wing any day now, I'd wager. You'll shed all pretence, just like Konrad, and succumb to the madness in your blood...*

Mannfred snarled. His hand flew to the hilt of his blade and he drew the sword, twisting around in his saddle to face the shade of his mentor. The tip of his blade narrowly missed Markos's nose as he rode up. The other vampire jerked back and nearly fell from his saddle. 'Are you mad?' he snarled.

'Mind your tone, cousin,' Mannfred growled. He fought to control his expression. 'You shouldn't sneak up on me while I am concentrating.' He looked about, and saw that every dead thing around was standing at attention, empty eyes fixed on him. He could feel the power of the Claw mingling with his own as it spread outwards and roused the inhabitant of every grave for miles around, be it skaven, human, orc or animal. More, he could feel them stumbling forwards at his call, answering his summons. Thousands of rotting corpses and tormented spirits were coming in response to his command.

'How many more cadavers do we require?' Markos muttered, looking around at the swaying dead who surrounded them.

Mannfred smiled nastily. 'Enough to drown the skaven in their burrows, cousin. I will bury them in the bodies of their kin. Come – time slips away, and I would not have my prize do the same!'

Quenelles, Bretonnia

When it came time to make camp, the village had seemed the best spot. It was still mostly intact, if all but abandoned. They had seen smoke rising up into the overcast and cloud-darkened sky, and Anark, the Crowfiend and the other vampires had ridden pell-mell to claim whatever living blood remained in the village. Unfortunately for them, all of the villagers who had not fled were piled up on a pyre in the centre of the market square, burned to a crisp.

Luckily, the vampires had glutted themselves during the battle several days before. But Arkhan had been hoping to add the inhabitants to his host. Too many of the dead had been irretrievably lost in that battle. If they were to take La Maisontaal Abbey, and then escape Bretonnia in the aftermath, they would need a host of considerably larger size than they currently had.

'No blood, no corpses of any worth – it's almost as if someone got here ahead of us,' Erikan Crowfiend said as he rode up to Arkhan to deliver his report. A gaggle of ghouls gambolled after his horse. The Crowfiend had an affinity for the flesh-eaters and he had begun to assert some control over the numberless cannibals that haunted the meadows of Quenelles. 'I've sent out scouts, but none of them have come back yet.'

Arkhan pondered his comment silently. Every graveyard and town they had come to since crossing the border into Quenelles had been razed to the cellar stones, and the bodies of the dead mangled or burned beyond use. Some of that, he knew, was down to the ghouls, who spilled across Bretonnia like locusts, feeding on the dead left behind by the civil war. But he could not escape the feeling that potential lines of supply were being cut one by one by unseen enemies.

In all the centuries of his existence, Arkhan had learned much of the arts of war. The back-alley gambler had become a hardened battlefield general, who knew the way of the refused flank, the feint and the coordinated onslaught. He knew when he was facing a planned attack, even if it looked like coincidence or random chance.

There was a mind working against his, and he suspected he knew where

it hid. More than once, he had caught the creeping moth-wing touch of
dark magics at the edges of his senses. Not necromancy, but something
older and fouler by far. The magics of ruination and entropy. The magics
of the Dark Gods. He could taste them on the air, as he had when he'd
breached the wall of faith in Sylvania. They were gathering their strength,
as the winds of magic writhed in torment. Even now, the air stank of the
breath of the Dark Gods. It hung thick and foul and close, obscuring his
sorcerous senses.

He glanced up, and saw a shape, circling far above. For a moment, he
mistook it for an unusually large carrion bird. Then, he realised that he had
seen that dim, flapping form before. It had harried his host for leagues.
It never drew too close, but it had pursued them relentlessly. It was this
thing that radiated the magics he sensed, he was certain. It followed him,
and a horde of beastmen followed it, the very beastmen who had led the
Bretonnians upon him, and now loped in his wake like wolves haunting
the trail of a dying stag. They had been shadowing the undead since the
battle with Tancred's forces.

Arkhan had dismissed the creatures at first, thinking them little better
than the ghoul packs that now loped in the wake of his host. But his scouts
had brought him reports that the creatures had followed them from the
battlefield, shadowing his forces, never engaging in conflict, and always
fleeing if challenged. The herd was also growing in size. Worse, it was doing
so more quickly than his own forces. He felt as if he were being driven forwards, like the beast before the hunters, and there was nothing for it but
to run as quickly as possible.

'Bah, we will find blood and corpses aplenty if we but follow Tancred's army
and destroy it. They'll make for Castle Brenache. With the forces at our disposal we can tear it down stone by stone,' Kemmler said. Arkhan ignored him.
'Are you listening to me, liche?' Kemmler snapped. He grabbed Arkhan's arm.

Arkhan knocked Heinrich Kemmler sprawling. '*You are a fool, old man.
Your obsession has almost cost us everything. We are done with your fantasies
of vengeance.*' The liche pinned Kemmler in place with his staff. Krell moved
towards them, axe not quite raised. Arkhan fixed the wight with a glare,
and the cat perched on his shoulder hissed at the wight. Krell hesitated,
seemingly uncertain who to strike. Arkhan decided not to press the issue.

He lifted his staff and stepped back. '*You have cost me an asset, and burdened us all, in the name of bruised pride and ego.*' Kruk had died in the
battle with the Bretonnians. Kemmler had abandoned his position to attack
his old enemy, leaving Kruk exposed to the lances of the knights, and the
little necromancer had been dislodged from his harness somehow. He'd
subsequently been trodden into a red pulp by the galloping hooves of the
knights' horses. Ogiers and Fidduci had been able to keep those dead under
the little man's control upright, but only just. With Kemmler distracted by
Tancred, Arkhan's army had nearly disintegrated.

If the Bretonnians had not routed when they had, Arkhan knew, it was very likely that his mission would have been over before it had even truly begun, so devastating had their initial charge been. Luckily, the core of his army was still intact – the wights and skeletons he'd drawn from the mole-hills and tombs of the Vaults, and the blood knights who Mannfred had foisted on him. And he too had recovered the ancient canopic jars that he had cached on the border of Quenelles, which housed the dust and ashes of the Silent Legion.

Over the course of centuries, Arkhan had carefully seeded many des-olate and isolated places with unliving servants, so that should he ever find himself in need, he would have warriors to call on. The Silent Legion were one such group. In ages past, they had served Nagash, and it was only the increasing strength of the winds of magic that would enable Arkhan to restore them to fighting vigour and control them. But he needed time to prepare the proper rites to do so. Time that Kemmler had cost them.

'You promised me Tancred's head,' Kemmler snarled as Krell helped him to his feet. The old man stank of blood and indignation, and he pressed a hand to his side, which was stained dark. Tancred hadn't died without leaving his enemy a painful reminder of their dalliance. That wound had weakened Kemmler, and slowed down their advance considerably. 'I was merely taking my due, and I won you the battle in the process.'

'*It should not have been a battle,*' Arkhan said. '*It should have been a slaughter. We should have drowned them in a sea of rotting flesh and mould-ering bone, and swept them aside in minutes. Instead, we were drawn out into a pointless struggle that lasted more than a day. We have no time for this.*'

'Maybe you don't,' Kemmler spat. 'But Bretonnia owes me a pound of flesh and I intend to collect!' He gripped his staff so tightly that the ancient wood creaked.

'*What you think you are owed is of no concern to me,*' Arkhan said. '*La Maisontaal Abbey is only a few days' march from here, and I would give our enemies no more time to prepare. I care nothing for Brenache, or your grudge. We have wasted enough time.*'

'Time, time, *time,*' Kemmler mocked. 'You act as if you still live, and that one day is different from another. What matters when we do it, so long as it is done. Let Nagash wait.'

The zombie cat twitched and fixed Kemmler with a glare that the old necromancer didn't seem to notice. Arkhan reached up to stroke its head. '*Nagash isn't what I'm worried about. How long do you think we have before the new king of this ravaged land notices that we've invaded? Or the rulers of Athel Loren? They are occupied, for now, but that will not last forever. And there are more enemies abroad than just men and elves.*'

'Who would dare challenge the most mighty and puissant Arkhan, eh?' Fidduci broke in, before Kemmler could spit what was certain to be an acidic reply. The Tilean took off his spectacles and began to clean them on the hem of his filthy robe.

The spear caught him just between his narrow shoulder blades and punched through his chest in an explosion of gore. Ogiers, who'd been standing beside him, fell back with a yelp. Arkhan looked up as a howl echoed through the air. The flying shape had drifted lower, and he saw then that it was no bird, but instead a winged beastman. It swooped upwards with a triumphant roar and he knew then that it had thrown the spear. Kemmler had distracted him, and he had not seen the beast's approach.

Fidduci coughed blood and reached out, weakly, towards Arkhan. The liche ignored him, and began to ready a sorcerous bolt. He intended to pluck the flying beast from the sky for its temerity. A shout drew his attention before he could do so, however. He saw Anark and the other vampires riding back towards him, smashing aside zombies in the process. 'Beware!' Anark bellowed. 'It's a trap!'

Horns wailed and Arkhan cursed as beastmen came charging out of hiding in a rush, exploding from the meadows around the village, and out of the seemingly empty shacks, howling and snarling. They tore through the ranks of the unprepared dead like starving wolves, with crude axes and chopping blades. Arkhan whirled around, and black lightning streaked from his eyes, incinerating a dozen of the malformed creatures. It wasn't enough. A gor, foam dripping from its muzzle, leapt over the burning, smoking remains of its fellows and brought a blade down on Ogiers's skull, splitting the Bretonnian's head from crown to jaw.

As the necromancer fell, Arkhan obliterated his killer. Power roiled within him, and spewed out in murderous waves, laying beastmen low by the score. But still they came on, their eyes bulging and froth clinging to their lips. They had been driven beyond the bounds of madness, and there was no fear in them. Magic had hidden their presence from him, magic wielded by the flying creature that even now circled above him, its jeering laughter drifting down like raindrops. It was all Kemmler's fault. The Lichemaster had tarried too long, playing his games of spite with Tancred, and been wounded for it. They'd lost half of their army at a stroke, as Fidduci fell, bleeding and hurting. And now, the children of Chaos were attempting to take advantage of their weakened state. He could almost hear the laughter of the Dark Gods, echoing down from the storm-stirred heavens.

Arkhan was forced to fall back. The cat yowled and hissed as it clung to his shoulder, and he drew his tomb-blade, only just in time to block a blow aimed at his skull. He spun, crushing his attacker's head with the end of his staff. For a moment, he won clear. But it didn't last.

The minotaur was the largest of its brutish kind that Arkhan had ever had the misfortune to see. It rampaged towards him, bellowing furiously, bashing aside its smaller cousins heedlessly as it came closer to him, the great axe in its hand licking out towards him. Arkhan thrust his staff and his blade up, crossing them to catch the blow as it fell. The axe was the same size as his torso, and it was all that he could do to catch the blade. The force of the blow drove him down to one knee. He strained against the weight of the axe as the minotaur hunched forward, trying to break his guard through sheer brute strength.

Then, suddenly, a red-armoured form bulled into the creature from the side, rocking it away from Arkhan. The minotaur stumbled back, lowing in confusion. Krell stomped forward, pursuing the creature. The two axes met in a crash of steel again and again as beast and wight fought. The minotaur was the stronger of the two, but Krell was by far the better warrior, and the wight's greater skill with the axe began to tell. The minotaur staggered in a circle, pursued by Krell, who opened wound after wound in its hide. Blood splashed onto the ground as the giant, bull-headed beast sank down onto all fours and gave a piteous groan. Krell planted a boot against its shoulder and sent it flopping over onto its back.

As Krell finished off the minotaur, Arkhan shoved himself to his feet and looked up, hunting for the flying creature he'd seen before. That one was the true danger, he knew. That one had the ear of the Dark Gods, else why would it be able to fly?

But the creature was nowhere to be seen. It had vanished, and, as Arkhan watched, its followers departed as well. Crude horns wailed and the beastmen began to retreat in ragged disorder, streaming back into the night, not altogether reluctantly. They had been eager enough for a fight when they'd arrived, but the dead made for bad sport.

He looked around. Fidduci had finally succumbed to the spear that had pinned him to the earth. His spectacles had fallen from his nerveless fingers to shatter on the ground, and his black teeth were wet with blood. Ogiers lay nearby, still twitching in his death throes. Arkhan felt the weight of his army settle on his shoulders, like a sodden blanket.

He wondered, as he leaned against his staff, if this had been his enemies' intent all along. His trusted servants were dead, and his effectiveness lessened. Now he had only Kemmler to help him. Kemmler, who had already proven himself as unreliable as ever. Kemmler, who was more powerful now than Arkhan had ever seen him.

Kemmler cackled nearby as he jerked Fidduci's and Ogiers's bodies to their feet. He appeared unconcerned about the state of affairs, and his coarse, chilling laughter echoed over what had, only moments before, been a scene of slaughter.

Arkhan watched him, pondering.

Castle Sternieste, Sylvania

Volkmar was on the plain of bones again, the stink of a hundred thousand charnel fires thick in his nose and lungs. His hammer hung broken and heavy in his hands, and his armour seemed to constrict about him like a giant hand clutching his torso. He was tired, so tired, but he couldn't give up. He refused to surrender.

Catechisms sprang unbidden to his lips and rattled through the stinking air. Passages and entire pages from holy books shot out into the grey emptiness. He shouted out Sigmar's name, and shrieked out the story of the Empire's founder.

Sigmar.

Sigmar.

Sigmar!

The name pierced the emptiness like a well-thrown spear, and it hung quivering there for a moment, gaining strength. Then, as it had before, the ground began to move and shift, as if something vast were burrowing beneath it. The bones rattled and fell as the thing drew closer to the surface and ploughed after him.

He heard Aliathra's voice, somewhere far above and behind him. Though he could not make out her words, he knew that she was calling out to him, pleading with him not to fight this time, but to run.

Volkmar hesitated, and then did as she bade. The thing, the force, the daemon, wanted him to fight. He knew it in the marrow of his bones. It wanted him to fight, so that it could sweep over him and bowl him under. So he ran. And it followed him. A hideous voice, as loud and as deep as the tolling of the monstrous bells of Castle Sternieste, smashed at him, trying to force him to make a stand.

Instead, he ran harder, faster, forcing his body to keep moving. And he shouted Sigmar's name as he ran. Every time the word left his lips, the terrible voice seemed to weaken a little bit. But it did not cease its hunt.

Bones slipped and rolled beneath his feet. The hands of the dead clawed at his legs as they always did, dragging him down. Fleshless jaws bit down on him, and bony fingers tore at him, and he swung about with his hammer, trying to free himself. Too late, though. Always too late.

A mountain of bones rose over him, blotting out the grey light. The bones shifted and squirmed, shaping themselves into a vast countenance, titanic and loathsome. Eyes like twin suns blazed down at him, and a breath of grave-wind washed over him, searing his lungs and withering his flesh. He felt his skin shrink taut on his bones, and his marrow curdle as the wind enveloped him. He lifted his hammer, too weak to do anything else.

And then, Volkmar the Grim woke up.

Volkmar stirred groggily in his chains. Sleep still held him in its clutches, and the faintest ghost of a distant howl rippled through the underside of his mind. He felt the air stir, and knew that they had a visitor. He smelt the stink of old blood, and stale perfume, and knew that the new mistress of the castle had come to visit.

Mannfred was gone. Where, he could not say, but he had suspicions aplenty. That left a castle full of vampires still, and there was no hope of escape. That realisation had come to him slowly but surely, with insidious certainty. There was no hope, of escape or even survival. But perhaps whatever Mannfred was planning could still be thwarted. Perhaps the Empire could be spared whatever monstrous evil the vampire sought to unleash.

Then, perhaps not.

He heard the vampire as she drew close, passing amongst Mannfred's collection. Did she linger over the Crown, perhaps, and let her fingers drift over the books?

'What would you give me, if I were to kill one of you?' the vampire asked, without preamble. She looked up at Volkmar with something approaching loathing. The Grand Theogonist hung in his chains like a side of beef, his eyes not quite closed, his breathing shallow. 'That being the only way to defeat our lord and master, of course. He had nine. Now he has eight. He can do nothing with seven.' She cocked her head like a falcon sighting prey, and her eyes slid towards Aliathra, who hung nearby, head lolling, her blonde locks spilling over her pale face, matted with blood and filth. 'I know that you are conscious, elf. I know that you are listening.' Her eyes slid back to Volkmar. 'As are you, old man. Pretending to be unconscious will avail you nothing.'

'Your kind only bargains for two reasons,' Volkmar rasped. *He had nine...* Lupio Blaze was dead, then. They had come and taken the knight in the evening. They had not brought him back. He had suspected that the Tilean was dead. 'Either you are bored... or afraid,' One blood-gummed eyelid cracked wide. 'Which is it, Elize von Carstein?' The old man laughed as her eyes widened slightly. He allowed himself to feel a brief surge of pleasure at her momentary discomfiture. 'Oh yes, I know you, witch. I know all of your cursed clan, root and branch. The witch hunter Gunther Stahlberg and I even made a chart, before Mannfred killed him. The Doyenne of the Red Abbey, Handmaiden of Isabella von Carstein, cousin to Markos von Carstein, of the red line of Vlad himself, rather than by proxy. You are as close to royalty as your kind gets.'

'Then you know that I can give you what you wish,' Elize said. 'I can help you, old man.' She turned towards Aliathra. 'I can help you as well, elf. I can free you. I can kill you now, to spare you pain later. I can kill your fellow captives, if you are too proud to ask for yourselves. All I require is that you ask.' She glided towards him and leaned close, her palms to either side of his head. Volkmar glared at her with his good eye. 'Ask me, old man. Beg me, and I will put you out of your misery, like an old wolf caught in a trap.'

'Frightened, then,' Volkmar coughed. His lips cracked and bled as he smiled. 'You are frightened, and I think I know of what. Something so dark and hungry that you pale in comparison. You can feel it, can't you? In whatever passes for your heart,' he said. He closed his eye. 'Mannfred has left you here, and now, like a rat that scents a snake, you want to squirm away. So be it, woman. Kill us, and run.'

'Beg me,' she growled.

Volkmar wheezed hoarsely. It wasn't quite a laugh, but it was as close as he could manage. 'No, no, I think not. Run away, little rat. Run and hide before the snake gobbles you up.'

Elize raised a hand, as if to tear out his throat. It trembled slightly, and then fell. Volkmar said nothing. He opened his eyes to watch the vampire leave. 'You should have let her do it, priest. You should have asked her to kill you,' someone croaked, as the chamber door rattled shut. 'You should have *begged*.'

'Be quiet, witch,' Volkmar rasped. It was hard to get air into his lungs, hung on the wall as he was. It was all he could do to speak. The manacles bit into his flesh, and he felt his blisters pop and weep as he shifted in his chains.

'Your arrogance has doomed us, Volkmar. And you most of all – I am damned, but you will be doubly damned,' the Bretonnian witch yowled. Volkmar heard her chains rattle. 'He is coming for you, old man.'

'I said be silent,' he snarled, trying to muster something of his former authority. He knew he'd failed when she began to laugh and wail.

There was no hope.

Volkmar closed his eyes and tried not to sleep.

Elize stood staring at the wall opposite the door to the chamber for some time. She could feel the burning gazes of the two wights, who now guarded the chamber, on her back, but she didn't move away. They were no threat to her. Mannfred had seen to that.

She considered simply going back in and killing one of them – the nature priest, perhaps. He was little more than a mindless husk, after all this time in captivity. There were ways that it could be done that would leave no one the wiser. Mannfred would assume that he'd simply expired, despite the sustaining spells he'd etched into the prisoners' flesh. Unless he didn't, in which case she'd have some explaining to do.

Elize didn't fear Mannfred's wrath any more than she had feared Isabella's incandescent and unpredictable tantrums, or Vlad's quietly menacing disappointment. She knew which strands to pluck to see her safely out of the von Carstein web, and which to pull in order to get back in, should it be necessary. Mannfred was guileful and cunning, but not especially subtle. He strode across the landscape like a warrior-king, and expected his opponents to fall at his feet in awe of his majesty and political acumen.

He was, in short, a barbarian. Vlad had been much the same – a man out of time. The difference between them lay in the fact that Vlad had had an almost childlike delight in learning the ways of the Imperial court, and navigating the choppy political waters of the Empire. Vlad had been subtle: patient and unswerving. Mannfred was not patient. He never had been. He was a creature of passions and selfish demands, and he only understood those things in others. Patience, to Mannfred, was simply fear. Dedication was foolishness. Subtlety was hesitancy.

But this time, Mannfred had bitten off more than he could chew. They could all see it, even if the sisters of the Silver Pinnacle hadn't been whispering it into every ear. It was madness, what he planned, and in everyone's best interests to see that he failed.

Elize looked back at the door, thoughtful now. The old man hanging on the wall in there was no different, really. An obstinate, obdurate relic, sitting athwart the stream of history, determined to bend it to his will. Again, the temptation to simply kill him rose. But... no. Best to wait, until there was no other option. Best to wait until all of the pieces were in place.

'Think carefully, child. Think, before you do something we will all regret.'

Elize turned. Alberacht Nictus lumbered down the corridor towards her, more or less a man. His wings had shrivelled to flaps that could easily be folded in the narrow corridors and he wore a set of armour purloined from somewhere. His face was still a tale of horror, but his eyes shone with kindly madness. He held out a taloned paw. 'Come away, my sweet girl. Come away, and let the Sigmarite rot in his tomb.'

Elize took his claw gingerly. Alberacht pulled her close, like a doting uncle. 'You always were a risk-taker, my little stoat. Always going for the throat,' he gurgled. 'That is why Isabella loved you best.'

'Unlike Mannfred,' Elize said. She allowed Alberacht to guide her away from the chamber. The big vampire chuckled harshly.

'Mannfred heeds your words,' Alberacht said. 'After all, we are here, are we not?'

Elize tensed. 'What do you mean? Speak plainly, Master Nictus.'

'Oh, is it Master Nictus now? Have I offended you, cousin?' Alberacht peered at her owlishly, and showed his teeth in a ghastly smile. 'You were here, at Sternieste, before the wall went up, and before Mannfred made his bid for secession. It was you who advised him to raise the Drakenhof banner and call the order to war. You asked him to set the black bells to ringing, while you rode out to find your pet and Markos.'

'Anark is hardly my pet,' Elize murmured.

'Was I speaking of him?' Alberacht leaned over and kissed the top of her head. 'You are as clear as glass to these old eyes, my girl.'

Elize pushed away from him carefully. They had come to one of the places where the wall of the keep had crumbled away, and she leaned against the gap, looking out over the courtyard far below and the plains beyond. The dead were still mustered amongst the barrows, waiting for an invasion that might never come. Screams echoed up from the courtyard, where Mannfred's court were engaged in their early evening amusements. She'd had to put a guard on the larder once Mannfred departed, to keep the greedy parasites from emptying Sternieste's dungeons of every breathing human in an orgy of indulgence and slaughter.

'He left me,' she said softly, after a few moments.

'Aye, he did,' Alberacht said. He loomed behind her, his claws on her shoulders. 'Though I think he regrets it. I think the Crowfiend regrets many things.'

'I care not whether he regrets it,' she hissed. 'He. Left. Me. I made him and he *left*. No one leaves me. I leave. I go where I will. Not him!'

'Ah,' Alberacht breathed. He was silent for a time. Then, he said, 'Sometimes, I think that Vlad did us a disservice. There is something in the von Carstein blood that encourages duplicity and madness. Konrad, Pieter, Nyklaus with his ambitions of admiralty... Isabella.'

'I am not mad,' Elize said.

'I am,' Alberacht said. 'Then, I was a von Drak, and they were all mad.' He leaned close. 'I was speaking of your duplicity, in any event. All of this, simply for the Crowfiend?' He leaned around her, so that he could peer up into her face. 'Tomas – dead. Anark elevated to a position he is unsuited for. Markos's predilections with succession encouraged, and Mannfred warned of that burgeoning treachery. Are any of us out of your web, my child?'

'You and the Vargravian,' she said, smiling slightly.

'Ah,' he murmured. 'Am I to feel slighted, then?' She tensed again. There was no way of telling which way the old monster would jump at the best of times. His mind was lost in a red haze.

'No,' she said carefully. 'But you are impossible to predict. And the Vargravian is an unknown quantity. I know him only by reputation. Tomas elevated him to the inner circle. The others I know.' She pounded a fist against the crumbling edge of the gap. 'They are fixed points, and I can weave my web, as you call it, about them.' She smiled thinly. 'Mannfred taught me that.' She looked at Alberacht. 'It is not all for Erikan. It is for us, as well. For the future. For too long we have clung to this place. Sylvania was a prison even before the wall of faith surrounded it. There is a whole world out there, past the borders, where we can spread and take root. But before we can flourish, certain branches must be pruned.'

'And what of Mannfred's plans, child? You know what he intends. You know what awaits us, when they return.'

Elize turned away. 'It will not come to that. Even Mannfred is not so blinded by ambition that he would risk unleashing the Undying King upon the world.' She smiled. 'Anark will do his part, and Markos as well. Nagash will not rise, but when this farce is done... *we will.*'

CHAPTER TWELVE

Beneath Mad Dog Pass, the Border Princes

The skaven screamed and died as the bodies of the Iron Claw orcs, torn and savaged by the ultimately futile battle that had seen the entire tribe decimated by the forces under Mannfred's command, launched themselves through the crude pavises of wood and rope, and hacked down the clan-rats manning the ballistae behind. More zombies shoved through the gap created by the dead greenskins, flooding the tunnels beyond the chamber where the skaven sentries had chosen to make their stand.

Mannfred urged his skeleton mount through the sea of carnage that his servants had left in their wake, his face twisted in an expression of disdain. This was the tenth such cavern he had ridden through in as many hours, and impatience was beginning to eat at him like acid.

Never before had he felt so pressed for time. It had always seemed a limitless commodity for him. But he felt it closing in on him now, cutting off his avenues of manoeuvre. It was as if he were being surrounded by enemies on all sides, trapped in an ever-tightening noose. He clutched Kadon's staff to him, and took comfort in the Claw of Nagash, its withered fingers twitching and gesturing mutely.

Power. That was what it was all about. That was what it had always been about. The power to see his journey to its end. The power to control his own destiny. Too often had he been at the mercy of others, his desires supplanted by the whims of those who considered themselves his superiors. Vlad, Neferata, his father... They had all tried to keep him from achieving his destiny. But no longer. He had outlived, outfought, outschemed them all. He had thwarted his enemies at every turn, and thumbed his nose at every empire.

That you have, my boy. Your famed subtlety has deserted you, it seems. Or perhaps you deserted it, eh? The skies are blood-red, the gallows scream hungrily and Mannfred von Carstein has come into his own, Vlad murmured.

Mannfred snapped his reins, causing his mount to gallop through the cavern. The drumming of its hooves blocked out Vlad's voice. Nevertheless, he could hear the quiet conversation of his Drakenhof Templars behind him, as they urged their steeds to keep up with his. They were talking about him, he knew. Scheming most likely, but then, they were von Carsteins. None of them would dare try anything, save perhaps Markos.

He scanned the cavern and caught sight of the latter, dispatching a squealing skaven warrior with a casually tossed sorcerous bolt. Markos was almost as good a sorcerer as Mannfred himself. He, like Mannfred, had learned much under the tutelage of the bat-faced nightmare known as Melkhior, when Vlad had employed the latter to teach them the finer arts of necromancy. Mannfred remembered the thin-limbed horror, in his stinking rags, with his fever-bright eyes as he showed them the formulas of the Corpse Geometries. There was much of W'soran, Melkhior's primogenitor, in him, from the way he spoke, to his apparent disdain for even the most basic aspects of hygiene.

It was from Melkhior that he had discovered the origin of the dark magics that empowered the ancient ring that Vlad wore, and it was from the old monster that he learned of how it held the secrets of the resurrection of the Undying King. Melkhior had whispered of certain rites that might stir Nagash, and of the shifting of the Corpse Geometries that had seen Nagash come back and wage an abortive campaign to reclaim his pilfered crown. Then the Night of the Restless Dead, in which Nagash's ravening spirit had managed only a single night of terror. Even diminished and shrunken, Nagash was the sort of power that caused the world to scream in horror. But he was a power without true thought. Nagash himself, as he had been, was long gone to whatever black reward awaited such creatures. All that was left of him was something less even than Arkhan the Black – blind impulse, and the fading echo of a once mighty brain.

Or so Melkhior had sworn. Mannfred knew better than to trust the words of any of W'soran's brood. He had felt a great sense of relief when Melkhior's student, Zacharias, had put paid to whatever subtle schemes his master had been weaving. Not that Zacharias was an improvement; if anything, he was just as devious and as arrogant as Melkhior, and W'soran before him. Indeed, Zacharias had openly opposed Mannfred's schemes from the moment of Melkhior's death, striving to unravel stratagems that had taken him centuries to forge. He could not fathom the other vampire's intent, save that Zacharias feared what Mannfred might do once he gained the power of Nagash. Or, perhaps he feared what would happen should Mannfred fail.

Mannfred frowned. He considered the Claw of Nagash, where it lay across his saddle. He could feel the power it held, power enough to carve out a nation, if he wished. Once, that would have been enough for him. He had vied for thrones before. But something had changed in him. A throne, a city, a province – these were no longer good enough. Even an empire was but a drop in the ocean of his ambition.

Those ambitions were the root of every plan he had concocted since he had dragged himself from the mire of Hel Fenn, revivified by the blood of a dying necromancer. They drove him on, into the reeking tunnels, and he, in his turn, drove on the dead with the lash of his will. Vlad was right. He had discarded subtlety; there was no use for it here. The only tools of worth were the press of bodies and the savage tactics of attrition.

In the hours that followed, Mannfred willed wave after wave of zombies into the labyrinthine network of tunnels. Through the eyes of his flesh-puppets, he mapped out the safest route for him and his Drakenhof Templars to take towards the heart of the festering pit. He lost hundreds of zombies, but gained twice their number in new recruits from among the skaven dead. Entire squealing tribes of the vermin were stifled and silenced beneath the tide of rotting meat, and then dragged upright to serve beside their slayers. It was necromancy as applied brutality, sorcery wielded like a blunt object, as Mannfred battered himself a path through the enormous burrow.

He led his knights deeper into the tunnels, which grew grand in scale. The burrow was a tumour of stone and darkness. Foul poisons dripped from filth-encrusted stalactites, and the rough walls of rock were marked by generation upon generation of crude skaven-scrawl; the caverns were choked with ramshackle structures of warped wood and rust-riddled metal. And everywhere, the skaven. Some fled his approach, others tried to resist. Sometimes they even fell upon one another in vicious displays of compulsive betrayal that startled even Mannfred, who took advantage of such incidents with bemusement.

Deeper and deeper he pushed his forces. He could feel the Fellblade now, like a wound in the world, pulsing, calling to the claw it had hacked from Nagash's wrist. It called to him, and Mannfred went gladly, driven by the devils of his ambition.

The Fellblade would be his, and with it, the power of Nagash.

La Maisontaal Abbey, Bretonnia

'It's a fairly innocuous sort of place,' Erikan Crowfiend murmured. He leaned over his horse's neck and ran his fingers through the matted mane of the ghoul crouched beside him. The rest of the pack swirled about him, yapping and snarling like dogs on the scent. There were hundreds of them, drawn from all over Bretonnia to the meadows of Quenelles by the scent of death. The other vampires seemed perturbed by the presence of so many flesh-eaters, especially Anark von Carstein, who glared at the Crowfiend with barely repressed fury.

'It is nothing more than a slightly fancy tomb,' Kemmler said. The ghouls gambolling about the legs of Erikan's steed avoided the Lichemaster and Krell, who stood just behind him, his Great Axe in his hands.

'*A tomb whose inhabitants are barred to us, thanks to Bretonnian witchery,*' Arkhan said. He stood on the back of his chariot and looked at his commanders, examining each one in turn. Then, he turned his attentions back to the object of their discussion.

La Maisontaal Abbey sat on the slopes of the Grey Mountains, its walls the same hue as the tumble-down stones of the cliffs around it. Its walls were half finished, but it was an imposing structure nonetheless, built to protect its inhabitants from any who might wish them harm. It had been built in the early years of Gilles Le Breton's first reign, its construction funded by a mysterious nobleman from the east, who had claimed that the abbey was the repayment of a debt owed. Arkhan, who had once lost his head to the sword of the nobleman in question, suspected that there was more truth to that tale than not.

In the fading, grey miasma of the day, the abbey was a flickering nest of fireflies as torches, lanterns and bonfires were lit. He wondered if the inhabitants thought that firelight would be enough to keep back the host he had arrayed on the plains before La Maisontaal. '*What do your spies tell you, Crowfiend?*' he asked, after a moment.

The vampire glanced down at one of the ghouls, who gave a warble and licked broken fangs in the parody of smile. The Crowfiend looked at Arkhan. 'Much meat,' he said, with a shrug. 'Asking them to count is useless. Past one, it goes "many", "much" and "most". That's as accurate as they get.' He straightened in his saddle. 'They're keeping close to the walls and the torches, however. That much they could say. Plenty of weak points, jammed with frail, trembling meat, ready to be torn and squeezed dry of life.' The Crowfiend smiled crookedly. 'A better sort of battlefield than Couronne, I will say.'

'*If you must,*' Arkhan said. He looked at Anark. '*You, vampire. Mannfred spoke of your military experience. Analyse and explain,*' he said.

The vampire grunted and shook himself. 'Traditional Bretonnian tactics. A shieldwall of peasantry in front of artillery, knights on the flanks to crush the attack once it becomes hung up on the fodder.' Anark lifted himself slightly in his saddle, and his brutal features slackened into something approaching consideration. 'Trebuchets and archers. The bonfires mean fire-arrows,' he added, his lip curling away from a fang.

'What is fire to the dead?' Kemmler asked, running his fingers through his tangled beard. 'Let our army carry an inferno into the heart of their army, if that is the fate they choose.'

Arkhan ignored the necromancer. He let his gaze drift across the ragged ranks of his army. The vast majority of it was composed of the graveborn victims of war and plague. He disliked relying on such chattel – zombies were little more than ambulatory shields for better, more reliable troops. Unfortunately, he had precious few of the latter.

The Silent Legion stood ready for battle, clad in ancient armour and bearing weapons not seen since the height of the Nehekhara. He had seen to their resurrection from their essential salts upon his arrival on the fields before La Maisontaal Abbey, and Nagash's nekric guard stood ready to wage war on the living once more.

Arrayed about the Silent Legion were the warbands Arkhan and Kemmler had dragged from their slumber in the Vaults. Composed of wights and skeletons, the warbands were possessed of a savage bloodlust second only to Krell's, and without the sorcerous chains that compelled them to obey Arkhan, they would have already begun the attack.

Beyond them, and scattered before and around the host were the ghoul packs that had followed them from the borderlands and into the hills. A harsh winter and a bloody spring had added to their numbers, as villages throughout southern Bretonnia became little more than haunts for newly christened cannibal clans. Such pathetic beasts were drawn to the stench of necromancy like iron filings to a lodestone. Like the zombies, they were of little practical use, but Arkhan was confident that they could readily take blows meant for more valuable troops as easily as any staggering corpse.

And last – the Drakenhof Templars. The armoured vampires were eager for war, none more so than the brute Mannfred had named Grand Master. Anark met his gaze and looked away quickly. Was he nervous, Arkhan wondered, or bored? Neither would surprise him. That Anark intended treachery was almost certain. The creature was barely competent, save in military matters, and openly defied Arkhan at every opportunity, eliciting chortles from his fellow leeches. All save the Crowfiend, whom he seemed to despise even more than Arkhan.

Arkhan dismissed the thought. He had no time to worry about traitors. He looked up at the night sky, and for a moment, immense, terrible shapes seemed to claw down towards him, like hungry birds. The cat on his shoulder hissed softly. He'd almost forgotten that the animal was there, so quiet had it become since they'd arrived. He stroked its greying flesh gently.

No time, he thought. There was no room for error now, not with the delays and losses they'd suffered. The beastman attack they'd fought off some days before had taught him that. Though they had driven the creatures off, the damage had been done. The unassailable horde he had assembled had dwindled to its current state. It was still an ocean of corpses, but he was forced to see to their control himself, along with Kemmler.

His options had been forcibly limited. There was no time for grand strategy now, only brute speed. '*So be it,*' Arkhan rasped. He swung his staff out and pointed it at Krell. '*Krell will take the fore. He will lead the Silent Legion, and the tribes of the dead into the centre of the enemy line. They shall be the head of my spear and the stumbling dead shall be the haft, driven forward by Kemmler and me.*'

'That is exactly what they are counting on,' Anark protested. 'Even a dried up old thing like you should have the wit to see that. The knights will fold into your flanks like the jaws of a trap!'

Arkhan looked at the vampire. '*That is what you are for, von Carstein. Besides, it would be rude of us to ignore such a heartfelt invitation, would it not?*'

Kemmler cackled wildly. 'Oh, there's hope for you yet, liche! Come, hurry! I have waited centuries to tear this rotting heap of stone apart, and I can wait no longer.' He gestured sharply, and Krell broke into a trot. As the wight moved, the Silent Legion fell into step with him. The skeletal warbands joined them, rasping battle-cries issuing from the long-withered throats of their chieftains.

Arkhan stepped down from his chariot and made to join Kemmler, where the latter waited amidst a knot of zombie knights, still clad in bloodstained armour and clutching broken weapons. He paused as the Crowfiend interposed his steed. Arkhan looked up at him.

'A word of advice,' the vampire said, not looking at him. 'Kemmler stinks of ambition.'

'*As does your companion Anark,*' Arkhan said.

'Not my companion,' the Crowfiend said. The vampire looked at him. 'The Drakenhof Templars were ordered to escort you to La Maisontaal Abbey. And that is what we shall do.'

'*And afterwards?*'

The Crowfiend kicked his horse into motion. He galloped away, followed by his ghouls. Arkhan watched him go. Then he joined Kemmler.

'What did the leech want?' the old man grunted.

'*Merely to pass on the compliments of Mannfred von Carstein,*' Arkhan said. The dead twitched into motion, lurching forwards. Arkhan and Kemmler moved with them, lending sorcerous speed to the slower corpses.

'Ha! That's a poisoned chalice if there ever was one,' Kemmler spat. He peered after the Crowfiend, eyes narrowed. 'I remember that one. He served in Mallobaude's army. He followed that fool Obald around. Fussed over the old pig-farmer like a nursemaid,' he sneered. He smiled nastily. 'If he's here, the Bone-Father must have finally died.'

'*You sound pleased,*' Arkhan said.

'Merely satisfied, I assure you,' Kemmler said, and tittered. 'Obald was a fool. Just like the idiot Ogiers, or that black-toothed sneak, Fidduci.' He glanced at Arkhan, his eyes sly. 'They were but pale imitations of their betters. Useless chattel, fit only to be used and discarded.' He made a fist. 'Power belongs only to those strong enough to wield it. It belongs to those who can survive its use, and those who can take it for themselves. I'm a survivor.' He licked his lips. 'Pity Nagash wasn't, otherwise we wouldn't be in this mess, would we?'

Arkhan said nothing. Kemmler laughed and turned his attentions back to the dead. The vampire had been right – Kemmler was up to something.

He couldn't help but to boast. He resolved to keep an eye on the old man, even as the night sky above was suddenly lit up by a rain of fire.

'*Arrows,*' he said, raising his staff. A quickly conjured wind plucked away those missiles that drew too close to him and Kemmler. But even as Arkhan readied himself to deal similarly with the next volley, he saw that they were not the target.

The forward elements of the undead host had crossed no more than half the field before the Bretonnian bombardment began. A second volley of flaming arrows pierced the darkness and tore into the ranks of skeletons and wights. Again and again, the Bretonnian archers fired. Only scant seconds passed between each volley, testament to the skill of the longbow-men. Peasants though they were, Arkhan was forced to admit that their skills were on par with the archers of Lybaras.

With a flick of his fingers, he willed those of his minions who possessed them to raise their shields. Nonetheless many were still set alight by glancing or lucky shots, and the shields were of little help against the larger fireballs launched by the massed trebuchets. As the great war engines found their range, more and more impacts occurred, tearing great ragged holes in the undead ranks.

But the undead marched on, driven forwards relentlessly by the combined wills of Arkhan and Kemmler. Dark magic flowed from the fingers of both necromancer and liche, rousing the fallen dead to continue the march, no matter how badly damaged they were. There were few in the world more attuned to the winds of death than he and his troublesome comrade, Arkhan knew. Dieter Helsnicht, perhaps or Zacharias the Ever-Living, but no others possessed the mastery of broken bone and torn flesh that he and Kemmler did.

The dead fell around him and rose again; shattered skeletons swirled and danced back into motion, to rejoin the unwavering advance. The attrition caused by the bombardment slackened, drew to a crawl and then ceased. Arkhan spat black syllables into the greasy air, and every iota of concentration he possessed was bent to thrusting his warhost forward, as if it were a single weapon, and his the hand that wielded it.

It would have been easier with the others – the battle-line more fluid, the tactics less primitive. But Arkhan was forced to admit that it would not have been nearly as satisfying. It had been decades since he had dirtied his hands with war in this fashion. He had stayed on the sidelines of Mallobaude's rebellion, a fact he regretted, if only for the squandered opportunities.

His attention was drawn by screams. Krell had reached the enemy. With a roar audible only to sorcerers and lunatics, Krell unleashed the Silent Legion upon the Bretonnian lines.

The killing began.

◄ CHAPTER THIRTEEN ►

Mordkin Lair, the Border Princes

'The dead-things... followed you,' Warlord Feskit hissed. He was old, for a skaven, and his fur was the colour of ash. He tapped the hilt of the wide, jagged-bladed cleaver that was stabbed point first into the bone dais supporting his throne. The latter was a trophy taken from a fallen dwarf hold in years past, and it overflowed with pillows and cushions made from the hair and beards of men, elves, dwarfs and unlucky skaven. Feskit himself wore a necklace of orc tusks, goblin noses and human ears, all of which he'd pilfered from the various battles he claimed credit for. 'You ran, and they followed.' Every word was enunciated slowly, drawn out like the flick of a torturer's knife across cringing flesh.

'No-no, Snikrat the Magni– Snikrat the *Loyal* came to warn you, mighty Feskit,' Snikrat chittered. He knelt before the throne, his loyal Bonehides arrayed behind him – far behind him – and gestured towards Feskit imploringly. 'They seek to invade our lair, oh perspicacious one, by which I mean our tunnels, the very heart of our fortress, this place here,' he continued, sweeping his arms out. 'That they followed me is only incidental, by which I mean unrelated, to my own headlong plunge to assure myself of your wellbeing, because you are my warlord and I am your loyal champion.'

In truth, Snikrat had no idea whether or not the dead had followed him. It was certainly possible, but he suspected otherwise, given his cunning and the stealthy nature of his retreat across the plains, back to the mountains. He had seen other clans attempt to match claw and blade with the undead, and he had, briefly, considered lending aid. But it was imperative that he warn Feskit about the enemy; and if that enemy was destroyed before he got back... Well, the credit would be ripe for the claiming, wouldn't it?

As it happened, he had managed to lead what was left of his warband past the undead at the entrance to Mad Dog Pass, while the charnel horde was otherwise occupied with the Iron Claw orcs. The greenskins hadn't been faring particularly well, the last Snikrat had seen. He decided not to mention it. Clan Mordkin and the Iron Claws had waged a war for control of the pass for decades, and Feskit respected their strength inasmuch as he respected anything. If he knew that they had been beaten, he might decide to abandon the lair, rather than fight, and Snikrat's continued survival hinged on the latter.

'Hrr,' Feskit grunted. He sat back, his eyes narrowed to mere slits. Snikrat tensed. He glanced at the armoured stormvermin, who crouched or stood arrayed about Feskit's dais, ready to lunge forward to slaughter at their claw-leader's command. The Mordrat Guard were Feskit's personal clawband and they were loyal to a fault, thanks mostly to Feskit's generous patronage, which ensured that they saw little in the way of actual combat while claiming the bulk of the loot. Feskit was too smart to risk them in open combat, where they couldn't protect him from treacherous rivals, or, in certain cases, each other. They were also indolent, lazy and far from as skilled as most thought them.

Snikrat knew all of this because he had, once upon a time, been the commander of the Mordrat Guard. He had profited from Feskit's indulgence, and then, when he had climbed as high as he could, he had made the obvious decision. Granted, it had been the wrong decision, and it had ended with him flat on his back and Feskit's teeth in his throat, but it had seemed obvious at the time. Snikrat rubbed his throat nervously. Feskit had spared him that day, though he'd never said why.

Snikrat thought – Snikrat *hoped* – that it was because Feskit was canny enough to know that he was getting old, and that if Clan Mordkin were to continue to flourish, it would need a suitable skaven to lead it. A magnificent skaven, a great warrior and cunning to boot. But that skaven had to prove himself worthy of Feskit's patronage. He had to acquire victories, follow orders and serve the clan in all those ways that most skaven simply could not, whether due to their inherent untrustworthiness or simple weakness.

As Feskit stroked his whiskers, deep in thought, Snikrat surreptitiously took in the gathered chieftains. Those Feskit considered the most loyal sat near the dais, surrounded by their bodyguards. The rest were scattered throughout the great cavern or hadn't been invited. There were more than a dozen missing. Some were likely still out plundering the Border Princes, he suspected. Which was just as well – more opportunities for him. He needed to reclaim his place at the foot of the throne, if he was to have any chance of successfully challenging Feskit a second time. He scratched at his throat again. Unless Feskit simply had him executed.

A sudden, discordant clamour of bells echoed through the caverns. The upper tunnels had been breached, Snikrat knew. A wave of relief washed aside his worries. He'd timed his return perfectly. Death shrieks drifted down from the vaulted roof of the cavern, slithering through the numerous flue holes that marked the rock. They echoed and re-echoed about the cavern, and a nervous murmur swept through the gathered chieftains. Snikrat, who was already far too familiar with the enemy even now bearing down on them for his liking, shivered slightly.

Feskit glared at him. Then he waved a paw at the knot of trembling slaves who cowered at the foot of his throne. 'Bring me my armour and weapons.' He gestured to the black-clad gutter runners who lurked nearby, waiting to carry forth Feskit's decrees to all of the small clans within his realm. 'Summon the conclave of chieftains. The burrow must be defended.' His eyes found Snikrat again, and his lips peeled back from his fangs. 'It is lucky that you returned when you did, Snikrat. Where would I be without my greatest champion?'

Snikrat stood, his chest swelling. 'Snikrat the Magnificent lives only to ensure the greater glory of Clan Mordkin, mighty chieftain,' he said.

'Of that I am certain, yes-yes,' Feskit said. He flung out a paw. 'Go then! Defend our lair from these intruders, Snikrat. Prove yourself worthy of my faith, yes,' he chittered.

Snikrat hissed in pleasure and whirled, gesturing to the gathered chieftains. 'You heard our most merciful and wise clan-leader! Gather your warriors and war engines. Awaken the beasts,' he snarled. 'It is time to drive these dead-things from the lair of Mordkin!'

Quenelles, Bretonnia

Anthelme slumped in his saddle, aching, exhausted beyond all measure, burdened by tragedy and fear alike. Nonetheless, the newest, and perhaps last, Duke of Quenelles led his companions north, to war.

He closed his eyes as he rode. His cousin's face swam to the surface of his thoughts, and he banished it with a curse. He had failed Tancred. It hadn't been for lack of trying, but it had been a failure regardless. At the battle's height, his steed had been struck with terror and had fled, taking him with it. By the time he'd brought the beast under control, Tancred was dead, and his muster shattered and shoved aside by the undead host as it made its way north.

Anthelme had made his way to Castle Brenache, where he'd found Fastric Ghoulslayer and Gioffre of Anglaron and the rest of the Companions of Quenelles attempting to rally the remaining knights. Their joyful greetings as he'd ridden shame-faced into the castle courtyard had torn his heart worse than any blade. They'd thought him dead; he wished that were so. More, he wished that Tancred were alive and that he had fallen in his cousin's place.

Instead, Quenelles was his, and the weight of it felt as if it would snap his spine. The province was in ruins – beset by beastmen and worse things. Calls for aid came every hour, and Anthelme was inundated with inherited troubles. He did not know what to do. Would the defences of the abbey hold, or would aid be required? He had sought the counsel of the Lady of Brenache, the Dowager of Charnorte. She had warned Tancred so many months before, and he'd hoped that she might help him now. And she'd tried.

Her scrying had proven a troublesome affair, marred by what he could only describe as daemonic interference. Anthelme shivered in his saddle as he remembered how the clear waters of her scrying bowl became as dark as a storm cloud, and leering faces formed in the ripples. Fell cries had echoed from the stones and the Lady's voice had been drowned out by the laughter of the Dark Gods.

He had been ushered from her chambers then, with a promise that she would find an answer for him, and for three days she took neither food nor drink. Her chamber had rocked with the sounds of madness – strange laughter, scratching on the stones and foul smells that lingered in the corridors of the castle. The knights began to mutter that the Lady had deserted them – why else would Tancred have fallen? Why else would the realm be beset by so many enemies at once?

As Anthelme sat and waited for the Lady Elynesse to come out of her room, knights had demanded that he ride out to face one foe or another. Anthelme refused them all, though it hurt him to do so. Some knights left, sallying forth alone to confront the horrors that afflicted their ancestral lands. Others stayed, their natural impetuousness tempered by the memory of Tancred's fall.

On the third day, their patience was rewarded. Lady Elynesse staggered from her chambers. The Lady's voice had at last pierced her fevered dreams, and given her a dire warning to pass on – if Anthelme did not go to La Maisontaal, Bretonnia itself would fall.

'Stop thinking,' a voice said, rousing Anthelme from his reverie.

'What?' he asked. Gioffre of Anglaron grinned at him, and slapped him on the back, causing his mail to jingle.

'I said stop thinking so hard. You're spooking the horses.'

'That doesn't make any sense.' Anthelme looked around.

'No, but it got you to pay attention, didn't it?' Gioffre said. 'We're but a day's hard ride from the abbey, and you look as if you'd rather be anywhere else.'

'It's not that,' Anthelme said quickly. Gioffre laughed.

'Oh I know. Anthelme, you are a true knight, as was Tancred. I fought beside you during Mallobaude's rebellion, remember? I know that you are no coward. Just as I know that you only fear failure.' He smiled. Gioffre wasn't especially handsome, but his face became almost pleasant when he smiled. 'We will not fail. Troubadours will sing of the day the Companions of Quenelles sent the dead back into the dark, and saved Bretonnia.' He clapped Anthelme on the shoulder. 'Now, heads up.' He pointed upwards. 'The Ghoulslayer and his flock of overgrown pigeons are back.'

Anthelme couldn't resist a smile. Gioffre had a distaste for the winged stallions that Fastric Ghoulslayer and his fellow pegasus knights rode. Anthelme suspected that it had less to do with the fact that he felt the surly beasts were unnatural, and more to do with their habit of befouling the ground beneath them as they swooped through the air. Horse dung wasn't pleasant, especially when it was coming at you from above, and very quickly.

'Ho, Duke Anthelme,' Fastric shouted as his steed swooped lazily through the air. The pegasus whinnied as it descended, and it tossed its head and trotted arrogantly towards Anthelme and Gioffre. Their own steeds snorted and pawed the ground as the beast fell into step with them. Normal warhorses didn't get along with pegasus, even at the best of times. Gioffre's stallion nipped at Fastric's steed, and the former planted a fist between his mount's ears. 'Keep that bad-tempered nag of yours under control, sirrah,' Fastric said.

'It'd be easier if that beast of yours didn't provoke the other animals,' Gioffre said.

Before the old, familiar argument could begin again, Anthelme said, 'What news, Ghoulslayer?'

'Beasts,' Fastric growled. 'Hundreds of them. They're moving north, but much more slowly than us.'

'Has Arkhan the Black made common cause with the creatures, do you think?' Gioffre asked. 'I wouldn't put anything past that creature, frankly.'

Anthelme frowned. 'They've been following us for days. If they were allies, wouldn't they have attacked us by now? Even creatures like that should have no difficulty in divining our destination.' He thought briefly of the beast-herd that had led Tancred into the ambush that had cost him his life, and wondered if this was the same one, before dismissing the idea. There were dozens of such warbands prowling the province now. 'No,' he said, straightening in his saddle. 'No, they're scavengers. They're following us in hope of an easy victory. Well, let them. All they'll find is death.'

He twisted in his saddle and looked back at the column of knights that followed him. Standards of every design and hue rose over the assembled force. Warriors from every province and city were counted amongst the Companions of Quenelles, and for a moment, just a moment, Anthelme felt the shadow that had been on his heart since Tancred's death lift. He felt a hand on his shoulder, and looked at Fastric. 'He would be proud,' the older knight murmured. 'As are we all. Where you lead, Anthelme, Duke of Quenelles, your Companions will follow.'

Anthelme nodded brusquely. 'Then let us ride. La Maisontaal Abbey is in need of defenders, and I would not have it said that the Duke of Quenelles fell short in his responsibility.' He kicked his horse into a gallop, followed by Gioffre. Fastric set spurs to his steed and the pegasus sprang into the air with a neigh.

Horns blew up and down the column, and the Companions of Quenelles hurtled north.

La Maisontaal Abbey, Bretonnia

Theoderic of Brionne growled in satisfaction as the line of shields buckled, but did not break. 'Hold, you filthy pigs,' he rumbled as he watched the peasants resist the undead advance. 'Hold.' The peasants did not love him. He knew this, and accepted it as a consequence of his position. But if they did not love him, they at least feared him, and they would do their duty, dreading the price of failure.

Tancred had cautioned him against meeting the enemy in open battle, should they arrive in his absence. The dead could not be smashed aside so easily, he'd said. But Tancred hadn't heeded his own advice, and now, if the message his cousin had sent was to be believed, his body was somewhere out there in that lurching horde.

It was almost enough to make him doubt himself. The newly christened Duke of Quenelles had sent riders from Castle Brenache, where he was taking the counsel of the Lady Elynesse, the Dowager of Charnorte. The riders had only just managed to outpace the dead, and they had brought word of Tancred's fall and of Anthelme's intention to ride to La Maisontaal's aid with the Companions of Quenelles. Anthelme had advised him to retreat behind the abbey walls, and to hold the dead back, but not to meet them in pitched battle.

A sensible plan; behind the walls, the muster of La Maisontaal could more readily rely upon the magics of the three sisters of Ancelioux. At the thought of the trio of damsels, he glanced towards the shieldwall, where they stood, clad in shimmering damask and furs against the chill of evening. He knew little of the women, and what he did know, he didn't like.

It was rare to have three daughters chosen by the Fay Enchantress, as poor Evroul of Mousillon had, and even rarer to see them after the fact. It hadn't been a happy reunion, by all accounts – Evroul, unlucky in fortune as well as family, had chosen the wrong side in the civil war, and his own daughters had killed him. Nonetheless, their magics would come in handy in the battle to come, he thought.

Anthelme's advice aside, Theoderic had no intention of waiting for rescue. Right or wrong, he was a man of tradition. The darkness was not to be feared, or avoided. It was to be confronted head on, and smashed aside with blade and lance. Under his command, the garrison at La Maisontaal was more active than it had been, even under Tancred's father. It was larger, with more men than had ever before manned its walls.

As soon as his scouts had reported the host approaching the cleared plains before the abbey he had sworn on the tatters of his honour to guard, he had known that the moment he had been seeking since he had given up his ancestral lands and titles had arrived. Before him was a chance for redemption, a chance to atone for the failings of mind and body that had tarnished his family name.

'This... is a glorious day,' he murmured. He looked around at the knights who surrounded him. Anticipation was writ on every face, and their horses shifted impatiently, as eager as their riders to be at the charge. He knew that similar looks would be on the faces of the knights waiting for his signal on the opposite flank.

He rose up in his saddle and lifted his axe over his head. On the other side of the field, a horn crafted from the tusk of a great wyrm wailed. Theoderic knew that horn, and the man who wielded it – Montglaive of Treseaux, slayer of the wyrm Catharax, from whose cooling corpse he had hacked the tusk he had made into his horn. Montglaive commanded the right flank, as Theoderic commanded the left. As the horns on the right sounded, so too did the horns on the left, and Theoderic felt his soul stir.

He was not a man for speeches, inspiring or otherwise. It was not in him to rouse or incite, but he knew that something must be said. He felt the weight of the world's attention on him. The air vibrated with some inescapable pulse, some fateful pull, which sharpened his attentions and tugged at his heart. He might die this day, but he would not be forgotten. He would not be remembered as a sozzle-wit or a failed knight, but as a hero. As a champion of the Lady, and of the realm. Songs would be sung, and toasts raised, and the name of Theoderic of Brionne would stand through the ages to come.

That was all he had ever wished.

'This is a glorious day!' he roared, spreading his arms. 'We honoured few stand between holy ground and a black host, and the Lady stands with us! Our fair land writhes in pain, assaulted by daemon, outsider and ill-roused corpse. But we few stand here, to prove not simply our courage, or our honour, but that though all Bretonnia is besieged, hope has not yet forsaken the realm eternal! Hope, which echoes in the rattle of swords and the thunder of hooves! Ride, defenders of La Maisontaal! Ride, knights of Bretonnia! Ride and sweep the enemy before you – ride for the Lady and the world's renewal!'

All around him, his knights gave a great shout, and then thrust back their spurs and joined the battle, Theoderic at their head. The ground shook as the pride of Bretonnia hurtled towards their enemy, lances lowered.

Theoderic bent forward over his charger's neck. He carried no lance, but instead wielded his axe. The weapon was his only reminder of who he had been, before his disgrace. He had carried it in glory and in folly, and he would not be parted from it save in death. Its blade had been anointed in the holy font of La Maisontaal, and as it spun in his grip, it began to shine with a blessed light.

The darkness retreated before him, and he could see the dead where they stumbled, mindless and remorseless. To him, in that moment, they were a sign of all that had afflicted Bretonnia. He raised his axe, roared out an oath and struck out as his steed smashed into the flanks of the dead and pierced them like a spear. His axe licked out, shining like a beacon, and took the head from a zombie.

Then the rest of the knights struck home, and the twelfth and final battle for La Maisontaal Abbey began in earnest.

◄ CHAPTER FOURTEEN ►

Mordkin Lair, the Border Princes

Markos von Carstein did not consider himself unduly ambitious. Indeed, he liked to think of himself as something of an idealist. Vlad had been an idealist, and Vlad was his model in most things. Vlad was a paragon, the vampiric ideal made flesh. The King of Blood, the Emperor of Bones, his ghost was tangible in every speck of Sylvanian soil.

Markos bent away from the thrusting spear, and flicked his wrist, bisecting the squealing ratman's skull with his sword. He twisted in his saddle, chopping another in half, and swatted away a smoke-filled globe with the flat of his blade, sending it tumbling back towards the skaven who'd thrown it. It shattered and the skaven died, choking on its own blood.

It was Vlad who had elevated him from the common muck, and made him a Templar of the Drakenhof Order. It was Vlad who had nurtured his natural gifts for sorcery and strategy. It was Vlad who had given him purpose.

And it was Mannfred who had taken it all away.

Mannfred the liar. Mannfred the schemer. Mannfred the acolyte. Mannfred, who had come from somewhere else to join Vlad, who was no Sylvanian, who sometimes spoke in an accent that Markos had yet to recognise, despite his travels.

Vlad should never have trusted him. But that too was part of the ideal. Vlad had worn his honour like armour, and it had dragged him down in the end. Markos had learned from Vlad's mistakes and when Mannfred had set his feet on the path of empire, Markos had absented himself. Mannfred was not Vlad, and he lacked Vlad's patience, something that inevitably led to his downfall. His attempt at conquest had ended with him sinking into Hel Fenn, and the shattering of the Drakenhof Order. They had all gone their separate ways, eager to put their defeat behind them.

Markos had spent years building up his own network of spies and informers. He had schemed and plotted dynastic marriages and political alliances, all to ensure his ultimate success. Elize, he knew, had been doing much the same, as had Tomas and the others. The Game of Night had lasted for centuries, as the remaining von Carsteins wove plot and counter-plot against one another and the Lahmians.

And then Mannfred had ruined it all by coming back.

Markos growled and parried a rust-edged cleaver. He thrust down, pinning the skaven to the cavern floor. There were seemingly thousands of the beasts, and they just kept coming in wave after wave of squealing fodder. He jerked his blade up out of the dying skaven and looked around. The cavern resembled the bowels of some vast, nightmarish engine – immense cogs, corroded pistons and acid-pitted flywheels projected from the walls at all angles, and rose from deep grooves in the cavern floor. The mechanisms were still in motion, despite the battle, and as Markos watched, a skaven warrior got too close to one and was whisked into a clanking maw, to be pulverised instantly.

The cavern was so choked with machinery that it was impossible for the combatants to fight more than five or six abreast, and the skaven suffered for this inability to bring their numbers to bear. Horns wailed and bells clanged somewhere far back in one of the tunnels, and those skaven closest to the exits began to flee the cavern.

Markos wheeled his horse about and galloped back towards the knot of undead horsemen who surrounded the Drakenhof Templars and Mannfred. As he passed through the ranks of the former, he examined them enviously. The Doom Riders had been legendary even in Vlad's time. Supposedly, they had first ridden forth from whatever barrow had held them at Nagash's command, and after his defeat at Sigmar's hand, they had ridden into the depths of the Drakwald, from whence they had haunted the surrounding lands for centuries until Vlad had sought them out and bent them to his will.

The undead horsemen wore corroded armour of a bygone age, and carried lances wreathed in cold flame. They watched him as he threaded through them, and his flesh felt as if it were covered in crawling spiders as they tracked his progress with hell-spark eyes. When he reached the others, Mannfred glanced at him. 'Well?'

'They're falling back,' Markos said. He leaned back in his saddle. 'We'll have the cavern cleared within the hour, unless they bring up reinforcements. Which they don't seem inclined to do, if you want my opinion.'

'I don't,' Mannfred said, turning away.

Markos bit down on the reply that sprang unbidden to his lips. He turned away from Mannfred and settled down to wait, one hand resting on the pommel of his blade. His anger simmered, but he wrestled it down.

Striking now would be disastrous, whether he succeeded or not. They were miles beneath the surface, and dependent on Mannfred for guidance to find their way through the seemingly endless labyrinth of twisted and reeking warrens. He'd considered trying his luck when the skaven had attacked Forzini's camp, but Elize's words of caution had restrained him. Mannfred was wary, ready for treachery right now. But, when he'd achieved his goal, Markos would have his chance, or so Elize swore. With the Claw and the Fellblade in his possession, Mannfred would be distracted, drunk on victory and his own power. It was a window of opportunity, albeit a narrow one.

Strike swiftly, before he has the chance to acclimate himself to the power of the artefact, she'd said, and he had to admit that it wasn't bad advice. Not that he trusted Elize farther than he could throw her. She was likely hoping that he and Mannfred would kill one another. So be it. He couldn't find it in his heart to blame her. Elize had her own games, just as he did.

Mannfred had ruined them all by coming back. Arrogant, assured of his superiority, he had smashed their delicately woven webs to shreds and tangles, and demanded that they kowtow to him, as they once had. As if their ambitions meant nothing compared to his own.

Well, Markos intended to show him the error of his ways.

Mannfred was as mad as Konrad had been. Oh his madness took a different form, to be sure, but he was just as much a lunatic. His time in the mire had rotted his brains, and he endangered them all with his current obsession. Markos shivered slightly as he looked at the staff Mannfred clutched, and the withered thing that occupied its head. He could feel the malignancy of the Claw in his bones.

Markos was not one to lie to himself. He knew what he was, and what he had done in his centuries of bloodletting. But there were things in the world far worse than him, and the Claw was the tool of one of them. Mannfred was caught up in its whispers and promises. They could all hear the voices – the voice – of the artefacts that Mannfred had gathered. A wheedling, demanding susurrus that permeated Castle Sternieste and haunted them. Every vampire felt the call of Nagash in their blood, whether they admitted it or not.

Most, however, knew better than to give in to it.

He looked at Mannfred again, and blinked. For a moment, in the flickering of the great globes of warpfire that hung from the roof of the cavern, he thought he'd seen something looming over the other vampire. A dark shape, far darker than any shadow, and colder than the depths of a mountain lake.

Markos shuddered and looked away.

La Maisontaal Abbey, Bretonnia

Heinrich Kemmler didn't flinch as the knights struck the vast sea of the dead. He felt the reverberations of that impact in his bones, but he ignored it. He had more important matters clamouring for his attention. His magics were growing less precise, and less effective. At first, he'd thought the culprit was Arkhan. He wouldn't have put it past the liche to strike while he was otherwise occupied, and try to wrest control of the dead from him.

Arkhan didn't trust him, Kemmler knew. Nor did he blame the liche. Kemmler had no intention of allowing Nagash to return, whatever Arkhan's desires. Nagash's time had passed and good riddance to the creature. Hundreds of arch-necromancers had risen and fallen with the tide of years since the Undying King had been gutted on his own basalt throne, each of them worth more than any old dead thing.

The very thought of it incensed him. The drumbeat – the heartbeat of the Great Necromancer – in his head threatened to drown out all of his hard-won coherency. It had driven him mad, that sound. He knew that now. It had forged him, and fed his hungers. It had been the rhythm that had guided his steps, and set him on the path he had trod for centuries. It was the voice inside his head, whispering the secrets of power and the wielding of it; and then, when he had needed it most, it had taken all of it away. That was something Kemmler could not forgive.

Fresh rage flooded him, and he clawed at the barely visible skeins of magic that flowed about him, trying to find the source of the interference. He could feel the heat of Krell's growing battle-lust, and he focused on it, using it as a touchstone. The wight had been his constant companion for more years than he cared to count, and he had woven innumerable spells with Krell at his side. The creature was at once a sump and a sponge for dark magic. Sometimes, he even thought that he could hear Krell speak. Or perhaps not Krell, but something that clung to his brutal husk like a shadow.

When Krell was near, the drumbeat was almost impossible to ignore. But that was not the only sound in his head. There were words as well, whispers and wheedling, plaintive murmurs, which rose and fell with the winds of magic. Kemmler had first heard those voices in the hour of Krell's resurrection, when they had offered him aid if he would bend the wight to certain tasks. And he had, and the voices too had grown quiescent. But now, as the drumbeat grew louder, so too did they, as if the initiators of each were attempting to drown out the other.

Strange currents of power flowed through him now, beneath the old familiar shroud of deathly sorcery. Like an adder beneath the water, this new power warmed him to his joints, and buoyed him. It had healed his mind and memory and soul, though it had taken centuries to do so. Centuries to clear out the rot of Nagash, Kemmler knew.

Nagash had used him. It was Nagash who had used him to build an empire, and Nagash who had guided him to Krell, but not for Kemmler's sake. That was what the whisperers had told him. And it was Nagash who wanted to use him now. It was Nagash who stalked him in the dark hollows of memory, hunting the tatters of his soul.

Fear, now, warred with rage. He flailed as a thread of magic slipped between his fingers. A nearby zombie flopped down, inert and inanimate. More followed suit, and Kemmler hissed in mounting frustration. Concentrate, he had to concentrate. Between the hammer of the drum and the mounting agitation of the whispers, he heard the telltale cackle of the skull atop his staff.

Kemmler turned, and his eyes narrowed. He caught a pale wisp of rising magics – not the ashy smoke of the wind of death, but the gossamer effluvium of the raw stuff of life – and saw a trio of women standing behind the embattled shieldwall of peasantry. His lips writhed back from his teeth in a snarl of disdain.

The women were marshalling the magics of life to counteract his sorceries of death. Behind them, moss and flowers crawled across the stones of the abbey walls, and thick vines and roots crawled across the battlefield about them. The impertinence of it assaulted his sensibilities, and he slammed the end of his staff down, planting it like a standard.

'This is my ground, witches,' he hissed. And it was, in every way that mattered. He had bought it in blood and time. Every time he had made war in this place, on the abbey, he had shed his life's blood and soured the ground with the stuff of death. They could plant all of the trees and flowers they liked, remove all of the bodies, weave every protective enchantment known to elf or man, but the ground was still his and would be forever more.

As if they had heard his words, three pairs of eyes, violet and alien, met his own dark ones. He felt a jolt as three minds, trained to think inhuman thoughts and bent to inhuman goals, reached out to him. They were powerful, these witches. The cursed elves of Athel Loren had taken their natural gifts and forced them down unnatural paths, moulding them into weapons to be used against their own kind.

Thoughts like claws tore at his connection to the winds of magic, severing his links with brutal efficiency. He snarled and champed like a beast in a trap, and every vein stood out in his neck and arms as he reached for his staff with his free hand. A wind sprang from nowhere, tearing at him, hot and cold all at once. His bones felt heavy, but hollow, and things that might have been maggots squirmed beneath his flesh and dripped from the unhealed wound that Tancred had dealt him. The soil churned beneath him, as if in pain, and there was moss growing on his staff. He swept it off angrily.

They had minds like trees with ancient roots: anchored and arrogant. He lashed out at them, attacking them mind to mind, and was rebuffed. Kemmler ground his teeth in growing frustration. His rage turned incandescent and burned away all hesitation.

The whispers rose, drowning out the drumbeat. Warmth – true warmth – flooded him, filling the cold emptiness that Nagash had left in him all those centuries ago when his voice, his spirit, had abandoned Kemmler on the eve of the Battle of Ten Thousand Skulls. *Yes,* they whispered. *Yes, yes, yes, it is all yours for the taking. You do not serve us, but we will serve you.* And he knew that they lied, because they were crafted from the very stuff of falsehood; but he also knew that what they offered was real – and that Arkhan, and his phantom master, offered nothing at all save the very thing that Kemmler had fled from down through the long, winding night-mare road of years.

No, better damnation than oblivion.

Better madness than servitude.

Better to fight and fail than surrender and be nothing.

'Mine – the abbey, the air you breathe, the ground you stand on, all of it mine,' Kemmler snarled, as the fire surged in him. He dug the end of his staff into the ground the way a torturer might dig a blade into the flesh of his victim. 'So listen and listen well to the master of La Maisontaal, witches.' Power flooded through him as he gripped his staff with both hands and channelled the new, destructive magics that hummed through his veins into the earth. Pockets of dark magic and old, sour death awoke at its touch, and the ground lost its colour as he sent the awakened power burrowing through the soil. 'I am not the intruder here. *You are.*'

He felt, rather than saw, the panic begin to creep in and undermine their inhuman calm. They could feel the very earth beneath their feet rejecting their petty magics. Steam escaped from the cracked and dying soil, rising up to mingle with the smoke of the fires. Three pairs of hands began to weave a complicated counter-spell, but it was too late.

Kemmler smiled as he felt their mystical defences fall away, as if they had built them on sand. Then, the sky spoke harshly, and a bolt of black lightning lanced down through the dark sky to strike the three women and the men who protected them. Kemmler felt their deaths and he threw his head back and expelled a cackle.

'Thus to all who would deny me my proper due,' he roared. 'Heinrich Kemmler yet lives!' He swept out his hands and felt his ebullience fill the dead around him, driving them faster and lending strength to their falter-ing limbs.

For a moment, he stood in an eye of calm amidst the chaos of battle. He felt strong – stronger than he had ever felt before. He was cloaked in magic, and his wound was healed. He sucked in a breath.

The dead hesitated. Empty eyes turned towards him, and lipless mouths flapped as though in warning. His skull staff was silent. The rush of confi-dence, of self-assurance, faded. Kemmler licked his lips, suddenly nervous. Though many corpses were looking at him, they were all doing so with the same set of eyes. And they were neither as dead nor as empty as he had first thought. They were dark with anger, and with promise.

Kemmler pushed through their ranks. One or two reached out for him, but he clubbed them aside with his staff and his will. More and more of them turned to follow him, but not in the way they had before. He felt his control slacken, and knew then what he had given up.

It was time to get what he had come for.

It was time to put an end to things.

◄ CHAPTER FIFTEEN ►

Mordkin Lair, the Border Princes

'Again! Burninate them again – quick-rapid!' Snikrat shrieked, beating one of the warpfire gunners about the head with the flat of his blade. 'Immolate, by which I mean set fire to, the cursed twice-dead, but still somehow moving and, more importantly, *biting,* things!'

Things were not going as well as Snikrat had hoped.

The gunner chattered curses as he aimed the warpfire thrower and unleashed a second belch of crackling green flames into the mouths of the tunnels that opened up onto the cavern. The fire lashed out indiscriminately, spraying the walls and those skaven too slow in retreating as well as the inexorable dead. Skaven flooded out of the tunnel past Snikrat and his warriors, squealing and slapping ineffectually at their fur as they sought to escape the hungry grasp of the flames.

The undead came on at a remorseless pace, pushing through the flames. Some fell, but these were replaced by more. And those that had fallen continued to crawl or slither forward until they were consumed entirely by the snapping flames. They inundated the upper tunnels, marching blindly into the spears and swords of the skaven, dragging down their destroyers as they were hacked apart. No matter how desperately the skaven fought, no matter how ferociously or cunningly, they could not match the dead, nor the unbending will that forced them on, metre by metre, tunnel by tunnel. Little by little, the warriors of Clan Mordkin were being driven back to the very heart of their domain.

'More! More-more-*more!*' Snikrat wailed, battering away at the unfortunate gunner with his blade for emphasis. 'Hotter! Faster! Quicker! Don't look at me idiot-fool – look at them!' The warpfire gunner snarled and hunched, trying to avoid the blows. The warpfire throwers burbled and a third roar of green flame spewed out, momentarily obliterating the mouth of the tunnel. 'Yes! Yes! Yes!' Snikrat bounced on his feet, sword waving over his head as the front rank of corpses vanished, utterly consumed. 'Fall and cease, dead-dead things. Snikrat the Magnificent commands you in his most commanding and authoritative manner to die, by which he means die again, and to thus stop moving!' Behind him, his Bonehides began to cheer in relieved fashion. The stormvermin hadn't been looking forward to fighting the undead again, especially in the cramped tunnels.

The cheers died away abruptly as the first stumbling, staggering torch lurched blindly out of the tunnel mouth. It was followed by another and another and another, until it seemed as if hundreds of burning corpses were squirming towards Snikrat's ragged battle-line. A snorting undead boar, still girded with the legs of the orc who had ridden it in life, barrelled towards the warpfire throwers.

Snikrat yelped and, in his haste to scramble out of the way, his sword accidentally chopped through the hose. Green liquid sprayed everywhere as the burning pig lunged at the hapless gunners. The resulting explosion picked Snikrat up by the scruff of his neck and sent him hurtling away from the tunnel mouth, his fur crisping and his flesh burning.

He hit the cave floor hard and rolled, snuffing the flames that had caught him in the process. The cavern rumbled as fire washed the walls. Timber props, weakened by the gushing warpfire, gave way, and some of the tunnels collapsed, burying the living and the dead alike.

As Snikrat scrambled to his feet, clutching his burned tail to his chest, he saw the few surviving warriors of the Bonehides fall, dragged down by the burning dead. The air stank of fear-musk as the remaining warriors began to stream away from the cavern, pelting into the various tunnels, swarming away from the groping dead.

The tunnels were lost. Feskit was not going to be happy. Nonetheless, it was Snikrat's duty to report on his sad failure, in person, to his liege lord. He ran with heroic alacrity, his injured tail whipping behind him as he pelted down the tunnel. He used his weight and strength to smash aside fleeing clanrats, and when the tunnel was so packed with squealing skaven that such tactics proved impossible, he scrambled up onto a clanrat's shoulders and bounded across the heads of the others as they fought and bit for space.

Snikrat burst out of the crowded confines of the tunnel and sprinted towards the Mordkin lair's final line of defence – a vast chasm, which split the outer tunnels from the great central cavern that was the rotten heart of the burrow. A long and winding bridge spanned the chasm. Composed of planks, spars, tar-clogged ropes and other detritus fit for purpose, including but not limited to panels of metal, bones and sheets of filthy cloth, it was the very pinnacle of skaven efficiency and engineering, and the sight of it lent Snikrat speed.

There was no other way across the chasm, not for leagues in any direction. Feskit had long ago ordered all other routes undermined to better prevent infiltration or attack by rival clans or ambitious greenskins. Skaven were clustered about the bridge, some trying to organise themselves into

something approaching military readiness, while others were squealing and
fighting to cross the bridge before their fellows. Snikrat charged headlong
into the disorganised knot of clanrats, laying about him with his fist and
sword until he reached the bridge and began to scramble across.

He heard the communal groan of their foes echo through the cavern
as he ran. Skaven began to scream and the bridge swayed wildly as clanrats followed him, pursued closely by the swarming dead. Snikrat whirled
as something grabbed his tail. A zombie, blackened by fire and missing
most of its flesh, had lunged through the confusion and latched on to him.
Snikrat shrilled in terror and lopped off the top of the thing's grinning skull.
It slumped, and its weight nearly pulled him from the bridge. As he extricated himself, he saw that those skaven who had been following him had
not been nearly so lucky. They fell or were hurled into the chasm by the
stumbling corpses, as the latter pressed forward, crawling along the bridge.
The whole ramshackle structure shuddered and swayed wildly, and Snikrat
had a sudden vision of himself plummeting into the darkness below.

Fear lent him wings, and he fairly flew towards the opposite side. A small
army of clanrat weaponeers were gathering there, beneath the watchful
eyes of several other sub-chiefs. Warpfire throwers and jezzail teams assembled along the edge of the chasm, weapons at the ready. As Snikrat hurtled
to join them, he screamed, 'Burn it! Burn the bridge – hurry, hurry, hurry!'

With somewhat unseemly haste, the warpfire throwers roared, the
tongues of green flame barely missing him as they struck the centre of
the span. He crashed onto solid ground and rolled to his feet, teeth bared
and sword extended in what he hoped was a suitably heroic pose. 'Yes, yes!
Watch, minions – my grand strategy unfolds! See how cunningly Snikrat
the Magnificent wages war,' he cackled as the bridge began to groan and
shift. Then, with a shriek of rupturing wood and tearing cloth, it toppled
lazily into the chasm, carrying the dead with it.

Snikrat's cackles grew in volume, and he was joined in his triumphant
laughter by the other skaven as more and more zombies flooded out of the
tunnels and were pushed into the depths by the mindless ranks coming
behind them. The dead were stymied by the chasm, just as he had cunningly planned. Now was the time to unleash the full fury of Clan Mordkin's
arsenal. He shrieked orders to that effect, and the warpfire teams and jezzail
gunners opened fire in a cloud of black powder and scorched air.

Snikrat watched in satisfaction as the dead were plucked from the opposite side of the chasm by a barrage of warpstone bullets, which whined
and crashed across the divide. Zombies slewed off the edge and spiralled
into oblivion, or collapsed burning. With a hiss of triumph, he sheathed
his blade and strutted back towards the tunnels that led to the fortress-lair
to inform Feskit of his triumph.

By the time Snikrat made it back through the gates of the fortress-lair,
however, his ebullience had begun to sour. The clangour of alarms still

choked the air, and clanrats scampered past him, running far more quickly than he would have expected. He could hear screams as well, and once, the dull crump of a warpfire thrower exploding.

Snikrat began to run. He had to explain to Feskit that whatever was happening wasn't his fault. The weaponeers had disobeyed his orders – the clanrats had broken and run – the chieftains were fleeing – only Snikrat was loyal enough to stand beside Feskit, as he had in times past. His hand clenched on the hilt of his blade, as, in the depths of his twisty mind, the thought surfaced that merciful Feskit would surely be distracted enough to accept Snikrat's blade at his back. He would need all of the loyal servants he could get, would old Feskit.

Snikrat had visions of himself courageously stabbing the tyrant of Mordkin in the back as Mordkin's arsenal of weapons and beasts exterminated the dead. They carried him all the way to Feskit's throne room, where chieftains and thralls scurried about in varying levels of panic. The alarm bells were deafening here, and they were ringing so ferociously that one snapped loose of its line and plummeted down, crushing a dozen slaves into a pulpy mess as Snikrat watched.

'You failed,' Feskit hissed from behind him. Snikrat spun, his paw still on the hilt of his sword. Feskit was surrounded by his Mordrat Guard, and Snikrat jerked his claws away from his sword as they levelled their halberds.

'No! Successes unparalleled, oh merciful Feskit! Snikrat the Faithful, Snikrat the Dutiful, was failed by faithless, cowardly clanrats and irresponsible underlings; I-I came to warn you that the dead-dead things advance towards the gates even now,' Snikrat babbled, his mind squirming quickly as he tried to stay on top of the situation. 'They-they have crossed the chasm somehow – magic! They crossed it with magic, foul sorcery – and Snikrat came back to see to your defence personally.'

'Did he?' Feskit said. 'I feel safer already.' His eyes glinted. He glanced at one of his stormvermin. 'Rouse the packmasters and the remaining weaponeers. Summon the turn-tail chieftains who enjoy my gracious hospitality, and scour the barrack-burrows for every stormvermin,' he snarled.

'And... and what of Snikrat, oh most kindly lord?' Snikrat squeaked hesitantly. He rubbed his scarred throat, and wondered if he should make himself scarce.

Feskit glared at him, and then said, 'You... Hrr, yes, I have a special task for you, Snikrat.' He turned and grabbed another stormvermin by his cuirass and jerked him close. 'You – tell the slaves to fetch... the Weapon.'

The stormvermin paled beneath his black fur. Feskit snarled again and shoved him back. 'Fetch it now, quick-quick!' Snikrat smelt the spurt of fear-musk that rose from the assembled stormvermin at the thought of the Weapon. The Fellblade, with its blade of glistening black warpstone. Could Feskit mean to give it to him to wield? He felt his courage return. With that blade in hand, Snikrat knew he would be invincible.

'I will not fail you, Lord Feskit,' Snikrat hissed, head full of the victories to come.

'No, you will not,' Feskit said. Then, with a lunge that would have put a wolf-rat to shame, he sank his yellow, chisel teeth into Snikrat's throat. Snikrat tumbled back, clutching at his ruined jugular. Through a darkening haze, he saw Feskit chew and swallow the lump of gristle and flesh. 'The Fellblade drains its wielder. You shall sustain me through the efforts to come, loyal Snikrat,' Feskit said, cleaning his whiskers as his stormvermin raised their blades over Snikrat, to complete his butchery. As everything went dark, he heard Feskit say, 'Thank you for your contribution.'

La Maisontaal Abbey, Bretonnia

Arkhan's mind was like a spider's web, stretched to its breaking point by a strong wind, covering the battlefield. In the north, he urged Krell on about his bloody business. In the south, he goaded the shuffling dead to keep pace with the rest of the army. What remained of his attentions were fixed on Kemmler, and when he felt the surge of power, he knew that his suspicions had been proven correct.

The Lichemaster was more powerful now than ever before, and that power had not come from Nagash. The decaying cat on his shoulder hissed as a bolt of black lightning cut down through the night sky and struck a point on the battlefield. '*What are you up to, necromancer?*' Arkhan said, out loud.

The winds of death suddenly thrashed about him, as if they were ropes that had been pulled taut. He felt the air pulse with indefinable motions and saw things not born of the world move through the shifting gossamer aurora of magics that hung over the battlefield. Daemonic voices cackled in his ear, and gloating phantom faces gibbered at him and vanished. His attentions snapped down, retracting to focus on Kemmler. But before he could do so fully, he was brutally interrupted.

'Death to the dealers of death!' the knight bellowed as his horse bulled through Arkhan's skeletal bodyguard and drove the blade of his axe down through the liche's ribcage, before the latter could react. The blow lifted Arkhan from his feet and sent him to the ground in a heap. The laughter of the Dark Gods roared in his head. He could see the trap now, in all of its crooked cunning. The beastmen, Kemmler, all of it... He was caught in the jaws of a hungry fate. Even now, with more than half of the knights who had crashed into the flanks of his host dead, there were still enough Bretonnians left on the field to carry the day, if Arkhan fell.

Something – not quite panic – filled him. It wasn't desperation either, but frustration. To have come so close only to be denied. He saw the cat streaking towards him. It had fallen from his shoulders when he was knocked down, and he felt bereft, though he could not say why. Above him, in the smoke, faces leered down at him, mouthing the vilest curses, and devilish shapes capered invisibly about the knight, kept at bay by the light emanating from his axe. The Dark Gods wanted Arkhan in the ground, and more, it seemed that they wanted to watch him being put there.

Under other circumstances, he might have felt flattered. As the knight urged his horse forward, Arkhan's shattered, brown bones began to repair themselves. The knight growled in satisfaction as he closed in. Arkhan tried to heave himself up. 'Oh no, evil one. That will not do. The Lady has tasked Theoderic of Brionne with giving you the long overdue gift of death, and you shall accept it in full,' the knight roared as he raised his axe. His armour was battered and stained, but the blade of his axe glowed brightly as the dawn broke over the battlefield.

Before the blow could fall, a blur of red iron interposed itself between axe and bone, and the knight was toppled from his saddle. Arkhan was somewhat surprised to see Anark von Carstein there, blade in hand, armour torn and stained with the detritus of hard fighting. Another slash and the knight's horse screamed and fell, hooves kicking uselessly in its death throes. Arkhan watched in satisfaction as the knight gasped as he tried to gather his feet under him. His fall had broken something in him, the liche knew. The man spat blood and groped for his axe. He caught it up, while Anark's blade descended for his skull. He swatted the blow aside and dragged himself to his feet.

'Give me your name, devil, so that I might tell it to the troubadours who will sing of this day in years to come,' Theoderic rasped, hefting his axe. Anark lunged without speaking, his blade moving quicker than the knight could follow. He interposed his axe, audibly swallowing a groan as whatever had broken inside him shifted painfully, and the edges of both weapons bit into one another. Arkhan watched the battle, somewhat amazed that the mortal was still on his feet. A raw light seemed to infuse him, as it had his axe, and it forced him up and on, lashing at him like a slave-driver's whip. The Bretonnians called it a blessing, but Arkhan knew it for what it was. Nagash had used similar spells to invigorate and drive forward the Yaghur in those dim, dark days of the past. Whatever the Lady was, whether she was some goddess of elves or men, or something else entirely, she was as desperate as the Chaos gods to see Arkhan stymied.

Theoderic smashed the vampire in the face with his elbow and knocked him to one knee. He drove his axe down, crumpling a blood-red pauldron and gashing Anark's neck. He drew his axe back and swung, knocking the vampire sprawling. 'Tell me your name, beast! Let it ring over the field!' he roared, swinging his axe up to take a two-handed grip on the haft as the beast clawed for its blade. The vampire moved so quickly, Theoderic's words had barely left his lips before Anark launched a blow that severed both of Theoderic's arms and his head as well.

'My name is Anark von Carstein, meat,' the vampire spat as he glared down at his fallen foe. Arkhan dragged himself upright. He touched the spot where the axe had caught him, and felt the bones click back into place. The weapon had been blessed, to do such damage, but he had survived worse in his time.

'*Indeed it is. It seems that I owe you a debt, von Carstein,*' Arkhan said as he retrieved his staff. The cat leapt up and hauled its way back onto his shoulder, its eyes glowing faintly. Most of the flesh was gone from its skull, and its spine rose above its sagging hide like a battlement. It felt as heavy as ever, and it gave an impatient miaow as it wrapped itself about his neck. He stroked its bony shoulder and set his staff. All around him the fallen dead, including what was left of Theoderic, began to slide and slither and stumble upright. Waste not, want not, after all.

'One that I will be only too happy to collect from you, but not until this affray is ended,' Anark growled. He gestured with his sword. 'Which shouldn't be too much longer, from the looks of things.'

Arkhan followed the gesture just in time to see the Bretonnian shieldwall shatter. Here and there, groups of men kept their order and fought against the tide that sought to overwhelm them. But most of them gave in to their terror and fled towards the dubious safety of the abbey walls. Krell's wights pursued, taking advantage of the breach in the line. The lines of archers and war engines were overrun by slavering ghouls, led by the Crowfiend, and embattled knights were surrounded by skeletons and clawing zombies. The battle was breaking down, becoming a slaughter.

The greater part of the Bretonnian army was dead or fleeing. Those who remained would not survive long. La Maisontaal Abbey was as good as theirs. The staff of Nagash would soon be on its way back to Sylvania, to be reunited with the other relics. Satisfaction filled him such as he had not felt in centuries.

The end was coming. The end of his road, of all struggle and strife. Lamps extinguished, story finished and finally... sleep. Blessed eternal sleep. He swept his staff through a curl of smoke full of silently snarling faces. '*Arkhan still lives, little gods. You have failed. And Nagash will shatter your petty schemes and hurl you back into the void that gave birth to you,*' he rasped, hurling his bravado at the wispy shapes like a javelin.

But his moment of satisfaction was brief. Kemmler was nowhere to be seen. And Arkhan knew where he had gone. He saw hazy daemonic shapes, small, stunted things, scampering towards the grounds of the abbey, invisible to all eyes but his. He looked at Anark. '*Finish this. Kill everything that lives.*'

The vampire looked at Arkhan as he started towards the abbey. 'And what about you?'

Arkhan didn't stop or turn. '*I go to claim our prize.*'

◄ CHAPTER SIXTEEN ►

Mordkin Lair, the Border Princes

'It's really quite amusing, in its way,' Markos murmured as he leaned against the tunnel mouth, arms crossed. 'They just keep wandering into the flames, don't they?'

'It's a waste of materials,' Count Nyktolos grunted. He plucked his monocle from his eye and cleaned it on the scorched hem of his cloak. 'We only have three thousand, six hundred and fifty-three zombies left.'

'Did you count them?' Markos asked, brow arched.

'No,' Nyktolos said. Then, 'Yes, possibly.' He put his monocle back into place and sniffed. 'There is very little to do down here but kill skaven or count zombies.'

Markos shook his head, and looked at Mannfred, where the latter stood in the tunnel mouth, hands clasped behind his back, gripping the staff of Kadon with the Claw of Nagash mounted atop it, held parallel to the ground. 'Well, cousin? You heard the Vargravian – we're running short on fodder. How do you intend to get us across that chasm?'

Mannfred ignored Markos. His eyes were fixed on the chasm ahead, rather than the group of vampires behind him. He heard the hiss of the bloodthirsty steeds of the Drakenhof Templars, and the soft clatter of his own skeletal mount. The former were as impatient to taste the blood of their enemies as their masters were.

He lifted the staff, and the Claw flexed. The power it radiated throbbed in him like the ache of a sore tooth. The Fellblade was close – too close to allow such a minor obstacle to stymie him. A slow smile crept across his face, as he came to the obvious conclusion. Ignoring Markos's pestering, he strode out of the tunnel, towards the chasm. The zombies ceased their mindless advance as he took control of them directly once more, the reins of his will snapping taut about the husks, and pulled them in his wake.

Mannfred could feel the dregs of raw magic that still lurked in the warpfire-blackened stones, and in the shards of expended warpstone fired from the skaven weapons. He went to the edge of the chasm, where the anchors for the bridge had been torn free of the rock. He held the staff in both hands, and focused on drawing the residual magics from the warpstone all about him. The air bristled with energy, which only grew as the skaven began to fire at him. Warpstone bullets whistled past his head, and he drew their energy from them as they drew close. A corona of crackling magics swirled about him, and the burned and shattered dead scattered in heaps and piles began to stir.

The dead behind him moved towards the chasm, their rotting bodies shuddering as Mannfred gestured sharply. The dead flesh of the zombies split and tore as their bones began to lengthen and grow. Hooks of bone sank into the rock as the dead toppled forward. More zombies, some little more than burned skeletons, climbed over these, their bones going through a similar transformation. A symphony of bursting flesh and cracking bone overshadowed the crack of skaven weaponry as the gruesome bridge took shape.

The skaven's rate of fire grew more intense, and Mannfred's smile grew as a warpfire thrower, pushed past its limits, exploded and consumed its crew. Pistols and jezzails snapped and snarled, and bullets struck the bridge or hissed past Mannfred. More weapons began to misfire. The skaven began to retreat in ragged formation as the bridge drew closer and closer to the opposite ledge. Some continued to fire as they fell back, but most simply dropped their weapons and ran.

'Oh well done, cousin,' Markos said from behind Mannfred. He led his own mount and Mannfred's by their reins. 'Not subtle, mind, but we've dispensed with subtlety, haven't we?'

'Markos... shut up,' Mannfred growled, fixing Markos with a glare. He hauled himself up into his saddle. 'All of you, mount up. We are close to our goal, and I would tarry no longer. I want this business done. I grow tired of these reeking tunnels.'

So saying, Mannfred jerked his mount's reins and galloped over the bridge. Markos and the others followed suit. The bridge squirmed beneath the pounding hooves of their fiery-eyed horses. Seeing the onrushing knights, the remaining skaven turned to flee. But not one of the vermin made it to the dubious safety of the tunnels as Mannfred and his followers laid about them with their blades, lopping off heads and tails, and shattering spines as they crushed the ratkin to a red mulch beneath their hooves.

The dead flowed after them. Howling spectres led the way, filling these new tunnels as they had the others, flowing through every flue, nook and cranny that the skaven had dug. Hastily erected barricades of wood and metal were no barrier to immaterial beings, and skaven clanrats died in droves, unable to fight back or even flee. Zombies too pressed forward, flooding those passages wide enough to accommodate their sheer numbers. The dead skaven left in Mannfred's wake staggered up to join the advancing host, adding to the sheer bulk of corpses that choked the inner tunnels of the skaven stronghold.

As the dead fulfilled their function, Mannfred led his Templars on through the crooked burrow, Kadon's staff held out before him like a standard pole. The Claw of Nagash pulled him on, drawn inexorably towards its nemesis. Over the hours that followed, Mannfred and his warriors fought their way through waves of mutated beasts, armoured stormvermin and limitless ranks of skaven warriors. Some vampires were pulled down, but even outnumbered seven to one, Mannfred and the others were more than a match for the best that the ratkin could throw at them. Where blade and muscle would not suffice, Mannfred, supported by Markos, unleashed volley after volley of devastating spellcraft, scouring entire tunnels and caverns of all life before drawing their victims to their feet and sending them ahead to attack their fellows.

So it went for hours, until at last, Mannfred, at the head of his host, stood before the walls of the fortress-lair of the skaven. The walls were, like all skaven constructions, a derelict mismatch of materials, most of which had never been intended for such a purpose. The gates were a different, and much more interesting, matter. They were made from the bones of what appeared to be a great dragon, and as Mannfred examined them, he smiled.

'We can take the walls,' Count Nyktolos said, calming his restive steed. Mortar fire and warp lightning began to streak from the lopsided towers, as if in reply to his statement. He whistled. 'Or not,' he added.

'I lack the patience for a siege,' Mannfred said.

'Then what – surely you don't mean to parley with vermin?' Markos asked. Mannfred's smile spread. The other vampire sounded affronted.

Mannfred lifted the Claw of Nagash, and black lightning began to spit and spark from the twitching, spidery fingers. He chuckled. 'No, Markos. I have a more... elegant solution in mind.'

La Maisontaal Abbey, Bretonnia

Erikan bounded through the line of trebuchets, his blade singing out to open up an unlucky peasant's throat. The man fell, gagging on his own blood, and the ghouls that had followed Erikan pounced on him, ending his troubles with a few well-placed bites. Erikan watched them feed for a moment, and then continued on, pursuing the fleeing peasantry. More ghouls followed him, baying hungrily as they knuckled across the uneven ground.

The true dead were barred from the abbey grounds for the moment, leaving only creatures like himself and the ghouls capable of crossing the boundary stones in pursuit of the peasants. He'd left his horse somewhere amongst the abandoned artillery pieces. He'd never been very comfortable fighting from the back of a steed. He felt like too much of a target. Let Anark and the others play at hammer and anvil with the flower of Bretonnian chivalry. He would hunt amongst the stones and take his share of scalps there.

The air sizzled with sorcery, and he heard a thunderclap, which shook the ground beneath his boots as he moved. In the next moment, Krell bulled into the line of archers, his great black axe chopping through armour, flesh and bone with ease. Men died screaming. Smoke coiled through the air, obscuring his vision for a moment.

When it cleared, he saw a hunched shape hurrying towards the abbey. Kemmler, he realised, after a moment. The necromancer was far ahead of them, and moving more quickly than Erikan had thought possible for such a broken-down wreck of a human being. Another curl of smoke obscured the Lichemaster, and when it cleared he was gone. Erikan considered pursuing him, and then decided that it wasn't even remotely his problem.

An armoured knight, unhorsed and bare-headed, charged towards him. He shouted unintelligible oaths and awkwardly swiped at the vampire with his blade. He was barely more than a youth, and his eyes were wide with fear and determination. Erikan parried his next blow, and for a moment, duelled back and forth with the young knight. He felt no satisfaction when his blade slid through his opponent's guard and crunched into his throat. He kicked the body off his sword and spun in time to chop an inexpertly wielded halberd in two.

He stepped back as the man who'd thrust it at him was bowled over by a ghoul sow and her mate. The two creatures smashed the wailing peasant to the ground, but didn't kill him. The sow shrilled a question at Erikan. He looked at her, and then at the cursing, struggling man she held down. Men just like him had taken Erikan from the only home he knew, and put his parents to the torch. The knights had ordered it, but men like this one... They had taken pleasure in it. They had enjoyed seeing his family die.

For a moment, as he stared down at the pale, frightened features, he remembered that night – the stink of torches cutting through the comforting miasma of the tunnels, his mother shrieking in anger and fear as his father bellowed and hewed at the invaders with his fine sword. He remembered his brothers and sisters fleeing into the darkness as men rode the slower ones down. He remembered a white sun on a red sky turning black. He remembered Obald saving him from the flames, and a red-haired woman – had it been Elize, even then? The memory was fuzzy and he couldn't be sure – tending his burns.

But mostly, he remembered fire and blood.

Erikan snarled and hacked the helpless man's head from his shoulders. He lifted his blade and licked the blood from it, as the ghouls fell to their feast. He looked about him, watching as the battle became a massacre. A new day was dawning, but the skies were mournful, as if the clouds were weeping for the fate of the defenders of La Maisontaal.

297

He smiled, amused at the thought. Let the world weep, if it wished. Crying never made anything better. The first drops of rain had begun to fall when he heard the horns. He turned, and his eyes widened. A curse flew from his lips as he saw the standards rising over the melee.

The new arrivals came by the south road, as if they'd followed in the footsteps of the dead. Ghouls scattered before them, and zombies were trampled beneath the hooves of their steeds as the column of knights plunged deep into the undead ranks, further fracturing an already divided army. The knights struck the dead like a battering ram, their lances thrust forwards to catch the enemy. When the lances had done their work, swords came into play, hacking apart rotting limbs and splintering ancient bone.

The undead reeled, and those with any spark of initiative converged on the newcomers. Erikan saw Anark and the other Drakenhof Templars fighting their way towards the knights, and Krell as well. Satisfied that he wasn't needed, he turned back, ready to order his ghouls into the abbey. Before he could do so, a shadow fell over him.

He looked up as the ghouls scattered, wailing. A lance crashed into his shoulder and knocked him sprawling. The pegasus swooped overhead as its rider released his shattered lance and drew his sword. 'Filthy flesh-eater,' the knight roared as his flying steed dived back towards Erikan. He scrambled aside, narrowly avoiding the blow. He snatched up his sword from where it had fallen and flung himself into the frame of a trebuchet. The pegasus galloped past, wings snapping like thunderclaps. More pegasus knights plunged through the air, attacking the ghouls and wights.

Out of the corner of his eye, he saw Krell swat one of the newcomers from the air, killing both pegasus and rider with a single blow. The wight was steadily chopping his way through enemy and ally alike as he fought his way towards the knight in the fanciest armour. From long, bitter experience, Erikan knew that one was likely the leader. He silently wished Krell luck, though he doubted the creature would either need or appreciate it.

Erikan skinned up through the frame of the trebuchet, climbing towards the arm. His attacker circled the trebuchet, rising back into the air as Erikan burst out into the open, and as quick as lightning, climbed the arm. He ran upwards, sword held low, and sprang into the air as the pegasus passed overhead. His hand snapped out and caught hold of the saddle.

With a twist of his shoulder, he flung himself up and landed on the back of the snorting, bucking beast. The knight twisted in his saddle but not quickly enough, and their blades locked. Erikan's lunge carried him and his enemy off the pegasus, and they hurtled towards the ground.

Erikan struck the earth first, and he shrieked as he felt bones crack. Thrashing wildly, he sent the knight flying. The man climbed awkwardly to his feet, his armour rattling. Erikan slithered to his feet, his body already healing. The knight had lost his sword in the fall, as had Erikan. The former scooped up a spear and lunged smoothly, faster than Erikan expected, and

caught him in the belly. With a single, powerful thrust, he shoved Erikan
back and up. Erikan howled and grasped at the haft of the spear.

'When you get to whatever damnation awaits you, tell them it was Fastric
Ghoulslayer who sent you,' the knight roared, shoving the vampire back.
The point of the spear burst out from between Erikan's shoulder blades,
punching through his armour and pinning him to the frame of a trebuchet.
He screamed in agony. The spear had only just missed his heart, but agony
sizzled through him, causing his limbs to spasm helplessly.

'Do it yourself,' Erikan spat, through bloody teeth. He kicked out and
knocked his enemy sprawling. He tore the haft of the spear to flinders and
fell to the ground. With a snarl, he ripped the splinter of wood from his
chest and flung himself onto the knight before the latter could get to his
feet. He clawed at the man's helm as the latter struggled, and shoved the
edge of it up, exposing a small expanse of flesh. With a triumphant howl,
Erikan plunged the splinter of wood into the soft flesh just below his opponent's jaw, and shoved until the tip scraped metal. The man shuddered
beneath him, and went still.

Erikan rolled aside and looked up into the cold, burning gaze of Arkhan
the Black. '*Kemmler... Where is he?*'

Erikan pointed weakly towards the abbey. Arkhan nodded and stepped
over him. Erikan watched the liche stalk towards the abbey. 'You're welcome,' he coughed, and shoved himself to his feet. Then he began to search
for his sword, one hand pressed to the wound in his chest.

There was still a battle to win.

◄ CHAPTER SEVENTEEN ►

Mordkin Lair, the Border Princes

The gates twisted and then shrieked, the dark spirit that still clung to the ancient dragon's bones giving voice to its frustration and rage. Ropes snapped and wood ruptured as the creature tore itself free of the fortress walls that rested upon it, and the dragon's skeleton rose to its full terrifying height for the first time since its death at the hands of the skaven. The walls sagged and crumbled as the great beast thrust itself into the lair of its murderers, seeking vengeance on the descendants of those who had long ago feasted on its flesh. Skaven died in droves as they tried to flee.

The reanimated dragon reared up and ripped an artillery tower apart. Its whip-like tail curved out, the sorcerously hardened bone cutting through stone and wood like a scythe through wheat, and part of the outer wall exploded into ragged fragments.

'Elegant, he says,' Markos muttered, as he stared at the ensuing devastation.

'Perhaps we have different definitions of the term,' Mannfred said, smiling thinly. 'Regardless, we have our path.' He raised the staff. 'For Drakenhof! For Sternieste! For Sylvania – ride!' He drove his spurs into the fleshless flanks of his horse of bones, and it shot forward, galloping faster than any living creature. His knights, vampire and wight alike, followed in his wake. They charged towards the shattered walls and on through, riding hard amidst the dust and smoke. Zombies poured through in their wake, hungry for the flesh of the living, as Mannfred allowed his control to lapse. Let the dead go where they would, and cause what mischief they wished. The more confusion, the better for him.

Skaven weapons overloaded and exploded as the gunners on the walls tried to bring down the reanimated dragon. Warp lightning arced out, destroying the ramshackle buildings and obliterating knots of skaven who rushed to repel the invaders.

Mannfred gave vent to a primal howl as he rode down a mob of clanrats. In the days since he'd entered the tunnels, he'd refrained from engaging in

battle more than was necessary. But now he was free to unfetter his accumulated frustrations. His knights scattered, similarly hungry for carnage.
Their lances and swords tore the life from the clanrats and stormvermin
who sought to keep them at bay, or else escape them.

Mannfred unleashed baleful magics and laid about him with his blade,
following the pull of the Claw. The Fellblade was close. He could feel it,
like an itch behind his eyes. He pursued the sensation, galloping down the
central thoroughfare of the fortress-lair, eliminating anything that dared
cross his path.

Then, at last, he saw it. The Fellblade seemed to blaze with a darkling
light, as its wielder swept it through the air in a gesture of command. The
skaven warlord – for so Mannfred judged the heavily muscled, grey-furred
beast to be – crouched atop a heavy shield, carried by four of its black-furred
bodyguards. It was surrounded by a phalanx of stormvermin, and as it
caught sight of him, its eyes bulged with rage. It gestured at him and chittered shrilly. The stormvermin began to advance cautiously towards him.
Mannfred brought his steed to a halt and watched them come.

He considered simply charging into their midst. Kill a few, and the rest
would flee. And, as big as the warlord was, it was little more than a beast
and no threat to him. But the presence of the Fellblade in its paw gave
him pause. Craven though its owner might have been, the blade was still
dangerous. Even a lucky blow might harm him greatly. So... the oblique
approach, then.

Mannfred slid from the saddle. Then, mustering the quicksilver speed
of his bloodline, he sped towards the advancing skaven. But rather than
attacking them, he sprang aside, skirting them and winnowing through
their ranks faster than their beady eyes could follow. He let his blade lick
out, and the shield-bearers who held the warlord's makeshift palanquin
aloft fell, blood spraying from their wounds. The warlord was spilled to the
ground with a wail. The other stormvermin reacted much as he'd predicted,
and panic swept through them. He ignored them, and circled the warlord
as the beast struggled to its feet.

It whirled with commendable speed, launching a blow that, under other
circumstances, might have split him crown to groin. But to Mannfred, the
beast was moving in slow motion. He watched the blow descend before
casually stepping into the arc of the swing. He grabbed the warlord's
forearm, and snapped it with a twist of his wrist as he slid the point of
his own blade through the creature's rusted breastplate and scabrous chest.

The skaven gave a shrill, agonised cry, and sank down to its knees. The
Fellblade fell from its worthless paws and clattered to the ground. With a
final whimper, the creature toppled forward, and kicked in its death throes.
Mannfred watched it die, and felt little satisfaction.

*Well, he was hardly a worthy opponent, was he? A bit anticlimactic, wasn't
it?* Vlad laughed. *More like pest control than a true battle.*

Mannfred ignored the shadowy presence and scooped up the Fellblade. It seemed to writhe in his grip for a moment, like a spiteful cat, before it grew still. He peered down the length of the sword, studying the eerie patina of the black blade. Then he shoved it through his belt without flourish and remounted his steed.

He summoned his remaining knights and Templars to him as he rode back through the ruined gates of the fortress-lair, ignoring the battle that still raged all around him. The reanimated dragon and the zombies would serve to keep the skaven occupied for several days to come, until the magic he had used to reanimate them at last faded. After that, let the skaven do as they would. He couldn't care less whether they survived, flourished or perished. Whatever their fate, they were no longer of any importance.

Mannfred bent low over his steed's neck as he began the long trek back to the surface. He had his prize, and there was much work yet to be done.

Nagash would rise, and Mannfred would rule.

La Maisontaal Abbey, Bretonnia

'*Kemmler!*'

The aged necromancer turned as Arkhan's challenge echoed through the darkened crypt that lay in the bowels of the abbey. The bodies of the brothers of La Maisontaal lay about him on the floor, slain when they'd made one last desperate attempt to defend the malevolent artefact long ago given into their care. Arkhan paid no heed to the crumpled corpses as he stepped into the chamber.

Kemmler smiled and lifted the Great Staff of Nagash, Alakanash, in triumph. 'Too late, puppet. Too late,' he said. 'I've found it, and I have claimed it.'

'*If I am a puppet, I am not alone in that,*' Arkhan rasped. He had foreseen Kemmler's betrayal. Subtlety had never been the Lichemaster's strong suit. But he had never expected the old fiend to possess enough courage to take up Nagash's staff for his own. He could practically hear the shard of Nagash in the staff writhing in animal fury, and Kemmler's knuckles were white as he tightened his grip on his prize.

'Indeed. I have been a puppet for more years than I care to remember, liche,' Kemmler said. 'Not as long as you, but long enough to know that I do not wish to end up like you – a hollow, thin thing of ashes and scraps, haunting its own bones. Nagash is as much a vampire as the von Carsteins. He feasts on us, taking and taking, until there's nothing left. And then he drags us up to take yet more. Creatures like you and Krell might have no will of your own left, but Heinrich Kemmler is no dead thing's slave.' He circled the sarcophagus slowly, leaning on Nagash's staff. Even now, he was playing the tired old man, though Arkhan could see the power flowing through his withered frame, and the invisible daemons that capered about him like eager children. 'I am the master here. Not you. And certainly not Nagash. He might have his hooks in you and in the fanged fop, Mannfred, but the Lichemaster is no dogsbody. I have found new patrons.'

'*New masters, you mean,*' Arkhan said.

'Partners,' Kemmler said, flashing rotten teeth in an expression that was as much grimace as grin. It was a lie, and a vainglorious one, and Kemmler knew it. 'They recognise my power, liche. They see me for what I am, what I have always been, and they shower me with their gifts where Nagash would grind me under.' He smiled in a sickly fashion. 'And oh, they hate him. They hate him more than any creature that has yet walked this world. They hate him for his hubris, and they hate him for what he would do to this world.'

'*They hate him. And they fear him,*' Arkhan said. '*Otherwise, this conversation would not be taking place. They fear him, and you fear him. The Dark Gods are mice, scrabbling in the holes of time, and Nagash is the cat who will drive them out.*' As he moved forwards, his thoughts reached out to the freshly slain bodies of the monks, and they began to twitch and scrabble at the floor. If he was quick, he might be able to overwhelm Kemmler before he became attuned to the power contained within the staff.

'Not without this he won't,' Kemmler said. He lifted the staff and brought it down, so that the butt struck the floor. The stones hummed with a black note as mortar and dust cascaded down. Several of the bodies flopped back into motionlessness. 'Answer me honestly, Arkhan... Do you truly want him back?'

Arkhan stopped. '*What?*'

'It's a simple enough question,' Kemmler said. 'Do you want him back? Have you ever questioned that desire? Are you even *capable* of doing so?' He shook his head. 'What am I saying? Of course you aren't.'

Arkhan said nothing. Kemmler's words echoed through him. That was the question, wasn't it? He had never truly considered it before. He wanted to throw the Lichemaster's assertions back into his face, but he couldn't. The cat dug its claws into his shoulder. It seemed to weigh more than it had, as if death had lent it mass.

Before he could muster a reply, the beast yowled and sprang across the distance between Arkhan and Kemmler, raking the latter's wizened face. The necromancer screamed and batted the animal aside with the staff. The cat's body struck the wall and fell in a tangle of broken bones and rotting flesh, but it had accomplished its goal. Arkhan threw aside his staff and lunged with all the speed his long-dead frame could muster. Skeletal palms struck the staff in Kemmler's hands and, for a moment, liche and Lichemaster stood frozen. Living eyes met dead ones, and a moment of understanding passed between them.

Arkhan understood Kemmler's rage, his fear and his obsession. But he could not forgive it. Once, maybe. But not now. For now, Arkhan understood what was truly at stake. There were only two paths available to the world as it stood here in this moment – one led to madness and the destruction of the natural order, as the world was remade by the Dark Gods in their image; the other led to a cessation of everything before those horrific changes could be wrought. Had he not already had his destiny chosen for him, Arkhan knew which he would have preferred. At least Nagash might let him rest, eventually.

'*You have always been a selfish, short-sighted creature, Heinrich,*' Arkhan rasped. Kemmler grimaced and began to mouth a spell, but Arkhan swung him about and smashed him back against the sarcophagus that had contained the staff. '*Driven by petty desires, unable to see the bigger picture even when it is laid out before you. The Great Work must be completed, and no turncoat beggar with delusions of grandeur will stop it. Nagash must rise, and if you must fall to serve that end, so be it. You call yourself the Lichemaster... Well then, prove it.*'

Kemmler howled and the raw stuff of magic erupted from him, cascading over Arkhan, searing his bones and blackening his robes. But the liche refused to release his grasp on the staff. His will smashed against Kemmler's, probing for some weakness. The old man's will was like unto a thing of iron, forged by adversity and rooted in spite, but Arkhan's was stronger yet. He had conquered death more than once, clawing his way back to the world of the living again and again. '*Prove it,*' he said again, dragging Kemmler towards him. '*Prove your boasts, old man. Show me the fiend who almost cracked the spine of the world at the Battle of Ten Thousand Skulls.*'

'I'll show you,' Kemmler screeched. He shoved Arkhan back, and they strained against one another, the staff caught between them. 'I'll not be your slave! I am Kemmler – I have broken cities and empires. I have slain armies,' he shrilled. 'And I will kill you, once and for all!'

Spell clashed against spell and magic inundated the chamber, splashing across the stones like blood. Arkhan could feel it building, growing in strength as the magic fed on itself and its surroundings. There were too many dangerous artefacts here, and they all resonated with the power that poured from him and Kemmler, even while the staff did.

The chamber around them began to shake. There was a thunderous crash as the windows upstairs succumbed to the growing pressure and exploded outwards. Green fire licked out from between the stones, rippling around them as they struggled. A tornado of wild magic swirled, and La Maisontaal Abbey shuddered like a dying man. One of the holiest sites in Bretonnia was being ripped apart from the inside out, but Arkhan spared no thought for such trivialities. It was all he could do to maintain his grip on the staff. Kemmler shrieked and cursed as magical flames caressed his flesh, billowing up around him and from within him as his new gods filled him with their power. Arkhan held on grimly, ignoring the sorceries that tore at him.

Kemmler's flesh bulged and split like a blooming flower, and shapes squirmed in the dark within the raw redness of him. They were strange, terrible shapes that cursed and railed as they lashed Arkhan with fires of many hues and sweetly scented lightning. Kemmler's eyes protruded, and the determination in them faded, swallowed by fire and intent. The skull-headed staff, which had been screaming the entire while, fell silent as it exploded into fragments. Caskets exploded out of the crypts around them, wreathed in fire. Arkhan felt ethereal talons tear at him and hideous voices wailed in his head, but he ignored them all, concentrating on the staff and his enemy. Kemmler's eyes widened still further, as if he'd seen something over Arkhan's shoulder, but Arkhan ignored the sudden babble of his voice.

And then, it was done. There was a roar, as of ocean waves smashing across rocks, and a great, sudden motion as if all of the earth had been thrown into the sky; a fire without heat filled Arkhan's vision. He heard Kemmler wail, and it was a sound full of horror and hopelessness and frustration. Then he was on one knee, leaning against Alakanash, amidst the crater that had once been the vaults of La Maisontaal Abbey.

Arkhan chuckled grimly and rose to his full height. Ash drifted off his ravaged robes. He heard the thunder of voices and the blare of horns, and knew that what was left of the Bretonnian army was retreating.

He looked around, searching for the cat. There was nothing left of the beast, save a pile of ash and, rising above it, an enormous shadow, which had been burned into the ravaged stones. There was something unpleasantly familiar about that shadow, and Arkhan felt a pang of unease. Then, with a skill born of long experience, he brushed the feeling aside.

Nagash would rise.

\blacktriangleleft CHAPTER EIGHTEEN ▶

The Black Mountains, the Border Princes

Mannfred coughed and rolled over onto his back, smoke rising from where the sorcerous blast had caught him. His fur cloak was burning and his armour was scorched. He knew by the taste of the magic who had attacked him, and he cursed himself. He had expected it to come sooner, and he had become distracted by the thrum of power that emanated from the Claw and the Fellblade. The hum of the ancient sorceries had lulled him, and now he was paying the price. His attacker strode towards him, casting aside his cloak of elegant haughtiness.

'I expect Anark has made his move by now, the sullen fool. He won't succeed, you know. And Erikan won't help him. The Crowfiend knows better than to get between creatures like you and the liche,' Markos said, stopping a short distance from Mannfred.

'A wisdom that you do not seem to share, cousin,' Mannfred said, as he rose to his feet. He cast a glance at the Fellblade where it lay, considering. Then, with a grunt, he turned away from it. He didn't need it.

'The Crowfiend knows his limits, as do I. Mine simply... extend a bit further than his,' Markos said, gesturing lazily.

'Have you chosen a side then, Markos? Picked a new master, perhaps?' Mannfred asked. He considered a spell, and then discarded the idea. Markos was not his equal, but there were certain traditions to be honoured. Markos had made his challenge, and the battle would be settled in the proper way – blade to blade.

'Hardly,' Markos said. 'If Anark fails, then I will see to the liche, never fear. Your rival will not long outlive you, Lord Mannfred.'

'My heart swells,' Mannfred said. 'You cannot win, Markos.'

'No? I rather fancy my chances.' He drew his sword. 'I had this forged for me, by a certain swordsmith in Nippon.' He smiled. 'You call yourself a god, cousin.' Markos extended his sword. 'In Nippon, they say that if you meet a god, if he is real, he will be cut by this steel,' Markos said. 'It is the finest, sharpest steel that can be made in this world. A man can be cut by it and not know for several hours, such is its keenness.' He smiled and spun the blade. 'Don't worry, cousin. I'll make sure you know when it's time to die.'

Markos moved forward smoothly, with a grace and poise that Mannfred couldn't help but grudgingly admire. He'd learned more than sorcery in his time in Cathay and Nippon, it seemed. His first slash came so quickly that it had opened up Mannfred's cheek before he saw it coming. Mann-fred scrambled to his feet, the taste of his own blood on his lips. He drew his blade, blocking a second blow.

'You choose the most inopportune times to exert yourself, cousin,' Mann-fred hissed as he and Markos circled one another. The other Templars were staying out of it, Mannfred noted. Vampires respected little, save for the sanctity of the challenge. 'We are on the cusp of ultimate victory, and you seek to rock the boat *now?*'

'*You* are on the cusp of ultimate victory, and so, yes, now seems like a good time,' Markos said. 'I've read the same tomes, cousin. I've read the scrolls and the grimoires, and what you're planning is madness. You can't con-trol what you intend to unleash, and I'll not be the slave of some long-dead necromancer, first of his kind or otherwise.' He fell into a defensive stance, blade angled parallel to his body. 'You would damn us, and the world that is ours by right of blood, to servitude at the feet of a dusty god. For the good of all of us, in the name of Vlad von Carstein, I will gladly, and cheerfully, strike off your head.'

Hark at him, the supercilious little weasel, Vlad's voice murmured in Mannfred's ear, as if he were right over his shoulder. *Familiar bit of rhe-toric, though, you must admit. It wasn't so long ago that you were framing similar arguments, right about the time my ring went missing, eh, boy?*

'Shut up,' Mannfred hissed. Vlad laughed. 'Shut up!' Mannfred howled, and flung himself at Markos. Their blades crashed together with a sound like a wailing wind, and sparks slid from their edges as they scraped against one another, separated and came together again. Markos laughed taunt-ingly and pressed Mannfred back.

'I'll be silent the day I lose my head, cousin,' he sneered. 'I was of Vlad's get, the same as you. My blood runs as pure as yours, and flows with the same power!'

'Your blood,' Mannfred spat. He caught a blow on the length of his blade and rolled into it, driving his shoulder into Markos's chest who staggered back. 'Your blood is gutter-froth, compared to mine. I was born in a palace, *cousin.* I was born the son of kings, and Vlad did not make me the creature I am. He merely honed me, the way that blade you boast of was honed.'

Vlad's laughter faded in Mannfred's ear drowned out by the sound of his own blood thundering in his veins, as he harried Markos back, wield-ing his sword as if it were a feather. His rage lent him strength, as it always had, and his arrogance as well.

He was not meant to fall here. He was meant for greater things. Better things. He had no illusions about the kind of man he was. He had sacrificed more on the altar of ambition than a guttersnipe like Markos could ever guess, all to reach this moment, this crossroads. He had been denied a throne once, in the dim, fell reaches of the past. And the world owed him a debt for that insult.

Markos's confidence began to crumble as they traded blows. He had squandered the advantage of surprise in order to grandstand. That was the perennial flaw in Vlad's blood, the urge to monologue, to make the enemy recognise your superiority, before the first blow had fallen. Mannfred fell victim to it himself, but he at least came by it honestly. Markos had been the son of a vintner, and not even a wealthy one.

'You think a sword, or a bit of knowledge, makes you special, Markos? You are not,' Mannfred said, sliding around a blow and catching Markos in the belly with a shallow slash. Armour peeled back like flesh as the blade danced across Markos's torso. 'You are no more special than Hans or Pieter or Fritz, or poor, sad Constantin, buried in his books. Just another funeral pyre to light the way of your betters.' He attacked Markos again and again as he spoke, striking him with all of the speed and strength he possessed. Blood poured down Markos's arms and legs, and his armour fell to tatters. Efficiently, ruthlessly, Mannfred cut ligaments and tendons, the way a butcher would ready an animal for sale.

Markos stumbled and sank to one knee, bracing himself with his blade. He coughed blood, and his free hand was pressed to his belly. His blood pooled about him, and the greedy earth drank it up thirstily. His lips began to move, and Mannfred felt the winds of magic stir. With a single word, he cut Markos off from them. He saw the other vampire's eyes widen. A pall of resignation crept over Markos's narrow features as he realised what had happened. 'I waited too long,' he said.

Mannfred nodded and said, 'The approach of death lends a certain clarity.' He caught Markos's chin with the flat of his blade and lifted his head. 'You went after me with a blade for the same reason Tomas did, all those months ago. You thought I was a better sorcerer than a swordsman.'

'No, I thought you were mad. I see no evidence to the contrary,' Markos coughed. 'You will destroy us – all that Vlad built, and for what?'

'For me,' Mannfred said. 'Always, for me. This world is mine. It did not belong to Vlad and it does not belong to Nagash or the Dark Gods. It was promised to me in my cradle, and I will have what I am owed.' He lifted his blade in both hands. 'Close your eyes, cousin. No man should have to see his body after his head has left his shoulders.'

Markos continued to stare at him. Mannfred shrugged and let the blade fall. Markos's head came away, and his body slumped. *Do you feel better now? Konrad always felt a bit better after a good bloodletting,* Vlad hissed. Mannfred looked down, and saw something that might have been Vlad's face – or perhaps a skull – reflected in the blood spreading away from Markos's body.

He didn't reply to the taunting voice. He had given in to that urge entirely too often, of late. It was stress and nothing more. The ghost of his fears and worries. Vlad's spirit was gone from this world.

True enough, though you especially should know that beings like ourselves do not go gently into the darkness. You came back, after all, Vlad murmured. Mannfred could almost see him, circling, hands clasped behind his back, speaking the way a master speaks to a pupil. *Then, perhaps I am not Vlad at all, and perhaps you did not come back all on your own, hmm?*

Mannfred cleaned his blade on his cloak and sheathed it. The presence continued to speak, as if it took his silence for an invitation. He wondered, briefly, if there might have been some truth to Markos's words. Was he going mad?

Do you care? Vlad asked.

Mannfred had no answer.

Beechervast, the Grey Mountains

The town had been called Beechervast. Now, it was nothing. Flames crackled and buildings collapsed with rumbling groans as the dead marched through the dying settlement, adding to their number. Erikan watched as a screaming woman was dragged from the ruins of a hostel by two of his order. Her screams faded to moans as the two vampires fed greedily.

Erikan let his gaze drift to where Arkhan the Black stood near his chariot, watching what his magics had wrought. After the wood elf ambush at Parravon, they'd lost most of what was left of their army, including Krell, who'd held off their attackers while Arkhan and the others made for the dubious safety of the mountains. Whether Arkhan had attacked Beechervast simply in order to replenish his forces, or to wait and see if Krell caught up with them, Erikan couldn't say, and hadn't asked.

They'd lost much to acquire the shroud-wrapped shape strapped to Arkhan's back. His eyes were drawn to it. It was a staff, he thought, much like the one Arkhan carried. To Erikan, it seemed to pulse with a sour light. It was like a wound in the world, and something in it pulled at the thing he was. There was power there, but he knew that if he tried to take it, it would consume him the way a moth is consumed by flame. Arkhan was welcome to it, whatever it was. He looked away from it, and saw Anark ambling towards Arkhan. Subtle as a brick to the head, he thought. He'd been wondering when Anark was going to give it a go.

Anark sprang into motion. He leapt towards the liche and shrieked a war-cry as he swung a wild, overhand blow. The liche whirled and swatted aside the tip of the sword with his staff and drove a bony fist into Anark's face, sending him flying backwards.

Erikan winced, as the Grand Master of the Drakenhof Templars hit the ground with a clatter. To his credit, Anark was on his feet a moment later. He charged towards Arkhan, who had stepped down from his chariot. Arkhan side-stepped the vampire's lunge and caught him in the back of the head with his staff, sending him stumbling to his hands and knees.

Arkhan looked at Erikan, who still sat atop his horse. *'Well, vampire?'* the liche croaked.

'Not me,' Erikan said, holding up his hands. 'Not my fight, Black One.'

'Traitor,' Anark snarled as he regained his feet.

'From here, it looks like you're the one attacking our ally for no reason,' Erikan said, settling back in his saddle, thumbs hooked in his sword belt. 'What would Lord Mannfred say, I wonder? Or Elize, for that matter?'

'I could hazard a guess as to what Lord Mannfred would say,' Arkhan said, planting his staff. *'Tell me, vampire... What did he offer you? What could possess you to act so foolishly?'*

'This is positively cunning for Anark, sad to say,' Erikan interjected. 'What happened, Anark? Did Elize bat her pretty lashes and ask you for one little favour? I remember those days, when I was her favourite.'

'Shut your filthy mouth,' Anark howled. He leapt for Arkhan again. There was no subtlety to him, only raw power. He was nothing but one big muscle, all killer instinct without the cunning to mediate it. His armour creaked as he swelled with murderous power. Arkhan caught the blow on his staff, and for a moment, liche and vampire strained against one another.

Then, the moment passed. Black lightning crackled along the length of Arkhan's staff and caught hold of Anark's sword. A moment later, the blade shivered into fragments, and its wielder was tossed back into the dust, bloody from the metal fragments that had spattered his face. Before Anark could get to his feet, Arkhan drove the end of his staff into his skull with all the precision of a trained spearman. There was a wet, unpleasant sound, and Anark went limp.

'Effective,' Erikan murmured.

'I have dealt with treacherous vampires before,' Arkhan said. He turned and looked at Erikan. *'I assume that you were not part of this less-than-devious stratagem, then?'*

'I had no idea that it was even in the offing,' Erikan lied. 'Thick-headed as he is, that blow won't keep him down long. Anark isn't much, but he's a fighter. I fancy he could keep going, even missing the whole of his head. And he won't give up.'

'What would you suggest?'

Erikan couldn't say why he was helping the liche. He thought, perhaps, it was simply that Anark had been a constant source of annoyance. Or maybe he'd grown tired of the way Elize seemed to shower the brute with affection. Let her get a new, hopefully smarter, pet. 'Chain him to the postern of the Sigmarite temple I noticed when we rode through the gates. Let the flames or the sun have him, and that'll be the end of it.'

'*A more merciful death than I intended,*' Arkhan said. He gestured, and a trio of wights came forward and hefted Anark's limp form. They carried him off.

'But still a death,' Erikan said.

'*Yes,*' Arkhan said. The liche examined him silently for a moment, and then turned away. They left Beechervast not long after, riding out at the head of an army newly swollen by the addition of the population of the town, slaughtered and resurrected.

No one seemed too put out by Anark's death. Then, he hadn't exactly gone to great lengths to make friends amongst the order. Neither had Erikan, but he supposed he was more tolerable than a swaggering bully any day. As a member of the inner circle, leadership of the remaining blood knights had fallen to him, and he rode at their head for lack of any better ideas. He wondered how Elize would receive the news of Anark's death. Would she be angry, sad, or... nothing. The latter, he thought, would be the most unpleasant. Vampires could love, but it did not come easily. And sometimes it was not recognised as such until it was far too late.

The Lahmians had songs, spread by the Sisterhood of the Silver Pinnacle, about lost loves and immortal tragedies. They turned troubadours and poets just to keep those songs and verses alive and circulating amongst the living. It made things easier, sometimes, if the cattle thought love, rather than thirst, was the norm for vampires.

As they rode towards the Sylvanian border, Arkhan communed with the spirits of the dead from atop his chariot, seeking any word on Krell. Wailing ghosts and shrieking spectres circled him like pigeons in an Altdorf plaza. Erikan rode beside him.

The spirits scattered abruptly. 'Any word?' Erikan asked.

'*Krell yet persists. He will rejoin us when he can. He is leading the Wild Hunt away from our trail.*' Arkhan shook his head, a curiously human gesture. '*Beastmen, wood elves, Kemmler... Enemies at every turn.*'

'Rats in a sinking barrel,' Erikan muttered.

Arkhan looked at him. Erikan shifted uncomfortably. '*Why do you serve the von Carstein, vampire?*' Arkhan asked suddenly. '*Love, fear... boredom?*'

Erikan didn't look at the liche. He didn't like the twin witch-fires that flickered in the dead thing's eye sockets. He'd only ever seen Arkhan at a distance; up close, the sheer wrongness of him, of something once human bent and twisted into something new, something abominable, something that should not walk upon the earth, was all too easy to see and to feel. Arkhan's presence, the undiluted necromantic energies that emanated from his skeletal form, made Erikan's head ache, as if he had a sore tooth.

But it wasn't simply the liche's noxious presence that made him hesitate. The question wasn't an easy one. Why had he answered the call? Why had he left Sylvania in the first place? The questions were like the strands of the same cloth; as he tugged each one, another came loose. Arkhan looked at him. *'Well? We have nothing but time, Crowfiend. Why not pass it in conversation, rather than silence?'* Arkhan cocked his head. *'Are you upset about the other? What was his name – Anark?'* The liche made a rattling sound that Erikan had come to associate with his attempts at humour. *'That one was not fated to find himself on the right side of history, I'm afraid. But you... You are a survivor, I think. A scrambler on the edge of destiny. When all is said and done, why do you serve von Carstein?'*

Erikan hesitated. And then, he said, 'Power. Not over the world, but over myself – my own fate. As long as others were stronger, I would never be master of my own fate. That is why I studied necromancy.'

'I smell no stink of grave sorcery about you,' Arkhan said.

'I was a terrible student,' Erikan said, smiling slightly. 'Plenty of inclination, but no aptitude. So I sought out the next best thing...' He bowed his head. Arkhan gave a raspy chuckle.

'A woman, was it? And then?'

'It wasn't enough. I climbed one tower, to find myself at the bottom of another. So... I left.' His smile faded. 'From the moment I was born it was a loveless life. I lived out of spite, and it wasn't enough. So I turned into something worse than death, and tried to take from the world until there was nothing left to take. But the world was bigger than I thought.' He looked up at the forest canopy overhead. 'I am tired of surviving. I am tired of the world. I want an end, and I want to watch it all fall into the grave with me. I do not want fire. I want ash, and silence. I want night, silent and eternal, stretching from pole to pole, heaven to earth.'

Arkhan looked at him for a long time. Then, as if uncertain of his own intent, he reached out and clasped Erikan's shoulder. *'You will have it. Nagash rises, and the world descends. We will all know the peace of oblivion.'*

'Will we?' Erikan asked softly. 'Or will we be puppets, for an eternity?'

Arkhan's grip tightened. *'No. Nagash despises anything that is not him, or of him. He hates and fears that which he did not create. We will be dust on a nightmare wind, vampire, when we have fulfilled our purpose. We will be nothing.'* He released Erikan's shoulder. *'Or so I hope.'* He turned away. *'I am tired, vampire. I am so tired, but I cannot lay aside my burden, until the end of all things. I was a gambler once. I gambled and lost. And this is my debt.'*

Erikan said nothing. Arkhan fell silent. They rode in silence, two weary souls, bound in chains of night and servitude.

◀ CHAPTER NINETEEN ▶

Castle Sternieste, Sylvania

'Treachery,' Mannfred intoned grandiloquently. 'Treachery most vile.'

'*Which treachery are we speaking of – yours, or mine?*' Arkhan asked, not bothering to look at the vampire. Mannfred glared at the liche's back. The two stood at the top of Castle Sternieste's tallest tower. Arkhan had arrived a few days before Mannfred, and had awaited his return at the tower's pinnacle, as if in anticipation of a confrontation. Mannfred saw no reason to deny him such, if that was his wish.

Despite the fact that they had both been victorious in their respective endeavours, and that both Alakanash and the Fellblade were now in their possession, Mannfred saw little reason for celebration. Neither, apparently, did Arkhan. Mannfred wondered whether the liche was even capable of such an emotion.

On the ride back through the Border Princes, Mannfred had managed to half convince himself that Arkhan had somehow encouraged Markos's failed coup. He hadn't thought the liche would actually admit it, but he'd hoped to see some sign of concern. Instead Arkhan had seemed almost... relieved? He wondered what had happened on Arkhan's campaign in Bretonnia. The vampires who had ridden with the liche spoke of a rain-lashed battle on the Lieske Road with a herd of beastmen, and an attack by the fierce elves of Athel Loren, which had seen the loss of Krell. Whether the ancient wight had truly been destroyed, or merely separated from his master for the moment, Arkhan had not seen fit to share. Mannfred shoved the thought aside. 'Yours is the only treachery I see, liche,' he snarled.

'*Then you are as wilfully blind as you are ignorant, vampire.*' Arkhan glanced over his shoulder. '*Your assassin failed.*' Mannfred let no sign of his annoyance show on his face. Elize had sworn to him that her pets could accomplish the task he'd set for them, but they'd failed. Anark was dead, and the Crowfiend had either thrown in with Arkhan or chosen discretion over valour. If it was the latter, Mannfred found it hard to blame him. If it was the former, he fully expected Elize to deal with it before he next saw her.

'As did yours,' Mannfred hissed. Arkhan didn't react. Mannfred glared at the fleshless face, and wondered what he had expected. Denial, perhaps, or denunciation. That was how a vampire would have reacted. Instead, the liche simply turned away. Mannfred shook his head, frustrated. 'And I am not speaking of overly ambitious underlings, in any event, as you well know.'

'*Illuminate me then, I beseech you.*'

Arkhan stared out at the horizon, his fleshless hands clasped behind his back. He stood at the edge of the crumbling battlement, at his ease and seemingly unconcerned. Mannfred's hands twitched, and he considered unleashing a spell to send the liche tumbling from the tower like a skeletal comet. But he restrained himself. If Arkhan wanted to play the fool, fine. He would treat him as such.

'The protective spells I wove about my land are failing,' he ground out. 'You told me that losing one of the nine would have no effect.' Elize had reported as much to him as soon as his mount clattered into the courtyard of Sternieste. She had practically flown to his side to warn him that the omnipresent clouds that swirled overhead, blanketing his kingdom, had grown thin in places. The cursed light of day was returning to Sylvania. Slowly, but it was returning. And when it had, so too would come the zealous priests and fanatical witch hunters, to harry his subjects and tear asunder all that he had worked so hard to build. Worse, Gelt's wall of faith still stood as strong as it ever had, and showed no sign of failing.

'*I told you that it would have negligible effect. And such is the case. Your enchantments still hold – the sun is kept at bay and your empire of eternal night yet stands. Rejoice,*' Arkhan said. Mannfred snapped at the air unconsciously, like a dog provoked beyond endurance.

'With every day that passes, the spell grows weaker, and I can do nothing to stop it. We have weeks, or perhaps only days, before the enchantment fails entirely. And then what, bag-of-bones?' Mannfred demanded, pounding a fist into the battlement. Stone cracked beneath the blow and fell, tumbling down, down, to smash onto the courtyard so far below. Arkhan watched the stone fall, and then looked at Mannfred.

'*By then, Nagash will have risen. By then, it will be too late.*'

'You knew,' Mannfred hissed. He leaned towards the liche. 'You knew. You tricked me.'

'*I am but a bag-of-bones. I am dust and memory. How could I trick you, the great Mannfred von Carstein?*' Arkhan gave a rattling laugh. He looked at Mannfred. '*How it must have galled you to take that name, eh? How it must have pricked that monstrous pride, that abominable vanity that you wear like a cloak. Tell me, did you weep bloody tears when you surrendered your silks and steel for wolf-skin and crude iron?*'

Mannfred heard Vlad's chuckle. He had hoped that he'd heard the last of the memory, or the ghost, or whatever it was, in the Border Princes. *You did. I remember it quite clearly. You whined for weeks – weeks! – and over a bit of frayed silk.*

'Quiet!' Mannfred snapped. He saw Vlad's face, hovering just behind Arkhan. His mentor's smile cut him to the quick, and he longed to unleash the most destructive spells he could bring to mind, just to wipe that mocking grin away.

'*Were you talking to me, or to him?*' Arkhan asked. The liche cocked his head. '*Who do you hear, vampire? I can hazard a guess, but I would not wish to offend you.*'

Mannfred spun away with a snarl, fighting to regain his composure. His hands balled into fists, and his claws cut into the flesh of his palm. 'You have already offended me,' he said, not looking at the liche. 'And I hear nothing but your hollow, prattling lies.'

'*Then I shall continue... Time is our enemy. It has turned on us. The enchantments I laid upon the Drakenhof banner yet hold. But they too will eventually fade. And our work is not yet done.*'

'The Black Armour of Morikhane,' Mannfred said. He closed his eyes. Somewhere behind him, he heard Vlad applaud mockingly. *Oh well done, boy. I see you were paying attention. Then, you always were a quick study,* Vlad said. Mannfred opened his eyes and turned. 'Heldenhame,' he said. He looked out over the battlements, towards the northern horizon, where Heldenhame Keep stood silent sentinel over Sylvania.

He felt a pang as he took in the realm he had claimed by right of blood and conquest. In the beginning, he had never truly thought of Sylvania as anything other than a stepping stone. It was a backwater, full of ignorant peasants, barbaric nobility and monsters. He had never seen its potential the way Vlad had. But as he waged war after war, shedding blood for every sour metre of soil, he had come to see what the other vampire had seen, all those centuries ago. He had come to understand why they had taken up new names, and sought to burrow into the vibrant, if savage, flesh of the young Empire.

There was a rough beauty to this land, with its dark forests and high crags. It was a cold land, full of shadows, as far and away from the land of his youth as it was possible to get. But where that land had cast him out, this one had taken him to its bosom, and he felt his pulse quicken as he gazed out over it.

This was his land now. He had died to defend his right to it, and its waters ran in his blood. Nothing would take it from him. Not Nagash, and certainly not Karl Franz. But they weren't his only enemies. He'd seen the portents, but hadn't truly believed, not until his march across the Border Princes. The world was in upheaval. Everything was changing. His spies had learned much while he prosecuted his campaign against the skaven. There was a war-wind blowing down from the north, and drums beat in the Troll Country, rousing the lost and the damned to war. Kislev was gone, and the northern provinces of the Empire were in flames.

As he stared out at his land, Mannfred thought of the being he had seen in his scrying, the one to whom even daemons bowed, and he felt a cold determination settle over him. If this was the end, better Nagash than nothing. 'Heldenhame,' he said aloud, again.

Heldenhame was the Empire's first line of defence against any army coming from his lands, and he had wasted more than one legion on its walls. But then, so had many others – including the barbarous orcs. 'Its walls are strong, but they have their weaknesses.'

'*And you know what they are?*' Arkhan asked.

'I have known what they are for the better part of a year. My spies within Heldenhame tell me that the city's western wall was badly damaged last year, during a greenskin attack. Leitdorf has spared no expense in conducting repairs, but such a thing cannot be rushed, especially when you have naught but frail men as your labourers. It will be easy to breach, with the proper application of force.' Before Arkhan could speak, Mannfred held up a hand. 'However, the garrison of that wall has been reinforced with cannons, fresh from the forges of Nuln, thus rendering any assault there costly.'

'*You have a plan,*' Arkhan said. It wasn't a question.

Mannfred chuckled. 'I have many plans. The western wall is the obvious point of assault. But to strike there is predictable, and sure to be more arduous than we would like. However, the appearance of predictability is as valuable as its absence, if properly employed. We must take the oblique approach to this.' He stretched out a hand, and curled his fingers. 'With one hand, we shall show them what they expect.' He raised his other hand. 'And with the other, we shall crack their walls.'

'*Your confidence is inspiring,*' Arkhan said.

'And your mockery is forgivable, this time,' Mannfred said, with a mildness he didn't feel. 'You were right before. We need each other, liche. We are surrounded by enemies, and time, as you said, is not on our side. So let us cease wasting it. We will march north, now. And we will rip the last piece of the puzzle from the guts of Heldenhame.'

He turned and set one foot on the battlement. He flung back the edges of his cloak, raised his hands and began to speak. Overhead, the clouds swirled as Mannfred cast his voice and his will to the winds. He called out to every creature, dead, alive or otherwise that owed him allegiance. In his mind's eye, he saw bat-winged monstrosities flop from dank caves and ghoul packs emerge from their burrows. He felt his mind touch the ephemeral consciousness of every chill-hearted spirit within his demesne, and rouse them to abandon their haunts and hurtle through the black sky towards Sternieste.

Before the ancient bells of Sternieste struck midnight, he knew that a mighty army would be assembled before the walls of the castle. And when it marched north, the world would tremble.

Amused by Mannfred's display of unbridled sorcerous dominion, Arkhan watched in silence as the vampire called his forces to war. He let his mind drift as Mannfred lashed the world with his will. He had more pressing concerns than Mannfred's petulance.

He had brooded on Kemmler's betrayal and what it meant since the obliteration of La Maisontaal Abbey. He had suspected Kemmler's treachery, but not the reasons behind it. Nagash's hold on the necromancer had not been as certain as Arkhan had thought, and that disturbed him. Kemmler's taunts haunted him.

That the Dark Gods would intervene so directly in order to prevent Nagash's resurrection seemed unbelievable. But he knew what he had felt and seen. And it hadn't merely been Kemmler. His return to Sylvania and Castle Sternieste had seen him lead what remained of his forces through the Great Forest. After departing Beechervast, Arkhan had taken the Lieske Road, and it seemed as if every Chaos-touched creature in those woods had been drawn to him, like moths to a flame. Howling, malformed monsters had pounced from the shadows, or swooped through the branches above. Chimeras and jabberslythes and worse things had thrown themselves into battle.

There had also been the beast-herds. Frothing, goat-headed beastmen had launched ambush after ambush, culminating in a final, bloody affray during a storm that Arkhan suspected was of no natural origin. During that battle, he had again seen the winged beast that he had first spotted in Quenelles. Clad in ragged robes, it had bellowed in a crude tongue as it tried to stem the inevitable retreat of the beastmen, once their courage had been broken by Arkhan's spellcraft and the ferocity of the Drakenhof Templars, led by Erikan Crowfiend.

Arkhan had recognised his winged foe, in that moment before it too had fled. Like Mannfred, he had his spies and for years he had gathered information about the powers that might place themselves in his path. The thing called Malagor was a true servant of the Dark Gods, in the same way that he served Nagash. Its presence would have spoken volumes as to their intentions, if he did not already suspect their meddling.

With betrayal, and obstacles, however, came clarity. Misfortune had dogged his trail for months prior to coming to Sylvania. And not only his. Every being, however removed or reluctant, who might serve Nagash had seemingly been marked for death by the Chaos gods. When he had first begun to groom Mallobaude for his task, even providing for the would-be king to receive the blood-kiss of vampirism from an old, long-established Bretonnian line of the creatures, his stronghold of Mousillon had been beset by a horde of daemons. Though the creatures had gone on to assail the realm at large, Arkhan's plans had nonetheless been interrupted. When he had arrived in Sylvania, he had learned that Mannfred had suffered similar attacks.

His study of the mystical wall of faith forged by Balthasar Gelt had also led him to wonder just how the wizard had come by the knowledge he'd used to forge the cage that now encompassed Sylvania. Brilliant as the Supreme Patriarch was, at least as far as mortals went, Arkhan couldn't help but question the timing.

Sylvania had been a thorn in the Empire's flank for centuries. Why suddenly move to contain it now? Unless, perhaps, Gelt was also an agent of the Dark Gods, in some capacity. Not an active, aware one of course, otherwise he could not have so effectively shackled the power of Sigmar. But he could easily be a pawn of other powers.

Had Kemmler been telling the truth – were the gods of Chaos so frightened of Nagash's return that they were actively attempting to prevent it? Was Nagash truly so powerful that he incited such terror in entities as vast and as unknowable as the Dark Gods? And if so, what was Arkhan truly bringing back into the world? Was it the Nagash he remembered, the petty, spiteful, stubborn Undying King, who had killed his own people because they refused to bow... Or was it something even worse?

Arkhan looked down at his hands. They had been free of flesh for more years than he could count. He had sacrificed his mortality, his flesh and his hope on the altar of Nagash's ambition. If it came down to it, he knew that he would sacrifice all that remained. He had no choice in the matter.

Or did he?

Elize von Carstein traced the rough bark of the dead tree with her fingers. The garden was empty, save for a few carrion birds perched here and there on the battlements. The castle itself was a hive of activity, as it had been since von Dohl's failed assault a week earlier. The self-proclaimed Crimson Lord had ridden right up to the gates and demanded that Elize turn Sternieste and all of its treasures over to him.

Von Dohl had been accompanied by Cicatrix of Wolf Crag, and the heir of Melkhior, Zacharias. The Necrarch, in particular, had seemed unusually intent on getting into Sternieste's vaults. When Elize had denied them entry, von Dohl had been beside himself with rage. The battle that followed had been brief but brutal.

Long-dead warriors had clashed amidst the barrow-fields as the Drakenhof Templars held their lord's fortress against his enemies. She had duelled with Cicatrix atop the gatehouse, trading sword blows with the other woman. Von Dohl had ever let his harlot fight his battles for him, and he had only retreated when Elize had struck her shrieking head from her shoulders. What was left of Cicatrix still decorated one of the stakes mounted on the gatehouse battlements, and had greeted the master of Sternieste when he returned.

Arkhan the Black had returned a few days after the battle, and Mann-fred not long before him. Their confrontation had been brief, and from what her spies claimed, heated, but now the great bells were tolling and the forces loyal to Mannfred were gathering. The time had come to take Heldenhame, and the murky air of the castle was tense with anticipation.

She heard Erikan Crowfiend enter the garden behind her. She knew it was him by the sound of his footsteps and the scent of him, sweet like over-ripe flowers or spoiling meat. She recalled that she had once tried to teach him how to use perfumes to mask his predator's scent, but he had never taken to it. 'Markos,' he asked, simply. His voice tugged at her. It was not a purr or growl, but placid like the burr of treacherous waters.

'Dead,' she said. 'Just like Anark.' She dug her claws into the bark. Impos-sibly, the tree had begun to flower. Its skeletal branches were covered in putrid blossoms, which stank of rotting meat. She turned away from it, and fixed Erikan with her gaze. 'Why didn't you help him?' she demanded.

'And how would I have helped Markos? I wasn't with him.'

'Don't play the fool,' she snapped. 'I meant Anark. Why didn't you help him?'

'Why should I have? He was attacking our ally – the very ally we were sent to protect, in fact,' Erikan said. 'He's lucky I didn't kill him myself.'

Elize snarled. 'Are you truly so foolish? Do you understand what you've done? *The liche is dangerous!*' She took a step towards him, her hands curling into fists. 'What could possess you not to seize that opportunity?'

'I did,' he said, flatly.

'Then why is he still here?'

Erikan smiled. 'I would have thought that was obvious.'

Elize stared at him. For the first time in a long time, she was uncertain. She had thought that Erikan would have seized his moment and struck Arkhan down, as Anark kept him occupied. Surely, she'd thought, he would see what was so clear to her – if Nagash returned, they were doomed. Perhaps not immediately, but soon enough. She knew enough about the Undying King to know what it was he wanted, and how badly that would end for her kind. When the last mortal had died, what would they feed on?

Mannfred had likely never even considered that, she knew. He thought he could control the force he sought to unleash. But Arkhan knew better, and that made him more dangerous. 'What do you mean?' she demanded. 'Speak sense!'

'Nagash must rise,' Erikan said. 'And I intend to see that he does. If that means I must keep the liche in one piece, so be it.'

Elize shook her head. 'Are you mad?'

He was silent for a time. She wanted to grab him, and shake him, to force him to speak. But something in his gaze held her in place. When he fin-ally spoke, his voice was rough. 'I think I have been. But I'm sane now.' He reached for her, and she jerked back. He let his hand fall. 'For the first time, in a long time, I see things as they are, rather than how I wish them to be.' He looked up at the sky. 'Can't you feel it, Elize? Can't you smell it on the air?' He looked at her. 'Then, maybe it's only obvious to someone who was raised by the eaters of the dead.'

'What are you talking about?' she growled, shaking her head. A lock of red hair fell into her face and she blew it aside impatiently.

'The world is already dead,' Erikan said. He stepped forwards swiftly, before she could avoid him, and he took hold of her. She considered smashing him to the ground, but stayed her hand, though she couldn't say why. 'All of our struggles, all of our games, have come to nothing. Whatever purpose you conceived for me the day you bestowed your blood-kiss upon me will never be fulfilled. The petty schemes of Mannfred, von Dohl and even Neferata in her high tomb are done, though they may deny it.' He pulled her close, so close, as he had done so many times before he had gone, before he had left her. 'The world is dead,' he repeated. 'Let Nagash have it, if he would.'

She stared at him. She tried to find some sign in his face of the young man she had turned so long ago, thinking to make him a king in his land the way Mannfred had made himself king in Sylvania. What had happened to him, she wondered, in all their years apart? What had made him this way? She reached up and stroked his cheek. 'Why did you leave?' she asked softly. 'Oh my sweet cannibal prince, why did you leave me?'

He looked down at her, his face twisting into an expression of uncertainty. 'I... wanted to be free,' he croaked, with what sounded like great effort. Then, 'I *want* to be free.'

She grimaced. Her lips peeled back from her fangs and her claws dug into his cheek, drawing blood. He staggered back, a hand clapped to his face. She lunged forward with a serpent's grace and struck him. He tumbled onto his backside, his eyes wide with surprise and shock. 'Freedom,' she spat. 'Freedom to – what? – slide into oblivion? That isn't freedom, fool. That is *surrender*.'

He made to scramble to his feet, and she kicked him onto his back and pinned him in place with her foot on his throat. She glared down at him, her fingers dark with his blood. 'If I had known that you would give up so easily, I would never have bothered with you in the first place,' she hissed. 'Fine, fool. Have your freedom, and enjoy it while it lasts.'

'I–' he began. She silenced him with an imperious gesture.

'Since you feel so strongly about it, you will stay here and guard Sternieste. I will lead our brethren to war in your place, Crowfiend,' she spat. Then Elize left him there, staring after her. There was an army to ready for the march, and the castellan of Sternieste had much to do. As she stalked through the corridors, snarling orders to scurrying ghouls and lounging vampires, her mind pulsed with dark purpose.

The world was hers, and she would not surrender it – or anything of hers – without a fight.

Nagash would not rise. Not if she could help it.

◄ CHAPTER TWENTY ►

Heldenhame Keep, Talabecland

Hans Leitdorf, Grand Master of the Knights of Sigmar's Blood, tossed the scroll aside with a weary curse, and rubbed his aching eyes. 'I'm not as young as I used to be,' he said.

'None of us are, old fellow,' Thyrus Gormann said, emptying a decanter into his cup. 'What was that one – bill of sale? An invoice for lumber, perhaps? Or something more interesting.' Gormann spoke teasingly. He was the only man who could get away with poking Leitdorf, and he indulged every opportunity to do so. He glanced towards the frost-rimed window. The sun was rising. It had been a long night, and they were almost out of ale. Still, it was nearly time for breakfast, a thought that cheered him considerably.

'Elves, actually,' Leitdorf said, leaning back in his chair. He and Gormann were in his office in the high tower of Heldenhame Keep. The office had a certain rustic charm, which spoke more to its owner's disregard for the subtleties of interior decoration than any longing for simpler surroundings. Gormann took a swallow of wine and gazed at the other man with keen eyes. The Patriarch of the Bright College was, despite his bluff exterior, a man of quick wit and political acumen. It was something he shared in common with Leitdorf, who was more a political animal than he let on.

Gormann grunted. 'Elves... in Altdorf?' he guessed. 'Ulthuani, I'm guessing.'

'Yes. They've come to petition Karl Franz for aid, apparently.' Leitdorf said. He rubbed his face. 'Fill me a cup, would you?'

Gormann did so. 'Well, they picked the right time, didn't they?' he asked, as he handed the cup to Leitdorf. 'It's not like we have a war to fight, after all.'

'I don't think they particularly care about our little disagreements with our northerly neighbours,' Leitdorf said. He emptied half the cup and set it aside. 'Karl Franz is keeping them at a distance, for the moment. He placated them by sending a rider to Karak Kadrin – I'm guessing to see if the dwarfs were interested in taking them off his hands.'

'Ha! That I'd like to see,' Gormann laughed. He tugged on his beard. 'Old Ironfist is no friend to the elves, nor in truth to us. We're allies of convenience, nothing more.' He cocked his head. 'Did your spies happen to mention what it is they want?'

Leitdorf gave Gormann a hard stare. 'I don't employ spies, Thyrus.'

'My mistake. Did your... friends happen to say what the elves wanted?'

Leitdorf made a face. 'No. Nor do I particularly care. We have enough troubles of our own.' He swept a heavy, scarred hand out to indicate the stack of reports scattered across his desk. 'Reports from the Border Princes, Bretonnia, Tilea... It's all going to pot.'

'When isn't it?' Gormann asked.

'This isn't a joke, Thyrus,' Leitdorf growled. 'If I didn't know better, I'd swear von Carstein had escaped Sylvania somehow.'

Gormann's mouth twisted into a crooked smile. 'No such luck, I'm afraid. Gelt's wall of faith still holds.'

Leitdorf sighed. 'Admit it, Thyrus. That was the whole reason you came to visit Heldenhame, wasn't it? To examine Gelt's thrice-cursed enchantment.' He shook his head. 'I know what goes on behind the doors of your colleges. They're worse snake pits than the Imperial court.'

'Well, I admit, it wasn't for your company, splendid as it is, Hans,' Gormann said, opening a second decanter. He gave the liquid within a sniff and filled his cup. 'Gelt's a funny one – always has been. Powerful, but dodgy. Even Karl Franz, Sigmar bless and keep him, doesn't like the scrawny alchemist much.'

'Which was it that saw him usurp your position as Grand Patriarch? The power or the dodginess?' Leitdorf asked. He held up a hand as Gormann made to reply. 'I know, I know – it wasn't a usurpation. It was a transition. That's what wizards call it, isn't it?'

'He beat me fair and square, Hans. Truth to tell, I was getting tired of the job anyway. There's precious little fun in it. The uptight little alchemist is welcome to it.' Gormann took a drink. His duel with Gelt was the stuff of legend, though not for the reasons he'd wish. Gelt had been more cunning than he'd expected, though he'd heard plenty of stories about the younger man's little tricks – turning lead to gold and the like. When the dust had cleared, he'd been out of the job, and the Gold Order had outstripped the Bright Order in prominence.

He didn't bear Gelt a grudge – not too much of one, at any rate – but he'd come to learn that the new Grand Patriarch wasn't adverse to cutting corners. He was cunning but sloppy, with a compulsion to tinker when he wasn't cheating his creditors. That sort of man needed someone trailing after him, making sure he wasn't causing too much of a mess. Gormann chuckled to himself. That he'd been elected to that position by his fellow patriarchs would be amusing, if it weren't so sad. Then, if Gelt grew suspicious, they could simply claim that Gormann was driven by vindictiveness.

He'd come to Talabecland to study the wall of faith. The magics that Gelt had employed to create his wall were old, and far outside of Gelt's area of study. Someone, it was assumed, had helped him. Gelt was keeping mum, but the other patriarchs, especially Gregor Martak, master of the Amber Order, were concerned, and Gormann didn't blame them. It wouldn't be the first time one of their own had used forbidden magics. Traitors like van Horstmann were few and far between, but their actions were indelibly engraved on the collective memory of the Colleges of Magic. Gormann didn't like to think of them, though. As much as he disliked Gelt, he didn't think the alchemist would willingly turn to the dark. He cleared his throat and asked, 'What news from the rest of the Empire?'

'The same as it's been for a year. Kislev is gone, and her people with her, save those who fled south to warn us of the invasion,' Leitdorf said. 'Only Erengrad remains yet standing, and that only because of von Raukov and the Ostlanders. Men from Averland, Stirland, Middenland and Talabheim march north to bolster our defences on the border.'

He looked tired, Gormann thought. Then, he always had. Being brother to a man like the deceased and infamously insane former Elector of Averland had a way of ageing a man prematurely. Leitdorf had stayed out of the succession debacle, claiming that his duty was to the Knights of Sigmar's Blood. In truth, Gormann was one of the few who knew that it was actually because Leitdorf was convinced that the Empire of his father and grandfather was being bled white by callow nobles and politicking aristocrats. He included Karl Franz among the latter, though he'd been wise enough never to say so where anyone important could hear him.

Gormann often feared for his friend. Leitdorf was a man of blood and steel, for whom patience and politesse were vices. Gormann had never been very good at the glad-handing his former position had required, but even his limited skills in that regard far outstripped Leitdorf's. If the Knights of Sigmar's Blood hadn't been so influential, it was very likely that someone would have put something unpleasant and surely fatal in Leitdorf's wine.

Leitdorf went on. 'Beastmen still rampage across ten states, including this one. Plague ravages the western provinces, and our sometimes allies across the mountains are beset by their own foes.' He drained his cup and stared at it. 'The dwarfs have shut their gates. Tilea and Estalia are overrun.' He smiled sadly. 'I fear that we are living in the final days, old friend.'

'Plenty before you have said as much, and as far back as Sigmar's time, I'd wager,' Gormann said. He drained his own cup. 'We're no more at the End Times than they were then.'

Before Leitdorf could reply, the clangour of alarm bells sounded over the town. The bells echoed through the room, and Leitdorf leapt to his feet with a curse. 'I knew it!' he snarled. He hurled aside his empty cup. 'I knew it! Gelt's wall has failed.'

'You can't know that,' Gormann said, but it was a half-hearted assertion. He could feel what Leitdorf couldn't – the rising surge of dark magic that caused a sour feeling in the pit of his gut. He knew, without even having to see, why the bells were ringing. He tossed aside his cup and snagged the decanter as he followed Leitdorf out of his office.

Outside, men ran through the courtyard of the keep, heading for their posts. Leitdorf stormed to the parapet, shoving men aside as he bellowed orders. Gormann followed more slowly. The sky was overcast, and a cold wind curled over the rooftops of Heldenhame. Flocks of carrion birds were perched on every roof and rampart, cawing raucously.

'You told me I didn't know that Gelt's wall had failed, Thyrus? There's your proof. Look!' Leitdorf roared as he flung out a hand towards the approach to the western wall. It was thick with worm-picked skeletons, clutching broken swords and splintered spears, and steadily advancing towards the wall. Further back, on the edge of the tree line, Gormann could make out the shape of catapults. Their silhouettes were too rough to be wood or metal, and Gormann knew instinctively that they were bone.

He took a long drink from the decanter. As he watched, the torsion arms of the distant war engines snapped forward with an audible screech. The air ruptured, suddenly filled with an insane and tormented cackle that cracked the decanter and made Gormann's teeth itch. Most of the missiles struck the wall. One crashed into the ramparts, and smashed down onto a regiment of handgunners who'd been scrambling to their positions. A dozen men died, consumed in eldritch fire or simply splattered across the rampart by the force of the impact.

'They're aiming for the blasted scaffold,' Leitdorf growled. 'The Rostmeyer bastion is still under reconstruction. There's no facing stone to protect the wall's core. It's nothing but rubble.' He whirled to glare at Gormann. 'If they destroy that scaffold, the whole wall will come down.'

'That's why you put the guns there, isn't it?' Gormann asked, taking another slug from the cracked and leaking decanter. 'See? There they are – happily blazing away.' And they were. The sharp crack of the Nuln-forged war machines filled the air, as in reply to the enemy's barrage. Round shot screamed into the packed ranks of skeletons, shattering many.

But even Gormann could see that it was like punching sand. Every hole torn in the battle-line of corpses was quickly and smoothly filled, as new bodies filled the breaches, stepping over the shattered remains of their fellows.

'Kross is a fool,' Leitdorf said, referring to the commander of the Rostmeyer bastion. 'They need to concentrate on those catapults. Infantry, dead or otherwise, will break itself on the walls. But if those catapults bring it down...' He turned and began shouting orders to his men. Gormann peered out at the battlefield. Gun smoke billowed across the walls and field beyond, obscuring everything save a vague suggestion of movement.

'I think they figured it out,' Gormann said. The smoke cleared for a moment, and the wizard saw one of the catapults explode into whirling fragments and flailing ropes as a cannonball struck it dead on. Men on the ramparts cheered. Leitdorf turned back, a fierce grin on his face.

'Ha-ha! That's the way!' he shouted. 'I knew Kross was the right man to command that bastion. Damn his pickled heart, I knew he wouldn't fail me!'

Gormann said nothing. He finished the bottle. His skin itched and his eyes felt full of grit as he sensed a tendril of dark magic undulate across the field. He heard the cheers began to falter and didn't have to look at the tree line to know that the shattered engine was repairing itself.

'By Sigmar's spurs,' Leitdorf hissed.

'All these years sitting on their doorstep and you didn't expect that, Hans?' Gormann asked dully. He examined the decanter for a moment, and then flung it heedlessly over his shoulder. He heard it smash on the cobblestones somewhere far below. 'This battle won't be as quick as all that.'

The cheering atop the battlements faded as the wind slackened and the fog of war descended on Heldenhame once more.

Wendel Volker staggered through the smoke, eyes stinging and his lungs burning. Flames crackled all around him. A shrieking fireball had crashed down onto the tavern, and it was ready to collapse at any moment. He resisted the urge to sprint for safety and continued to clamber through the wreckage, stumbling over bodies and searching for any signs of survivors. So far he'd found plenty of the former, but none of the latter.

The roof groaned like a dying man, and he heard the crack of wood surrendering to intense heat. Fear spurted through him, seizing his heart and freezing his limbs, but only for a moment. Then his training kicked in, and he whispered a silent prayer of thanks to the man who'd taught him swordplay. He knew the fear was good, and it had sobered him up. He had a feeling he was going to need to be sober. He could hear the bells of the keep, and the roar of the cannons on the western wall, punctuated by the harsh rhythm of handguns firing at an unknown enemy.

Kross would be up there, he knew, unless he was still sleeping off his drink from the night before. A brief, blissful image of Kross, asleep in his bunk as a fireball landed atop his quarters, passed across the surface of Volker's mind. His joy was short lived. A burning mass of thatch tumbled down, nearly striking him. Ash and sparks danced across his face and clothes, and he swatted at himself wildly. He heard someone scream, and a flurry of curses. He wasn't the only one in the tavern. He'd led as many as would volunteer into the burning building.

That they'd been close to hand was less luck and more circumstance – Volker and the men he'd led into the inferno had only just left the tavern, after all. He'd wasted an entire night swilling cheap beer rather than dealing with the stacks of make-work that the seneschal of Heldenhame, Rudolph Weskar, insisted his underlings produce. Those who could read and write, at any rate. Since Kross could do neither, his records and logs were handed over to Volker, who suspected that Weskar was still attempting to stir the pot. The seneschal had made his disdain for both men clear in the months since their last confrontation, and Volker had done all that he could to avoid Weskar and Kross, as well as Kross's lackeys, like Deinroth.

Volker saw a bloody hand suddenly extend from beneath a fallen roof beam and flail weakly. He shouted, 'Here!' He coughed into a damp rag and shouted again. Uniformed men swarmed forwards through the smoke and Volker helped them shift the roof beam. He recognised the barmaid from his previous night's carousing and scooped her up. Ash and sparks washed down over him as he grabbed her, and he heard the groan of wood giving way. 'Everyone out,' he screamed. The barmaid cradled to his chest, he loped for the street. Men bumped into him as they fled, and for a moment, he was afraid that he would be buried and immolated as the tavern roof finally gave way and the building collapsed in on itself.

Volker hit the open air in a plume of smoke. His skin was burning and he couldn't see. Someone took the girl from him and he sank down, coughing. A bucket of water was upended over him and he gasped. 'Get his cloak off, it's caught fire,' a rough voice barked. 'Someone get me another bucket. Wendel – can you hear me?'

'M-Maria,' Volker wheezed. 'Is she...?' More water splashed down on him. He scraped his fingers across his eyes and looked up into the grim features of Father Odkrier.

'Alive, lad, thanks to you.' Odkrier hauled him to his feet. 'Can you stand? Good,' he said roughly, without waiting for a reply.

'We're under attack, aren't we?' Volker asked. The streets were packed with people. Some were trying to put out the spreading fires, but others were fleeing in the direction of the eastern gate. Volker didn't blame them.

'Sylvania has disgorged its wormy black guts and the restless dead have come to call,' Odkrier said. Volker saw that he held his long-hafted warhammer in one hand.

Volker shuddered and looked west. The boom of the cannons continued, and he saw men in Talabecland uniforms hurrying towards the Rostmeyer bastion. He swallowed thickly, and wished that he'd managed to save a bottle of something before the tavern had gone up in flames. 'Kross isn't going to be happy.'

'No one will be happy if our visitors get in, captain,' a harsh voice said. Rudolph Weskar glared about him, as if he could cow the burgeoning inferno by sheer will. Then, Volker wouldn't have been entirely surprised if it had worked. 'Especially you, captain. Why aren't you at your post?' He raised his cane like a sword and tapped Volker on the shoulder. Excuses flooded Volker's mind, but each one died before reaching his lips. Weskar frowned. 'Never mind. Go to the eastern walls and bring as many men as you can. We'll need them if the western wall comes down.' Weskar's hard eyes found Odkrier. 'The men at Rostmeyer bastion are in need of guidance, father.'

'I'll wager they could use my hammer as well,' Odkrier growled. He slapped Volker on the shoulder. 'Take care, lad. And don't dawdle.' Then the warrior priest turned and hurried off.

Volker watched him go, and wondered if he would ever see the other man again. He looked at Weskar and asked, 'How bad is it, sir?'

Weskar looked at him, his eyes like agates. 'Get me those men, Volker. Or you'll find out.'

Hans Leitdorf cursed for the fourth time in as many minutes as a merchant's cart was crushed beneath the thundering hooves of his warhorse. The man screamed curses from the safety of a doorway as the column of heavily armoured knights thundered past. Leitdorf longed to give him a thump for his impertinence, but there was no time. Instead, he roared out imprecations at the running forms that blocked the path ahead. 'Blow the trumpets!' he snarled over his shoulder to the knight riding just behind him.

The knight did as he bade. Whether the blast of noise helped or hindered their efforts, Leitdorf couldn't actually say. He felt better for it, though. No one could say that the knights hadn't given fair warning. Anyone who got trampled had only themselves to blame.

Still, it was taking too long to reach the southern gate. When the messengers from the Rostmeyer bastion had reached him, Leitdorf had already been climbing into the saddle. A sally from the southern gate was the most sensible plan – it would enable the knights to smash into the flanks of the undead unimpeded. If they ever got there. A night soil cart was the next casualty of the horses, and Leitdorf cursed as bits of dung spattered across his polished breastplate.

He'd brought nearly the entire order with him. Those who remained he'd left to watch over Heldenhame Keep, or were abroad on the order's business elsewhere. He felt no reluctance in bringing every man who could ride with him. He'd left the defences of the city and the keep itself in Weskar's capable hands. Even if the enemy got into the city, the keep would hold. The walls were thick, and the artillery towers manned. No barbaric horde or tomb-legion had ever cracked those defences, and this time would be no different.

Fireballs shrieked overhead, striking buildings. Bits of burning wood, thatch and brick rained down on the column as they galloped through streets packed with panicked people. Men and women were scrambling for safety like rats, and the roads were becoming progressively more impassable. The rattle of handguns echoed through the air. The dead had drawn within range then, which meant they were close enough to scale the wall.

The enemy had no siege towers and no ladders for escalade, but Leitdorf had fought the undead often enough to know that they had little need of such. If there was a way in, they would find it. 'Damn Gelt and his gilded tongue,' he spat out loud.

'You're not the first to say that,' Gormann said. Leitdorf looked at the Patriarch of the Bright College. The wizard rode hard at his side, clad in thick robes covered in stylised flames. He wore no hood, so his white-streaked red hair and beard surrounded his seamed face like the corona of the sun. He carried his staff of office, and he had a wide-bladed sword sheathed on his hip.

'Nor will I be the last, I think, before our travails are over,' Leitdorf said. 'I knew his blasted cage would fail. I knew it.' He looked away. 'I argued long and hard that his sorcery was only a temporary measure at best – that it afforded us an opportunity, rather than a solution. We should have seized the moment and swept Sylvania clean with fire and sword. And now it's too late. The muster of Drakenhof is at our gate, and the Empire is in no fit state to throw them back if we fail.' He pounded on his saddle horn with a fist.

'Doom and gloom and grim darkness,' Gormann said. A fruit vendor's stall toppled into the street as people made way for the knights, and cabbages and potatoes burst beneath his horse's hooves. He looked up as another fireball struck home. 'If this is an invasion, it's a fairly tentative one. A few mouldering bones and artillery pieces do not a conquering force make. Where are the rest of them? The rotting dead, the cannibal packs, the spectres and von Carstein's detestable kin?'

'Sometimes I forget that you've been living in Altdorf, getting fat all of these years,' Leitdorf said. He ignored Gormann's outraged spluttering. 'You are fat, Thyrus. I'm surprised you fit into your robes. Those dead things out there are to soften up our walls for the rest of them, when night falls. Then we'll be on the back foot, unless we smash them here and now, and send von Carstein back over the border with our boot on his rump.'

'You never told me you were a poet, Hans,' Gormann said.

Leitdorf growled and hunched his shoulders. 'Will you for once in your sybaritic life take things seriously?'

'I take everything seriously, Hans,' Gormann said. 'I'm more concerned about *how* von Carstein circumvented Gelt's cage. That enchantment was like nothing I've ever encountered, and if von Carstein managed to break it, then old Volkmar's wild claims about that leech getting his claws on the thrice-cursed Crown of Sorcery might be more than some dark fantasy.'

'Or Gelt's spell wasn't as permanent as he claimed. I ought to wring that alchemist's scrawny neck,' Leitdorf barked. He looked at Gormann. 'Of course, you've considered the obvious...'

Gormann made a face. 'I have.'

Leitdorf frowned. 'What do we really know about Gelt, Thyrus? I'd always heard that he cheated you of the staff of office, but you've never said what really happened.' He snapped his reins, causing his mount to rear as a pedlar scurried out of his path. 'Out of the way, fool!' he roared. He glanced at Gormann. 'There are rumours about Gelt. Dark ones... What if this is part of some scheme? He caged Sylvania, right after Volkmar – one of his most influential critics – vanishes into its depths, and then claims that nothing can escape. As soon as we've turned our eyes and swords north, that inescapable cage is suddenly no more effective than a morning mist.'

Gormann didn't look at him. Leitdorf had known the Bright Wizard for a long time. He could tell that what he was saying wasn't new to Gormann. Even knowing as little as he did of the internal politics of the Colleges of Magic, he knew that Gelt's eccentricities weren't as universally tolerated as Gormann's had been. Why else would they have sent Gormann to investigate the wall of faith, unless they suspected that something was amiss?

Before he had a chance to press his friend further, he saw the blocky shape of the southernmost gatehouse and barbican rising over the tops of the buildings to either side of him. His trumpeter blew another note, and the men manning the gate hurriedly began raising the portcullis. He spurred his horse to greater speed, and pushed aside his worries.

There would be time to worry about Gelt after the dead were successfully driven back.

'Well?' Mannfred hissed, from where he lurked beneath the trees. His eyes were pinpricks of crimson in the shadows, and his fingers tapped against a tree trunk impatiently.

'*Well what?*' Arkhan asked. He gestured and a shattered catapult began to repair itself. An easy enough task when the engine in question was composed of bone, dried flesh and hair. It was child's play for a creature like Arkhan – barely worth the effort it took to accomplish it. In fact, none of what he was now doing was worth his attention. Any halfway competent hedge-necromancer could keep the mass of skeletons attacking a wall, and the catapults and their crews functioning.

'Don't taunt me, liche.'

'*I wasn't aware that I was. I am trying to concentrate, vampire. You are disrupting that concentration. Unless you have something pertinent to say, I'll thank you to keep quiet.*' Arkhan gestured again, resurrecting a pile of shattered skeletons moments after a cannonball tore them to flinders.

He'd spent most of the night before stalking the steep slopes beneath the distant western wall of the city, drawing those selfsame skeletons to the surface. The worms had fed well the previous year, and thousands of bodies, both human and orc, had been buried in mass graves on the field before the wall. Their spirits, only barely aware, were restless and eager to rise and fight again. Arkhan was only too happy to give them that opportunity.

The catapults had been a stroke of genius on his part. He had found a spot where the dead had lain particularly deep, and manipulated their remains to form his war engines, as he had so long ago in the Great Land. Frames of twisted bone and ropes of hair and stretched ligament worked just as well as iron and wood. His magics supplied the ammunition as well – great, cackling balls of witch-fire.

'Do not bandy words with me, sirrah,' Mannfred snapped. 'Have we drawn them out?'

'*You can hear the trumpets as well as I,*' Arkhan said. In his mind's eye, he could see what the dead saw. Balls of lead hammered into the dead ranks as they advanced up the muddy slope towards the western wall, fired by the increasingly desperate ranks of handgunners on the parapet. The men loaded and fired with an almost mechanical precision and, for a moment, Arkhan almost admired them. They displayed a courage and dedication that rivalled that of the legions of Khemri at their height. But it would buy them nothing. '*The knights are exiting through the southern gates, as you predicted. They will crush my fleshless legion and the artillery with ease, when they get around to charging.*'

'Not too much ease, one hopes,' Mannfred said, glaring up at the sun. It was riding low in the sky, and obscuring clouds clawed at its edges. 'We need to keep them occupied for another few hours.'

'*Easily done. You know where the Black Armour rests?*' Arkhan looked at him. Mannfred's cruel features twisted into a smile.

'I've known for months, liche. It is sequestered in the vaults of the castle from which this detestable little pile takes its name. While you keep them occupied here, I shall seize my– Your pardon, *our* prize. My forces but await the weakening of the sun's gaze.'

'*Good,*' Arkhan said.

'That said, you should keep an eye socket tilted further west,' Mannfred said, watching the skeletons march into the teeth of a cannonade.

'*Reinforcements?*'

Mannfred's smile widened. 'Of sorts,' he laughed. 'A herd of beastmen are gambolling towards us, even as I speak. I have set wolves, bats and corpses on them, to occupy them for the nonce, but they are heading this way.' He examined his nails. 'They've come a long way, for such blissfully primitive creatures. Almost as if they were looking for something, or someone.'

Arkhan felt a cold rush of frustration. '*Was there a winged creature leading them?*' he demanded, after a moment's hesitation. Mannfred's gleeful expression told him that the vampire had been expecting that question.

'Oh yes, your crow-winged pet is amongst them. Why didn't you tell me you'd made a new friend in Bretonnia? My heart aches,' Mannfred said as he placed a hand over his heart. 'It simply bleeds for the distrust you continue to show me.'

'*Now who's mocking who?*' Arkhan said. Frustration lent strength to his magics. He raised his hands, the sleeves of his robes sliding back from the bone. Black smoke rose from the pores that dotted the bones of his forearms, and drifted towards the battlefield. Where it drifted, dead things moved with renewed vigour. '*I did not tell you because it was not important.*'

Mannfred drifted towards him. He drew his sword and Arkhan felt the edge of the blade rest against the bare bone of his neck. 'Oh, I believe that it is, liche. We are so very close to our goal, and to have it endangered thus... aggravates me sorely.'

'*Is the Grave Lord of Sylvania afraid of a few mutated beasts, then?*' Arkhan ignored the blade and kept his attentions fixed on the western wall. At a twitch of his extended fingers, the skeletons closest to the wall surged into fresh activity. Gripped by Arkhan's will, they climbed over one another like a swarm of ants, building ladders of bone that grew taller and taller by the moment. Soon, skeletal hands were grabbing the ramparts. Handguns and cannons barked and flamed, shattering sections of the growing constructs, but Arkhan's magics repaired them as quickly as they were broken. The pace of the ascent barely slowed.

'It is not the beasts that concern me, but what they represent,' Mannfred said. 'You were attacked by beastmen and the cursed inhabitants of Athel Loren on your journey, liche.' He did not lower his sword. 'We are seemingly beset by enemies.'

'*I told you that time was not on our side. The Dark Gods fear Nagash. They fear his power and his wrath. The events which even now grip this world are a sign of that.*' He looked at Mannfred. '*Did you think it was coincidence that saw Sylvania caged right at the moment that Kislev fell to northern steel? Did you think the daemon-storms that ravaged your lands were but an odd turn of weather? Those were distractions, just like this is a distraction. Of course we are beset, fool... We seek nothing less than the unmaking of the world, and the overthrowing of the old order. They will do everything in their power to delay and hinder us. They will send beasts and even men and elves to assail us. They will aid our enemies, and undermine our allies, all to buy a few more hours of existence.*'

Arkhan turned away. In his mind's eye, he saw what was taking place on the distant wall. A doughty man, old and steeped in faith, whose aura blazed like the light of a comet, had thrust himself into the fray, sweeping the dead aside with great swings of his warhammer. Men cheered, heartened by his presence. Arkhan knew him for what he was – a priest of Sigmar – and at his impulse, the dead turned their attentions to dealing with this new threat. The warrior priest was plucked from the bastion and torn apart. The defenders began to flee, in ones and twos at first; and then, all at once, organised fighting men became frightened cattle, stampeding for the dubious safety of the second bastion on the western wall. Satisfied, Arkhan turned his attentions back to Mannfred.

'*We are at war with life itself, vampire. All life, however corrupt and insane. Without life, the Dark Gods do not exist. Without life, they will gutter like candles in the wind, and as the gods of men and elves do. They must stop us, or they face extinction.*'

Mannfred stared at him. Then, almost absently, he lowered his sword.

His head tilted, as if he were listening to some inner voice berate him. Mannfred shook himself. In a quiet voice, he said, 'I do not wish the death of all things.'

'*What you wish is inconsequential*,' Arkhan said, after a moment of hesitation. Mannfred looked at him, and for a moment, the mask of von Carstein slipped, and was replaced by an older, yet somehow younger, face. The face of the man who became the vampire. The face of one who had known grief and strife and eternal frustration. Of one who had seen his hopes dashed again and again. Some spark of pity flared in Arkhan. He and Mannfred were more alike than he had thought. '*Nagash must rise,*' he said.

The mask returned crashing down like a portcullis, and Mannfred's eyes sparked with fury. 'At the moment, Nagash is dust, liche. And my wishes are anything but inconsequential. He will rise, but at *my* behest, at *my* whim,' he snarled, striking his chest with a closed fist. He flung out a hand. 'Bring that damnable wall down. I would be done with this farce.'

'*As you wish,*' Arkhan said.

◄ CHAPTER TWENTY-ONE ►

Heldenhame Keep, Talabecland

Volker and the men he'd procured from the eastern bastions reached the foot of the inner wall just in time to see the entirety of the western wall give way. The battlements lurched like a drunken giant, and Volker could only stare in mounting horror as, with a great rumble and an explosive gout of dust, the centre of the wall collapsed in on itself, scaffolding and all. Rubble and crushed bodies spilled across the ground in front of him.

'Back!' he yelped, waving at his men. 'Get back!' With the scaffolding's support removed, destruction rippled along the sturdier sections of the wall, buckling the ramparts and causing them to collapse. Men and skeletons alike were hurled from the battlements, their bodies vanishing into the ever-expanding cloud of dust and smoke.

Shock was replaced by fear, as Volker saw skeletons clamber through the dust-choked breach. He tore his sword from its sheath and lurched forward. His men followed, forming up around him more out of well-drilled instinct than inclination. As he moved over the rubble, he brought his sword up. It was made of the finest Kriegst steel, and had been a gift from his mother. He quickly kissed the twin-tailed comet embossed on the hilt and, without a word, pointed the blade at the approaching skeletons.

Someone shouted something vile, and a litany of epithets and curses boiled out of the ranks around him. It wasn't quite the sort of battle cry the bards sang of, but it would do in a pinch. Volker gave voice to his own string of curses, firing them from his lips like shots from a helblaster volley gun as he began to run up the newborn slope of rubble towards the invaders.

A skeleton hacked at him with a broken blade and he swept it aside with a blow from his sword. As Volker reached the top of the slope, he wondered if he ought to shout something inspiring. He opened his mouth and got a lungful of dust, so he coughed instead. His men followed him up, battering aside skeletons in order to join him at the crest of the breach, where they formed a ragged line of spears and swords. Sergeants bellowed orders and a defensive formation took shape. Volker, who knew better than to interfere with sergeants, settled for looking heroic. Or as close to heroic as he could get, covered in dust and blood, and smelling of the previous night's booze-up.

The line was barely formed when the next wave of skeletons ploughed towards them through the breach. Volker swung and chopped at the undead until his arm and shoulder were numb. For every three skeletons they hacked down, six more replaced them. They attacked in total silence, providing an eerie counterpoint to Volker and his men, who expelled curses, cries and wailing screams as they fell to ragged spears and rusty blades.

Volker stumbled, sweat burning his eyes, his lungs filled with dust. The rubble beneath his feet was slick with blood and covered in fragments of shattered bone. The enemy catapults continued to launch shrieking fireballs into what was left of the walls and the city beyond. Most of the artillery fire was directed at what was left of Rostmeyer bastion, where the surviving handgunners fired down into the melee in the breach. Volker felt bullets sing past his head and wondered which would get him first, the skeletons or his own comrades. He pushed the thought aside and concentrated on the work at hand.

A fireball struck the side of the breach and crackling flames washed over the line of men. Soldiers screamed and died. Volker screamed as well as fire kissed the side of his face and body. He staggered into a soldier, slapping at the flames that clung to him. The man stumbled as Volker fell, and nearly lost his head to a skeleton.

By the time he put the fire out, half of the men he'd brought were dead. Volker pushed himself to his feet, using his sword as a crutch. A skeleton lunged out of the smoke to thrust a jagged spear at the man Volker had fallen into. Volker intercepted the blow, catching the spear by the haft. He jerked the dead thing towards himself with a yell and smashed its skull with his sword. He heard men cheer, and looked around blearily, thinking Leitdorf or Weskar had finally arrived with reinforcements.

It took him a moment to realise that they were cheering for him. He shook his head, bemused. He dragged the man he'd saved to his feet and propelled him back into line. 'Form up,' he shouted. 'Back in line, back in line!'

More skeletons stalked through the breach, and many of the shattered ones began to twitch and rattle. The cheers died away. Volker spat and raised his sword. 'Sigmar give me strength,' he said, even as he wondered where Leitdorf was – where were the Knights of Sigmar's Blood?

'Sound the trumpet,' Leitdorf growled. 'Let the cursed dead know that the hand of the god is here to send them back to the grave.' He drew his sword and levelled it at the mass of thousands of skeletons advancing on the breach in the western wall. When the knights of the leading brotherhoods had rounded the southwestern corner of the city wall and beheld the horde that awaited their lances, not one had hesitated, which caused the gloom that enveloped Leitdorf to abate slightly.

The loss of the city's outer wall was a failure on his part. He had been too distracted to see personally to the repairs, as he should have done. He'd left it to the fat pig, Kross, and Weskar, when he knew the former was allergic to hard labour and the latter had no interest in such menial tasks. It was his fault that it had come to this. It was his fault that men – his men – had died. But he could see to it that no more did so. He could see to it that the dead were punished and thrown back across the border into their dark county once more.

Mannfred von Carstein's head would be his. He would take it in a sack to Altdorf and hurl it at Balthasar Gelt's feet, just before he took the alchemist's lying tongue as well.

'Sound the trumpet again,' he bellowed. 'The Order of Sigmar's Blood rides to war!' The world became a whirl of noise and sensation as the knights around him began to pick up speed. There were nearly twelve hundred warriors gathered, spreading to either side like the unfolding wings of an eagle as they urged their horses from a canter to a gallop. Once loosed to the charge, they were nothing short of a wall of destruction that could level anything in its path.

The ground shuddered beneath them. He caught sight of Gormann hunched over his horse's neck, his staff held up like a standard, a swirling ball of fire floating above it. The wizard caught his eye and grinned widely. Leitdorf couldn't help but return the expression. It had been too long since they had fought side by side – the Battle of Hel Ditch, he thought, and the razing of the Maggot Orchard – and he looked forward to seeing his old friend in action once again.

The closest skeletons had only just begun to turn when the charge struck home with a sound like thunder. To Leitdorf, it was as if he and his men were the curve of some vast reaper's scythe. One moment, there was an unbroken sea of bleached or browning bone, marching beneath ragged, worm-eaten banners; the next, a wave of shining steel crashed into and over the dead in a massive roar of splintering bone and pounding hooves.

Leitdorf roared out the name of Sigmar as he hewed a corridor through the dead, making way for the knights behind him. As he took the head of a grinning skeleton, he jerked his stallion about and raised his sword. His standard bearer, close by, raised the order's banner in response, and the trumpeter blew a single, clarion note. The men who'd been with Leitdorf wheeled about and smashed their way clear of the skeletal phalanxes that sought to converge on them. They would reform and charge again, each brotherhood picking their own targets in order to render the horde down to a manageable size and destroy it piecemeal.

He'd learned from hard experience that the dead didn't care about numbers, or morale. If his knights became bogged down amidst the mass of corpses, they'd be swarmed under in short order. The only way to defeat the dead was to pummel them to nothing with mechanical precision. To hit them again and again, until they stopped getting back up. He looked around for Gormann and saw that the wizard's horse had gone down in the first charge. Gormann was on his feet, however, and fire swirled about him, like silks about a Strigany dancer. His face was flushed, and his eyes looked like glowing embers as he spun his staff about, conjuring dancing flames. The air about him thickened, becoming the eye of a nascent firestorm.

Leitdorf found himself unable to tear his eyes away. It had been years since he had seen Gormann's power unleashed. Normally the wizard contented himself with parlour tricks – lighting his pipe or conjuring a fire in the fireplace. But here was the true majesty of the Bright College, the searing rage of an unfettered inferno.

He pulled his men back with oaths and furious gestures. The knights formed up and cantered to what he hoped was a safe range. The dead closed in all around Gormann, who did not appear concerned, and for good reason. Even at a distance, Leitdorf felt the heat of what came next.

There was no sound, only fury. No flames, only incredible, irresistible heat. Bone and rusty armour fused into indeterminate slag as the heat washed over the ranks of the dead. Bleached bone turned black and then crumbled to fragments of ash as Gormann began to stride forward, encased in a bubble of devastation. The bubble shimmered and began to grow, as if every skeleton consumed by it was a log added to a fire. Tendrils of flame exploded outwards from his palms at Gormann's merest gesture, and consumed the dead in a maelstrom of fire and smoke.

Leitdorf looked up as one of the enemy catapults fired at the wizard. Without looking up, Gormann raised his hand and his fingers crooked like claws. The cackling fireball slowed in its descent and finally stopped right above its intended target. Gormann gave a great, gusty laugh, wound his arm up and snapped it forward, like a boy hurling a stone. The fireball careened back towards its point of origin, and the catapult and its crew were immolated instantly.

More catapults fired, and Gormann slammed his staff down. The fireballs jumbled before him like leaves caught in a strong wind. He raised his staff and they followed the motion of it. With a sharp gesture, he sent them hurtling back the way they'd come. Gormann turned as smoke rose from the tree line behind him and called out, 'Well? What are you waiting for, Hans? Get to work.'

Leitdorf laughed and signalled his trumpeter. Another note, and two unengaged brotherhoods galloped towards the tree line and the remaining artillery pieces, crushing any skeletons who tried to bar their path underfoot.

The catapults fell silent a few moments later, and he allowed himself to feel a flush of victory. The battle had been costly, but he had done it.

He made to call out to Gormann when the wind suddenly shifted. The breeze, which had played across the city all morning, increased in speed and strength, becoming a roaring gale. The sun faded as dark clouds gathered, filling the sky. Instinct made him turn in his saddle.

The clouds were thickest and darkest around Heldenhame Keep. 'No,' he said, in disbelief. The enemy had got past them, somehow, some way, and they were in his city. He thought of Weskar, and the few men he'd left on the walls and knew that they would not be enough, brave as they were. 'Sound the retreat,' he snarled to his trumpeter, jerking his horse about and driving his spurs into its flanks. 'We have to get back to the city – *now!*'

But as he said it, he knew it was too late.

The vargheists went first, as was their right and their duty. They hurtled down from the teeth of the storm onto the battlements of Heldenhame Keep, unleashing a frenzy of blood-soaked death upon the men who manned them. Handguns flamed, and here and there, a bat-like shape plummeted with an animal wail. But such occurrences were few and far between. The remaining vargheists took the fight across the battlements and into the passageways and barrack-rooms of the towers, drawing defenders after them into a nightmarish game of cat and mouse, just as Mannfred had intended.

Astride his steed of twisted bone and leathery wings, Mannfred watched the battle unfold with a cruel smile. His strategy had worked to perfection. Leitdorf and his cursed knights had been unable to resist the bait Arkhan had dangled before them, like meat before a lion. They had denuded the castle of defenders, and he intended to make them pay for that error in blood. 'You thought me caged, Leitdorf? There is no cage built or conjured that can hold me!' he roared, spitting the words down at the battlements as his mount swooped over them.

Well that's simply not true, now is it?

Mannfred grimaced. Even here, amidst the fury of the storm, Vlad haunted him. Or perhaps not Vlad. Perhaps something else, something worse. He shook his head. 'I say what is true. I make my own truth, ghost. Go haunt Arkhan if you wish to play these games. I grow tired of them and you.'

Clouds billowed around him, and he could almost see the outline of a face, the same face he'd glimpsed so many months ago in the garden, and from out of the corner of his eye many times since. It smiled mockingly at him and he snarled in annoyance. Vlad's voice was loud in his head, as if the long-dead Count of Sylvania was right behind him. *This isn't a game, boy. It's a warning from a teacher to a student – do you remember that night? The night it all began, the night I opened the Book of Nagash and set us on this path? Do you remember what I said then?*

Mannfred twitched and tried to ignore the voice. At his unspoken command, spectral shapes descended through the storm or flowed up through the rocks of the castle. These were the ghosts of madmen, warlocks, witches and worse things, conjured by his skill and impressed into his service by his will. He felt their cruel desire to abate their own sufferings by inflicting pain and death, and encouraged it. At a thought, they swept into battle with those who still manned the walls and artillery towers, killing them in droves. Such things could not be harmed by mortal weapons and as such made effective shock troops.

I asked you a question, little prince... Maybe you didn't hear me. Or maybe you are afraid to answer...

'I am fear itself, old man. I cause fear, I do not feel it,' Mannfred hissed, watching as the defenders of Heldenhame died in their dozens. He longed to join the battle, to drown out Vlad's needling voice in blood and thunder, but he had to be patient. He could not risk himself, not now. He was too close to victory.

He could feel the Black Armour calling to him as the other artefacts had. It longed to rejoin them, and he could hear its whispers in his mind, imploring him to come and find it. Luckily, he didn't have to. That was what the ghosts and vargheists were for. They would locate the armour, and when they had, he would strike.

You see it, don't you? Or are you so blinded by ambition that you cannot temper it with common sense? Vlad hissed. *What did I tell you? Answer me!*

Mannfred closed his eyes and ground his fangs together. 'You said that Nagash was not a man, but a disease that afflicted any who dared use his works. A pestilence of the mind and soul, infecting those who sought to use his power.' His eyes opened. 'And maybe he is. But just as he used a plague to wipe the Great Land from the ledger of history, I will use him to clean off the world and remake it in my image. His Great Work shall be superseded by mine, and I shall do what you never could – what Ushoran and Neferata never could. I will seat myself on the throne of the world and rule unto eternity. My people will worship me as a god and I shall serve them as a king ought,' he said. 'I have waited so long for this moment. I shall wait no more.'

Then you will be broken on his altar, as Kemmler was. As Arkhan is, so shall you be, my son, Vlad said, softly.

'I am not your son,' Mannfred shrieked, bending forward in his saddle, his eyes glaring at the clouds about him.

But you might have been. Now you are... what you are, and I am dead. Yet still, you conjure me to beseech me for my advice, as a son would. I am you, boy. I am your wisdom, your wariness given voice. In this moment, you know that you can still escape the trap that yawns before you. You can still be free of the shadow of Nagashizzar and its legacy, Vlad said intently. Only now, it wasn't Vlad's voice he heard, but his own. His own thoughts, his own worries and suspicions given shape and voice.

'I am free,' he said.

The words sounded hollow.

In his head, something laughed. Not him, not Vlad, but something else. Something that had shadowed him since he'd returned from the muck and mire of Hel Fenn. He closed his eyes, glad that he had left the Drakenhof Templars to safeguard Arkhan.

Freedom is an illusion, his voice murmured. *Power carries its own chains. But you can slip this one now... Run. Retreat... Go anywhere else. Fly to the farthest corner of the world until its reckoning. Live out what remains of these final days as your own master. Leave Nagash to rot in whatever hell holds him. Just... leave.*

'I will not die,' Mannfred said. 'I shall not die. I shall not perish a beggar. I was born for greatness...'

Your mother was a concubine. You would never have ruled your city of jewelled towers and tidy streets, and you know it, his voice said. *You were born and you died and you returned. You have ever meddled and sought to control the uncontrollable, and what has that brought you, save strife and madness?*

'I am not mad. Konrad was the mad one, not me!' he shouted.

Then why are you talking to yourself? Why pretend it was Vlad's ghost haunting you when it was your own fear? Run, fool. Fly from here. Leave everything behind. Do not die again for a fool's dream!

Down below, there was a flash of light. Aged blades, blessed long ago, blazed like torches as the castellans of the castle rallied. The blessed weapons drove back the confused spirits, cutting their ethereal flesh. It was time for Mannfred to take a hand, if he still wished for victory.

Did he still wish it? That was the question. Some part of him, wiser perhaps than that to which he'd given voice, screamed that it was already too late, that he was being pulled in the wake of a black comet that could not be stopped from reaching its destination. An undercurrent of laughter greeted this and he looked up, trying to read the future in the skeins of the sorcerous storm clouds he had summoned.

He saw the moments of his life, spread across the tapestry of the wind-wracked sky. Every scheme and hope and mistake. A life lived in pursuit of one overriding goal.

If he gave it up now, what was he? What could he ever be?

The voices fell silent. The laughter faded. Determination replaced hesitation.

'It is not the dream of a fool. It is not a dream at all, but destiny. I was born to rule, and I shall, one way or another,' he said as he raised his hand. At his gesture, two massive shapes cut through the swirling storm clouds and dropped down into the castle courtyard below with twin shrieks so piercing that every window, goblet and mirror in the structure shattered all at once. The two terrorgheists had no fear of the blessed weapons that some of the defenders wielded. Driven by a ravenous hunger that could never be sated, the two beasts knuckled and lurched their way across the courtyard, snagging swordsmen and handgunners, and dragging the screaming men into their decaying gullets.

Mannfred's mount touched down on the blood-washed stones a moment later. He could feel the song of the Black Armour trilling through his mind, washing aside his suspicions and fears. He would not die again. He would triumph and stride the world like a colossus. Still in his saddle, he turned as one of the terrorgheists squalled.

He saw a limping knight duck under a flailing wing and bring his sword around in a brutal two-handed blow, which shattered the beast's malformed skull. As the creature collapsed in a shuddering heap, the knight extended his blade towards Mannfred in challenge. 'You shall defile this place not one second more, vampire. So swears Rudolph Weskar.'

'I'd be inclined to worry, if I had any idea who you were,' Mannfred said, leaning back in his saddle. He laughed. 'Well... come on. Some of us have a schedule.'

Weskar charged. And men followed him, knights and swordsmen. A desperate rabble, making their last stand. Mannfred was only too happy to oblige them. He kicked his steed into motion and rode to meet them, drawing his sword as he did so. He gave a mocking salute with the blade as he met them. Then, with barely a flicker of effort, he took Weskar's head. His next blow cleaved through two of the knights, his sword ripping through armour and flesh with ease. For a moment, he crested a wave of violence as he took out his frustration and worry on the men who sought to bring him down.

He slid from the saddle as the last of them fell. The castle echoed with the sounds of horror and butchery as those defenders who yet lived fought on against his servants. He ignored them all, his eyes fixed on the great iron-banded doors that marked the entrance to the castle's vaults, where his prize sat waiting for him to come and fetch it.

Nagash would rise, and the world would kneel at last to its rightful ruler.

PART THREE

Return

Autumn 2524

⚔ CHAPTER TWENTY-TWO ⚔

Castle Sternieste, Sylvania

'*It is almost time,*' Arkhan said as he joined Mannfred in the garden. Mannfred didn't turn around. Instead he continued to examine the worm-pale tree, whose blossoms had sprouted, flowered, and now drifted across the garden like snowflakes. He was reminded slightly of the cherry orchards of far Nippon, and the colours of their blossoms as they swirled in a breeze. There had been a beauty there that even he recognised.

'This tree has somehow blossomed, despite being quite dead,' Mannfred said. He plucked a fallen blossom from his pauldron and held it up. 'They smell of rot, and of grave mould. Is that a sign, do you think?'

'*Perhaps the land is telling you that it is ready for the coming of the king,*' Arkhan said. He held Alakanash, Nagash's staff, in one bony hand. He leaned on it, as if tired. '*Or perhaps it is merely a sign of things to come.*'

Mannfred popped the blossom into his mouth and smiled. 'A parody of life. A good omen, I should say.' He turned to Arkhan. 'I can feel it as well as you, liche. The winds of death are blowing strong. Geheimnisnacht will soon be upon us.' He cocked his head. 'Where is it to be, then? I suppose it's too much to hope that here will do, eh?'

'*I have located the site. A stone circle.*'

'This is Sylvania,' Mannfred said. He gestured airily. 'We have many stone circles.'

'*East of the Glen of Sorrows,*' Arkhan said.

Mannfred smiled. 'Ah, the Nine Daemons. Legend says that those aren't stones at all, you know, but the calcified bodies of daemons, imprisoned for eternity by the whim of the Dark Gods.' He plucked another blossom from the tree and sniffed it. 'Are you developing a sense of humour in your old age?'

'*Legends do not concern me. Those stones sit upon a confluence of the geomantic web. The winds of magic blow strongly about them.*'

'Legends might not concern you, but our enemies should,' Mannfred said. 'My spies–'

'*Your spies are your concern, as are our enemies,*' Arkhan said. He tapped the ground with the staff. '*My concern is with our master.*'

'Your master,' Mannfred spat. He calmed. 'But you are correct. They are my concern. This is my realm, after all, and I will deal with them as I see fit. And you, my friend, will see to the preparations for our eventual triumph.' He smiled unctuously. 'Do not hesitate to ask, should you need any help in your preparations. My servants, as ever, are yours.'

'*Of course,*' Arkhan said. The witch-fires of his eyes flickered slightly and he inclined his head. Then, without a word, he turned and departed. Mannfred watched him go. His smile thinned, turning cruel. He turned back to the tree.

'Well?' he asked.

Elize stepped out from behind the tree, her hand on the pommel of the basket-hilted blade sheathed on the swell of one hip. She'd been there the entire time he'd been speaking with Arkhan, listening. 'He's planning something,' she said.

Mannfred laughed. 'Of course he is, gentle cousin. We have come to the end of our journey together, after all. Our paths diverge, come Geheimnisnacht and what was begun at the Valsborg Bridge will at last be finished.' He looked at her. 'What else?'

'He's already begun transporting the artefacts. Three wagons of bone and tattered skin left by the main gate not an hour ago, accompanied by those desert-born dead things he summoned from those blasted canopic jars of his.'

'And the sacrifices?'

'They are still in their chamber,' she said, leaving the obvious question unspoken.

Mannfred shrugged. 'Let him take them, if he wishes. The ritual protections I wove about our fair land have grown so thin and weak that they are no longer necessary in that capacity. It is past time we disposed of them.' He gestured flippantly. 'Now, what of our visitors, sweet cousin?'

Almost every eye and ear in Sylvania was his to command. He knew the size and composition of each of the forces that had, in the past few weeks, begun to encroach on his realm, but he thought it best for Elize to consider herself useful, and so had left the particulars of scouting out the invaders to her.

Other than Nictus, she was one of the last of Vlad's get remaining in Sylvania. One last link to the old order. He had considered dispatching her soon after his return from the Border Princes for what he suspected was her part in exacerbating Markos's regicidal tendencies. He had reconsidered after seeing how she had defended Sternieste in his absence. Such loyalty was to be rewarded, and such commitment to his cause was to be husbanded against future treacheries. She made a fine castellan, and a fine Grand Mistress of the Drakenhof Order.

Elize cleared her throat. 'A force of men and elves approaches from the east,' she said. 'They crossed through the wall of bone a few hours ago, and are marching towards Templehof.'

'Our old friend Leitdorf and the hounds of Ulthuan, come to punish me for my many transgressions against their respective empires,' Mannfred said. He clasped his hands behind his back and examined the tree, watching the blossoms flutter in the cold breeze that coursed through the garden. He had known that the war in the north would only occupy the men of the Empire for so long. And after Nagashizzar, he had expected another rescue attempt on behalf of the Everchild from the High Elves. But given the way their island nation was currently beset by daemons and dark kin alike, he was surprised that they had sent the forces they had.

'There are beastmen in the Hunger Wood,' Elize went on. 'The herd is undisciplined, but it's enormous – it eclipses all of the other invaders combined. It's as if something – or someone – has browbeaten every filthy pack of the brutes within several leagues into joining together.'

'Yes, and I'll bet Arkhan knows who,' Mannfred said. He rubbed his palms over his skull, considering. The identity of Arkhan's be-winged nemesis was obvious in retrospect. He had long heard the stories of the enigmatic creature known as the Dark Omen; the beast was a lightning rod of sorts for its primitive kin, drawing them together to do the will of the Chaos gods. In this case, their desire was plain. Arkhan was right – the Dark Gods were intent on stopping Nagash's resurrection. He lowered his hands. 'Still, it's of little matter who's behind it. They're here and we must see them off. Who else comes uninvited to my bower?'

'More elves, from the south west,' Elize said.

Mannfred's eyes narrowed. 'Athel Loren,' he murmured. 'Arkhan was nearly taken by them, as he crossed the Grey Mountains. Krell moved to lead them away, costing us his strength in this, our hour of need.'

'We do not need a mere wight to defend our ancestral lands, cousin,' Elize hissed.

'Krell is no more a mere wight than I am a mere vampire,' Mannfred said, scratching his chin. 'He is a weapon of Nagash, as Arkhan is. One of his oldest and best. How large is their host?'

'Infinitesimal,' Elize said dismissively. 'It is barely a raiding party.'

'Nonetheless, we must take care. Elves are always dangerous, no matter how few they are,' Mannfred said. He raised his fingers and ticked them off one by one as he spoke. 'Men, elves, beasts, yet more elves and... Who am I forgetting?'

'Dwarfs,' Elize said. 'A throng, I think it's called. Coming from Karak Kadrin.'

Mannfred closed his eyes and hissed in consternation. The dwarfs were the only invaders who truly worried him. The warriors of Athel Loren were too few, the beasts too undisciplined, but the dwarfs were neither. For a century he had stepped lightly around Ungrim Ironfist, and taken care not to antagonise either him or his folk. Now, it seemed as if all of that was for naught. 'The Slayer King is at our gate,' he murmured. 'Tch, where is he stumping, then?'

'Templehof,' Elize said tersely. 'I think that they are attempting to join forces with Leitdorf and the Ulthuani.'

'That... would be unfortunate,' Mannfred said. He stared at the tree, thinking. None of this was surprising, though the timing was problematic. Still, he had prepared for this from the beginning. Everything had led up to this point. He had known the moment that he had kidnapped the Everchild, the moment he had seceded Sylvania from the shambolic Empire, that he would eventually face an invasion from one quarter or another. Now, at last, on the eve of his certain triumph, his enemies were making their final stab at stopping him.

He took it as a compliment, of sorts. All great men could be judged by the quality of their enemies, and after all, wasn't it the sad duty of every new empire to eradicate those older, stagnant empires that occupied its rightful place before it could take the stage?

He plucked another blossom from the tree. 'When I was but a headstrong youth, with more bloodlust than sense, a warrior came to my city. He was a terror such as no longer walks this world, thankfully. We called him "the dragon". He taught me much about war, and the waging of it, and despite our... falling out some years later, I am grateful to him.' He smiled slightly. 'His folk often waged wars on multiple fronts, so fractious was their land. Division and conquest, he said, were as good as the same thing. When your enemies converge, you take them apart one... by... one.' As he spoke, he began to shuck the petals from the blossom. 'Men are like water. They can be redirected, contained and drained away with the proper application of tactics and strategy.' He held what was left of the blossom out to her.

She stared at it for a moment, and then looked at him. 'You have a strategy, cousin?'

'Oh many more than are entirely necessary for the conflict to come, I assure you.' He dropped the denuded blossom. 'Our task is simplified by our goal – we are buying time for the inevitable.' He pointed at Elize. 'We must peel them away, one by one. And here is how we shall do it...'

The Broken Spine, Stirland-Sylvania border

Hans Leitdorf stared morosely over his shoulder at the distant and now crumbling edifice of bone and sorcery that had, until a few hours ago, barred his path into Sylvania. It had begun to collapse, even as had the walls of Heldenhame so many months ago, but it had still required sorcery to clear a path for his army. Luckily, his new allies had provided a certain amount of aid in that regard.

He surreptitiously examined the silvery figures as they studied the territory ahead from a nearby rocky knoll. Three of them – two in the ornate and delicate-looking armour characteristic of Ulthuani nobility, and the third in flowing robes of blue. All three carried themselves with the haughty surety of their folk, an arrogant confidence that no human could hope to match.

That it had come to this was a sign of the times, in Leitdorf's opinion. Dark times made for strange allies, as Thyrus was wont to say. Thinking of Gormann brought back memories of those terrible, final days at Heldenhame, after the undead assault had melted away.

He remembered finding Weskar's head, mounted on the butt of a spear that had been stabbed point first into the centre of the castle courtyard. He remembered the blood that slopped thickly down from the battlements, and the gory remains of the castle's defenders, heaped carelessly where they had fallen. He and Gormann had personally cleansed the bestial filth from the upper barracks and towers, burning and killing those shrieking vargheists that had not fled with Mannfred.

During the cleansing of the castle, they'd discovered that the vaults of Heldenhame had been torn asunder and scoured by sorcery. Ancient treasures, gathered from Araby in the time of the Crusades, had been melted to glittering slag as a sign of Mannfred von Carstein's disdain. There was no way to tell if anything had been taken, though Gormann had had his suspicions. Leitdorf had found them hard to credit at the time, but as the year wore on, and he had seen the current state of the Empire for himself, he had begun to believe.

Worse even than the desecration of his order's citadel had been what happened afterwards – as he had readied his surviving forces to pursue von Carstein back into his stinking lair to accomplish what the Grand Theogonist, Sigmar bless and keep his soul, could not, a massive herd of foul beastmen had blundered through the line of trees only just recently vacated by the undead. The children of Chaos had thrown themselves at the newly breached western wall with no thought for the consequences.

The battle that followed had done little to assuage the fury Leitdorf had felt at the time, or indeed still felt. It had, however, gone much better than the first. A single charge by Leitdorf and his vengeful knights had sufficed to set the howling rabble to rout. When the beastmen had been thrown back, he had seen that the defences were repaired. Then, leaving Captain Volker in command of the forces of Heldenhame, Leitdorf, Gormann and a handful of knights had ridden for Altdorf, looking to procure reinforcements.

The journey had been nightmarish. Beastmen ran wild across Talabecland and Reikland, despite the efforts of the knightly orders who hunted them relentlessly. Every noble, innkeeper and merchant with whom Leitdorf spoke whispered of darker monstrosities than just beasts lurking beneath the trees, and of villages and towns obliterated by fire from the sky.

Doomsayers and flagellants were abroad in ever-swelling numbers, agitating the grimy, plague-ridden crowds that clustered about every temple however large or small, begging for respite from gods who seemed deaf to even the loudest entreaty.

Things had been little better in Altdorf. Karl Franz had played his usual games, stalling and refusing to commit himself openly, and Leitdorf had waited for an audience for three days before being informed that the tide had turned for the worse in the north. It seemed as if Balthasar Gelt's magics had proven as useless there as they had in Sylvania, and the Emperor had ridden north to inspect the war effort personally, along with the Reikmarshal. Gormann had ridden out after them, to see what aid he might provide, leaving Leitdorf to scrape up what additional troops he could for the long march back to Heldenhame.

That was when he had met the elves.

Leitdorf felt a begrudging respect for Karl Franz's politesse even now – he had arranged events so that two annoyances satisfied one another, at no cost to himself or the war effort in the north. It even placed both him and the elves in the Emperor's debt, for having done so. Each had what they sought, more or less. Awkward compromise was the soul of diplomacy, or so Leitdorf had been assured by men who knew more of such things.

Leitdorf and his new allies had ridden out that night. As they reached the eastern border of Sylvania, the silvery host of Ulthuan had been joined by the full might of the Knights of Sigmar's Blood. A mightier host Leitdorf could not conceive of. Nonetheless, such a joint effort came with its own particular difficulties.

The elves were cautious to the point of hesitation, or so it seemed to him. For a race that moved so swiftly and gracefully, they seemed inclined to tarry overmuch for Leitdorf's liking. Irritated, he spurred his horse forward to join the elves on the knoll. His horse whinnied at the smell of the griffon, which crouched nearby, tail lashing. The great brute hissed at him as he drew close, and his hand fell to his blade instinctively. All three elves turned to face him as his fingers scraped the hilt.

'Stormwing will not harm you,' the woman, Eldyra, said, her voice high and musical. She spoke in an archly precise and archaic form of Reikspiel, and the harsh, jagged words sounded odd coming from her mouth. She was a princess of Tiranoc, he recalled, though he knew little of the distant island home of the elves, and so could not say what the human equivalent might be. A countess, perhaps, he thought.

'If he tried, it would be the last thing he did, I assure you,' Leitdorf growled, eyeing the beast warily. The elf woman smiled, as if amused.

'I have no doubt,' she said. 'Are your men rested?'

'Rested?' he repeated, feeling as if he had missed some vital part of the conversation.

'We stopped to allow them to rest. Humans are fragile, and lacking in endurance,' the older elf, Belannaer, said, as though he were lecturing a particularly dense child.

'Are we?' Leitdorf asked, through gritted teeth. 'My thanks. I was not aware of our limitations, or your consideration for such.'

'I could make a list, for you, if you like. For future reference,' Belannaer went on, seemingly oblivious to Leitdorf's growing anger. Then, maybe he was. Sigmar knew that Leitdorf was having trouble reading anything on the marble-like faces of the Ulthuani... Maybe they had a similar difficulty with human expressions. The thought didn't allay his anger, but it calmed him slightly.

'That won't be necessary. We are ready to continue on, when you are,' Leitdorf said, addressing the third of them, the grim-faced elf prince called Eltharion. The Prince of Yvresse was plainly the leader of the expedition, yet he had not spoken one word to Leitdorf in their travels to date. Nevertheless, Leitdorf suspected that the prince could speak and understand Reikspiel well enough. He was beginning to get the impression that Eltharion resented the indignity of having to ally with men. It was all the same to Leitdorf, in the end. As long as Sylvania was a smoking ruin by Geheimnisnacht, he could indulge the elf's pettiness.

'Excellent,' Eldyra said. Her eyes sparked with humour. 'We were just discussing whether we should slow our pace so that the dawi have time to reach– What was it called again?'

'Templehof,' Leitdorf said. He tugged off his glove with his teeth and reached into his cuirass to retrieve a map. He tossed it to Eldyra, who caught it gingerly, as if it were something unpleasant. 'A foul little town, located on a tributary of the Stir. It's not far from Castle Sternieste, which is where the vampire is currently skulking, if the survivors of the Grand Theogonist's ill-fated crusade can be believed.' He cocked his head, considering. 'It might be wise. Ungrim is going to be fighting his way west, through the heart of this midden heap of a province. Von Carstein will be throwing every corpse between Vanhaldenschlosse and Wolf Crag at the dwarfs, if he's smart.'

'And is he?' Eldyra asked.

Leitdorf laughed bitterly. 'Oh he's a cunning beast, that one. But he's still a beast. And we have him trapped in his lair.' Which was true enough. Despite all evidence to the contrary, Gelt's wall of faith seemed to still be intact. Objects of veneration still hung in the air like a chain of holiness about the borders, shining a clean light into the murk of Sylvania. Still, he hoped Gormann was giving the weedy little alchemist an earful of it, wherever they were.

'Yes, very inspired that,' Belannaer said idly, looking at the horizon. 'I would not have expected a human mind to grasp the complexities of such an enchantment. It was crude, of course, but that cannot be helped.'

'No, it cannot,' Leitdorf said, biting off the rest of his reply. The worst of it was that he didn't think that the elves meant to be insulting. They simply assumed he was too thick to tell when they were being so. Well, all save Eldyra. The elf woman shook her head slightly and rolled her eyes. Leitdorf grunted. Unnatural as her beauty was, she nonetheless made him wish he were a few decades younger, and less cautious. 'And no, we should not. Templehof lies in the shadow of Castle Templehof, which has long been claimed by Mannfred. It is a centre of power for him, which is why I chose it for our meeting place.'

'You wish to make our intent clear to him,' Eldyra said, after a moment. She nodded and her odd eyes flashed with understanding. 'We will take it, and show him what awaits him.'

'It is a waste of time,' Eltharion said.

Leitdorf was surprised. The elf's voice was no less musical than Eldyra's, but it was filled with contempt. 'What do you mean?' he asked.

'We care nothing for centres of power, or clarity of intent. All that matters is rescuing the one we came for. Let the stunted ones catch up with us, if they can.' He looked at Leitdorf. 'We are not here to subjugate your lands for you, human.'

'No, of that I am quite aware, thank you,' Leitdorf snapped. The griffon hissed again, but he ignored it. 'What are you here for then? You still haven't even mentioned the name of the one you are supposedly here to rescue.'

'Such is of no concern to you,' Eltharion said bluntly. He looked away.

'You are right. It is of little concern to me. But we are allies, and such things should be shared between allies,' Leitdorf said. He longed to swing down out of his saddle and drive his fist into the elf's scowling face. 'I have fought these devils for longer than any other. We must take their places from them. We must burn their boltholes and dens. Otherwise they will vanish again and again, and the object of your mission with them.' He looked hard at Eltharion. 'I appreciate your desire for haste – I share it myself – but we need the dwarfs. Sylvania must be put down, once and for all, for the good of all of our peoples.'

Eltharion didn't respond. Leitdorf felt himself flush, but before he could speak, Eldyra handed the map to Belannaer and spoke to Eltharion in their own tongue. It sounded strange and off-putting to Leitdorf's ear. He hoped she was speaking on his behalf. Eltharion ignored her, but she persisted, fairly spitting words at him. Belannaer held up the map and unrolled it. He looked at the land ahead and then back at the map. He looked up at Leitdorf. 'This is Templehof here?' he asked, tapping a place on the map.

Leitdorf nodded. 'Yes. As I said, it's close to our destination. It will make an adequate staging area for the assault to come,' he said. 'We're only a few days away.'

Belannaer nodded and handed him the map. The mage said something to the others. He spoke sharply and hurriedly. Eltharion made a face and shook his head. Leitdorf looked around in frustration. 'What is it?' he barked.

Eldyra looked at him. 'Belannaer says that the route you've chosen is dangerous. There are many...' She trailed off and made a helpless gesture, as if trying to pluck a word from the air.

'Sepulchres,' Belannaer supplied.

'There are many sepulchres and places where the dead rest uneasy on this route,' Eldyra said. Leitdorf laughed.

'This is Sylvania,' he said. 'The whole province is an affront to Morr. Dig anywhere and you'll find a layer of skulls beneath the soil. The trees are nourished by mass graves, and every town is built on a burying ground.' He leaned over and spat, trying to clean the foul taste of the air out of his mouth. 'If we get to Templehof, we can more readily defend ourselves for when Mannfred inevitably rouses the dead to stop us.'

'It is better to delay or stem the tide, than merely weather it,' Belannaer said. 'I can seal or cleanse these places as we march.' He looked at Eltharion. 'We are but a small force, Warden of Tor Yvresse, and in enemy lands. Think of the fate you inflicted on Grom, Eltharion. Haste did not save the greenskin from the death of a thousand cuts.'

'Grom?' Leitdorf muttered. The only creature he knew of by that name was a historical footnote. He peered at the elves, suddenly all-too aware of the vast gulf of time that sat between them. How old were they? He pushed the thought aside. He didn't want to know. 'Most of what you're talking about is near Templehof, if not actually within its boundaries. As I said, it is a centre of power for our enemy. Taking it from him will weaken him considerably.'

Eltharion looked at him for long moments. Then, with a terse nod, he said, 'Templehof. But we will not wait long. If we have finished cleansing the place before the stunted ones arrive, they shall have to catch up.'

'I wouldn't have it any other way,' Leitdorf said.

◄ CHAPTER TWENTY-THREE ►

The Hunger Wood, northern Sylvania

Count Alphonse Epidimus Octavius Scaramanga Nyktolos of Vargravia, Portmaster of Ghulport and its waters, hunched low in his saddle as he urged his terrorgheist to greater speed. Around him, several more of the great, bat-like corpse-beasts flew, the sound of their wings echoing like thunder. Fellbats and rotting swarms of their normal-sized cousins kept pace. Every so often, Nyktolos would catch sight of a screeching varghe-ist amidst the swarms and even a single bellowing varghulf, as the latter lurched awkwardly through the air. It had taken him nearly a day to rouse the denizens of the deep caves, but he thought he had managed to drag forth every flapping thing and night-flyer that made its home there.

It was an odd sort of army, this, but he had commanded worse in his peculiar career. There had been the time he had led a force of brine-soaked zombie sea turtles against the harbour guard of Tor Elasor. Or that incident with the mimes. Nyktolos shuddered and looked down. The vast expanse of Hunger Wood spread out below him like a shroud of green, and he could hear the crude drums and horns of the army marching through those woods.

Lord Mannfred had tasked him with the eradication of two of the invading forces currently assailing the heartland. It was a job that Nyktolos was more than capable of accomplishing, but he nonetheless felt a certain concern.

He had learned early on that the best way to survive the continuous cycle of incessant purges and inevitable betrayals that marked one's entry into the inner circles of the von Carsteins was to become part of the background. Show no ambition, and rarely offer more than an amusing *bon mot,* as the Bretonnians put it. If that failed, stand around looking stupid, busy or stupidly busy. In truth, it wasn't much different than being a mortal aristo-crat. The von Carsteins were vicious but the von Draks had been monsters.

Below, the trees cleared momentarily, and he saw the galumphing, hairy shapes of beastmen. They were still following him, as they had been since his first attack several days ago. It had taken no great effort to antagonise the creatures. His forces had struck again and again at the flanks of the great herd before retreating ever eastwards, and drawing the beasts away from the Glen of Sorrows and the Nine Daemons.

Nyktolos hawked and spat. He could feel the world grinding to a halt, deep in the marrow of his bones. The sky boiled like an untended cauldron and the earth shuddered like a victim of ague. He wasn't a learned man, but he knew what it meant well enough. Still, the lessons of his wild youth held – stay in the background and stay alive, or as close to it as a vampire could get. Markos and Tomas and Anark had all made that mistake. They'd thought of themselves as main characters, when really they were only bit players in the story of another. Well, he wouldn't make that mistake.

No, he would play his part to perfection. And at the moment, that part was as a distraction. The beastmen composed the largest group of invaders, and were thus the most dangerous. They could be beaten in open battle easily enough, but it would take time and effort better spent elsewhere. If, however, the brawling mass could be redirected at another of the invading armies – say, for instance, the disciplined throng of Karak Kadrin – then they could leave them to it, and get on with more important matters.

A day before he had encountered the buzzing mechanical contraptions the dwarfs called gyrocopters, and swatted them from the sky with little difficulty. He'd lost a terrorgheist and more than a few fellbats in the process, but the dwarfs had been too few and too slow. He still recalled how one of the doughty little creatures had made a terrific leap from the cockpit of his machine, axe in hand, even as a terrorgheist crushed it. The dwarf had gone right down its gullet, hacking away in a most amusing fashion. Well, amusing right up until the terrorgheist had exploded.

Nyktolos shook his head, banishing the memory. He wanted no part of the dwarfs and their explosives and cannons, thank you all the same. Better to let them vent their petty grudges on more deserving targets.

Down below, horns wailed and the beastmen slowed in their tramping. That wouldn't do. The dwarfs were still several leagues away, and marching towards Templehof. Nyktolos clucked his tongue and set his spurs to his mount. 'Come, my dear. It is feeding time, I expect,' he said as the terrorgheist shrieked and dived down towards the trees. The rest of the swarm followed him, screeching and chittering. Nyktolos drew his sword as the terrorgheist crashed through the canopy and landed atop a squalling centigor. Several more of the snorting quadrupedal beastmen charged towards Nyktolos, who flung himself from his seat with a yowl. He chopped through a hairy midsection as he landed, separating the centigor's top half from its lower body.

Quicker than thought, Nyktolos spun and blocked a club that would have dashed his brains across the forest floor. The centigor reared, and Nyktolos slashed open its belly as he ducked aside. The beast fell with a squeal. Beastmen rushed headlong out of the trees, covered in bats, and the terrorgheist lunged forwards, making a meal of two of the closer ones.

Nyktolos killed another, opening its throat to the bone with a casual flick of his blade. More creatures poured out of the trees. He surged amongst them for a moment, like a tiger amongst goats, killing them with wide sweeps of his sword and his own talons. Then, satisfied that he had regained their attentions, he leapt back onto the terrorgheist and swatted it between the ears with the flat of his blade. 'Up, you great, greedy beast! Up!'

The giant bat-thing heaved itself up into the air with an explosive shriek, tearing apart the forest canopy as it clambered into the sky. Nyktolos guided the creature in a low swoop across the tops of the trees. 'Follow me, little beasts. Your playmates await you!'

Malagor roared in fury as his herd rampaged out of control through the forest. They were going the wrong way and there was little even he could do about it. The horde was driven by its primal appetites. The cloven-hoofed warriors had left a trail of devastation in their wake, burning and pillaging a path right into the heart of Sylvania, and Malagor felt little impetus to control their baser urges, so long as they kept moving in the right direction.

What lay at the end of their trail was a mystery even to him. He knew only that though he was the truest of servants, he had failed to fulfil the desires of the Dark Gods three times. Three times Arkhan the Black had slipped away from him, and three times Malagor had given chase. He had pursued the bone-man across the world, from mountain to forest to plain and back again, and always, always the dead-thing escaped. With each failure, the whispers of his gods had grown in volume, until he thought his brain would be pounded to mush inside his vibrating skull. But they had not punished him, as he'd feared they might.

The Dark Gods knew that even though he was their truest child, his kin were less so. They were too wild to ignore their primitive urges and too feral to be organised for long. His failures had been no fault of his, but a weakness in the tools he'd been gifted. The gods knew this, and they whispered their endearments to him, urging him towards Sylvania. As he'd driven what was left of his horde after the debacle at Heldenhame into the lands of his enemy, more and more beastmen emerged from the forests and submitted to his will. By the time he'd reached Sylvania's northern border, and the crumbling wall of bone that protected it, the tumult of his horde could be heard for many leagues in all directions.

It had been a simple enough matter to gain entry after that, between his magics and the brute strength of his followers. They'd poured into Sylvania like a flood, following the pull of the Dark Gods. Now, however, that pull was being disrupted yet again by his followers' bestial instincts. No matter how many he killed, order could not be restored and they still pursued the flapping abomination that had harried them for some days.

It attacked and retreated, drawing his followers ever further away from their true goal, playing on their bloodlust and stupidity. He'd come close to killing the vampire more than once, but the creature was almost as slippery as Arkhan. It avoided open battle, and seemed content to bloody his flanks and slip away, just out of view.

Malagor flew over his loping warriors, easily dodging through the twisted woodland, his frustration bubbling away inside him. If he could get ahead of them, he might be able to head them off. That hope died a quick death, however, as he exploded out of the trees and saw what awaited him in the open ground beyond.

Arrayed about an irregular circle of standing stones the colour of freshly spilled blood, was a force Malagor recognised easily, though he'd never seen them before. Gold-topped standards rose above a wall of shields, and the air was cut by the stink of gunpowder. Malagor rose into the air, his black wings flapping, and tried to understand what he was seeing.

There were dwarfs ahead, thousands of them. Their numbers were nothing compared to those of his followers, but they should not have been there, and certainly not arrayed for battle. It made no sense – why were the stunted ones here? Was this part of the Dark Gods' plan? Or was it something else?

As he tried to come to grips with it, he heard the first of his followers burst through the tree line. The big gor, a chieftain called Split-Nose, snorted in incredulity as his watery, yellow eyes fixed on the distant shieldwall. Then he brayed and raised the axe he held over his head. Malagor growled in realisation. He had to stop them. If he failed again, there would no next chance.

'No,' he roared, and fell out of the sky like a rock. He crashed down onto Split-Nose and crushed the gor's broad skull with the end of his staff. He swung the staff like a club, battering another beastman off his hooves as they began to straggle through the trees in small groups. 'No! Go back – Dark Gods say *go back!*'

A bellow greeted his cry and the ground trembled beneath his feet. A moment later an enormous doombull smashed a tree into splinters with its gargantuan axe as it charged out of the forest. Its piggy eyes were bulging redly with blood-greed, and slobber dripped from its bull-like jaws as it charged forward. Malagor bleated in anger as he thrust himself skywards, narrowly avoiding the doombull. Minotaurs, centigors and beastmen followed it. It was as if some great dam had been cracked, and a tide of hair and muscle flowed out, seeking to roll over everything in its path.

Malagor could only watch as his lesser kin charged towards the dwarf shieldwall, heedless of anything save their own desire to kill, defile and devour that which was in front of them. He could feel the displeasure of the Dark Gods beating down on him, and with a strangled snarl, he flung himself after his followers, eager to drown out the voices of the gods in the noise of slaughter.

* * *

Red Cairn, northern Sylvania

'Come on then, scum! Come kiss my axe,' Ungrim Ironfist roared hoarsely. His voice was almost gone, and his limbs felt like lead. Nevertheless, he and his bodyguard of Slayers bounded out from amidst the dwarf shieldwall as the pack of bellowing minotaurs and bestigors charged towards the dwarf lines stationed around the blood-red standing stones. From behind him, volley after volley of cannon fire tore great, bloody furrows in the ever-shifting ranks of the children of Chaos, but the hundreds who died only served to make room for those who thundered in their wake. The air shuddered with the roar of the guns and the maddened braying of the horde, as it had for days.

'I'll crack your skulls and gift my wife a necklace of your teeth,' Ungrim shouted, as he ploughed into a mob of bestigors like a cannonball wrapped in dragonscale. He lashed out with blade, boot and the brass knuckles on his gloves. 'Hurry up and die so your bigger friends can have a turn,' he snarled, grabbing a bestigor by the throat. The beast bleated in fury and struck at him with a cut-down glaive, but Ungrim crushed its throat before the blow could fall.

Momentarily free of opponents, Ungrim clawed blood out of his face and looked around. The beastmen had flowed around the Slayers and smashed into the shieldwall, where many were thrown back in bloody sprays. Thunderers loosed destructive volleys at point-blank range over the shoulders of clansmen as minotaurs hacked at their diminutive opponents, stopping only to gorge upon the fallen. Skulls were cracked, and blood ran in thick streams across the lumpy ground.

Ungrim hesitated. All around him, Slayers were fulfilling their oaths as they savaged the belly of the enemy horde, and part of him longed to hurl himself even deeper into the fray alongside them, axe singing. But he was a king as well as a Slayer, and a king had responsibilities. He spat a curse and lifted his axe as he started back towards the dwarf lines. He picked up speed as he ran, and he smashed aside any beastman who got in his way without slowing down.

When the Imperial herald had come to Karak Kadrin so many weeks ago, Ungrim hadn't been surprised. It was just like the Ulthuani to go running to the humans when the dawi weren't feeling charitable. Given what he'd learned at the Kingsmeet the year before, and what tales his own folk brought east, from the border country, it wasn't difficult to see that something foul was brewing in Sylvania. Despite the fact that the thought of helping the feckless elgi sat ill with him, Ungrim had decided to set an example, to show Sylvania and the world, including his fellow kings, that the dwarfs were still a force to be reckoned with. Over the numerous and vociferous complaints of his thanes, he had gathered his throng and marched west. He had made arrangements to meet Leitdorf, the Imperial commander, at Templehof. His siege engines and cannons had easily shattered the petty defences the Sylvanians had erected – walls of sorcerous bone were no match for dwarf ingenuity and engineering – but his progress had slowed considerably as they reached the lowlands.

Dead things of all shapes and sizes had come calling, and the throng had been forced to shatter one obscene army after the next. A necklace of vampire fangs rattled on the haft of his axe, taken from the masters of each of those forces. But it wasn't just the living dead that attacked his warriors. Even the land itself seemed determined to taste dwarf blood – bent and maggoty trees clawed at them as yellowed grasses clung to their boots and sucking mud tried to pull them down. But the dwarfs had trudged onwards, until they'd reached the standing stones where they now made their stand.

They'd heard the cacophony of the horde from leagues away, and Ungrim, knowing what the noise foretold, had ordered cannons unlimbered and the oath stones placed, as the Slayers sang their death songs and his clansmen gave voice to prayers to Grimnir. Three times they'd driven the beasts back, and three times the creatures regrouped and charged again, as if the scent of their own savage blood on the air only served to drive them to greater ferocity.

Again and again and again the beasts had thrown themselves at the shieldwall of Karak Kadrin. Though it was almost impossible to tell, thanks to the sunless skies overhead, Ungrim thought that the battle was entering its second day. The dead were piled in heaps and drifts, and the dwarf lines had contracted more than once, shrinking with their losses.

Ungrim bounded over a fallen centigor and launched himself at a towering bull-headed monstrosity that was hacking at the shieldwall. It was larger than any of the others, and it stank of blood and musk. He gave a triumphant yell as his axe sank into the thick muscles of the minotaur's back. The monster bellowed in agony and twisted away from its former opponents. Ungrim was yanked off his feet and swung about as the minotaur thrashed, but he clung to his axe grimly. He reached out with his free hand, grabbed a hank of matted hair and hauled himself up towards the creature's head. 'You'll do, you oversized lump of beef,' he roared. 'Come on, let's see if you can kill a king before he boots you in the brains.'

Ungrim tore his axe free in a spray of blood and chopped it down, hooking the screaming minotaur's shoulder. He snagged one of its horns and drove his boot into the back of its skull. The minotaur reared and clawed for him, trying to drag him off. Ungrim hung on, anchored by his axe, and continued to kick the beast in the head. It wasn't particularly glorious, as tactics went, but they were good, tough boots, and the creature's skull was bound to give before his foot did. It caught hold of his cloak and began to yank at him, and Ungrim lost his grip on his axe. Flailing wildly, he caught hold of the brute's horn with both hands and, with a crack, he snapped it off.

The minotaur wailed and tore him from his perch. It smashed him down and so powerful was the blow that he sank into the soil as all of the air was expelled from his lungs. Drool dripped into his face as the minotaur crouched over him, its hands squeezing his barrel torso. Unable to breathe, Ungrim rammed the broken horn into one of the beast's eyes. It reared back with a scream. Ungrim tried to rise, but it smashed him from his feet with a wild blow. Dazed, he glared up at the monster as it loomed over him. Then, there was a roar and the minotaur's head vanished in an explosion of red. It toppled over.

'Och, are you dead then, yer kingship?' a voice shouted.

'Damn you, Makaisson,' Ungrim spluttered as a burly Slayer dragged him to his feet. 'What's the meaning of cheating me out of a perfectly good death?'

'Was that yers, then? I hae noo idea, yer kingship,' Malakai Makaisson said. A pair of thick goggles, liberally spattered with blood, covered his eyes, and he wore a peculiar cap, with ear flaps and a hole cut in the top for his crest of crimson-dyed hair. A bandolier of ammunition for the handgun he carried in one gloved hand crossed his barrel chest, and a satchel full of bombs dangled across it. As Ungrim watched in consternation, the engineer-Slayer grabbed one of the bombs, popped the striker-fuse and slung it overhand into a mass of confused beastmen.

'Stop blowing all of them up!' Ungrim roared. He kicked and shoved at the minotaur's body as he tried to retrieve his axe. If he didn't get his hands on it quickly, there was every likelihood that Makaisson would blow up the lot of them.

'What? I cannae hear you, what wi' the bombs,' Makaisson shouted as he lit and hurled another explosive. 'They're loud, ya ken.'

'I know,' Ungrim snarled. He tore his axe free in a welter of brackish blood and shook it in Makaisson's face. 'Why aren't you with the artillery?'

'Beasties are falling back, ain't they?' Makaisson said. 'They've had enough, ya ken?'

'What?' Ungrim turned and saw that the engineer-Slayer was correct. The beastmen had broken and were fleeing into the trees, as if the death of the giant minotaur had been a signal. Behind them, they left a battlefield choked with the mangled and half-devoured bodies of the dead. The throng of Karak Kadrin had control of the field.

But, as he looked at the battered remnants of his once-mighty army, Ungrim was forced to come to the conclusion that though they had won the battle, they had lost this particular war. As he moved through the weary ranks of his warriors, his mental abacus tallied the losses – with a sinking heart, he saw that almost eight in ten of them had fallen in the battle. Though they'd won a great victory – perhaps the greatest victory in the annals of Karak Kadrin against the foul children of Chaos – they had failed their allies.

He looked west. Part of him longed to push on, but there would only be death for his remaining warriors if the march continued. Perhaps Kazador had been right after all. What purpose had his march served, save to cast his warriors into the teeth of death? He had a feeling, deep in his bones, that he was going to need every warrior who remained in the coming days. And that meant he had to save those he could. He had to return to Karak Kadrin, and ready himself for whatever came next.

He closed his eyes, and felt the old familiar heaviness settle on him. Then he opened them and pointed his axe at Makaisson, who was filling his pipe nearby. He shouted, startling the Slayer into dropping his tobacco. 'On your feet, Makaisson! You just volunteered to go west and see if you can find the manlings and the elgi before they move on. They need to know that we're not going to make our appointment.'

'Me?' Makaisson said.

'You,' Ungrim said. He smiled thinly. 'Consider it your reward for saving my life.'

Ghoul Wood, southern Sylvania

'Oh, my sweet Kalledria, you do this old beast the greatest of honours,' Alberacht Nictus said as the rag of filthy silk drifted towards him through the dusty air of the crumbling tower. He extended a talon, snatched it out of the air and brought it to his nose. 'See how she teases me, lad? She was ever a woman of passion, our Queen of Sorrows,' he said, glancing at Erikan. 'Much like our Elize, eh?'

Erikan stood back warily, his gaze darting between the hunched, bulky shape of Nictus and the hovering, ghostly shade of the banshee that faced him, her hellish features contorted in a ghastly parody of affection. 'I wouldn't know,' he said.

'Ha! Do you hear him, love? He denies what is obvious even to the blind and the dead,' Nictus chortled as he threaded the silk rag through his hair. 'Hark at me, whelp, you are her Vlad and she your Isabella, or I am a Strigoi. She will have you before the century is out, my lad, see if she does not.'

'Elize has no more interest in me, old monster,' Erikan said, sidling around the banshee. 'She never did. Only in her schemes and games.'

'Ha, and what do you think you are, boy, but the culmination of both?' Nictus asked slyly. He watched the other vampire's face assume stone-like impassivity and grinned. He had been there the day Elize had brought the scrawny little ghoul-pup into the fold, and he had seen then what both of them now insisted on denying.

Shaking his shaggy head, he looked up at Kalledria. She had been a beautiful woman once, during the reign of Sigismund. Now she was nothing more or less than malevolence given form. Her skull-like features were surrounded by a halo of writhing hair, and she wore the gauzy tatters of archaic finery. Innumerable spirits floated around or above her, all dead by her hand. There were hundreds of them, and they crowded against the cracked dome of the tower roof, their ghostly shapes obscuring the ancient, faded mural that had been painted on the underside of the dome oh so many centuries ago.

Nictus laughed. He remembered that mural well, for he'd stared up at it often enough, in his youth. He'd visited the tower often, on behalf of Vlad. Kalledria had always been welcoming. Some stories said that she had been sealed away in the tower that her shade still inhabited, but he couldn't remember if those were the true ones or not. His mind was like a storm-tossed sea, and his memories were like helpless vessels caught away from safe harbour. Whatever her origin, he'd always thought her loveliness personified. He extended his other claw, the edges of his wings dragging on the floor. 'Oh, my sweet, you have done so well. You have collected so many new souls for your harem,' he gurgled as she drifted towards him, her ghostly fingers wrapping about his claw.

The hovering souls above were not merely men, but wood elves now, as well. She had taken them in the dark and the quiet of the forest, while her honour-guard of blood-hungry spectres had shadowed the others, snatching those who strayed too far from the host that even now impinged on the sovereign soil of Sylvania. She had drawn the invaders off course, and deep into the Ghoul Wood, just as Lord Mannfred had planned.

'Oh, my lovely lass, how you do chill these crooked bones of mine,' he said, trying to brush her fingers with his lips unsuccessfully. Some days, she was more solid than others. Her other hand passed through his face, and her mouth opened in a soft sound, like the cry of a dying hare. 'And your voice is as lovely as ever. Music to my ears, oh my beauteous one...'

'Master Nictus,' Erikan said softly. Nictus turned, annoyed.

'What is it, boy?'

'They are here,' the other vampire said, one hand on the hilt of his blade. He stood near the tower's lone window, staring down into the trees below.

Nictus sighed. He could hear the sounds of battle, now that he was paying attention. Elven-forged blades clashed with poisonous claws beneath the dark canopy that spread out around the tower. The elves had corralled one of Kalledria's servitors and traced the ancient tethers of dark power that bound the spirit to its mistress. He looked up into her hollow eyes. She had been banished before, his dark lady, and had always returned. But this time...

He was not as observant as he had once been. The weight of his centuries of unlife rested heavily upon him, and there were days where he wanted nothing more than to slip into the red haze of a varghulf and drift from kill to kill. No more plots and schemes, no more betrayals or fallen comrades. Only sweet blood and the screams of his prey. But he could feel the long night stirring deep in the hollow places of him now. Lord Mannfred, impetuous and haughty, was dredging something up out of its sleep of ages, and the world would crack at its rebirth. The Drakenhof Templars would be at the forefront of the war that was sure to follow, and so would Alberacht Nictus, broken-down old beast that he was. He had sworn an oath to the order, and his word was his bond, for as long as he remembered it.

'We must go, my love,' Nictus said, reaching up to not-quite touch Kalledria's writhing locks. 'You will do as you must, as will we.' Her mouth moved, as if in reply, and her ethereal fingers stroked his jowls briefly, before she turned and floated upwards, trailing her harem of spirits. Nictus watched her go, and then moved to join Erikan at the window.

Beneath the trees, elves and ghouls fought. There was nothing orderly about the battle. The participants fought as individuals, and the combat swirled about the sour glen below. One of the wood elves drew Nictus's attention. He was a lordly sort, clad in strange armour and a cloak the colour of the autumn leaves, wearing a high helm surmounted by a stag's antlers. He wielded his blade with a grace and skill that Nictus knew even a vampire would be hard-pressed to emulate. That one was more trouble than he was worth, Nictus suspected. He stank of strange gods and even stranger magics.

'Should we take him?' Erikan hissed. His eyes were red as he watched a ghoul lose its head to the elven lord's blade.

'That is not our task, boy,' Nictus said. He peered up at the sky. 'Come, the Vargravian will be here soon, to take us to the Glen of Sorrows. Let Kalledria deal with the elves in her own fashion, eh? A woman's fancy, and all that.'

Araloth, Lord of Talsyn, spun about, his sword trailing ribbons of red as he sent ghouls tumbling into death. He danced among the cannibals, avoiding their claws and striking them down in turn. It was a mercy, of sorts. Grubbing in graves was no sort of life for a thinking creature. He sank down into a crouch, his cloak settling about him, and spitted a charging ghoul. The beast grasped his blade and gasped out its life, its eyes wide in incomprehension. Araloth rose to his feet, jerking the blade free as he did so.

From somewhere far above him, he heard the shriek of his hunting hawk, Skaryn. Then he heard the chanting of the spellweavers, as they sought to bind the monstrous spirit that had plagued them so much in recent days.

He felt a pressure on his chest and grasped the locket the Everqueen had given him. It hummed urgently, pulling them ever towards the captive Everchild. But there were matters that needed dealing with before they could continue. Dead grass crunched behind him and he pivoted, his blade sliding upwards. The ghoul split apart like rotten fruit as his sword tore through its body. More of the grey-fleshed cannibals loped out of the trees, swarming like flies to a corpse.

'Protect Keyberos and the others,' he shouted, as his warriors retreated before the onrushing ghouls. 'They must be given time to seal the beast in her lair.' He glanced back at the small group of spellweavers who yet remained. Clad in dark robes, their flesh marked by savage tattoos, the mages flung every iota of the power that was theirs to command at the spectral creature that had emerged from the crumbling tower at the centre of the glen. Surrounded by a host of wailing spirits, the banshee drifted towards the spellweavers, her mouth open in a scream, which only Keyberos's magics kept the other wood elves from hearing and succumbing to.

Of the ten spellweavers who'd volunteered to accompany him on his mission, only four remained now, including Keyberos. Three had died in the attempt to discover the lair of the creature their fellows now confronted, and three more had gone mad. Now those who remained pitted their magics against the fell power of the thing that had stalked Araloth's warband since they'd crossed the border into Sylvania.

Blood-hungry spirits had shadowed the wood elves' every step since they'd crossed the Corpse Run. Scouts had vanished into the dark woods never to return, or else were found strewn across the trail ahead, their bodies drained of blood. Terrible dreams of long-dead kin and courts of dancing corpses had haunted the survivors, and an unlucky few had been lost to those night-terrors, never to awaken again.

Those who remained were as tense as drawn bowstrings, their faces pale with something Araloth was unused to seeing on the faces of the warriors of Athel Loren – fear. He could not feel it himself, for fear had no purchase on his heart, thanks to his connection with his goddess and the gift she had shared with him the day that she had crossed paths with a callow lordling and made him into a hero. Since that day, he had shared a portion of her prophetic gift, and was blessed with the ability to see hope in even the most perilous of days.

But now, he saw nothing ahead save darkness. It did not frighten him, for all things ended, even his folk and their works, but it did make him more determined than ever to complete his mission. If the darkness awaited them, then it would not be said that the Lord of Talsyn had gone into it a failure. He would wring one last victory from the world or die in the attempt. Hope cost nothing, and it could be purchased on the edge of a blade.

His warriors arrayed about him, Araloth met the undisciplined charge of the ghouls. His blade licked out, glowing like a firebrand. Blood soaked the thirsty ground, and bodies tumbled upon one another in heaps as the warriors of Athel Loren reaped a toll from the inhabitants of Ghoul Wood. The ghouls were driven back again and again, but they always returned with slavering eagerness as their monstrous hunger overcame their natural cowardice.

A shrill sound rose up behind him. Araloth glanced back and saw a spellweaver topple over, black smoke rising from his eyes, nose and mouth. The banshee thrust herself forwards, as if she were trying to fly through a strong wind. Keyberos gestured, and the soil at his feet began to shift and shuffle. Vines and strong green shoots burst out of the seemingly dead ground. The nearby trees shed their withered bark and bent pale, strong branches down. Wailing spirits were brushed aside as branches and vines began to encircle the banshee. Some blackened and disintegrated as she tore at them, but others caught her insubstantial form somehow.

A second spellweaver stumbled, her hands pressed to her ears. She screamed and pitched forwards, her body turning black and crumbling to ash as she fell. The air reverberated with a faint hum, as the magics that contained the banshee's wail began to crumble. Any moment now, he suspected that the creature would break free of Keyberos's magics and launch itself at the hard-pressed wood elves. 'Any time now, Keyberos,' he shouted.

'Keep your eyes on your own prey, Araloth,' the spellweaver snarled, his fingers curling and gesturing. More vines and branches shot towards the struggling banshee.

A wash of foetid breath alerted Araloth to the wisdom of Keyberos's words, and he turned. His sword separated a lunging ghoul's jaw from its head. He used the crook of his arm to hook its throat as it stumbled past, and broke its neck before flinging the body aside. As it fell, the remainder broke and fled, scampering away with simian-like cries of dismay. A moment later, he felt a rush of noisome air and a clap of thunder. He spun, his sword raised to fend off an attack from the banshee.

His eyes widened as he took in the large cocoon of vines, bark and leaves that hung suspended above the ground. Steam rose from the mass, wafting up into the sunless sky. Keyberos sat on his haunches, his hands dangling between his knees and his head bowed. The other spellweaver sat nearby, her face covered in sweat and her eyes hollow with grief. Keyberos reached out and gripped her shoulder for a moment. Then he pushed himself to his feet and looked at Araloth. 'It's done.'

'Will it hold?'

'For as long as this forest lives,' Keyberos said, his thin face twisting into an expression of grief. 'Which will not be long, I think. Sylvania is dying, Araloth. I can feel its death rattle echoing through me.'

'All the more reason for us to hurry,' Araloth said. Keyberos gave him a look of dismay, and Araloth caught the back of his head. He brought his brow against the spellweaver's in a gesture of brotherly affection. 'We must press on, my friend. If for no other reason than I would not have the lives we have already spent in pursuit of this goal wasted.'

He caught the locket and held it up, so that all of his warriors could see it. 'This is a promise, my brothers. A promise we made to our cousin, the Everqueen of Ulthuan. She has sworn to aid our queen in her hour of need and we must do all that we can to earn that oath. Even unto death...' He trailed off, as he realised that no one was looking at him. Even Keyberos was looking away, at something that even now approached them through the trees.

Somehow, the moon had broken through the darkness above, and its silvery radiance illuminated the form of a slender elf woman, who moved towards the weary warband through the dark trees. The Ghoul Wood seemed to sigh and draw away from her, as if her presence pained it. She was paler than death, but beautiful beyond measure, and clad in robes that gleamed with starlight.

Araloth gave a great cry of joy. He knew her face, and her name – Lileath – echoed through him like the voice of a lover. He raced towards his goddess, all weariness forgotten, ignoring the cries of his fellows. She caught him, and began to speak before he could even begin to compose a greeting.

Her words were not things of sound, but rather fragments of memory, thought and image, which coalesced across the surface of his mind, showing him what had been, what was, and what must be.

Araloth could not say for how long they stood, minds and souls inter-twined, but the moment passed and he knew then what she had come for, and what he had to do. He stared at her in disbelief, his every warrior's instinct rebelling. 'Is there no other way?' he asked.

Lileath shook her head and held out her hand. Reluctantly, he placed the locket into it. With no sign of effort, the goddess crushed it and flung the shimmering dust into the air, to create a portal of purest starlight before him.

Araloth turned. Keyberos took a step towards him. 'What does it mean? What is she here for?'

Araloth glanced back at Lileath, squared his shoulders and said, 'The Everchild's fate is written, my kinsmen. And we have no power to change it.' As the elves raised their voices in protest, he held up his hand. 'But there is a task for us elsewhere. On a distant shore, a great battle will be waged and the warriors of Athel Loren must go and wage it. Lileath intends to take me there. Any who wish to follow may. There is no shame to those who do not.'

Keyberos looked around at the gathered warriors, and then smiled sadly. 'I think you know our answer, Araloth. We followed you this far. And one battle is as good as the next.'

Araloth smiled, turned and took Lileath's outstretched hand. There was a flash of light, and the host of Athel Loren passed from Sylvania and mortal sight.

Klodebein, central Sylvania

'Five leagues,' Mannfred murmured, as he watched the dead fall upon the Knights of Sigmar's Blood. He stood on the edge of the vast garden of Morr, which occupied the southern edge of the village of Klodebein, and leaned on the hilt of his sword. 'Five leagues between him and his allies.' He glanced at Elize, his eyes wide in mock surprise. 'Not even my doing. His own impatience brought him here. I merely seized the moment,' he said with some bemusement. 'Would that all our enemies were so foolish, eh, cousin?'

'One could argue that any who choose to invade Sylvania on the edge of winter are prone to foolishness,' Elize said. She sat atop her horse, and looked past the tombs that crowded the garden, to where the ramshackle houses of Klodebein sat. Mannfred followed her gaze. He could hear the terrified communal thudding of the hearts of the inhabitants as they waited out the massacre occurring just past their walls. Barely a quarter of the living population of Sylvania yet remained, most in villages like this, close to the Stir. He'd wondered for a moment if the folk of Klodebein might try and warn the knights of the danger they were riding into, but instead they hid in their homes, waiting for it all to end and the never-ending night to become silent once more. He smiled and turned his attention back to the battle.

He'd have thought a seasoned campaigner like Leitdorf would know better than to lead his column through what amounted to a very large graveyard in Sylvania, but then maybe wearing all of that armour gave some men an inflated sense of invincibility. Or maybe it was Leitdorf's infamous impatience in action. It was that same impatience that had seen him leave Heldenhame Keep undefended, and it had finally got him killed. Or so Mannfred intended to ensure.

When his scouts had reported that the joint force of knights and elves had left Templehof, he'd thought perhaps that they were planning on attacking Sternieste. Or worse, they'd somehow discovered his plan for keeping their allies at bay, and were rushing to the aid of the dwarfs at Red Cairn. Instead, they'd begun to march slowly through Sylvania's heartlands, making for the Glen of Sorrows. That alone would have been enough to prompt Mannfred into taking action; Arkhan had not yet completed his preparations for the Geheimnisnacht ceremony, and if their enemies reached the glen before then, everything they had accomplished until now would be for naught.

Luckily, Leitdorf and his ironmongers had ever so obligingly ridden right into the jaws of a trap. As the knights rode through the closely packed tombs of the garden of Morr, the vargheists Mannfred had roused from a nearby well had struck. The Klodebein Brothers had betrayed Vlad at the Battle of Fool's Rest, and they and their equally treacherous sister had been sealed in their coffins at the bottom of the village's well since Konrad and Mannfred had run them to ground in the days following their disastrous ambush. The centuries had not been kind, but it had built in them a ferocious hunger, which they duly vented on the hapless knights.

As the newly freed vargheists revelled in a maelstrom of blood and death, Mannfred gestured and incited the death-magics that had long since seeped into the tombs and graves of the garden. As the first blindly clutching hands thrust upwards through the damp soil, Mannfred turned to Elize. 'How long do you think it'll take them to realise there's no escape?'

'A few minutes, if ever,' Elize said. 'Men like these do not admit defeat easily. The original Drakenhof Templars went to the grave assured of eventual victory, if you'll recall.'

'Would you care to place a wager, dear cousin?'

'What would we wager?' Elize asked carefully.

'I'm sure we can think of something,' Mannfred said, and laughed. His mind stretched out, awakening the dead in the sparse forest that surrounded Klodebein. Soon there were hundreds of shambling cadavers filling the garden, attacking the already embattled knights with worm-eaten fingers, brown, broken teeth and rusted blades. Soon there were ten corpses for every knight, and Leitdorf's warriors began to die.

A vargheist shrieked, drawing Mannfred's attention. He recognised Hans Leitdorf as the latter smashed his shield into the monster's face, rocking it back. The vargheist reared, wings flapping, and Leitdorf rammed his sword through its throat.

'Von Carstein!' Leitdorf roared, twisting in his saddle to face Mannfred. He spurred his horse into a gallop, and several knights followed him, smashing aside any of the dead that got in their way.

'Oh dear, he's seen me. Whatever shall I do, cousin?' Mannfred asked.

'You demean yourself with such flippancy,' Elize said softly.

Mannfred looked up at her. 'Do I? How kind of you to let me know, cousin. Wherever would I be without your words of wisdom?'

Elize continued as if he hadn't spoken. 'Leitdorf has killed many of our kind, cousin. Do you recall Morliac? Or the Baron Dechstein? What of the Black Sisters of Bluthof? They were von Carsteins, cousin, and Leitdorf slew them all. You would do well not to underestimate him.'

Mannfred laughed. 'You sound like someone I used to know.'

'Did you listen to her?'

Mannfred didn't answer. His amusement faded as he watched Leitdorf gallop towards him. Elize was correct, whether he wished to admit it or not. After Volkmar, Leitdorf was his greatest foe in the region, and he had expected to feel a certain sense of satisfaction at his destruction. Instead, he felt... nothing. Annoyance, at best. He should have been at the Nine Daemons, overseeing Arkhan's preparations. Instead, he was wasting valuable time dispatching a fool. He was so close to ultimate victory that he could taste it, and he was as impatient for Geheimnisnacht as Leitdorf was to get to grips with him.

The ground shook as Leitdorf drew closer. Mannfred watched him come, impressed despite himself by the mixture of bravado and stupidity that seemed to drive men like Leitdorf. Had he ever been so foolish? He glanced at Elize, and knew that she would say 'yes'. She had seen him at his worst, skulking in Vlad's shadow and scheming away against his kith and kin. Neferata too would have agreed with that assessment, he suspected. Then, the Queen of the Silver Pinnacle had never been shy about sharing her opinion on things that did not concern her.

Mannfred shook the thoughts aside. What Elize or even Neferata thought of him mattered little enough, and would matter not at all come Geheimnisnacht.

He stretched out a hand and drew up the skeletons that slumbered beneath the ground at his feet. They rose in shuddering formation, and at a twist of his hand, they formed a tight phalanx immediately before him, directly in Leitdorf's path. Timeworn spears of bronze were levelled at the approaching knights.

Leitdorf raised his sword and bellowed in defiance as he and his order struck the phalanx. The air rippled with the screams of men and horses as the impetus of the charge carried them onto the spears and in some cases, beyond. Leitdorf was thrown from his saddle as his steed collapsed, a spear in its chest. The Grand Master of the Knights of Sigmar's Blood was thrown deep into the ranks of skeletons. He crashed through them, but was on his feet with remarkable speed for one who ought to have been dead from a broken neck at the very least.

Mannfred watched as Leitdorf waded through the ranks of bleached bone, his sword flashing as he fought to reach his prey. Spears sought and found him, but he refused to fall. Mannfred found himself enraptured by the spectacle. Leitdorf's face was not that of a berserker, or a man driven insane by fear. Rather, it was the face of one determined to see his desires fulfilled, regardless of the cost. Mannfred could almost admire that sort of determination. For a moment, he considered swaying Leitdorf to his way of thinking. Vlad had always been fond of that – turning foes into, if not friends, then allies. A brave man was a brave man, he'd always said.

Then, Leitdorf broke free of the phalanx, and his blade chopped down, narrowly missing Mannfred's face. Mannfred sprang back, a snarl on his lips. From behind him, Elize said, 'I told you.'

'Yes, thank you, cousin,' he spat. He brought his blade up as Leitdorf, wheezing like a dying bull, staggered towards him. 'Anything else you'd like to add? No? Good. Shut up and let me have this moment, at least.' He extended his sword towards Leitdorf in a mocking salute. 'Well, old man, is this it then? Come to die at last?'

'The only one who'll die tonight, vampire, is you,' Leitdorf said hoarsely.

Mannfred brought his blade up. 'Well, we'll see, won't we?' He crooked his fingers in a beckoning gesture. 'Come, Herr Leitdorf... One last dance before the world ends, eh?'

CHAPTER TWENTY-FOUR

Glen of Sorrows, Sylvania

Eldyra looked up at the dark sky. Morrslieb and Mannslieb waxed full and bathed the world in an unpleasant radiance. She leaned back in her saddle and fingered the pommel of the runeblade sheathed on her hip. She said a silent prayer of thanks to Tyrion for all that he'd taught her. She'd used every ounce of skill and every swordsman's trick she'd learned in the days since they'd found what was left of Leitdorf, hanging from a tree south of the gutted and stinking ruin that had been the village of Klodebein.

She felt a pang of sadness as she thought of her mannish ally. She hadn't known him long, or well, but Leitdorf had seemed a good sort as far as humans went. But he had been as impatient and reckless as men invariably proved to be.

They'd lost the dwarfs as well – Ungrim's throng had not made the rendezvous. Belannaer had cast a spell of far-seeing and discovered that the throng had come into conflict with the largest beast-horde Eldyra had seen this far from the Wastes. She couldn't tell whether Eltharion was pleased or disappointed. He was no dwarf-friend, but even the Warden of Tor Yvresse could see that that their nigh-hopeless quest had become a suicidal one.

Nonetheless, they had not turned back. The Stormraker Host had fought its way through every obstacle Mannfred von Carstein had placed in its path – snarling packs of dead wolves, swarms of ghouls, shrieking spectres, and vampire champions clad in armour reeking of the butcher's block. Eldyra had taken the heads of more than a few of the latter, including a particularly stupid creature who had dared to challenge her to single combat.

Belannaer, guided by Aliathra's silent song, had guided them at last to this place, where the final fate of the Everchild, and possibly the world, would be decided. 'To think that it all comes down to such an uninspiring place,' Belannaer murmured from beside her. The mage stood on the edge of the slope looking down into the immense crater, at the centre of which lay their destination: nine great standing stones, arrayed on a bubo of rock and soil. And spread out around it, in all directions, was the vast and unmoving army of the dead. Eldyra doubted that they could have defeated that army even with the aid of the men and the dwarfs.

'You would prefer Finuval Plain?' Eldyra asked.

'As a matter of fact – yes,' Belannaer said. 'The air here is thick with the stuff of death. It is their place, not ours, and they have the advantage in more than just numbers.'

'Then we shall have to fight all the harder,' Eltharion said. They were the first words he'd spoken in days. He sat atop his griffon, his fingers buried in the thick feathers of the creature's neck. He leaned forward and murmured soothingly to the restive beast as it clawed at the hard ground impatiently. Eltharion's face might as well have been a mask, for all the expression it showed.

Eldyra thought that somewhere beneath that impassive mask, the Grim One blamed himself for Leitdorf's death. The man had tried several times to convince Eltharion to move faster, but he had been rebuffed every time. Eltharion had thought speed secondary to ensuring that their path was clear of potential enemies.

He had dispatched Eldyra to cleanse dozens of ruined mansions, abandoned villages and ancient tombs. And with every day, Leitdorf had grown more and more impatient, until at last he had simply given up trying to nudge his allies along and marched on ahead, to his death. Eltharion had said nothing either way. He'd shown no emotion when they found Leitdorf's body, and he hadn't mentioned the man's name since.

If Eltharion had a fault, it was that he was arrogant enough to think that the world was balanced on his shoulders. Eldyra had always wondered if that strange arrogance was the common bond he shared with Tyrion and Teclis. Heroes always thought that the world would shudder to a halt if they made a mistake.

Then, given what they'd seen recently, maybe they were right.

'Then perhaps it is time to tell them what we are fighting for,' Eldyra said softly. Belannaer's eyes widened. Eltharion didn't look at her. None had known the identity of the one whom they sought to rescue, save she, Eltharion and Belannaer. They had hidden that information from their own folk, as well as the men and the dwarfs, for fear of what might happen were it to be known. For long moments, Eldyra thought Eltharion might refuse.

Then, as if some great weight had settled on him, he sagged. 'Yes,' he said.

And he did. Once a decision was made, Eltharion would not hesitate. Eldyra watched from her horse as the warriors of Tiranoc and Yvresse mustered on the edge of the crater, and Eltharion, standing high in his saddle, addressed them. He spoke long and low, with deliberate plainness. Rhetoric had no place here, only the plain, unvarnished truth.

Eldyra watched silently, wondering what the result would be. She wasn't afraid to admit, to herself at least, that the Ulthuani had no more love of truth than their dark kin. The world coasted on a sea of quiet lies, and the truth was an unpleasant shoal best avoided.

Eltharion finished.

For a time, the assembled host might as well have been statues. Then, one warrior, a noble of Seledin by the cut of the robes beneath his armour, swept his curved blade flat against his cuirass in the ancient Yvressi salute. '*Iselendra yevithri anthri*,' he said. 'By our deaths, we do serve.'

As Eldyra watched, the salute was echoed by every warrior in turn. Eltharion stared, as if uncertain how to respond. She nudged her horse forwards to join him and drew her blade. She laid the flat of it over her heart as she gazed at him. 'You heard them, Grim One,' she said.

The briefest hint of something that might have been a smile rippled across his face. 'Yes. I did.' He drew his own blade and laid it against his cuirass as he hauled back on Stormwing's reins. The griffon, never one to miss a moment to spread its wings, clawed at the air with a rumbling screech. '*Iselendra yevithri anthri*,' Eltharion shouted. 'For Yvresse! For Tiranoc! And for Aliathra! Let us bring light into this dark place!' He pulled Stormwing about and the great beast leapt into the air with shrill roar.

And with an equally thunderous noise, the Stormraker Host marched to war.

'By Usirian's teeth, look at them,' Mannfred hissed. He laughed and spread his arms. 'Look at them, my Templars! Look upon the pride of Ulthuan, and know that we have come to the end of this great game of ours. Our enemies lie scattered and broken, and only this last, great gasp yet remains.' Despite his bravado, Mannfred recognised the warrior leading the elves – Eltharion the Grim, whom he had faced in the battle beneath Nagashizzar two years before. Of all the warriors of Ulthuan, only Tyrion worried him more.

He and the Drakenhof Templars stood or sat astride their mounts in the lee of the Nine Daemons. The ancient standing stones sat atop a bare knoll, overlooking the Glen of Sorrows. Nothing grew on the knoll, and even the raw, dark soil looked as if it had been drained of every erg of life. At the foot of each of the standing stones, one of the nine Books of Nagash had been placed, and Arkhan the Black moved amongst them, awakening the power of each eldritch tome with the merest tap from Alakanash, the staff of the Undying King.

The prisoners had been gathered amongst the stones, broken and unawares. All save Volkmar were unconscious, for Arkhan had been insistent that the old man be awake for what was coming. Mannfred was only too happy to acquiesce to that demand. He turned from the new arrivals and stalked to where Volkmar was held by a pair of wights. The old man cursed weakly and made a half-hearted lunge for the vampire. Mannfred caught his chin and leaned close. 'They are too late to save you, old man. The heat of a black sun beats down on you, and the end of all things stirs in your blood. Do you feel it?'

'I feel only contempt, vampire,' Volkmar croaked.

'That particular feeling is mutual, I assure you.' Mannfred looked past Volkmar. A scarlet light had begun to pulse deep within the standing stones, and he hesitated, momentarily uncertain. Now that the moment was here, was he brave enough to seize it? He shook himself and looked at Arkhan. The liche stood before an immense cauldron, which had been set at the heart of the stone circle. More wights stood nearby, holding the other artefacts: the Crown of Sorcery, the Claw of Nagash, the Fellblade, and the Black Armour. 'Well, liche? Are you ready to begin?' Mannfred asked.

'*I am,*' Arkhan said. He set the staff aside and hauled the first of the sacrifices up by his hairy throat. The Ulrican stirred, but he was too weak to do anything more. Arkhan drew his knife as he dragged the priest towards the cauldron. '*Do not disturb me, vampire. I must have complete concentration.*'

Mannfred was about to reply, when the winding of horns made him turn. The elves struck like a thunderbolt from the dark sky, singing a strange, sad song as they came. They drove deep into the ranks of the mouldered dead, fine-wrought steel flashing in the ill light emanating from the Nine Daemons. The elven mages, led by one in startlingly blue robes, who surmounted the battlefield atop a floating column of rocks, wrought deadly changes upon the withered vegetation of the glen, urging it to vicious vibrancy, and roots, briars and branches grasped and tore at the dead.

Mannfred lashed his army with his will, driving them forwards against the invaders. The reeking ranks closed about the elves, trapping them in a cage of the seething dead. Rotting claws burst from the sour soil, clutching at boot and greave, holding elves in place as rusty swords and broken spears reaped a bloody harvest. Mannfred flung out a hand. 'Crowfiend! Summon your folk to war!'

Erikan threw back his head and let loose a monstrous shriek, which bounced from standing stone to standing stone and shuddered through the air. As his cry was swallowed by the clangour of war, monstrous ghoul-kin, larger than their packmates scurrying about their legs and broader than ogres, hurled themselves into battle, trampling the dead in their eagerness to get to grips with the living. Bowstrings hummed and spears thrust forward, catching many of the beasts, but not all of them, and elves screamed and died as poisoned claws tore through silver mail and the flesh beneath.

Mannfred turned as scale-armoured steeds and swift chariots punched through the leftmost ranks of his army. Elven riders gave voice to rousing battle cries as they swept over the dead in a crash of splintering bone. Skeletons were ground to dust and ancient wights were burst asunder and freed from their undying servitude by the force of the thunderous charge. Mannfred cursed.

'Nothing for it now,' Count Nyktolos said. The Vargravian drew his blade. He looked at Mannfred. 'Do we charge?'

'Not all of us,' Mannfred said. He looked at Elize. 'Guard the liche,' he said softly, so that only she could hear. 'Arkhan's treachery will come at the eleventh hour. If he should try anything, confound him.'

'Do not worry, cousin,' Elize said. She blew an errant lock of crimson hair out of her face. 'The day shall be ours, one way or another.'

'Good,' Mannfred said. He climbed into the saddle of his skeletal steed and looked about him, at the assembled might of the Drakenhof Templars. A surge of something filled him. A lesser man might have called it pride. These were the greatest warriors in Sylvania, the backbone of all that he had built. It was fitting that they would be the blade that earned him his final victory. 'Know, my warriors, that this day is the first day of the rest of eternity. This day is the day we drag a new world, screaming and bloody, from the womb of the old. Your loyalty will not be forgotten. Your heroism will be remembered unto the end of all things. Now ride,' he shouted. 'Ride for the ruin of the living and the glory of the dead!' He drew his blade and extended it. 'Ride!'

And they did. Hell-eyed nightmares snorted and shrieked as night-black hooves tore the sod, and a wall of black-armoured death descended into the glen with Mannfred at its head. As he rode, he tried to gather the skeins of magic about him for an incantation, but found that the currents of sorcery shifted in his grasp, as if to thwart him. He knew at once that it wasn't merely the fickle nature of the winds of magic that prevented him from weaving his spells. His eyes were drawn to the distant figure of the elven mage on his dais of floating rock, and he snarled. He was too far away to deal with the creature himself, but was he not the master of every dead thing?

Mannfred reared back in his saddle and let slip a guttural howl, and the air above him was suddenly thick with the ragged shapes of spectres and ghosts. The spectral host shot towards the distant column of floating rocks. They flowed over the mage's bodyguard of Sword Masters like a tide of filthy water, chill fingers stretching towards the mage. The mage flung out his hands, and cleansing fires roared to life, surging in all directions. It left the living untouched, but the dead were consumed utterly. Spirits burst into clouds of ash, and zombies blazed like torches. Soon, the elves were surrounded by a ring of fallen, blackened corpses.

Mannfred laughed, despite the failure of his minions to kill the elf. They had served their purpose regardless. The elf mage had been outmanoeuvred, and his obstruction of Mannfred's sorcerous undertakings faltered as he was forced to see to his own defence. Mannfred seized the moment, and swept out his sword, carving an abominable glyph on the quivering air even as he urged his mount to greater speed. All across the battlefield, the newly dead began to twitch to life. Whatever losses his army had suffered would be replaced within moments.

Yet he could feel the elf-mage attempting to undo what he had just wrought. He gnashed his teeth and jerked his steed about. He raised his blade and the strident shriek of a horn sounded from behind him as the Drakenhof Templars wheeled about and formed up around him with supernatural discipline. It was time to deal with the sorcerer personally. Mannfred chopped the air with his blade.

As one, the Drakenhof Templars charged.

Arkhan did not bother to bid Mannfred a fond farewell. The battle did not concern him. He drained the blood of another of the sacrifices into the cauldron, and reflected on the days to come. He did not know what awaited him come Nagash's return, but he did not fear it, whatever it was. He hurled the body aside and chose the next.

Behind him, the vampire made little sound as she drew her basket-hilted blade from its sheath. Arkhan heard it regardless but did not turn around. '*Do you think that he will thank you, woman?*' There was a grim sort of humour to it – Mannfred, ever alert to treachery, had placed as Arkhan's guard the least trustworthy member of his entourage.

'At this point, what Mannfred does or does not do is of little concern to me, liche,' Elize said. The spurs on her boots jangled softly as she strode towards him, the blade held low by her side. She stepped over the bodies of the previous sacrifices, where Arkhan had flung them – the Shallyan, the Ulrican, the Ranaldite. He held the last of the preparatory sacrifices over the bubbling cauldron, his knife to the dead-eyed young man's throat.

'*I was not speaking of Mannfred,*' Arkhan said, as he drew the knife across the waiting flesh of his captive. The young priest of Morr gave a gurgling moan as his life's blood ran out to join that of the others bubbling in the belly of the cauldron. When he was satisfied that it had been drained to the last drop, Arkhan let the body fall, careful that no blood should splatter on him. The consequences of even a small drop touching him would be disastrous.

Elize stopped. 'Erikan will thank me, when he comes to his senses. Ennui is but a passing madness – a flaw in his blood. I will draw it from him, when this madness is past, and I will make him know his proper place.'

'*How like a woman, to think that only she knows what is best for a man,*' Arkhan rasped.

'How like a man, to think that a woman does not know what is best for him,' Elize said. 'Are you going to try to stop me, old bag-of-bones, or are you content to watch as I bring your plan to an untimely end?' She raised her sword to Morgiana's neck. The Fay Enchantress's eyes flickered and she tilted her head back.

'Do it,' she hissed. 'Kill me, before it's too late.'

'Quiet,' Elize snarled. She met Arkhan's gaze without flinching. 'Well, liche... Try your hand, if you would. You will get no second chance.'

'*Do it, and damn the world to madness and ruin,*' Arkhan said, his knife dangling loosely in his grip. '*If Nagash does not rise, the world burns. And you will burn with it, whatever your schemes and plans.*'

'And if he does rise, what then? Servitude and eventual oblivion? No, I'll not accept that,' Elize said. 'Better to be consumed by the fire, than to suffer a puppet's fate.'

'*Fate is a mocker,*' Arkhan said. '*A woman once told me that. Like you, she refused to surrender to Nagash. She told me that there are no certainties, save those you make for yourself. I still do not know if she was right or wrong.*' He looked down at the cauldron. '*Nagash will rise. The world will shudder. But the sun will still come up tomorrow. Sylvania will still be here, and Bretonnia as well. But if he does not rise, the sun will go dark and Sylvania will be consumed in fire, blood and Chaos. These are my certainties.*' He raised his hand and pointed to the battle raging outside of the Nine Daemons. '*That is yours.*'

Elize glared at him suspiciously for a moment, and then glanced back in the direction he'd indicated. The battle was a maelstrom of carnage; elves and vampires both lost their hold on eternity as two lines of knights crashed into one another. 'I don't see what–' she began.

'*There,*' Arkhan said. '*The Crowfiend fights alone against a hero of Ulthuan. A woman who has fought daemons and worse things than any suicidal blood-drinker.*'

Elize turned back to face him, her eyes narrowed to crimson slashes. 'You lie,' she hissed. 'No elf can kill him. I trained him myself. He is better with a blade than any among the order.'

'*Will he win, you think? Or will she take his head, as she has already taken the heads of those who fought beside him? Will your cannibal prince stand alone... or will you go to his aid one last time?*' Arkhan continued, as if she hadn't spoken.

'If he dies, he dies,' Elize snarled.

'*Then why do you hesitate?*'

He knew what she would do before she did. He had seen such looks before, in other places at other times. Some people possessed a pragmatic ruthlessness of spirit that outstripped even Nagash's histrionic malevolence. Vampires were often blessed with this quality, if they survived long enough. The drive to see their goals through at any cost. They would lie to themselves, rationalising that obsession into entitlement.

But some could only go so far.

Some went to the edge of that night-dark sea and then turned back.

Elize lowered her sword, turned and sprinted away, towards the battle.

'*Run fast, little vampire,*' Arkhan said, as he turned to the Fay Enchantress. '*We come to it at last, Morgiana.*'

'She was right, you know... Better the fire than the dust,' Morgiana whispered, her eyes closed. 'Better death than what is coming.'

'*And you shall have it, I swear to you. Your spirit will not rise at his command or mine,*' Arkhan said, drawing her to her feet. '*You shall be dead, and will suffer no more.*'

'Do you promise?'

Arkhan hesitated. Then, he nodded. '*I do.*'

'Why?'

'*It seems some small touch of mercy yet remains to me,*' he said.

Morgiana smiled as Arkhan cut her throat.

Overhead, the dark sky turned ominous as strange clouds began to gather. Screeching spirits swarmed about the stone circle. The wind began to howl, like a dying beast. Turning from Morgiana's body, Arkhan gestured, and his wights dragged Volkmar to his feet.

'Do what you will, corpse, but Sigmar will have you, in the end,' the old man spat. 'Your bones will be splintered by his hammer, and the dust he makes of you scattered on the wind.'

'*I am certain he shall, and it will,*' Arkhan said. '*You were born for this, you know. All of your years and deeds are the foundation of this moment. The blood that flows in your veins is the same as that of your god. It is the blood of the man who destroyed Nagash, and set the world on its current course.*'

Volkmar's eyes widened. Arkhan gestured, and the wights began to place the Black Armour upon the old man. Volkmar struggled and screamed and cursed, but he was too weak to break the grip of his captors. He called down the curses of his god on Arkhan's head. Arkhan looked up, waiting. Now would be the time for Mannfred's enchantment to fail at last. If this were a children's story, that is how it would go. When nothing happened, he looked down at Volkmar. '*Nothing. Proof enough that destiny holds us all in its clutches, I'd say. This was always meant to be. This moment is an echo of a promise of a thought cast forward through a thousand-thousand years. And we must all play our part.*'

The last clasp was tightened and the armour was attached. Volkmar sagged beneath its awful weight as the wights stepped back. Arkhan gestured, and a pile of iron chains, discarded when the prisoners were killed, rose at his command, clinking and rattling. The chains rushed forward and ensnared Volkmar, binding him and dragging him to his feet again. Arkhan motioned towards the cauldron, and the chains rose into the air, carrying Volkmar with them. As they deposited him feet-first into the cauldron, Arkhan reverentially lifted the Crown of Sorcery up and placed it upon the old man's bloodstained brow.

Volkmar moaned, and his eyes rolled up in his head. Arkhan could hear the crown's whispers start up as the voice of Nagash murmured in the old man's mind. Arkhan retrieved Alakanash and began to chant the ritual of invocation and awakening.

Elize sprinted across the battlefield, moving quicker than any black steed from the stables of Drakenhof. She swept her blade out, cutting down anything, living or dead that sought to bar her path. Erikan had been with the Templars. She had seen them charge before she made her move to stop the ritual, and she saw that the elves had met the assault at full gallop. Now the centre of the glen was a whirling melee of screaming horses, splintered shields and falling bodies.

She charged into the melee, her blade sweeping the life from an elven knight as the warrior rose up in front of her. She saw the Drakenhof banner, flapping in an unnatural breeze, and knew that that was where Mannfred was; and where he was, Erikan and the other members of the inner circle would be as well.

She caught sight of Nyktolos a moment later, duelling with an elven knight, his too-wide jaws agape in laughter. Nictus hurtled through the air on leather wings, plucking enemies from the saddle and dashing them to the ground, mangled and broken. And there, beneath the banner, Mannfred and Erikan, fighting back to back. But even as she caught sight of them, she saw a flash of painful light as the Drakenhof Templar bearing the battle standard fell. The source of the light was a sword, held in the hands of an elf woman, who leapt into the air while the standard fell, her blade clutched in both hands.

Mannfred turned, but too slowly. The blazing sword swept down, searing the air white in its wake. And then Erikan was there, parrying the blow. He and the elf swayed back and forth, their blades ringing as they connected. Elize fought her way towards them through the press of battle, Arkhan's words ringing in her head.

In that moment, nothing else mattered. All of her hopes and dreams and schemes turned to ash and char, consumed by the fire that drove her forward towards the man that she loved. And it was love, for all that it was built on hate and blood and deception. Perhaps that was the only kind of love available to creatures like them. Love was the reason she had schemed to bring him back in the only way she knew how, to show him that he still needed her, that he belonged with her. And she had failed. All of her lies and deceptions had done nothing save drive him even further away from her, down a dangerous path.

She bashed an elf to his knees and chopped down on him. As she jerked her blade free, she saw Erikan lose his blade and snatch up the Drakenhof banner to fend off his opponent. The elf hacked down through the standard pole as he tried to block her blow. Her sword scraped against his cuirass, and he fell.

'No!' Elize howled. She flung herself towards the elf, her lean frame moving like quicksilver. The elf woman pinned Erikan to the ground and raised her blade. Elize intercepted the blow and rocked the woman back with a wild slash. 'He's mine,' she snarled, extending her blade. She glanced down at Erikan. His eyes were closed, and his cuirass had been split open by the blow that had felled him. Dark blood welled up from within it, and he lay limp and unmoving. Elize turned her attentions back to her opponent as the elf woman spat something in her native tongue.

Elize studied her, sizing up her opponent. Her armour was battered and her robes torn and stained. But her face was composed, with no sign of weariness or fear. Her sword was steady. She lunged smoothly, and Elize was hard-pressed to parry the blow. They circled one another, feeling each other out.

They crashed together a moment later, like lionesses fighting over a kill. The elf woman was strong, surprisingly so, and more vicious than Elize expected. Even Cicatrix hadn't been as ferocious. She was forced to give ground, step by step.

Something caught her foot and she slid backwards. Her legs were tangled in the tatters of the Drakenhof banner and she almost laughed at the foolishness of it. She fell, and her sword was jolted from her hand. The elf lunged, blade raised.

Then, something dark rose up behind her and smashed into her, bearing her to the ground with a roar. Elize scrambled to her feet, snatching up her sword. Erikan had his fangs sunk into the elf woman's neck, and he tore her sword from her grip and flung it aside. She screamed and tore a dagger from her belt. The blade caught him in the chest and he staggered, clawing at its hilt. The elf woman sank down to one knee, a hand clasped to her throat. Her eyes were dull with pain as she scrabbled for her sword. Elize stepped on it and pressed the tip of hers to the elf's throat. She tensed, ready to thrust it home.

Somewhere behind them, Elize heard a monstrous roar and the earth trembled. She felt a wave of excess magic wash over her. Then something was dropped to the ground beside her. She looked down and saw a blackened corpse, clad in the burned remnant of blue robes. 'My thanks, sweet cousin. You gave me the respite I needed to deal with that pestiferous mage,' Mannfred said from behind her.

'One moment more, and I'll add another to your tally,' she snarled. She made to ram her blade home, when she felt Mannfred's hand on her shoulder.

'No, I think not. This one has spirit. Most elves are nothing more than trembling knots of vanity and fragile ego, but this one is something... wilder, I think,' Mannfred purred. 'She killed several of your fellow Templars, and nearly killed you both as well.' He stepped forward and crushed the charred skull of the dead mage. As the elf woman tried to get to her feet, Mannfred slapped her to the ground. She did not get up. He looked at Elize. 'I leave her in your tender care, sweet cousin. You and the Crowfiend can finish what you started with her. Be gentle, I beseech thee.'

A moment later, his smile faded. His face twisted in an expression of panic and he clutched at his head. Elize felt something like a wasp's hum in her head, but as soon as it had sounded, it faded. 'What was that?' she spat.

'Nagash,' Mannfred snarled. He sprang past them, running flat out back towards the Nine Daemons. As he ran, his skeletal steed seemed to appear from nowhere, galloping beside him. Without pausing, Mannfred reached up and swung himself into the saddle. Elize watched him go, and then turned back to Erikan. Count Nyktolos had joined them, and Nictus as well. Both vampires looked as if they had waded through a sea of blood, and the former had plucked the blade from Erikan's chest. He held it up. 'Barely missed his heart. He has the luck of a von Carstein, if not the name,' he said, grinning.

'He'll live, child,' Nictus gurgled comfortingly. 'He is tough, your ghoul-prince.'

Elize sank down beside Erikan and caressed his cheek. He looked at her. 'W-why did you come for me?' he croaked.

'Fool,' she said gently. 'No one leaves me. Especially not you.' She leaned forward and kissed him. She could taste his blood and that of the elf woman. She sat back on her heels and tucked a stray strand of hair behind her ear as she looked back towards the Nine Daemons. The winds about the stones had reached a howling crescendo, and the stones themselves glowed with an eye-searing light. Whatever was happening there, it was too late for her to do anything about it. It was up to Mannfred now. She looked back down at Erikan and smiled sadly.

'Freedom is overrated, my love,' she said, and kissed him again.

Mannfred rode madly towards the Nine Daemons, his fangs bared in a snarl. Elize had failed him. He would punish her later, her and her pet. But for now, he had to reach the stone circle before Arkhan completed the ritual. Nagash could not be allowed to return unfettered.

So intent was he on his destination that he barely noticed the shadow that swept over him. A moment later, pain tore through him as large talons pierced his armour. Mannfred flung himself forwards, over his mount's neck, and hit the ground hard. He rolled across the hard-packed earth as his mount came apart around him, showering him with bones and bits of flesh. As the dust cleared, he saw Eltharion's damnable griffon swooping towards him like an immense, spotted bird of prey. Its shriek cut through his skull and he jerked his sword from its sheath as the elf's lance dipped for his heart.

Mannfred snarled and ducked. The lance point skidded over his pauldron and tore through his cloak as he lunged upwards to meet the griffon's descent. His blade smashed through its furry ribcage and the great beast shrieked in agony. It tore away from him, knocking him from his feet with a flailing talon, and crashed into the ground right at the foot of the slope upon which the Nine Daemons stood.

Mannfred, bloody-faced, sprang to his feet and loped towards the fallen beast. As he reached the creature, Eltharion rose, battered but unbowed. He spared a single, inscrutable glance for his fallen mount, and then he extended his blade towards Mannfred. 'You're in my way,' he said.

Mannfred grinned. 'So I am, elf.'

Eltharion strode forward. 'I haven't got the time for you today, beast. It would be best if you walked away, and lived to fight another day.'

'Make time,' Mannfred spat. Here was a creature whose arrogance rivalled his own, and he found himself stung by the sheer gall of the elf. How dare they invade his lands and presume to treat him as anything less than what he was! He interposed himself as the elf charged towards the Nine Daemons.

Two blades, one forged by the greatest artisans of an empire long since fallen, the other by the mightiest civilisation to ever walk the world's white rim, came together with a sound like the roar of tigers. Mannfred stamped forward and shrieked, a war-cry not heard in the world for ages undreamt of slipping instinctively from his lips. Eltharion made no sound, and his face betrayed no effort as he met the vampire's blow and blocked it.

Mannfred moved quicker than he ever had before in the entirety of his accumulated centuries. He moved faster than the human eye could follow, so fast that his flesh was rubbed raw by his speed. Nonetheless, Eltharion parried every blow with a grace that stung Mannfred's eyes. Every blow save one. Mannfred gave a hiss of satisfaction as the tip of his blade slid across the elf's arm, slicing easily through armour and cloth to bite the flesh beneath. Eltharion staggered, and a second blow sawed at his side, tearing at his cuirass. Mannfred laughed as the sweet smell of elf blood filled his nostrils. 'Death, warrior – death is all that you'll find here. Death and an eternity of servitude after.' He circled Eltharion and continued to spew taunts. 'You'll be my bodyguard, I think. I'm running short on those, thanks to you. Would you like that, elf? I'll let your mutilated husk lead my legions when I burn the pretty white towers of your people and make them my chattel.'

He'd hoped to provoke the elf. To spur him into attacking wildly, and without concern for his own wellbeing. Instead, the elf came at him with a chilly meticulousness. He parried Mannfred's next blow and the edge of his blade came close to opening the vampire's throat. Eltharion fought with machine-like precision, every blow calculated for maximum effect and minimum effort. If he hadn't suddenly found himself on the defensive, Mannfred would have been impressed.

He realised, as they traded blows, that for the first time in a long time he was the less-masterful combatant in a duel. For too many years, he had relied upon old skills and sheer brute strength, but here, at last, was an opponent whom he could not simply overmatch.

A blow from Eltharion's sword tore open his cuirass and sliced through the flesh beneath. A second blow smashed into Mannfred's forearm with hammer-like precision, shattering bone and shearing muscle to leave the limb hanging from a single agonised strand of muscle. Mannfred howled and staggered back, clutching at his wounded limb, his sword lying forgotten in the dust. The world spun around him, and he could see all of his hopes and dreams turning to ash before him.

'No,' he hissed. 'No! I've fought too long, too hard to be beaten now, by you!' he roared as he flung out his good hand. Deathly magics coalesced in the air before the grimly advancing elf, forming into a sextet of black swords. Eltharion weaved through the blades, parrying their every blow.

Mannfred, crouched on the slope, watched the elf fight his way through the blades. The sable swords had only been a distraction. They would fade in moments, leaving Eltharion free to attack again. He had only moments in which to act. Ignoring the pain of his mangled arm, he summoned the energy to unleash a bolt of raw, writhing magic. He rose on unsteady legs, the scope of his world narrowed to Eltharion's graceful form. If he could kill the elf, it would be done. He extended his hand, black lightning crackling along his forearm and between his curled fingers.

But before he could unleash the spell, he heard a guttural snarl. A heavy body lunged across the slope, trailing blood and feathers. The griffon's beak snapped shut on his extended arm, its talons smashing into his chest and thigh. Mannfred screamed as he was borne to the ground by the monster's weight. It was no consolation that his spell had killed the creature as it struck it.

'No! Damn you, no!' Mannfred screamed, pleading with fate as he tried to extricate himself from the dead animal's claws and beak. 'No! Not now! Eltharion – face me, damn you!' he shrieked as Eltharion started up the slope with only a single backwards glance. 'Eltharion,' Mannfred wailed, squirming beneath the corpse of the griffon.

Eltharion strode towards the standing stones, seemingly gaining strength with every step. As he reached them, light crackled between them. Mannfred cackled weakly. Of course Arkhan had cast some defensive enchantment, of course!

His cackles died away as Eltharion raised his sword in a two-handed grip and thrust the sword into the mystical barrier. The magic crackled and spat, writhing around the blade like a thing in pain. The runes upon the elvish blade glowed as red as coals, and then Eltharion pushed his way into the ring of the Nine Daemons.

With an agonised snarl, Mannfred freed himself from the dead griffon, leaving behind more flesh and blood than he liked to think about. Bleeding heavily, he staggered up after the elf and, with a last surge of strength, he pounced at the gap the elf had made.

He was too slow. He struck the mystic barrier and staggered back. Wailing spirits whirled about him as he pounded his now-healed fists against the barrier. He saw Eltharion toss away his smoking and melted blade.

Arkhan had his back to the elf, standing before the cauldron, one hand wrapped in the golden tresses of the Everchild, forcing her head and torso over the cauldron's rim. In his other hand, he held his knife in preparation for slashing her throat, as he had with all of the other sacrifices. In the centre of the cauldron, Volkmar hung limp in a mystical web of chains.

Eltharion lunged with a roar worthy of his slain mount. Arkhan released his captive and spun. Eltharion slammed into him, his hands closing about the liche's bony neck. Arkhan glared at the elf. '*Release me, warrior.*' Eltharion slammed him back against the cauldron as if to snap the liche in two. '*Very well. I have no more time for mercy.*'

Arkhan's hands snapped up and caught the elf's wrists. Instantly, a cloud of rust billowed up from Eltharion's vambraces. As Mannfred watched, the entropic curse consumed him. It rippled across metal and flesh with equal aplomb, warping and cracking armour as it withered flesh. The elf's hair turned white and brittle, and his flesh took on the consistency of parchment, but he did not release his hold on Arkhan. To the last, his gaze held the liche's.

Then, with barely a sigh, Eltharion the Grim, Warden of Tor Yvresse, burst apart in a cloud of dust.

Arkhan staggered back, the witch-lights of his eyes flashing with something that might have been regret. Mannfred began to pound on the barrier anew as Arkhan turned back and jerked Aliathra to her feet. He reclaimed his dagger. 'My father will destroy you, liche,' she said. Mannfred was impressed. There was no fear in her voice, only resignation.

'*Your father is already dead, child. My allies have seen to that.*'

'Allies? What allies?' Mannfred shouted. 'Arkhan – let me in!'

Arkhan ignored him. He looked at Aliathra as she said, 'For all of your power, you know nothing.'

'*We shall see,*' Arkhan said. He glanced at Mannfred. '*Stop striking my barrier, vampire. It's becoming annoying.*'

'Let me in, you fool,' Mannfred snarled. His mind probed at the sorcery that protected the stones, trying to find a weak point. He had to get in there.

'*Why? So that you can try and subvert this moment for your own ends? No – no, I think not. You have played your part, and admirably so, vampire. Do not ruin it now with petty antics.*' Arkhan stepped forward and dragged Aliathra towards the cauldron. She struggled for a moment, then pressed her hands against the liche's chest. Arkhan threw up a hand as a white, painful light flared suddenly. He recoiled as if burned, and then swung the elf maiden towards the cauldron. '*What have you done, witch?*' he rasped.

'You'll find out,' she said.

Arkhan hesitated, staring at her. Then, with a dry rasp of anger, he cut her throat.

As her blood spilled into the already bubbling cauldron, Arkhan began to speak. The words had a black resonance that caused the air to shudder and squirm, as if in fear. Mannfred began to pound on the shield again, howling curses at the heedless liche as he continued to chant.

As Mannfred watched in mounting frustration, Arkhan placed his knife against one of Volkmar's wrists and, with a single, efficient motion, severed the hand. Volkmar screamed and writhed in his chains. Arkhan, still chanting, lifted the Claw of Nagash and pressed it forcefully against the Grand Theogonist's pulsing stump.

Volkmar's screams grew in pitch and volume, spiralling up into the tormented air to mingle with the unpleasant echoes of Arkhan's chanting. Arkhan stepped back and snatched up Alakanash. He lifted the staff high and tendrils of dark magic burst from the stump of the Claw. The tendrils writhed about Volkmar's arm and burrowed into the old man's abused flesh. Volkmar screamed and shook in his chains, convulsing with a suffering that even Mannfred had trouble imagining.

He took no pleasure in the old man's pain, though he might have, under different circumstances. He slid down, suddenly weary, as the tendrils began to expand. As they grew, they lashed and flailed and spread across Volkmar's frame, winnowing into him and leaving only a cancerous mass of dark magic in their wake. Soon, the only thing of Volkmar that Mannfred could see were his eyes, bulging in agony.

Then, there was nothing save the mass, which swelled like an abominable leech as it feasted greedily on the blood in the cauldron. Chains snapped as the mass thrashed about, drawing sparks from the stones around it. It continued to swell as Arkhan held the Fellblade extended, point-first towards the cauldron.

Arkhan spat words like arrows, piercing the air with the hateful sound of them. The Fellblade rose from his hand as if plucked by invisible fingers. It hung in midair for a moment and then, with a loud crack, it shivered into a thousand steaming fragments, which swirled about the mass like tiny comets before striking it and burrowing into its surface.

Outside the circle, Mannfred hunched closer to the stones as the wind picked up, and the howling of the spirits grew deafening. The stones trembled and glowed with daemonic fire. Thunder rolled across the sky above, and he screamed in pain as the enchantment he had laid across the land – *his* land – was torn asunder. Something vast and terrible descended into the stone circle with a volcanic sigh.

His head was filled with fiery wasps, and his bones felt as if they would tear from his flesh to join the maelstrom swirling about inside the circle. His heart swelled and wrenched in his chest, and he crawled forward as the spell that had barred him entry shattered like glass. Something spoke in a voice that echoed through his mind.

'*YOU HAVE DONE WELL, MY SERVANT.*'

Nagash.

It was the voice of Nagash and it tore through him like a blade, cutting through his arrogance, his ambitions, his hopes and his vanities. Mannfred shuddered in his skin as he crept towards the cauldron. He felt sick, as though a great pressure had settled on him. He knew then that his dreams had only ever been that – dreams. Arkhan had been right, in the end. There was no controlling what had come back into the world. What now spoke in a voice like sour thunder. '*THE GREAT WORK CAN BEGIN.*'

He saw that Arkhan had prostrated himself and he could not stop himself from doing the same. He bent low, hoping that the thing that now gazed at him with eyes as deep and as empty as a hole in the world could not sense the bitterness in his heart.

'*DO YOU SERVE ME?*' Nagash asked, looking down at him.

Mannfred von Carstein closed his eyes. 'Yes,' he croaked, 'I serve you... master.'

EPILOGUE

Geheimnisnacht

Mannfred von Carstein screamed.

For the first time in a long time, he truly screamed. Not a howl of frustration, or the cry of a wounded warrior, but the shriek of a frightened beast, caught in a trap. Nagash's servants had stripped his cuirass and cloak from him, leaving him bare-chested. They held his wrists pinned, and skeletal hands sprouted from the ground like hellish mushrooms to grasp his feet and ankles.

'No, I refuse – I will not let you do this – I forbid it!' Mannfred screamed, struggling vainly against the withered grip of the ancient, long-dead warriors who held him.

'*YOU... FORBID?*' The sickly green witch-lights of Nagash's eyes flickered. The fleshless jaw sagged in what might have been laughter. Nagash loomed over the vampire. '*YOU FORBID NOTHING, LITTLE FLEA. YOU SIMPLY SERVE.*'

'Then you don't need him! You have me,' Mannfred howled, jerking in his captors' grip. 'I have always been loyal to you! I brought you back – me, not him!'

Nagash took Mannfred's chin in one black claw. 'LOYAL. YOUR KIND DOES NOT KNOW LOYALTY. DO THEY, ARKHAN?' The witch-lights flickered towards Arkhan, where the liche stood watching.

'*Loyal or not, he has served you,*' Arkhan said, one hand still pressed to his chest where the Everchild had struck him. He could feel something there, as if she had passed something to him, but he could not say what. '*As have I.*'

'YES. AS YOU WILL CONTINUE TO DO, UNTIL THE GREAT WORK IS COMPLETED. AS THIS ONE WILL DO. AS ALL HIS KIND WILL DO.' Nagash leaned towards Mannfred. 'YOU WERE CREATED TO SERVE ME. YOU ARE AN EXTENSION OF MY WILL, NOTHING MORE. AND I WILL DASH YOU DOWN OR CALL YOU UP AS IT PLEASES ME.'

With that, Nagash sank his fingers into Mannfred's chest and wrenched a gobbet of flesh free. Mannfred screamed and thrashed as Nagash turned and squeezed the bloody hank of meat onto the pile of dust and soil his servants had created earlier. When the last drop of blood had been wrung from it, he tossed it aside without a second glance.

'RISE,' Nagash said. It was not a request. The air, murky and foul, twitched like an inattentive cat. 'RISE,' he said again.

The air twitched again. Dust billowed, mixing with Sylvanian grave soil and Nehekharan sand. Something vague was beginning to take shape. Mannfred's howls of denial grew louder as the pool of his blood began to bubble and froth.

Arkhan watched, curious. The blood of all vampires was, at its base, the blood of Nagash, albeit diluted by poison and sorcery. The black brew devoured and replaced all that was human in them, making them over into something else. It made a dreadful sort of sense that Nagash would know how to manipulate it.

For as long as he could recall, the vampires had thought themselves separate and superior to beings such as himself. They had thought themselves the inheritors of Nagash's legacy, rather than merely another sort of servant.

Today, Nagash proved them wrong.

The blood began to spread, increasing in volume, and rising upwards like a geyser to encompass the dust. The vague shape became less so. To Arkhan, it was as if someone were swimming towards him across a great distance. A sound drew his attention.

Mannfred was weeping. Great red tears rolled down his cheeks, and his mouth was open in a soundless howl of fury and fear. He'd been forced to his knees by Nagash's servants, and he'd ceased his struggles. He stared at the pulsing column of blood as if it were the end of the world.

Then, maybe it was.

Arkhan turned back as Nagash stepped close to the blood and, without hesitation, plunged his arm in. There was a sound like the ocean's roar and the crash of thunder, and then Nagash jerked something out of the blood and tossed it aside. As it struck the ground, Arkhan saw that it was a human figure, flesh stained red.

The blood splashed down and lost all cohesion. The figure lay on the ground, curled into a ball. Nagash reached for it, as if to shake it to wakefulness. A bloodstained hand snapped out, seizing his wrist. Nagash paused.

A voice, hoarse with disuse, said, 'I... live.' The figure uncoiled and rose awkwardly, as Nagash jerked his wrist free and stepped back. Beneath a mask of dried blood, feral, handsome features twisted in confusion as dark eyes gazed down at clawed hands in incomprehension. 'I live? I-I... Isabella?'

The eyes flickered up as Mannfred at last tore himself free of his captors and lunged towards Arkhan. Unprepared, Arkhan could only stumble back as Mannfred tore his tomb-blade from its sheath and shoved him back.

'No,' Mannfred wailed, 'No, not again, never again!' He hurtled towards the newcomer, his stolen sword licking out to remove the latter's head.

The newcomer sprang aside, stumbled and dived for one of Nagash's warriors. He ripped the archaic blade from the wight's belt and whirled about, bringing his newly procured weapon up just in time to block Mannfred's next blow.

'You,' he said, eyes narrowing as they fixed on Mannfred's contorted features. Thin lips peeled back, revealing an impressive mouthful of fangs.

'I killed you once, old man. *I can do it again,*' Mannfred shrieked.

Arkhan moved to break up the duel, but stopped at an imperious gesture from Nagash. The Undying King wanted to see what happened next. The two vampires lunged towards each other, their blades connecting in a screech of metal. They spun in a tight circle, their swords locked together. For a moment, Arkhan thought Mannfred had the advantage. The other vampire seemed weak, uncertain... But then, slowly, steadily, he began to gain the upper hand. Arkhan realised that he'd been feigning weakness, in order to draw Mannfred in.

Mannfred was too blinded by rage to see what his opponent was up to. He lunged, and the other vampire performed a complicated manoeuvre that Arkhan had last seen on the proving grounds of Rasetra more than a thousand years before, blocking the blow and disarming Mannfred all in one smooth motion. Mannfred, unable to halt his lunge, stumbled forward. His opponent's blade was suddenly there to meet him, and it slid into his belly with a wet sound. Mannfred coughed and his eyes bulged in shock as he clawed at his opponent's blade.

He forced Mannfred down to his knees, the sword still in his gut. With his free hand, he grabbed the back of Mannfred's scalp and dragged his head up. 'Where is Isabella, boy? Where is my ring?' he hissed, glaring down at Mannfred.

'Dead, and gone,' Mannfred spat weakly. 'Just as you were.'

'You should know better than that, boy,' the other vampire growled. He kicked Mannfred off the blade, and raised it over his head, as if to split Mannfred's skull. But before the blow could fall, Nagash raised his hand.

'*HOLD, VAMPIRE. YOUR STUDENT STILL HAS HIS USES, AS DO YOU.*'

The vampire turned, his eyes widening in shock. 'Usirian's teeth,' he hissed. 'Nagash...'

'*YES. AND IT IS NAGASH TO WHOM YOU OWE YOUR FEALTY, VLAD VON CARSTEIN.*' Nagash loomed over the two vampires, his eyes burning like twin infernos, the air turning sour around him. '*KNEEL, VAMPIRE. KNEEL AND RECEIVE MY BLESSING. KNEEL, AND JOIN ME.*' Nagash raised his claws as Vlad sank slowly down to one knee, his sword planted blade-first into the ground. There was a great roar, as of a thousand-thousand voices raised in agonised protest, and the world contracted like a beast in pain. The earth trembled, and the sky wept oily rain. And Nagash found it good.

'*THE GREAT WORK CAN NOW COMMENCE.*'

THE FALL OF
ALTDORF

Chris Wraight

THE FALL OF ALTDORF

The Monstrous Horde

The Tattooed Tribes

REIK RIVER

The Tattooed Tribes

Altdorf
Undead

Altdorf
Undead

Altdorf
Undead

Altdorf
Undead

Altdorf
Undead

Hammerplad

South Road

Leon
Sk

The Crusades of
Bretonnia

Road to Montfort

REIKWALD
FOREST

DRAKWALD
FOREST

Drakwald
Beasts

Dragon
Ogres

Reiksguard
Assault

Knightly
Orders
and State
Troops

Road to Middenheim

Golden Plaza

RIVER TALABEC

Road to Talabheim

The Empire's
Blades

Sigmarsen Street

Dampfplatz

Steam
Tanks

The
Tallyman's
Host

Fleischmark

Altdorf
Undead

RIVER RE

DRAKWALD
FOREST

PART ONE

Heffengen

Late Winter 2524-2525

◄ CHAPTER ONE ►

The tent's walls flapped in the cold west wind, making the fires in the torches spit and gutter. Its lone occupant knelt on mud-slick grass, bowing his head before a makeshift altar. A rich red cloak hung, rain-heavy, from his armoured shoulders. His gauntlets were crossed on the hilt of a proffered sword, thrust naked and point-down into the earth in the knight's fashion.

His eyes remained closed. He was un-helmed, exposing a lean, noble face lost in prayer. His hair was close-cropped and mottled with the marks of the battlefield – mud, blood, lines of old sweat.

The altar was small, and had been carried with his baggage ever since his first days as a squire. It was made of rosewood, with a carved representation of twin griffons facing one another across the battered top face. It was a cheap thing, in truth. He could have had it replaced with a gold-plated one by now, or employed priests to pray on his behalf, but he had prayed before that same altar for thirty-two years, and was not about to change now. Not today, of all days.

'My lord Heldenhammer,' he whispered, his breath steaming in the dawn's chill. 'As I have ever been faithful, remember Your servant this day. I fear no death, no pain, no trial, if it be in Your service. I admit only one fear: to prove unworthy of the sword I bear, the armour I wear, the men I command.'

From outside the tent, the noises of a preparing army could be heard – horses being led to their riders, artillery pieces being hauled across the furrowed earth on iron-rimmed wheels. He could hear the muffled roaring of battle-priests, rivalled only by the parade-ground shouts of sergeants and captains.

He had heard such sounds all his life. Ever since childhood, the instruments of war had been around him. In that, if in no other way, this day was little different.

'When I slay, let it be in Your name. When I face the darkness, let it be in Your name. And when the hour comes, and when my service ends, let it be that I reflected honour to You in the time that I was given.'

Rain started up again, drumming on the already sodden canvas. The downpour would make the earth well with water, hampering the charge of the warhorses.

'Let it be,' he prayed, near-silently, 'that no man has cause to doubt my devotion, and that they will say nothing more of me, after I am gone, but that I fulfilled my vows.'

He opened his eyes, and stood stiffly. He took up his sword and sheathed the blade, then made the sign of the comet across his breastplate and bowed a final time. As he did so, the wind whipped around the tent-walls, brushing ice-cold rain under the skirts.

He reached for his helm, held it loosely in his left hand, and turned to the entrance flaps.

Outside, they were waiting for him.

Schwarzhelm glowered massively in the drizzle, his heavy broadsword already unsheathed, his great beard dank and draggled. Huss stood in his shadow, scarce less brutal in mien, moisture running in trickles down his bald pate. The boy Valten was beside him, grasping Ghal Maraz one-handed as if it weighed less than a stick of straw. Helborg stood apart, magnificent in his war-plate, steel-clad, hard and hawk-like.

Behind them were the generals, the warriors, the foot soldiers, the knights, the halberdiers, in white and red and yellow and chequered black and carrying the serried weapons of the Empire in readiness.

As one, they raised those blades.

'*Karl Franz!*' they roared.

At that, the Elector Count of Reikland, the Prince of Altdorf, the Bearer of the Silver Seal and the holder of the *Drachenzahn* runefang, Emperor of all Sigmar's holy inheritance between the Worlds Edge Mountains and the Great Sea, nodded in acknowledgement.

'Gentlemen,' he said. 'Let us begin.'

Heffengen, like all towns in the upper Ostermark, was fortified. Thick stone walls enclosed its tight streets of wattle-and-daub dwellings, overlooked by steep tiled roofs. Those walls, though, had been left to rot by a neglectful burgomeister, whose body now swung from a high gibbet over the gates.

Perhaps the burgomeister had done the best he could. Perhaps the plague or the heavy draft of fighting men had made his job impossible. It hardly mattered now – an example had to be set.

With the walls in their state of disrepair, Karl Franz had decided that a defence of the town itself was impossible. In any case, the army he had mustered would have struggled to fit inside, and so the coming battle would be fought on the plains, out in the open, under the rain and the watchful eyes of whatever gods deigned to observe.

Squalls continued to drive hard from the north-west, bearing more moisture with them. The land stretched away to a steel-grey horizon, glistening with standing water atop soft black earth. A few blasted trees hunched over here and there, dark against the water-heavy sky.

Karl Franz had drawn his forces up on the wastelands a mile north of Heffengen's limits. The battlefield was bounded on the east by the deep cleft of the Revesnecht river as it snaked north towards the greater flood of the Talabec. Over to the west, open ground slowly gave way to the straggling fronds of marginal forest.

The enemy would come at them from the north, just as they always did. They would sweep over the moors, fresh from their slaughter at the Auric Bastion, tearing up sodden ground under brazen hooves. The hounds would come first, loping with jaws agape; then the cavalry on their red-eyed mounts; then, striding on cloven hooves, the armoured behemoths with spiked helms and skulls hanging from blood-glossed armour.

Their formations would be ragged, powered onward by lust for slaughter. The one defence, the only advantage possessed by mortal men, was discipline. Just as had been the case for a hundred lifetimes, raw mania would be met by ordered lines of Imperial steel.

General Talb had petitioned hard for the honour of guarding the eastern flank. His ranks of Ostermarkers stood in place, arranged into squares of halberdiers and pikemen. They were supported by units of gunners and swordsmen, including a contingent of mercenary ogres who towered over the warriors around them. Huss had taken his fanatics with him to bolster Talb's lines, though the warrior priest's presence alone was worth more than all the zealots he brought with him. Valten, as ever, accompanied his mentor.

Karl Franz had watched them go. It remained uncomfortable to see the holy warhammer borne by hands other than his own. Gelt had counselled against it from the start, but the decision had not been his to make.

What brought you down? thought Karl Franz, ruminating on Gelt's disgrace and departure. *Pride? Weakness of will? Or just, like so many before you, despair?*

So much had changed, and in so short a time. The mighty defensive bastion Balthasar Gelt had raised across the Empire's northern borders had been breached at last, freeing the hordes of the Wastes to pour into Ostermark like blood fountaining from a wound. The strain of maintaining it had turned the Gold Wizard's mind in the end, damning him to association with fallen souls he would not have so much as spat on while sane.

Gelt had not deserved his sudden fall from grace, not after the service he had rendered, but then so many did not deserve the fates that had befallen them, and there was no leisure to mourn them all.

You could have fought here with us. Your spells might have turned them back.

'You will not ride out,' grunted Schwarzhelm.

Karl Franz smiled. His bodyguard had been fighting solidly for weeks, first on the Bastion, now as part of the long retreat south from the breach at Alderfen. He was caked with grime, much of it flecked amongst the curls of his immense beard.

'The choice is mine, Ludwig,' he reminded him.

'Ludwig is right, my lord,' said Helborg. 'They wish to draw you out. We may fall in battle, you may not. You are the Empire.'

You are the Empire. Those words always gave Karl Franz a cold twinge of unease, though he had heard them many times before.

It was a comfort, though, to hear his two lieutenants in agreement. Such had not always been the case.

'The judgement will be mine,' Karl Franz said, firmly. 'As ever, Sigmar will guide.'

The three of them stood at the very centre of the Empire battle lines, set some way back from the front ranks. Ahead of them was arrayed the main force of Reiklanders, decked in white and red. Three whole regiments of the Palace guard had been assembled, flanked by greater numbers of regular troops. Like the Ostermarkers to the east, the halberdier squares formed the backbone, supported by ranged weaponry – bowmen, handgunners, light artillery pieces. The elite of the entire army, the Reiksguard cavalry, had formed up to the left, waiting for their lord Helborg to join them. Proud banners bearing the Imperial griffon and black cross of the knightly order hung limp in the drizzle.

It looked solid. Rows and rows of steel glinted dully in the grey light, close-serried and well-drilled. Sharpened stakes protruded from the earth in steed-killing lines, dripping dankly in the morning mist.

'And Mecke?' asked Schwarzhelm.

The west flank was held by Lord General Mecke of Talabheim, whom Karl Franz thought was an ambitious bastard with an unseemly enthusiasm for the coming slaughter. Still, his men were as disciplined as any of the others, and he had numbers. The red and forest-green livery of his infantry squares was just visible to the west, part-shielded by fringes of foliage. The greater part of the artillery pieces were there too, lodged on higher ground and with a commanding vantage over the open field.

'He knows his business,' said Karl Franz. 'Nothing more to be done, now.'

Helborg wiped a sluice of rainwater from the visor of his hawk-winged helm. Karl Franz could see he was anxious to be gone, to saddle up and join his men. That man was only truly happy on the charge, his runefang in his fist and the thunder and crash of arms around him. He would have made a poor statesman, so it was fortunate he had never been charged with that role. Killing suited him better than bartering.

'I can smell them already,' said the Reiksmarshal.

Karl Franz turned his gaze north. Beyond the furthest ranks of the central defence, the land ran away, bleak and empty. Eddies of rain whipped across the mud.

'You should go, Kurt,' said Karl Franz.

Helborg pushed his cloak back, drew his sword and saluted. 'This day will see the line restored.'

Always confident, always brash.

Karl Franz acknowledged the salute. 'Should we lose the field–'

'We cannot lose,' muttered Schwarzhelm.

'Should we lose the field, they will press for Altdorf. We discussed what is to be done then.'

'Middenheim is closer, and stronger,' said Helborg, repeating what he had argued in the war council two days ago. 'I still think–'

'I have spoken,' said Karl Franz, holding the Reiksmarshal's gaze calmly. 'These are desperate times. I have no faith in electors, wizards have proven themselves unreliable, and I barely understand Huss's motives.' He smiled, clapping an armoured hand on Helborg's shoulder. '*We* are the Empire. *Men*. Altdorf is the key. It always has been, and they know it too.'

Helborg looked, for a moment, like he might argue the point. Then he bowed. 'It matters not – we will drive their bones into the earth. Here is where the tide turns.'

'Well said,' said Karl Franz. 'Now go in faith.'

'Always.'

Helborg strode off. As the Reiksmarshal walked down through the ranks, attendants hurried after him. Soon he would be mounted, blade in hand, poised at the forefront of the Reiksguard's formation.

Schwarzhelm stayed put. His unsmiling eyes strayed over to the stockade behind them, where Deathclaw had been chained. The griffon's scent penetrated through all the others – a wild, bitter aroma, suggestive of raw meat and frenzy.

'I know what you're thinking, Ludwig,' said Karl Franz.

'Listen to Kurt, if you will not listen to me,' grumbled the old warrior.

Karl Franz laughed. 'I don't know what to worry about more – them, or the fact you're both speaking with one voice. It's almost as if Averland never happened.'

Schwarzhelm's face did not so much as twitch from its mask of belligerent certainty. His trials in the south were almost forgotten now, washed away by the greater war of the north. Combat with an enemy he understood had restored him to his former self, it seemed.

He looked about to say something else, no doubt some plea for the Emperor to remember his place at the rear of the army, and not to go charging off into the fray like some avatar of Sigmar reborn. Such counsel was Schwarzhelm's duty, of course, just as it was Karl Franz's prerogative to make his own damned mind up.

In the event, Schwarzhelm said nothing. Any words he might have uttered were snatched from his lips by a clamour rising up out of the north. It started off low, like the growl of beasts at bay, then picked up in volume, carried by the skirling winds and wafted across the empty land.

Soon it was a *howl*, a mass of screaming and roaring. Drums underpinned it, making the standing waters shiver. The northern horizon darkened, as if storm clouds had boiled into existence in defiance of the law of nature.

Then Karl Franz saw the truth – the clouds were birds, thousands of them, flocking unnaturally. They blotted out the meagre sunlight in a fast-moving scab of ragged black, sweeping out of the mist and circling clear of arrow-range.

The howling continued, muffled by distance for the moment, but that would not last. All along the Empire lines, sergeants bellowed at their men to hold fast, to grip their halberds ready, to remember their vows, to take no damned backward step or their bones would be first to feel the crack of the maul.

Schwarzhelm's grizzled face tightened. His burly hand crept automatically to the hilt of his great blade, the *Rechtstahl*, the famed Sword of Justice.

'Here they come,' he murmured.

Karl Franz heard Deathclaw's agitated growling from behind the stockade. The war-griffon was eager to tear at the foe. The beast might not have to wait much longer.

'Unto death,' he breathed, feeling the weight of the runefang at his belt. 'Never yield.'

The enemy charged under the shadow of crows.

The birds wheeled and dived across the Empire defences, cawing maddeningly. Detachment captains forbade the wasting of arrows against such fodder, and so the birds were left unmolested to crash and flap into the waiting soldiers. They clawed at faces and fingers, and soon the halberdiers were flailing at them, their exposed flesh running with lacerations.

Runners broke out of the mist next, hundreds of them, isolated and without formation. From atop his mount, Helborg watched them come. No Imperial gunner opened up at them yet, giving the runners an unimpeded charge at the Empire positions. They careered mindlessly, limbs cartwheeling, eyes staring. Some were naked and daubed with inks across their snow-pale flesh; others were riddled with disease, their eyes staring and red-rimmed. All were lost in battle-fury, triggered by the poisons they had been fed by their shamans.

Helborg curled his lip in disgust. The first of the baresarks hurled themselves into the outer lines of pikemen. He saw one skinny lunatic impale himself on the stakes designed for the cavalry, and writhe there in a kind of wild-eyed ecstasy. Others slammed into the waiting defenders, and the halberds rose and fell, slewing up tatters of plague-sick gore.

Helborg felt his steed twitch under him. The warhorse knew what was coming, and was eager for it. Cold wind, still laced with fine rain, hissed up against its barding, chilling the muscles beneath.

'Easy,' he murmured, keeping a light hold on the reins.

More runners emerged from the mists, screaming as they came. They charged down the centre of the battlefield, ignoring the flanks. Still the handgunners restrained themselves, letting the infantry squares deal with the threat as it emerged. The real enemy was still to show itself.

It did not take long. Norscans strode out of the grey haze, rain bouncing from thick, bronze-lipped armour. They carried heavy axes, or mauls, or gouges, or double-bladed swords with obscene daemon-headed hilts. Some had helical horns twisting from their helms, others tusks, or spikes, or strips of flayed skin.

As the mist flayed into tatters around them, the front rank of Chaos warriors broke into a lumbering charge. There was still no formation to speak of, just a broken wave of massive bodies, swollen and distended by disease and mutation. War horns, carved into crude likenesses of two-headed dragons and leering troll-faces, were raised amid the throng.

The Norscan infantry brought the rolling stink with them – like charnel-house residue, but thicker and more nauseating. It seethed across the battlefield, pungent and inescapable, making mortal soldiers gag and retch. Even before the first of them had entered blade-range, the Empire's defensive formations began to suffer.

'First rank, fire!' came the cry, and the first squads of handgunners opened up. A second later, and the long rifles sent a curtain of shot scything out. A few Chaos warriors stumbled, borne down by those coming behind and trodden into the mud.

After frantic reloading, the gunners opened up again, then again, taking aim as soon as they could, and the air became acrid with the drifting stench of blackpowder. The great cannons opened up from Mecke's western position, booming with thunderous reports and driving gouges into the emerging horde. They were more effective: dozens of warriors were dragged to a bloody ruin by the iron balls.

Even the thickest plate armour was no defence against such disciplined fire, launched in wave after wave. Norscans and baresarks alike were blasted apart, their armour-shards spiralling into the swooping flocks of crows. One huge champion, antler-horned and clad in overlapping iron plates the width of a man's hand, took a cannonball direct in the throat, severing his head clear. He rocked for a moment, before the momentum of the charge dragged his body under.

It still was not enough. The howling screams became deafening as more warriors strode onto the battlefield. Soon the cacophony was so loud that it was impossible to hear the shouts of the captains. The earth reeled under the massed treads of iron-shod boots, and the northern horizon filled with the rain-shrouded shadow of thousands upon thousands of Chaos fighters.

By then the foremost of the Norscans had caught up with the baresarks, and they crashed into the static defenders. Most detachments initially held out as the battle-blinded enemy charged straight into thickets of angled

halberds. Every impact, though, drove the defenders back a pace, until gaps
began to form. Halberd-shafts snapped, arms were broken, legs slipped in
the mire, and the squares buckled.

The blood would flow freely, now. The preliminaries were over, and the
hard, desperate grind had begun.

'Reiksguard!' roared Helborg, raising his blade *Klingerach*, the fabled
Solland runefang. Rain bounced from the naked blade. 'On my word.'

Behind him, he heard the stamp and clatter of five hundred knights prepare for the charge. They drew their swords in a glitter of revealed steel,
flashing against the darkening pall ahead.

Helborg looked out, tracing a path into the storm. A mass of Reikland
halberdiers stood to his right, the artillery positions and Mecke's contingent to his left. The knights would charge through the gap, emerging into
the Chaos hordes just as the last of the cannon volleys rang out. After that,
the fighting would be closer, grimier, harder – just as he liked it.

'For Sigmar!' he roared, brandishing his sacred blade in a wild circle
before pointing the tip directly at the enemy. 'For the Empire! For *Karl
Franz!*'

Then he kicked his spurs in, and the mighty Reiksguard, driving on in a
wedge of ivory and black, thundered into the heart of the storm.

⊲ CHAPTER TWO ⊳

Karl Franz strode up the wooden steps of the stockade, his armour clanking, and Schwarzhelm followed him up.

The Emperor could hear the incessant chants of the warrior priests. Huss had taken the best of them with him to the front, and those left behind to lead the prayers to Sigmar were the old and the wounded. Their dirges, normally strident with martial vigour, sounded feeble set against the horrific wall of noise to the north.

The Emperor reached the stockade's summit, where a fortified platform rose twenty feet above the battle-plain. Standards of the Empire, Talabheim, Ostermark and Reikland hung heavily in the drizzle, their colours drab and sodden. Guards in Ostermark livery saluted as he approached, then withdrew to allow his passage. The only other occupants of the viewing platform were a group of extravagantly bewhiskered master engineers, peering out through long bronze telescopes before issuing orders for the artillery teams via carrier pigeon.

Karl Franz walked over to the platform's edge and stared out across the windswept vista. His entire field of view was filled with the vast, sluggish movements of men. Whole contingents were advancing into the grinder of combat, trudging through an increasingly ploughed-up mud-pit to get to the bitter edge of the front.

The bulk of the fighting was concentrated in the centre, where the Reikland detachments held firm. Some infantry squares had already buckled under the force of the first charge, but others had moved to support them, sealing any breaches in the defensive line. The Chaos horde beat furiously at a wall of halberdiers, causing carnage but unable to decisively break the formations open.

With the enemy charge restricted to the centre, both Empire flanks had cautiously edged forward. Mecke's gunners continued to launch their barrages, winnowing the reinforcing Norscan infantry before they could reach contact. Karl Franz fancied he could even hear Huss's wild oratory rising over the tumult, urging the fanatics under his command to hold fast.

The eastern flank had come under a weaker assault than the centre thus far, but an undisciplined charge by the flagellants so early would undermine the integrity of the whole defensive line.

Karl Franz gripped the rough-hewn edges of the platform's railing, waiting for what he knew was coming. Then he heard the harsh bray of war-trumpets, and saw Helborg's Reiksguard charge out at last.

He caught his breath. As ever, the Imperial knights were magnificent – a surge of pure silver fire amid the bloody slurry of battle. The packed beat of the warhorses' hooves rang out as they powered through the very heart of the battlefield.

Karl Franz leaned out over the edge of the platform railing, peering into the rain to follow their progress. He saw Helborg's winged helm at the forefront, bright and proud, glittering amid a flurry of Reiksguard pennants. His knights hit the enemy at full-tilt, cracking them aside and driving a long wedge into the horde beyond. Lances shattered on their impaled victims. Any who evaded the iron-tipped wave were soon dragged under by the scything hooves of the warhorses.

'Glorious,' murmured Karl Franz.

Shouts of joy rang out from the Empire ranks. The Reiklander infantry squares pushed back, given impetus by the Reiksguard charge. Huss at last relaxed the leash, and his zealots entered the fray from the east, followed more implacably by Talb's state troopers. Mecke's gunnery continued to reap a swathe from the west, now angled further back to avoid hitting the advancing contingents of Empire infantry.

The enemy reeled, struck by the coordinated counter-attacks. From west to east, Empire defenders either held their ground or advanced. The foot soldiers marched steadily through the angled cavalry stakes, held together in tight-packed formations by the hoarse shouts of their captains.

'Not too far,' warned Karl Franz, watching the detachments begin to spread.

Schwarzhelm nodded, and passed on the order. Runners scampered out again, tearing from beneath the stockade and out towards the command positions. An army of this size was like a giant beast – it needed to be constantly reined-in, or it would run away with everything.

Schwarzhelm rested a heavy gauntlet on the wooden parapet. His watchful eyes roved across the scene, probing for weakness. Like Helborg, he would have preferred to be in the thick of it, though his duty as the Emperor's bodyguard prevented him entering the fray – for the moment.

'They're holding,' the huge bodyguard said, cautiously.

Even as the words left his mouth, the sky suddenly darkened. Lightning flickered across the northern horizon, and the jagged spears were green and sickly.

A sigh seemed to pass through the earth, as if giants rolled uneasily underneath. Men lost their feet, and the beleaguered Norscans found fresh heart. The Reiksguard charge continued unabated, crashing aside swathes of Chaos foot soldiers and crunching them down into the mire.

'Call him back!' cried Karl Franz, watching Helborg's momentum carry him deeper into the gathering shadow.

The storm curdled further, dragging ink-black clouds across a tortured sky and piling them high. More lightning skipped and crackled across the horizon, now a violent emerald hue and boiling with unnatural energies.

Shrieks echoed across the invading army – not mortal shrieks this time, but the fractured, glassy voices of the Other Realm. Karl Franz felt his heart-rate increase. No matter how many times he faced the creatures of the Outer Dark, that raw sense of *wrongness* never dissipated. No other enemy had such power over men's souls. To fight them was not just to fight physical terror, it was to face the innermost horrors of the mortal psyche.

Schwarzhelm tensed as well. 'The damned,' he growled, balling his immense fists.

It was like the very ground vomited them up. They boiled out of the earth, seething and hissing with foul vapours. Tiny malicious sprites swarmed from the mud, clutching and snickering at the legs of mortal men. Stomach-bloated horrors lurched into existence amid gouts of muddy steam, their jaws hanging open and their lone rheumy eyes weeping.

Such apparitions were the least of the denizens of the Other Realm, mere fragments of their gods' diseased and febrile imaginations. *Maggotkin*, they were called, or plaguebearers, or Tallymen of Plagues. As they limped and slinked into battle they murmured unintelligibly, reciting every pox and canker their addled minds could recall.

Beyond them, though, the skies drew together, laced with febrile flame-lattices. A crack of thunder shot out, shaking the earth, and the crows scattered.

Somewhere, far out across the boiling hordes of enemy troops, something far larger had been birthed. Karl Franz could feel it as a cold ache in his bones. The rain itself steamed as it fell, as if infected by the torture of the heavens themselves.

Karl Franz called for his helm-bearer.

'My liege–' began Schwarzhelm.

'Say nothing,' snapped Karl Franz. A servant brought over the Imperial helm – a heavy gold-plated lion-mask with sun-rays radiating out from the rim. 'What did you expect, Ludwig? I fought at Alderfen. I fought at the Bastion. I am Sigmar's heir, and by His Immortal Will I shall fight here.'

Schwarzhelm glowered down at him. Despite the vast gulf in rank, the grizzled bodyguard was physically far bigger than his master. 'That is what they wish for,' he reminded him.

Karl Franz glanced back towards the stockade behind him. He could hear Deathclaw raking against his prison. The creature was desperate to take wing, and instinctive war-lust permeated through the driving squalls.

With difficulty, he turned away. The battlefield sprawled before him again, shrouded in churning clouds and punctuated by the screams of men and the clash of arms. The stink of blood rose above it all, coppery on the rain-drenched wind.

He swallowed down his fury, and remained where he was. Schwarzhelm, satisfied, took the war-helm again.

'For now,' murmured Karl Franz, watching the clouds swirl into grotesque tumours. 'For now.'

The impact of the first lance strike nearly unseated Helborg, but he dug his heels into the stirrups and pushed back, driving the iron point through the heart of a barrel-chested Norscan champion. The force of his steed's momentum carried the creature of Chaos high into the air before the lance broke and the broken halves of its body crashed to earth again. By then, Helborg's warhorse had already carried him onward, treading down more disease-encrusted warriors under its churning hooves.

The charge of the Reiksguard was like a breaking tide, sweeping clean through the very centre of the raging tempest and clearing out the filth before it. Helborg's knights rode close at his side, each one already splattered with bile-tinged gore. Their pennants snapped proudly, their naked swords plunged, the horses' manes rippled. There was no standing up to such a concentrated spearhead of fast-moving, heavily armoured killing power, and the enemy infantry before them either fled or were smashed apart.

Consumed by the power and fury of the charge, Helborg felt the change in the air too late. He did not see the clouds of crows rip apart and fall to the earth, thudding heavily into the mud. As he drew his runefang and sliced it down into the neck of a fleeing warrior, he did not see the columns of marsh-gas spew from the earth itself, coalescing rapidly into the fevered outlines of witchery.

The Reiksguard drove onward, scattering their foes before them. The air stank with blackpowder and blood, flecked with flying mud and storm-rain. By the time Helborg smelled the rank putrescence simmering on the air, his knights were half a mile beyond the Imperial reserve lines and far beyond the advancing ranks of halberdiers. He pulled his steed around, and the vanguard of his cavalry drew up in his wake.

Ahead of them, half-masked by shuddering walls of miasma, the rain was spiralling away from something. Like a glittering curtain of twisting steel, the deluge bulged outwards, veering clear of a scab of shadow at its core. Dimly, Helborg could make out a vast profile beyond – a heaped, piled, bulging mountain of flesh and blubber, crowned with antlers and split near the summit by a thousand-toothed grin. Flabby arms emerged, pushing out from swelling muscle with wet pops, followed by a rust-pocked cleaver that left trails of mucus hanging behind it.

Helborg's mount reared, its eyes rolling, and he had to yank hard on the reins to pull it back into line. The remaining Reiksguard fanned out, forming up into a loose semicircle about their master. On the edges of the formation, cowed enemy troops regrouped and started to creep back into range, emboldened by the gathering diabolical presence in their midst.

Helborg stared at the abomination, and an icy wave of hatred coursed through him. 'Knights of the Empire!' he roared, throwing back his cloak and holding his blade high. 'Break *this*, and we break them *all*! To me! For Sigmar! For Karl Franz!'

Then he kicked his steed back into the charge, and his warriors surged forward with him. Ahead of them, the enormous swell of the greater daemon fully solidified, shuddering into the world of the senses with a snap of aethyr-energies releasing. The ground rippled like a wave, rocked by the arrival of such a glut of foetid, corpulent flesh-mass. Cracks zig-zagged through the mud as it *schlicked* open, each one spilling with clumps of scrabbling roaches.

The Reiksguard charged into contact. As they tore along, the ranks of enemy foot soldiers closed on them, narrowing their room for manoeuvre. Some succeeded in waylaying knights on the flanks, and the force of the charge began to waver. The rapidly undulating landscape accounted for several more, causing the horses to crash to the earth and unseat their riders.

Helborg, though, remained undaunted, his eyes fixed resolutely on the hell-creature ahead. He careered through the screaming hordes, his companions struggling to stay on his shoulder, his blade already whirling.

'For Sigmar!' he bellowed.

Ahead of him, still masked by the after-birth tendrils of the aethyr-vortex, the scion of the Plaguefather gurgled a phlegm-choked laugh, and licked a long, black tongue along the killing edge of its cleaver. Its grotesque body shivered with cold laughter.

Beckoning the mortals forwards like some obscene grandfather, it raised a flabby arm to strike, and vomit-coloured aethyr-plasma flickered along the cleaver-blade.

Karl Franz paced to and fro across the platform, never taking his eyes from the unfolding struggle ahead of him. His stockade felt less like a privileged viewing tower and more like a prison, keeping him from where he needed to be. Schwarzhelm remained silently at his side, offering nothing but a grim bulwark for his growing anger to break against.

'Order Mecke to angle the guns higher!' Karl Franz bellowed, sending messengers scampering through the rain. 'And get Talb's reserves further up! They're useless there!'

The situation was dissolving before his eyes. Pitched battles always degraded into messy, confused scrums after the first few hours – form-ations collapsed and orders were misheard – but the foul conditions

north of Heffengen were turning the encounter into a formless crush. He
could only watch as Huss's flagellant zealots tore headlong at the enemy
Skaelings, losing all shape as their fervour carried them far beyond Talb's
supporting infantry. Karl Franz was a powerless spectator as the Reiksguard's spectacular success took them out of reach of the Reiklanders in
their wake, and as the daemon-allied northerners finally brought carnage
to Mecke's west flank.

The air vibrated with febrile derangement. Clouds of flies had taken the
place of the crows, blotting out the thin grey light of the sun and turning the
air into a grimy dusk. Artillery strikes had blasted apart some of the more
prominent tallymen, but ravening knots of daemon-kind still stalked among
the living, bringing terror in their noxious wake. The Norscan bulk of the
army had been reinforced by fresh waves of other tribesmen, and already
the dull mantra of *Crom, Crom* could be heard over the choir of screams.

Huss still stood firm, as did his protégé Valten. While they still laid about
them with their warhammers, hacking through whole companies of Chaos
troops, the eastern flank still had a fulcrum about which to turn. For all
that, the balance of the battle still hung by a fragile thread. The bulk of the
mortals could not stand against daemons – even being in proximity to one
was enough to threaten madness – and so the bulk of the state troopers
teetered on the brink of collapse.

'They need me,' said Karl Franz, unable to watch the killing unfold.

Schwarzhelm, this time, said nothing. He gazed out across the battlefield, his head lifted, listening. He sniffed, drawing the air in deep. Then a
shudder seemed to pass through his great frame. 'They are here again, my
liege,' he rumbled, looking utterly disgusted.

For a moment, Karl Franz had no idea what he was talking about. He
followed his Champion's stare, screwing his eyes up against the drift of
smoke and plague-spoor.

Over in the east, where Talb's troops struggled heroically amid a slew of
shifting mud, a chill wind was blowing. The ragged clouds summoned by
the daemon-kin blasted back across the wide field, exposing a clear sky. All
along the horizon, black figures crested a low rise. Tattered banners hung
limp in the drizzle, dozens of them, standing proud above whole companies of infantry. The figures were moving – slowly, to be sure – but with a
steady, inexorable progress.

Karl Franz turned to one of the engineers and snatched a telescope
from his trembling hands. He clamped the bronze spyglass to one eye
and adjusted the dials.

For a moment, all he saw was a blurred mass of winter-sparse foliage. Slowly,
his vision clarified, resting on an outcrop beyond the curve of the Revesnecht.
As he examined it, he understood why Schwarzhelm had been so appalled.

Again, he thought, bleakly. *But why, and how? And for whom do they
fight?*

He moved the telescope's view down the long line of unkempt figures, resting on none of them for long. He swept north, aiming for their leader. Eventually, he found him, and the spyglass halted.

Karl Franz clutched the bronze column tightly. The rumours had swirled since Alderfen, and he had not wanted to believe any of them. It had been *so long ago*. The chroniclers and scholars could have been wrong – it might be an impersonator, a shadow, a lesser demagogue assuming the mantle of an older and more sinister soul.

As he nudged the dials to bring the focus into line, Karl Franz felt a hollow sensation in his guts. There could be no mistake. He saw a long, arrow-straight mane of pure white hair, hanging from a still-noble head. Eyes of purest obsidian were set in a flesh-spare visage, drawn tight across sharp bones. He saw armour the colour of a flaming sunset, blackened with old fires and old blood; a long, ebony cloak lined with finest ermine; fangs jutting from a proud, cruel mouth; a longsword, sheathed in an ancient scabbard.

And, most of all, the ring. Even at such a distance, its garnet-stone glowed like an ember, leaking smoke from its setting.

Karl Franz put the telescope down. 'Then it is true,' he murmured, leaning against the balcony railing heavily. 'Vlad von Carstein.'

Schwarzhelm's face was black with fury. He looked torn between rival hatreds – of the Chaos hordes that hammered at them from the north, and the undead blasphemers that had crept into view in the east. 'There were rumours at Alderfen,' he rasped. 'They say the dead fought with us.'

Karl Franz felt like laughing at that, though not from mirth. 'What surety can we place on that?' He gazed up at the heavens, as if some inspiration might come from there. In days long past, it was said that the comet would appear to men at the times of greatest darkness, such as it had done for Sigmar and for Magnus. Now, all he could see was the scudding of pestilential clouds.

He reached again for his war-helm, and this time Schwarzhelm made no move to stop him. The undead continued to gather along the ridge. With every passing moment, their numbers grew. Soon there would be thousands. Between them, the armies of Chaos and undeath outnumbered the mustered Imperial forces.

'What do you command, my liege?' asked Schwarzhelm.

'Talb's flank is close to collapse,' said Karl Franz, placing the helm on his head and fastening the leather straps around his neck. 'Take any reserves you can find, join Huss and pull him out of there. Salvage what you can, stage a fighting retreat.'

Schwarzhelm nodded. 'And you?'

Karl Franz smiled dryly, and his hand rested on the hilt of his runefang. As if in recognition of what was about to happen, Deathclaw let fly with a harsh caw from its enclosure.

'We are between abominations,' he said, his voice firm. 'This is my realm. Once again, we must teach them to fear it.'

Then he started moving, ignoring the supplications from his field-staff around him. As he went, his mind fixed on the trial ahead. The whole army would see him take to the air. All eyes would be on him, from the moment Deathclaw cast loose his chains and ascended into the heavens.

'Hold the line for as long as you can,' he ordered, descending from the viewing platform with long, purposeful strides. 'Above all, the daemon is *mine*.'

Helborg charged straight at the daemon, spurring his steed hard. The vast creature towered over him, a swollen slag-pile of heaving, suppurating muscle. It was now fully instantiated, and its olive-green hide glistened with dribbling excreta.

The stench was incredible – an overwhelming fug of foul, over-sweet putrescence that caught in the throat and made the eyes stream. Every movement the thing made was accompanied by a swirl of flies, sweeping around it like a cloak of smog. Under its hunched withers the earth itself boiled and shifted, poisoned by the sulphurous reek and ground down into a plague-infused soup. The daemon wallowed in its own filth, revelling in the slough it had created around it.

Helborg's horse nearly stumbled as it galloped into range, betrayed by the shifting terrain, but its head held true. The daemon saw him approach and drew its cleaver back for a back-breaking swipe. Helborg drove his mount hard towards the target. The cleaver whistled across, spraying bile as it came. Helborg ducked as he veered out of its path, and felt the heavy blade sweep over his arched back; then he was up again, raised up in the saddle and with his sword poised.

Others of the Reiksguard had followed him on the charge, some still bearing their long lances. Two of them plunged the weapons deep into the daemon's flanks, producing fountains of steaming mucus. The daemon let slip a gurgling roar, and swung its bulk around, tearing the knights from their saddles and flinging their bodies headlong across the battlefield.

Helborg's warhorse shied as it tore past the wall of trembling hide, and Helborg plunged his sword into the daemon's flesh while still on the gallop. It was like carving rotten pork – the skin and muscle parted easily, exposing milk-white fat and capillaries of black, boiling blood beneath.

The daemon's cleaver lashed back towards him, propelled by obese and sagging arms, but Helborg was moving too fast. He guided his steed hard-by under the shadow of the other daemonic arm, slashing out with the runefang as he went. More gobbets of flesh slopped free, slapping to the earth in smoking gouts.

The Reiksguard were everywhere by then, riding their steeds under the very shadow of the daemon's claws and hacking with their longswords. The creature throttled out another echoing roar of pain, and flailed around more violently. Its cleaver caught two Reiksguard in a single swipe, dragging them from the saddle. Its balled fist punched out, crushing the helm of another as he angled his lance for the cut.

The clouds of flies buzzed angrily, swarming around the beleaguered daemon and rearing up like snakes' heads. They flew into visors and gorgets, clotting and clogging, forcing knights to pull away from the attack. Maggots as long as a man's forearm wriggled out of the liquidised earth, and clamped needle-teeth to the horses' fetlocks. Swarms of tiny daemon-kin with jaws as big as their pulpy bodies spun out from the greater creature's armpits as it thrashed around, clamping their incisors onto anything they landed on and gnawing deep.

The Reiksguard fought on through the hail of horrors, casting aside the lesser creatures in order to strike at the greater abomination beyond, but the creature before them was no mere tallyman or plaguebearer – it was the greatest of its dread breed, and the swords of mortal men held little terror for it. Its vast cleaver whirled around metronomically, slicing through plate armour like age-rotten parchment. Helborg saw three more of his men carved apart in a single swipe, their priceless battle-plate smashed apart in seconds.

He kicked his steed back into contact, riding hard for the daemon's whirling cleaver-arm. As he went, he pulled his runefang back for the strike, and the sacred blade shimmered in the preternatural gloaming.

The daemon saw him closing in, but too late. It tried to backhand him from his mount with the cleaver's hilt, and Helborg swerved hard, leaning over in the saddle. As the eldritch blade whistled past again, Helborg thrust out with his own sword, ramming the point up and across. The runefang plunged in up to the grip, sliding into the putrid blubber as if into water.

The daemon roared out a gurgled cry of outrage, affronted by the audacity of the attack. Helborg grabbed the hilt of his sword two-handed, fighting to control the movements of his mount, and heaved. The rune-engraved steel sliced through sinews, severing the daemon's arm at the elbow. A thick jet of inky blood slobbered across his helm visor, burning like acid, and he pulled harder.

With a sickening *plop*, the daemon's entire forearm came loose, trailing long strings of muscle and skin behind it. Weighed down by the cleaver, the chopped limb thudded to the earth, sinking into the slurry of saliva and pus underfoot. The daemon *bellowed*, this time in real agony, stretching its wide mouth in a gargantuan howl that made the clouds shake.

The surviving Reiksguard pressed their attack. Noxious fluids slapped and flayed out from the stricken daemon, each lashing tendril studded with clots of biting flies. Helborg pulled his steed around for another pass, his heart kindling with raw battle-joy.

It could be hurt. It could be *killed*.

But then, just as he was about to kick his spurs back into his mount's flanks, he heard it. War horns rang out across the battlefield, cutting through the surge and sway of massed combat.

Helborg had heard those horns before – their desiccated timbre came from the age-bleached trumpets of another era. No Empire herald used such instruments – they were borne by armies that had no right to still be marching in this age.

Helborg twisted in the saddle, trying to scry where the sounds came from. For a moment, all he saw were the grappling profiles of knights and plague-horrors, locked in close combat around the raging mass of the greater daemon. Swirling rain lashed across them all, masking the shape of the hordes beyond.

Then, as if cut through by the harsh notes of the war horns themselves, clouds of milk-white mist split apart, exposing for a moment the whole eastern swathe of the battlefield. Helborg caught a glimpse of huge crowds of mortals and aethyr-spawn, grappling and gouging at one another across the vast sweep on the eastern flank. And then, beyond that, on the far bank of the Revesnecht, he saw the cursed banners of Sylvania hoisted against the squalls, each one marked with the pale death's head of that cursed land. At the head of the revenant host stood a lone lord clad in blood-red armour, his long white hair standing out as starkly as bone in a wound.

A shudder of disbelief ran through him. He knew who had worn that armour. He also knew how long ago that had been. It was *impossible*.

Vlad von Carstein.

The shock of it broke his concentration. As he gazed, spellbound, on the host of undead advancing into the fray, he forgot his mortal peril.

The daemon lumbered towards him, dragging its vast weight forward in a rippling wall of wobbling flesh. Its lone claw scythed down, trailing streamers of smoking poisons. Helborg's horse reared up, panicked by the looming monster bearing down on it.

Helborg fought with the reins, trying to pull his steed away from danger, but the creature had been maddened and no longer heeded him. The daemon's talons slammed into Helborg's helm, ripping the steel from his head and sending it tumbling. Long claws bit deep into his flesh, burning like tongues of flame.

The impact was crushing. The horse buckled under him, screaming in terror, and he was thrown clear. Helborg hit the earth with a bone-jarring crash, and blood splashed across his face. He tried to rise, to drag himself back to his feet, but a wave of sickness and dizziness surged up within him.

He gripped his sword, trying to focus on the pure steel, but the dull ache of his wounds flared up along his flank. He saw the blurred shapes of his brother-knights riding fearlessly at the daemon, and knew that none of them could hope to end it.

He cried out in agony, trying to force his limbs to obey him. A wave of numbness overwhelmed him, racing like frost-spears through his bones. He heard the deathly echo of the war horns as if from underwater. The wound in his split cheek flared, and he smelled the poison in it.

Then his head thudded against the mud, and he knew no more.

Deathclaw soared high above the battlefield. The griffon's huge wings beat powerfully, shredding the black-edged tatters of cloud around it. Its bunched-muscle shoulders worked hard, pulling the heavily built beast into the air.

Karl Franz leaned forward in the saddle, his blade already drawn. The griffon, once released from its shackles by fearful keepers, was a furnace of bestial power. Both of them had saved the life of the other more than once, and the bond that connected them was as strong as steel.

'You have been kept collared for too long,' Karl Franz murmured, running the fingers of his free gauntlet roughly through Deathclaw's feathered nape. 'Let your anger *flow*.'

The war-griffon responded, emitting a metallic caw that cut through the raging airs. Its pinions swept down, propelling it like a loosed bolt over the epicentre of the battlefield.

Karl Franz gazed out at the scenes of slaughter, trying to make sense of the battle's balance amid the confused movements of regiments and warbands. The bulk of his forces were now locked close with the Chaos warriors, gripped by brutal hand-to-hand fighting. The western flank was still largely intact and Mecke had ordered his veteran Greatswords into the fray, where they grappled with ranks of plate-armoured warriors bearing twin-headed axes and skull-chained mauls. The centre remained contested. The bulk of the Reiklanders had no answer to the seething tides of daemonic horrors, though the Reiksguard knights still fought hard amid the raging centre of the field. Over to the east, the Ostermarkers were fighting a desperate rearguard action against utter destruction. Beyond them, the army of the undead was drawing closer to the battlefield, advancing in terrifyingly silent ranks.

Karl Franz's task was clear. Mecke still held position. Schwarzhelm, Huss and Valten would have to salvage something from the wreckage of the eastern flank, whether or not von Carstein came as an ally or an enemy. The malign presence at the core of the Chaos army, though, was beyond any of them, and its baleful aura was spreading like a shroud across the whole army. From his vantage, Karl Franz could see its bloated bulk squatting amid the shattered Reiksguard vanguard, laying about with a gore-streaked fist. Such a monster was capable of ripping through whole contingents of mortal troops, and nothing else on the field was capable of standing against it.

There was no sign of Helborg. No doubt the Reiksmarshal had charged the creature, hoping to bring it down before its full strength was manifest. It was a typically reckless move, but the daemon still lived, despite the gouges in its nacreous flesh and an arm-stump spurting with ink-black blood.

'That is the prey, great one,' urged Karl Franz, pointing the tip of his rune-fang towards the daemon's blubbery shoulders.

The griffon plunged instantly, locking its huge wings back and hurtling towards the horror below. Karl Franz gripped the reins tightly, feeling the ice-wet air scream past him. The landscape melted into a blur of movement, all save the bloated monstrosity below them, which reared into range like a vast weeping boil on the face of the earth.

Deathclaw screamed out its battle-rage, bringing huge foreclaws up. At the last moment, the daemon's vast head lolled upward, catching sight of the two of them just as their fearsome momentum propelled them into it.

The griffon dragged its talons across the daemon's face, slicing into its eyes. Its rear legs raked across the daemon's slobbering chest, churning the foetid flesh into putrid ribbons. Karl Franz hacked out with his rune-fang, feeling heat radiate out from the ancient blade – the runes knew the stench of daemon-kind, and they blazed like stars.

Just as the daemon reached for them with its lone arm, Deathclaw pounced clear again, circling as expertly as a hawk. The daemon's talons slashed at it, but the griffon ducked past the attack and surged in close again. Deathclaw's beak tore at the daemon's shoulder, ripping more skin from its savaged hide.

The daemon twisted, pulling its obese haunches clear of the slough below and reaching to pluck the griffon from the sky. Its claw shot out, and clutching fingers nearly closed on Deathclaw's tail.

The griffon shot clear with a sudden burst of speed, and circled in for a renewed strike. As it did so, Karl Franz seized the hilt of his sword two-handed and held it point-down. He knew just what his steed was about to do, and shifted his weight in the saddle in preparation.

The daemon reached out for them again, and Deathclaw plummeted, evading the creature's claws by a finger's width before clamping its own talons into the daemon's back. The griffon scored down the length of the daemon's hunched spine, ripping through sinews and exposing bony growths.

Karl Franz, poised for the manoeuvre, waited until the nape of the daemon's neck loomed before him. It was a foul, stinking hump, studded with glossy spikes and ringed with burst pustules. He aimed carefully.

The daemon twisted, trying to throw Deathclaw loose, but Karl Franz plunged the sword down. The tip bit clean between vertebrae, driving into the bone and muscle beneath. The magic blade exploded with wild

light, spiralling out from the impact site and tearing through the drifting
filth around it.

The daemon arched its blubbery neck, choking out cries of blood-wet
agony. Karl Franz was nearly torn loose, caught between the sway of his
prey and the bucking movements of Deathclaw.

He held firm, grinding the blade in deeper. Thick blood raced up the
blade, crashing over his gauntlets and fizzing against the metal. Clouds of
flies swarmed in close, trying to clog Karl Franz's visor, but he held firm.

Deathclaw roared with bloodlust, steadying itself on the heaving spine
of the daemon, and Karl Franz gained the leverage he needed. With a
huge heave, he wrenched the sword across, severing the daemon's neck.

With a coiled spring, Deathclaw leapt clear. The huge daemon reeled
in a torment of snapping sinew. Weeping from a hundred lesser wounds,
it thrashed and jerked, spewing vomit and bile. Rancid coils of greenish
smoke spilled from its eyes as the dark magicks required to keep it on the
physical plane unwound.

Deathclaw climbed higher. Karl Franz sensed its raucous joy, and shared
in it.

'The blood of Sigmar!' he cried, gazing in triumph at the horror he had
ended. Its death-throes were ruinous, carving up the earth and mingling
it with gouts of acidic blood. The plaguebearers thronging around it held
their elongated heads in their hands, and wailed.

Upon such moments did battles turn. Whole hosts could lose heart with
the death of their leader, and the momentum of entire campaigns could
falter with the removal of a talismanic figurehead. Deathclaw soared above
the sea of fighting men, screaming its elation at the heavens.

Karl Franz scoured the ground below, searching for any sign of Helborg.
He was about to order the griffon to circle about and swoop lower when a
harsher cry echoed out across the battlefield. His head snapped up, and he
saw a new terror sweeping in from the north. The Chaos ranks had been
sundered by a vanguard of heavily armoured knights on brazen steeds,
their pauldrons rimmed with gold and their helms underpinned with iron
collars. They thundered towards the surviving Reiksguard, ploughing up
the ground on spiked metal hooves. These newcomers rode with greater
discipline and verve than most servants of the Fallen Gods, though their
livery was as foul as any blood-worshipping fanatic from the frozen north.

Above them all came a truly vast flying creature that bounded through
the air with an ungainly lurch. It was the size of a war-dragon, and its
colossal wings splayed across the skies like motley sheaves of blades. Unlike
a true dragon, no sleek hide of jewelled scales clad its flanks and no flames
kindled against its twisting neck. Where tight flesh should have stretched,
raw bone glinted from between a lattice of age-blackened sinews. Gaping
holes punctured an open ribcage, exposing nothing but coiled shadow
within. A heavy skull lolled at the end of a bleached spine, wreathed in

wisps of inky smoke, and awkwardly flapping wings were held together by mere ribbons of atrophied muscle.

The monstrosity's rider was scarcely less extravagant in grotesquerie – an ivory-white face, elongated to accommodate protruding fangs, jutting from heavy armour plates. Bat-wing motifs vied for prominence on the armour-curves with chain-bound skulls and stretched skins. The rider carried a straight-bladed sword as black as the maw of the underworld, and it rippled with blue-tinged fires.

Karl Franz smelled the foul aroma of death roiling before it, and arrested Deathclaw's swoop. The griffon thrust upward violently, already eager to tear at a new enemy.

Karl Franz hesitated before giving the order. The daemon had been a daunting foe, but it had already been weakened by Helborg and the Reiksguard, and Deathclaw was lethal against such earth-shackled prey. The huge creature tearing towards them, carving through the sky with sickening speed, was far larger, and had the advantage of being battle-fresh.

Moreover, something about the rider gave Karl Franz pause. He looked into those dark eyes, still a long way off, and his heart misgave him. He looked down at his blade, drenched with the blood of the slain daemon, and saw the fire in the runes flicker out.

With a glimmer of presentiment, a terrible thought stole into his mind. *This foe is beyond me.*

Karl Franz knew he could refuse combat. He could do as Schwarzhelm had advised, saving himself for another fight, one that he could win. He was the *Emperor*, not some expendable champion amid his countless thousands of servants. His captains would understand. They would come to see that the Empire came first, and that his preservation, above all, held the promise of survival into the future.

He imagined Altdorf then, its white towers rising proudly above the filth and clamour of its tight-locked streets. He saw the river creeping sluggishly past the docks, teeming with all the burgeoning trade and industry of his people.

That place was the fulcrum about which his Empire had always revolved. He had always assumed that if death were to come for him, it would take him there.

Deathclaw screamed at the approaching abomination, straining at the reins. Karl Franz looked out across the battlefield, at the desperate struggle of the faithful against the closing ranks of horror. With every passing moment, more of his subjects met a painful, fear-filled end, locked in terrified combat with a far greater enemy than they had any right to be taking on.

I will not leave them.

'Onward, then,' ordered Karl Franz, shaking the blood from his runefang and angling the tip towards the skeletal dragon, 'and strike it from the skies.'

* * *

◄ CHAPTER FOUR ►

Schwarzhelm strode out into the heart of the battle. As he went, he drew soldiers about him, and the solid knot of swordsmen advanced under the shadow of the racing clouds.

The last of the reserve detachments had been committed to the fighting. Whole infantry squares were being hurled into the maw of the oncoming storm, in the desperate hope that sheer weight of numbers could do something to stop the tide of plague-daemons.

Schwarzhelm advanced immediately towards Talb's eastern flank, roaring out orders to the semi-broken warbands he encountered as the fighting grew fiercer.

'Form up!' he roared, brandishing his longsword and raging at the Empire troops around him. 'You are *men!* Born of Sigmar's holy *blood!* Fight like men! Remember *courage!*'

His words had an instant effect. Schwarzhelm's voice was known to every last halberdier and pikeman in the army, and though he was not loved as Helborg's flamboyance made him loved, no living fighter was more respected. Schwarzhelm was a vast bear of a man, clad in plate armour and bearing the fabled Sword of Justice before him, and the mere rumour of his presence on the field kindled hope in men's hearts again.

With his trusted swordsmen beside him, Schwarzhelm cut a channel towards Talb's last known position. The enemy came at them in waves – Skaelings, for the most part, an unruly rabble of fur-clad barbarians carrying the first signs of the sickness and staring wild-eyed from their shaman's ravings. Under Schwarzhelm's direction, the Empire halberdiers managed to restore something like proper defensive lines, and pushed back the hammering cycle of attacks. Ground was regained, and the momentum of the onslaught lessened.

The respite did not last long. Up through the ranks of the enemy came sterner opponents – Kurgan warriors in dark armour and chainmail, bearing axes and long-handled mauls, followed by the scrabbling flotsam of gibbering daemon-kin. Behind them lumbered the obscene bloat of the plaguebearers as they limped and stumbled into battle. Their rancid stench came before them, a weapon in itself, making men retch uncontrollably even before reaching blade-range.

Schwarzhelm laid eyes on the closest of the daemonic plaguebearers, and marked it out with a furious sweep of his blade. 'To *me*, men of the Empire!' he thundered, breaking into a heavy jog towards the scabrous horror. 'They can be killed! *Believe!* Believe in the holy Empire of Sigmar, and *fight!*'

The Empire troops surged after him, smashing into the incoming Kurgans in a flesh-tearing, armour-denting, blade-snapping flurry of limbs and fists. Eyes were gouged, sinews torn, throats cut and throttled, ankles broken. A whole band of halberdiers was ripped apart by a single Kurgan champion; a massive Chaos warlord was dragged down by a dozen sword-wielding state troops, hacking away at their huge opponent like wolves on a bear.

Schwarzhelm drove them onward, kicking aside the scuttling daemon-kin that raced along the earth to sink fangs into his boots. A Kurgan chieftain squared up to him, hefting a twin-bladed axe in iron-spiked gauntlets. Barely breaking stride, Schwarzhelm slashed his sword crosswise, cutting him across the midriff. Before the Kurgan could bring his axe to bear, Schwarzhelm jabbed the sword back, ripping through addled flesh, then crunching his leading shoulder guard into the reeling Kurgan's face. The warlord staggered, and Schwarzhelm punched him hard with his gauntleted fist, breaking his neck and sending his body crunching to the earth.

The men around him bellowed with renewed bloodlust, and surged after him. All around him, emerald lightning continued to spear down from the heavens. The ground underfoot seethed with a vile mixture of blood and rainwater, pooling in boot prints and gurgling in rivulets.

'Onward!' roared Schwarzhelm, eviscerating another barbarian with a lone thrust of his blade, clearing the last obstacle before the plaguebearer.

The daemon's weeping body pushed past the armoured warlords around it, stalking eerily on painfully elongated limbs. Its whole torso ran with rivers of pus, dripping onto the mud at its cloven feet in boiling clumps. Its olive-green skin had burst open, exposing loops of entrails. It had no eyes, ears or other features, just a face-encompassing jaw rammed with incisors. As it sensed Schwarzhelm, it let out a phlegmy cry of challenge, and swung a long staff topped with rust-pocked spikes. Every time the spikes were jangled, foul vapours billowed out, creeping across the ground like morning mist.

Schwarzhelm charged straight at it, holding his breath as he closed in, whirling his sword around in a blistering arc. The plaguebearer swung its staff to intercept, and the two weapons clanked together with a deadening *thunk*. Schwarzhelm lashed out again, feeling vile gases creep up his armour. The daemon lurched towards him, snapping its distended jaws, and Schwarzhelm ducked to one side as the saliva slapped against his helm. He shoved out with one fist, catching the daemon in the torso. His hand passed clean into disease-softened tissue, disappearing up to the wrist. He tried to shake it free, but the daemon caught him by the throat with its free claw, and squeezed. Schwarzhelm hacked back with his blade, carving deep into the plaguebearer's raddled body, but the wounds just resulted in more suffocating waves of corpse-gas pouring forth.

Schwarzhelm began to gag, and lashed out furiously, aiming to sever the creature's stringy neck. He missed his aim, hampered by the plaguebearer's cloying embrace, but something else impacted, and the daemon's skull was ripped from its shoulders in a welter of mucus and brown blood-flecks.

The headless body loomed over Schwarzhelm for a moment, held upright by its staff. Then it toppled over, bursting open as it hit the ground. A swell of brackish fluid swilled over his boots.

Schwarzhelm staggered away, momentarily blinded by the spray of thick pus. He wiped his visor and saw the robed form of Luthor Huss standing over the daemon's prone corpse. The warrior priest's warhammer was slick with bodily fluids, and his bald pate was covered in a criss-cross of bloody weals.

Schwarzhelm bowed clumsily. 'My thanks, lord priest,' he muttered gruffly.

Huss nodded curtly. 'And there are more waiting.'

The fighting raged around them unabated. Empire troops grappled with Kurgan, Skaelings and worse. The air no longer stank of blackpowder, for the artillery had long ceased firing. In its place came the rolling stench of long-rotten bodies.

Schwarzhelm's entourage pressed on, sweeping around him and clearing a little space amid the close-packed battlefield. He shook the worst of the bile from his sword, feeling the dull ache of weariness stir in his bones.

'The Emperor sent you?' asked Huss, already searching out the next fight. From nearby, Schwarzhelm could hear the clear-voice war cries of Valten, the mysterious boy-champion who was wielding Ghal Maraz with a youthful vigour.

'This flank cannot hold,' rasped Schwarzhelm. 'We must fall back.'

'Impossible,' scowled Huss.

'We are outnumbered.'

'By faith we shall pre–'

'Vlad von Carstein is here.'

That stopped Huss dead. He turned his baleful gaze onto Schwarzhelm. 'That cannot be.'

Schwarzhelm snorted impatiently. 'Use your *eyes*. The dead march against the damned, and the living are caught between them. I have my orders – we must fight our way to the Reiksmarshal, rally what we can, then hold the centre until we can fall back in good order.'

Huss looked agonised. Retreat was anathema to him – only surging onward against the foe was sanctified by his austere creed, and he would fight on until the end of the world, unwearied, his warhammer dripping with the gore of the fallen.

But even he was not blind to what was happening. As Schwarzhelm spoke the words, realisation dawned across Huss's face. The stench was not that of disease, but of *death*.

'Where is Helborg?' the priest asked.

Schwarzhelm was about to answer, when a fresh roar of challenge rang out. The voices were different again – not the bestial screams of the Norscans, nor the chill war horns of the Sylvanians, but a bizarre amalgam of aristocratic human and blood-crazed baresark. Both warriors lifted their eyes to the north.

Fresh troops were piling into the fray, their armour arterial red and their steeds towering behemoths of iron and bronze. They were still a long way off, but they were driving all before them. Above the vanguard soared a hideous creature of the darkest myth – a dragon, emaciated and splayed with bone and talon, cawing like a carrion crow and ridden by a lone red-armoured knight. It flapped through the heavens, its vast body held aloft by ancient magic.

In the face of that, even Huss's mighty shoulders sagged a little. Then, with a defiant curl of his mouth, he hefted his warhammer again. 'You will stand beside me, Emperor's Champion?'

'Until the ends of the earth, priest,' snarled Schwarzhelm, brandishing the *Rechtstahl*.

Huss cracked a thin smile then. 'We will smash some more skulls before they drag us down.'

Schwarzhelm nodded grimly. Already the hordes around them were pushing back again, slaughtering as they came.

'That we will,' he growled, striding back into the fight.

Deathclaw surged towards the dragon. The undead creature saw it coming, and reared up in the air, its scythe-like claws extended. Skeletal jaws gaped wide, and a noxious gout of corpse-gas burst from its gaping innards.

Karl Franz brandished his sword. The blade was still inert, bereft of the fire that usually kindled along its runic length, and even amid the rush on oncoming combat, that troubled him. Perhaps the daemon's blood had quashed its ancient soul.

The dragon rider hailed him then, his voice ringing out through the rain like a raptor's shriek.

'You are overmatched, warmblood!' he cried. 'Flee now, while your bird still has feathers!'

Deathclaw screamed in fury, and hurtled straight into close range. Its wings a blur, the griffon swept under the hanging streamers of yellowish gas and plunged straight at the dragon's exposed torso.

The two creatures slammed together, both sets of claws raking furiously.

The griffon's fury was the greater, and whole sheets of age-withered flesh were ripped from the dragon's flank. The abomination lashed back, tearing a bloody line down Deathclaw's back, nearly dragging Karl Franz clear from the saddle. As the bone-claws scraped past him, Karl Franz cut down sharply with his blade, taking two talons off at the knuckle.

Then the two creatures, powered by momentum, broke apart again, each angling back for a return pass.

'Do you see what is happening here, warmblood?' came the dragon rider's mocking voice. 'Your world is ending. It is ending before your eyes, and still you fail to grasp it.'

Karl Franz had caught a glimpse of his enemy as their steeds had grappled, and what he had seen had been unsettling. The rider wore heavy plate armour of rich blood-red, gilded with fine detailing and bearing the ancient seal of the lost Blood Keep. His jawline was swollen with fangs, and his voice bore the archaic, prideful accent of Empire nobility. Everything about him, from his cursed mount to his imperious bearing, indicated that he was an undead lord, a powerful vampire of the knightly bloodline.

Yet Karl Franz had never faced a vampire like this one. He had never seen tattoos carved into a face like that, nor heavy bronze collars adorning such armour. The rider wore a crude eight-pointed star on his breast, as black as ichor, and his sword-edge flamed as if alive with violent energies.

Can the dead fall to corruption? he wondered as Deathclaw banked hard and sped towards the dragon again. *Can even they succumb?*

The two beasts crashed into one another, writhing and lashing out in a twisting frenzy of mutual loathing. Deathclaw clamped its hooked beak into the dragon's neck and tore through weak-shackled vertebrae. The dragon pushed back with a blast of poison-gas before plunging down at the griffon's powerful shoulders, whipping a barbed tail to try to flay it from the skies.

Deathclaw shook off the dragon's foul breath and thrust back up, all four claws extended. The two riders were propelled close to one another, and for the first time Karl Franz was near enough to strike at his adversary with *Drachenzahn*.

The vampire was fast, as blisteringly fast as all his damned kin, and the two blades clanged together in a glitter of sparks. Despite his heavy armour, the undead lord switched his blade round in a smear of fire and steel, thrusting it point-forward at Karl Franz. The Emperor evaded the strike, but only barely, and the killing edge scraped across his left pauldron.

Deathclaw and the dragon were still locked in a snarling duel of their own, keeping their riders close enough to maintain a flurry of sword-blows. The blades collided again, then again, ringing and shivering from the impacts.

The vampire lord was a consummate swordsman, capable of the refined viciousness of his breed and animated by the unnatural strength that was the inheritance of that fallen bloodline. In addition to that, the marks of ruin emblazoned on his armour made the air shake – they were bleeding corruption, as if leaking dark magic from the Other Realm itself.

'For Sigmar!' Karl Franz roared, standing in the saddle and bracing against Deathclaw's bucking flight. He rammed his blade down two-handed, aiming to crack the vampire from his mount.

The undead lord parried, but the strength of the strike nearly dislodged him. Karl Franz followed up, hacking furiously with a welter of vicious down-strikes. The vampire struggled to fend them all off, and his armour was cut from shoulder to breastplate. The contemptuous smile flickered on his tattooed face, and for a moment he lost his composure.

But his steed was nearly twice the heft of Deathclaw, and even in its deathly state was a far more dangerous foe. The dragon's claws cut deep into the griffon's flesh, tearing muscle and ripping plumage from its copper-coloured back. Karl Franz could feel the fire ebbing in his steed, and knew the end drew near. If he could not kill the rider, the dragon would finish both of them.

'*Why?*' Karl Franz hissed as the swords flew. 'Why do *you* fight for these gods?'

The vampire pressed his attack more savagely, as if the question struck deep at whatever conscience he still possessed. 'Why not, mortal?' he laughed, though the sound was strained. 'Why not take gifts when offered?' His fanged mouth split wide in a grin, and Karl Franz saw the iron studs hammered into his flesh. 'They give generously. How else could I do *this*?'

The vampire's armour suddenly blazed with a gold aura, and the flames on his sword roared in an inferno. Karl Franz recoiled, and the dragon rider pounced after him. Their blades rebounded from one another, ringing out as the steel clashed. A lesser sword than the runefang would have shattered; even so, it was all Karl Franz could do to remain in position. Fragments of his priceless armour cracked free, and he saw gold shards tumbling down to the battlefield far below.

He pressed the attack again, resisting the overwhelming barrage of blows with blade-strikes of his own, when the dragon finally broke Deathclaw's guard and plunged a man-sized talon of bone into the griffon's chest.

Deathclaw screamed, and bucked wildly in the air. Karl Franz was thrown to one side, nearly hurled free of the saddle, and for a fraction of a second his sword-arm was flung out wide, exposing his chest.

The vampire needed no more than that – with a flicker of steel, he thrust his blade into the gap, unerringly hitting the weak point between breastplate-rim and pauldron.

The pain was horrific. Flames coursed down the length of the fell blade, crashing against Karl Franz's broken armour like a breaking wave. His entire world disappeared into a bloody haze of agony, and he felt his back spasm.

He heard roaring, as if from a far distance, and felt the world tumbling around him. Too late, he realised that Deathclaw had been deeply stricken, and was plummeting fast.

Karl Franz looked up, fighting through the pain and fire, to see the rapidly diminishing outline of the vampire gazing down at him.

'You could have had such gifts!' the dragon rider shouted after him, his voice twisted and shrill. '*You* chose the path of cowardice, not I!'

Karl Franz barely heard the words. Deathclaw was trying to gain lift, but the griffon's wings were a ravaged mess of blood-soaked feathers, and the creature's great chest rattled as it strained for breath.

He fought to remain conscious, even as a hot river of blood ran over his own armour. As the two of them whirled and spun earthwards, Karl Franz caught a blurred view of the entire battlefield. He saw the limitless tides of the North hacking their way through what remained of his forces. He saw the deathly advance of the Sylvanians from the east, covering the Revesnecht valley in a veil of darkness. The rain hammered down, shrouding it all in a bleak curtain of silver-grey, drowning the Imperial colours in a sea of plague-infested mud.

He reached out, as if he could grasp it all in his fist and somehow reverse the tide of war.

I have failed, he thought, and the realisation was like poison in his stomach. *There will be no return from this. I have failed.*

Even as the earth raced up towards him, his pain-filled mind recoiled at the very idea. He felt the great presences of the past gazing down at him, lamenting his great negligence. He saw the stern faces of Magnus the Pious, of Mandred, of Sigmar himself, each one filled with accusation.

I was the custodian, he thought, his mind filled with anguish. *The duty passed to me.*

The foul wind whistled past him. Deathclaw was struggling to fly on, to evade the heart of the Chaos horde, but his pinions were broken, and with his last, blurred sight Karl Franz saw that they would not make it.

Karl Franz did not feel himself slip from the saddle, dragged clear by his heavy armour. He never saw Deathclaw try to retrieve him, before the griffon finally collapsed to the earth in a tangle of snapped bones and crushed plumage. He never even felt the hard thud of impact, his face rammed deep into the thick mud even as his helm toppled from his bloodied head.

His last thought, echoing in his mind like an endless mockery, was the one that had tortured him from the first, as soon as the vampire's corrupted blade had pierced his armour and rendered the outcome of the duel inevitable.

I have failed.

From the beleaguered western flank to the shattered east, every Empire soldier saw the Emperor fall. A vast ripple of dismay shuddered through the ranks. They all saw the skeletal dragon tear Deathclaw from the skies, casting the war-griffon down amid a cloud of gore-stained feathers. They all saw the creature valiantly try to drag itself clear of the battlefield, fighting against its horrific wounds. For a moment, they dared to believe that it might reach the precarious safety of the stockade again, and that even if the Emperor was sorely wounded that he might still live. For a moment, all eyes turned skywards, hoping, praying fervently, *demanding* the salvation of their liege-lord.

When the griffon's flight at last dipped to earth, still half a mile short of safety and surrounded by the raging hordes of the North, those hopes died. They all saw Karl Franz fall from the saddle, dragged down into the mire, far from any possible rescue. They saw the war-griffon follow him down, the proud beast dragged to earth as if weighed with chains.

A wild howl erupted from the Chaos armies. Even the undead, now fighting their way west through turbulent formations of Skaelings, paused in their assault. The remaining Empire formations buckled, folding in on themselves as if consumed from within. The weakest soldiers began to run, tripping over bodies half-buried in the mud. The stoutest detachments fought on, though their positions were now exposed by the cowardice of lesser men.

The undead dragon ran rampant, sweeping low over the Empire lines, scooping defenders up in its emaciated claws and hurling their broken bodies far across the plain. The other fallen vampires crashed into contact, borne by monstrous creations whose eyes smouldered with forge-fires and whose hooves were lined with beaten iron. Ranged against them were the last of Huss's zealots, a horrifically diminished band, and what remained of Talb's hollowed-out forces. The Reiksguard still fought on, guarding their fallen captain, but were separated from the rest of the Empire army by a swirling tempest of daemons and fanatical fighters. Even Mecke's western flank now crumbled, its defenders panicking and turning on their tyrannical commander. The army of Heffengen finally subsided, sinking into the morass.

Schwarzhelm fought like a man possessed by the spirit of Sigmar, single-handedly accounting for scores of Kurgan scalps. Huss was scarcely less brutal, shouting out war-hymns as he laid into the enemy with his war-hammer. For a time, those two warriors defied the encroaching tides, bolstered by the vital energy of Valten and Ghal Maraz. Amid a sea of seething corruption, the lights of faith endured for a little while.

But even that could not last. Schwarzhelm fought to within a hundred yards of where Helborg had been felled, but as the Empire formations around him melted away, he was forced to turn back at last. Gathering what remnants he could, he hacked his way south, veering east as he reached the curve of the Revesnecht. He, Huss and Valten were harried all the way, though the pursuit faded once the prize of Heffengen itself loomed on the southern horizon.

A few other scraps escaped the carnage – a kernel of the Reiksguard cut their way free, bearing the sacred Imperial standard and taking control of the army's baggage trains before they could be looted. Many of the wagons were set aflame to prevent the enemy taking on fresh supplies, but a few were driven hastily south. The remnants were joined by the shattered Reiklander companies, plus any outriders from the Ostermarkers and Talabheimers who managed to escape the slaughter.

For those that could not escape, the end was swift and brutal. Champions of Chaos stalked across the war-scorched battlefield, breaking the necks of any who still lived. Spines were ripped out of the corpses and draped over the shoulders of the victorious. Daemonic grotesques capered and belched amid the charnel-debris, sucking the marrow from the bones and spewing it at one another. Though the greater daemon had been slain, its lesser spawn survived in droves, sustained by the crackling magicks animating the air.

The last to quit the field was the spectral Vlad von Carstein, whose presence at the conclusion of the battle remained as enigmatic as his arrival. His undead host had reaped a terrible toll on the Chaos army's eastern extremity, but after the Empire contingents had scattered, they were exposed to the full force of the victors' wrath. Whole regiments of skeletons and zombies were smashed apart by charging warbands of Kurgan, adding to the tangled heaps of bones already protruding from the blood-rich mud.

It did not take long for their dark commander to give the silent order to withdraw. The winds of death were driven east by the stinking fug of decay, and the black-clad host melted back beyond the riverbank just as mysteriously as they had arrived, their purpose still unclear.

Only one duel of significance remained. Few witnessed its outcome, for a strange vortex of shadow swept suddenly across the skies, its edges as ragged and writhing as a witch's cloak-hem. The undead dragon tore into the heart of the vortex, its empty eye sockets burning with an eerie green light. Flashes of sudden colour flared from within, as if a whole clutch of battle wizards had been trapped in its dark heart.

At the end of whatever had taken place in that sphere of magicks, the dragon took flight again, lurching as awkwardly as ever over the bleak plain and following the undead army east. Its rider still wore crimson armour, though not the same as earlier, and he carried a severed, fanged head in one gauntlet.

With that, the legions of the dead quit the field, leaving the plaguebearers to scavenge and plunder what remained. A peal of corpulent thunder cracked across the vista, echoing with faint echoes of laughter. The tallymen trudged through the dead and dying, taking note of the contagions they came across on long rolls of mouldering parchment. Insects of every chitinous variety buzzed and skittered across the rows of corpses, seeking out juicy eyeballs and tongues to feast on.

Across the whole, drab vista, the rain continued to fall, as if the flood could bear away the filth that had infected Heffengen. No natural rain could wash such plagues clean, though, and the sodden earth reeked from it, steaming in the cold as a thousand new virulences incubated in every bloody puddle.

The Bastion was broken. The Empire had been routed across its northern borders, exposing the long flank of the Great Forest to attack. Not since the days of the Great War had the wounds been so deep, so complete. Even in those dark times, there had been an Emperor to rally the free races and contest the Dark Gods.

Now there was nothing, and the winds of magic were already racing. Not for nothing did men say, in what little time of sunlight and happiness remained to them, that the end of all things had truly begun. Not in Praag, nor in Marienburg, but in Heffengen – the dank and rain-swept battlefield where Karl Franz, greatest statesman of the Old World, had fallen at last.

◄ CHAPTER FIVE ►

Helborg woke into a world of agony.

He reached up with a shaking hand, pressing cautiously against the seared flesh of his raked cheek, and even his old warrior's face winced as the spikes of pain shot through him. He tried to rise, and a thousand other wounds flared up. After two failed attempts, he finally pushed himself up onto his elbows, and looked around him.

He was in a canvas tent, the walls streaked with mud and heavy with rainwater. He had been placed on a low bunk of rotten wooden spars, little better than wallowing on the sodden ground itself. From outside the tent he could hear the low, gruff voices of soldiers.

He reached for his sword, but it was gone. With a jaw-clenched grunt, he sat up fully on the bunk and swung his legs over the edge. His armour was gone, too – he was wearing his gambeson, covered in a mud-stained cloak.

He could not make out what the voices outside the tent were saying – it might have been Reikspiel, it might not. He searched around him for something to use as a weapon.

As he did so, memories of the final combat with the daemon flashed back into his mind. He remembered the *stench* of it, spilling from the wide, grinning mouth that had hung over him at the end.

I should be dead, he mused to himself. *Why am I even breathing?*

Then he remembered the clarion calls of the dead, and a shudder ran through his ravaged body. If *they* had taken him, then the outlook was even bleaker. The servants of the Fallen Gods might torture their prey before death, but at least death would come at last. If he were in the hands of the grave-cheaters then the agony would last forever.

The entrance flaps of the tent stirred, and Helborg searched for something to grasp. The tent was empty, and so he grabbed one of the rotten ends of a bunk-spar and wrenched it free. Brandishing it as a makeshift club, he prepared himself to fight again.

The canvas was pushed aside, and Preceptor Hienrich von Kleistervoll limped inside.

'Awake then, my lord,' he observed, bowing.

Helborg relaxed. As he did so, he felt a trickle of blood down his ribs. His wounds had opened. 'Preceptor,' he said, discarding the spar. 'Where are we?'

Von Kleistervoll looked terrible. His beard was a matted tangle, and his face was purple from bruising. He was still in his armour, but the plate was dented and scored. The Reiksguard emblem still hung from his shoulders on what remained of his tunic, soiled by the wine-dark stains of old blood.

'Ten miles south of Heffengen,' von Kleistervoll said grimly. 'Can you walk? If you can, I will show you.'

Helborg was not sure if he could reliably stand, but he brushed his preceptor's proffered arm away brusquely and limped past him into the open.

The sky was as dark as river mud. A bone-chilling wind skirled out of the north, smelling of ploughed earth and rust. Helborg shivered involuntarily, and pushed up the collar of his gambeson tunic.

Ahead of him, over a bleak field of bare earth, men were moving. They limped and shuffled, many on crutches or carrying the weight of their companions. Some still had their weapons, many did not. All of them had the grey faces of the defeated, staggering away from the carnage with what little breath remained in their cold-torn bodies.

Helborg watched the long column trudge along. So different from the bright-coloured infantry squares that had marched up to Heffengen, their halberds raised in regimented lines. There could not have been more than a thousand in the column, perhaps fewer.

Von Kleistervoll drew alongside him. The preceptor's breathing rattled as he drew it in.

'This is all we retrieved from the Reiklander front,' he said. 'Some of Talb's men, too. Mecke was driven west. No idea where he ended up.

'Schwarzhelm?'

'He was still fighting at the end. Huss too, and the boy-warrior. They dragged together what they could and headed east.'

Helborg hesitated. 'And the Emperor?'

Von Kleistervoll's stony visage, scabbed with black, did not flicker. 'You did not see it?'

Helborg could not remember. His last hours of awareness were like a fever-dream, jumbled in his mind. He thought he recalled fighting alongside Ludwig, dragging their heavy blades through waves of enemy daemon-kin, but perhaps that was just his damaged imagination.

He dimly remembered a skeletal dragon breaking the clouds, a nightmare of splayed bone and tattered wings. He recalled a rider in crimson armour, surrounded by spears of aethyr-lightning. He saw the grin of the daemon again, bubbling with the froth of madness. All of the images overlapped one another, fusing into a tableau of fractured confusion.

'Could he have survived?' Helborg pressed.

'The day was lost,' said von Kleistervoll. 'If we had stayed a moment longer... I do not know. We could not remain.' The preceptor's voice was strained. 'You were wounded, Huss had been driven east...'

'I understand,' said Helborg. Von Kleistervoll was a seasoned fighter and knew his warcraft – if he had judged that retreat was the only option, no doubt he had been correct. 'What are your plans?'

'You gave the order, lord: Altdorf, with all haste. The enemy tightens its grip on the north, fighting with what remains of the living dead over the ruins. Heffengen is no place for mortal men now – we must save what remains.'

Helborg remembered his final words with Karl Franz.

Altdorf is the key. It always has been.

He pulled the ragged cloak around him. He would have to don armour again, to find a steed strong enough to bear him. The men needed a leader, someone who *looked* like a leader.

'My sword?' he asked.

Von Kleistervoll smiled, and gestured towards a line of heavy wagons struggling through the mud. 'We have it, and your battle-plate. Now that you are restored to health, the runefang will lead the army once more.'

Now that you are restored to health. Helborg felt hollowed-out, his body shriven and his mind tortured. He was sweating even in the cold, and the hot itch of blood under his clothes grew worse. 'I saw him, preceptor,' he murmured, watching as the grim procession of wounded and bereft wound its way past. 'A legend from the past, standing under the world's sun. What times are these, when the princes of the dead walk among us?'

Von Kleistervoll looked at him doubtfully. He did not know to whom Helborg was referring. There was no surprise in that – so many horrors had assailed them over the past few months that it had become hard to choose between them.

'Von Carstein,' explained Helborg, spitting the words out. 'The eldest of the line. It was he that broke us.'

'They say the dead fought the northmen,' replied von Kleistervoll, carefully.

Helborg laughed harshly. 'Do they? Who are *they*? Who still live who witnessed this thing?'

The preceptor had no reply. The bitter wind moaned across the land, cutting through the scant protection of their cloaks. The whole world seemed drained of life and colour, sunk into a rotting mass of corpse-earth.

'He came to feast on the remains,' Helborg said. 'I felt his fell magicks even at the heart of the fighting. These are our darkest enemies, preceptor – the corrupted and the undead. The day has come when they march in tandem.'

Von Kleistervoll looked unconvinced, but said nothing. Helborg's voice was becoming firmer. The pain in his wounds still flared, but he would recover. He would grip the *Klingerach* again. Karl Franz had gone, but there were other powers in the Empire, and there had been other Emperors. A successor would be chosen, and new armies raised. The war was not over.

'My order remains,' Helborg told him. 'We gather what we can, and we march on Altdorf. The other electors will gather now. In the face of this, they will put their rivalries aside. They will have to.'

As he spoke, a banner-bearer walked across the land before them, dragging a limp trailing leg through the mud. His face was a mask of effort – every last scrap of energy was devoted to keeping his rain-heavy standard aloft. The banner itself hung solidly, blackened from mould-spores but still bearing the griffon icon of the Empire on the fabric.

Helborg watched him go. Other marching men looked up at the rumpled griffon, and their glassy eyes fixed on it in recognition.

'We must get that standard cleaned up,' Helborg said. 'Find other regimental flags, and find men to bear them. We will march with the sacred images held before us. We will not enter Reikland like thieves, but rightful owners.' For the first time since awaking, he felt the urge to smile – to let slip with that wolfish grin he wore in combat. '*We* do not matter, Heinrich. *That* matters. When we are long gone in our graves, men will still carry those signs, and they will still fight beneath them. We are but their custodians. There are no End Times, there are only *our* times.'

The pain in his wounds was like a goad, giving him energy again. The road would be long, but the prize at its end was worth fighting for.

'To Altdorf, then,' he ordered, turning on his heel and walking towards the wagon where his armour had been stowed. 'The eternal throne of Sigmar. If there is to be an end to us, we will meet it there.'

Only the living dreamed, he had discovered.

Death was a kind of dream all of itself, so there was no escape there. In truth, he remembered very little about being dead – just vague and horrifying impressions of an absolute, eternal nothingness that extended beyond imagination.

He had once heard it said, a long time ago, that the only thought a mortal was truly unable to entertain was that of his own oblivion. Now he was able to reflect on the deep truth of that. Perhaps it was still true even of him, even after all he had experienced beyond the gates of the living.

There were many levels of oblivion, after all. As far as the faithful of the Empire were concerned, he himself had been dead for a very long time indeed, but that supposition was based on a fearful level of ignorance. There was all the difference in the world between the cold, hard existence of the Curse and the utter, profound oblivion of bodily annihilation.

He was free to dream again, now. His mind had knitted together, and with it had come all the old images, all the old desires and lusts and fears.

Preeminent among them was, of course, *her*. She had come to him in his dreams, dressed in bridal white, her smooth neck exposed, her dark eyes glinting wetly in the light of candles. She still moved in just the way she had done in life. Isabella had never been capable of a clumsy gesture. The sight of her again, after so long, was just as intoxicating as it had ever been. He found himself extending a withered hand into the depths of his own visions, trying to pull her towards him.

Perhaps that was the only preferable aspect to oblivion – the torment of seeing her had been spared him.

Vlad rolled a near-empty goblet in his palm idly, watching the dregs pool in its base. The fingers that cradled the silver bowl were pearl-grey and as dry as dust. Since being restored to existence by Nagash, his body had not entwined together in quite the way he might have wished. Some aspects of his earlier presence had not carried over, others had changed in subtle ways.

He felt... *scoured*. Learning to use muscles again had taken a long time. First, there had been the numbness, which brought on its shameful concomitant clumsiness. Then the pain had come, the raw, burning pain of reincorporation. That had been welcome – it had proved his body was his own again. He had drawn breath, and felt the damp air of the Old World sink into his lungs, and known that it was no illusion, and that he was back again, alive, and with unfinished tasks in the world of the senses.

For a long time, he had wondered whether his heart might beat. He had lain awake during the long nights, expecting to feel the hot rush of blood around his veins, pulsing with the old immutable rhythm he could barely remember.

It never came. He had been restored to the state of semi-life, just as he had been in the last days with Isabella. He still felt the Thirst, and still commanded the same strain of dark magic, and still felt at home in the shadows and the dank hearts of decay. The souls of the living were still translucent to him, burning like torches in the dark, and he still salivated at the sight of a bared vein.

I am an instrument, he ruminated sourly, pondering the time that had passed since his restoration.

In his earlier incarnation, Vlad had been master of his own destiny. Armies had risen and marched at his command. Sylvania, the Empire itself, had trembled before his name.

Much of that old power still remained. The unquiet dead still rose at his bidding, but he knew, in his silent heart, that his will was now a mere proxy for a greater intelligence.

There was no resisting the Master. There never had been. Some souls were so great, so bloated with power, that they transcended the standard order of things, and even a pride-driven aristocrat like Vlad felt little shame in bending the knee to *that*.

Still, it rankled. Deep in his stomach, where the last vestiges of human pride lingered, it rankled.

He lifted his goblet to his grey lips and drained the last of the wine. It was foul. In his former incarnation, even Sylvania had produced better vintages. Truly, the Empire was a shadow even of its earlier, rotten, decadent and miserly self.

Around him, candles burned low, their thick stumps heavy with molten tallow. The stone chamber was dark, and the ever-present north wind moaned through the cracks.

Before him, set on a bronze table, was a severed head. Walach Harkon's eyes had rolled up into his skull. His once elegant features had been defiled by tattoos and scarification, something that made Vlad's lip curl in disgust. Only the fangs gave away his proud bloodline; everything else had changed.

When Vlad had spied Harkon bringing his Blood Dragons into combat during the climax of the battle at Heffengen, he had assumed that the task was near completion – the Chaos forces would be broken between his own and those of the Empire, crushing them utterly. It should have been a great victory, the first step in the long road of bringing the living and the dead together to fight the damned. He had already rehearsed his speech before the mortal Emperor, demonstrating how only an alliance of former enemies could hope to staunch the tide of corruption spilling through the Auric Bastion.

No one, least of all him, could have guessed that Harkon had turned. Somehow, during the Blood Dragon's enforced exile north of the Bastion, his battle-hungry mind had been twisted to the service of the Blood God.

It was shameful. *Embarrassing.* Mortal cattle could have their heads turned by every petty shaman raving under a standing stone, but a lord of undeath, one of those capable of delivering the Kiss, one of the mightiest servants of Death in the entire world...

The thought made him furious. Harkon had driven a wedge between that which should by now be in unity. Far from gaining the trust of the mortal Emperor, he had *slain* him. Such rebellion, propelled by weakness, had earned him the torment of a thousand years. It had given Vlad some little pleasure to crush him, taking control of his draconian mount and using the tortured beast to end its own rider.

By then, though, the damage had been done. The Empire army had been routed, handing the servants of the Ruinous Powers an unbreakable momentum. Vlad himself had been forced to withdraw, an ignominy he had suffered too many times over his many lives.

He placed the goblet on the table next to Harkon's shrivelled head and glowered at the blank-eyed face. 'Glory-hunting *fool,*' he hissed.

The setback was a grave one. Every day saw more corrupted souls flock to the hosts of the North. The Empire was in no condition to offer more than a token resistance – for all Gelt's boasts, the Bastion was entirely breached now, and the hordes would soon pour through it like blood through a sieve. The scattered cities of the northern Empire, over which he had once cast covetous eyes himself, were as good as lost. No doubt the remnants of Karl Franz's army would attempt to make some kind of stand at Talabheim and Middenheim, but if there was to be genuine resistance, a chance to recover something before all was lost, it would have to be mounted further south.

'Altdorf,' he murmured, remembering his last sight of those white towers. He had got close enough to smell the fish being landed on the quays. For a glorious moment, many lifetimes ago, he had stood on the battlements and seen the entire city spread out before him, supine as a lover, tense for the ushering in of a new age of living death.

He did not know how he would feel when he saw it again. Perhaps the old passions would stir, or perhaps that was all behind him now. That was the strange thing about being reborn – he had to learn about himself again.

He sighed, and shoved Harkon's head from the table. It hit the stone floor with a wet thud and rolled away.

There could be no postponing the matter now. He had tarried long enough, uncertain how to break the news. There were few souls in the world that could make Vlad von Carstein hesitate, but the Master was one of them.

He sighed once more, pushed himself from his chair and arranged his cloak about him. The fine ermine settled on the polished crimson war-plate. He ran his fingers through his snow-white locks, ensuring not a strand of hair was misplaced.

From the chambers below, he heard the screams of living sacrifices as the last of the rites was completed. It was a waste to end mortal souls in such a way, and he took no great pleasure in it, but establishing a link with the Master over such distances could not be done without some trivial hardship.

Vlad made his way from the chamber and towards the lower levels of the tower. The disaster at Heffengen had to be recounted, and Nagash was not one to be kept waiting.

It was well, then, that he had something else to tell him – a new path to tread, and an old one to revisit. The future was just another aspect of the past, after all, which was yet another lesson his slumber in the halls of eternity had taught him.

The dead did not dream. Neither, it so happened, did their dreams ever die.

PART TWO

The Road to Altdorf

Spring 2525–Autumn 2525

PART TWO

CHAPTER SIX

Gregor Martak, Supreme Patriarch of the Colleges of Magic, awoke from a fevered dream of ruin and terror.

He had done likewise for the past three weeks, and it made him exhausted and irascible. Previously, he had slept phenomenally well. Wizards of the Amber Order were accustomed to deep slumber – they had little to trouble their unwaking minds, and so they slept like the beasts they emulated: in brief, deep snatches, as dreamless as the empty vistas of the underworld.

Martak yawned and scratched his unruly beard. Then he lifted his coarse robe and scratched the rest of himself. Tufts of hay stuck out from every crevice of his makeshift nightshirt, a result of taking his bed in the Imperial Stables. As one of the three most powerful men in the Empire, he could have occupied the most opulent chambers of the Palace. He could have had a staff of hundreds, a whole series of willing and creative companions, and barrel-loads of fine victuals carted into his personal kitchens every morning.

His predecessor, the avaricious and brilliant Balthasar Gelt, had taken full advantage of such opportunities. Martak had always had a sneaking admiration for Gelt, in the way only a man of such completely antipathetic character could. The two of them had never been rivals, for Martak had spent most of his life in the wilds of Taal's boundless forests, far from the labyrinthine conspiracies of the capital city. Where Gelt had been an accomplished puller of Imperial levers, Martak had been content to remain an uncultured savage, scavenging around the margins while his powers over beast and bower grew steadily stronger.

When news had come in concerning Gelt's fall from grace, Martak had not been one of the many who had secretly rejoiced. Subsequently being named as Supreme Patriarch had come as a complete surprise. He had been stalking through the wildwoods of the northern Reikland when the summons had come. Six messengers had been dispatched to find him; only one made it, and he had been white from primal fear when he had turned up. The deep forest was no place for ordinary men.

Martak was under no illusions why he had been chosen: he was the least offensive candidate to the largest number of people. The Amber College was a filth-ridden backwater compared to the lofty Gold, Light and Bright Colleges, from whose precincts the Supreme Patriarchs were normally drawn, and that made him a non-contentious choice, particularly as the Emperor was not around to oversee a protracted dispute.

The Amber reputation did not worry him. If his colleagues were too pre-occupied by their incessant feuding to see just how powerful the Lore of Beasts could be, and just how completely he had mastered it, then that was their fault to remedy. So he had taken the honour when it had been offered, even putting on a largely fresh robe to receive his staff of office. Then he had left the Palace for the stables, bedding down in the straw and breathing in the thick aroma of horseflesh.

For a while, surrounded by thoroughbreds, he had slept well. Then the dreams had come.

Martak ran his calloused hands through his long greasy hair, and belched. Moving stiffly after his troubled night, he staggered over to a water trough and splashed his face. He walked out of the stable doors, yawning again widely. It was the hour just before the dawn. The eastern sky was a deep blue, casting a weak light across the entire cityscape. Mist rose up from the ground, as white as cream and nigh as thick.

The stables were situated on the southern edge of the vast Imperial Palace complex, not far from the upper curtain walls. Martak strolled through courtyard after courtyard, loosening his limbs and rolling his shoulders as he went. By the time he reached the outer parapet, the first rays of the sun were slipping over the distant eastern hills.

He leaned on the stone balustrade, and took in the view.

Below him, a tangle of roofs tumbled away down the steep slope towards the river. Thin columns of dirty smoke spiralled up from the streets, bearing the wet, dirty aroma of Altdorfers' hearths. Ahead of him, a quarter of a mile eastwards, the huge dome of the Temple of Sigmar thrust up from the clutter of houses, its copper skin relatively unscathed by the grime that affected every other building in the city.

Beyond the temple lay the wide curve of the river. The rising sun cast rippling lines of silver across its turgid surface. Barges were already plying the trade-ways, sliding like whales through the muck. Martak could hear the calls of merchants as they unloaded their cargo onto the wharfs.

Altdorf had a kind of rough, unregarded beauty to it. Perhaps Martak was one of the few to appreciate that, for he liked rough, unregarded things. The poet Heine Heinrich had once described Altdorf as having the looks of a toad-dragon combined with the charm of a threepenny harlot. Being strictly chaste, Martak could not attest to the latter, but as for the former, toad-dragons had their own kind of magnificence. They had certainly been around a long time, something that could also be said of the City of Sigmar.

He drew in a long, deep breath. The nightmares were fading. Soon the Palace would begin to stir in earnest. Night-watch soldiers would slope back to their barracks, hoping none had witnessed their snoozing in the shadow of the battlements, to be replaced by bleary-eyed, unshaven day-watch regulars. The great fires would be lit in the hearths, banishing the worst of the night chill, and pigs would be rammed on spits for the evening banquets. The refuse-strewn streets would fill with the harsh, jostling press of unwashed bodies, replacing the cutpurses and petty cultists who had stalked the night shadows.

Until then, Martak's view would be largely untroubled by interruption. The city lay before him peacefully, barely touched by the burnishing rays of the world's sun, as dank and sullen as fungus.

In his dreams, he had seen the city burning. He had seen the cobbled streets erupt in foul growths, and the walls collapse under the weight of rampant vegetation. He had seen monsters stalking through the ruins, their eyes bright green in the flame-lit dark. He had seen the river clogged with strangle-weed and the proud towers of the Imperial Palace cast down in flaming destruction.

He had seen the Emperor, alone, wandering across the lands of the dead, surrounded on all sides by the hosts of the damned. His armies were gone, and the sky had been alive with light of all shades, some hues having no name in the languages of mortal men.

Perhaps, if he had had such dreams a year ago, he would have disregarded them, putting them down to the strange ways of the wizard's mind, but things had changed since then.

The city ran with rumour of imminent invasion. Armies had been sent north months ago under the command of the Emperor, who had taken his finest captains with him and most of the capital's standing army. Since then, the news had been fragmentary and confused. Some reports had it that Kislev had been overrun, just as in the time of Magnus the Pious. Others faithfully recounted tales of carnage across Nordland and the Ostermark, where the dead pulled themselves from the earth to aid the ravening hordes of the Fallen Gods. Those stories had been the most numerous of all – that the necromancers had entered into unholy alliance with the practitioners of Chaotic magic, and that each faction planned to feast on the bodies and souls of mortal men.

None could be sure of the truth of such tales. Those few messengers who claimed to come south from the far north said contradictory things. Some had been driven mad by the journey, and others had always been, so all they brought were fragments – half-truths and whispers, none of which might be true, or all of which might be.

If Martak had not had the nightmares, he might have been inclined to dismiss the refugees as the usual doom-mongering End Times fanatics. He would have left the city and returned to the wilds, leaving the ordering of the Empire to its usual masters, the elector counts. Though they were as squabbling and infuriating as ever, they understood the deep complexities of Imperial government, something that Martak knew he would never comprehend.

In the light of his visions, though, he stayed his hand, and waited in the Imperial Palace, holding on for tidings he could trust. The Emperor would surely return soon, to whom he needed to give his tokens of allegiance as Supreme Patriarch. The latest rumours told of devastation in Marienburg, and the imminent return of the Reiksmarshal to the city. If either of those things were true, then even the most sanguine of the Empire's servants would do well to worry.

Martak coughed up a gobbet of spittle and spewed it over the balustrade. His bodily aroma was strong, mixed in with faint overtones of horse-dung and mouldy straw. That was as it should be. The bestial spirits were strong in his blood, coursing like fine wine. As he drew in the cold, briny air, he felt his wilderness-toughened muscles respond. He would stay, observing, waiting for a signal, doing what he could to live up to the foreign responsibilities placed on his shoulders.

Below him, the city was waking up. He heard the first calls of the stall-holders setting up, the heavy clang of temple doors unlocking, and the clatter of quayside cranes unloading goods.

They were good sounds. They were *human* sounds, in all their inextinguishable variety. Altdorf was home to every vice and cruelty, but it also harboured joy, mirth and generosity. If you wanted to gain a picture of the race in all its messy, fragile and marvellous splendour and folly, there was no better place.

This is the heart of it all, Martak mused, leaning heavily on the stone railing. *This is our soul.*

By then, the sun had risen indeed, casting its thin grey light over the tops of the distant forest and gilding the temple dome. It was a faint, uncertain light, but just enough to lift the murk and fear of the long night.

Martak let it warm his limbs for a little while, before stomping back off to the stables. He had appointments with powerful men later on that day, which meant that he should make at least some effort to scrape the worst of the grime from his hands and face. He did not like the thought of it, but it had to be done.

As he padded back across the stone flags, his bare feet brushing soundlessly like a hunting cat's, he felt the final shreds of terror dissipate from his soul. As the sun strengthened, he knew the memory would fade entirely.

Until the next night, when the visions would come back again.

The lamps were lit in Couronne every night. Teams of armed men patrolled the streets of the stone-walled citadel, keeping the fires going and banishing the shadows.

Bretonnia had become a land of nightmares. Witches were abroad, hideous apparitions crept across the devastated fields, daemons squatted in the ruins of burned-out watchtowers. The new king, the reborn Gilles le Breton, had restored a shell of order to the realm, but he presided over a shattered caste of exhausted knights and half-starved peasantry. Since announcing the start of a new Errantry War, he had been abroad for months at a time, hunting down the dregs of the Chaos armies that had vomited forth from Mousillon.

His regent at Couronne remained Louen Leoncoeur, master of the realm no longer but still a Paladin Champion of the Green Knight. The duke knelt in his private chapel at the summit of his ancestral castle. Tapestries hung in the candlelight, each one depicting great deeds of his ancient House across the generations. A stone altar stood before him, surmounted by a lone marble figurine of the Lady.

Leoncoeur knelt in his full plate armour. He clasped his naked sword, resting it point-down on the stone before him and crossing his gauntlets at the hilt. His long blond hair hung about his armoured shoulders, lank from the battlefield. Like all the knights of the realm, he had been at war near-ceaselessly since the times of strife had descended. On one such sortie, he had nearly met his end under the blade of his own bastard son Mallobaude. For a long time, lost in the far reaches of the Bretonnian wild country, he had walked a fragile path between death and life, teetering on the edge of oblivion.

It had been the Lady who had guided him back – she had spoken to him in the depths of his fever. Her voice, as soft as ermine and yet as firm as the blade he carried, had whispered to him throughout those dark, lost times, refusing him permission to yield. Leoncoeur dimly remembered begging her to let him go, to cast him loose, to let his service die even as the land around him died.

She had never relented. He could recall her stern face looming over him, refusing the command that he yearned for. A lifetime of chivalry and pious devotion had sealed his fate – he could never have refused a boon from her, and so he clung to life, refusing the seductive embrace of the underworld even as it grasped for him. His senses returned in time, and he wandered the lands, near-starved, barely more than a shade himself. When he at last found his way back to Couronne, he was nearly slain for a wraith by a grail knight, and only his mud-splattered emblems saved him.

By then, Mallobaude had been destroyed and Gilles le Breton was the new king, feted by all across the realm as a harbinger of a new dawn for Bretonnia. Leoncoeur had recovered his strength and his wits, recovering under the auspices of the white-robed Sisters of the Lady. It took longer for him to recover his pride. He had ridden out to face Mallobaude as unquestioned monarch of his domain. He had returned to find a legend from the past sitting in the throne-room to accept the acclamation of the masses.

There was no contesting the will of le Breton. The green-eyed king's magisterial presence was unquestionable. A fey light shone in his ageless face, and his countenance bore the raw weight of centuries. All bowed the knee before him, including Leoncoeur himself.

That did not assuage the bitterness. In the long, sleepless nights as his body was restored to health, he found himself gnawing away at the injustice of it. He prayed, over and again, asking to be shown what fault he had committed, what aspect of chivalry he had transgressed that would warrant his kingdom being taken from him and his bloodline disinherited.

If le Breton himself was aware of such anguish, he did not show it. He was one of the Immortals, the avatar of the Green Knight himself, and matters of pride and propriety no longer concerned him. Even his voice was otherworldly, an archaic, haughty speech that belonged to another world. He existed now to take the war to the enemies of the realm: he was a weapon, forged from the myths of the past and given life by the unfathomable will of the Lady. Leoncoeur could not gainsay such commandments; neither, though, in truth, could he understand them.

So he knelt before the altar as the lamps burned, murmuring the words of faith he had known since childhood, seeking the answers that eluded him even in the midst of battle. Every night he did the same, and every night his prayers went unanswered.

As the first stirrings of fatigue ran through his battle-weary frame, his lips finally stopped moving. He opened his frost-blue eyes, and looked up at the image of the Lady.

A chill breeze rattled through the loose stained-glass windows, making the candle-flames shiver. The benign face of his divine mistress gazed down at him, serene and pitiless.

It was as he looked up at her, just as he had done in the dream-lands of his long near-death, that realisation dawned. There would be no answers from Her in this place. It was no longer his. Whether for good or for ill, the realm had been taken from him and given to another. To linger in Couronne like a ghost over its grave was pointless, and only grief could come of it.

Leoncoeur clambered to his feet, bowing again as he addressed the altar. He sheathed his sword.

'Where, then?' he asked, his deep voice soft. 'What path shall I take?'

The figurine of the Lady gave no answer. The flames flared a little, stirred by the wind, but no other sign revealed itself. The faces on the tapestries, picked out by long-dead fingers and faded by time and trial, gazed sightlessly down on him.

Leoncoeur smiled faintly. The ways of the Lady were never easy. That was the point of Her – She was the trial, the anguish, the test. Weakness had no place in Her service, only undying devotion.

'I will discover it, then,' he said. He looked around him. He had prayed in the same chapel since boyhood, and the stones were as familiar to him as his own flesh. 'This is no longer my realm. As you will it, I will find another.'

He bowed again, and turned away. Limping still from his last cavalry charge, the deposed king swept from the chapel, and the great oak doors slammed shut behind him.

In his absence, the candles still burned, and the draughts still swirled around the bases of the pillars. The figurine Lady stood in the flickering dark, her face still serene, her thoughts, behind the sculptor's smooth smile, unknowable.

Marienburg had already fallen, but its torment was not yet over.

The streets that had once bustled with the commerce of a dozen realms were now knee-deep in reeking effluent. The great docks were shattered, their steam-cranes tilting into the brine, the loading chains already rusting into nothingness. The mighty sea-wall built atop the foundations of ancient elven ruins was smashed into lumps of subsiding masonry, and foul slithering creatures with many eyes and splay-webbed feet slapped and slid across its remains.

Bodies lay stretched throughout the ruins as far as the eye could see, and every corpse was swollen with a different strain of pox. Many cadavers had burst open, spilling nests of maggots and black-limbed spiders over what remained of the cobbled thoroughfares. The corpses were piled high at the strategic choke-points, their blood mingling with the dribbling sputum of the Plaguefather's foul gifts. The sea itself was polluted, turned from a choppy grey into a dark-green slurry, as thick as tar and crowned with a crust of yellowish foam. The mixture lapped sluggishly against what remained of the old quay-walls, sucking and wheezing against the disintegrating stone blocks.

Above the fallen city, the clouds hung low, just as they had at Heffengen. The air carried a greenish tinge, and clouds of flies buzzed and droned through the miasma.

Everything was ruined. Every building was a hollow shell, bursting with rotting, preternatural growths. The great guild buildings in the dock-quarter were now temples of decay, draped with putrescent vines like giant entrails pulled from a body. The dull crack of thunder still echoed from the northern horizon, though the spell-summoned storms that had ravaged the city during the worst of the fighting were ebbing at last.

Through the very heart of the devastation, a vast army marched. Just as at Heffengen, they were drawn from the corrupted hosts of the North, and every tribe was represented in their tormented ranks. Norscans strode out, clad in thick furs and bearing ornately crafted axes with runes of ruin carved on the daemon's-head steel. Skaelings and Kurgan came with them, as well as Khazags and Vargs and Kul, a collection of the whole of the Realm of Chaos's sundered peoples, thrown together under a panoply of skull-topped banners.

It took a full day for the huge host to pass from the waterfront, through the dead city and out of the ruined eastern gates. As they marched, daemons flickered and wavered in the mournful half-light, hissing and drooling as they danced. All manner of pestilential beasts, from roaches to rats, scuttled under their feet, welling up like oil from the bubbling sewer-grates.

The host was beyond counting. Every soldier in it bore some mark of the Plaguefather, whether merely a pale pallor scored by throbbing rashes, or an entirely changed body, bloated with pox and bursting with mutations. Thick armour plate buckled outward over tumours, and ragged shirts of chainmail barely concealed festering wounds. Some clearly revelled in their diseases, leering as they crunched the bones of mortal men under their boots. Others limped along in agony, their ribcages protruding as they were consumed from the inside.

For hour after hour, the banners swayed past, each one daubed with a fresh sign of pestilence. The army was larger by far than the one that had broken the Bastion. It had been sent south by Archaon, hurled far out into the trackless ocean before sweeping back towards the Empire coastline. Ship after ship had disgorged its contents into Marienburg's stricken harbour, overwhelming the defenders in a remorseless wave of foul sorcery and dogged blade-work. For many hours the resistance had been heroic, and the fighting had been heavy in the streets.

But the result had never truly been in doubt. Archaon had unleashed his armies on the effete lands of the South in such quantities that even Asavar Kul would have blenched to see them. Two more allied hordes were already grinding their way south, tearing through the Great Forest like blades ripped under the skin. Each one alone was larger than any prior army sent to bring punishment to the unbelieving. Taken together, there could be no stopping them.

The force sent to shatter Marienburg was the mightiest of them all, a tumultuous rabble of pustular, addled, filth-spreading, contagion-fanning glory. As rank after rank trudged east, demolishing the few remaining walls as they went, they were observed by three pairs of eyes.

In the semi-remembered past, those eyes had belonged to mortal triplets, born under the midnight sun of the frozen tundra. Their family name was Glott, though that had meant little at the time and nothing to them now. The eldest, though only by moments, was Otto, who came closest of all of them to being a warrior in the traditional sense – he was a pot-bellied monster with marsh-green flesh and the tripartite marks of the Plaguefather scraped in black ink across his pocked forehead.

Otto stood atop the ruins of the Oesterdock Temple, leaning casually against the broken cupola of the Chapel of Manann. His clammy fingers pressed against the stone, causing mould-spores to spontaneously spider out across it. He laughed throatily, watching his troops lurch and swagger, then reached down for a strip of moss that had sprung up between the bricks of the temple wall. He pressed the wiry fuzz to his slobbering chin in a mockery of an Empire Greatsword's beard, and grinned.

Ethrac, the second triplet, saw him do it, and rolled his rheumy eyes in disgust. Like his brother, he was a wiry, spare figure, emaciated under blotchy robes of coarse wool. He clutched at a gnarled staff of oak heartwood, desecrated with columns of twisting runes, and picked his way through the rubble of the temple's roof. As he moved, bronze bells shackled to the staff-tip clanged dully, and flatulent vapours wafted out from the hem of his torn robes. He kicked aside a few clumps of rubble, and spat at them as they tumbled down to the street below.

'We could have lost this,' Ethrac muttered.

'No, we couldn't,' said Otto casually, picking flecks of plaster from what remained of the cupola.

Their voices were strange, wet rasps, almost like that of beasts, and filtered through mouths of blackened teeth. When they spoke, they overlapped one another constantly, as if each were just a part of one confused mind.

'I did not foresee the dead,' Ethrac said, pausing in his scrabbling search. 'Why did I not foresee the dead?'

Otto picked at his nostril. 'Does it matter?'

'It matters, o my brother. Yes, yes, it *matters*. We are not seeing everything. There are portents withheld. Why? I do not know. I should be seeing the world turn, the minds of men open. I did not see the dead. I did not *see* them.'

Just as at Heffengen, the defenders of Marienburg had been bolstered by the sudden intervention of undead warriors, though, just as at Heffengen, the reinforcements had not proved enough to halt the onward march of Chaos. That bothered Ethrac. He had sent tidings north, hoping to warn Archaon's war council that the Law of Death was proving more mutable than in past ages, and that it posed complications, but he had little hope of any of his messengers arriving alive. The Great Forest was as unforgiving to the damned as it was to the faithful.

'You should learn to calm yourself,' said Otto, scratching at a new and beautiful boil that had emerged under his chin. 'Nothing stands between us and Altdorf now. Nothing of any note, anyway.'

Ethrac shook his bald head impatiently. 'Does not *matter!* Mortals do not matter. But something has changed.' He screwed his eyes into a frown, and the scabby skin of his forehead broke out in bloody cracks. 'They are rising from the earth like new shoots. Why? Why is the wall between living and dead broken?'

Otto sighed and walked over to his brother. He took Ethrac's cheeks in both hands and squeezed affectionately. 'They are *desperate*, o my brother,' he whispered. 'Every witch-rattler between the Great Gate and the Hot Lands is flailing around for something to call up. You know why? Because *we* are here. They know this is the end. What if a few skeletons are thrown into our path? Do you think they will last longer at the White City than they did here?'

Ethrac nodded reluctantly, some of his agitation subsiding. 'And there is Festus,' he murmured. 'We must not forget him.'

Otto released Ethrac. 'It has been sewn up, tight as a burst stomach. The Leechlord is with us. Brine is with us, the Tallyman is with us. Stop worrying.'

Ethrac started to root around with his staff again, only half placated. 'Festus has been working hard. I can smell it from here. Much joy, to see him again.'

Otto walked back over to the edge of the temple ruins. 'Never forget, my favoured loin-brother, that we are *three*, and that we have not seen the finest of the Father's plague-pots yet.'

As he spoke, a vast, rolling mountain of scabrous flesh lumbered into view. As tall as a guilder's townhouse, the third of the triplets stomped past the teetering shell of the temple. His skin glowed a violent green, as if lit by weird lantern-light. Vast, muscle-thick arms hung, simian-like, from swollen shoulders. One terminated in a long, greasy tentacle that trailed along in the dust behind it. Catching sight of Otto and Ethrac, the monster cracked a wide grin, and a semi-chewed leg dropped from his jaws.

'Good feasting, o my brother?' asked Otto, reaching out to stroke the creature's bald head.

Ghurk, the final triplet, nodded enthusiastically, and more half-chewed body parts slopped from his slack lower jaw. Eating made Ghurk happy, and eating warm human flesh made him even happier. Several hapless victims were still clutched in his clawed hand; some of them still struggling weakly.

Otto took a short run-up, and launched himself from the temple's edge and into mid-air. He landed heavily on Ghurk's shoulders, and shuffled into position. Ghurk gurgled with pleasure, and started chewing again.

'Can anything stand against *this*, o my brother?' called out Otto to Ethrac, proudly surveying the scene from atop his sibling's unnaturally huge bulk. In every direction, the rampant desecration of the Plaguefather ran wild. Soon the last of what had been Marienburg would be overwhelmed entirely, a festering jungle on the western seaboard of the Empire, the first foothold of what would become Father Nurgle's reign of corpulence on earth.

Ethrac gazed at his two brothers with genuine fondness, and his withered face cracked a toothy smile. 'No, my brother,' he admitted, making ready to join Otto on Ghurk's back, from whence the two of them would begin the long march east. 'You are quite correct. *Nothing* can stand against it.'

◄ CHAPTER SEVEN ►

Drakenhof was not how Vlad remembered it. The centuries had not been kind to the ancient structure, and whole wings had fallen into ivy-covered ruin. The ice-cold wind from the Worlds Edge Mountains cut straight through the many gouges and gaps in the walls, skittering around the dusty halls within and shaking the ragged tapestries on their wall-hangings.

Since returning to Sylvania from the far north, he had done what he could to restore something like order to the ruins. He had raised the cadavers of the old castle architects, and they had soundlessly got back to work, ordering work-gangs of living dead to haul stone and saw wood, just as they had years ago.

There was no time to make the necessary repairs though, and so Vlad's throne stood in an empty audience chamber with the chill whistling through open eaves. Sitting in his old iron throne gave him no joy, for his surroundings were scarce better than any common bandit-lord.

He deserved better. He had always deserved better, and now that he was a mortarch, one of the Chosen of Nagash, his surroundings were little more than a bad joke.

Beyond the castle's crumbling walls, out under the sick light of Morrslieb, the entire countryside was alive with movement. A thousand undead did their dread master's bidding, dragging old sword-blades from graves and fitting them with spell-wound hilts. Armour was pulled from cobwebbed store-chambers and dug out from long barrows, all to arm the host that would take Vlad from the margins of the Empire and back into its very heart.

Mortal men worked alongside their dead cousins, swallowing their horror out of fear of the new seigneur of Castle Drakenhof. In truth, it was not just fear that made them work – the old ties of loyalty still had purchase, and there was no doubt in their slow, brutish minds that their true lord had returned.

Vlad did not despise them for that. They were only performing what their station demanded, and he held no contempt for his subjects. When he slew them in order to drink their blood, he did so cleanly, taking libation through the magics of his sword rather than sucking the flesh like an animal. They were *cattle*, as necessary to his kind as meat and water were to the mortal lords of the Empire, and if they served him faithfully then their lives would be no worse than any other of the toiling peasantry across the hardscrabble badlands of the outer Empire.

Some, of course, refused to see that, which required more punitive action to be taken. Thus it was that the witch hunter hung before him, suspended in a writhing aura of black-tinged flame. His arms were locked out wide, his legs clamped together, his head thrown back.

Vlad regarded him coolly from the throne.

'What do you think will happen to you?' he asked.

The witch hunter, his scarred face taut with pain, could only reply through clenched teeth. 'I will... resist,' he gasped. 'While I live, I will resist.'

'I realise that,' Vlad sighed. 'But when your resistance ends, what do you think will happen then?'

'I will be gathered into the light of Sigmar. I will join the Choirs of the Faithful.'

'Ah. I am afraid not,' said Vlad, feeling some genuine sadness. 'Perhaps, in the past, you might have done, but the Laws of Death are not what they were. Perhaps you have not felt the change.' He got up from the throne, and his black robes fell about him as he stepped down from the dais towards his victim. The witch hunter watched him approach, his face showing little fear but plenty of defiance. 'The world is running out of time. My Master has wounded the barrier between realms. The long-departed will soon stir in the earth, and nothing your boy-God can do will have the slightest effect. I admit that, for a time, our kind were troubled by your... faith. Those days, I am happy to say, are coming to an end.'

Vlad walked around the witch hunter, noting with some appreciation how the mortal controlled the trepidation that must have been shivering through him.

'You think of me as your enemy,' Vlad said. 'How far from the truth that is. In reality, I am your only hope. The paths of fate are twofold now: servitude before the ravening Gods of the North, or servitude before the Lord of Death. There is no middle way. I do not expect you to see the truth of it immediately, but you will, in time. All of you will. I merely hope the realisation comes before all is lost.'

The witch hunter struggled against the black flames, but they writhed more tightly, binding him as firmly as chains. Vlad needed to exert the merest flicker of effort to maintain them. Sylvania's soil was now such a fertile breeding ground for magic that his powers were greater than they had ever been.

'Lies,' spat the witch hunter, with some effort. 'My faith is unshakeable.'

'I can see that,' said Vlad. 'And so I am willing to extend a great gift to you. You may join me freely. You may follow me as a mortal man, and learn the ways of my Master. Your life will be extended many times over, and you will accomplish far more against the Dark Gods than you ever would have done while in your current service. The pain can end. You can still fight evil. I have ever been a generous liege-lord – even your annals must tell it so.'

The witch hunter's eyes narrowed, and the muscles on his jawline twitched. Vlad could feel the man's willpower eroding – he had been tormented for hours, and every man, no matter how well-prepared, had his breaking point.

'Never,' he said, his voice nearly cracking with effort.

Vlad drew close to him. He extended a finger to the man's throat, tracing the line of a raised vein. 'Your Empire is *over*, mortal. I say that not to crow, for I take no pleasure in seeing the ruin of what I once aspired to rule. It is merely a fact. I saw your Emperor slain at Heffengen. I saw the Bastion break, and I saw what was behind that wall. You are an intelligent man: you can see for yourself what is happening. Plagues run free, wiping out whole villages in a single night. The forest comes alive, churning with unnatural growth. The rivers clog, the crops fail.' He slid his finger alongside the man's ear. 'They say that Marienburg has already fallen. Talabheim will be next. Your house is crumbling around you – I offer a new home for your loyalty.'

The witch hunter's face creased in agony. His fists balled. He was still fighting. Lines of magic-heated sweat ran down his temples and slipped to the floor, fizzing as the drops hit the cold stone.

'*Never,*' he said again, screwing his eyes closed as he struggled to fight on.

Vlad regarded him bleakly. The offer had been magnanimous, but even the patience of lords came to an end. 'One thing, then,' he said. 'Just one scrap. Tell me your name. I will need it.'

The witch hunter's eyes snapped open. He stared up at the open rafters, his expression proud. 'Jan Herrscher,' he said. 'By the grace of our Lord Sigmar, that is the name I have always borne. I never hid it, and may it give honour to Him forever.'

Vlad nodded. 'Herrscher,' he murmured. 'A fine name. And believe me, you have given him honour. Truly, you have.'

Then he withdrew, and snapped his fingers. The black flames flared into a coil, and fastened themselves around Herrscher's neck. The coil contracted, snapping the man's spine. For a moment, his eyes continued to stare upward, then he went limp in his bonds. Vlad gestured again, the fires flickered out, and the witch hunter's body thudded to the stone.

Vlad gazed down at the corpse for a moment. It was a shame. Herrscher was the kind of man that made the Empire worth fighting for.

His thoughts were interrupted by a low cough at the chamber's entrance. He looked up to see one of his white-faced servants hovering anxiously. This one was a living soul, and Vlad felt an involuntary pang as he watched the man's blood vessels throb under his skin.

'You pardon, lord,' the servant stammered, clearly terrified, 'but the first brigades are ready for inspection.'

That was good. It would be a long and arduous task to create the army that Vlad required, even though Nagash had been quite insistent on the need for haste. The hosts of the North were converging on Altdorf already, and Sylvania was far further from Reikland than Marienburg. Even the expedience of raising the fallen to fight again would scarce suffice to meet the need, and so the scouring of Sylvania for living troops had begun in earnest.

'Very good,' said Vlad, pulling his robes about him, preparing to descend the winding stairs to the parade ground below. 'I will attend shortly.' His gaze alighted again on the body of Herrscher. 'And do something with this while I am gone.'

The servant hesitated before complying. Even in death, a witch hunter could inspire terror in a Sylvanian. 'Shall I burn the body, lord?' he asked.

Vlad shook his head. 'Do no such thing,' he said. 'Take it to my chambers and give it every proper burial rite.'

He swept imperiously out of the chamber. As he did so, the last of the black flames guttered out.

'He is too good to waste,' Vlad said. 'We shall have to find ways for him to serve again.'

The Grand Chamber of Magnus Enthroned stood near the summit of the Imperial Palace's main basilica. Vast walls of granite and ashlar stone soared above a wide marble floor. The pillars that held up the high vaulted roof were many-columned and banded with silver. Torches blazed, sending clouds of soot rolling into the heights. Statues of fallen heroes stood in alcoves along the walls, each graven from black veined stone. Magnus himself had been carved from a solid block of dark grey granite, depicted sitting in judgement on a massive throne. His image dominated the far end of the hall, fully twenty feet high, as stern and unbending as he had been in life.

Overlooked by such grandeur, the chamber's few living inhabitants were dwarfed into near-insignificance. They stood in the empty centre in a loose circle, clad in the robes of finest silk and linen and bearing heavy gold artefacts of office – chains, amulets, crowns.

All but one. Martak had not had the time or the will to find something to wear less filthy than the robes he had slept in, and so stood apart from the others. He guessed that he smelled fairly bad to them. That was simply reciprocal – each of the others smelled truly repellent to him, with their thick-wafted perfumes and armour-unguents.

'None have suffered more than I,' said the sturdiest of them, a tall man wearing a fur-lined jerkin and long green cloak. His leonine face was crested with a mane of snow-white, and he wore a goatee beard on his age-lined face. Despite his advanced years, he carried himself with a warrior's bearing, and his flinty eyes gave away no weakness.

Of all of them, Martak liked him the most. This was Theodoric Gausser, Elector Count of Nordland, and there was something attractive about his unflinchingly martial demeanour.

'We have *all* suffered,' replied a woman standing to his right. She was as old as Gausser, and draped in lines of pearls over a fabulously opulent gown of grey and silver. Her face was gaunt, though liberally rouged and slabbed with whitener. She carried herself perfectly erect, as if her spine might snap if she curved it.

This was Emanuelle von Liebwitz, Elector Count of Wissenland, as fabulously wealthy as her subjects were grindingly poor. Like Gausser, she was no one's fool, though her imperious manner even with her peers made her hard to warm to.

'Nordland has borne the brunt of the enemy for centuries,' reiterated Gausser. 'We have fought them longer and harder. I know what it takes to beat them.'

'None of us knows what it takes to beat them,' said a third figure, quietly. He was thinner than the others, as tall as a crane and with a pronounced nose. His attire was less flamboyant – a drab green overcoat and travel-worn boots. That would have come as little surprise to any who knew his province – Stirland was miserably poor, and far from the Imperial centre from which all patronage flowed. This one was Graf Alberich Haupt-Anderssen, a grand name that did little to disguise the poverty of his inheritance. 'If we did, their threat would have been eradicated long before this day. They are unbeatable. All that remains is survival for as long as we can muster it.'

The other two glared at Haupt-Anderssen contemptuously. The first two were warlike electors, and their cousin's blood was too thin for their liking.

Martak said nothing, but took some enjoyment from the incongruity of the situation. None of those assembled could remotely have been described as the finest the Empire had to offer. The greatest names were dead or missing – Gelt, Volkmar, Schwarzhelm, Helborg, the Emperor himself. Other Electors, such as the great Todbringer of Middenheim, were looking to their own defences. What remained in Altdorf were the outriders, those still obsessed enough with the Great Game to seek political advancement even as the wolves scratched at the door.

'Your cowardice damns you, Graf,' spat von Liebwitz.

Haupt-Anderssen shrugged. 'There is no virtue in hiding behind fantasies.'

'You shame this hall,' said Gausser, gesturing to the towering image of Magnus.

Haupt-Anderssen sniffed, and said nothing.

A fourth figure cleared his throat then – Hans Zintler, the Reikscaptain. In Helborg's absence he was the highest ranking military officer, and carried himself suitably formally, with a brass-buttoned jerkin and short riding cloak. His black moustache was neatly trimmed across a broad-jawed face.

'With your pardon, lords,' he interjected. 'Only one task requires our attention this day. The news from Marienburg requires a response.'

'Deserved everything they got,' growled Gausser. 'Dirty secessionists.'

'Maybe so, lord,' said von Liebwitz, 'but the question is what to do about the army that laid them low.'

'Nothing,' said Haupt-Anderssen. 'Look to our walls. That is the only hope.'

'Carroburg stands in their path,' pointed out Zintler. 'If it is not to fall in turn, it must be reinforced.'

'With what?' grunted Martak, his first contribution to the debate. All eyes turned to him, as if the others had only just noticed his presence. Von Liebwitz's elegant nose wrinkled, and she pressed a scented handkerchief to her mouth. 'We can barely man the walls here. Send men to Carroburg and they'll just die a little earlier.'

Gausser bristled. 'We have wizards advising us on military matters now?'

'You invited me,' shrugged Martak. 'I'd have been happier with the horses.'

Zintler coughed nervously. He was a good man, a fine soldier, but he did not like discord amongst his superiors. 'Then, Supreme Patriarch, what would you suggest?'

Martak laughed harshly. 'Gelt was Supreme Patriarch. I'm just a filthy bird-tamer.' He looked at Gausser shrewdly. 'Call the Carroburg garrison back here. Call them all back. Surrender the forest – it can look after itself. You can't weaken this army, not out there. All we have are walls.' He shot a glance at Haupt-Anderssen. 'You're right. We need to use them.'

Von Liebwitz took a short breath, trying not to sniff too deeply. 'It is clear to me, master wizard, that you have little understanding of war. There are *three* armies making their way towards us. Once they reach the Reik valley, we will be without hope of reinforcement. If nothing is done to hamper their progress, the noose will tighten before the solstice falls.'

'They won't hurry,' snorted Martak. 'Do you not see it yet? Geheimnis-nacht is the key. They will arrive then, when their powers are at their height and the daemon-moon rides full.' He crossed his arms. 'That is the hour of our doom. We can neither delay nor hasten its coming, so we should just make ready for it.'

Zintler looked uncomfortable. In normal times, Martak's advice would have been balanced by the Grand Theogonist's, but, as with so many others, Volkmar was missing, presumed dead, and the arch-lectors had not answered his summons.

'Superstition,' muttered Gausser, though with no great certainty.

Martak raised a dirty eyebrow. 'You think so? I'll remind you of that when the wind is screaming and the earth beneath our feet begins to move.'

'That is already taking place,' observed Haupt-Anderssen archly.

He was right – reports had started coming from across the city. Panicked residents had begun to flee the poorer quarters after wells had sprouted foul weeds overnight, and gutters had burst open with broods of writhing rats. The nights had been filled with unearthly screams, though the City Watch had never been able to track them down. Some even said that the river itself was changing, thickening up like broth over a stove.

'And that is *your* task, wizard,' accused von Liebwitz. 'Let us look to the defences – your kind should be cleansing the city.'

Martak glared at her darkly. 'We're doing our part. It would help if I weren't summoned to all these damned councils.'

'We need to determine the order of defence,' insisted Gausser, his cheeks reddening.

'So you can master us all,' sniped von Liebwitz.

Haupt-Anderssen laughed at that, and Gausser started to shout something about the noted cowardice of Wissenlanders, to which their elector vigorously responded.

By then, though, Martak was not listening, and neither was Zintler. Heavy crashes could be heard from outside the chamber, echoing up the long corridors. The Reikscaptain drew his blade, and slowly moved towards the double-door entrance. Two guards on either side of the portal did likewise. The commotion drew closer, growing louder on the far side.

Then the twin doors slammed back, and a band of heavily armed men broke in. They were plate-armoured, and bore the marks of a hard road on travel-worn garb.

'Stand down!' shouted Zintler, barring their passage with commendable bravery, seeing as how he was outnumbered eight to three. 'This is a private council – who dares to interrupt?'

The intruders parted, allowing one of their number to stride to the forefront. Unlike the others, he was helm-less, exposing a hawk-like visage barred by a long, carefully lacquered moustache. There could be no mistaking the proud features that adorned coins and devotional lockets from Helmgart to Middenheim, though they had been badly disfigured by clawmarks along one cheek. The lines were still raw and bloody, making the Reiksmarshal look half daemonic.

'What is this rabble?' rasped Kurt Helborg, striding up to the electors. 'Where is Todbringer? Where are the Reikland generals? And who is this beggar?'

Martak bowed clumsily. 'The Supreme Patriarch, my lord. Or so they tell me.'

Helborg stared at him, incredulous, before turning to Gausser. 'My lord elector, tell me this is some foul jest.'

Gausser shot him an apologetic look. 'Times are not what they were, lord Reiksmarshal.'

Von Liebwitz drew up to Helborg then, a rapt expression on her aged face. 'You are *alive!* Thank the gods. Now we can plan our defence in earnest – what of the Emperor? What of Lord Schwarzhelm?'

Helborg briefly looked lost then, as if the questions confused him. His gaze ran around the chamber, from Gausser to von Liebwitz to Haupt-Anderssen to Martak. '*This* is the war council?'

Martak sniffed noisily, dislodging a troublesome clot of dried mucus that had been plaguing him since waking. 'Who were you expecting? You took every blade worth having north.'

Helborg repeated his incredulous stare, before shaking his head with resignation. 'Then these are the tools I have. They must suffice.' He turned to Gausser, the only figure in the room he seemed to have any rapport with. 'I bring hard truths with me. The Emperor is slain. Our northern armies are scattered, and the enemy follows hard on my heels. We do not have much time, and the city must be secured. What preparations have been made?'

Gausser glanced at von Liebwitz, whose eyes strayed towards Haupt-Anderssen, who quickly deferred to Zintler.

'We were debating our first moves, my lord,' said the Reikscaptain, haltingly. 'The news from Marienburg is just in, and we had not yet determined just where to concentrate–'

'Taal's teeth,' swore Helborg. He beckoned to his preceptor. 'Find out what forces are still in the city. Order the gates closed – no man leaves without my order. Secure the armouries. Appoint a quartermaster-general and place all water-sources and food-stores under his protection. See the Imperial standard is flown from the Palace summit, and spread the word that the Emperor has routed the enemy at Heffengen and will soon return. Make sure this is believed.'

His preceptor saluted, and departed to carry out his orders, taking the remaining knights with him. As he left, Martak chuckled softly. This was why Kurt Helborg was Reiksmarshal, and why fighting men worshipped the earth he trod. For the first time since his appointment, Martak wondered whether he actually might survive this war.

'May I say, sir, your return seems timely,' Martak said.

Helborg looked back at him doubtfully.

'We will see,' he muttered. 'We will see.'

Deep in the foundations of the old city, far below the streets and avenues, the vapours never ceased. They curled along the brick-lined sewers, steaming from the surface of the foetid waters. They pooled in the dank, dark recesses of ancient cesspits and long-buried catacombs, curling like hair amid the endless shadows.

No natural light penetrated so far down, and the only illumination was the pale glow of phosphorescent mosses clambering all across the crumbling masonry. The moss had spread quickly since its introduction, racing down the winding shafts and choked tunnels, feeding on the filth that sank to the city's base. It was everywhere now, smothering all other growths and lending the forgotten ways of Altdorf a ghostly sheen.

It got worse the lower one went, until the waterways were a thick soup of throbbing spore-clumps and the luminous tendrils hung from the low ceiling like stalactites. At the very bottom, in the deepest shafts of the under-city, the infestation was so complete that it felt like the entire structure was built from nothing more than fronds of softly iridescent lichen.

Down there, behind a locked door under a low stone archway, the noise of bubbling and hissing never ceased. The vapours poured out from the cracks in the door, seething out from between planks of long-rotten wood before drifting off down the myriad tunnels of the labyrinth beyond.

Within the chamber lay a bizarre panoply of instruments – copper kettles, alembics, condensers, cauldrons and mixing-pots. Concoctions bubbled in a dozen bronze jars, sending lurid coloured steam twisting up to the low chamber roof. Further in, the contents became more grisly – corpses, as thin and wasted as rabbits, hung from iron hooks on the wall, each one bearing the signs of horrific illness. Some had burst torsos, their entrails hanging from the rupture and dripping steadily onto the filth-strewn floor below. Others had no eyes, or obscene growths suspended from their agonised flesh. All bore expressions of unbearable horror on their drawn faces, the marks of their final struggles against the poxes that had killed them.

Further down, moving along narrow passageways, the sounds of bubbling and gurgling grew louder. Gouts of steam hissed from tangled iron piping, and an immense pendulum ticked back and forth as if counting time towards the end of the world. More jars and phials cluttered every surface, each one fizzing and boiling with an endless variety of lurid liquids.

Right at the far end of those chambers, deep down in the basement, a hunched figure worked steadily over a long, low bench. He was grotesquely fat, and the jowls of his under-chin wobbled as he moved. A thick-lipped mouth murmured and drooled, sending lines of yellowish sputum coursing over a boil-encrusted face. Perhaps once he had been a mortal man, for he still wore the remnants of Imperial garb amid the folds and sags of his overspilling corpulence. Now, though, he was changed, given unnatural bulk beyond the dreams of even the most assiduous glutton. Tiny creatures, no more than jaws and eyes attached to slug-like sacs of blubber, crawled all over him, wriggling between the grease-stained fabric of his clothes.

He hummed to himself as he worked, transferring frothing potions from vial to vial, mixing them, testing them, observing the results on a long, ink-stained ledger before stacking the glassware back amid the racks on the walls and starting again.

Behind him, huger than any of the others, a black iron cauldron stood, squat as a gravid sow and thick with the patina of ages. A daemon's face had been hammered onto the swollen curve of the bowl, spewing excreta from a fanged mouth. Within that cauldron bubbled the strongest broth of all – a noxious brew that made the air above it tremble. The fat-slick surface broke, and a desperate hand burst out, clutching at the side of the cauldron and gripping tight.

The grotesque alchemist saw the fingers scrabbling for purchase and chuckled wetly.

'Oh, no,' he chided, reaching over and prising the hand from the cauldron's edge. 'Not again. Stay down, and drink it up. It will be over quicker that way.'

He shoved the arm back under and held it there. A flurry of bubbles plopped up, accompanied by what sounded like desperate gagging. After a while the bubbles ran out, and the alchemist withdrew his hand. He brought it up to his mouth, and licked the liquids from it with a long, prehensile tongue.

'Almost there,' he murmured, savouring the taste.

From further along, past the cauldron and into the shadows beyond, came the sound of desperate, furious weeping. The alchemist frowned, and looked up.

'What is this?'

He shuffled past the cauldron, squeezing his heft past the cluttered work surfaces, wobbling over towards a series of iron cages bolted to the walls. Living men and women huddled inside them, their faces stark with terror. Most already showed signs of sickness. All were famished.

'No more of this!' the alchemist warned, brandishing a huge ladle like a weapon. 'You are the *lucky* ones. You have been chosen. Show some respect.'

The captive mortals stared back at him, some with disbelief, some with rank fear, a few with some residual defiance.

They had seen what had happened to the others. They knew what was coming for them.

'We are *nearly there* now,' said the alchemist, his phlegmy voice almost tender. 'Nearly there.'

He shuffled back to the cauldron, and started to stir. As he did so, the surface steamed and bubbled, filling the air with a hot, sweet, overpowering aroma of putrescence. Translucent slops hit the floor as the ladle stirred. Some of those slops were moving.

The alchemist leaned over the cauldron's edge and took a long, deep sniff. As he did so, something stirred under the surface – a shadow moved, as if a creature of the deep had made its home amid the greasy soup of flesh and fat.

'Quicken, now, great one,' cooed the alchemist. 'Festus calls you. The Leechlord smoothes the way between the worlds.' His grin broadened, exposing flattened, butter-yellow teeth. 'Altdorf awaits. It has no idea of the delights in store.'

He stirred faster, making the broth ripple.

'But it will soon,' he slurred, growing sweatily excited. 'Oh, yes. It will very soon.'

⫷ CHAPTER EIGHT ⫸

Leoncoeur rode out, feeling the harsh wind brush against his face. His sword was already slick with the blood of the slain – no excursion into the countryside around Couronne passed without encountering the dregs of Mallobaude's corruption. The land still crawled with sorcery, as dark as oil and stained deep into the soil.

Ahead of him, barren fields marched away to the north. To his right stood a scraggy mass of forest, choked with briars and bearing the dank smell of decay. The land fell away sharply as the trees clustered, tumbling towards the river Gironne as it wound its uncertain way towards the distant coast.

Leoncoeur leaned forward in the saddle, scouring the landscape ahead. His quarry could not be far off.

Then he saw it – a ragged bundle of robes, scampering madly, haring for the cover of the trees. Leoncoeur recognised the long pointed hat, the trailing wisps of a ruddy overgrown beard.

He kicked his steed into a gallop, hoping to run the hedge-witch down before he vanished into the shadow of the trees. Such wizards were petty necromancers and curse-pedlars, but in such straitened times even their trivial malice was cause for concern.

The hedge-witch sprinted hard, knowing his danger, nearly stumbling as he careered down the slope towards the woodland. He was already close to safety.

Leoncoeur spurred his mount on, kicking up mud as he went, tearing towards the rapidly approaching line of trees. He pulled his blade back, readying for the lean and swipe that would take the witch's head off.

Just at the last moment, the man swerved aside, darting as if alerted by premonition, and scampered under the protection of the first gnarled branches.

Leoncoeur did not hesitate. Crouching low, he crashed through the forest's edge after his prey, ignoring the whiplash branches across his face and arms.

'Yield yourself!' he commanded, made angry by the missed chance.

He could still see the hedge-witch ahead of him, swerving desperately between black-barked tree-trunks and slipping on the greasy leaf-litter. Soon the forest would grow too dense for the pursuit, and Leoncoeur's charger would become useless.

With a savage kick of his spurs, Leoncoeur goaded his steed into a final burst of speed, sending it thundering across the rapidly closing terrain. Just as the hedge-witch made for a screen of wickedly thorned brambles, Leoncoeur's sword lashed down, raking across the man's cloaked back and cutting down to the bone beneath.

The witch screamed, dropping to the ground and writhing. Leoncoeur pulled his steed around tightly and spurred it back towards the stricken wretch. The wizard tried to rise, to drag himself to his feet and somehow stagger out of danger, but it was too late. Leoncoeur rode him down, crushing his bloodied frame into the mire and silencing the shrill screams. Then he drew his horse to a halt, working hard to calm the enraged steed, before dismounting and striding over towards the remains.

He gazed down with disgust. The man was just another impoverished village trickster with delusions of power. It would have been better to have made an example of him, to have drawn his guts slowly out in front of a crowd of appreciative peasants. Out here in the wilds, the lesson was wasted.

Leoncoeur plunged his sword into the twitching corpse, just to be sure, then pulled the blade free, noting with distaste the stains along the steel.

He felt soiled. Running down such filth was a task barely worthy of his station. He needed something better, something *grander*, befitting the station he had once enjoyed.

Ahead of him, the Gironne churned at the base of a deep creek, its banks thickly cloaked with trees and creeping vines. The leaves had an unhealthy sheen to them, as if rot had penetrated down to the sap.

Leoncoeur tied his horse up and trudged down to the water's edge. He slithered down the muddy bank and knelt down, dipping his sword into the murky water. Grabbing tufts of grass, he wiped the gore from the blade, working slowly and patiently. His sword was his life, and had been ever since he had been a raw novice with more bravery than sense.

He had always done things diligently. He had always served, and yet the reward had been snatched away.

His blade now a little cleaner, he replaced it in the scabbard. Then he knelt over the water's edge, thirst kindling in his throat. He stared at the scummy surface, and changed his mind. Something foul was getting into the rivers – they were beginning to smell like sewers.

Just as he was about to pull away, he caught sight of his reflection gazing up at him. He looked haggard, his noble bearing thinned out by Mallobaude's treachery and le Breton's acquisition of his birthright.

Then, looking closer, he saw that it was not his reflection at all – he had not lost *that* much weight. The golden locks were too long, the face too slender. A face clarified below the filmy surface, one he remembered from the distant past.

'My Lady,' he breathed, falling to both knees.

The waters stirred, bubbling into a froth, then broke. A figure rose from the river, lithe and translucent. She wore a gown of purest emerald, and it flowed across her like cataracts. Her face was hard to look at for long – it had a fey, dangerous quality, as if touched by elven magic. She remained standing in the river, the weeds draped around her ankles, gazing benevolently down at the kneeling knight before her. The sunlight became a little less grey, and the leaves were touched with a golden sheen.

Leoncoeur felt his heart-rate pick up, and his face went hot.

'Lion-heart,' the Lady murmured, her voice as ephemeral as the wind in the reeds. 'You were ever my favourite. My *champion*.'

Leoncoeur looked up at her, and the sight of her unfiltered beauty pierced his heart. 'Then *why*, lady?' he asked.

She knew what he meant. Her face did not give away pity – it would never do that – but understanding shone in her emerald eyes.

'All things are changing,' she said softly. 'The world turns faster, and the old gods are passing. This realm is only one of many, lion-heart – you could not be contained by it forever.'

Leoncoeur struggled to hear her. When they had spoken before, so long ago that it seemed like a dream of infancy, she had been proud and imperious, a queen in her invincible realm. Now, she whispered as if sick, her otherworldly voice as faint as an invalid's.

'My *soul* is Bretonnia,' Leoncoeur said, not understanding what she was telling him.

'It was. The Green Knight has come to claim his kingdom. It has always been his. Your destiny is different. You will die alone, my champion, far from home. You will never take the throne again.'

The words were harsh, and they cut him deeply. Deep down, Leoncoeur had never quite lost the half-hope that le Breton was an apparition sent by the fell gods, some terrible shade who would be exposed in due time, leaving the throne free for him again.

'Once, you told me different,' he said, unable to keep the ghost of reproach from his voice.

'I never tell false,' she said. 'I told you that you would lead your people into glory. That remains your destiny, should you be strong enough to seize it. Are you strong enough, lion-heart? Or has this bitterness quenched your fire?'

'Never. Command me.'

A chill breeze made the river ripple, stirring the trees around them. The Lady shivered, and her impeccable features creased. 'Great powers are moving. They converge on Sigmar's city. The Fallen covet it, as do the Dead.

Those who remain will not stand unaided. That is where the hammer will fall, and that is where the world will change.'

'But my realm–'

'It is no longer your realm.'

'My people are hard-pressed.'

'The Green Knight is their guardian now,' the Lady said, almost sorrow-fully, as if that alone presaged the end of her hopes for something better. 'I tell you the truth. Is that not what you have been praying for?'

Leoncoeur looked at her intently. The beauty was still there, as was the ethereal power, but both were diminished. She was fighting against some-thing. This apparition was costing her, and the price would be steep. 'All lands are dying,' he said, realising what made her sick. 'They have poisoned the rivers.'

'You asked for a way to serve,' she said. 'I have given it to you.' She gave him a fond, faint smile. 'If you spurn the offer, you might yet live. There might be some kind of service for you in safer places, of a meagre sort.'

Then it was Leoncoeur's turn to smile. When their faces cast off the most oppressive lines of care, they looked so alike. 'I never craved meagre ser-vice. I was a king.'

'You still can be.' The Lady began to sink, sliding down into the brackish waters. 'The City of Sigmar, my champion. Already its foundations tremble. That is the anvil upon which the fate of man will be tempered.'

'Then will you live, Lady?' asked Leoncoeur, watching with concern as she slipped towards the Gironne's tainted waters. 'Can you be saved?'

'Ask only of mortal fates,' she whispered, her tresses sliding under the surface. 'Look for me in pure waters, but the games of gods do not con-cern you.'

But they did. They always had. As Leoncoeur watched her subside into nothingness again, as the golden edges faded from the leaves and the air sunk once more into mud-stinking foulness, he felt as if his heart had been ripped out. He remained immobile for a long time, his knees sinking steadily into the mire, his hands limp by his sides.

'The City of Sigmar,' he murmured.

No force of the Empire had stirred itself when Bretonnia had been riven by war. Very rarely had the great and the good of Karl Franz's realm given much thought to their chivalrous cousins over the Grey Mountains. Then again, it was foolish to assume that they had not been hard-pressed themselves. Leoncoeur had heard the rumours running through court – that disaster had overtaken Marienburg, that the north was aflame, that even the green-skins were terrified of something and remained hidden in their forest lairs.

He felt icy water creep under the skin of his armour plate, rousing him from his lethargy. He stood cumbersomely, hauling on looped creepers. No remnant of the Lady's presence remained, and the Gironne looked as turgid and weed-choked as before.

Leoncoeur trudged back to his mount, slipping on the mud-slick river-bank as he went.

'Altdorf,' he said, musingly, already gauging the distances. 'If that is where the fates are to be written, we must not be missing.'

He thought of the hot blood of his countrymen, and their desire to exchange the grim hunts after petty quarry for the blood-and-thunder of a real war. Many still looked to him; if he ordered them, they would ride with him still.

He reached his horse, and untied it.

'So be it,' he said to himself, smiling dryly as he prepared to mount again. 'I asked for a path. I have been given one.'

He vaulted into the saddle. He turned one last time, gazing back to where ripples still radiated, and saluted.

'Thank you,' he said.

Then he kicked his mount up the slope, and was soon gone.

In his absence, the riverbank sunk into silence once more, broken only by the faint slap of the river-current against the shore, and the mournful wind in the twisted branches.

The deathmoon rode in the eastern sky, glowing with a sick greenish sheen. Its wholesome companion was nowhere to be seen.

Such as was foretold, Vlad thought, looking up into heavens.

The land around him was limned with a ghostly light, tainted as stomach-bile. Morrslieb had ever cast a corrupted illumination, but now its noxious effluence seemed worse than ever. Its scarred face was bloated, presaging the onset of Geheimnisnacht.

That should have made him glad. In the old days, when the deathmoon rode high on bitter, cloudless nights he had gloried in the visions it had brought him. He had raised scores of unliving to march under his black banners, and their bones had shone under the glow of the tainted heaven-spoor.

He stood before Castle Drakenhof's ruined gates, his long cloak snapping in the night wind, and gazed out over the host he had summoned. As yet it did not compare to the vast armies he had once marched west with, but it was grand enough for now. Crowds of Sylvanian troopers, shivering in the cold, stood in decent approximations of Imperial infantry squares. They were dwarfed by the clattering ranks of skeletons and zombies, some pulled from the dark soil just hours ago by Vlad's necromancers. Skinless horses walked silently along avenues between ghostly regiments, their skull-faced riders showing no emotion as they surveyed the lines of the undead host. Black banners flew, their tattered edges pulled by roving winds.

'Will it be enough?' Vlad asked.

No one answered. He stood alone. On his first such crusade, Isabella had been by his side, counselling him, encouraging him. Her absence made his heart ache – to the extent he had a heart, at any rate. The grief was real enough.

In the far distance, thunder cracked along the eastern horizon. The sawtooth edge of the mountains briefly became visible, black against the outer dark. Carrion crows cawed as they flocked above in huge swarms, ready to fly west ahead of the main host.

Vlad watched them mob and swirl. There were many hours left before the dawn, and they could make good time under cover of night. Though he planned to drive the army onwards even during the daylight hours, he knew they would struggle under the sun's harsh glare. The mortals would need to be fed and rested, and even the dead would require constant supervision from his covens of spell-winders.

They would make for the Stir, taking any towns and villages on the way and turning their impoverished inhabitants to the cause. Since the Law of Death had been loosened, the many graveyards of his cursed province would readily yield up more fell troops for the host, and so the numbers of both mortal and unliving would swell with every league they marched. Once at the river, they would take barges downstream, riding the flood as the dark waters foamed and rushed west.

He did not expect any serious resistance before reaching the borders of Reikland. The Empire was like a rotten fruit – still intact on the outside, but eaten hollow within. The fortified city of Wurtbad might prove a temporary delay, but he had already taken steps to ease that potential barrier.

Behind him, he heard the howls of vargheists as they loped and swooped amid the ruins. He sensed the shuddering movements of ghouls, and saw the shimmer-pattern of unquiet spirits. Those spectral presences would soon send the entire realm into paroxysms of fear, just as they had done so long ago. And yet, this time he was not marching to bring the Empire to its knees. Far from it.

He looked down at the roll of parchment in his left hand, sealed with a great wax glob and marked with the signet-device of the von Carsteins. He remembered how difficult it had been to find the words to use.

I am aware that the mutual enmity between our peoples will make this proposal a hard one to entertain fairly. I have no doubt, though, given the circumstances, you will see past ancient prejudices and buried grievances. You will have seen the same auguries as we have, and you will know what is at stake. And, after all, do I not have some prior claim to this title? Or does right of conquest count for nothing in these debased times?

Vlad was not sure about those lines, but he had left them in. The detail of the law could be hammered out in person – the important thing was to make the approach now, before the city was cut off by the hosts of the North.

He looked up, just in time to see an enormous bat flutter down from the castle rafters. Its body was as big as a wolf's, and its leathery wings had a downdraft like a hunting eagle's. More bats followed their leader down, hovering in pack formation, until nine pairs of red eyes glowed before him in the night.

Vlad wrapped the parchment tightly in oilskin and tied the bundle with twine. He held it up, and the hovering bat took it in its powerful jaws.

'Go swift, go safe,' whispered Vlad, reaching up to caress the animal.

Then the whole flock of fell creatures shot upward into the night, spiralling high over the assembled army and heading west.

'Their pride will be the greatest obstacle,' he mused aloud. 'Can the Empire humble itself enough to see sense? That is yet to be decided.' Then he smiled coldly to himself, feeling his long fangs snick on his lower lip. 'All men can change, and every mortal has a turning-point. We just have to find where that is. Would you not agree, Herrscher?'

The witch hunter stepped from the shadow of the gates, flanked by ashen-faced guards. His own skin was as white as bone, shrivelled dry onto his prominent skeleton. The clothes he had worn when fully alive now hung from him loosely, and his pistol-belt had slipped almost comically about his thighs.

Herrscher stared out at the host before them. Then he looked down at his hands. He was trembling.

'The shock will pass,' said Vlad, not unkindly. 'You forget the worst of the pain, in time.'

Herrscher looked at him, a mix of horror and hatred on his face. For all that, he did not reach for his weapon. 'How is it... *possible?*' he rasped, and his once-powerful voice was as thin as corpse-linen.

Vlad sighed. He would have to get used to many such initiations into the half-life of undead servitude. 'You do not need to know that. All you need to know now is that my will gives you breath. You will accept that. You will come to cherish it. The power of resistance you once commanded has gone, and you are my lieutenant now.'

Vlad regarded Herrscher with something approaching fondness. The witch hunter would never truly know it, but his position was one of the highest honour – other captains would be appointed, but he was the very first.

Herrscher looked like he wanted to scream, to dash his own brains out, to launch himself at Vlad and wring his neck, but of course none of those things were possible now. The witch hunter might be screaming on the inside, but he would do the bidding of the one who had raised him, just as Vlad did the bidding of Nagash who had raised *him*.

'Now come,' said Vlad, placing a gauntlet on Herrscher's shoulder and leading him out from the gate's shadow. 'We march within the hour. Let me show you your new servants.'

Helborg woke with a jolt. He was still on his feet, propped up against a wall. He did not remember falling asleep. He had hardly been able to close his eyes for the three days since he had been back in Altdorf, and when he did his mind swiftly filled with nightmares. He saw, over and over, the Emperor felled above Heffengen, plummeting to the earth in a deathly spiral before disappearing from view.

The grief was still raw. Karl Franz had been the undisputed master of the sprawling Empire, the only man with the patience, the guile and the sheer presence to hold the fractious provinces together. Only Karl Franz could have faced down Volkmar in one of his tirades, or kept Gelt from flying off into another half-considered magical endeavour, or resisted the grim implacability of Schwarzhelm in his worst moods. Karl Franz had kept them all in line.

If Helborg was honest, only in the past few days had he truly understood what a titanic achievement that had been. The demands of electors, courtiers, wizards, engineers and generals were endless. Every hour brought new demands to his door, burdening him with both the vital and the trivial. For the moment, he had cowed the three electors into submission and ensured his mastery over the city defences, but it would only be a matter of time before they started scheming again. Both Gausser and von Liebwitz saw the present crisis as an opportunity for advancement, and even Haupt-Anderssen sniffed the chance to profit from the flux. Only the wizard Martak seemed to understand the Empire's desperate straits, and he was little better than a pedlar, looked down on by his more elevated kin in the colleges and disregarded by the Palace staff who served him.

Helborg pushed himself from the wall he had been leaning against, cursing himself for losing consciousness. He was still in full ceremonial armour. He wore his Reiksguard symbols at all times to remind the populace – and, in truth, himself – that he was the last remaining link to the past. Out of all the great heroes of the Empire – Gelt, Volkmar, Schwarzhelm, Huss – only he remained, isolated and cut off from what remained of the northern armies. There was no knowing if any of them still lived, and to even contemplate mounting a significant defence without them felt alien and uncomfortable.

Helborg blinked heavily, hoping none had seen his lapse. The corridor around him was empty, a stone shell lined with torches. Through narrow slit-windows he could see that it was nearly dark outside, and the night's chill was creeping through the granite. For a moment he could not remember why he had come this way, then it all came back – inspection of the northern gate with Zintler. He had made it as far as the fortified citadel above the gatehouse. He must have just paused for a moment.

He shook himself down, still feeling groggy from lack of rest, and went quickly up towards the parapet level. He climbed two spiral staircases, strode down a long archer's gallery, then finally emerged into the open air again.

Zintler was waiting for him on the open summit of the gatehouse, a wide courtyard ringed with shoulder-height battlements. A huge flagpole stood in the centre of the space, hung with an Imperial standard. As he passed it, Helborg could smell the mould-spores on the fabric.

Even here, he thought grimly.

Zintler saluted as Helborg approached, not giving any indication that he had been kept waiting.

'How stands it?' asked Helborg, joining him on the northern edge of the courtyard.

'Plague has reached the city,' said Zintler. 'Barely two-thirds of the men capable of carrying a sword can still lift one. It will only get worse.'

Helborg nodded grimly. Similar reports were coming in from all across Altdorf. Despite guarding the water supplies tightly, something was infecting the poorer quarters and spreading out to the garrisons. The air itself was foul, and carried an edge of bitterness when the wind blew.

'The walls?' Helborg asked, peering over the edge to look at them for himself.

The northern gate had been built up and augmented over hundreds of years, and was now a vast pile of age-darkened stone, crested with gunnery emplacements and the snarling golden gargoyles of griffons and lions. Bulwarks and kill-points jostled with one another in a cunning series of funnelling formations. By the time an enemy got anywhere close to the gates themselves, they would have been pummelled by artillery and ranged magic, doused in boiling oil and pelted with building rubble, then finally overwhelmed by sorties streaming out from hidden posterns all along the ingress way.

At least, that was how it had been in the past, when the Empire's armies were more numerous than the sands on the grey Nordland shore. Now Helborg doubted whether he had enough able bodies to occupy more than half the defensive positions available to him.

'The walls are crumbling,' said Zintler flatly. He reached over to the top of the battlements and prised a section of mortar from the joints. It disintegrated between his finger and thumb. Once again, Helborg smelled the stench of rot.

'It can't be crumbling,' Helborg muttered. 'This is granite from the Worlds Edge peaks.'

'The Rot,' said Zintler, as if that explained everything.

They were already referring to the Rot in the streets – the malaise that seemed to spread through everything, spoiling milk, fouling foodstuffs, infecting living flesh.

'Enough of that,' snapped Helborg. 'Summon the master engineer and get him to shore up the foundations. The gates must hold.'

'Master Ironblood is already engaged–'

'Summon him!' Helborg snapped. 'I don't care what he's tinkering with – the gates must hold.'

Zintler bowed, admonished. The Reikscaptain had the grey lines of fatigue around his eyes, just as they all did. Helborg wondered if he had had any sleep either.

'What reports from the west?' Helborg asked, running a weary hand over his cropped scalp.

'The enemy draws close to Carroburg.'

'Have the Greatswords been pulled back?'

'The messages were sent.'

'That is not what I asked.'

Zintler looked rattled. 'I do not know, lord. We send messengers out along the river, and never hear from them again. We send fortified contingents in barges, and they disappear. I do not have enough men to chase them all down. We do what we can, but–'

'So be it,' growled Helborg, not wanting to hear any more excuses. Zintler was doing his best, but the inexorable tide of work was getting to them all. Carroburg housed some of the finest regiments in the Reikland – if they could be salvaged, then the city's defences would look a lot more secure. If they decided to make a doomed stand at the western city, then things looked even bleaker. 'There is nothing more to be done.'

Helborg's cheek flared with pain. The daemon's claws had bitten deep, and though the wound had closed over, it had never truly healed. He was aware how it made him look. He could feel poisons at work under the scabby skin, and knew that no apothecary would be able to salve them.

It is my penance, he mused bleakly. *For failing my liege.*

Zintler's face flushed. 'I can try again,' he said.

'Too late now,' growled Helborg, cursing the luck that seemed ever against them. 'If they come, they come. Until then, look to the walls. Organise details to begin work on the gatehouse this night, and bring me reports from the watch. We need clean water from somewhere, and I cannot believe *all* the shafts are tainted.'

Zintler saluted smartly, and walked across the courtyard to the stairwell. Helborg watched him go, noting the stooped line of his shoulders.

Karl Franz would have handled him better, he thought to himself. *He would have handled all of them better.*

Helborg limped over to the very edge of the parapet, and gazed moodily north. Out under the cover of the encroaching dark, the tree line brooded like a vast slick of tar. The foliage had been allowed to creep closer to the walls than it should have done. Everything seemed to be growing at a burgeoning rate, blooming in a mire of foulness far more quickly than it could be cut down again.

Above the jagged lines of the firs, Morrslieb rode low, its virulent orb glowing yellow-green. As Helborg's eyes strayed towards it, the wound in his cheek throbbed harder.

Behind him, the soft light of lanterns flickered into life, one by one, as the citizens began the nightly chore of warding against the night-terrors. Bonfires would be lit at every street intersection, and patrols doubled up. That did not stop the regular disappearance of citizens, nor the growing spread of the pox, nor the uncontrollable nightmares that made children and adults alike scream in their sweat-sodden cots.

Out there, somewhere, the hordes of the End Times were coming, burning and hacking, and with only one goal in mind.

'I will *resist* you,' murmured Helborg, fighting against exhaustion, knowing how much labour still lay ahead of him. 'We will not retreat. We will meet you with our blades and our hearts intact, for we are *men*, and you have never extinguished us, not after three thousand years of trying.'

As he spoke, his gauntlets curled into fists. He stood atop the pinnacle of the northern gate, with the entire city at his back, and cursed the darkness.

Out in the gathering night, nothing changed. The trees rustled in the distance, rubbing branches against one another as if they were greedy hands clutching weapons. The eerie calls of night-birds shrieked into the gloom, and the uncaring stars came out, just as they had done since the world was made.

Slowly, his body shot through with the gathering weight of exhaustion, Helborg turned from the vista, and limped back into the gatehouse. His tasks for the night were only just beginning.

The river Reik had once flown strongly west of Carroburg. It had plunged into a narrow gorge, foaming and hissing, before reaching the cataracts that sent it tumbling down forty feet of rock-strewn white water. The cliffs on either side of the valley soared up precipitously, clad in dark firs and dripping with a constant mist of spray. The famed citadel itself had been raised on the northern shore – a spur of black rock, wound about with tight circles of inner walls and close-packed towers. Carroburg perched above the drop like a crow poised for scavenging. The banners of Middenland hung from its sheer-angled tower roofs, bearing the device of the white wolf atop a blue ground.

Dominating the city was its fortress, built for defence, with soaring outer walls jutting from sheer cliffs of rain-slick rock. Only two gates broke the circle of the citadel's lower walls, one looking east towards Altdorf, the other west towards Marienburg. In normal times both were kept open during the daylight hours, though for many weeks they had been barred and locked tight. A meagre force of Greatswords had issued out along the great western road to relieve Marienburg once news of its siege had come in, but no news had returned regarding their fate, and the city's burgomeisters had feared the worst. After that, no living soul passed the cordon of the walls, and the populace huddled within their protection even as the nights were filled with lurid screaming and the waters around them seemed to thicken and spoil.

Travelling at the head of their vast host, Otto and Ethrac paused at the point the Reik curved steeply north towards the Carroburg gorge. They were both riding Ghurk, and had to yank his ears hard to get him to stop lumbering.

'What do you make of it, o my brother?' asked Otto, licking his lips.

'Satisfactory,' replied Ethrac, running a wizened finger around the lip of his plague-bells. 'Better than I hoped for.'

In years past, they would have been staring up at a daunting defensive position, a natural funnel-point overlooked by formidable gunnery and backed up by the feared garrison of Greatswords. Now, the Reik was clogged with great mats of grey-fronded moss. In defiance of the strong current, the mats had floated upriver, lodging against the bank and blocking the flow. As the flood around them ebbed, more clots of foliage bumped and twisted upstream, further silting up the power of the waters.

Even as the river had choked on the thick layers of unnatural vegetation, the forest on either bank had burgeoned and burst its bounds, sending meandering tendrils snaking out into what had once been open ground. Tree-trunks had burst, exposing thick smears of throbbing mucus within. Briars had shot from the boiling earth, tangling and throttling anything they came across. The naked cliffs below Carroburg were now writhing with tentacles, spikes and suckers. The cataract itself was gone, replaced by a slithering slop of viscous algal slime.

Otto gazed up at the fortress. The base of its still-mighty walls was a hundred feet away. He reached for a copper spyglass at his belt, and placed it against his bloodshot eye. As he did so, the lens blinked.

'They are locked up within it, o my brother,' Otto observed, moving the spyglass across the battlements. He could see spear-tips moving across the parapets. There were still artillery pieces on the high battlements, and some of them might do a little damage. 'They are not getting out now. Ghurk will feast on hot flesh this night.'

Ghurk chortled, making his rolling shoulders shudder. Ethrac stood up, shaking his bell-staff. 'The foundations will moulder,' he muttered, invoking the dark magic that welled up all around him so easily now. 'The stone will break. The bones will snap.'

Otto joined his brother's chuckling. He had not slain in earnest since Marienburg, and the blood on his scythe was almost dry. 'It will be a *mercy* for them,' he said. 'Your medicines! They will splutter on them.'

Ghurk started to lumber onwards, his cloven hooves sinking deep into the muddy mulch below. He waded across the channel where the river had been, and sank barely up to his shins. All around him, the vanguard of the pestilential host advanced in turn, surging across what should have been a raging torrent. Norscan warriors strode out, swinging their cleavers in armoured fists, followed by the long ranks of disease-addled plague-zombies.

The trees around them shivered, and strange beasts crept out from the shadows – wolves with swollen bellies and sore-thick jowls, bears with split torsos and glistening ribcages, goat-like horrors with eyeless faces and dribbling withers. The whole of nature had been perverted, and the coming of the Glottkin roused them all from whatever dank pit of misery they had curled into.

Otto felt a savage joy kindle in his rotten heart. Ethrac's magicks would do their work soon, and the citadel's foundations would begin to crack. He could already see the results – poison-vines prising the block apart and freezing it into powder. The air stank with glorious virulence, ushering the numberless hordes up the gorge mouth and towards the high gates.

'Faster, Ghurk-my-brother,' Otto urged, slapping his brother on his shoulder. 'We are dallying. Show some speed!'

Ghurk issued a joyous bark, and started to pick up the pace. His hooves splashed deep as he rolled up the choked riverbed. In his wake, the entire horde did likewise, shambling and surging like some colossal tide of incoming filth. A thousand parched throats croaked out battle-cries, and sonorous war horns boomed a hoarse, echoing dirge.

Far ahead, from atop the tallest tower, the trumpets of the Empire issued their counter-challenge. Puffs of white smoke rippled along the parapets, presaging the blackpowder volleys that would soon be cracking and spitting among them.

Otto cared nothing for that. The seamy air coursed through his lank hair as he held tight onto Ghurk's yawing body. Soon they would be up among them, breaking skulls.

There were times when the resistance of mortals genuinely puzzled him. What could be better than indulging in the glorious foulness of the Plaguefather? What could be better than to be blessed with such noxious, bountiful gifts?

Still, for whatever reason, they failed to grasp the possibilities and held on to their dreary, grey lives surrounded by fear and privation. He could not be too miserable about that – it meant that there were wars to be fought, and so his scythe would always run with glutinous fluids, melting from the body and ready to be slurped down quick.

He grinned, seeing how quickly Ghurk ate up the ground and brought the doom of Carroburg closer. Ethrac continued to mutter, and inky clouds roiled across the beleaguered fortress, spinning out of the lead-grey sky like bile dropped into spoiled cream.

'Onward, my creatures!' Otto croaked, waving his scythe wildly and straining to catch the first sight of a terror-whitened mortal face. 'Climb fast! Drag them down! Suck their marrows and squeeze their eyes!'

The host answered him with a chorus of eager roars. Like some enormous, unnatural flood breaking in reverse, the host of the Plaguefather surged up the gorge mouth, clambered up the rocky cliffs and swarmed up towards the walls, its eyes already alight with slaughter.

Leoncoeur stood on the balcony of the old stone tower south of Couronne and gazed out across the assembled throng. The rain hammered down, just as it seemed to do all the time these days, turning the turf below into a quagmire. The eastern horizon grumbled and snapped with thunder, heralding the latest storm to blight the eastern marches. It was just as the Lady had told him – the world was coming apart at the edges, torn like a worn saddlebag.

He had chosen to make his appeal outside the boundaries of the city. Gilles le Breton had given him leave to make the case for Errantry, but it would have been discourteous to do so within the confines of Couronne. So the tidings had gone out to every keep and knightly hold between the coast and the mountains. Despite the weariness of the long and grinding war, those tidings had been answered handsomely, and knights had ridden through the wild nights to answer the summons.

That alone gave Leoncoeur some respite from the doubts that had plagued him. He may not have been king any longer, but they still responded to the House of Couronne when it called.

'My brothers!' he called out, shouting hard to make his voice carry across the crowds. Several hundred faces, many wearing open helms, others with their long hair lank from the rain, looked up at him expectantly. A riot of colours was visible on the collected tabards and tunics – a chequerboard of knightly houses in azure, sable, argent and crimson. Beyond the crowd, squires stood with the horses, enduring the ice-cold rain with grim fortitude.

'Much has changed since I last addressed you,' said Leoncoeur. 'The traitor Mallobaude is dead, and the kingdom rests again with its founder. We have seen signs and wonders in the night sky, and the curse of foul magic creeps across our realm. You know in your hearts that this is no ordinary war, such as we have endured for time immemorial. For once, the prophecies of End Times strike at the heart of it. My brothers, the final test is coming.'

As he spoke, he studied their reactions carefully. Bretonnian knights were hard-bitten warriors, some of the finest and most dangerous cavalry troops in the entire Old World. They were not given to flights of fancy, and took tales of woe and prophecy in their stride.

'Daemons are abroad again, and the servants of the foul gods march south with the storm at their backs. But as the winds of magic stir, other powers rise to contest it. I have seen the Lady, my brothers. She came to me from the waters and told me of the trials to come. This is why I call you here, so that her summons may be answered. I call Errantry, a crusade to strike at the heart of the new darkness.'

The knights watched him intently. From any other mouth, they might have scoffed at claims to have spoken with the Lady, but they knew Leoncoeur's past and none raised so much as a sceptical smile. As Leoncoeur spoke, he thought he even detected something like longing in their steady expressions. They had endured so much over the past months, and the prospect of something turning the tide of long, slow defeat spoke to their martial hearts.

'The axe will fall, not here, but on the City of Sigmar,' Leoncoeur told them. 'Even now, the enemy burns its way south, turning forests into haunts of ruin. We do not have long. If we muster as quickly as we may, even an unbroken ride across the mountains will scarce bring us there in time.'

Some scepticism showed on their faces now. The Empire was far away, and far removed from the concerns of Bretonnia. Relations between the two foremost kingdoms of men had ever been distant, riven as they were by both tongue and custom.

'I know what you feel!' Leoncoeur urged, forcing a smile. 'You say to yourselves that Altdorf is distant, and has armies of its own, and that the Emperor did not send his own troops to aid us when we were staring devastation in the face. All these things are true. If you refused this summons then no Bretonnian would blame you. None of your ladies would scorn you, and your people would not whisper of your honour in the shadows of their hovels.'

Leoncoeur leaned out, clutching the railing of the stone balcony.

'But consider this! The fire is coming. The war that will end all wars is breaking around us, and no realm on earth will be free of it. The anvil, the *heart* of it, is Altdorf. Here will the fates of men be decided, and here will the trials of the gods play out. Would you miss that contest? Would you wish to tell your children, if any future generation still lives in years to come, that the flower of Bretonnia was given the chance to intervene, and turned aside?'

The crowd began to murmur. Leoncoeur knew what stirred their hearts, and what kindled their ever-present sense of honour.

'There is *glory* to be had here!' he thundered, striking the railing with his gauntlet. 'When we swore our vows, we swore to guard the weak and cast down the tyrant. We swore to ride out against any creature of darkness that threatened our hearth and home, and to take the vengeance of the Lady to every last one of them.'

Shouts of agreement now, and a low murmur of assent. Their spirits were roused.

'In these times, every realm stands as our hearth, and the whole *world* is our home!' roared Leoncoeur. 'The corrupted will make no distinction between them and us. If Altdorf falls, who can doubt that Couronne will be next? When we shed blood on the Reik, we shed it for Bretonnia; when we shield the Empire from the storm, we shield the vales and towers of Quenelles and Bordeleaux!'

'Leoncoeur!' someone cried out, and the chant was taken up. *Leoncoeur! Leoncoeur!*

'I can promise you nothing but hardship!' Leoncoeur went on. 'We may not return from this adventure, for I have seen the hosts of the north, and they are vast beyond imagination. But which of us has ever shied from the fear of death? Which of us has ever shown cowardice in battle, or refused a duel against the mightiest of foes? If we are to die, then let it be where the storm breaks! If our souls are forfeit, then let it be fighting in the last battle of the Old World, where our sacrifice shall echo down the ages! And when the tally of years is complete and the reckoning made for all nations, let no man say that when the call came, Bretonnia failed to answer!'

They were roaring now, drawing swords and crying out for vengeance. Leoncoeur felt savage joy rise up within his gorge.

They are still my people, he thought. *And I am still their master.*

'For the Lady!' he cried, raising both arms high in defiance of the tempest that raged about the tower.

The knights before him replied without hesitation, shouting out their fealty in a single massed roar.

The Lady!

Leoncoeur relaxed at last then, knowing the first task was over. Errantry had been called, and the heavy cavalry that made Bretonnia feared throughout the world had been unleashed. The road ahead would be dark, but at least the path was set.

The Lady had spoken. Her crusade had begun.

The vampire army travelled fastest by night. Only the weakest of Vlad's servants suffered under the glare of the sun, but as the skies were relentlessly overcast and dark with rain even they were able to make some progress. In any case, the forest around them had burst into incredible growth, and the trees snaked and throttled one another in an orgy of tumescence.

Vlad rode at the head of his skeletal vanguard, looking about with distaste at the corruption of his land. Creepers twisted across the road, all bearing virulent fruits that burst with acid when trodden down. The soil itself seethed with fungi and clinging mosses, all striving with perverted fecundity to assert themselves against the foul growths around them.

This was *life* in all its disgusting, liquid excess. Even as a mortal man he would have found such violent displays of fertility alarming. As a lord of undeath, committed to the austere night-world of his Master, it was almost more than he could bear to endure it.

If he chose, he could have halted the army and summoned his necromancers and lesser vampire lords. They could have shrivelled the growths and bleached the fruits white. If they committed themselves for long enough, they could have parched the land from the Stir to the mountains, draining it of the noxious mucus that leaked from every suppurating pore and returning it to the barren waste it deserved to be.

But there was no time, and his energies needed to be husbanded for the trials ahead, so he grudgingly suffered his homeland to be overrun.

Not forever, he thought darkly, running his ancient eyes over the tangle of vines. *The cold fire will come, once all is accomplished.*

Herrscher rode beside him. Both their steeds were skeletons, their bones knitted together by dark magic and held in place by Vlad's will. The undead witch hunter looked a little less miserable than he had done, though he still slumped in the saddle.

'How do you find your gifts?' asked Vlad, trying to take his mind off the filth around him.

Herrscher shot him an incredulous look. 'Gifts?' He shook his emaciated head. 'You have poisoned me.'

'Learn to appreciate what you have been given. You are stronger than you were. You hear better, see better, and you will endure against all magic. Scorn this, and you remain a greater fool than when you lived.'

'This is what you wish for,' muttered Herrscher. 'Slaves, all of us.'

'Not quite. I wish for *order*. I wish for the weak to know their place, guarded over by their betters. Do sheep resent their shepherds? Or would they rather take their chances with the wolves?'

'I would have done,' retorted Herrscher, his face a picture of resentment.

'And that would be a terrible waste,' said Vlad. 'You are better at my side, where your talents can flourish. Do not resent the past – soon you will have trouble even remembering it.'

'So the past does not trouble you?' asked Herrscher, his lips curling sardonically. 'That is not what I heard.'

Vlad's anger rose, and he made to turn on Herrscher, when he suddenly noticed a flash of white in the road ahead. In an instant, he saw Isabella riding to greet him, alone under the trees, a look of admonishment on her perfect alabaster face, and he froze.

The illusion faded. More than one figure emerged from the arboreal gloom – eight shades, each as thin and drawn as dried fruit, carrying between them a palanquin of shimmering glass. Silently, they set the carriage down, and three women emerged, all of them wearing lace-edged gowns of purest white. They seemed to glow like moonlight, and their footfalls left no tracks in the sodden earth. They curtsied archaically, and shuffled closer.

Vlad mastered himself. He knew the names of the ladies well enough, and which master they served, though he had not expected to encounter them so soon.

'My lord von Carstein,' said the foremost of the pale creatures, her voice as dry and hollow as a coffin-echo. 'We had begun to worry. This land has become an abomination.'

'All lands have,' said Vlad, offering his hand for the lady to kiss. 'Why are you here, Liliet? I did not seek to find you for days hence.'

The white lady gave him a dry smile. 'Your servant Mundvard failed. Marienburg is a nest of writhing horrors, and the Empire has been driven back like whipped curs to Carroburg.'

'They are moving fast, then. What strength do they have?'

'They are led by three siblings – foul triplets, each blessed with grotesque gifts. One is the size of a house, and chews his way through fortifications like a fat child through sweetmeats. Their host is swollen beyond counting. Your servant did his best – I can vouch for that – but they will not be halted.' She shuddered distastefully. 'Such numbers. I would not have believed it, had I not seen it.'

Vlad pursed his fleshless lips together. 'And where is Mundvard now?'

'Gathering what forces he can. He sent us to you, and begs leave to join his army with yours north of Altdorf. He says that no action further west can delay the enemy now, and only a combined stand at the city holds the hope of resistance.'

'Oh, he said that, did he?' Vlad was irritated. Mundvard was a supreme fighter, but a poor general. More than that, it was not his place to dictate tactics to his betters – he should have delayed the Chaos forces for longer at the coast, giving time for Vlad to gather the greatest host he could. Now the need for haste, already pressing, had become overwhelming.

'He fought skilfully, lord,' said Liliet, a little coquettishly, given her cadaverous appearance.

'Not skilfully enough,' snarled Vlad. 'You do not need to return to him. Remain with me, and together we will cut a faster path. I will send messages via other means, and if he still commands more than a rabble of zombies, he can meet us in the Reikland.'

Liliet bowed, then looked sidelong at Herrscher. 'And who is this, my lord? Surely you have not been doling out the Kiss to mortals without the consent of the Master?'

Herrscher was looking at the three women with a mix of horror and fascination on his face. That was good – in the past, it would merely have been horror.

'My new lieutenant,' said Vlad kicking his horse into motion again and forcing the ladies to give way. 'Ride with us awhile, and tell us tales of old Marienburg. We make all haste to Wurtbad, and I am sure he can learn much from you on the way.'

◄ CHAPTER TEN ►

Captain Hans Blucher felt the stone crack before he heard it, and it made his blood freeze. The flags beneath his feet sprouted paper-thin fractures, which then widened to a blade's width.

'Maintain fire!' he bellowed, striding along the ranks of gunnery pieces. 'Let no man leave his station, or by Taal's beard I shall break his head apart with my own hands!'

The walls of Carroburg had been under sustained attack for over an hour. In his worst nightmares, Blucher could not have imagined such an assault. The earth itself seemed to have been roused against them, and the forest in every direction now rang with the tramp of hooves and iron-shod boots.

The rain had started to fall soon after the enemy had arrived. At first it had been like any other deluge, though soon the drops became heavier and heavier, until it was like trying to fight under a hail of mud splatters. Every exposed surface became greasy and treacherous, fouling the cannon wheels as they were rolled out and making men slip and stagger.

Blucher was stationed on the south wall, in command of many of the bigger artillery pieces. Helblasters jostled on the narrow parapet alongside the bigger Great Guns, each one christened by their foundries in Nuln – *Grosse Bertha, Todslingeren, Trollsbane*. They had been firing without pause since the first emergence of the enemy, hurling their shot out at the horde and blasting great channels through the oncoming ranks.

'Ulric damn you all!' hollered Blucher, not paying too much attention to which god's wrath he invoked, so long as it inspired a faster work-rate from his men. 'Reload! They are pouring into the outer curtain!'

The blackpowder guns had reaped a terrible swathe, but it had merely sliced a tithe from the oncoming masses. They showed no fear, clambering over the twitching corpses of the felled, whooping and gurgling with glee. The driving mud-rain should have slowed them, washing them back down the steep cliff edges and into the grimy channel that had once been the Reik, but they seemed to thrive on it, slithering up through the deluge with the effluent streaming down their calloused faces.

Blucher's guns were arranged on the inner wall, high up above the first ring of courtyards. From their vantage they had been able to rain mortars and cannonballs with impunity, but now it felt as if the fortress's very foundations were shaking under them.

Blucher ran to the edge, skirting carefully around the red-hot maw of *Grosse Bertha* and taking care not to touch the metal. He reached the lip of the parapet and peered down.

What he saw took his breath away. The curtain wall was gone – overwhelmed, lost under a simmering carpet of limbs and tentacles. Shocked to his core, Blucher nearly lost his footing, and grabbed hold of the battlement's edge to steady himself.

Mere moments ago, the outer perimeter had been held by companies of archers and handgunners, bolstered by the few Greatswords Aldred had left behind before marching out on his doomed attempt to relieve Marienburg. It had been a diminished company, to be sure, but it should have held out for longer than that. Now the walls' summits were crawling with all manner of mutants and daemon-spawned horrors. Even as he watched, he saw the remaining defenders caught up in a rolling wave of tortured flesh, hacked apart and absorbed by the racing riptide of green and brown.

The enemy ranks were a bizarre assortment – some mortal men in plate armour and matted furs, some grotesque plague-victims carrying hooks and spike flails, some forest-beasts swollen to obscene proportions and slavering with unnatural hungers. Amid them all shimmered the faint outlines of daemons, screaming and shrieking amid the downpour.

There was no fighting against those numbers. They swarmed like rats, scrabbling up the sheer walls along living briars and thorn-tendrils. The stone underfoot gave way, crushed by their weight, but still they came on, chortling as they trod on the tumbling bodies of their own kind.

They would be across the inner courtyard in moments, and after that the great doors to the keep would not hold them for long, not if the outer walls had been demolished and surged over so ruthlessly.

'Belay that!' Blucher cried, unholstering his pistol and cocking the hammer. As he did so, he noticed his hands were trembling. He had been a captain for twenty years and a trooper for ten more, and was used to the sights and sounds of battle, and they had never shaken before. 'Fall back to the towers!'

There is no resisting this, he found himself thinking even as he retreated across the parapet towards the tower beyond. *This will be over within the hour.*

All around him, men deserted their stations and fled for the last bastions of defence. As they did so, more stone flags cracked and splintered, sending shattered masonry flying high. The rain intensified, splattering green gobbets across the tortured citadel.

Blucher resisted the urge to run. The main gate to the tower was less than twenty yards away, and already clogged with gunnery crews trying to cram their way in.

'In good order!' he cried, trying to give his orders a clarity that his mind lacked. 'Up to the top level, form up in the Great Hall!'

He was almost there – he could see the safety of the archway before him. Then, just as the last of the artillery crews slipped inside, the ground beneath him erupted.

He was thrown back, landing on his back several yards away. Dazed, he looked up, trying to make out what had felled him.

The parapet's stone floor had burst open, and a fountain of mud and earth was jetting from the breach. Something huge was clawing its way to the surface, flinging aside stone flags as if they were children's toys.

The entire wall-section groaned and tilted, listing out over the court-yard below. Blucher grabbed hold of a stone railing and hauled himself to his feet, bracing unsteadily as the world swayed and cracked around him.

The beast flailed its way into the open, tunnelling up from where the gunnery level had just been. It was vast, a leviathan of earth and rubble, surging up with the bulk and weight of a river-barge and slewing debris from its massive shoulders.

For a moment, Blucher did not have anything to aim at, just a shower of loose soil and broken stone pieces, but then the beast itself shook loose and turned on him.

He had never seen a monster so big. It was the size of the officer's mess at his old parade ground, a nightmare of bulging veins and fat-slick limbs. Its pocked flesh was the green of rotten fruit. A tiny head protruded from absurdly muscled shoulders, drooling with butter-yellow saliva and grinning inanely. A low *hhurr, hhurr* rattled out from its vast lungs, and an overpowering stench of un-sluiced night-pans wafted out from its sweat-moist haunches.

Blucher raised the pistol, holding it two-handed to quell the shakes, then fired. The shot spun out, perfectly aimed, and hit the creature square in the forehead.

The monster stopped dead. For a moment, Blucher dared to believe that he had felled it, as a line of thin blood ran down the monster's face. He saw it begin to topple, swaying amid the ruin of its ascent, before it blinked heavily, shook its head, and grinned again.

Blucher tried to reload. He scrambled for another shot, pulling it from the wallet at his belt and tipping it into the palm of his hand.

The monster lumbered towards him, shattering what remained of the stone floor under its tread. With a lurch of pure horror, Blucher saw that there was no stopping it. He could fire again and again, and still make no impression on that thick hide.

He pushed himself back towards the edge of the tilting parapet, and glanced down over his shoulder. Below him, a drop of over thirty feet, the courtyard filled with enemy troops. He could see Carroburgers being pulled limb from limb amid the cackling laughter of daemons. Others were being dragged before cauldrons of boiling liquid and forced to drink, gagging and screaming as the corrosive poisons boiled their innards away. Huge booms rang out as the enemy got into the blackpowder storerooms, sending cracks racing up the flanks of the tortured fortress.

It was already over. In the space of just a few hours, one of the oldest and proudest garrisons in the Empire had been overrun. Blucher's fear was replaced by a deadening sense of shame. They should have done better. They should have fought *harder*.

By then, the behemoth was nearly upon him. Blucher cast his pistol aside and reached for a short sword, staring up at the monster as it loomed over him. As he did so, he saw two twisted figures crouching on the beast's shoulders, one in dirty robes and carrying a bell-bearing staff, the other wielding a scythe. Neither of them seemed to have noticed him – they were both absorbed in the carnage bursting out all across the reeling citadel.

'This is *not* the end!' cried Blucher, holding his blade as firmly as he could. 'The Emperor will have his vengeance! Sigmar protects the faithful! The fate of the fallen is–'

His tirade was cut off by a single down-stomp of the monster's hoof. His body was smashed into the stone, crushed into a bloody pulp as the earth beneath was shivered into scree.

Atop Ghurk's shoulder, Ethrac paused and turned to his brother. 'Did you hear something?' he asked.

Otto was in a frenzy of war-lust, barely sensible to anything outside his own world of slaughter. His red-rimmed eyes sparkled with delight as he surveyed the volume of destruction around him. 'Hear what, o my brother?' he asked, absently.

'Never mind it,' muttered Ethrac, preparing the next phase of the noxious deluge that would rip the roofs from the towers and expose the last of the cowering defenders within. 'Press on, Ghurk. Break and shatter, snap and wither.'

Ghurk barked with enthusiasm, too enraptured with the joy of destruction even to scrape the remains of his last kill up to his mouth. Turning cumbersomely, he swayed drunkenly towards the pinnacles of Carroburg.

The sky above them lanced with flashes of green, exposing the shimmer-pattern of daemons in the air. All around them, a symphony of screams, flesh-*schlicks*, ribcage snaps and eyeball-pops swelled in the storm.

The battle was won. Now the true carnage could begin.

Another day dawned over Altdorf, as dank and rotten as all the others. The Reik's flow had slowed to a grimy halt, and the stagnant waters now lapped at the edges of the streets above the quaysides. Insects multiplied on the filmy surface, and their massed buzzing drowned out even the cries of the merchants on the loading wharfs.

Martak strode down the winding streets through the poor quarter, trying not to slip on the grime-soaked streets. Altdorf's thoroughfares were filthy places at the best of times, but the endless rain and damp and plague and misery had turned them into little more than rivers of mud. The drenched and half-starved populace shuffled around in the margins, hugging the dripping eaves of the wattle-and-daub townhouses and shivering in the cold.

For Martak, used to the wilds of the Great Forest, the confinement and the stink were especially trying. He had long since given up trying to get used to it, and had actively turned his finely honed sense of smell towards the task of detection. The plagues were being borne by foul winds from the north, that was certain, but there had to be a source within the city as well. Every chaplain of Sigmar was chanting nightly to banish the contagions, and the fact that they had failed suggested either that the power of faith was waning, or a greater power was at work, or both.

There was no shortage of places to look for the plague's root – the City of Sigmar was built upon a warren of alleys, cesspits, warehouses and thieves' dens, all of which were suitable nesting places for the Rot. There might be just one source or hundreds – it was impossible to know, not without tearing the entire poor quarter apart, brick by rotting brick.

Ahead of him stood the Temple of Shallya. It had been deliberately placed in the darkest and most impoverished district of the old city, and stood like a shaft of sunlight amid piled-high tenements. Very few inhabitants of Altdorf were free of the fear of being assaulted or pick-pocketed while abroad in that district, but the Sisters of the Goddess lived their lives unmolested in the very heart of the lawless slum-city. Every day they would receive long lines of supplicants, desperate for relief from the panoply of maladies that afflicted them. Since the full onset of the Rot those lines had grown fourfold, and the temple was now permanently besieged by a throng of blistered and scarlet-faced sufferers.

As he neared the temple precincts, Martak pushed them aside, using his staff to drive them from his path.

Sister Margrit, the head of the order in Altdorf, watched him struggle. Her stern, matronly face showed some disapproval as she waited for him at the top of a wide flight of stone stairs. By the time Martak had reached her, he was sweating like a hog in midsummer.

'Tell me, sister,' he panted, wiping his greasy forehead, 'how do you stand it?'

'Stand what?' Margrit asked.

'The smell.'

'You are not that clean yourself.'

Martak ran his fingers through his clotted beard. 'True enough. But you know why I'm here.'

Margrit nodded. 'Come.'

The two of them passed from the crowded courtyard and walked under an open colonnade. Beyond the pillars lay a shaded cloister, free from the worst of the clamour outside. A fountain played amid a knot garden of carefully tended herbal plants. Martak felt like he had stepped into another world, and took a deep breath. The faint tang of corruption still laced the air, but it was less overpowering than outside.

'It is rare, for one of your kind to come here,' said Margrit, walking slowly along the cloister paths. 'Wizards and priests – we have not always seen the world the same way.'

'Times are changing,' said Martak. 'And I'm not a very grand sort of wizard.'

'You are the Supreme Patriarch.'

Martak winced. 'Come, you know that means nothing. The Reiksmarshal has more than a dozen better battle wizards on his roster.'

Margrit stopped walking, and regarded him carefully. 'But they are not here.'

'No, they are not.'

Margrit considered that. Then she swept a pudgy hand around her, demonstrating what she presided over. 'We dwell in an island now – a drop of clear water amid a sea of pain. We guard it, and we tend it, but it cannot last forever. Mark it well, my lord. All gardens wither.'

'Where is the sickness coming from?' asked Martak. 'Helborg has his eyes on the walls, on the Great Guns and the Knightly Orders. He looks out from the ramparts, searching for the coming storm, but he is blind to what is happening *here*. What is the source?'

Margrit smiled sadly. 'Our masters are military men. What do you expect?' The smile faded. 'I cannot tell you where the Rot wells up from. We have made enquiries. The people tell us things, as long as we bandage their sores and listen to their sorrows.'

'You have nothing?'

'It comes from the sewers, but that will not help you. There are miles of them down there, and the City Watch does not send its men under the streets.'

'They might need to.'

'None would come back.' Margrit looked at him sympathetically. 'You don't spend much time in the city, do you, wild-man? There are things under Altdorf that have lain undisturbed since the time of the old Emperors. Only a fool would venture far down there.'

Martak shrugged, scratching his neck. 'Wise men have not got us very far. Perhaps fools are needed.'

'Then take armed men,' said Margrit, seriously. 'Take whole bands of them. Flush the tunnels with fire – if you have a Bright magister or two, all the better. I would not venture down beneath the streets with less than a hundred troops at my back.'

'A hundred,' said Martak, amused by the thought of this stout, severe-jowled woman leading an expedition into Altdorf's hidden underbelly. 'I think you'd need less.'

'This is just the beginning,' Margrit warned, starting to walk again. As she went, she trailed a hand along the tops of severely-harvested medicinal herbs. There were not many fresh leaves left. 'We can feel it growing. Shallya, may She be blessed forever, does not answer us. We have a gifted sister, a young woman from Wurtbad whose power for prophecy and healing is the most powerful I have ever known, and even she hears nothing now.'

'Why not?'

'She hears nothing because she dashed her head against the fountain you see over there. Before we got to her, she had polluted the sacred spring with her own blood. She had been sent mad, they tell me. She had seen what was coming, and it turned her mind.' Margrit looked close to angry tears. 'She would have been so *powerful*. She would have done much good.'

Martak halted her, placing his burly hand on her arm. 'Listen, I have to speak to the Reiksmarshal,' he said, his gruff voice as soft as he could make it. 'I will tell him what you told me. He has men. I will tell him we need to purge the sewers, and I will tell him to send no less than a hundred men in each party. Plus a couple of Bright mages, which I can handle.'

Margrit nodded, looking grateful. 'If you can do that, it would help. We need our health back. If the enemy comes on us now, we will be too weak to man the walls.'

Martak knew the truth of that. As much as Helborg struggled manfully with the thousand tasks at hand, he was blind to the fundamental truth. Altdorf was not like a Reiksguard regiment, full of superbly trained men in the prime of condition – it was home to the weak, the ragged and needy. They were being given nothing, and in the final test that would cost them.

'Lord Patriarch, tell me one thing,' said Margrit, glancing up at him with an odd expression in her eyes. 'We were told the Emperor will return. If he were here, I could believe that the storm will pass, but the days go by and we hear nothing. Have you any news to give me?'

Martak looked at her for a long time. They were all under strict instructions to maintain the fiction that Karl Franz was on his way south, riding at the head of his armies with Schwarzhelm at his side. Helborg had been insistent on it, fearing uncontrollable panic if the truth of his loss got out.

Martak understood the strategy. He saw the need for it. Still, the falsehood stuck in his craw.

'You want the truth?' he asked, hoping to evade giving an answer.

Margrit's gaze never wavered. 'Tell me,' she said. 'I need to know.'

Martak thought of his dreams. They had grown more vivid with every night, and he had seen the Emperor in them all, alone and cast adrift in the benighted north.

Then he thought of the young sister, smashing her skull against the stone

fountain, all through despair. He thought of the deathly faces in the streets
outside, all desperate for something to believe in. If the gods had deserted
them, then all they had was each other. In the end, perhaps the stories now
told by the city's generals were as good as those once told by its priests.

'He will return, sister,' Martak told her, doing his best to smile. 'He *is* the
Empire. In the hour of greatest need, how could he not be here?'

All across the north, the campfires still burned.

A frigid gale howled over the blasted lands, tearing straight from
conquered Kislev across the shattered provinces of Ostland and the Ostermark. The settlements of men in those places were now no more than
smouldering mazes of half-walls and gaping lintels, their inhabitants slain
or enslaved. Nightmare creatures limped across the far horizon, some as
tall as watchtowers and carrying heavy crowns of antlers on their bulbous,
swaggering necks. Thunder cracked across an uneasy horizon, echoing
with the half-heard laughter of glowering gods.

The realm of dreams was expanding. Spreading like a cancer in the wake
of its victorious armies, the warping misrule of the Realm of Chaos was
gradually twisting and carving through the Realm of Nature. Rivers dried
up, or turned to blood, or boiled into poisonous smog. Birds fell from the
sky to roll blindly in the muck, and creatures of the earth sprouted wings
and flapped around in pathetic confusion.

In the wake of the great victory, Heffengen had been plundered down
to the bone. The armies of Chaos, freed from the attentions of the undead
and with the Empire forces destroyed, had been given free rein to sack the
city, and had applied themselves with gusto. Very little now remained, save
the long rows of gibbets and wheels that lined the road south, each bearing
the broken, twitching corpse of a hapless defender. The Revesnecht still
ran red, though the cloying mats of greymoss and throttlevine had already
started to knit together from its silty banks, choking what flow remained.

It had been that thirst for plunder that had saved him. For a long time
he had lain insensible at the base of a pile of rotting bodies. The course of
battle, as confused and blind as it ever was, had raged about him, driving
south and fixing on the walled prize of living flesh. If fate had been otherwise, he would have been trampled by cloven hooves, his neck broken and
his spine crushed into the mud.

But the fates had not abandoned him entirely. A huge, bloat-bellied
champion had seen him come down and had charged over to finish him off.
A massed volley of musket-shot had felled the champion before he could
swing his cleaver, just as the barrages mowed down a whole warband of
marauders on the charge. Their bodies *thunked* into the mire, overlapping
one another in a bloody carpet of limp flesh.

The champion had been the one to preserve him, masking his prone
body with a heavy, rotten corpse. The sweep and ebb of battle had passed

over them both, tearing south with all its grinding momentum, leaving behind the corpse-gardens of the dead and dying.

He awoke much later, while the broken walls of Heffengen still rang with the screams of the captured and the battlefield itself had not yet been plundered of its riches. He pushed the still-warm cadaver from him, grunting from the pain as his cracked ribs creaked. He dragged himself out from under its shadow, feeling the sharp pang of a broken arm. His helm had gone, lost on the dreadful plummet earthwards. For an awful moment he thought *Drachenzahn* had gone as well, then he saw the hilt protruding from beneath the doubled-back arms of a slain Norscan.

Hobbling to his feet, he took up the blade again. If the weapon's spirit recognised him, it gave no sign – the rune-etched steel remained blank and lifeless.

After that he trudged north, knowing the danger, grateful for the night's cold shadows as they stole across the fields of slaughter. He found a ditch to shelter in, part-masked by brambles and with a sliver of blood-foul water at its base. He shivered there for the rest of the night, plagued by the howls and shrieks of raucous joy, parched and yet unable to drink.

Karl Franz, Sigmar's Heir, lay shuddering in the filth, listening to the sounds of Heffengen's agony. Only as the eastern sky brightened to a death-grey dawn did he creep forth again, trusting that the aftermath of the night's debaucheries would give him some cover. He limped north again, then west, skirting the city and hugging the sparse patches of undergrowth that still remained.

In the days that followed, he brushed against death a dozen more times. He was almost discovered twice by armoured patrols. His wounds festered in the dank air, and he passed out from hunger and thirst more than once. He was forced to drink brackish water that made him vomit, and gorge on spoiled grain from plundered storehouses.

Only the amulet kept him alive – the silver seal at his neck that had been imbued with sustaining magic by the magister Tarnus. In the dark of the frigid night, he could feel its aethyric energies warming his chest, staving off the worst of the injuries that threatened to overwhelm him.

A few times, when the sickness raged and despair mounted, he was tempted to cast it aside. As fever raged thickly through his mind, tormenting him with visions of the laughing vampire lord, he listened to the voices that echoed within.

You do not deserve to live. You were slain, and now only prolong the agony. Let it go! Give it up!

He grasped the chain with sweaty hands, intending to rip it clear. Only weakness prevented him – he could barely lift his arms, let alone break the links.

So he lived. He kept walking, each day a fog of pain and confusion, somehow avoiding the enemy columns as they marched south around him. The enemy's own contagions helped him, for the rampant vegetation that erupted across the conquered land soon gave ample cover.

Slowly, painfully, he recovered himself. The amulet worked its subtle power, and his body dragged itself back from the edge of death. He was still wracked with pain, and as weak as any of his sickly peasant subjects, but the worst was past.

He no longer entertained thoughts of giving in – that had been the fevers polluting his mind. He no longer considered heading away from the danger. In fragments, his memory came back, and with it his certainty.

Nothing substantial had changed. He was the Emperor. He was alive. His duty was to fight.

With that, and for the first time, Karl Franz's thoughts turned from survival, to revenge.

CHAPTER ELEVEN

Otto lashed out with his scythe, ripping through the chest of the state trooper and ending his challenge. It had always been an unequal contest – Carroburg had been reduced to little more than rubble, and the only sport remained hunting the last holed-up defenders and rooting them out.

The man tottered for a moment, his legs not getting the message immediately that his heart had been ripped out, before he crashed face-first onto the stone floor. As soon as he did so, a dozen tiny daemon-kin leapt onto the corpse, tearing at it with their teeth and squeaking like excitable kittens.

Otto watched them indulgently. Twenty more corpses lay prone around the basement of the old brewery, all of them leaking guts onto the stone flags where the scythe had whirled. Their bodies would be dragged off at some point and added to the vast cauldrons simmering in Carroburg's old town square. The army had to eat.

As he gathered his breath, Otto reflected coolly on the futility of opposing powers such as his. The fall of Carroburg had been achieved with almost embarrassing ease. Marienburg, a city over three times the size, had not been much more arduous. Perhaps the Empire had finally lost its spine. Perhaps there were no more mortals truly capable of standing against the destiny that, in truth, had always been theirs.

A frog-like daemon the size of Otto's fist pounced onto the state trooper's face and started to suck the eyes from their sockets.

'Greedy, o little one!' laughed Otto, feeling a wave of affection for it.

He watched it feed for a while, before turning from the scene of slaughter and retracing his steps up a long, winding stair. The brewery building he was in was a towering edifice of many levels, and the resistance there had been stouter than almost anywhere else in Carroburg.

The men of the Empire value their beer, Otto mused, as he clambered methodically towards the top level, his scythe-blade dripping over his shoulder as he went.

From outside the thick brewery walls, he heard the ongoing crash and thud of Ghurk's rampage through the town's shabbier regions. There were still morsels of living flesh to be found in some of the hidden pockets, and his corpulent brother's hunger knew no limits.

He would have made his mother proud.

After a long haul, Otto reached the summit and entered a large vaulted chamber. Once it had been lit by rows of tall mullioned windows under a high ceiling, though now the windows were all smashed and the roof sagged. Great copper kettles stood on the tiled floor, each one capable of holding hundreds of gallons. A thick slime of grease and bloody lumps churned and bumped in them now, boiling amid a soup of altogether nastier fluids.

Otto sniffed deeply, appreciating the complex fug of aromas. He could have spent whole days in that place, revelling in the creations his brother had painstakingly piped and funnelled together, if only time allowed. Already, though, the appeal of Carroburg was beginning to wane, and the need to keep moving was making him impatient.

'Where are you, o my brother?' Otto called out, unable to see the far end of the chamber through the clouds of steam.

'Here, o my sibling!' Ethrac replied from the far side of the largest of the kettles, his voice muffled from chewing.

Otto sauntered over to him, noting the elaborate array of tubes that had been strung between the old brewery's impressive range of glass vials. 'What keeps you busy here?' he asked. 'Must be on the move soon.'

'Come,' said Ethrac, beckoning Otto over to where he stirred a thick slop of acrid matter. 'This was worth the effort. We are far from home now, and need all the help we can get.'

Otto joined him at the cauldron's edge. Ethrac mumbled a few incantations, and shook his bell-staff over the liquid. The cauldron's contents popped and seethed, sending a lumpy lip of froth over the edge. At the very centre, shapes began to shimmer into life.

'Observe our cousins,' said Ethrac eagerly. 'We are not alone.'

For a few moments, Otto struggled to see what he was being shown. The cauldron's contents morphed into bubbling shapes, like wedges of the moss that had brought the Reik to a standstill. Then he understood – he saw the wriggling path of rivers, and the crumpled mounds of mountains. He was looking at a map, albeit one that fizzed like molten metal on the forge.

At the centre lay the object of their march – the city of Altdorf, clustered in a wobbling series of towers by the shore of a trembling Reik. Otto peered closer, leaning low over the cauldron.

'Do not break the water!' snapped Ethrac. 'Ignore the city. It is the others I will show you.'

He extended his clawed fingers over the vista, and it began to zoom out. Forests and mountains swept into view, all of them picked out by the foaming bubbles of Ethrac's sorcery.

'We were three, when we set off,' said Ethrac, pulling the portal expertly.

'Autus Brine, Lord of Tentacles, hacks his way through the Drakwald, slaying the greenskin as he comes.'

As Ethrac spoke, Otto made out a long wound in the vast face of the forest. It might have been his imagination, but he thought he even saw tiny figures crashing their way through the thick foliage.

'Is that–?' he began, but Ethrac shushed him impatiently.

'He has been slowed, but he picks up his pace now. He brings the Harbinger with him. You know of this?'

'Who is it?'

'A shaman. Beast-kind.'

Otto wrinkled his nose in distaste. 'Reduced to such. Brine will be angry.'

Ethrac chuckled. 'Allies are allies. They make a good pace now. The Drakwald is emptied, and they tear south with haste.' The scope of the cauldron's roving eye switched east, passing over more overabundant tracts of deep forest. 'And the third of all – the Tallyman himself.'

Otto sniffed again. It was not good to be reminded of their rivals for the Urfather's affections. If Archaon had not been so insistent on the need for an overwhelming, three-pronged attack, he would have preferred to have had no supporting armies at all. 'Epidemius is foundering, it must be so,' he said, grudgingly.

'Wish it not, o my brother,' chided Ethrac, shifting the cauldron's eye over a vast crater set within the forest. 'We will need his daemon-horde. Dharek rides with him, and they tear apart Taal's city even as we linger here.'

Once again, Otto fancied he could make out infinitesimally small figures struggling across the face of the conjured map-face. It looked like driving rain was hammering against the walls of the rock-bound city. A great swathe of glimmering daemons was assaulting a beleaguered force of mortals. Otto screwed his eyes up, trying to gain a better view. 'They are winning,' he murmured.

'That they are,' said Ethrac, with some satisfaction. 'Old allies fade, new allies arrive. Dharek will be at the walls of Altdorf in good time to meet us.'

Otto scratched a pustule on his cheek absently. 'So many,' he muttered. 'Who will take the prize?'

'Prizes for all,' said Ethrac. 'We should shackle Ghurk again – if he spends his strength on gluttony, we shall be late.'

Otto nodded. 'I shall loop the chains around his neck. He will not be happy.'

Ethrac snapped his fingers, and the map zoomed out again, exposing the whole vast panorama of the Empire. In that instant, it was clear what was happening – the three great arms of the northern host were converging with inexorable, steady progress on the Reikland, smashing aside every obstacle in their path. It was unfolding just as the Everchosen had ordered, and the heart of the Empire was being slowly torn inside out.

'And the dead?' asked Otto, remembering Ethrac's concern at Marienburg.

'No skeletons here,' said the sorcerer, sending the boiling visions slopping back into the cauldron. 'Perhaps they have been seen off.' He grinned at his brother. 'Or maybe they turn on the living. What matter? What could stand against the three of us?'

Otto grinned back. Ethrac was right. It helped to be shown the full majesty of the plan. It helped with the nagging doubts that, every so often, snagged in his feverish mind. 'That is good to see, o my brother,' he said, clapping Ethrac on the shoulder. 'So we should be off now.'

'That we should,' said Ethrac, gazing around himself wistfully, no doubt speculating what sport he could have had in such a place. 'Festus will be waiting for us.'

Otto blurted a throaty laugh. He always forgot about Festus, but, in truth, the Leechlord was the pin around which the whole scheme revolved.

'Then all hastens towards the purpose,' he said, satisfied.

'It does,' said Ethrac. 'Now fetch our brother, and feed the armies until their stomachs swell.' He shot Otto a smile of pure, lascivious darkness. 'Just one more march. That is all. One more.'

The knights of Bretonnia on the march was a sight unequalled in the Old World. Each warrior took with him three or four warhorses, all draped in fine caparisons and marked with the heraldic signs of a hundred different bloodlines. Squires and grooms came with them, and reeves, cooks, heralds, priests and a hundred other officials and servants. A vast train of baggage followed them all, carrying all the supplies and weaponry for a long campaign in the saddle. The whole cavalcade coursed through the countryside in a single, vast column, winding its way east from the fens of Couronne and into the highlands north of the Pale Sisters range.

Leoncoeur rode at the head of the column, pushing the pace hard. He had studied the maps long in the vaults of Couronne while the army had mustered, debating with his counsellors which path to take. Throughout, the mysterious Gilles le Breton had held his silence, offering neither blessing nor condemnation of the Errantry. Towards the end, exasperated, Leoncoeur had asked him outright what his counsel was.

'The Lady ordained you,' le Breton had told him, his green eyes as unfathomable as the sea. 'I have no part in this.'

Le Breton spoke to him as if he were already dead – a walking ghost, just like so many that had been loosed across the realm.

So Leoncoeur had plotted his own course – south-east, across the highlands of Gisoreux, before descending into the borderlands of Montfort. They would cross the Grey Mountains at Axebite Pass, heading swiftly north and emerging into Reikland south of Altdorf.

That path was not the swiftest, but the news from the wasteland was now unequivocal – Marienburg had been destroyed and daemons loosed across the marshes. There was no profit in getting bogged down in fighting with such creatures when speed was of the essence. Since his vision of the Lady, Leoncoeur's dreams had become ever more vivid, and he needed no scouts to tell him the scale of the host that was grinding its way east across the lower Empire.

Still, if the Bretonnians could maintain the blistering pace that he had set, the prospect still survived of reaching Sigmar's city before the enemy had it completely surrounded and beyond hope of rescue. Once clear of the Grey Mountains, the race would truly begin.

For now, they picked their way up from the plains and into the granite highlands. Huge outcrops jutted into the sky on either side of them, pocked and striated from the racing winds. Lush pastures gave way to thinner grass-land, littered with chalky boulders.

It was a relief to get away from the low country. The air became fresher as they climbed, rippling the pennants and making the colours flow across the flanks of the steeds. The skies above them never cleared of the oppressive grey mantle they had worn since the coming of Mallobaude, but the rains held, and the worst of the thunder growled away in the far north.

As he rode, Leoncoeur was joined by his lieutenant, Yves Jhared of Couronne, who had fought alongside him on many previous engagements and was as trusted a companion as the king had ever had. Jhared had the flaming red hair and ice-pale skin of a native of Albion, though no one had ever dared to suggest such ancestry to his face.

'Hail, lord,' said Jhared, pulling his horse level with Leoncoeur's. 'We make good progress.'

'Needs to be faster,' Leoncoeur replied, still preoccupied with the pace. With every passing day, the prospect of missing out on the battle loomed a little larger.

Jhared laughed easily. 'We are the best of the realm. Command greater speed, and we will answer.'

'I have no doubt of it,' said Leoncoeur, scouring the skies ahead. The clouds remained blank and unmoving, which troubled him. He had not chosen the route across the Pale Ladies idly, but his hopes had not yet come to fruition.

'Do you search for spies?' asked Jhared, half-seriously. 'Have the Dark Gods turned even the birds of the air?'

Leoncoeur snorted a bitter laugh. 'Do not jest.' He inclined his head a little, sniffing the air carefully. 'But do you not sense them? You disappoint me.'

Jhared looked amused, then uncertain, and peered up into the skies in turn. 'Pray, what am I looking for?' he asked, just as the question became superfluous.

Ahead of them, where the land rose steeply towards a forked granite peak, the clouds suddenly swirled, like cream stirred in a pail. Leoncoeur held up his gauntlet, and the column clanked to a halt. He drew himself up in his saddle, turning to address the long train of knights behind him.

'Stand fast, brothers!' he cried. 'You are not the only warriors to answer my summons.'

As the words left his mouth, the clouds were pierced by a dozen winged horses, swooping earthwards with the poise and grace of swans in flight. Their outstretched pinions gleamed like pristine ivory, and their proud heads tossed and bucked. More pegasi emerged in their wake, flying in formation. They wheeled around in a wide arc, galloping through the high airs just as their earthbound cousins did on the charge.

Jhared whooped with joy, as all Bretonnians did at the sight of such rare and prized steeds. 'Never so many!' he exclaimed, eyes shining. 'In the name of the Lady, how did you achieve this?'

Leoncoeur could not stifle a laugh himself. It felt good, after so many months of brooding. The sky-host circled above them, four-score of the semi-wild pegasi of the mountains, each of them answering the call he had sent out, trusting to the Lady's influence that the summons would be answered. 'I was lord of this realm, once,' he said, watching them soar. 'That still counts for something.'

Jhared looked at him wonderingly. 'So it does. But how did you give them the summons? These are wild creatures.'

Leoncoeur smiled. 'I have one loyal servant who never lost faith.'

As the last of the pegasi emerged from the cloudbanks, they were followed by a far huger creature, a bizarre amalgam of raptor and horse, with a greater wingspan and a bulkier, more powerful body. Where the pegasi soared across the skies with an acrobat's grace, this creature plunged through the air like a galleon crashing through breakers. It dropped rapidly, folding its huge wings as it extended four huge clawed legs beneath it.

Leoncoeur's mount reared up, panicked by the plummet of the monstrous beast. 'Fear not!' Leoncoeur commanded, yanking hard on the reins. 'This is your cousin, and it would no more eat horseflesh than I would.'

The huge hippogryph landed heavily before them, flexing its shaggy limbs and cawing harshly. Leoncoeur dismounted and raced over to it. The beast lowered its beaked head and nuzzled against its master's embrace. Leoncoeur breathed in the familiar aroma again, and it instantly reminded him of past wars and past victories.

'Beaquis,' he murmured, feeling the plumage brush past. 'Now I am complete.'

Then he turned to the assembled knights, and laughed again. It was a pure laugh, a warrior's laugh, free of the care that had trammelled it for so long.

'Can any doubt the favour of the Lady now?' he cried. 'With weapons such as these, what enemy will dare stand against us?'

The knights roared back their approval, hammering on their shields with the hilts of their blades. At the head of the column, Jhared saluted his liege.

'Smartly done, my lord,' he said, bowing as the pegasi circled above them all protectively.

Leoncoeur gave Beaquis a final affectionate thump on the thickly muscled neck, then strode back to his stamping, wide-eyed mount. 'They will fly before us over the mountains. They will take saddle and halter when Altdorf is in sight, and not before. I will not have them wearied before time.'

Then he mounted once more, and kicked his horse back into motion. 'Until then, the march continues. Ride on.'

The sun slanted weakly through the high windows of the Imperial Chamber of War, striking the veined marble floor in thin grey streaks. Columns soared up around the chamber's circular perimeter, enclosing a vast auditorium of concentric seats. The hall's capacity was considerable, for it had been designed to hold representatives from every elector's staff, every senior ranking magister from the Colleges, the Grand Theogonist and representatives of the sanctioned Imperial Cults, the Engineering Colleges, the Knightly Orders and the standing regiments of the Empire, plus trading guild observers and members of the various diplomatic corps from all over the known world.

Looking up from his throne at the very centre of the chamber, Helborg noted how sparsely it was filled. Fewer than two hundred seats were occupied, and most of those by deputies and functionaries. The three resident elector counts sat in the inner circle, along with their official staff and some minor Imperial courtiers. The Colleges of Magic had sent four delegates, including the peasant-stock charlatan Gregor Martak, whose presence in the Imperial Palace continued to baffle Helborg. Zintler was there, as well as von Kleistervoll and a few dozen high-ranking generals. The Knightly Orders were headed by the brute figure of Gerhard von Sleivor, Grand Master of the Knights Panther, who sat brooding with eight of his peers in full plate armour. Several other delegates were unknown to Helborg, which in itself was an eloquent statement of how far the defenders' numbers had been thinned.

'Very well,' he said thickly, feeling the weight of his eyelids as he looked down the long agenda. 'What is next?'

'The forest draws close to the walls,' said Magister Anne-Louisa Trinckel of the Jade College, her grey hair falling messily around a droopy face. 'It must be culled, for the growths are not natural.'

'It is scheduled to be done, Herrin Magister,' said Helborg, wondering how on earth such a woman came to be the head of her Order. 'We are short of men, and the rebuilding of the outer walls takes priority.'

'That is a mistake,' said Trinckel, looking around her for support. 'The enemy will use the trees. There is *power* in the trees. We have long counselled that the felling of the forest has been neglected – now the consequences have come to haunt us.'

Helborg shot a dark glance at Zintler. 'Do we have any work details that can be spared?'

Zintler raised an eyebrow. 'Spared?'

Helborg nodded, understanding his frustration. Every able-bodied man and woman in the entire city was being worked to exhaustion just to keep on top of the landslide of tasks. The state troopers were being drilled relentlessly, the engineers spent hours atop rickety scaffolds working on the fortifications, the gunnery crews ceaselessly practised running out the great cannons and re-arming the mortar launchers.

'I am sorry, magister,' Helborg said, remembering the courtesies with some difficulty. 'At this time, we just do not have the hands for the task.'

Trinckel was about to protest, when she was overruled by Arek Fleischer, the acting Arch-Lector of the Church of Sigmar. 'Forget the trees!' he blurted impatiently. 'The temples are falling into ruin. We are nothing without *faith*. My priests have been pressed into the service of the army, even those who do not carry the warhammer. This is unacceptable – they are not trained for war.'

Von Sleivor slammed his armoured fist on the table before him. 'Where is Volkmar?' he hissed. 'He would have had you drawn and quartered for less – priests must do their part.'

'The temples will be restored, arch-lector,' explained Helborg, as patiently as he could. 'Now, though, is not the time. All must take their turn on the walls. Surely you can see our weakness is in numbers?' Fleischer did not look convinced. Helborg attempted to smile, knowing that it was more likely to emerge as a grimace. The arts of persuasion, rather than brute force, did not come easily. 'I myself fought with Luthor Huss, your brother-in-arms. There is no finer warrior in the Empire. Surely *he* is the example we should be following here.'

At the mention of Huss, Fleischer's face reddened, and he started to shout something unintelligible about heresies even in the bosom of Sigmar's congregation. This was angrily contested by Magister Willibald de Champney, the ludicrously coiffured magister of the Celestial College, appointed following the departure to war of his superior Raphael Julevno. His fellow wizards soon piled in on his behalf, following by Haupt-Anderssen's chief of staff and the Grand Master of the Knights of the Sable Chalice.

'Silence!' roared Helborg, standing up and smashing his gavel on the lectern before him. His voice rang around the chamber, quelling the restive quarrels before they became unstoppable. Looking down, he realised he had snapped the small hammer with the force of his strike.

A broken hammer. Oddly appropriate.

'This is a council of *war*, my lords,' said Helborg, his darkening visage sweeping the rows of occupied chairs before him. Not for the first time, he wondered just how Karl Franz had kept such a disparate and dysfunctional body politic operational for so long. 'With every passing day, the enemy comes closer. Marienburg has already fallen. We have no word from Talabheim or Middenheim. The river-passages are closed to us, and our attempts to contact Nuln and Couronne have yielded nothing. If we are to survive this, we will have to start worrying less about *trees* and *temples* and more about *blades* and *blackpowder.*'

For the first time, Helborg let a little of the parade-ground earthiness into his speech, and his voice assumed the rasping quality it took on when ordering his knights into the charge. Some of the assembled worthies, like von Kleistervoll and Sleivor, appreciated that. Others, the electors among them, murmured unhappily among themselves.

'Now,' said Helborg, deliberately inflecting his words with as much calm, clear authority as he could, 'let us take stock of what we have determined here. The remaining grain supplies will be removed to the main barracks, as will the surviving quantities of ale and unspoiled water. We will carry out the levy in the poor quarters, drafting any man who can stand into the reserve battalions under General von Hildenshaft. There will be *no exemptions* from the watch rotations. When the enemy gets here, I wish to see every able hand clutching a sword.'

Then he fixed his eyes on each of the delegates in turn, daring them to question the scant resolutions that had been painstakingly agreed. 'Is there anything else?' he asked.

Only one man had the gall to stand. With a sinking feeling in the pit of his stomach, Helborg recognised Martak.

'I come to speak of the Rot,' said the Supreme Patriarch, speaking haltingly in his strangely accented Reikspiel. 'It does not matter how strong we make the walls – the plague spreads from within. We must purge the undercity.'

Martak's voice fell flat in the huge echoing spaces of the chamber. As soon as he mentioned the Rot, irritated muttering started up again.

'There is no such thing,' said von Liebwitz confidently. 'If the peasants only bathed more and ceased their rutting, all this sickness would cease.'

'It is carried by the air,' opined de Champney, to much nodding from his fellow magisters. 'It cannot be eradicated while the foul winds blow.'

'It comes from the river,' said Fleischer. 'And we will not dam that.'

Helborg felt a vice of weariness settle like a yoke on his shoulders. Was there *nothing* they could agree on? 'And just what do you suggest, my lord Patriarch?' he asked. 'As you can clearly see, every ready hand already has a task to perform.'

'I need teams of armed soldiers,' said Martak. 'A hundred strong each, all to be led by a magister of my colleges. The Rot rises from the sewers. Only by purging them all can we reach the source.'

'Purge them all?' blurted Elector Gausser. 'You are mad, Supreme Patriarch.'

'It cannot be done,' added one of the master engineers, a bearded man with a bronze-rimmed monocle and gold braids on his epaulettes. 'The undercity runs for dozens of miles.'

Martak remained calm in the face of the scorn. Throughout the uproar, his steady gaze never left Helborg. 'Something is working against us down there,' he insisted. 'Something that grows stronger. It must be rooted out.'

Helborg struggled to control his irritation. Martak had not bothered to pull out the straggles in his filthy beard. Helborg could smell the man from twenty paces away, and his robes, such as they were, were streaked with dirt. 'I do not doubt you,' Helborg said, trying not to let his jaw clench. 'But there is no question of those numbers. They are needed on the walls.'

'Just one company, then,' said Martak, stubbornly. 'I will lead it myself.'

'Out of the question.'

Martak bristled. 'You're... *banning* me?'

The insolence was intolerable. For a moment, fatigue made Helborg think he was addressing some dishevelled soldier out on the fields of war, and he nearly drew his blade. 'This is not a priority,' he growled.

'Have you been down to the poor quarter?'

'Of course not. Do not deflect this to some-'

'They are dying down there. Dying like dogs.'

'I cannot be concerned about that now.'

'Your whole city is dying, Reiksmarshal.'

'Silence. You have had your-'

'The city is dying before your eyes and you cannot see it.'

'I said, silence!'

'If the Emperor were here-'

'*Enough!*' Helborg's raw shout echoed from the high vaults, shocking even the hardened warriors into startled looks. 'Who *are* you? What pit of filth were you drawn up from, to be thrust into my face like some mockery of your ancient office?'

The words poured like water from Helborg's mouth. The anger made him feel *alive*, after so many hours, so many days, biting his tongue and abasing himself before men he would have slain on the battlefield without a second thought. Once he started, he could not stop – it was cathartic, to vent his spleen again, to pour out all his pent-up fury and frustration at a single source.

'You come here dressed like some peddler from the backwoods of Stirland's foulest shit-hole and dare to address the Reiksmarshal of the Empire? You *dare*? I walked these streets for decades while you rolled in the muck of the Reikswood and sniffed the spoor-trails of beasts. This is *my* city! It is *my city!* If you wish to challenge that, then Sigmar damn you and you may leave it!'

The echoes lingered for a while after the spittle-laced tirade had ceased. No one spoke. A few mouths hung open.

Martak himself remained icily calm. His brown eyes never left Helborg's, who stood, trembling with rage, his chin jutting defiantly.

Then, very slowly, Martak drew in a long breath. 'So we understand one another,' he said, his gruff, uncultured voice heavy with contempt.

He shuffled from his place, and clumped heavily down to the chamber floor. As he left, his shoulders held stiffly, his clogs clanked noisily against the marble. It took a long time for him to leave, and the clanks rang out uncomfortably until at last he had been ushered into the corridors outside.

Gradually, Helborg recovered his composure. Almost immediately, the loss of control shocked him. Part of him wanted to rush after Martak, to apologise, to explain that he had not slept for days and that the burden of wresting an entire city from its indolence and dragging it into a war that every instinct told him could not be won was more than any man could bear.

But he could not, not with the eyes of the entire council on him. He was still the Reiksmarshal, and a display of weakness now, any weakness, would see the electors onto him like wolves on a lamb.

There were always disagreements. They could be overcome later. For now, what mattered was *control* – keeping Altdorf together just long enough to give it a chance.

Moving stiffly, he sat down again. The silence in the chamber was total.

Clearing his throat, Helborg turned a leaf of parchment over, moving to the next item on the long agenda.

'Now then,' he said, forcing his voice once more into calmness, as if nothing untoward had just happened. 'Where were we?'

◄ CHAPTER TWELVE ►

It look Karl Franz a long time to find his quarry. Something had changed since his fall, and a kind of prescience seemed to have lodged in his mind. The world around him seemed a little more vivid than it had done, as if the colours and smells had somehow cranked up. He saw more, he felt more, and his dreams were as startlingly immediate as anything that happened when awake.

Chief among those dreams was the figure of the great antlered god, reeling under the influence of a thousand cuts. Like some stricken stag, the god stumbled in a fog of darkness, assailed from every side by hidden foes. When Karl Franz saw the wounds in the god's flanks and limbs, he wanted to weep.

He saw other things, too. Every night he had the same vision – a bearded man in dirty robes pacing on the battlements of a far city. In the depths of his slumber, he would call out to that man, not knowing why. He never answered, lost in struggles of his own.

In his waking hours, Karl Franz nursed himself back to something like strength. The wilds of the north were vast beyond imagining, and even with the hordes of Chaos marching through them, there were still blank tracts where he could hide and gather strength. There was even food to be found for those with sharp eyes and a searching mind, and since his rebirth Karl Franz had never had sharper eyes.

He knew he needed to head south, tracing the path of whatever remained of his once-mighty armies. He had no idea how many of his generals had survived. Helborg, surely, was dead, since the greater daemon at Heffengen had been a foe beyond him. He could not quite believe that Schwarzhelm was also gone, nor Huss, but there were no clues as to where they had been driven by fate and the currents of war. His thoughts turned to Valten often. That youth had been the great hope for so many – an image of Sigmar for troubled times. Perhaps he still would be, though it was hard to see what he could accomplish now.

For the time being, though, Karl Franz did not hurry to quit the wasteland.

He followed the trails of warbands, creeping close to the bonfires at night and doing what he could to divine the movements of the fractured hosts. He understood some of what they said to one another, picking up meaning from the guttural speech of the north in a way he had never been able to do before. One word was repeated over and over again – Glottkin – though he had no idea what it meant.

He heard other words he did recognise – Talabheim, Drakwald, Altdorf. The plan of attack was simple – striking towards the Empire's heart, just as he had told Helborg.

He would never make it to the city, though, not alone and on foot. The leaguer had been broken, and he was already a long way north of the rolling battlefront. He was isolated, cut off in a desolate land of refugees and broken corpses.

As the sun set on another lonely day of foraging, Karl Franz crouched low amid a thicket of briars. With a twinge of wry amusement, he wondered how he must have looked – the Emperor of the greatest realm of men on earth, crouching like a beggar amid thorns, his beard ragged and his clothes torn.

Ahead of him, blood-red in the gathering dusk, burned another campfire. Armed men sat around it, grunting and slurping. Something turned on a spit above the coals, too big to be a hog, though with a similar stench to burning pork. There must have been over twenty warriors there, hulking tribesmen from the far reaches of the Chaos Wastes with bones hammered through their cheeks and god-marks inked on nearly every inch of exposed flesh.

They were careless, marching through a land they had scoured of enemies, and the watch was lax. Karl Franz saw a ramshackle corral on the far side of the camp, and noted the lack of guards. Just one sentry, half-asleep and resentful at being banished from the fireside, huddled against the driving wind, wrapped in a thick, fur-lined cloak.

Going silently, keeping low, Karl Franz crept away from the flickering light-circle and skirted around the edge of the campsite. Hugging the scant cover of the thorn-bushes, he edged closer to the lone sentry. Once within strike-range, he crouched down again, his hand on the hilt of his blade, and waited for the moment.

The sentry was a balding, bearded man with boiled leather armour and an iron ring through his nose. His head slid forward, his eyes half-closed.

Karl Franz moved. Padding softly, he sprinted over to the half-aware guard. Before he had had time to look up, *Drachenzahn* had slipped silently into his neck, killing him instantly. Karl Franz lowered the body to the ground, casting a wary eye over at the campfire.

The tribesmen were still eating, tearing chunks of meat from the spit and ripping it with their teeth. Karl Franz propped the sentry back up, making it look as if he was simply slumped against the cold earth, then moved towards the stockade.

It was a clumsy, makeshift thing, no more than shafts of wood nailed loosely together and crowned with a crude fence of twisted thorn-vines. By rights it should not have held its prisoner for more than a few moments. Karl Franz could already smell the familiar musk, though there was something else there too – the over-sweet tang of muscle rot.

He prised the planks of the stockade apart, and squeezed inside. Deathclaw immediately hissed, and tried to rise, but long leather bindings held the creature down. Karl Franz hurried over to the griffon, sheathing his blade.

'Calm, great one,' he whispered. 'You know your master.'

The huge creature immediately relaxed, and the hissing turned to a low rumble within its cavernous chest.

The creature had been sorely abused. Both wings looked broken, and dozens of arrow-shafts protruded from its flanks. Clumps of plumage had been ripped from its haunches, leaving bloody weals glistening wetly in the faint light. It had been tied to stakes hammered into the ground, its limbs compressed into a permanent crouch.

As soon as Karl Franz had severed the last of the leather bindings, the griffon nearly collapsed, issuing a strangled caw of pain as its tormented muscles gave way.

Karl Franz hurried over to its head, cradling the thick neck in his arms. He reached for the amulet and pressed it against the creature's rapidly beating heart.

Gradually, the griffon's yellow eye regained focus. Its heartbeat slowed to normal, and something like firmness returned to its stance.

'This will be painful,' said Karl Franz, hearing the first noises of alarm from the campfire. 'But it is better to be alive and in pain, yes?'

Deathclaw hissed an angry response. From outside the stockade, Karl Franz heard the tramp of boots running and the cries of the blasphemous northern tongue.

'You have the strength for this?' he asked, brandishing his runefang.

By way of answer, Deathclaw dragged itself to its haunches, staggered over to the corral's wall and hurled itself into it. Freed from its bonds, it smashed through the wooden staves, ripping them up and tossing them aside with an imperious flash of copper-gold plumage. The Norscans halted in their charge, suddenly faced with a freed griffon, one whose anger they had stoked over long nights of torment and who now faced them with the flash of bestial fury in its eyes.

'The vengeance of Sigmar!' roared Karl Franz, charging into battle alongside the enraged Deathclaw. Even wounded, the unshackled creature was more than a match for its captors, and Drachenzahn knew it would drink deep before the night was done.

The Norscans charged straight back at them, bellowing their strange war-curses with flamboyant bravery. As Karl Franz scythed his blade around for the first strike, cracking heavily against a blunted axe-face, he felt a strange euphoria thrill through his ravaged body.

I am fighting again, he thought, as the runefang danced and the shrieks of the enraged war-griffon split the night. *May it never cease.*

The town of Wurtbad clung to the southern shore of the Reik, a sprawling conurbation built by the trading guilds who plied the great river barges down to Altdorf and the coast beyond. It was not distinguished by grand buildings or fine fortifications – it was a functional place, built by practical men for practical purposes. A thick stone wall ringed a motley collection of townhouses, inns, warehouses and loading derricks. Even by the standards of the provinces, it had always had a shady reputation, the kind of place a cunning man would make a fortune and a simple one would lose it. Taverns and bawdy-houses crowded the streets, jostling alongside temples, barracks and customs stations.

Since the start of the troubles, Wurtbad had been hit hard. First the barges had stopped coming down from the north. No explanation for the stop in traffic had ever been forthcoming, so the burgomeister sent members of the City Watch upriver to investigate. They came back on a single, empty vessel, hanging from meat-hooks amid piles of rotting pig carcasses.

Then news of the war in the north had come in, carried by draggled refugees from Stirland and the Ostermark. As the Empire's creaking war-machine responded, some of the cannier Wurtbad merchants made a quick profit hawking supplies to desperate generals at inflated prices. For a time, the passage of arms wending its way up the river from Nuln and Altdorf kept the taverns and brothels in roaring business, and, also for a time, a steady flow of regiments kept coming to replace those ordered onwards.

Then the flow dried up. Every company due to be sent to the distant front was deployed, hollowing out the defences along the Reik and the Stir. The streets fell quiet and the warehouses were locked. Barges stood empty at their berths, waiting for trade to resume, just as it always had when the worst was over.

Except that, this time, no soldiers returned from the north. No proclamations came out of Altdorf celebrating deliverance in Sigmar's name. The temples began to fill, as a previously ambivalent populace suddenly remembered its piety.

The plagues came next. No one knew from where – perhaps the thick miasmas churning in from the east, or the lines of impoverished peasants fleeing the blight in the fields, or the curdling waters themselves as they lapped the empty wharfs. Soon the bodies were piling up, and every dawn a new cart left the town gates, heaped high with cloth-covered lumps. After a while even those stopped – no one dared venture out to where the forest sprouted unnaturally under the endless sheets of rain, and so the dead lay festering in the rubbish pits where they had been dragged.

By the time the watchmen on the southern wall caught sight of black banners on the far horizon, few believed the newcomers brought salvation with them. A few zealots started chanting, taking a kind of perverse, vicious pleasure in the vindication of their endless prophecies of the End Times. The rest of the city's survivors grimly took up arms. The gates remained locked and barred, and every surviving militia member was called to the armouries to equip. Then they waited, watching the sable-clad host creep closer through the cloying mists.

The new arrivals did not advance further while the sun shone. They waited south of the river, issuing no challenge and making no demands. Inside the town, a vociferous and terrified faction argued that the burgomeister should sue for peace, since the garrison was in no condition to resist a siege and the Empire, such as it still was, had clearly abandoned them. By nightfall, as the true nature of the attackers became horrifyingly clear, those voices subsided, and a gnawing, crawling fog of despair took over.

Ghouls flickered through the frigid air, screaming at a gravid Morrslieb above. Flocks of bats raced across the sky, their blood-red eyes glowing in the velvet dark. Rank upon rank of bone-white warriors advanced under death's-head banners, never issuing a sound. Some warriors stalked by their own will; others glowed luminously from within with the flickering light of corposant, impelled by the necromancers who cried out in grave-scraped voices and whirled staffs hung with clattering human skulls.

Black-armoured knights nudged bony steeds through the undead throng, and wights wearing ancient tomb-garb limped and shuffled in their wake. Most horrifying of all were the vargheists, which loped into battle with huge, ungainly strides, half-flying, half-running, their animalistic faces twisted with bloodlust and their claws already extended.

At the sight of that onslaught, many of Wurtbad's mortal defenders lost heart and fled, wailing that the gods had abandoned them, trying to find somewhere in the shadowy maze of the narrow streets to hide. Others stood firmer. The burgomeister, Jens Bohr, was a veteran of the state levy and had faced down larger armies of greenskins in his time. His warrior priest, a fervent Sigmarite by the name of Kalvin Wolff, whipped the remaining troopers into a frenzy of pious defiance. Huge fires were kindled across the walls, flooding the land beyond in a writhing aura of crimson. Every captain on the walls was given a flaming brand, and teams of runners kept the stores of wood replenished. Desperate battle-hymns rose up from the battlements, competing with the shrieks of the living dead.

That did not stop the vice closing. Gradually, the undead host spread out, moving up the southern bank of the Stir and crossing the flood on either side of the town. The still-living troops traversed using barges looted from further upstream, while the truly dead simply waded across the river bed, emerging on the far bank covered in a thick layer of slime and weeds.

Then, once Wurtbad had been fully surrounded, the assault began.

The night's cacophony was broken by the snap and rattle of trebuchets. The warped machines, looking more like giant ribcages than engines of war, hurled clusters of human skulls high over the walls, and where they impacted, they exploded in gouts of greenish gas. Any defenders too close to the impacts immediately succumbed to the blooms, their skin falling in shreds from their bones. They died in agony, clawing at their own sinews as their bodies fell apart around them.

Next came the bats. Some were taken down by hurried volleys of arrows, but most got through, grabbing men from the parapet and sending them tumbling, their chests torn out. Ghouls and grave-shades followed, floating eerily over the defensive perimeter in shimmering clusters and latching their cold magic around any who dared face them.

As the walls were ringed with horrors, the greater mass of skeletons and zombies reached the base and started to raise siege ladders. Dozens were cast down by the defenders, but more were immediately hoisted up. Whenever a weakness was isolated, deathly warriors surged up into the breach, falling into soundless combat with the troopers who rushed to repel them.

For all the ferocity of the initial assault, however, the main ring of defence held firm. The roaring fires did their job, daunting the undead horde and preventing them from advancing recklessly. Wolff kept up his furious defiance, showing the way by smashing swathes of skeletons apart with his warhammer. Bohr used his limited corps of gunners well, picking out champions with as much accuracy as the fire-flared night would allow.

Ladders were cast down, smashing amongst the seething masses below. The zombies moved too slowly to evade the blades of determined defenders, who fought with the ferocity of men who knew their lives were forfeit if they faltered. Some of those who had fled at the first sign of the undead recovered their spirits and returned, shamefaced, to the fray, shuddering with fear but still able to clutch a weapon in their clammy hands.

Combat raged on the wall-tops for over two hours, with neither side able to land the killer strike. The fires continued to crackle, the hymns rang out, but the undead could not be shaken from their grip, and just kept on coming.

If any Imperial chronicler had been present on that night to witness the battle of Wurtbad, he would have noted, perhaps with some grim pride, that the end did not come from outside. Freed from the need to guard their backs, the defenders of Wurtbad might have held out through the darkness, perhaps using the dawn to clear their besieged walls and restore a solid line of defence. But just as the undead attack began to lose momentum, a fell prince in blood-red armour rose up in his saddle, standing high above the town on a rise north of the river. He raised a lone, clawed hand, holding it palm-upward, and cried out words in a language of the distant hot sands. Those words somehow cut through the clamour of fighting, piercing the soul of every mortal and sending the undead advancing with renewed energy. A ring blazed from his withered finger, sending coils of smoke churning out into the night.

For a few moments, nothing else happened. The deadly struggle continued, and the battle-cries kept coming. Wolff even managed to clear the enemy from the summit of the southern gatehouse, felling a vargheist with a savage blow from his hammer before launching himself at the lesser troops.

But then the earth began to boil. Sodden soils shifted, churning like molten oil. A wild snap rang out across the city, and the air buckled with actinic lightning.

The first hand shot up from the ground, withered and pale. Then another, then a dozen more. Corpses pulled themselves free from their graves, hauling their etiolated bodies out of the mire. The tottering cadavers swayed for a moment, then set off, shuffling blearily towards the noise of combat.

The people of Wurtbad had not been foolish – they had always buried their dead outside the city walls, facing down and with the marks of Morr set over their graves. But now the Law of Death had been breached, and those many hundreds who had died on the site of the town before Wurtbad had been established as an outpost of Sigmar's Empire suddenly shifted in their cold slumber. With a shiver and a sigh, they came scratching and scrabbling back into animation. Arcane armour of lost ages and blades long-rusted into stabbing stumps cracked up through the topsoil, followed by creaking bodies slaved to a new master.

It took a while for the new arrivals to be noticed. Intent on keeping the walls free of attackers, the troops of Wurtbad resolutely devoted their attentions to the host at their gates. By the time the screaming from the heart of the town could no longer be ignored, it was too late.

Hundreds of living dead had been wrenched from their ancient graves, and they thronged in Wurtbad's alleys and backstreets, twittering and hissing. With blank, rotting faces, they dragged themselves towards the living, their only desire now to drink the hot, dark liquor of mortal blood. They crept out of the town's central courtyards and fanned out through the crooked streets, feasting on any unfortunates they were able to overwhelm. Even the river-rats, which had clustered in Wurtbad's river-front, ran before them, streaming out towards the outer walls in a rippling wave of panicked grey.

Wolff was the first to notice the tumult. Dispatching a final skeleton into a clattering pile of bones, he plunged down from his position over the gates, leading a charge against the growing crowds of living dead within the town's perimeter. Others joined him, and the fragile bodies of the newly-raised were soon being cracked and smashed apart.

That left the walls depleted, though, just as the shot for the gunners began to run low and the fires lost their vigour. The hordes outside sensed the presence of their kin on the inside, and the assault redoubled in ferocity. The real killers among the skeletal army took their chance, and armour-clad warriors wearing tattered cloaks and ornate liveries of forgotten, cruel ages pushed up the siege ladders and on to the parapets.

Dark magic raced across the night, reaching a crescendo in tandem with the greater mass of human screaming. The fires began to die one by one, doused and chilled by the advancing dead, and shadows welled and pooled more thickly, plunging Wurtbad into a slick of oily darkness.

The battle-hymns rang out right until the end, growing fainter as more and more defenders were cut down. Those mortals who were slain did not rest easily, but soon got up again, this time taking the fight to their erstwhile comrades, and so the advance of the undead grew ever stronger as the will of men was eroded.

Bohr was eventually killed after his position at the northern gate was overrun by ghouls. He died shouting in outraged defiance even as icy fingers were plunged into his thick chest and his heart was ripped out. With the death of the burgomeister, the last organised defence of the northern walls collapsed, and those who could ran for whatever temporary refuge they could find.

Knowing the futility of flight, and knowing too that hope had gone, Wolff was the last one standing. He cut his way back to his temple, gathering a few dozen of the stoutest defenders around him as he went. They made a stand before the dome of the Sigmarite chapel, overlooked by granite statues of griffons and with the final bonfires guttering about them.

Waves of undead swept towards them, chattering excitedly as they sensed the prospect of drinking the blood of the valiant, but all were repelled. Wolff's band held the outer precinct against them all, hacking and smashing with desperate strokes until the ground at their feet was knee-deep in broken bones and parchment-dry flesh.

One by one, though, fatigue and ill-chance took their toll. The relentless numbers could not be defied forever, and in the end Wolff stood alone, his throat raw from war cries and his hammer as heavy as lead in his bloodied fists.

Just as the vanguard of the undead host was poised to launch a final push, though, a chill voice rang out. The undead fell back instantly, shuffling into the shadows and clearing a space before the temple gates.

Wolff stood under the lintel, his forehead sheened with sweat, breathing heavily. Between the parted crowds of lesser warriors, the Master of the Host strode out, his black robes rustling in the wind. Ice-white hair rippled about his shoulders, part-obscuring the scarred and cracked mask of his skin. The ring he had used to raise Wurtbad's dead still smouldered on his finger.

The warrior priest did not flinch. His eyes fixed on the vampire lord's, and never moved. He murmured battle-curses in an endless litany, and prepared to lift his hammer once more. He knew he was overmatched, but he could at least die on his feet, taking the fight to the enemy just as his immortal patron demanded.

Then Vlad von Carstein spoke.

'You too may serve,' said the vampire, coming to a halt before the priest and folding his arms. He made no attempt to defend himself, even though he was in range of the warhammer's strike. 'This is why we do this. You are too good to be sacrificed to gods who appreciate nothing but mania.'

Wolff's lip pulled back in contempt. 'Your kind has come this way before,' he snarled. 'You were always turned back. You will be again.'

'By whom?' Vlad sighed. 'There is nothing left. Look around you – you can see what ruins remain.'

'From ruins come glory. From the darkness comes light.'

Vlad smiled thinly. 'Come, you have fought enough. I always offer the valiant a place at my side – take the offer, priest. You can still fight against the greater darkness.'

'At your side?' Wolff laughed. 'You know so little that you would even ask?' He spat at the vampire, and the spittle landed on the crimson armour, sliding across its lacquered surface. 'You have come amongst *men*, abomination. You may crush us for a time, you may tread across our broken bodies and burn our temples and strong places, but we will always come back at you. If I were given a thousand lifetimes, I would choose the same path every time – to *smite* you with the holy fire of my calling.' He smiled with contempt. 'And you came too close.'

He swung his warhammer. It was a fine strike, one that Huss himself would have been proud of – fast, hard, well-aimed. The hammer-head flew out, angled at the vampire's neck.

At the same time, a single shot pierced the night, just as well-aimed. It struck Wolff clean in the forehead, penetrating the bone and punching a clean, round hole through his skull. The warhammer clanged to the ground, and the warrior priest tumbled backward, collapsing under the lintel of his own temple before coming to rest amid the shattered bones of his victims.

Vlad looked down at the corpse thoughtfully. The man's zeal had been striking. Had he himself been capable of such fervour, once? Of course he had, but it was hard to remember just how it felt.

Herrscher emerged into the light, his pistol still smoking. The witch hunter had a tortured look on his face.

'There,' said Vlad, turning away from Wolff to look at him. 'That was not so hard.'

'I could not let you be harmed,' said Herrscher, his voice shaking. 'I killed... my own.'

'He is not your own,' said Vlad, impatiently. 'Look around you. *We* are yours, you are ours. You have killed for us, and we will kill for you.'

Herrscher looked like he wanted to vomit, though his body was no longer capable of it. Before he could reply, the sound of overlapping laughter wafted across the temple courtyard.

Liliet and her sisters had climbed on to the dome of the temple. Their

gowns were streaked with blood, and it dripped from their long finger-
nails like tears.

'Rejoice!' they chorused. 'A thousand new blades for the army of the
night-born! A thousand more to come before dawn-fall!'

All across Wurtbad, those of Vlad's army with the self-command to
respond lifted their parched voices in victory-cries.

Vlad laid a gauntlet on Herrscher's shoulder. 'The Empire trains its hunters well – that was a good shot.' Then he turned on his heels, his cloak
swirling about him, and strode away from the temple, back towards the
river-front where the empty barges had been tethered, ready for the passage
of the Reik. 'Do not dwell on it. The night is still dark, and we have work to
do. By the dawn, our new servants must be on the move.'

Martak's fury took a long time to ebb. He had stormed up to his barely used
chambers in the Imperial Palace and smashed a few things up in there.
He gave a glimmering simulacrum of Helborg's gaunt face to every item
he hurled across the room before it smashed into the wall.

No one dared interrupt him. By then, every servant in the Palace had
all heard tales of the half-feral Supreme Patriarch, and kept their distance.
Gelt had been capable of rages, but at least he was vaguely understandable.
Martak, deprived of even that measure of respect, took a grim satisfaction
in causing fear instead.

Let them fear me, he snarled to himself. *They deserve what is to come.*

He did not mean that. No one deserved the horrors that lay ahead, not
even the stiff-necked Reiksmarshal, and certainly not the flunkeys who
struggled to do his impossible bidding.

By the time he had calmed down, his personal chamber was a mass of
ripped parchment and broken crockery, and he was a sweaty, panting mess.

Martak cracked his knuckles, stomped over to the chamber's narrow
window and pushed the lead catch open. The window faced east, giving a
view out over the great mass of the city.

He took a deep breath. The stench was becoming unbearable, even at
such a height. He thought again of Margrit – sensible, dutiful Margrit. He
had promised her that something would be done. Every hour that the Rot
was allowed to swell and grow was another hour for the temple's supplies
to run down and the energies of the sisters to ebb a little further.

He propped his elbows on the sill and rested his chin gloomily on locked
hands. Far below, the Reik was the colour of spoiled spinach and barely
flowed at all. He could make out the sullen blooms of algae lurking just
under the surface, and could smell the acrid stink of its steady fermentation.

He had made a mess of his short time as Patriarch. Helborg was making
a mess of the city defences, and the electors were making a mess of assist-
ing him. They were like children caught by the glare of a predator, frozen
and witless, unable to do more than bicker in the face of oncoming disaster.

It is the city.

The realisation came to him so suddenly and so easily that he immediately wondered how he had not seen it before.

It is the poison.

Martak was a creature of the wilds, of the windswept tracts of unbroken forest. He had been known to spend months in the wilderness, kept alive by his arts and native cunning, eschewing all comforts and embracing the idiosyncratic path of his college's disciplines.

I have allowed them to cage me. This is their world, not mine, and they have made me useless in it.

He was a sham Patriarch in a sham Empire, playing out his role in dumbshow as the world unravelled around them. He could not command men, and had no desire to. Helborg had been right about one thing: this was *his* city, not Martak's.

He stood up again, and shuffled over to the writing desk he had just half-smashed. After a few moments scrabbling around, he found a scrap of intact parchment and a near-empty jar of ink. He pulled a quill from under a disarranged collection of broken-spined tomes, and started to write. Once he had finished, he folded the parchment and sealed it, stowing the letter in his grimy robes.

Then he moved over to Gelt's old Globe of Transmigratory Vocalisation within a Localised Aethyric Vicinity – a bronze-bound sphere set atop an iron web of intricately-woven threads. It was a meagre device for one of such talents, but it had its uses.

Picking it up and setting it before him on the floor, Martak placed both palms on the cool surface of the sphere. Something like clockwork clicked inside it, and he felt the tremble of moving parts. Previously hidden runes glowed into life on the bronze, welling softly with a sudden heat.

Martak concentrated. This was Gelt's toy, and he still was not sure he had mastered it properly.

'Search her out,' he whispered gruffly, imposing his will on the machine's. 'The soul of Sister Margrit.'

It resisted him. The device knew its gold-masked master, and resented being used roughly by a stranger. In the end, though, Martak's presence prevailed, and the Globe performed its function. The air above it trembled, warmed, then parted, revealing a blurred and translucent image of Margrit's garden. The priestess herself was standing with her back to the Globe's view. As soon as Martak laid eyes on her, she stiffened, turned, and made a warding gesture.

'Be at ease, sister,' said Martak, knowing that he would appear to her as nothing more than a ghost, hanging above the herb-garden like a puff of steam in summer.

'Patriarch,' said Margrit, her voice muffled and distorted. She looked at him through the Globe's portal, peering as if into murky water. 'Could you not come in person?'

THE FALL OF ALTDORF

'I am leaving the city,' said Martak. A soon as he saw her face fall, he regretted his clumsy way with words.

'All is lost, then,' she said.

'No, you were right – the Emperor is master. While he remains lost, we cannot stand. I go to find him.'

Margrit's expression brightened into an almost childlike hope. 'You know where he is?'

'He is coming, sister. The stars foretell it, and the elements gather to witness it.' Martak had no idea whether this was true. All he had to go on were his dreams, which had been getting more vivid with every sleepless night. He had dismissed them for too long, and knew now that he should have listened to the whispered voices much earlier. 'It will not be easy, but yours will be the harder road. I can give you no promise the Reiks-marshal will act. I would stay, if I could, but...' He struggled for the words. 'This is not my place.'

Margrit nodded, accepting what he told her. 'Then you can give me no sign.'

Martak racked his mind for something that would appeal to her. 'When the hour is darkest,' he said, hoping he sounded vaguely plausible, 'look to the heavens above the Imperial Palace. Look for the sign of Sigmar reborn.' It was poor stuff, this deception and fakery, but it was all he had. 'In advance of that, *endure*, sister. Endure for as long as you are able.'

Margrit looked satisfied, and Martak found himself marvelling once again at her quiet resolve. Given the tiniest sliver of hope, she would hold fast to her station until the very ending of the world. If the Empire deserved any kind of salvation, it was for the ones like her – the faithful, the decent, the selfless.

'Do not be long gone, Patriarch,' Margrit said. 'I liked the colleges better with a wolf at the helm.'

Martak laughed, and bowed at the compliment. He would have been happy betting that Gelt had never walked the streets in the shadow of the temple. 'Go with Shallya, sister,' he said, and lifted his hands from the Globe. Margrit's image rippled into nothing, and the runes on the sphere faded back to blank bronze.

Back in the realm of the senses, Martak looked about him. His chamber looked as if an animal had got in and destroyed everything in its frantic efforts to escape again. Perhaps that was not so far from the truth.

He walked over to the heavy oak door and pulled it open. The corridor outside was empty, and he had to walk through two more antechambers before he found an official. The servant, wearing a crimson tunic marked with the sign of the griffon, looked startled to see the Supreme Patriarch back on the prowl.

'My lord?' he asked, shrinking from Martak's malodorous presence.

'Send this to the Reiksmarshal's office immediately,' said Martak, handing over the ink-stained letter. 'Ensure that it is placed before him at the first occasion – he will want to read it.'

The servant handled the letter nervously, as if it might be a mortar primed to go off in his hands. 'Very well, my lord. Where shall I tell him he may find you?'

Martak snorted. 'Find me? He'll have trouble.' He looked around him. The corridors and chambers of the Palace were still mostly a mystery to him, a vast web of tunnels and spirals and shafts and towers. 'But you can help me with one small thing.'

The servant looked up expectantly. Martak smiled darkly, already enjoying the thought of what he was going to do.

'Tell me,' he said, 'what is the quickest path to the Imperial Menagerie?'

◄ CHAPTER THIRTEEN ►

The wind was bitter and never-ending, driving down from the high peaks with the shrieks of fell voices echoing in its wake. The skies had turned from a screen of blank grey into a churned mass of violent thunderheads, surging and boiling as if some immeasurably vast pair of hands was tearing the heavens apart.

As Leoncoeur rode up to the head of the pass, wrapped in his cloak, the deluge drummed on the rocks around him. Rivulets poured down from the rising land ahead, slushing and bubbling as the torrent picked up pace, and the stony track up to the entrance to Axebite Pass was now little more than a stream of gushing water.

Ahead of the Bretonnian column reared the mighty peaks of the Grey Mountains, piled up into the tortured sky in ranked visions of granite-headed immensity. To Leoncocur's left soared the double-headed summit of Talareaux, called Graugeleitet by the Imperials. To his right was the colossal bulk of Findumonde, which the Empire dwellers called Iceheart. Both summits were lost in the haze of storms.

Gales were always strong in the passes, but those during this passage had been unreasonably ferocious. Baggage wains and valuable warhorses had been washed away on the precipitous pathways, and at times every footfall had been treacherous. Progress had slowed to a grim crawl. Each night, Leoncoeur had sat sullenly around the campfires with his lieutenants, noting the growing gap between where they were and where they wanted to be.

Still, they had persevered. The highlands had slowly fallen behind, replaced by the jagged, hard country of the mountains proper. The last of the pasture disappeared, replaced by a stone-land of sheer, hard-edged severity. The rain stung like ice, and the wind whipped it into wicked eddies, creeping into every fold of fabric and armour-joint.

The raw enthusiasm of the crusade was hard to sustain in such conditions. Battered by the ferocity of the elements, the knights kept their dripping heads low, saying little. The hundreds of peasant workers in the baggage train suffered worse, their coarse woollen garments offering little protection, and many succumbed during the frozen nights, left behind in scratched, shallow graves by the roadside.

As the head of the pass loomed before them at last, Leoncoeur called a halt. He peered ahead towards the high entrance. Slushy snow lay in grey-white drifts higher up, draped across the striated shoulders of the mountains. The winding road ahead was overlooked by near-vertical cliffs of broken-edged stone, narrowing near the summit to a gap of less than thirty feet across.

His eyes narrowed. He sniffed. It was near-impossible to sense much in the shifting gales, but *something* registered. Something he felt he ought to recognise.

Jhared drew alongside him. Of all of them, the flame-haired knight had retained his humours the best, but even he looked windswept and rain-soaked. 'Why are we halting, lord?' he asked, shivering as the driving sleet bounced from him.

'Can you hear it?' asked Leoncoeur, inclining his head a little.

Jhared listened, then shook his head.

Leoncoeur was about to speak again, when a hard, massed roar suddenly broke out from up ahead.

Every knight in the entourage knew that sound – it had been engraved on their minds from their earliest days. The ancestral enemies of the Bretonnians could be purged, burned and driven back a thousand times, but they would always come back.

'To arms!' cried Leoncoeur, drawing his sword in a spray of rain.

The column's vanguard formed up immediately, kicking their horses into a line and drawing weapons. Each knight carried a heavy-bladed broadsword, and they threw back their cloaks to expose moisture-slick breastplates marked with the livery of their houses.

Before the knights could charge, the gorge before them filled with what looked like a rolling tide of earth and rubble. It was accompanied by throaty bellows of challenge, rising quickly to a deafening crescendo that ripped through the scything curtains of sleet.

'Charge!' roared Leoncoeur, digging his spurs into his steed's flanks.

With a hoarse battle-cry, the Bretonnian vanguard surged along the throat of the gorge, picking up speed rapidly despite the treacherous footing. Accelerating to the gallop, ten horses abreast, they thundered towards the landslide hurtling towards them.

Except that it was no landslide. A host of green-skinned monsters had burst from cover, their red eyes blazing with fury. The rubble that came with them was flung from their backs as they emerged from the ambush, and stones the size of fists *thunked* and rolled about them. There must have been hundreds of orcs before them, all jostling and tearing down the funnel of the gorge, sliding on the slippery rock and trampling their own kind like cattle on a stampede.

When the two forces collided, it was with a sick, hard smash that sent the bodies of both orc and human flying. Bretonnian warhorses were huge, powerful beasts, and their whirling hooves were quite capable of cracking skulls and snapping ribcages. The greenskins were battle-hardened monsters, each of them far larger than a man and with corded, muscled limbs that hurled axes and mauls around with plate-denting force.

Leoncoeur crashed through the hard glut of the toughest of the orcs, laying about him in flamboyant sweeps of his blade. He rode his mount with imperious perfection, compensating for every buck and rear. As the greenskins clawed for him, he laid waste to them, hammering with all the pent-up strength of the long ride.

Jhared remained close by, working his own blade furiously. 'For the dead of Quenelles!' he thundered, his lank hair thrashing around his un-helmed head. 'For the dead of Lyonesse!'

Every knight of the company fought in the same way – with a cold anger generated by the many humiliations suffered by their realm. They were devastating on the charge, as pure and violent as the cascades around them. The orcs died in droves, and soon the rivulets at their feet ran black with blood.

Leoncoeur wheeled his steed around and thrust his sword point-first into the open maw of a slavering greenskin. He ripped the blade free in time to meet the swiped challenge of another, and a dull clang of metal on metal rang out. Two swift parries, and he had dispatched the next challenger.

The impetus of the orc attack was already failing. They began to retreat back up the gorge, desperate now to escape the close-serried Bretonnian onslaught. There was no escape for them that way, though, for the pegasi plummeted from the clouds, drawn by the scents and sounds of battle. Even without riders they were deadly, swooping low to lash out at the stumbling herd of greenskins.

'Let none escape!' shouted Leoncoeur, riding down a stumbling orc and spurring his mount towards the next. The Bretonnians loosened their formation as they gained momentum. Gilles de Lyonesse, a rider with a love of the chase that exceeded even his hunt-obsessed brethren, broke clear with a small band of like-minded brother-knights and galloped up the gorge's flanks, aiming to cut off the rearmost greenskins. Leoncoeur and the main body of warriors advanced up the centre, cutting into the heart of the orc herd. The pegasi continued to dive and swoop, bludgeoning the slow-moving greenskins with impunity, and so the orcs were soon assailed from all sides.

The remainder of the fighting was little better than a slaughter, with the last of the creatures surrounded by a ring of stamping horses. Leoncoeur killed the last orc himself, as was his right, and lifted its severed head high in triumph. Gore slopped in a torrent from its serrated neck-stump, mingling with the deluge of crimson foam below.

'First blood of the crusade!' he shouted, and his knights returned the cry with genuine gusto. After so long suffering from the grinding cold, it was good to indulge in their proper calling again.

De Lyonesse soon returned, and the slower-moving infantry of the baggage train caught up, hauling their wagons over the broken ground.

In normal times the peasants would have been employed to drag the bodies of the slain for burning, for allowing the corpse of a greenskin to moulder in the open air was asking for trouble. On this occasion, though, Leoncoeur suffered none of them to waste time. The way was cleared for the passage of the largest wains, and the bodies of fallen knights were retrieved and buried with all honour, but no funeral pyres were lit.

Less than two hours later, the cavalry column was on the move again, snaking higher up into the mouth of Axebite Pass. The clouds above did not relent, but poured out their violence ever more intensely, washing the blood from the rocks and sending it tumbling down the throat of the killing ground.

Leoncoeur let his knights pass first, led by de Lyonesse, who had started singing hymns of praise to the Lady for deliverance. The old king remained at the site where he had slain the last of the greenskins, lost in thought.

'You were right,' said Jhared, nudging his mount past Leoncoeur's and preparing for the final push towards the summit. 'First blood. A good omen.'

For a moment, Leoncoeur did not reply. The severed head of his victim lay on the near-frozen earth, gazing blankly up at the heavens. 'I do not recognise them,' he said at last.

Jhared looked down at the piles of corpses, then back at Leoncoeur, then shrugged. 'They look much the same as any I've killed.'

Leoncoeur leaned down in the saddle, poring over the piled heaps of the slain. Jhared's confidence was misplaced – the orcs' wargear was like nothing a greenskin south of the mountains would have worn. Leoncoeur had travelled far across the Old World and had fought in a dozen different lands. The different tribes of greenskin fought amongst themselves even more than they warred with other races. Each strain had their own territory, which was only breached on the rare occasion when an exceptional warlord would unite them into the rare explosions of aggression that gouged trails of carnage across the civilised lands.

This was not one of those occasions. The slain orcs' wargear was in poor shape, and their armour – to the extent it could be called that – hung from their bodies in tatters. It was clear that many of them had been wounded before the fighting had even begun, and their bulk was far less than it should have been.

'They did not come here to attack us,' said Leoncoeur.

Jhared laughed. 'Then why were they here?'

'They are from north of the mountains. The Drakwald, I'd warrant. They have been driven south.' Leoncoeur looked steadily at Jhared, letting him be in no doubt what had happened. 'They were fleeing. Whatever waits for us, it has cleansed the forest of orcs.'

Jhared started to laugh again, but the sound trailed off. He forced a smile. 'The forest can never be cleansed.'

Now that the fervour of battle had faded, Leoncoeur could reflect on how poorly the greenskins had resisted. He had never seen them give up, not so completely, not so quickly.

'They were hunted,' he said, finding himself strangely appalled by the thought. 'They were scared.'

'Of us.'

Leoncoeur smiled wryly. 'Believe that if you wish.' He kicked his horse's flanks, and it began to move again. 'I do not.'

He looked up, to where his knights wound their way ever northwards, passing under the night-dark shadow of Talareaux. It looked like they were snaking their way into the underworld.

Perhaps that is so, he mused. *In which case, the Lady willing, we will soon set it alight.*

The sun had only just risen, and its light was grey and diffuse, barred by the heavy layer of cloud that had hung over Altdorf for weeks. The parade ground was sunk into a kind of foggy twilight, part-masking the movements of the men out on the sand.

Helborg barely remembered the last time he had seen a clear sky. Ever since the first stirrings of the hosts in the north, the heavens had been masked by a grimy curtain, washing all the colour out of the world and plunging it into a dreary fog. Everything was dank, wet, sopping and grime-encrusted. Under such a constant weight of oppression, it was easy enough to believe that the gods had deserted the world of mortals at last, and that the little remaining light and heat was draining out of reality one sodden day at a time.

It got under the skin after a while, the lack of blue in the sky and freshness on the breeze. When the air tasted foul for day after day, and the nights were clammy and the days were humid, and the rain kept coming in a fine drizzle that made everything mouldy and turned the earth underfoot into a spore-infested mire, it crushed the spirit. Even if the tensions of the impending battle had not been there, the city's people would have suffered badly under such unrelenting misery – their sleep would have been as fitful, and their nightmares just as vivid.

Reports were coming in of rioting in all quarters. Brawls started up over the most trivial of disputes, triggered by hunger, or despair, or the kind of futile anger that came simply from waiting for the axe to fall. Food shortages made the situation worse – unspoiled grain supplies were running low, despite the heavy guard placed on the remaining stores, and water was little better. Most of the populace avoided water in any case, preferring the strong beers brewed by the alemasters and the few dwarf refugees still lingering in the taverns. They said that beer warded against the Rot. Perhaps they were right.

Helborg had not had a decent drink in days, and it made his nerves brittle. The wounds across his face still had not healed, and the pain was getting worse. Whenever he found a scrap of sleep, the lacerations would flare up, waking him in sudden pain. His apothecaries could not do anything – their old remedies, never reliable, had long since ceased to work at all, and the best they could offer was to bandage the lacerations and apply a soothing salve.

Helborg refused. He would not walk around the Palace with linen strapped to his face, and nor would he seek to dampen the raw pain of the daemon's wound with potions. The pain was a reminder to him of the price of weakness. Moreover, it kept him awake, which with his chronic lack of proper rest was becoming essential.

'Make them do it again,' he rasped, running his hands through days-old stubble and resisting the urge to scratch the itching weals.

Von Kleistervoll, standing by his side, barked out the orders, and together, he, Helborg and Zintler watched the drills unfold.

They were standing on a narrow balcony overlooking the parade ground. The sandy surface had begun to go black from rot, despite the incessant raking from the groundskeepers and near-endless prayers from the arch-lectors.

Down below, formations of men began to move. Sergeants yelled out the drill orders, and troopers formed up into squares and detachments. The orders kept coming, just in the same sequence as they had been for the past two hours, rehearsing the various defensive tactics set down in Robert de Guilliam's great compendium of martial lore, the *Codex Imperialis*, that had provided the cornerstone of Imperial defence since the time of Mandred.

Helborg watched the detachments wheel around one another. He watched the halberdiers shuffle together, keeping tight in the first rank and holding their blades stiffly. He watched them perform the feints, the fall-backs, the rallies, all under the hoarse expletives of their taskmasters. Five hundred men moved across the parade ground, their every movement orchestrated like a masque in one of the old grand balls.

Except that there were no grand balls anymore, for the gowns had rotted away and the ladies' rouge and face-paints had mouldered in their tins, and the glittering halls where they would once have been worn were carpeted with dust.

'They are holding up,' remarked von Kleistervoll, looking for the positives.

The Reiksguard preceptor had taken a personal interest in improving the readiness of the standard Altdorfer garrisons since the defeat at Heffengen. Cohesion was everything to an Empire army – in any conflict, an individual human trooper was likely to be weaker and less well equipped than his enemy, but coordination with the warriors on either side of him made up for this deficiency. A Chaos horde charged into battle in ragged bands of berserk ill-discipline, against which the only defence was tight-ordered rows of steel. If the enemy managed to breach Altdorf's outer walls, as it surely would before the end, then such disciplined ranks would be needed to hold them up for as long as possible.

Zintler looked less sure. 'They grow weary,' he said, watching one squadron of pikemen fall out of step, and stumble as they tried to make it good.

'We're all weary,' snapped Helborg, observing the proceedings with a critical eye. 'Keep them at it.'

Then he turned away from the balcony's edge and stalked back inside, followed by Zintler. Von Kleistervoll remained where he was, scrutinising his charges like a kestrel hovering over its prey.

Helborg strode down the long corridor leading away from the balcony and into the Palace interior, and Zintler hurried to keep pace.

'How stands the gate repair?' Helborg demanded.

'The work was complete,' said Zintler. 'As soon as they finished, more defects were found. The engineers are working through the night. The West Gate will be complete by the end of this day; the others, a little longer.'

Helborg grunted. It was like trying to build with gravel – as soon as one wall was shored-up, another opened with cracks. 'Did the Gold magisters answer the summons?'

'They are working on the problem,' said Zintler. 'But in Gelt's absence–'

'Do not talk to me of Gelt. I do not want to hear his name.'

'Understood. His deputy is Gerhard Mulleringen. I will speak to him again.'

Helborg felt light-headed as he walked. Chambers passed him by, one by one, their edges blurred and their doors gaping. He was vaguely aware of functionaries and knights bowing, and the muffled sound of orders echoing from other corridors, and the clatter of running feet. It might as well have been a dream – all that mattered was the army, the walls, the supplies and the defence plans. He had to remain *focused*.

Suddenly, he realised that one of the vague shadows flitting about him was not moving. He blinked, to see one of the Palace servants standing directly in his path. The man looked terrified, but remained where he was.

'Your pardon, lord!' he stammered, bowing low. 'I was charged to deliver these as soon as I could, but you have been... hard to find.'

Helborg glared at him. The servant held two rolls of parchment, one in each hand. 'What are they?' he demanded, wondering whether he could face more ledgers and dockets to sign.

'Letters, lord. One is marked with the seal of the Supreme Patriarch. The other was delivered from the Grey College.'

Helborg shot Zintler a dry look. 'The shadow-mages. What have they laid hands on now?' He grabbed both rolls, and broke Martak's seal first. As he read, his reaction moved from curiosity, to disbelief, to fury.

'He's gone,' Helborg said flatly.

'What do you mean?' asked Zintler.

'He's left the city. The *damned traitor*. I'll have his eyes. I'll rip his throat out and hang it from the Imperial standard. I'll punch his–'

'I can send a search party. We'll bring him back.'

Helborg rolled his eyes. 'He's an Amber battle wizard, Zintler. Your men would limp back as green-eyed hares, if they came back at all. It's too late – he broke into the Menagerie and worked some trickery on a war-griffon. They're both long gone.' He leaned heavily against the nearest wall, putting out a hand to support himself. Martak had been a pestilential fool, a peasant of the worst and most scabrous order, but he had been gifted, and his staff was needed. His loss was just one more blow amid a thousand other lesser cuts.

Zintler looked shocked, and for a moment did not say anything. When he did, his voice was weak. 'Why?'

Helborg laughed harshly. 'He thinks the Emperor lives. He's gone to *find him*.' His voice dripped with sarcasm. 'The pressure's got to him. I knew he was weak. Damn it all, what were they *thinking*, appointing a man like that?'

Zintler shook his head sympathetically. 'Anything else?'

'He advises me to perform a purge of the sewers – still on that old saw.' Helborg snorted another bitter laugh. 'Even now, he still presumes to advise me.' He screwed the parchment up and hurled it away. 'We do not need him. We still have magisters, and we still have priests, and I will not waste men on a fruitless trawl of the undercity.'

Even as he said the words, he realised how he sounded.

Desperate. I am clutching at any morsel of hope now.

He unravelled the second roll of parchment, finding himself yearning for some better news.

'From the Grey College, you say?' he asked, breaking the seal.

The servant nodded. 'They told me it was found on the roof, surrounded by blood. They do not know how long it was there.'

Helborg raised a weary eyebrow – just one more portent of doom. The tidings had been so relentlessly horrific over the past few days – Carroburg lost, Talabheim silent, Nuln cut off. In the deep of the night, when he struggled for just an hour of sleep, he feared that even his iron-hard defiance was beginning to crack at the edges.

Let it be news of reinforcements – from somewhere. Anywhere!

He started to read.

To the most sublime and majestic Karl Franz, Prince of Altdorf,
Count of the Reikland, Emperor of the Eleven Provinces and

Heir of Sigmar (Or his deputy, given the uncertain times that have overtaken us.)

I have no doubt you will not wish to read a letter such as this, and from one such as me. You will be tempted to throw it into the fire as soon as you see the signature. I urge you to resist – I do not make this communication lightly, nor do I wage this war without urgent cause.

Your scryers will by now be telling you what all men of reason can see for themselves – the order of the world is changing. The Law of Death has been broken, and the remaining Seven Laws are straining at the edges. Powers that have stood firm for millennia are fading, while others are growing with unseemly haste.

Can any now doubt that the Gods of Ruin have put aside their ancient quarrels, and are now acting in concert? And, if that is so, can there be any further doubt that they must be victorious? The great heroes of the past are with us no more, for we dwell in a time of lesser souls.

And yet, not all is foregone. There is another way. Only one soul stands a chance of enduring the storm of Chaos: my Master, who even now strives to return from the banishment of ages. Already he has struck down enemies older than the stones you stand on, and soon he will turn his gaze northwards.

Your great ancestor once ended him in a duel that still echoes through the ages. And yet, if you wish to see the forces of Order prevail in this time, you will need to welcome him now. I am but an emissary, a forerunner of this greater soul, and I offer my services to you. My armies have already marched at the side of yours, though you may not have known it then. They will march alongside you again, should you consent to my offer, freely given and motivated by nothing more than mutual need.

The living and the dead have ever been at odds, but we are more alike to one another than to the corruptions of the Outer Dark. Where they would turn the world into a howling maelstrom of perpetual flux, we understand the principles of order, of command, of endurance. There is a future taking shape, one in which the foundations of reality are made firm again, where the weak are protected and the strong given dominion. It is not the future your priests were wont to pray for, but it is one in which humanity is preserved, and that, let me assure you, is the very best that can be hoped for now.

Make no mistake, my lord, this is the choice: alliance, or oblivion. Just as your ancestor Magnus swallowed his pride to make common cause with the elves of Ulthuan when they were

*denounced as witches by the ignorant, so must hard choices be
made in our own time.*

*I demand nothing but that which has always been my
birthright: Electorship of Sylvania, a province which has
unfairly been denied its existence for too long. The rights and
privileges of this station shall be the same as the others of that
rank: a runefang, a place at the Imperial Council, the old
exemptions from the common law and the freedom to raise and
keep men-at-arms. I only ask one more boon of you: the chance
to search the Reikland for the resting place of one who was
dear to me. If the world is to be remade, then I must discover
her before all is cast anew.*

*I am aware that the mutual enmity between our peoples
will make this proposal a hard one to entertain fairly. I have
no doubt, though, given the circumstances, you will see past
ancient prejudices and buried grievances. You will have seen
the same auguries as we have, and you will know what is at
stake. And, after all, do I not have some prior claim to this title?
Or does right of conquest count for nothing in these debased
times?*

*I trust that this missive will reach you, despite all the
turmoil that even now seeks to overwhelm us. By the time you
read it, I will be on the march, heading along the path of the
Stir towards Altdorf. By the time I arrive, I will command a
host larger than the last time I camped outside your walls. I
earnestly hope that I do not arrive too late, and that you will at
least have the opportunity to make your judgement under clear
skies and with a free heart.*

*Until then, I remain, as I ever have been, your loyal and
ever-obedient servant,*

Vlad von Carstein

Helborg took a long time over the words. When he had reached the end,
he read it again, hardly able to believe what was before his eyes.

If he had not been at Heffengen, he might have assumed the letter was
some malicious forgery, despite the authentic-looking seal and appropri-
ately archaic hand. But he had been at Heffengen, and so could believe
only too well that the provenance was genuine.

He remembered von Kleistervoll's words after the battle.

They say the dead fought the northmen.

Helborg had not believed that then. He had seen von Carstein emerge,
just as the battle remained in the balance. He had seen the skeletal dragon,

and the onrush of the fanged knights in blood-red armour. Until *he* had arrived, the day had not been altogether lost.

Zintler hovered at his side, clearly itching to know what had been written. Helborg let him wait. His mind was racing.

Could he be trusted? Could I have been wrong?

As soon as the treacherous words entered his mind, he cursed himself for even thinking them.

He lives for nothing more than destruction! All of his kind do! They sense weakness, and circle for the kill.

Zintler could not restrain himself, and coughed delicately. 'My lord?'

Helborg did just as he had done with Martak's letter, and crumpled the parchment into a tight ball. He stuffed it into a pocket sewn on the inside of his half-cloak, and shoved it down deep. It would not do to have any but him aware of its contents. Just as with so many other things, he would have to bear the burden alone. Even the electors could not be told.

'It is nothing, Zintler,' he said, pushing himself clear of the wall. He dismissed the servant with a curt wave and started walking. 'Nothing worth a damn.'

Zintler trotted to keep up. 'And Martak? Can we do nothing?'

Helborg whirled on the Reikscaptain, fixing him with his hawk-dark eyes. As he did so, the wounds on his cheek spiked with fresh pain.

'We do what we have to do,' he snarled. 'We prepare. We train. We fight the darkness. We never give in. And we do so *alone*. There is no salvation from outside these walls, Zintler – you understand that? We have everything we are going to be given, and it must suffice.'

He felt the thrill of mania begin to run away from him then, and he tripped over his words. When these dark moods came on him, he felt almost like laughing.

Zintler shrank back, anxiety written on his dutiful features. 'Just so, my lord. But – forgive me – we are all mortals. There is also need for rest. When did you last take any?'

Helborg's eyes flared at the impudence. 'Rest?' he blurted. '*Rest?* Did Mandred take rest? Did Magnus? Would Schwarzhelm, or Karl Franz?'

He started walking again. He could feel his joints ache, his ribs creak, his wounds leak blood in a thin trickle down his neck.

'To the walls,' he croaked, keeping his shoulders back, his neck stiffly upright. 'Our labours are not yet done, and neither are the stonemasons.' I will see the works for myself, and if they have slackened from the task I will gut them with their own trowels.'

The cauldron overflowed, sending frothy, fatty matter splatting on the stone floor.

Festus stirred more vigorously, knowing the delicate juncture he had reached. He had been working for so long now, so patiently and so carefully that even a minute error now would be more than he could bear. As his flabby body sweated from the fires, the alembics and glassware funnels bubbled violently.

From one of the cages he could hear a woman weeping. Those cages were almost empty now – he would have to find a way to step up procurement before the final stage, which would not be easy. The City Watch was getting vigilant, and he had seen evidence of those damned Shallyans poking their noses around the margins of his domain.

The Shallyans were the only thing Festus truly had anything like fear for. A normal mortal could be so easily corrupted, since their appetites were so typically gross and their fear of sickness so habitually complete. The inhabitants of Altdorf were just like the inhabitants of any other Imperial city – petty, spiteful, grasping and timorous. Being turned into vessels of a greater sickness was the best thing they could possibly have aspired to, not that they ever evinced much gratitude for it.

But the sisters – they were tricky. They did not fear illness. How could they, since they spent their whole lives immersed in it? They did not suffer from gluttony, and they had no crippling fears. They accepted the world for what it was, and felt no need to change it, other than to ease the suffering of those stricken by its more painful aspects.

That, frankly, was perverse, and was just what made the Leechlord shudder. When his work was done here and the Tribulation was complete, Festus knew exactly where he was going and exactly what he was going to do. He could already hear the screams of the sisters as they writhed on the tip of his scythe. He would take his time killing them, one by one, letting them experience the full strength of what they had always denied.

It did not matter how strong or stoical they were – when confronted with the utter inevitability of defeat, they would all crack. They would be lapping up his potions sooner or later, and they would be *thankful* for it.

He sniffed a slug of mucus up and swallowed. Tiny daemon-kin scurried around at his hooves, licking the drops of yellowish sweat that coursed from his bulging muscles. They were excitable now. They could sense what was in the cauldron, and they knew what it meant.

All along the walls of the subterranean chamber, vials and jars rattled and shivered. The drones of tumour-sized blowflies hummed through every vaulted cavity and undercroft. His realm had spread quickly, and now occupied hundreds of forgotten shafts and pits beneath Altdorf's foetid ground-level streets.

This was his kingdom, a foretaste of the greater kingdom of contagion to come, but it was still fragile. If he were discovered, if the mortals chose to look beneath their blocked noses and seriously try to track down the source of what ailed them, he might yet be vulnerable.

He stirred harder. Beneath the cauldron's surface, the dark shape grew ever more solid. A misshapen antler-prong briefly broke the brackish water, before sinking again. A gurgling sigh echoed from underwater, potent enough to make Festus shiver with anticipation.

They were all looking to him. The Glotts, the Tallyman, the Lord of Tentacles, the beasts, the damned and the god-marked – they were all looking to *him* to unlock the Great Tribulation.

He sweated harder. He was no longer chortling as he worked, and he no longer took any pleasure in his allotted task.

Time was running out. The deathmoon was riding low, and would be full soon. The massed hosts of the Urfather were crashing through a tangled, twisted forest of nightmares, and would be hammering at the gates uncomfortably quickly.

If he failed... if any of them failed...

Festus wiped his forehead. A diminutive toad-creature nipped his foot, and he kicked it irritably away. From the cauldron, a bubbling fountain briefly erupted, but did not sustain.

'Come on,' Festus muttered, putting more energy into the endless stirring. 'Come *on*...'

◄ CHAPTER FOURTEEN ►

Martak hung onto the griffon's neck and gritted his teeth. A range of terrors coursed through him.

This is the realm of birds, he thought grimly. *I have no place in it.*

It had been easy enough to break into the Menagerie. With the attention of the city locked on the walls and the impending arrival of the enemy, the internal watch had grown slack and undermanned. Martak had slipped into the vast array of pens and cages during the night, using every ounce of his art to placate the creatures that slavered at him from behind iron bars.

Initially he had hoped a Bretonnian pegasus might have been held there – he knew how to ride a horse, and guessed it would be much the same to control one of their winged brethren – but the only creatures capable of flight were the colossal Imperial dragon and the select herd of Karl Franz's war-griffons. He had not even got close to the dragon before gouts of sulphurous smoke had forced him back, and even he was not boastful enough to think he could master that living furnace of scale and talon – the world would have to be ending around his ears for him to contemplate rousing *that*.

The griffons were scarce less fearsome, though, rising to over twice the height of a man at the shoulder and with flesh-ripping beaks that curved like scimitars. They all growled and hissed at him as he passed their pens, pawing at the straw beneath them and watching him with beady, unblinking yellow eyes.

In the end, he had selected a russet beast, marginally leaner than the others and with bands of crimson and gold on hawk-like wings. He had held its gaze and whispered words of control and reassurance. It had taken a long time before the griffon was calm enough for him to break the locks and dare enter, and then it still reared up, cawing furiously, and Martak was forced to delve deep into the Lore of Beasts to prevent it clawing his eyes out.

Eventually the creature suffered him to lead it by the halter, and the two of them walked out of the Menagerie's main cage-chambers and into the dung-strewn exercise yards beyond. It took him three attempts to mount, during which the noble beast glared at him coldly with a mix of irritation and contempt. Eventually the commotion, punctuated with earthy swear-words of dubious origin, roused the less soporific members of the watch, and the thud of footfalls echoed down from the watch towers around the yard.

Cursing, Martak hauled on the reins. 'Fly, then, damn you,' he hissed, having no idea how such a creature was ridden. Griffon riders were vanishingly rare in the Empire's armies, and they trained for years before mastering the tempestuous natures of their wild mounts. Very quickly Martak felt the spirit of the beast defying him – it was perfectly aware what he wanted, and perfectly aware that he had no power to compel it.

Faint lights blinked into life from the summit of the watch towers as torches were lit. A bell began to clang somewhere in the depths of the Menagerie's guardhouse, and doors slammed.

Still the griffon remained on the ground, its wings unfurled, but resolutely unmoving. Martak cried out every word of command in his lexicon, racking his mind for the correct cantrip or word-form. Perhaps there was not one – griffons were not like the dumb beasts of the deep wood that could be charmed with a gesture, they were ancient and proud scions of the mountains, with souls as fiery and untamed as the peaks they circled.

'Fly!' he growled again, brandishing his staff over the creature's neck as if the splinter of gnarled wood would intimidate such a colossal mount. The griffon hissed back at him, and strutted around the yard aimlessly. More shouts came from the surrounding buildings, at ground level this time, and the red glare of firelight spread from the barred windows. Men burst out of the doors leading back to the beast-chambers, each carrying a long spear and clutching nets between them.

A huge, burly figure, bald-headed and with an iron stud in his nose, roared up at them, his face puce with anger. 'Get back in there, you flea-ridden fly-hog!' he bawled, gesturing frantically at the other men to fan out and surround the griffon. 'Sigmar damn you, you will suffer for this!'

At the sight of that man, the griffon immediately reared again, nearly throwing Martak from its back. Its forelegs scythed, and it let rip with a piercing shriek of fury.

The first net, weighted with iron balls, was thrown. With a coiled pounce, the griffon leapt into the air, flapping powerfully to gain loft.

More nets were thrown, then spears, but none reached the target. The griffon powered upward rapidly, climbing higher with every powerful down-beat of its huge wings.

Martak hung on, his heart racing, clutching to the beast's plumage with fear-whitened knuckles.

'Taal's teeth,' he swore, realising belatedly what he had taken on.

Altdorf fell away below him, a patchwork of faint lamplight amid the overcast gloom of the night sky. The griffon banked, and Martak saw the baroque sprawl of the Imperial Palace stretched out, glistening faintly from the light of a thousand lanterns. Even in the midst of his blind terror, it was hard not to be awed by the spectacle.

'*North*, damn you,' he hissed, trying again to impose his will.

The griffon did not listen, but headed east, instinctively heading for the mountains where it had been hatched. Martak persevered, reaching out to the beast's mind and trying to quell its wilfulness.

Slowly, painfully, it began to respond. Martak whispered every scrap of the Lore of Beasts into its ears, piling on the words of command.

Eventually, with a frustrated caw of defeat, it began to listen. It toppled to one side and angled north, heading over the seas of dark-limbed trees and flying steadily.

Ever since that moment, Martak had battled with it, forcing it to obey him through sheer bloody-mindedness. There was no beautiful meeting of souls and no mutual respect between them – every wing-beat was a struggle, a draining battle of psyches. The griffon toiled through the air as if mired in it. Just staying mounted was a challenge in itself, and Martak nearly slipped from his perch more than once.

Somehow, though, they flew on until the sunrise, by which time they were far out over the forest and the Reik valley was a long way behind them. Both of them were exhausted, bad-tempered and stinking with sweat.

Martak gazed out over the vast expanse of land below. Although he had often tramped far and wide into the Great Forest, it was only from the air that one could appreciate just how immeasurably immense the Empire was. During the long flight they had barely passed any settlements, and yet the forest still stretched off towards the four empty horizons in an unbroken, daunting mass. Night-mists curled and boiled atop the crowns of the trees, spiralling into eerie columns that twisted up to meet the weak light of the sun. The eastern horizon was a weak strip of pale gold, glistering faintly under heavy bands of iron-grey.

The griffon cawed harshly. Ahead of them reared several outcrops of dark rock, thrusting clear of the canopy like leviathans breaking the ocean surface. Martak sensed the beast's desire to set down, drawn perhaps by a landscape that reminded it of its mountainous home.

Martak allowed it to lose height, and soon they were circling down towards the nearest column of stone, angling with surprising dexterity through the chill dawn air. The griffon crouched as it touched down.

Martak gripped it tightly by the nape of the neck, and hissed into its ear. 'You are mine, now. I do not release you. One way or another, we are bound to one another, so do not get any ideas.'

The griffon hissed back at him, and scraped its talons along the rock, but did not make any further protest. They understood one another, and a bond, however tenuous and irascible, had been established.

Martak dismounted stiffly and hobbled to the edge of the stone island.

He stood fifty feet above the tallest of the trees, and could see nothing but a landscape of leaves in every direction – no rivers, no castles, no cultivated land. The forest reeked of slowly mouldering fruit. The more he looked, the more he felt the marks of slow corruption. The Great Forest had always been a perilous and dank place, but now it was truly festering.

Martak slumped to his haunches. He would have to make a fire soon. Somehow, he would have to find something to eat – if anything that still lived in the forest was worth eating.

He gazed out to the north, and at the sight of the endless ranks of trees, his heart faltered.

Is this a mistake? he ruminated. *Should I have stayed? My absence will make Helborg spit blood.*

He smiled grimly. That, on its own, probably made it worth the labour.

Behind him, the griffon began to preen itself, pulling at its tangled feathers with its hooked beak. Martak shuffled away from the precipice, and started to look for dry tinder. The fire would do more than keep them warm – it was the precursor to a spell, one that would allow his sight to roam far beyond the confines of his mortal vision.

It would not be easy to summon up the requisite power – scrying was not his strength, and the dreary tang of mutation hung in the air, thicker and more durable than the rolling mist.

'But I *will* find you,' Martak said aloud, startling the griffon. 'By the Eight Winds, this journey will not be wasted.'

He hobbled across the bare stone, limping from muscle-ache and the cold, muttering to himself. Out in the wilds, the clouds hung heavily, and the plague-wind moaned.

It would be a long, cold day.

'Consider it, o my brother,' said Otto, softly.

'I do so, o my brother,' replied Ethrac, his voice hushed in awe.

Neither of them spoke for a little while after that. The two of them sat on Ghurk's shoulders, lost in thought. Below them, their army waited for orders. They waited for a long time.

Ghurk stood at the summit of a bald, windswept hill on the north bank of the Reik. The close press of thorn and briar had given way a little there, exposing the vista to the east in all its untrammelled glory. Ahead of them, at last, lay their goal.

Just below Ghurk's hooves, the terrain fell away sharply in terraces of foliage-clogged undulation. The Reik valley had widened since Carroburg, and was now a broad, shallow bowl. The land had once been cultivated across the flat floodplain, but now the crops rotted in their drills, reeking with a subtle aroma that Otto found immensely pleasing. Everywhere he looked, the forest had crept past its ancient bounds, smothering everything. The new growths had taken on a wild variety of hues – pus-yellow, olive-green, the pulsing crimson of blood-blisters. Above it all, the clouds still churned, making the air as thick and humid as half-warmed tallow.

A mile away, Altdorf lay, rising from the tormented plain like a colossus, straddling the wide river and thrusting its towers up towards the uncaring heavens. Far bigger than Marienburg, far bigger than Talabheim, it was the greatest of prizes, the jewel of the southern Empire.

It had never been a beautiful place, even before the Rot. It had none of the soaring grandeur of Lothern, nor the stark geometry of the Lustrian megalopolises. What it had was *solidity* – the huge, heavy weight of history, piled atop layer after layer of construction until the final ramshackle, glorious heap of disparate architectural and strategic visions reached up to scrape at the lowering rainclouds themselves. Mighty buttresses reinforced vast retaining walls, straining amid the lattice of bridges and causeways and spiral stairs and gatehouses and watchtowers, all surmounted by slender tiled roofs that poked upward like fire-blackened fingers. A thousand hearths sent sooty trails snaking over the tiles, casting a pall of smog that hung like pox over the entire gaudy display. Copper domes glistened dully amid the tangle of dark stone and grimy daub, and the noise of forges and manufactories could be made out even from so far away, grinding away somewhere deep in the bowels of the vast, vast city.

Its walls were intact. Otto permitted himself some surprise at that – he had been told to expect the masonry to have crumbled away. Perhaps the defenders were more capable than he had expected. They had certainly worked hard.

It mattered not. Walls of stone were of little impediment to the hosts he commanded. Altdorf was just a microcosm of the Empire itself – the true rot came from *within*. There was no point in reinforcing borders and bastions and parapets if the flesh contained beyond them was withering away with every passing hour. They were weak, now. Terribly weak. How many of them could still lift their weapons? How many even had the desire to?

A low crack and growl of thunder played across the eastern horizon. Great pillars of cloud were gathering, driven west by gales from the Worlds Edge Mountains. Stray flickers of lightning briefly flashed out across the grey, drab air, glinting on the Reik's dreary surface.

The river had almost entirely turned into a glutinous slurry, and it barely lapped its own banks any more. Huge vines had slithered out of the encroaching tree-cover and extended into the water, making what remained even more viscous.

Otto smirked as he saw the transformation. The god he served was a mighty god indeed. The very earth had been poisoned, the waters thickened, the growing things perverted and sent thrusting into feral parodies of themselves. There was no resisting this – it was the wearing weight of entropy, the corruption of all purity, the glorious potential of the sick, the foul, the decaying.

'We march now,' Otto breathed, knowing how little time it would take. The army would sweep east, filling the valley before them from side to side, surrounding the city as the ocean surrounded its islands.

'Not yet,' warned Ethrac. 'We wait for the others.'

Otto felt like snapping at him. Ethrac could be tediously particular. He loved his brother – he loved *both* his brothers – but Ghurk's pleasing enthusiasms never ceased to be endearing, whereas Ethrac could, on occasion, be harder to like.

'We may crush it *now*, o my brother,' said Otto, forcing a smile. 'Crush it like Carroburg.'

'No, no.' Ethrac waved his staff to and fro, and the bells clanged. 'Not long to wait. The others grow closer. We will need all three – the Lord of Tentacles, the Tallyman, the beasts of the dark wood, the hosts of the far north.'

Otto rolled his eyes. 'They are *starved*, o my brother! They are timorous.'

Ethrac shot him a crooked smile. 'Not as starved as they will be, o my sibling. Not as timorous as they *will* be. While they still have a little of their native strength left, we must creep with caution. How many battles have been lost to impetuosity? Hmm? You can count them all?'

Otto was about to retort, knowing the argument was futile, when the clouds parted overhead. The fine drizzle that had accompanied them since making landfall at Marienburg guttered and trembled. A new light flooded across the valley, weaker than the shrouded sun, like a pale flame.

The hosts of ruin looked up. Otto did likewise.

He saw the flames of the comet flicker, masked by the shifting airs and made weak by the filth in the skies, but there nevertheless. Tongues of fire glimmered in the heavens, just as they had done in the half-forgotten days only recorded in forbidden books.

Otto made the sign of ruination. 'The twin-tailed star,' he muttered.

Ethrac chuckled. 'It surprises you, o my brother? You have not listened to me. The comet was there to witness the birth of Sigmar's realm, and it will be there to see it out. Such signs and portents were written into fate's tapestry since before you or I were woven into it.'

Otto continued to stare at the comet uneasily. He could barely catch sight of it, and its light was washed out by the gloom of midday, but the brief snatches he did perceive made his stomach turn.

'It presages nothing,' he muttered, to convince himself as much as anything else.

'That is right,' said Ethrac, satisfied.

'The full deathmoon is due.'

'That it is.'

Otto drew in a phlegmy breath. He could sense the tension from the thousands of warriors waiting behind him. All they needed was an order.

'Then we wait for it,' said Otto. 'We wait for the Night of Souls.'

'We do.'

Otto grinned. His mood was oddly changeable. Why was that? Nerves? Surely not – he had been shown the future, and it was gloriously, infinitely putrid.

'Not long now, then,' he said, drumming his fingers on Ghurk's leather-hard flesh.

Ethrac smiled contentedly, and looked up at the heavens.

'Not long at all, o my brother.'

The wait was over. The scouts had returned from the forward stations, and the reports had been sent down from the Celestial College's scrying towers.

In a way, it was a relief. The sham-war was over, the real one could begin. Whatever Helborg might have done better, it mattered not now. All that remained was the fight itself, the clash of steel against iron, and in that at least the Reiksmarshal had never been found wanting.

At the first sound of a warning clarion, he had donned his full battle-garb. Three menials were required to help him into it, and when they were finished he was encased from neck to knee in plate armour. They had polished it furiously hard over the past week, and the steel gleamed like silver. The scabbard of his runefang had been lovingly restored, and the icons of the griffon and the insignia of Karl Franz looked as pristine as they ever had done. The menials draped a new cloak over his shoulders, and it brushed against the stone floor with a sigh of fine fabric.

He banished them once all was done, and remained for a moment in his private rooms, donned for war.

From outside, he could hear the growing clamour of the city readying itself. Bells rang out from every temple tower, sounding the alarm and rousing the sick and the exhausted from their beds. Great arcs of lightning crackled across the rooftops as the magisters of the colleges readied their arcane war machines. Trumpets sounded in every garrison, calling the thousands of troops still in the employ of the Palace to their stations. Scaffolds cracked and groaned as huge cannons were winched into position and rolled forward on their parapet mounts.

Helborg smiled. They were the sounds he lived to hear. The troops were responding as he had drilled them to. They might have learned to curse him since he returned from the north, they might have spat his name with hatred when he had forced them into another exercise or commandeered another water-supply or made the engineers work through the night to keep the battlements intact and the foundations strong, but they were *ready*. The standards still flew from the turrets, and the cancer of fear had not undone them just yet.

He walked over to the door. As he did so, he caught sight of his reflection in a grimy window-pane, and paused.

He looked much the same as he had done in the past – the lean, aquiline face with its hook nose and flamboyant moustache. When he turned to one side, though, he saw the long rakes along his cheek, still flecked with scab-tissue. As if aware of the attention, the wounds flared again, hot as forge-irons.

'Keep it up,' Helborg snarled. 'Keep the pain coming. It'll only make me angrier.'

He swept out of the chamber and into the corridor outside. He walked swiftly, banishing the fatigue that had dogged him for so long. He still had not managed to sleep, but the adrenaline of the coming combat sustained him, flooding his muscles and making him itch to draw his blade.

As he went, commotion built around him. Palace officials ran to and fro, carrying orders and last-minute requisitions. Knights in full armour stomped from the armouries up to their stations, saluting smartly as they caught sight of the Reiksmarshal. Helborg saw the sigils of the Sable Chalice, the Hospitallers, the Knights Panther, the Order of the Golden Wolf, and there were no doubt more already stationed across the city.

And, of course, there were the surviving Reiksguard, restored to combat readiness following von Kleistervoll's punishing regimen. Nine hundred were ready to deploy, counting those that had remained in Altdorf prior to Heffengen – a formidable force, and one that he would personally command when the time came.

He neared the high doors of his destination. When they saw him coming, the door-guards hurriedly pushed them open, bowing as he strode through.

On the far side, the circular Chamber of Ghal Maraz opened up in all its many-arched splendour. In times of peace, the priceless warhammer itself was hung on chains of gold from the domed roof, guarded by four warrior priests and ringed with wards from the Light College. Only the mightiest or the most faithful were ever permitted access to the chamber while the weapon hung suspended over its iron war-altar. That altar had been forged from the guns used in the defence of the city against the vampire lords of legend, and was as black and sullen as pitch.

Now the chains swung emptily, for Ghal Maraz, like so much else, was lost, borne by the boy-warrior Valten somewhere out in the wilds of the north. The city's defenders still mustered before the altar nevertheless, as if some lingering aura of power still hung over the empty hooks.

They were all there: von Kleistervoll in his full preceptor's regalia, Zintler looking very different in his ceremonial Reikscaptain's war-plate, the grand masters of the Knightly Orders, the masters of the Colleges of Magic, the arch-lectors and the master engineers and the Imperial generals with their captains and lieutenants in tow. Von Liebwitz, Haupt-Anderssen and Gausser were present, all in their own ancestral battle-gear. They might have been quarrelsome, power-hungry schemers, but they each carried a runefang and had been tutored since infancy on how to use it.

The display of collected power was comforting. It would have looked better with Schwarzhelm there, or Huss, or Volkmar or Gelt, but it was still a daunting panoply. As the doors slammed closed behind Helborg, all head were lowered in deference.

'So, the enemy has been sighted,' said Helborg, standing before them and fixing each in turn with his gaze. 'We know now that they are three: an army to the north that still marches; an army to the east that is almost upon us, and the largest host of all, fresh from the sack of Marienburg and within sight of the walls. They will wait until Morrslieb is full, or so the arch-lectors tell me.'

Fleischer bowed. The head of the Celestial College nodded in agreement – they all knew the power of the witching-night.

'They outnumber us many times over,' Helborg went on, his harsh voice echoing strangely in the huge chamber. 'They bring foul creatures from the wilds on the edge of the world, and think to break us as easily as they broke Marienburg and – so we fear – Talabheim.' He smiled wolfishly. 'But they have not reckoned on the soul of this place. It is Sigmar's city. It is *our* city.'

Gausser grunted approvingly. All the true fighters – the grand masters, the Reiksguard – appreciated words like this. They had spent their lives going into battle, often against horrific odds, and only needed to know that their liege was with them; that he suffered alongside them, and that, in the final test, he would stand in the mud and blood with blade in hand.

'This is the heart of the Empire,' growled Helborg, gesturing to the golden pilasters and columns surrounding the empty altar. 'This is where the seat of power has always been, where the Emperors rule, where the Law was set down and where the source of our greatness was first delved. While Altdorf lives, the Empire lives. As fortune's wheel turns, it is we who have been charged with the sacred task of keeping it secure for the next thousand years.'

As he spoke, Helborg could see doubt in the eyes of those he addressed. If even half the scouts' reports were accurate, than the enemy was almost ludicrously vast – a host greater even than the swollen armies of Kul.

Let them doubt. What mattered was whether they stood up or fell to their knees, and there had never been a day of Helborg's life when he had not faced his enemy on his feet.

'Even as I speak, our troops are reaching their stations,' he said. 'They will remain firm so long as *we* remain firm. They will look to us, the masters of men, to lead the defence and show just what stuff the Empire is made of. They will not be afraid if we do not feel fear. They will not retreat if we hold fast, and they will not contemplate defeat if we do not let it enter our minds. So I say to you all this day: stand firm in Sigmar's image! As night falls and the terror grows, stand firm in Sigmar's image. As they bring fire from the firmament and summon horror from beyond the grave, stand firm in Sigmar's image. He has not abandoned us, for He is a god of *battle*. Wish not for a world in which there is no strife or bloodshed, for that would be a pale reflection of the world of glory we have been given to dwell in.'

He grinned, feeling the seductive mania return, and his wounds broke open on his cheek. 'And this will be the most *glorious* of days! Men will sing in after-ages of the heroes of Altdorf, and will curse their fortune not to have witnessed the deeds that will be done here. They will look up at the white towers of this city, standing prouder than they do today, and marvel at their eternal strength, just as they curse the darkness that thought to bring them low.'

Helborg drew his sword. 'You know what this is!' he said, brandishing the blade before them. 'This is the Sword of Vengeance, the *Klingerach*, and it has drunk the blood of the faithless across every province in the realm. I have driven you hard, and I know the burden has been heavy, but now the Sword of Vengeance marches to war, and you will march with it.'

He lifted the sacred runefang towards the empty altar. Ghal Maraz may have been missing, but his own weapon was ancient enough to honour the sacred space.

'And so, on this day, when the fates converge on Altdorf and we become the fulcrum of the war to end all wars, I pledge this,' he swore, feeling the lines of blood trickle down his neck. 'I will take no backward step. I will not retreat, I will not cower, I will not relent. I will *fight*. I will fight for this place with every breath and with every drop of blood in my body. And if the world is to end and if all is to be cast in the fire, then I will die in the service of the Empire as I have lived, as a *warrior*.'

He raised the sword high.

'For the Empire!' he roared.

As one, the assembled warriors raised their own weapons towards the altar.

The Empire! they cried in unison, and the massed voices soared into the dome above, echoing in fractured harmony. *The Empire! For Karl Franz!*

Helborg looked at them all, his blood pumping. They were as ready as they would ever be, each of them filled with the zeal of combat. This was what made the Empire great – that, for all its folly and corruption, when the storm broke they had never refused the challenge.

'Now then,' he snarled, feeling the dark swell of battle-lust throbbing through him. 'The time for words and prayers is over. Take your positions, and may Sigmar guide your blades.'

◄ CHAPTER FIFTEEN ►

More orcs came over the mountains after the first gang, jogging in loose bands, their maws drooling and their eyes rimmed with madness and fatigue. Every time they were dispatched, another herd would follow, not in huge numbers, but enough to slow the Bretonnians further.

The knights rode in full battle-gear all the time, keeping lances to hand and changing horses often. Snow began to fall, dusting the bare rock with a grey slush that made the horses' hooves skid and slip, and they lost more precious steeds and men during the vicious, short-lived brawls.

'They just run onto our blades,' Jhared remarked. 'It is as if...'

They no longer wish to live. Leoncoeur could have finished the sentence for him. That, beyond all he had seen since the rise of Mallobaude, filled his heart with foreboding. An orc was a crucible of nature's wrath, a furious avatar of martial excess. They lived to fight, to scrap, to roar out their feral abandon into the world as they tore it apart. An orc feared nothing.

And yet now they were broken. Just as Jhared said, they stumbled blindly into combat, going through the motions in a kind of dumb rehearsal of their old terrible glory. For the first time in his life, Leoncoeur took no pleasure in slaying them. It began to seem... cruel.

The series of skirmishes slowed their passage through Axebite Pass, but did not halt it. Leoncoeur gave the column no respite, and they trudged on through the swirling, snow-laced squalls. Peasants who succumbed to the grinding cold were left where they fell, and the baggage train became steadily more and more undermanned. Soon they would have scarce enough hands to keep the carts rolling and the teams of warhorses guarded, but the pace never slackened.

Eventually, they cleared the worst of the bitter high path, and the road began to snake downhill again. The vast peaks of the Grey Mountains still rose impossibly high above them, their distant heads blocked by thick cloud, but the hardest portion of the traverse was over. The knights began to pick their way down the gravelly paths of scree and boulders, going carefully lest more horses go lame.

The purity of the high airs soon collapsed once more into the thick filth they had breathed in Bretonnia, except it was far, far worse on the northern side of the range. On the second day of the descent, the vanguard rounded a tight bend in a narrow gorge, and beheld for the first time the land beyond the mountains.

Barring their path a few dozen yards away was a thick snarl of tangled briars. Beyond that lay a seething glut of vines and throttle-weeds, all gently moving as if propelled by intelligences of their own. Trees studded the congested road, looking like they had sprouted from the living rock just moments ago, their gnarled roots frozen onto the cracked stone and their crowns gasping for air and light.

From his vantage at the head of the column, Leoncoeur could see that the thick undergrowth extended for miles. It ran away from them, close-bound and endless. To their right reared the old fortress of Helmgart, once a mighty citadel, but now abandoned to the clutching vines, its walls crumbled and its keep hollow. It looked like it had been empty for weeks.

Leoncoeur sensed the dismay from the warriors around him. The way was blocked, and it would take days to hack through just a tithe of it. The pegasi would soar above it all, of course, but they were merely the spear-tip of his force.

Leoncoeur whispered an order and his horse walked on, approaching the first clumps of moss that marred the stony path. As the rank wall of growths neared, he smelled the over-sweet stench of fermenting fruit.

This is the spawn of corruption, he mused, watching the polyps flex and swell under his mount's hooves. *If it comes from magic, it can be dispelled with magic.*

To the left of the path, an ice-white cataract plunged down the mountainside, swollen from the storms in the peaks above. It remained pure when all around it was foetid. Leoncoeur halted before it, remembering the words of the Lady.

Look for me in pure waters.

The white river ran on ahead of him, foaming in its narrow course and throwing up a fine spray. Far ahead, it plunged under the shadows of the trees, hissing as if angered by the contagions around it.

Leoncoeur drew his blade, stained from greenskin blood, and held it high.

'By the Lady we march!' he cried. 'And by Her grace will all taint be cleansed from the world!'

His warriors remained at a distance, unsure. They had been sorely tested by the passage of the pass, and Leoncoeur was not so deaf that he had not heard the mutterings of discontent. They had been promised glorious battle, not an endless slog through poison-vines.

They would need to be reminded just who they served.

Leoncoeur pointed his sword towards the river, holding the tip just above the gurgling surface. 'They have not removed you from the waters just yet, my queen,' he murmured. 'I can sense your power here, just as it was in Couronne. Their faith wavers. I beseech you, humbly, restore it.'

Nothing happened. The rain started up again, drizzling down from the grey sky and making the standards heavy. The thick filigree of branches and vines seemed to tighten, drawing across the path ahead in a heavy wall of interlocking boughs.

Leoncoeur held his weapon in place, and closed his eyes. *What do you demand of me, Lady? I have already pledged everything. What is there left?*

He saw her then, in his mind, just as she had been in Bretonnia. If anything, her slender face seemed even more careworn.

Everything, my champion? she whispered back. *You have barely been tested.*

That hurt. He had lost a kingdom, and forfeited any chance of taking it back by following her command. He had already lost more than most men would ever have to give away.

The way is barred, he said.

All ways are barred, she breathed, her voice little louder than a child's whisper. *Are you sure you wish me to unlock it? If this road is made straight, you will never return along it.*

Leoncoeur stiffened. She had already warned him of this. What did she expect – that he would forget his vow?

Do you wish me to live?

That startled her. She looked at him, a sudden desire playing in her immortal eyes. *Of course, beloved*, she insisted. *I desire that of all things. Turn aside, and I will preserve you for as long as my power lasts. When you die, my heart will break.*

Leoncoeur nearly opened his eyes. For a moment, he saw a future unravelling before him – the two of them, mortal man and wife, riding out across a wide grassland, the sun rising swiftly in a dew-fresh dawn. He saw her face turn to his and smile, the care wiped from it. She reached out, and their hands touched.

The vision made his heart ache. It had been forbidden even to countenance such a thing, and here she was, *showing* it to him.

He looked down, still locked in the dream-image. His steed's hooves trod in the damp earth. In the marks of the hooves, tiny worms wriggled. They were white and blind, and their mouths were ringed with fangs.

There would be no escape, he told her, letting go of her hand. *It would pursue us to the ends of the earth. You know this.*

The Lady nodded, smiling sadly. *And now you do, too. So ask me again, my champion. You wish me to give you a path to Altdorf?*

He did not. He wished for nothing but the vision, even in its falsity and its deception. He wished only for a scrap of time alone with her, just as he had always dreamed of, even if it meant an eternity of damnation thereafter.

But wishes were for peasants, and he was a knight of the realm.

If it lies within your power, Lady, he breathed, *make the road straight.*

She bowed, her expression a mix of sorrow and satisfaction, and the vision ebbed away. Leoncoeur opened his eyes again.

Nothing had changed. His warriors gave no sign of impatience – however long the exchange had seemed to him, it had clearly been no time for them.

He straightened in his saddle, and turned to the foul morass ahead.

'Your reach does not yet compass the world,' he announced, gazing out at it with his fierce, blue-eyed glare. 'While we may yet contest you, we will.'

His words rang out, echoing strangely on the air. The vines shivered, and straggling roots withdrew. The entire forest seemed to falter, as if stirred by a sudden gust of wind.

Leoncoeur smiled coldly. He could feel the divine power now, warm against his flesh like summer sun. She was weakened, to be sure, but not yet destroyed.

'Rise,' he commanded, raising his blade and pointing it ahead.

The waters began to surge, let loose like a dam breaking. The river burst its banks, welling up and flooding the path ahead. Leoncoeur backed up, never letting his blade waver, as the road ahead dissolved into foaming silt.

The trees immediately shrank back, and a thin hissing broke out from among the branches. The waters kept on rising, boiling up out of the ground in defiance of all natural law. Fresh springs burst through the open rock, gushing in plumes of white before crashing to the ground again and sluicing down the slope.

Leoncoeur backed up further, watching with some satisfaction as the river's banks crumbled away, unable to accommodate the roaring torrent that now coursed through it. Boulders were dislodged, rolling along with the flow and crashing into the twisted trunks ahead. The roar of the waters mingled with the snap and crack of wood breaking.

Where the Lady's water-magic hit the sorcerous forest, great gouts of smoke leapt into the sky, fizzing and spitting with emerald aethyr-energies. The raging river seemed to carve straight through whatever it touched, burning the foul woods away as if acid had been poured onto them. A stench like burning flesh rose up, harsh and acrid.

'Stand firm!' commanded Leoncoeur, working to keep his steed from panicking. The waters frothed and swirled around its hooves, causing no more harm to it than a non-magical river. Ahead of them, the torrent gouged deeper, cutting a path through the woodland and leaving ragged wound-edges on either side. The up-swell of water kept on rising, roiling and churning out from the fractured earth. The forest was ripped open, its roots torn up and its tight-wound growths carried away. As the waters smashed onwards, tearing ever deeper into the country beyond, the sound of a woman's laughter could be heard over the thunder, faint but unmistakable.

Soon the sounds faded away, heading north as the magically roused river cut its way onward. An empty road stood in its wake, dripping and sodden, overlooked on either side by the surviving trees. The path was like a tunnel, overhung and hemmed in on all sides. The Lady's power had only been sufficient to rid the river's path of its filth, and the clear route extended no further than the road's edge.

Leoncoeur looked into the shadows, his heart thumping. Witnessing the extreme release of such magic had been a mixed experience for him. On the one hand, being in close proximity to the divine strength of his lifelong queen was what gave him the reason for living. On the other, he was under no illusions that this march would be his last. The brief, snatched vision of another life had made the choice even crueller, though he knew the purpose of it.

She had to be sure. Even the slenderest chance that he would turn aside had to be discounted. He did not resent her testing him, for his whole life had been a test, and the knowledge that he had passed it made up for some of the grief.

Not all of it, though. It would take him a long time to forget the vision.

'You have been shown the way,' he announced, lowering his blade at last and sheathing it. His horse stamped in the waters. Ahead of them, the river level gradually subsided as the tide-face worked its way further north. 'Now we begin the final march. Ride on, for Bretonnia and the Lady.'

The warriors about him saluted piously, and began to move. One by one, trooping in file, the knights of Bretonnia passed under the shadow of the plague-wood, and trod the last road to Altdorf.

The host of the undead grew ever larger, feeding from the slain of the battles and pulling corpses out of the ground every passing hour.

It was all so familiar. Vlad remembered doing the same thing just the previous year – gathering the lost souls to himself, giving them purpose, making them far greater than they ever had been in their first life.

Then he smiled to himself, embarrassed by the false recollection. It had not been last year – it had been over a thousand years ago, and everything in the world had changed. It was so easy to forget how long he had been away. His old enemies – Kruger of the Order of the White Wolf, Wilhelm the Theogonist – had been dead so long that no mortals outside the dusty archives still remembered their names. And yet, to him, it felt like mere months ago. He could still see the walls of Altdorf reeling before him, ripe for destruction. He could taste the blackpowder on the air, and feel the pressure of Isabella's hand in his as they jointly planned the final assault.

She had been his strength, back then. Everything he had done had been through her, driven onwards by the raw passion that had so surprised him. To be alone, truly alone, never lost its bitter aftertaste. He could summon as many courtesans to his side as he liked, taking his pick from the cadavers of a thousand years of ossified beauty, and it would make no difference.

Perhaps, he had thought to himself in the lonely hours of the night, that was why the Master had been able to pull him back. In true death, Vlad must have been an unquiet soul, ripped untimely from the world and still hungering to return for the love he had left behind.

'Now I am a *mortarch*,' he said to himself dryly. 'The titles he has given us, to usher in the reign of eternal order. I would have preferred *Emperor*, but such is fate. Perhaps I shall still be *elector*, which will be a decent consolation.'

He had not heard from Altdorf since sending his letter. He had not expected to, though to have no response at all, not even a denunciation, wore at his pride a little. As far as he was concerned, the offer remained open. He might have to wait until the walls were broken and the mortal armies were reeling, but waiting was something he had always been good at.

'My lord,' said Herrscher, sounding concerned. 'Regard the river.'

Vlad snapped out of his thoughts, and looked up.

He sat on a throne mounted atop the high quarterdeck of a shallow-hulled river cruiser. Ranks of oars dipped and hauled into the murky waters around, dragging the ship south and west along the course of the Reik. Behind him, in a long procession of bleak ugliness, trade barges followed on, each one stuffed with the bodies of his servants. Every barge carried several hundred soldiers, and there were dozens upon dozens of them now, plundered from the destroyed Imperial settlements along the Stir and the upper Reik. The sable banners of Sylvania hung from every one, held aloft by cold hands. No sound came from those barges, save for the slap of oars in the water and the thump of reed clumps hitting the solid bows.

Since taking to the river, progress west had been rapid. With the need to negotiate the clogged and treacherous forest paths negated, the entire army had slipped towards their goal without obstruction, travelling just as well by day as by night, pausing only to sack any of the riverside towns they came across. Kemperbad had been the last big one, a walled fortress to rival Wurtbad, and the fight to subdue it had been just as vicious. The outcome had been much the same, in the end – a cohort of newly dead and newly cowed to bolster the truly huge host now under his thrall.

Vlad had begun to relax then, safe in the knowledge that they would be there in time. He should have known better – the forces of Ruin were not led by fools, and they had formidable powers of their own.

'I have never seen the like,' said Herrscher.

Ahead of Vlad's position, in the bows, the Pale Ladies stood on the very edge of the deck railing, peering into the gloom and exchanging exclamations of outrage. Even the reanimated Wolff, still sullen and moody, looked out at the approaching vista.

Half a mile downstream, where the broad flow of the river expanded into a wide, slate-grey expanse of choppy, wind-whipped froth, the forest had crept from its bounds. It had started a mile or so back – heavy clods of moss floating in mid-channel, fouling the oars and bumping against the hulls. As they had made headway, the clots and mats had grown more numerous, breaking free of the tree-lined banks even as he had watched them.

The barrier before them, though, was something else. The trees themselves had burst open, throwing obscene spears of rotten wood into the water. More had followed, building on those sent before. Vines had snaked into the splintered bulwark, binding it all tightly. More mosses had latched on to that frame, swelling and pulsing under the perpetual twilight.

Somehow, the forest had managed to block the entire river, throwing out tentacles and sinking deep into the main flow. Backed up by the obstruction, the Reik had burst its banks, filtering into the woods on either side and welling up in pools of fly-encrusted muck.

Vlad stood up. The blockage was not a temporary thing. It looked like the unnatural outgrowths continued far beyond the first barrier, breaking the flow of the Reik entirely. Leeches wriggled across the top of the arboreal dam, pale-skinned and red-eyed. The stink was even worse than it had been higher up the river, magnified by the standing water that now mingled with rotten roots.

'We cannot break that, lord,' said Herrscher.

The witch hunter at least had the grace to sound concerned. Herrscher had long since given up the pretence of anger at his predicament, and was now a loyal member of Vlad's entourage. They all gave up caring, sooner or later, and settled into their new life. It was hard to sustain the old angers when one owed one's existence to one's enemy.

'Of course we can,' said Vlad, irritably, watching the twisted dam drift closer.

'We should order the barges to halt.'

'They will keep going.'

Herrscher looked exasperated. 'We will run aground!'

From the bows, the Pale Ladies had started to laugh. Their chins were all glossy with blood. They had drunk too deeply the night before, and it made them giddy.

'Who do you think you are with, Herrscher?' asked Vlad, pushing his cloak back and raising a clawed hand. 'I was mighty when I lived before, and I am mightier now. Nagash does not just give life, he also gives *power*.'

Vlad extended his arm before him. Knowing what was coming, the Pale Ladies giggled and scrambled for cover. Wolff and Herrscher looked on, one sourly, the other with interest.

The clouds above the forest-dam began to curdle. Thick slabs of stone-grey shifted, and flickers of silver lightning rippled across the horizon. The wind picked up, whipping the tips of the waves and making them froth.

Vlad began to recite words in a language he had never understood in his previous life. Now, though, they came easily, tripping from his dry tongue as if he had been chanting them since childhood.

The air shuddered, and the colour slopped out of it. Virulently green leaves crackled and shrivelled, turning black as if burned by fire. There were no flames – just a cold, cold gust as if from the maw of the underworld. The water turned slate-dark, and the trees beyond snarled and curled up. The wood dried and cracked, ageing lifetimes in mere moments. Vines unravelled from their clutch-holds and sprang back, their sap hardening and making them brittle.

With an echoing snap, the first of the bulwarks broke. Mighty tree-trunks, turning grey-white as if made of embers, dissolved away, splashing into the river below. Massive shivers ran through the entire structure. It began to give way, breaking back up into desiccated chunks. The leeches scurried for the safety of the banks, or plopped messily into the water below, scream-ing blindly.

Vlad smiled coldly. The unlocked Wind of Shyish surged through him, as chill as pack-ice. In the face of its limitless power, the perverted corruptions of life had no choice but to wither and collapse. In the end, that was the fate that awaited all mortal creation. The vagaries of life were impressive in their variety, but ultimately nothing compared to the bleak majesty of eternal death. Vlad had always guessed at the power of the Shyish Unlocked, but it had taken Nagash to truly reveal its potency to him. When victory came, as it surely would, *this* would be all that remained – empty lands, bled dry of filth and squalor, populated by the meek, whispering armies of the mortarchs. Even the sun and the moon would obey the new Law, bound into new circles and following regulated paths. There would be no more rebellion, no more misery, no more *fecundity*.

Herrscher shook his head in disbelief, watching the river-path open up once again. The waters rushed to fill the void, sweeping away the tinder-dry wreckage, and the river cruiser's deck trembled as the current picked up once more.

The Pale Ladies laughed uproariously, pointing out to one another where the leeches thrashed in the waves, slowly drowning.

Vlad maintained the pressure. There were miles of matted effluent to clear, and the closer they got to Altdorf the worse it would become. 'They are scared of us,' he told Herrscher, as his ring boiled and coughed with magic. 'They did not expect this on their eastern flank – all their prophe-cies were bound up with mortal men.'

Herrscher nodded slowly. 'They know we are coming, then.'

'Of course they do. They will rouse every pestilence against us, just as they always have done, and they will fail, for the dead do not sicken.' He smiled at the witch hunter. Then he gazed across the deck of his comman-deered vessel and smiled at all of his servants. They were so lucky. 'Nothing will stop us, my friend. We will sweep towards Sigmar's city like the cold wind over graves, and when we arrive they will see just how badly they have miscalculated by ignoring the scions of Sylvania.'

'Who, lord?' asked Herrscher. 'The corrupted, or the mortal?'

'In time, both,' said Vlad evenly, resuming his place on the throne and keeping his claw extended before him. 'But if the Emperor has the sense to take my offer, then all things are possible.'

He settled into position, watching the forest crumple and deteriorate before the waves of grave-magic. The display pleased him, just as it did the Pale Ladies, who still cackled like urchins.

'Send orders to the barge commanders to row faster,' he said. 'I smell the first whiff of rotten fish on the air – the city must be close.'

The greater part of the enemy hosts had already moved south, but that did not make the north safe.

Deathclaw had partially recovered from its wounds, but not yet enough to take wing, and so Karl Franz and the griffon remained earthbound and vulnerable. They travelled by night, trusting to the overcast darkness to hide them against the iron-dark earth. The unlocking of ancient Law had freed all manner of foul spirits from their long-established shackles. Ghosts floated across the lurid skies, shrieking in long-forgotten tongues. Cadavers pulled themselves from the ground without the aid of necromancers, and limped off in search of living flesh to gnaw. Splinter warbands from the main Chaos armies roamed the ruined lands, hunting down what little mortal prey remained for food and torture.

Every village Karl Franz passed through was abandoned, its houses empty and its fields standing fallow. Even the fauna had fled, excepting those bloated, dull-eyed mutations that flapped and limped in place of birds and beasts. Deathclaw would kill them, but not eat them. All they had for sustenance were the rotting remains in grain-stores or the trodden-down remnants of bread and pastries in looted taverns.

Karl Franz had long since stopped hoping to meet any survivors. At first, soon after he had rescued the war-griffon, he had entertained dreams of coming across resistance fighters. He would rally them, day by day, and the news would spread. Soon he would find a way to link up with Helborg and Schwarzhelm, who surely still fought on somewhere, and jointly they would take the fight to the invader again. The enemy may have been mighty, but this was *his* land, and they were *his* people.

It had become slowly apparent, though, that there were no fighters left. The invaders had driven every one of them away, or killed them all, or had dragged them all into slavery. Every hovel was empty, and every townhouse echoed with silence. Karl Franz trudged through them all, rooting through the remains under the yellow light of Morrslieb, now a mere whisker from fullness.

It was the little things that struck at his heart – the broken looms, the cold anvils, the tin plates half-buried in the straw. He soon realised that he could not have faced any of his subjects, had they still lingered by their cold hearths. He would not have known how to meet their gaze. He was their protector, and he had failed more completely than any Emperor in the annals ever had.

During the day, when he fitfully slept, he would see them come up to him in his dreams, their plague-ravaged faces accusatory.

'We toiled for you,' they would say. 'We cut land from the forest, and scraped crops from it. We built chapels, and armed ourselves, and served in your armies. We looked to you when the winter storms came, or the beasts tore up our fields, or the greenskins broke from the deep wood with blood in their eyes. We would say your name as we reached for our swords. That gave us all the hope we ever had. We would say your name.'

He would wake then, his breathing shallow and his heart pounding. He would lie in the twilight of the cloud-bound day, shivering as his body lay against the cold ground, wishing he had not seen those faces.

We would say your name.

Deathclaw was able to travel for miles without tiring, though his wings still hung broken by his harrowed flanks. Every night, they would break from whatever cover they had found the morning before, and set off. If they found stragglers from the Norscan hordes, they would kill them, and for a few moments the grief would be forgotten in the sudden heart-rush of combat. Karl Franz's runefang would flash in the dark, wielded by angry hands, and the blood of the Fallen would spill on lands that still hated them.

He knew it could not last. Sooner or later, word of a lone griffon and its rider abroad in the wastes would filter back to whatever dark mind controlled the conquest of the north, and more serious forces would be sent to hunt them down.

Karl Franz found himself hoping for that day to come quickly. Better to die fighting than wither away from starvation, lost and unmourned amid an Empire he had allowed to pass into the hands of its ancient foes. Until then, though, he never stopped searching. He never stopped praying, even though the petitions became steadily bitterer. At the end of each fruitless day, he would kneel against the sickened soil, pressing his knees and fists into the earth, and offer his soul to Sigmar.

'Anything,' he would whisper. 'Any suffering, any pain, just to be *worthwhile*. To serve again. The runes on my blade remain dark, the sun does not shine. What power remains in your people? Is Ghal Maraz still carried? I would know, surely, if it had passed into darkness.'

Silence. Always silence. He would fall into exhausted sleep with no answers being given, just the skirl of the wind and the stink of the foul woods.

He had lost track of how long it had been since Heffengen. On one particularly cold night, the clouds underlit with yellow-green and distant thunder crackling away in the far south, the two of them crawled along a choked river bed, hugging the shadow of the rising banks. Above them, strange lights played across the heavens, dancing like flames poured from an alchemist's vial.

Deathclaw suddenly froze, crouching low against the ground. Karl Franz tensed, recognising his steed's threat-posture, and gripped the hilt of his sword tight.

He sniffed. Experience had taught him it was easier to smell the enemy than see them in the dark. All he could detect was the filmy muck trickling at the bottom of the riverbed.

'What is it?' he whispered, reaching up to rub Deathclaw's neck. 'What do you sense?'

The griffon's head rose. Its golden eyes glittered, and it opened its hooked beak. One wing extended, but the broken pinions did not unfurl. With a muffled cry of agony, the creature started to shuffle up the broken riverbank.

Karl Franz cursed. The land above the dry gulch was open, offering precious little cover, and a griffon was a big creature to hide, even at night. 'Wait!' he urged, struggling up after it.

They broke into higher ground, and the earth ran away from them in all directions, empty and featureless. The strange lights in the sky were more visible up there – they were like ripples of ink across the heavens, and it made him nauseous to look at them.

There were no troops marching across the ink-black wasteland, only the wind, as frigid and merciless as ever.

Deathclaw, however, remained agitated. It tried to flap its wings again, only to give up in agony. By then, Karl Franz could hear something for himself – a rhythmic beating on the air, followed by a faint tang of foulness.

He advanced warily, peering up into the unquiet skies, seeking out the source. He saw nothing, but the beating became stronger. The air shifted, stirred by some powerful force above him.

He gripped his sword-hilt two-handed.

So it comes at last, he thought, knowing that whatever approached would be far more powerful than the scattered warbands he had previously encountered. The word must have got out – he had a sudden mental flash of the zombie dragon tearing towards him, its empty eye sockets flaming.

Then something huge and dark burst from the clouds, plummeting fast. Deathclaw hissed, and rose up, its claws extended. Karl Franz crouched, his sword held point-up, coiling for the spring.

'My liege, put your weapon down, if it please you!' cried a gruff, part-panicked voice from above.

A second later, and the huge profile of a war-griffon emerged above them, holding position awkwardly less than twenty feet from the ground.

Karl Franz straightened. He knew that beast. He knew all the griffons stabled in the Imperial Menagerie. It was young, barely broken-in, hellish to control. It should have been unrideable.

With a sudden flare of joy, he realised what that meant – loyal men still lived. Even if all else had failed, even if his northern armies had been utterly destroyed, something still remained.

'Declare yourself,' Karl Franz ordered, keeping his blade raised. Death-claw remained at his side, hissing angrily.

'Gregor Martak, Amber College,' came the voice from above, as harsh as rotten tree-bark. And then, as if he were strangely embarrassed by the addition, 'Supreme Patriarch.'

Karl Franz remained wary. There had been too many deceptions for him to take him at his word, and he did not even recognise the name. 'Supreme Patriarch, you say. Who authorised this?'

'My fellows, as is the way of the colleges,' came the defensive reply. 'De Champney, Reichart, Theiss.'

Karl Franz frowned. 'Those are deputies.' The true Heads of the Colleges had accompanied him to the war at the Bastion, including Gormann, Starke and Kant. If they were no longer involved in decision-making, then that hardly boded well.

'These are confused times, my liege,' said Martak. 'We do what we can. May I land?'

Karl Franz almost laughed at that. The wizard was a comically bad griffon rider, and his mount was quick to display its contempt, nearly throwing him from his seat as it laboured in position. 'If you can manage it,' he said, sheathing his sword and reaching out a calming hand to Deathclaw.

Martak's mount crashed to earth, and the wizard slipped awkwardly from between its wings, losing footing as he landed and sprawling onto the ground. He picked himself up, swearing under his breath as he brushed himself down.

Karl Franz observed the man coolly. He was dishevelled, even for one of his wild Order. A matted beard hung from a grimy face, and his loose robes were streaked with mud. He hardly bore himself with the demean-our of a magister. Gelt would have descended from the heavens wreathed with coronets of fire and accompanied by a glittering staff of gold.

This is what we have been reduced to, Karl Franz thought grimly.

'My pardon, lord, for taking so long,' muttered Martak, retrieving his own knotted mage-staff from amid his griffon's ruffled plumage. 'The Winds are disarranged, and searching for a single soul, even one as mighty as yours, is no longer as easy as it was.'

Karl Franz folded his arms. 'You come from Altdorf. It still stands?'

'When I left it, it did. I don't know for how long, what with an idiot of a Reiksmarshal in charge.'

'So Helborg lives.' The relief almost made his voice shake.

'He does, aye.'

'And Schwarzhelm? Huss?'

'They were not there.' Martak fixed him with a half-guilty, half-anxious look. 'To be frank, it matters little – the city will fall. I have seen it, and I have seen the state of the defences. I could have stayed and died, but I chose to find you. While you live, something can be salvaged. There may be armies still intact somewhere. Middenheim, or Nuln, perhaps.'

Karl Franz lost his smile. 'You are not speaking seriously.'

Martak sighed. 'I knew this would be your response, but please, *believe* me. There is nothing to be done for Altdorf.' His brown eyes stared out at the Emperor from the dark. 'I have witnessed your death there, lord. Night after night, and the visions do not lie.'

'Then why come to find me at all?'

'Because fate can be cheated,' said Martak, almost desperately. 'You were never destined to die out here, alone. Nor do you need to die in the city. There will be other ways.'

Karl Franz smiled thinly. It was interesting how other men regarded their fate within the world. Some, he knew, cared greatly for their own preservation, or for glory, or for evasion of duty. He had never so much disapproved of those men as found them baffling. Not to be governed by duty – the iron vice of obedience to a higher power – was so far removed from his philosophy as to be almost unintelligible.

'I thank you for searching me out, wizard,' said Karl Franz, sincerely enough. 'You have done what none of your fellows managed, and that alone earns you your rank. But if you have come here to persuade me to abandon the city, you are more a fool than you look. It is my place. I instructed Helborg to hold it, and if there is any chance I can join him in its defence, I must take it.'

The wizard stared back at him, looking like he was earnestly thinking of a way to change his mind. Then he shook his shaggy head. 'You will not be persuaded.'

'Persuasion is for debutantes and diplomats, wizard, and I am neither.'

That seemed to remind Martak of just who he was talking to. The wizard nodded wearily. 'Don't think I was running away,' he muttered. 'I'd have stood and fought, if I thought I couldn't find you. There are... good people there, ones who don't deserve to be abandoned.'

'Good or not, none deserve that.' Karl Franz turned to look at Death-claw. The griffon was wheezing in pain, just as it had done since its rescue. It looked barely able to remain on its feet, let alone take to the skies. 'But I fear your quest has damned one of us to remain in the north. My steed will not fly.'

Martak limped up to the griffon, studying it hard. He reached out with a calloused hand, and Deathclaw bucked.

'Steady,' whispered Karl Franz.

'I can heal your creature, if it will let me,' said Martak, running his hand down Deathclaw's snapped pinion.

Karl Franz raised an eyebrow. 'Really?'

'I am a magister of the Lore of Ghur. I may be a weak scryer and a poor judge of visions, but I know beasts.'

'You do not know how to fly them.'

Martak grimaced ruefully. 'My feet were never meant to leave the earth.' Then he looked more serious. 'Come to that, I should never have been elected. If Gormann or Starke had been in Altdorf when the news of Gelt's fall had come in, I would not have received so much as a vote. But consider this: as fate has it, you were found by an Amber wizard. None of them would have been able to make this creature whole again, but I can.'

Karl Franz considered that. Good fortune had been thin on the ground since his reawakening. For a long time, it had felt as if his immortal patron had vanished, withdrawing His presence from the world just as it was overcome by darkness.

And yet, the filthy wizard standing before him, scratching his cheek and running his thick fingers through Deathclaw's flight-feathers, had a point.

Do I dare believe again?

He drew in a long breath. Above him, the vile lights danced in the skies, proof of the deep corruption of the world. Much of the situation had not changed – his Empire was overrun, his armies were shattered, he was far from refuge, and even if he were to make it to some safe city, it was not clear how the tide of war could possibly be turned back.

Still, it was a start.

'Heal him, then,' Karl Franz said, walking over to the other griffon and taking it by the halter. 'Where we are going, we will need both.'

PART THREE

The City of Sigmar

Geheimnisnacht 2525

◀ CHAPTER SIXTEEN ▶

Festus cracked a wide grin as he sensed the elements come together at last. Somewhere up above street level, the last of the paltry sunlight was fading and the stars were beginning to come out. The clouds would be splitting open, ready to usher in the sick light of the deathmoon, bathing the land below in the yellow glare of putrescence.

He had stopped stirring, staggering back in exhaustion from the cauldron's edge. The last of the mortal sacrifices had been added to the infernal stew, dragged from their cages by drooling daemon-kin. Smoke poured out from the bubbling surface, as green as bile and thick like rendered fat. The flames reared up, licking the sides of the vast kettle and making the liquids inside seethe.

Festus wiped a sweaty hand across his forehead, wincing as pustules on his skin burst. After toiling for so long, he hardly knew what to do. Should he just watch? Or was there some other rite to perform, now that the power had been unleashed?

A child-sized daemon with webbed feet and a head entirely taken up by jaws capered in front of him, laughing uncontrollably. Festus chuckled himself, finding the laughter contagious.

'I know it, little one!' he agreed, reaching out with a burly hand. The daemon clasped it tight, and together they danced a lumbering jig around the laboratory. 'I share your joy!'

All through his subterranean kingdom, vials were shattering, spewing their steaming contents across the brick floors. The glassware ran with bubbles, and the valves burst their sleeves in puffs of skin-curling heat.

Festus cast off the attentions of the little daemon, and wobbled over to the next chamber along. The cages stood empty where he had left them, their doors swinging open and the soiled straw within buzzing with flies. Beyond the final set of arches, a wide shaft ran upwards, lined with mouldering brickwork and heavy with moss.

Festus entered the shaft, standing at the base and looking upward. The circular vent soared straight above him, unclogged and ready to vent his fumes into the world beyond.

'Are you ready?' he cried, his throaty, phlegm-laced voice echoing up the circular space. 'Do you know the bliss that awaits you? Are you *prepared?*'

Of course they were not. They would be retreating to their tiny hovel-rooms now, ready for the night terror to begin. They should be out on the streets, ready to witness the coming storm. They should be *revelling* in it.

From the cauldron chamber, huge booms were now going off. The reactions had started, bringing to fruition months of work. Every carefully placed jar of toxins was now exploding in sequence, kindling the baleful smoke that even now surged and blundered its way along the interconnecting tunnels.

Festus pressed himself to the shaft's edge, breathing heavily. His jowls shivered as he began to get the shakes, and a mix of terror and pleasure shuddered through his flabby body.

'You are coming!' he cried. 'At last, you are coming!'

The sound of metal snapping resounded down the tunnels, followed by the hard clang of the fragments bouncing from the keystones of the arches. A vast, earth-shaking roar boiled up from the depths of Festus's realm, making the water in the sewer-depths bounce and fizz.

Festus spread his arms wide, pressing his fingers into the mortar, and closed his eyes. Steam rushed past him, coiling and snaking up the shaft. He felt the heat of it blistering his skin, and relished every pop and split of his facial boils.

'It begins,' he breathed.

The bells tolled across the poor quarter, puncturing the increasingly fervid air. The Bright College had sent menials to light pyres at every street corner in the hope of rallying the populace in the face of the mounting terror, but all that did was send more smoke pluming up into an already polluted dusk.

Margrit dragged herself up to the balcony overlooking the Rathstrasse, feeling the age in her bones begin to tell. She had been working non-stop for weeks, coping with the gradually mounting toll of sick and dying. After so long resisting the contagion in the air, the endless filth had begun to overwhelm her at last. She wheezed as she leaned against the railing.

Below her, the city was burning. Bonfires blazed in every platz and strasse, throwing thick orange light up against the grime-streaked daub of the townhouses. She watched as a regiment of Reikland state troopers marched through the street immediately below the temple's east gate, clearing the lame from their path with a brutal military efficiency.

She hardly had the energy to be outraged anymore. They were just doing their job – strutting off to wherever they were destined to die – and the sick were everywhere, blocking the doorways, the drains and the marketplaces.

She breathed deeply, feeling her heart pulse. She felt light-headed, and the charnel stink in the air made it worse. Something was coming to a head. Whenever the clouds briefly split, the sickening illumination of Morrslieb flooded the rooftops, making Altdorf look like a forest of spikes set against an ocean of yellow-green.

Where are you? she found herself wondering. *For a moment, I believed you were different. You came down here, at least. Perhaps that told you all you needed to know.*

The image of the bearded wizard still hung in her mind. There was something about him – a rawness, a lack of cultivation – that she had found appealing.

Too late, now. This thing, whatever it is, is beginning.

Her head started to ache. The air was like it was before a summer thunderstorm, close and clammy. The smoke of the fires made it worse. She looked down at her hands, and saw that they were trembling.

Then she sniffed. There was something else in the air. Something... alchemical. She looked up, screwing her eyes against the drifting smog. Over to the north-east, across the Unterwald Bridge and towards the slaughterhouse district, a column of smoke was rising. Unlike all the others, it glowed green from within, glimmering in the night like phosphor. While the fires of the Bright magisters burned fiercely, this column rose into the sky like oil poured in reverse, slinking and sliding upward in violation of nature's order.

'There you are,' she said out loud, vindicated, though far too late. The column continued to grow, piling on more and more girth until it loomed over the entire district. Flashes of light flared up inside it, flickering and spinning, before guttering out. The hunchbacked roofs of the abattoirs were silhouetted, flashing and swinging amid the riot of colour. 'It was under us the whole time,' she murmured. 'Just one regiment would have sufficed.'

A dull boom rang out, making the earth shake, and plumes of emerald lightning lanced upward, shooting like geysers in the gathering dark.

Margrit swallowed, trying to remember the words of the Litany Against the Corruption of the Body. She knew, perhaps better than anyone else in the city, just what strain of magic had been unleashed in the depths of the city. It had been there for months, cradling slowly, growing like an obscene child in the dripping sewers, and now it had been birthed under the light of Morrslieb and with the hosts of Ruin camped outside the walls.

'Blessed Mother,' Margrit whispered, watching the column lash and unfurl, 'preserve us all.'

Ethrac was the first to see it.

'There it is!' he shrieked, jumping up from his long-held crouch and nearly losing his position on Ghurk's back. 'He has done it!'

Otto roused from a half-sleep, in which dreams of sucking the marrow from living victims had been making him salivate, and looked blearily at his brother. 'Who has done what?'

Ethrac cracked him over the head with his staff, making the bells chime. 'Festus! His spell breaks!'

Otto clambered to his feet, rubbing his forehead absently, trying to see what the fuss was about.

Then he did. Altdorf lay under the night's thick cover, lit up along its walls by a thousand grimy lanterns. The towers soared darkly into the void, black on black, each crowned by a slender tiled roof. Just as before, he was struck by the sheer vastness of it, like a mound of rotting fruit ready for gnawing on.

The roofs were overhung by lines of smoke, just as always, except that one of them was glowing green and curling like burning parchment edges. It towered over the city, rearing up like a vast and vengeful giant, swelling and bloating into flickering excess. Its green light, as gloriously lurid as anything Otto had witnessed, sent shadows leaping across the landscape. Half-defined faces rose and sank in the smoke, each one contorted into mutating expressions of agony and misery.

'It is beautiful,' he murmured, absently letting his hand fall to his scythe-stave.

A low rumble from below told him that Ghurk agreed. The triplets stood, lost in admiration, as the first mark of Festus's Great Tribulation began.

'I can feel the aethyr bending,' said Ethrac appreciatively. 'He has been working on this for a long time.'

Otto chuckled darkly. 'He enjoys his labours.'

'As do we all.'

The column continued to grow. The clouds above the city responded, sending down tendrils like stalactites, and soon a vortex began to churn over the battlements, glowing and flickering like embers. The growl of thunder rocked the valley, though this time it was not the world's elements that stirred. Lightning snapped down from tormented clouds, flooding more emerald light over the sacrificial city.

'It is fitting, is it not?' mused Ethrac. 'That the first strike should be self-inflicted? The City of Sigmar will gnaw its own innards out, and all before the first standard is lifted.'

Otto was barely paying attention. The column of smoke was twisting like a tornado, only far vaster and slower, rotating ominously as it gathered girth and momentum. The rain started up again, as if triggered by the pillar of aethyr-energy churning up out of the city's innards. Droplets pinged and tumbled down Ghurk's vast bulk.

A rumble drummed across the land, lower than the thunder, like the unsteady foundations of the world grating together. The rain picked up in intensity, sheeting down in thick, viscous gobbets of slime.

Otto lifted his head and grinned, feeling cool mucus run down his cracked features.

'And do you see them?' asked Ethrac, his bony face twisted into a look of ecstasy. 'The others? Look out, o my brother, and observe what the beacon has summoned.'

Otto blinked the slime from his eyes and peered out into the gloom. The sun was nothing more than a red glow in the far west, but all across the northern horizon, crimson pinpricks were emerging from the forest. First a few dozen, then hundreds, then thousands. 'I see it, o my brother,' he said. 'That is the Lord of Tentacles, and the scions of the beast-forest. So many! So, so many.'

'And, though you do not see it yet, Epidemius is closing from the east. The river will be blocked from both compass points.' Ethrac reached down to playfully tug at Ghurk's lone eyebrow. 'You will be feasting on live flesh again soon, great one!'

Ghurk chortled eagerly, and his shoulders rolled with mirth.

Over Altdorf, the column of green fire burst into ever more violent life, revealing a twisting helix of luminescent power coursing at its heart. The heavens responded, and the storm overhead rotated faster in sympathy, a vast movement that spread out over the entire forest.

Altdorf was now the fulcrum on which the heavens themselves turned. As the thunder ramped up and the slime-rain fell ever more heavily, a delicious air of terror lodged firmly over the Reik, seeping up from the slime of the earth and bleeding into the churn of the ruptured skies. The column of green fire punched a hole through the heart of the swirling vortex, fully exposing the damaged face of Morrslieb, hanging at the very heart of the heavens like a severed tumour set among the stars.

'My people!' Otto cried out, turning from his vantage to face the colossal army that had waited for so long within sight of the prize, held in place by the triplets' peerless command. Ranks of grizzled Norscans, wild Skaelings, gurning lesser daemons, plague-afflicted mortals and corrupted beast-mutants lifted up their sore-pocked faces and waited for the order. A thousand banners were hoisted into the dribbling rain, each one marked with a different aspect of the Urfather. Cleavers were pulled from leather slip-cases, mauls unhooked from chains, blunt-bladed swords from human-hide sheaths. 'The sign has been given!'

Otto raised one arm, holding his scythe aloft in triumph. The heavens responded with a violent crack, and green lightning exposed him in sudden vividness, his mutated face broken by a manic grin of pure battle-lust. 'You have waited long enough! The deathmoon swells full, the Tribulation has begun. Now for the final neck to snap!'

A guttural snarling broke out from the limitless hordes, and they began to shuffle forward, impatient for the command.

Otto laughed out loud, and lowered his scythe towards the epicentre of the maelstrom.

'To the gates!' he commanded.

* * *

Helborg stood with Zintler on the towering summit of the North Gate, overlooking the walls below. The two of them were surrounded by a twenty-strong detachment of Reiksguard, as well as the usual panoply of senior engineers, battle-mages and warrior priests. Below then, the parapets were stuffed with men. Every soldier on the walls held a bow or long-gun, and all eyes were fixed to the north, where the plague-forest had crept ever closer. They felt the tramp of massed boots long before they saw the vast array of torches creep towards the perimeter. They heard the brazen blare of war horns, and the low chanting of dirges to the god of decay.

When the rain began, Helborg had initially ignored it. The droplets felt heavier than normal, and splatted wetly on his helm's visor before trickling down the steel edges. His gaze remained fixed outward, ready to give the command to open fire.

The great cannons had been wheeled into position. Many were manned by the infirm and the elderly, for the plague had thinned out the gun-crews terribly. He would never have tolerated such a state of affairs in the normal run of things, but this was not, as had long been evident, in any way normal.

'Ready for the order,' he said, watching the enemy emerge from the tree-cover, barely three hundred yards from the outer walls.

Zintler passed on the command, which was relayed to the master engineer, which was sent down to the gunnery captain in the firing vaults, which was dispatched by the wall-sergeants, which was finally picked up by the dozens of crews standing ready by the piles of shot and blackpowder kegs.

Helborg's mind briefly ran over the order of defence for the final time. He and half of the Reiksguard had been stationed in the north, where the assault from the Drakwald was expected. Von Kleistervoll had taken the West Gate with most of the remaining Reiksguard force, bolstered by the sternest of the Altdorfer regiments. The East Gate defence was dominated by the Engineer's School, which stood just inside the walls to the north of the gate itself. The engineers had somehow coaxed four steam tanks into operation, which stood ready inside the gate itself, surrounded by companies of handgunners and artillery pieces. Magisters had been deployed in every formation, mostly drawn from the Bright College where possible, as well as warriors of the Church of Sigmar and priests of Ulric. The Knightly Orders had been mostly stationed in the north, though, as in all things, Helborg had been obliged to spread them thinly.

The vast majority of the state troop defenders were arranged on the walls, and given any ranged weapons that could be drummed up. The scant reserve forces stood further back, ready to be thrown into the fray whenever a section looked in danger of being lost. Scattered bands of pistoliers stood ready at all the main platzen, operating as a fast-reaction force.

It was as well-organised as it could have been, given the time and circumstances. Most regiments stood at no more than two-thirds strength, but every man who could stand on his own feet had answered the summons.

Even those that could not had dragged themselves into the streets, clutching a sword and preparing, with feverish minds and sweaty hands, to do what they could to staunch the onslaught. They knew that there would be no prisoners taken, and nowhere to flee to if they failed.

'My lord,' said Zintler, hesitantly.

'Not now,' growled Helborg, scrutinising the growing horde ahead as it crawled into position. He saw trebuchets being hauled into position, and heavier war engines grinding through the forest, dragged by teams of obscenely huge creatures with slobbering jaws. There were so many of them, more than he had ever seen in all his years of battle.

'My lord, you should see this,' insisted Zintler.

Helborg whirled on him, ready to tell him to stand down and attend to his own station, when he caught sight of the green light flooding the parapet.

He turned slowly, dreading what he was about to see.

A massive tornado had erupted from the heart of the poor quarter, over in the cramped south-eastern sector of the city. The rain whipped and danced around it, seeming to fuel the accelerating movement of the immense aethyr-walls. Already it had snaked high up into the skies, glowing like corpse-light and casting a foul sheen to every surface under it.

'What, in the name of...' Helborg began, lost for words.

Lightning scampered down the flanks of the enormous pillar. It boiled and massed and thrust ever upwards, making the rainfall heavier, driven by ever-faster winds that howled with the voices of daemons. The dense cloud cover above it broke, exposing the sickening light of the deathmoon. As the two lurid lights mingled, a booming crack rang out across the entire city, shaking it to its foundations. The war horns of the enemy rose up in answer, and a deafening wall of noise broke out from every quarter. Drums began to roll wildly, and the rain started to slam down with ever greater intensity.

'Where are the magisters?' roared Helborg. 'Order them to shut it down!'

He had a sudden, terrible recollection of Martak then, but there was no time to dwell on it – the column exploded into light, thundering into the heavens with the roar and crash of aethyr-tides breaking. Huge streamers of blistering coruscation shot down in answer from the skies, laced with white-edged flame, and he had to avert his eyes.

The rain now thudded around them in thick eddies, pooling and sliding on the stone. It was not water but a kind of milky slime that loosened footing and seemed to dissolve the surfaces it slopped over.

A vast, rolling laugh broke out across the city, resounding from one end to the other. No mortal being laughed like that, nor even the daemon-servants that stalked among the enemy armies – it was the laugh of a horrific, eternal and infinitely malevolent presence of the divine plane.

The twisting column broke open, bursting like a lanced boil, spilling multi-hued luminescence into the night and banishing the last of the natural shadows. The entire city swung and lurched with crazed illumination, dazzling the eyes of any who looked directly into it.

The battle-mages were already sending counter-spells spinning up at the raging tempest, but their hastily contrived wards had little effect on the gathering inferno.

The laughter picked up in volume, but this time it spilled from more than one mouth. Within the writhing pillar of steam and fire, dark clots emerged, galloping into reality with terrifying speed. They burst from their aethyr-womb and were flung out over the city, their limbs cartwheeling and their mouths wide with mirth. Every contorted, wizened and twisted denizen of the Other Realm vomited forth – horned-faced, bulbous-bellied, wart-encrusted, boil-bursting, cloven-hoofed and rheumy-eyed, the daemons had come. They spilled out of the gap in reality like a swarm of insects dislodged from the darkest corner of the deepest dungeon, snickering and dribbling as they came.

There was no time to respond. Before Helborg had a chance to rally his forces to resist the horrors capering among his own streets, the charge was sounded from outside the walls. The war horns reached an ear-ripping crescendo, and tens of thousands of hoarse voices lifted in lust and expectation. The trebuchets opened up, hurling strangely glowing projectiles into the walls, where they shattered in foul gouts of marsh gas. The enemy hosts to the west, north and east charged simultaneously, crashing towards the perimeter in a sweeping tide that soon joined up into a seamless scrum of jostling, hard-running, weapon-brandishing hatred.

The numbers were overwhelming, both inside and outside the walls. It was as if the world had split open and thrown every monstrous servant of the plague-god into the same place, replete with daemons and half-breed terrors and mutated grotesques. It was unstoppable. It was never-ending. They would just keep on coming, smashing aside any resistance, fuelled by the unclean magicks that played and burst above them in vortices of pure destruction.

Zintler froze. The gunnery captains looked to him, lost in shock. Even the warrior priests seemed uncertain how to react to such sudden, shattering force.

Helborg, his heart beating hard, his armour running with slime-rain, thrust himself to the very edge of the parapet where he knew he would be seen by the greatest number of his troops.

'Open fire!' he roared, bawling into the inferno with every ounce of strength. 'By Sigmar's blood, *open fire!*'

That seemed to galvanise the others. Zintler shouted out orders to the captains, most of whom were now moving again, relaying instructions to the firing vaults. The first of the great cannons detonated, sending its shot whistling out into the seething press beyond the walls. The crack of pistol and long-gun fire rippled down the walls, followed by the hiss of arrows leaving bows.

The magisters responded to the sea of sorcery with spells of their own, and soon the raging skies were riven with the arcs and flares of unleashed magic. More cannons boomed out, shaking the walls with their recoil and hurling lines of iron balls deep into the heart of the onrushing enemy. Whole sections of the walls disappeared behind rolling curtains of black-powder discharge, further adding to the cacophony.

The heavens were broken. The laws of reality were shattered. Men and daemons fought on the streets, while the engines of war blazed at one another across a battlefield already choked by death and madness. The rain scythed down, drenching everything in curtains of sickness, and the deathmoon presided over a lightning-flecked, smoke-barred picture of devastation.

At the heart of the storm, Helborg stood proudly, his fist raised in defiance of the arrows that already clattered and rebounded from the stone around him.

'Stand fast!' he bellowed, knowing he would need to stay visible. This was the hammer-blow, the hardest strike. If they faltered now, it could be over in hours – they needed to fight back harder than they ever had, and keep fighting harder. They were all that remained, the final redoubt, and that knowledge had to keep them on their feet. 'Men of the Empire, *stand fast!*'

◀ CHAPTER SEVENTEEN ▶

The Bretonnians rode clear of the worst of the plague-forest as the sun was setting. They had been moving without pause the whole time, unwilling to make camp under the eaves of such diseased trees. The knights had remained in full armour, ever watchful for attacks from the shadows. In the event, none came. It was as Leoncoeur had surmised – even the greenskins had been driven from the woodland, something he would have thought impossible had he not witnessed it himself.

The harsh pace had taken its toll, but they were now in range of the city. The pass was behind them, as was the worst of the Reikwald. Each knight could call on no more than two horses each, and some now rode the mount they planned to take into battle. They would arrive weary from the road and scarred from repeated encounters with the orcs. It was not ideal preparation for the battle to come, but the need for haste had always been the overriding concern.

As Leoncoeur rode out from under the plague-forest's northern fringe, he whispered a silent prayer of thanksgiving. The last of the river waters had dissipated, sinking back into the earth in gently steaming wells, leaving the original watercourse just as it should have been. At least this stream still ran clear – so many were now little more than polluted creeks, black with drifting spores and mutated, blind inhabitants.

The standards of Couronne and the other principalities were raised under the twilight, unfurled to the full once more as the trees gave way. A bleak land of scrub and heath undulated away from them, looking more grey than green under the failing light. Behind them rose the now-distant crags of the Grey Mountains.

One by one, the Bretonnians emerged to join him. The knights removed their helms and ran tired hands through sweat-slick hair. The peasantry did as they always did – hauled on their loads, shouldering the brute burden of the now much-diminished supplies.

Leoncoeur watched his fighters assemble, and let himself feel a glow of pride. They were intact, and still ready to fight. Their losses had been regrettable, but containable. Several thousand knights of the realm still marched with him, enough to count against any conceivable foe. When displayed in such concentrations, it was easy to forget the Lady's warnings.

These are my brothers, Leoncoeur thought. *There is no certainty in any fate. We will fight, and, who can tell? We may prevail.*

Above them, the pegasi still flew, shepherded by Beaquis. They had remained in close contact through the long trek, swooping low so as to remain visible through the filigree of clutching briars. They circled lazily now, saving their strength for what was to come. Beaquis snarled and snapped at the winged horses, as much their master as Leoncoeur was master of his men.

Jhared was one of the last to emerge, having ridden to the rear of the column to guard the vulnerable supplies. He greeted his liege with a rakish grin.

'A place to sleep, at last,' he said, saluting. 'I had begun to forget what that felt like.'

Leoncoeur smiled tolerantly. Resting his head against moss and grass rather than dozing in the saddle would be a welcome change.

'We must ride a little longer yet,' he said, casting a wary glance back towards the brooding forest-edge. 'I will not rest this close to those woods.'

'And you will have no argument from me.'

The last of the big wains trundled into the open, hauled by lines of peasants. The carthorses that should have pulled them had been lost in the passes.

Leoncoeur and Jhared rode on. The air smelled... foreign. It was not just the taint of corruption on the wind – this was a land as alien to them as any other, populated by strangers with strange ways. Many of those who rode with him would never have strayed across the border before. Their lust for adventure would be enough to fuel them over the last leg of the trek. Whether it was strong enough to make them fight as they would for their homeland, that had yet to be tested.

'All this way, for visions,' he murmured.

Jhared looked at him, surprised. 'Doubts, my lord?'

Leoncoeur smiled. 'No, not doubts. Never doubts.' That was not quite true. He had had plenty. 'And you saw Her power for yourself. Can any doubt that we were meant to be here?' He lost his smile. 'But still, the sacrifice. I do not remember the Empire being so swift to come to our aid.'

Jhared shrugged. 'This war would have come to us, in the end. So you said, at any rate, back home.'

Leoncoeur was about to reply, to agree, when the north-eastern sky was suddenly illuminated by a flash of pale green.

Every warrior immediately went for their weapon, and the horses whinnied in alarm. A cold gust of wind rustled across the brush, making the gorse shiver.

'In the name of the Lady...' began Leoncoeur, spurring his horse onward.

In the distance, to the north-east, a slender line of emerald was snaking up into the heavens. More flashes of pale light burst out, accompanied by the sporadic dart of lightning.

'What *is* that?' asked Jhared gazing up into the sky with uncharacteristic trepidation. Even as he did so, the earth shuddered underfoot, causing the warhorses to stumble. The bloom of unearthly green grew stronger, streaming heavenwards in a slender column.

'The city,' breathed Leoncoeur, feeling a terrible fear strike at him. 'We are come too late.'

Though far away, the luminescence kept growing, spreading across the fast-moving cloud cover in vile shades of pale jade. It must have been massive. It must have been more than massive.

'Hold firm!' ordered Leoncoeur, unable to resist looking at the baleful flame. As he did so, it seemed as if the storm above it coalesced into a vast, misshapen face, leering earthwards with lust in its blurred and fractured features. If it was a storm, then it was no storm of the earth.

Some of the peasants threw themselves onto the ground then, burying their heads under their arms and whispering hurried prayers. Even the seasoned warriors were unsettled by the vision, and struggled to control their steeds.

For a moment, Leoncoeur himself was unsure what to do. He had planned to make camp for the night, giving the chargers and their riders precious rest before leading them into battle. That was no longer possible – if they waited even an hour more, they would arrive at Altdorf to see nothing more than charred stone.

As he vacillated, Beaquis swooped down from its position, cawing furiously. There was no uncertainty in its feral eyes, just a rapidly kindled battle-lust. The hippogryph was under no illusions about what had just taken place, or what to do about it.

Leoncoeur reached up to grasp the beast's reins, which hung below its feathered jowls. The hippogryph flapped down lower, coming level with Leoncoeur's mount, and he leapt across the gap and hauled himself into position. Once righted, he drew his blade.

'We are *not* too late!' he cried as Beaquis gained loft. 'Had it not been for the Lady's grace, we would still be hacking through the forest, but we have been given a *chance.*'

Every warrior in his entourage looked up at him as he circled higher. The pegasi, following their master's lead, remained in close formation. None of them yet had a rider, but that would quickly change.

'You are weary,' Leoncoeur told them. 'You have already ridden hard. If you were any other people, I would not dare to ask more of you now.' He shot them a savage smile. 'But you are not *any other people* – you are the finest knights in the world, and you have been given one final chance to prove your mettle.'

By now every rider had controlled his steed, and the column was already forming up into battle order. The sky continued to glow with an ever more intense shade of sickness, but the first shock was already wearing off.

'We ride *together!*' Leoncoeur roared. 'The winged and the earthbound, united unto the walls of Sigmar's city!'

It would be brutal riding. The ground between them and the city walls was unknown and no doubt crawling with the enemy. By the time they arrived, they would have to move straight into battle, with no rest and no chance to prepare. It would be a desperate race.

'You have followed me this far,' Leoncoeur thundered, climbing into the tortured heavens. 'If we stumble now, then all is for naught, so ride now, with me at your head, and we shall yet break the darkness with our valour!'

Vlad sensed the build-up of sorcery before he saw the tempest erupt over Altdorf. For over an hour, as the river had slipped past, he had felt the gathering of an almighty conflagration. It was like the beating of some immense heart, just beneath the surface of the world, but gathering strength with every pulse.

When the towers of smoke poured up at last from the western horizon, accompanied by the distant sound of war-drums, his fears were confirmed in full.

They have worked some great spell, he thought to himself grimly. *Well then, what did I expect? That they would walk up to the gates and beg for entry?*

Herrscher still had the presence of mind to be shocked. It was a difficult time for him – still caught between his old residual ties to the Empire and his new allegiance to Nagash. Vlad remained confident he would fall on the right side of the argument when the test came, but his transition had taken place in such a short period, and he had had much to absorb.

'What *is* that?' the witch hunter asked, appalled.

Vlad sat back in his throne, drumming his fingers on the armrest. 'Your first sight of the enemy. Mark them well – if we fail here, you will be seeing a lot more of this.'

The smoke curled and writhed over the tops of the trees, burning its way into the sky. Vlad's army was still many miles away, hampered by the Reik's sluggish pace. As fast as his magic had cleared the river-path, more creepers and moss-mats had reached out to drag them back again.

Even the Pale Ladies looked impressed by the fires ahead. They gazed up at the gently turning storm, mouths open, watching as the heavens burned.

'We must go faster,' hissed Herrscher, his voice tight with impatience.

'Calm yourself, witch hunter,' said Vlad. 'Look at what else approaches.'

The cavalcade of barges was still in convoy, a huge train of heavily-laden troop carriers, following like cattle in the wake of Vlad's flagship. The entire convoy was passing around a wide bend in the river, curving from right to left as the watercourse opened up for the long straight passage towards Altdorf's eastern wharfs.

As they neared the curve's outside bank, a grey strand appeared, pale under the dusk shadow of the trees beyond. It widened rapidly, exposing a marshy beach on the northern shore, dotted with mottled reeds and studded with plague-webs.

The plain was not empty. Ranks of soldiers stood waiting, organised into disciplined infantry squares and carrying flaming torches. Black banners fluttered in the contrary winds, exposing old devices of Marienburg and silver death's-head emblems against a sable ground.

One lord stood apart from the others. Even for one of his lineage, he carried himself with a studied arrogance, his cloak flung back over one shoulder and his pale chin raised.

Vlad sighed, and motioned for his ghoulish steersmen to ground the cruiser on the shoals ahead. The vessel ground to a halt, and undead menials immediately splashed into the knee-deep water and locked their hands together. Vlad rose from his throne and descended a wooden stairway hastily lowered over the side, then used the interlocking arms of his servants to avoid getting his boots wet. He alighted at the far end of the silent processional, stepping lightly onto dry sand. Behind him came Herrscher and the Pale Ladies, who were already cooing with delight.

'My dear Mundvard,' said Vlad, extending his ring-finger.

The vampire lord before him looked at the garnet jewel with distaste, before stiffly bowing and kissing it. 'We are in danger of missing the party,' he said.

Mundvard the Cruel was one of the most powerful vampires outside Sylvania. For years uncounted he had plied his grisly trade in Marienburg, only leaving once the doom of that city had become assured. He bore the marks of the degenerate aristocracy he had once been a member of – an excessively thin frame, sharp bone-structure, decayed attire harking back to a forgotten age of elegance. His lean fingers were studded with golden jewellery, and he wore a velvet frock-coat.

'I had expected you to bring more guests,' said Vlad, casting his eye over the forces Mundvard brought with him. Some were the dead of Marienburg, still arrayed in tattered remnants of their old uniforms. Others must have been raised on his march east, and others still were creatures of Mundvard's old hidden retinue. At the rear of the throng, hissing under the leaves, lurked a greater beast, one that had once terrorised the Suiddock, and now slithered abroad again under new magical commandments.

Mundvard affected a look of disinterest. 'We do what we can. Times are not what they were.'

Vlad shot his deputy a dark look. Mundvard was a skilled killer, one of the finest exponents of the dagger-in-the-dark school of murder, but his long sojourn in Marienburg had made him flighty and high-strung. If there had been time, Vlad might have been tempted to give him a lesson in command, a painful one, but Morrslieb was now full and the gaps between the worlds had already been punctured.

He withdrew his claw.

'Tell me what you know.'

'Three hosts assail the city,' said Mundvard. 'They have already started the assault. Some hex has been enacted, and daemons are falling from the sky.' He wrinkled his slender nose in distaste. 'Altdorf is a rotten corpse. It will not last the night.'

'And that is why we are here,' said Vlad, patiently. 'Is your army ready to march?'

'Whenever I give the word.'

'Then give it.'

Mundvard looked at the barges, which were coming in, one by one, to ground on the beach. 'Should we not take the river?'

Vlad shot him a contemptuous look. 'I will enter the city when I am invited.' He drew closer to Mundvard, pleased to find that he was a half-head taller than his lieutenant. 'Let me instruct you in how this thing is to be done. I will not sneak into Altdorf like some beggar, fighting up from the quays and the sewage-bilges. I will demand my electorship before I raise so much as a sword to aid them. When their desperation finally forces them to crack, I will ride through the gates atop a war-steed, my head held high, and I will take the salute of the Emperor himself. They will *invite* me in. Do you see this? Nothing less will suffice.'

Mundvard looked at him doubtfully. Vlad could read the thoughts flickering across his elegant face. *Is this what Nagash intended? Can it be worth the risk?*

Eventually, though, the vampire nodded in acquiescence. 'So be it,' Mundvard said, as if he cared not either way. 'The North Gate is the quickest route from here. The forest is crawling with daemons, mind.'

Vlad raised an eyebrow, and gestured to where his troops were making landfall. Shades fluttered overhead, their long faces breaking into piercing moans. Ghouls slipped between the shadows of the trees, and hulking undead champions trudged through the lapping surf, uncaring if the brackish waters slopped over the tops of their age-crusted boots. Greater beasts were waiting on the barges in iron cages – skeletal leviathans, raving vargheists, crypt horrors wearing bronze collars marked with runes of control. Thousands had already landed, and thousands more would come.

'Daemons are but the dreams of mortals,' Vlad said, witheringly. 'Just wait until they clap eyes on *us*.'

The underworld kingdom was breaking apart. Sewer arches collapsed under the strain, showering broken bricks into the steaming channels.

The air burned, throbbing with released magic that bounced and swerved through the honeycomb of chambers.

Festus went as quickly as his sagging muscles would carry him, sloshing through the turbulent slurry and making his way back to the cauldron chamber. It had been a magnificent thing to witness – his Great Tribulation, soaring up the shaft and breaking into the city above, rupturing the skin of the heavens and ushering in the deluge of daemon-kind. He could feel unreality flex and buckle around him, warping the very fabric of the undercity.

Such complete success did not come without risks. He had unleashed forces that now ran far beyond his capability to control. If he did not get out soon, he would be buried by the destruction he had caused. All he had been charged to do was start the process, and like fermentation in a barrel, it would now bubble away without his further involvement, taken over by an intelligence far greater and subtler than his own.

He stumbled along the sewer-path, kicking past a gurgling gaggle of half-drowned daemon-kin. More of the masonry around him collapsed, sending dust spiralling through the echoing tunnels. Ahead of him stood the cauldron chamber, still lined with popping vials.

This was the crowning achievement of his long art. Most of the petty daemons summoned by the Tribulation would be ripped from the tortured skies by the plague-tempest, but that would not suffice for the greatest of the breed. For such titans of contagion, a more direct route was required.

Festus hurried over to the cauldron, wincing as more glassware exploded above him. The liquids within still bubbled as violently as ever, even though the fire at the cauldron's base had long gone out. Truly gorgeous aromas spilled from the lip, exuding freely as globular slush dribbled down the obese flanks.

A vast hand thrust up from the boiling broth. That hand alone should have been far too large to fit inside the vessel – it was a scaly, clawed and mottled hand, steaming gouts from its immersion and still wrinkled from the moisture.

Festus clapped his palms together in joy, watching as another claw shot out from the far side of the cauldron. Two enormous fists clamped onto the edges of the vessel, and flexed.

The broth spilled over, cascading to an already swimming floor, and a pair of antlers burst into view. Two enormous yellow eyes, slit-pupilled like a cat's, blinked at Festus.

'Plaguefather!' cried Festus, taking a hesitant step towards the emerging monster.

Like all its kind, the daemon had many names in many realms, all of which were but a distant mockery of its true title, which was unpronounceable by all but the most studious of mortal tongues. In Naggaroth it was cursed as Jharihn, in Lustria feared as Xochitataliav, in destroyed

Tilea hated as Kisveraldo the Foul-breathed, in distant Cathay reviled as Cha-Zin-Fa the Ever-pustulent. In the Empire it had earned the moniker Ku'gath the Plaguefather, and its ministrations had ever been most virulent in those lands.

Festus cared little for true names, for he was no scholar of the dark arts, just a meddler in potions and the delicious fluids of sickness. He *did* recognise the enormous power erupting before him, though – an unstoppable mountain of gently mouldering hides, crowned with a grin-sliced face of such exquisite ugliness that it made him want to reach up and chew it.

Ku'gath looked around, seemingly a little bewildered. It hauled itself up higher, and a truly colossal bulk began to emerge, flopping over the side of the now absurdly tiny cauldron. The daemon's bulk was far greater than the mortal vessel could possibly have contained, a conceit that Festus found particularly amusing.

'Where... is this?' growled the daemon, its slurred, inhuman voice resonating throughout the gradually disintegrating kingdom.

'Altdorf, my prince,' said Festus, wobbling for cover as a whole rack of vials crashed to the floor, scattering the glass in twinkling fragments. 'The Tribulation. You remember?'

That seemed to clarify Ku'gath's mind. The giant mouth curled as it snorted up remnants of the broth, before it vomited a pale stream of lumpy effluent straight at Festus. The Leechlord revelled in the slops hitting him, sucking up as many as his purple tongue would reach.

Then Ku'gath dragged its quivering flanks clear of the cauldron. A vast foot extended, terminating in a cloven hoof and trailing long streamers of pickled gore. Laboriously, puffing and drooling, the enormous creature extracted itself from its tiny birth-chamber, standing tall before its summoner.

Unfurled to its full extent, the greater daemon was immense. Its antlers scraped the high arched vault, and its withers slobbered over broken potion-racks. When it turned around, whole shelves of priceless liquors were crushed against its sloping flanks, streaking down the steaming flesh like thrown dyes.

'We have to leave,' said Festus, shuffling out of the daemon's path and knocking over an empty prey-cage as he did so. 'This place is no longer... commodious.'

Ku'gath grunted, and started to shuffle through the chambers, smashing and crushing as it went. 'I can smell the fear,' it slurred, spitting through the flecks of vomit still clinging to its lower lip. 'They are... *above.*'

'Yes, yes!' agreed Festus, doing what he could to usher the beast towards the only exit large enough to accommodate it. 'Follow the stink! They are lucky to have lived to witness you.'

Ku'gath spat a gobbet of mucus the size of a man's fist, and it splattered stickily against the wall. 'I *hunger,*' it gurgled.

Festus smiled lasciviously. 'As do I, bringer of ruin, but it is just a little way now.' He thought ahead, wondering how he would direct such a leviathan to its true target. 'Plenty of souls to suck up, plenty of guts to slip down your gullet. They are lining up, one by one.'

'I *hunger*,' the daemon drawled, as if it were incapable of saying anything else.

'I know you do,' said Festus, rubbing its lower spine affectionately. 'Your ache shall be sated.' His smile broadened as his plans crystallised. 'To the temple, great one. To the Temple of Shallya.'

CHAPTER EIGHTEEN

The army of the Urfather tore across the final stretch of open land, charging en masse towards the reeling walls. Altdorf was directly ahead, just a few hundred yards away, looming up into the madness of the Tribulation. The Glottkin's hordes spread out into an immense swarm of churning bodies, bearing torches as they ran and screaming the death-curses of the uttermost north.

Ghurk was at the forefront, leaping and blundering towards the vast West Gate. His breathing was already frantic and wheezing, his lust for flesh overtaking everything. His distorted right arm flailed around, and in his other hand he clutched an enormous maul that was still viscous with blood from older battles.

The city reared up before them, a soaring black silhouette amid the sheeting plague-rain. The towers starkly framed a cracked sky beyond, shrieking with daemon cries and the swirling power of the aethyr unlocked. Banked ramparts flashed and smoked with blackpowder weapons, and the hard *snap* of cannon-fire, followed by the boom of the report, briefly punctured the background roar of the winds and the flames and the screaming. Petty mortal magic flared in the night, shimmering with every colour of the spectrum, something that made Ethrac snort with derision.

The first ranks were already at the walls. Teams of plate-armoured Norscans strode up to the foundations bearing siege ladders. Wooden poles were hoisted up, swaying in the gales, before being shoved back by desperate hands on the high battlements. Boiling pitch was hurled down at the first rank of attackers, sending huge columns of steam spiralling up as the liquid burst over its targets.

The fighting quickly spread all along the western walls, before joining up with Autus Brine's assault from the north. Soon the outer perimeter, extending for miles in both directions, was completely besieged. The Chaos host surged up to it, bearing yet more siege ladders, crashing against the thick stone base like the tide.

War horns rang out, one after the other, overlapping in a maddening, glorious assault on the senses. The horns were soon matched by the bellows of the fell beasts that had been driven out of the forest – scaled and tusked monsters with flame-red eyes that ground their hooves into the mud and blundered in their madness towards the looming behemoth ahead of them.

In all directions, across the churning fields of war, battle-standards swung and swayed, crowned with skulls and lined red by the fires that had already kindled in defiance of the hammering squalls. Massive war engines were dragged out of cover and into range – trebuchets with thirty-foot throwing arms, lashed by chains to the ground and daubed with runes of destruction; bronze-wheeled cannons shaped with snarling wolf's-head barrels; siege towers pulled by teams of massive, six-horned oxen that lowed and thundered from shaggy throats even as they inched their immense burdens towards the distant target.

Otto gazed out across the measureless horde, and raised his scythe in salute. His heart was full to bursting, his whole body animated by a raw war-lust that made him want to scream aloud to the lightning-scored heavens. His forces compassed the earth in every direction, mile upon mile of battle-maddened warriors, each with only one purpose – to maim, to slay, to choke, to break bones.

Aethyric thunder snarled across the skies, making the tormented earth shake further.

'Death to them!' Otto bawled, waving his scythe around him wildly as Ghurk galloped towards the beleaguered gates. 'Death! *Death!*'

The cry began to spread through the army, and the myriad different tribal chants and curses moulded into one, repeated, terrible word.

Death! Death! Death!

The drums matched the beat, thudding like hammers on anvils, driving the hordes on and making their eyes roll and their mouths froth with drool.

Death! Death!

Further north, where the Reik's broad flow poured westward under the shadow of the great watchtowers, the Chaos forces leapt into the sludge and started wading towards the gap between the walls. The defenders had blocked the way with slung chains, each the width of a man's waist, and had lined up ships, hull-to-hull, to deny passage across the unnaturally viscous Reik. Otto saw the first warriors reach their target, braving showers of arrows and blackpowder shot to clamber across the chains. They died in waves, but the tide of corpses crept closer with every surge, clogging the river further and turning it into a semi-land of trodden cadavers.

Death! Death!

The first of the big hellcannons opened up, ripping the night apart and sending flaming streamers arcing high above the toiling masses. Enormous iron-spiked balls crashed into the walls, smashing the parapets apart and showering the ground below with powdered masonry.

Death! Death!

A siege tower reached the walls, the first to do so, and drawbridges slammed down onto the battlements. A team of wild-eyed Skaelings tore across the narrow span, charging straight into the defenders on the high parapet. They were repulsed, and the siege tower was stricken with flame-bearing arrows, going up like a torch in the fervid night. Otto laughed as he watched his slaves leap from the burning tower, smashing into the ground thirty feet below before being crushed by the iron-shod boots of the advancing thousands.

Death! Death!

The West Gate drew closer, and Ghurk began to wade through the screaming bodies of his own forces, shoving them aside to get closer. Two mighty towers thrust out from either side of the massive gatehouse, each one flying the Imperial standard from iron poles. The rounded battlements were ringed with furiously firing cannons, causing angry weals of smoke to tumble and drift across the raised portcullis.

Death! Death!

Beyond the blackened walls, already charred from the sorcerous fires flung against them, Festus's aethyric column was now glowing bright green, leering maleficently like some eerie phosphorescence thrust into the night. Otto could hear the knife-thin screams of the daemons as they tumbled from the rift, slapping and thudding onto the streets beneath and causing terror.

He could smell that terror most of all – more than the blood, the black-powder, the stink of the corrupted river and the Rot that ran through the city's arteries. The mortals were gripped by it now, frozen by it, and with every second the vice twisted tighter.

Death!

For the first time, Otto saw torches on the far eastern side of the valley. That meant Epidemius the Tallyman had thrown his forces into the fray. Altdorf was surrounded on all sides, brought low like a stag being dragged down by hounds.

Death!

He looked up, sweeping his joyous gaze to the summit of the gatehouse tower. A huge Imperial standard flapped wildly in the preternatural gales, half-tearing free from its pole. Men clustered beneath it, firing pistols and letting fly with arrows. There must have been dozens on the battlements, given heart by the image of the griffon that rippled above them.

'O my brother,' said Otto, turning to Ethrac.

The sorcerer nodded, seeing what was intended. He raised his scrawny arms, lifting his staff above his head. The bells clanged, spilling dirty smoke from their insides as the hammers hit. Ethrac mumbled words of power, the first that he had uttered since the assault had begun, then shook the staff a second time.

The standard, over two hundred yards away and separated by howling gusts of plague-rain, burst into green flames. It flared brightly, dropping fragments of its disintegrating fabric over the defenders at its base. Every scrap seemed to kindle where it landed, and the battlements were soon in confusion as men ran from the fires or tried to stamp them out.

Otto grinned. Few had died, but the mortals attached great importance to their little flags. One by one, they would all be turned into crisped piles of ash, and each loss would be like a dagger-strike to their weak hearts.

'Very good, o my brother,' Otto murmured, running a finger along the edge of his scythe. The gate was now close, and Ghurk was pushing his way towards it with ever greater zeal. 'Now for the doors.'

Ethrac was already preparing. Battering rams were being brought up, dragged by blind and diseased river-trolls. The portal itself, twenty feet high and barred with crossed iron over age-seasoned oak, waited for them. It might resist force for a while, or even magic, but not both, and not in such strength.

It had stood for so long, that gate. Otto could sniff out the age in the timbers, in the granite foundations, in the ancient ironwork that clad and bound it. He could sense the waning power of faith stained deep in its fabric, and could feel the spells of binding laid across it by Empire magisters. The mortals still manned every battlement and pinnacle above it, furiously determined to hold on to it.

The very idea made him smirk.

'Break it,' he ordered.

The North Gate had been hit as hard as the rest. The army raging against it was a mix of Chaos warriors and beastmen dragged out of the Drakwald's deepest pits, and the infernal alliance poured out of the storm-lashed gloom in an endless torrent.

Helborg paced the battlements, his fist clenched tight on his undrawn sword-hilt, his cheek almost unbearably painful, his mood black. The foul slime-rain continued to lance down from the churning skies, swilling across every stone surface and making footing treacherous. Archers slipped when they loosed their darts, gunners lost their footing with every recoil. The deluge got into eyes, wormed its way under collars and beneath breastplates. When it touched bare skin, it burned like acid, and several troopers had fallen to their deaths while frantically trying to rip the armour from their bodies.

'Tell the master gunner to angle his great cannons by two points,' ordered Helborg, furious at the delays.

The cannon crews were struggling just like everyone else. Aside from the plague-rain and the almost unbearable howl of the vortex above them, they could all hear the agonised screams of men being torn apart by daemons within the city. Helborg had dispatched every wizard and warrior priest he could to try to buy some time against them, but it was a desperate gambit, and it weakened the wall defences further.

Out in the dark, the enemy started to chant a single word, over and over again.

Shyish! Shyish! Shyish!

He knew what it meant, and needed no Amethyst magister to tell him.

Huge creatures were now stalking to the forefront of the host, barging aside or treading down any that barred their path – hulking, misshapen beasts with lone eyes and twisted horn-crowns, bellowing in cattle-harsh voices. They were followed by grotesque amalgams of dragon and ogre, which were so horrific that even the Chaos warriors around them gave them a wide berth. The stench of rotting meat washed over the whole army, sending those defenders still able to fire a pistol gagging and retching.

Helborg screwed his eyes up, leaning against the battlements, and peered into the tempest. Out in the murk, past the first detachments of infantry, colossal engines were being pulled into position. He recognised a gate-breaking ram in the centre of the cluster, hauled by centaurs.

He turned to Zintler. 'If that gets close...'

Zintler had seen the same thing, and nodded, wiping a patch of plague-mucus from his helm's visor. 'We're losing the battlements around the gate,' he noted grimly.

On either side of the vast gatehouse, men were struggling under the relentless onslaught of the slime-rain and thick clouds of projectiles from the trebuchets and war engines. Some sections already looked close to being abandoned. If the enemy managed to get siege towers closer, then the remaining defence would be hard-pressed to hold out.

Helborg drew in a deep breath. They were assailed on all sides, and any hope he had of maintaining a tight grip on the outer walls was fast dissolving. 'It had to come,' he said grimly. 'Just sooner than I'd have liked. The Reiksguard are ready?'

Even amid the carnage, Zintler could still smile at that. Of course they were.

'General, you will oversee the defence of the gatehouse,' shouted Helborg to Graf Lukas von Mettengrin, the grizzled Altdorfer assigned to the wall defence once, as they had always planned, Helborg was called to take the fight directly to the enemy. 'May Sigmar be with you.'

The general saluted, as did his staff and the other members of the field command still on the parapet. De Champney was one of the few magisters still present on the outer walls, though he was far too busy summoning up pyrotechnics to respond.

Helborg and Zintler hurried down from the parapet, jogging down winding stairways into the heart of the gatehouse. Once away from the edge, the sounds of battle became muffled by the thick stone, but there was no dousing the lingering screams and cries from within Altdorf itself.

'This must be swift, and it must count for all,' said Helborg, testing the straps under his helm and pulling the leather tight.

'The Knights Panther and of Morr are assembled,' reported Zintler, rolling his lance-shoulder in readiness for the sortie.

'Good,' said Helborg, noting, almost for the first time, how quietly efficient Zintler had been throughout. He was unassuming in the flesh, but once in his Reikscaptain's armour and given an order, he was the model of quiet resolve. 'Well done.'

Zintler looked at him, startled. He did not seem to know how to reply.

He did not need to. The two men broke out at ground level on the inside of the gatehouse, into a wide marshalling yard. The full strength of the North Gate's inner defence waited for them: nine full companies of Imperial knights, all saddled up and bearing lances. The white of the Reiksguard mingled with the black of the Knights of Morr and the blue and gold of the Knights Panther. Their warhorses were arrayed in full barding, each one adorned with the gilt emblems of their order. Every rider saluted as the Reiksmarshal and his captain emerged, and two chargers were led towards them.

Beyond the Knightly companies stood the reserve regiments of state troopers – some of the best men still at Helborg's command, several thousand of them, drilled mercilessly in repulsion manoeuvres, almost all armed with halberds and pikes.

Helborg mounted, adjusted his battle-plate, flicked down his visor, and took his lance. His heart was hammering hard, driving blood around his battered body. For the first time ever, he felt a spasm of guilt at leaving the command station to take the charge. In the past, there had never been any conflict – he had been there to fight, to break the enemy's will, to drive them from the field. Now his duties were many. The city needed him. They all looked to him, and he could not be in all places at once.

He remembered his last words with Karl Franz, back in the cold morn at Heffengen.

We may fall in battle, you may not. You are the Empire.

Would he be as indispensable? Surely not. Once again, Helborg felt the burden of measuring up to the real Emperor.

'Open the gates,' he growled, turning his horse around to face the coming tempest.

As he did so, every knight in every company readied himself. Lances were lowered, visors were closed. Final prayers were whispered, and the sign of the comet was made across breastplates and leather jerkins.

A huge *clang* broke out as chains were hauled over iron wheels. The mighty gears of the gate-doors shunted into position, and steam vented from the brass valves. The doors ground open, running on their iron rails across stone flags. The heavy portcullis was released, and fell open with a dull thud against the earth.

On the far side was a vision of pure madness. The sky danced with fell energies, and the earth boiled with countless bodies. The front ranks of the enemy saw the gate opening, and surged towards it, weapons in hand. They looked infinite.

Helborg picked his target, lowered his lance, and tensed.

'For the honour of the Empire,' he roared, '*charge!*'

'Seal the gates!' shouted Margrit, hurrying from the garden and towards the temple's entrance. 'For the love of the Lady, seal the gates!'

The order wrenched her heart – there were thousands still trying to push their way into the temple enclosure, praying that the building could give them some kind of respite from the hells unravelling outside the walls. When the plague-rain had started, the sisters had done what they always did – ushered as many wounded and infirm into the healing gardens, assessing the grades of sickness, binding wounds and whispering prayers of restoration.

But then the daemons had come, gibbering and slobbering, dropping out of the sky like hailstones. They were flung from the shrieking walls of the vortex, crashing into the sides of houses and smashing straight through mould-weakened walls. Shards of green-edged lightning danced amid the tempest, skewering men even as they ran for cover, and the sound of maniacal voices rang down every reeling alleyway.

The defenders had been caught wanting. With the emphasis on the walls, whole areas of the city had been stripped of watch-patrols and state troopers. Margrit had been forced to watch from the safety of the temple as swell-bellied grotesques had chased down and slain those who were left behind – the old, the children, the weak. Her every instinct had been to storm out onto the streets, raging, doing what she could to banish the stalking nightmares that were literally falling out of the sky.

She resisted. The powers of Shallya ran deep, but they were not martial powers. Her duty was clear – to endure, to resist, to remain pure. Once the storm hit in full, Margrit ordered the shutters to be locked, the doorways to be sealed, the precincts to be purified. The last of the temple's priceless blessed water was handed out to the remaining sisters, carried in earthenware vials to be sprinkled around the temple's perimeter. That might halt them for a while – as painfully insignificant as it looked, such gestures had proved their worth in the past.

All was at risk, though, as the panicked crowds outside surged towards the temple walls, ripping down the tents in which they had been tended to and wailing for sanctuary. The outer doors had been forced open, and the mob now beat at the gates to the inner courtyard, which were only lightly barred.

Margrit rushed along the walls, crying out more orders. From her vantage on the top of the battlements she could see down into the inner courtyard, where the temple guards were struggling to barricade the gates with whatever they could find – wooden planks, heavy metalware from the sacred

chapels. She could also see outside, across the heads of the milling crowds
and over the roofs of the houses beyond. The volume of screaming was terrific, and the stench of human fear nearly masked the ever-present musk
of the Rot.

As she neared the main gatehouse, the air was ripped apart once again
by the stink of magic. Bright magisters, three of them, had appeared on the
far side of the grand platz before the temple, and were unleashing withering
bursts of flame against the daemons that ran amok. At the same time, finally, a troop of soldiers charged into the square from the north, where the
streets ran towards the river's-edge. They bore the white and red of Altdorf's
own, and looked disciplined and prepared. Defying the slime-deluge, they
barged their way through the crowd towards the clots and gluts of daemonic
creatures, crying out prayers to Sigmar and Ulric as they came.

The new arrivals broke the momentum of the crowd. Caught between the
battle wizards and the aethyr-creatures, many of the sick broke for easier
cover, limping into the shadows of the burning townhouses. Those that
remained were easier to repel, and the pressure on the inner gates lessened.

Margrit reached the gatehouse, where Gerhard, her guard captain, and
many of her priestesses were gathered. All of them had pale faces.

'Will they hold?' asked Margrit, panting heavily.

'For now,' said Gerhard, watching the battles breaking out across the
square with some trepidation. 'But if they rush us again...'

Margrit turned to one of the sisters, a dark-skinned woman named Elia
from the distant south whose Reikspiel had never been perfected. 'And
the well?'

Elia shook her head. 'Some waters remains. We did not wish to make
all dry now.'

'Draw the rest. All of it. Take every last drop and make a seal around the
inner sanctum. They will not cross the line, not if the ring is unbroken.'

Elia bowed, and was about to rush off down to the sacred wellsprings,
when a fresh bellowing broke out from the far side of the square. All faces
on the gatehouse snapped around, ready to witness whatever fresh terror
had been unleashed.

Something was emerging from the eastern end of the platz, pouring out
of the narrow, overlooked streets and into the rain-drenched open. Margrit
saw petty daemons spill from the shadowed openings of burned-out houses,
their jaws streaked with blood and their claws dragging clumps of entrails.

The Bright wizards, who had by now taken the fight to the centre of the
square, rushed to staunch the new invasion. Flares of crimson flame shot
out into the gloom, making the daemons squeal and pop as they were
caught. The Altdorf state troopers rushed to support them, forming a ring
of halberds around the three magisters.

'My place is there, sister,' said Gerhard, strapping his helm tight and
making ready to descend to ground level.

'Your place is *here*, captain,' said Margrit, her voice hard. She could sense something coming, something far greater than the squalid daemons that had so far shown themselves.

'They are fighting back,' protested Gerhard, gesturing to where the Bright wizards were going on the offensive, backed up by their company of bodyguards.

'Stay in the temple,' Margrit ordered. She turned to the other assembled sisters. 'No one leaves. We have done what we can – now we tend to the wards and keep the gates locked.'

As she finished speaking, a great crack rang out from the square's eastern end. With a boom, one of the massive wooden-framed houses disintegrated, its beams snapping and its brickwork dissolving into a cloud of reddened dust. Something was thrusting up *through* it, tearing it apart from the foundations. The wizards retreated, launching bolts of fire at the house's carcass. As the smoke and dust cleared, something enormous waddled into view.

Its girth was phenomenal, far greater than any mortal creature had any right to possess. Slabbed flanks of grey-green, pocked with warts and sores, overflowed in a pyramid of scarce-contained blubber. The monster crashed through the remains of house, crushing the rubble under two stump-like legs. An obese belly dragged in its wake, mottled with sticky residues. A flat, grinning head emerged from the ruins, topped with a heavy coronet of slime-slicked antlers. In one claw the creature carried a thick-bladed cleaver; the other was free to clutch, rip and maim.

Gerhard's mouth fell open. The wizards immediately launched all they had at the greater daemon, bombarding it with flurries of starburst pattern flames. It roared at them, flooding the entire square in yellow spittle. The flames would not catch on its hide, and the wizards retreated steadily, loosing more bolts as they fell back.

The monster lumbered after them, accompanied by the last remnants of the house it had crashed through. Despite its phenomenal size, it moved with unnerving speed, seeming to flicker and shift out of reality, suddenly lurching closer before rearing up high again.

It lunged, managing to catch one of the magisters as he fled. The daemon picked up the struggling wizard effortlessly, breaking his spine with a squeeze of his massive claw.

The remaining two redoubled their efforts, dousing the creature in a rain of rippling liquid fire, causing clots of ink-black smoke to curl from its hide. That seemed to hurt it, and it wobbled backward, hurling aside the broken body of the slain wizard and roaring angrily. The halberdiers rushed in close, displaying insane bravery, poised to thrust their long staves into the daemon's flesh.

They never made it. Before they had got within twelve feet of the monster, their torsos burst open, spraying entrails across the rain-drenched flagstones. Screaming, they fell to the ground, rolling and clutching at their shredded skin.

A second figure emerged from the shadow of the fire-bound daemon. This one was still massive, more than twice the height of a normal man, though barely a quarter the size of the greater beast beside him. He was dressed in a parody of normal garb, though torn apart by his flabby belly and wobbling jowls. A similarly crooked grin disfigured a bloated face, stuffed with yellowing and rotten teeth. Pots hung from straps over his sloped shoulders, each one boiling with noxious fluids or stuffed with bloody clumps of human flesh.

The newcomer gestured to the two remaining wizards, and their bodies were instantly consumed with fronds of clutching vines. The strands burst from the ground below them, grasping and clutching at their throats. The wizards fought back furiously, crying out counter-spells and tearing at the tendrils.

By then, it was too late. Freed from the wizards' fiery attentions, the daemon surged back towards them. It did not even use its claw this time – it simply rolled into them, crushing them both under thick skirts of suppurating flesh. Even then, half-wrapped in clutch-vines and crushed under the oncoming avalanche of stinking daemon-hide, they fought back, but only for a few, futile moments. With a sickening snap of bones breaking, they were both sucked under the daemon's foul bulk.

The creature sat atop them for a moment, grinding itself over their pulverised bodies, gurgling with what looked like vile pleasure.

Margrit looked on, her jaw set defiantly. The surviving mortals in the square below, whether soldiers or supplicants, scattered. Lesser daemons scampered and scuttled after them, licking cracked lips in anticipation of the feasting to come.

The two larger horrors remained where they were. The lesser creature gazed up at Margrit, catching her directly with his rheumy gaze. His grin never went away, and a thin line of excited drool spilled from his lower lip.

'Hide while you can!' the creature screamed. 'Walls will not aid you!'

Then the two of them started lumbering towards the gate, crunching bodies underfoot as they came, a leering light of conquest in their addled faces.

Margrit could sense Gerhard's fear. She could sense the terror in her sisters. She thought of the rows of bunks inside the temple, each one occupied by at least two sick charges. She thought of the gardens, and the young acolytes fresh from the villages, all of whom she had trained herself.

It was all so, so fragile.

She made the sign of Shallya across her chest, then clutched the battlements with both hands. 'Faith is always to be tested,' she said. 'We fight for every last chamber.'

That seemed to rouse the others. Gerhard barked orders to his men, and the other sisters hurried down the stairwells to draw more sacred water from the wells.

Margrit barely noticed them go. Her temple was now a lone bulwark against a miasma of degradation. In every direction, the creatures of Chaos had free rein, burning, stabbing, infecting. Flames licked ever higher, reaching up like questing fingers to the pus-thick storm above. The vortex continued to twist and curl, bringing more destruction in its wake.

The two daemonic horrors began to move again, dragging corpulent bodies ever closer. The jowly creature with the jangling collection of plague-pots was laughing uncontrollably. He looked deranged by hatred, and drew a wickedly spiked meathook from a loop around his straining waist.

'In all things,' Margrit murmured, working hard to control her fear, trusting even then, against the face of pure loathing, that something would intervene to save them, 'Shallya be praised.'

◀ CHAPTER NINETEEN ▶

Martak lurched awake, panting like a terrified animal, his skin clammy. Shadow lay heavily on him, and he could smell burning. He scrabbled for his staff, and his hands clutched at nothing.

Then, finally, his fingers closed over the reassuring weight of the wood, and he clutched it tight. The smell of burning came from the night's fire, which they had let smoulder down as they slept. He was lying on the floor of a cave, little more than a scratch in the side of a moss-overhung cliff.

The dream-visions remained vivid. He saw Altdorf burning, and knew that all he was being shown was reality. More than that, he saw the antler-crowned god again, writhing in agony, his body covered in lesions. He saw vistas of pure devastation, mile after mile of land tortured and twisted into sickening pools of endless decay.

And, as always just before waking, he saw Karl Franz dying, his agonised face lit by the light of the deathmoon. That was the worst of all. It was all futile – such dreams did not lie.

Martak hacked up the night's phlegm, and dragged himself up onto his haunches. When he looked up to the cave-mouth, he saw the huddled silhouette of the Emperor, staring out over the forest below their vantage. Did he ever sleep? Had he taken any rest since Martak had rescued him?

Martak shuffled up to join him, hawking and spitting to clear his throat.

'Bad dreams?' asked Karl Franz.

Martak reached for the gourd of water they shared. It was almost empty, and neither of them had dared refill it from the polluted forest streams they had passed. He poured a dribble of it down his parched gullet, and felt the temporary pleasure of the liquid against his cracked lips.

'No change,' he said, settling down on the rock and rubbing his hands against his face.

They were high up above the forest. Since Deathclaw's recovery they had made use of every exposed patch of stone and earth amid the mind-bending vastness of the forest. The outcrops were like tiny islands, ringed by impenetrable overgrowth and sundered from one another by almost unimaginable distance. If they had not had the two griffons to bear them, they would be far to the north still, trudging through the brambled mire, hopelessly distant from their destination. As it was, Martak reckoned they were less than a day away.

'Even a wizard may dream without it coming true,' said the Emperor.

'I never dreamed before,' grumbled Martak. 'Perhaps it comes with the position.'

Karl Franz looked at him carefully. 'You are a strange Supreme Patriarch. I ask myself, would I have let them choose you?'

'It would not be your choice – the colleges decide.'

'What a quaint idea.' Karl Franz stretched out. His face was still gaunt from the long sojourn in the wilds, but he had gained in strength during the flight south. There was a steely light in his eyes, something that both impressed and worried Martak.

He knows he won't survive this. Does he look forward to death? Is that what this is about?

'I will not ask you again, lord,' said Martak, gathering himself for a final effort. 'For all we know, Middenheim still stands. Schwarzhelm may have made for it. Of all your cities, it has the greatest defensive potential.'

'Defensive potential? You sound like an engineer.' Karl Franz shook his head. 'We have been over this. I will not skulk around the margins. It is my city, and I will be there.'

Martak considered asking again, but decided against it. Once the Emperor's mind was made up, he had no doubt it was impossible to shift.

He watched the sun struggle to rise, its wan light filtering slowly through the grimy soup of the night's cloud cover. Palls of mist boiled clear of spiny conifer tops, tinged with yellow from the poisons now gnawing the roots. The stench was getting worse, like fungus unearthed from dank cellars.

The southern horizon had glowed throughout the night, a sick green that flickered and pulsed without rest. The clouds were being pulled towards the source like a gigantic blanket, rippling and furrowed in a vast, gradual rotation. At least there was no doubt over where they were headed.

'And here they come,' remarked Karl Franz, who had studiously avoided looking south. The two griffons were on the wing, returning from whatever hunting they had been able to find in such ravaged country.

Martak watched them approach. He took a little pride in seeing Death-claw restored to something like its full prowess. The Emperor's beast was far larger than his own, with a raw power to its movements that betrayed an enormous aptitude for killing. If it was still in pain from his earlier ministrations, it gave no sign of it, and now flew as strongly as an eagle.

With a whirl of claws and feathers, the two creatures landed on the ledge just below the cave-mouth, cawing at them both in what Martak guessed passed for a greeting. The Emperor acknowledged his mount's arrival gracefully. Martak scowled at his, already dreading the prospect of riding it again.

'You have seen the light, I take it?' asked Karl Franz, almost casually.

Martak grimaced. 'How could I miss it?'

'Not the burning. The other light.'

Martak looked up. The skies were just as they always were – a sea of dirty, dingy grey, tinged with an unhealthy bruise pallor. Not knowing if he were being made fun of, he searched for something more. When he failed, he shot Karl Franz a suspicious look. 'You mock me?'

Karl Franz shook his head, looking quite serious. 'The twin-tailed star scores the heavens. I see it even when my eyes are closed. They can mask its light for a while, but it will burn through eventually.' He smiled wryly. 'What do you suppose that means? A sign of hope?'

Martak snorted. 'What you propose is not hope but folly.'

Karl Franz looked at him tolerantly. Perhaps, in the past, wizards would have been put to the rack for such impertinence, but there were no henchmen out in the wilds, and the Emperor had proved surprisingly indulgent of Martak's irritable ways.

'It would not be here if our course were not sanctioned. I would perceive that.' Karl Franz nodded towards his sword, propped up in its scabbard against the cave wall. 'The runefang no longer answers, my armies are scattered, the sun's light is quenched, but Sigmar's star still burns. That is something to be cherished, I think.'

Martak did not say exactly what he thought of that. His empty stomach growled, souring his mood. They would have to be gone soon, straddling their half-feral mounts and heading towards deaths that were as certain as the rising of the moons. His counsel to head to Middenheim had been scorned, and the only consolation was that he stood a chance of fulfilling his vows to Margrit, which was very little to cling onto, since the chance of her being alive when they returned was slim indeed.

'I am sure you are right, lord,' he muttered, pulling his dirty cloak around him, thinking of what lay ahead, and shivering.

The knights of Bretonnia crested the last rise to the south of the city, and beheld the end of the world.

The vortex unlocked by the Leechlord was now a raging tornado, twisting its way through the lower city, ripping up roofs and throwing the tiles around in hailstorms of shattering clay. Flames roared around the walls, leaping up against the towering stone like sails in a gale, fuelled and spread by racing winds. Blooms of rot and canker flourished in spite of the inferno, glowing eerily in the fervid night and matching the unclean glare of the deathmoon, which presided over the carnage like some obscene god peering through the torn curtain of the skies.

Dawn was close, but the nearing sun made no impression on the mottled patchwork of magicks and sorcery. Altdorf was a lone rock amid a raging furnace of unrestrained madness. The Realm of Chaos had come

to earth, and to witness it was to witness the birth of a new and horrific order.

The first rank of warhorses lined up on the ridge, marshalled by Jhared,
de Lyonesse and the other knight commanders. The fleur-de-lys standard
was unfurled, and it snapped madly in the tearing winds.

Leoncoeur himself flew above the vanguard, mounted on Beaquis. The
remaining pegasi all now carried riders, each one hand-chosen to command the powerful beasts. The last of the lances had been distributed, and
the clerics had cried out their benedictions. Every horse was already lathered with sweat from the desperate ride, and now yet more trials awaited
them. The foremost were already stamping impatiently, tossing their manes
and itching for the charge.

Leoncoeur urged Beaquis to climb, surveying the battle. The West Gate
was closest, and was already tightly surrounded. An army of such immensity
that it defied the senses stretched all around the walls, hammering at the
perimeter amid a storm of projectiles and flashing spell-discharge. Trolls
lumbered through the swarms of lesser warriors, crazed by mushrooms and
waving flaming brands, only matched in ferocity by the towering, one-eyed
beastmen from the deep forest. The noise was incredible – a wild chant of
Shyish! bellowed out to the roll and slam of endless drums.

Already the defences were reeling. Leoncoeur could see the gates begin to
buckle, the first siege ladders hitting their mark, the great engines crawling
closer to unload their lethal contents. The topmost towers rose precariously
above the tumult, looking impossibly fragile set against the hurricane that
had enveloped them.

There would be no returning from this. To enter that maelstrom was to
give up hope, to strike a single blow before the tide crushed them.

Leoncoeur looked down at his army, forged in haste and driven mercilessly across the mountains. Knight after knight took his place on the ridge,
resplendent in plate armour and bearing the sigils of his heritage. It was
a devastating force, one that Leoncoeur would have trusted to match any
foe of the known world – until this day.

Now all had changed. The old rules had been ripped up and discarded,
lain waste before the all-consuming hunger of the Ruinous Powers.

'Jhared, lead your blades west!' he cried. 'Cut to the gate, and slay all
before you! Teach them the fear of Bretonnia!'

The flame-haired knight saluted, still grinning as he slammed his visor
down.

'De Lyonesse, ride east, cutting off the assault on the southern walls!
Hold them as long as you can, then break for Jhared's position. Hit them
hard! Hit them *fast!* They shall die choking on their laughter!'

The last of the vanguard drew up, over a thousand fully armoured
warriors, each bearing a heavy lance. More waves readied themselves
behind, forming a devastating series of thundering charges.

Leoncoeur surveyed the lines one last time, feeling pride mingle with raw grief.

They were beautiful – brave, vital and vivid, a flash of flamboyant bravado amid a world of gathering decay.

You will die alone, my champion, far from home.

Leoncoeur pulled Beaquis's head north, facing the burning city head-on, and flourished his blade.

'Now, the final test!' he roared. 'Unto death! Unto the end! Ride, my brothers! *Ride!*'

The charge took them clear of the gate, hurtling northwards under the first pale rays of the shrouded sun. Helborg lead the vanguard, driving his steed hard and balancing the long lance against the buck of the gallop. The Reiksguard came with him, just as they had in the north, an ivory wedge of steel-tipped murder carving its way through the heart of the mustered enemy.

For a few moments, it looked as if the beastmen did not see the danger. They lumbered towards the walls as before, roaring and bellowing in a stinking fug of battle-madness, but then even they seemed to see their fate unravelling, and sudden fear kindled in their feral eyes. By the time they recognised their peril, the lances were among them.

'Sigmar!' Helborg cried out, taking a raw pleasure from the surging pace of the charge.

Behind him, a thousand knights spread out across the battlefield, sweeping in an all-consuming line across the fire-flecked plain. Every rider lowered his lance, selecting a target and guiding his steed with unerring precision.

The two forces collided with a crack and whirl and thud of limbs breaking, shafts splintering and bones shivering. The Reiksguard vanguard hit as one, smashing into the ragged lines of beastmen and northmen, driving a long wound through the body of the horde.

Helborg speared a raging gor in the heart, and felt the impact radiate along his arm as he lifted the monster bodily from the earth. The shaft plunged deep, eviscerating it cleanly, before breaking mid-length under its weight. He discarded the remnants and drew his runefang, circling it into position before plunging it into the neck of another war-gor.

The Reiksguard were followed out by more Knightly Orders, each sweeping after the Reiksmarshal's spear-tip in successive waves. Most rode mighty warhorses, but some lumbered into battle astride the ferocious demigryphs, land-bound scions of the larger griffons, with all their cousins' furious temper and scything claws.

The main charge thundered on, plunging further into the rotten depths of the limitless hosts. The momentum was savage, carrying the horsemen in a wild hunt of speed, flair and unshackled bloodlust. Having had to watch powerlessly for days as their city was slowly consumed by Rot and sorcery, the pride of Altdorf's mighty armies was now cut loose.

Helborg pressed northwards, slashing out with his blade to slice down two fleeing beastmen, before his steed trod three more into the slurry underfoot. Ahead of him, he could see greater concentrations of heavily armed warriors trudging into battle, each company bearing a skull-topped standard bearing sigils of the plague-gods. The truly vast creatures of Chaos – shaggoths, ogres, cygors – bellowed as they swayed towards the interlopers who dared to take the fight to the open.

Then the direction of the charge veered westwards, bludgeoning its way out towards the straggling fringes of the forest. Helborg guided them away from the core of the enemy host, leading his squadrons of knights among the rumbling war engines.

As they galloped through the towering constructions, each rider sheathed his sword and reached for a gift from the College of Engineers – a small spiked ball, stuffed with blackpowder and crowned with a small brass lever. The warhorses weaved between the trundling battle-towers, evading the flame-tipped arrows that shot down from the topmost platforms.

Helborg waited until the last of his cavalry warriors was under the shadows of the siege machinery before giving the order.

'Let fly!' he roared, hurling his own device at the skin-wrapped flanks of a battering ram.

As one, the knights loosed their tiny spheres. Where they hit the edges of the war machines, tiny clamps locked them fast, and the faint tick of clockwork started to whirr down.

Helborg maintained the ferocious pace, drawing the vanguard ever further west and breaking clear of the main enemy advance. Out on the flanks, the killing became easier, as the bulk of the heavy warriors remained north of the main gates.

With a flurry of sharp bangs, the grenades thrown by the horsemen went off, cracking into multi-hued explosions. Those devices were the final creations of the colleges – an ingenious fusion of engineer's art and wizard's cunning. An unholy concoction of blackpowder mechanics and Bright magic resulted in violent explosions far out of proportion to the devices' size, and the hulking battle-engines rocked under the assault. Chain reactions kicked off, crippling heavy artillery pieces and sending trebuchets folding in on themselves, hurling smoke up into the lightening skies.

Helborg hauled on the reins then, bringing the long charge to a halt. He was joined by the vanguard of Reiksguard, and quickly followed by the other Knightly Orders. Their numbers had been thinned during the perilous ride, but they still remained cohesive. The charge had punched through the enemy vanguard and taken them a long way west of the horde's core advance, a fact which had not been lost on the heavy concentrations of Chaos infantry and warbands of Drakwald beastmen. Assuming the knights were breaking for safety, they had continued to advance south, leaving their siege towers to burn and opting to press the assault on the city. The gates, now undefended, lay before them, too far away for the Imperial knights to give defensive cover to before the infantry got within blade-range.

With a lustful roar, the bulk of the northern host's infantry broke into a shambling charge, heading towards the undefended gates. Isolated out on the western flank, Helborg could only watch them go. Zintler rode up to him, flicking his bloodstained visor open as his exhausted mount whinnied and stamped. 'They could not resist,' he observed.

Helborg nodded. The northmen were brutal foes, but they could never leave easy bait alone. 'Give the signal.'

Zintler drew a long-barrelled pistol and aimed it above his head. He fired, sending a blazing flare spiralling into the twilit murk above.

The signal was received. The infantry held in readiness inside the walls now advanced en masse, pouring through the open gates and out onto the battlefield beyond. Whole sections of artillery, concealed until that moment, suddenly opened up from the parapets, sending cannonballs and rockets ploughing into the onrushing hordes. The defence that had looked so shaky now presented its true shape – ruthlessly drilled, impeccably disciplined, and marching in the knowledge that only the most desperate fighting would stave off their encroaching fate.

The Chaos vanguard had advanced too readily, trusting in the flightiness of the mortals and deceived by the knights' sham bolt for freedom. Despite their huge numbers, they were now poorly positioned – caught between a stern defence at the walls and a powerful cavalry force on their right flank already mustering for the return strike.

'Now we take them,' said Helborg.

Zintler shouted out the orders, and the knights quickly formed up again. As soon as they were marshalled, the counter-charge began, driving back towards the exposed flank of the enemy.

Helborg did not lead the charge this time, opting to survey the battlefield more fully before following the Reiksguard back into the fray. He rode a short way towards higher ground, accompanied by his immediate bodyguard of Reiksguard, then pulled a spyglass from his saddlebag and placed it against his eye, sweeping across the expanse of the field.

As he did so, a sick feeling grew in his stomach. The manoeuvre had been executed impeccably, and he watched thousands of enemy troops being ripped apart by the combination of high-density artillery fire from the walls and the returning cavalry attacks. The pressure on the gates had been relieved for the moment, allowing the entire northern battle line to recover and restore a semblance of order.

But even as he watched the carnage unfold, he knew it would not be enough. He could see the west gates burning, and the enemy pouring in through the gap. He could see evidence, from the far side of the city, that the east gates had gone the same way. Pillars of smoke from all over the interior of Altdorf betrayed the desperate fighting taking place in every street and every courtyard. The Palace itself was wreathed with the greatest plumes of oily smoke. With the first shafts of sunlight angling through the murk, the whole edifice seemed to be covered in a film of grasping vegetation.

Helborg felt his heart sink. He might have saved the North Gate, but he could not be everywhere. The Reiksguard were spread too thin, the magisters were overwhelmed by the daemons in their midst, and the fragile protection of the outer walls was breaking apart.

'Lord, what are your orders?' asked Zintler.

The Reikscaptain was anxious to be riding again. They were exposed, and if they did not return to the battle soon then they risked being cut-off entirely. Already, enemy reinforcements were massing on the forest's edge, creeping out from the shadows and lining up along the northern horizon. Their numbers seemed to be limitless – for every warband that was destroyed, three more took its place.

Helborg slammed his spyglass closed and stowed it away. He took up the reins and prepared to give the order to fall back to the gates. If death awaited him, he would meet it inside the walls, fighting alongside those he had worked so hard with to avert the inevitable. Perhaps they could still salvage something, a last-ditch defence of the Palace, retreating in the face of the hordes but preserving just a fragment of defiance until some relief force – he had no idea where from – could somehow reach them.

It was then, just before he spoke, that he noticed the strange devices on the armour of the reinforcements steadily bleeding out of the forest. Unlike the first wave of attackers, their banners were pure black, with none of the sigils of contagion. Their troops were neither bloated nor mutated, but looked painfully thin in ill-fitting armour. They came on silently, with none of the feral roars of the wild tribes of the Chaos Wastes.

And then, finally, he realised the truth. Just as at Heffengen, he was staring straight at the armies of the undead. With a cold twinge of horror, he recognised the fell prince at their head, wearing crimson armour and riding a skeletal steed. Helborg froze, compelled to witness the same forces that had brought down Karl Franz, and the same monster that had broken the Empire armies while the Auric Bastion still stood.

'My lord...' urged Zintler, increasingly anxious to be gone.

Fury gripped Helborg. He still had the letter, crumpled up on the inside of his jerkin. The daemon's wounds, forgotten about in the heat of battle, suddenly spiked again, sending agonising bursts of pain flooding through his body.

Now his failure was complete. Now there could be nothing – *nothing* – preserved. He felt like screaming – balling his fists and raging at the heavens that had gifted him such an impossible task.

He gripped the runefang's hilt, and drew it shakily. He could still ride out, alone if need be, and bring vengeance to the slayer of his liege-lord. Slaying von Carstein would do nothing to arrest the collapse of the city's defences, but it would be a tiny piece of revenge, a morsel of sheer spite to mark the passing of the greatest realm of men between the mountains and sea.

Before he could kick his spurs in, though, his mind suddenly filled with a new voice, one he had never heard before but whose provenance was unmistakable. Von Carstein was addressing him from afar, projecting his mind-speech as amiably and evenly as if he had been standing right beside him, and the dry, strangely accented tones chilled him more than anything he had seen or heard until that moment.

'My dear Reiksmarshal,' the vampire said, somehow managing to sound both agreeable and utterly, utterly pitiless. 'It is time, I think, that you and I came to terms.'

CHAPTER TWENTY

Leoncoeur swooped low, plunging into the horde below and tearing it up. The hippogryph extended its claws, tearing the backs of the mutants that shambled to get out of its path. It picked up two, one in each foreclaw, ascending steeply, then flung them back to earth.

Leoncoeur watched the bodies tumble away before crashing into the seething mass of filth below. The pegasus riders were doing the same – tearing into the horde from the skies, skewering the enemy on lances or letting their steeds crush skulls with flailing hooves.

To the west, Jhared's cavalry had already struck, smashing hard into the main bulk of the enemy host. The Chaos forces had seen them approach too late, caught up in the slaughter ahead and desperate to reach the broken gates to the city. They were attempting to turn now, to form up in the face of the brutal assault from the south, but it was too little, too late. Jhared's knights ran amok, slaughtering freely.

Leoncoeur pulled Beaquis higher, angling across the battlefield and gaining loft. He hefted his bloodstained lance, still unbroken despite the kills he had made. Over to his right stood the towering mass of Altdorf, still deluged by the driving squalls and burning furiously from a thousand fires. The west gates had been driven in, overwhelmed by the concerted charge of hundreds of vast, plague-swollen horrors. The stones themselves seem to have been prised apart, and now boiled with tentacles and obscenely fast-growing fungi. The Chaos host was so vast that only the prized vanguard creatures had yet squeezed through the ruined gates, leaving the miles-long train of lesser warriors outside the stricken walls.

This was the filth that the Bretonnians now preyed upon, reaping a horrific harvest as their lances and blades rose and fell. Over to the extreme east of the battlefield, the second wave had already hit, with de Lyonesse leading a valiant charge into a shrieking mass of daemons and mutated soldiery. They were having equal success, cutting deep into the enemy and laying waste.

But the momentum of the charge could not last forever – the sheer

numbers would slow them in time. Sensing the tide about to turn, Leoncoeur dived again, aiming for a great plague-ogre stumbling in a blind,
spittle-flecked rage towards the breach. Beaquis folded its wings, plunging
straight down like a falcon on the dive. The creature only pulled up at the
last moment, sweeping low over the heads of the marching warriors and
streaking towards the greater beast in their midst.

Leoncoeur leaned over in the saddle, gripping his lance tight. The plague-
ogre turned to face him, swinging a heavy warhammer studded with
smashed skull-fragments, and bellowed its challenge.

Beaquis adjusted course, darting up and out of reach. Leoncoeur adjusted
his aim, going for the creature's throat. The lance-tip punched cleanly,
severing arteries, before the hippogryph's momentum carried them swiftly
out of reach of the whirling hammer-head.

The ogre clutched at its severed gullet, staggering on now-fragile legs,
dropping its hammer from twitching fingers. Then it crashed onto its back,
choking for air, crushing more than a dozen mutant warriors beneath it.

By then Leoncoeur was already searching for more prey. Riding through
the foul mucus-rain was hard work, and it was difficult to see more than a
few dozen yards in any direction. Beaquis's wings began to labour as the
beast struggled to gain height.

'Stay strong,' urged Leoncoeur. He need a better vantage. Slaying mutant
beasts was satisfying, but it would not halt the momentum of the assault –
there were too many of them, and they were not in command.

The hippogryph beat harder, climbing high above the swirl and crash of
combat. Leoncoeur twisted in the saddle, peering out over the beleaguered
city, trying to make some sense of the pattern of battle.

He had expected to find the enemy hammering at the gates, expending
its rage against the walls that had stood for over two thousand years, but
it was clear that fighting was already rampant across the entire city. Whole
sections were burning, collapsing in piles of stinking rotten timbers. He
saw daemons swarming over the ruins, chasing down the last of the mortal
defenders or fighting furiously with dwindling bands of battle wizards
and priests. They were everywhere, as profligate as the rain-showers that
splashed around them and covered the streets knee-deep in slime.

We come too late, he realised.

He drove Beaquis even higher, desperately searching for something to
use to his advantage. The earthbound knights were committed now, locked
in combat with a far greater foe, but he could still choose his prey.

The vast bulk of the Imperial Palace reared up out of the gloom. It was
still immense – a mighty gothic pile of imposing stone and iron, ringed with
huge statues to the Imperial gods – but already thick with corrosion and
unnatural growth. Just as the forest had been, the Palace was raddled with
foetid plant-matter, and the austere walls and domes were heaving with
clinging grave-moss. The causeways leading to the Palace precincts were

rammed tight with advancing warriors, led by a truly enormous troll-like creature bearing two lesser warriors on its back. The surviving defenders were doing what they could to halt it, firing the last of their blackpowder weapons from the high walls, but it would not be enough.

Leoncoeur considered swooping down on that horror. He might be able to pluck the riders from their mounts and break their backs. Then his gaze swept east, over the tight-packed rooftops and towards the wan light of the rising sun.

The concentration of daemons was greatest there. They were streaming towards a lesser temple dome, one surrounded by the slumped hovels of the poor. A truly titanic greater daemon was lumbering directly for the temple, its echoing bellows of rage rising above the tumult.

As soon as he saw it, he knew that was the prize. Time seemed to slow down around him, isolating the creature of darkness as the true quarry of his long hunt.

He could not save the city – that was beyond any mortal now – but battles could still be won.

He wheeled back to where the pegasi still plunged and dived into the hordes below. Their attacks were lethal, but isolated, and they were doing little to blunt the momentum of the colossal army below.

'Brothers!' Leoncoeur bellowed, straining to make himself heard even as he raced back into their midst. 'The prize lies within the city! Follow me!'

He banked hard, dragging Beaquis back towards the burning walls. The pegasus riders immediately fell in behind him, and the sky-host shot over Altdorf's flaming walls.

Leoncoeur looked over his shoulder as he flew over the shattered gates, over to where Jhared's knights fought on. They were still causing devastation, but the net was closing on them. It was only a matter of time before their unity was broken. A pang of guilt struck him, and he almost turned back.

They will die as they lived, came a familiar voice in his mind then. *As warriors. They slow the attack on the Palace, and thus their sacrifice will serve.*

Leoncoeur flew on, and Altdorf blurred below as Beaquis picked up speed. The pegasus riders caught up, and the phalanx burned towards its target.

And me? he asked, almost without meaning to. Just to hear Her voice in his mind again gave him comfort.

But She did not speak again. Beaquis started to plunge earthwards, and the grotesque daemon lurched up to meet them, still unaware of the danger from the skies. Lesser daemons rampaged around it, tearing at the walls of the temple and beating on the locked gates. The dome itself seemed to have some power to resist them, and alone of all the structures in that quarter of the city remained free of the creeping vines and grave-moss.

Leoncoeur fixed his eyes on the daemon, trying not to fixate on its sheer size and aura of terror. This was what he had come to slay – just one contribution amid a host of other duels that would seal the fate of humanity. Next to that, the loss of kingship felt like a trivial thing indeed.

'Follow me down!' he shouted to his fellow knights.

Then he shook the blood from his lance, crouched for the strike, and spurred his steed down towards the horror waiting below.

On a blasted hill to the north of the burning city, Kurt Helborg and Vlad von Carstein stood alone. Helborg's bodyguard, fewer than a dozen mounted knights, waited further down the slope on the Altdorf-facing side. The vast army of the undead waited to the north, arrayed for the advance but still making no move. In the distance, Altdorf's spires stood starkly against the plague-rain, now lit grey by the slowly strengthening light of the sun. Spidering strands of dark-green could be made out across the stone, strangling and crushing the ancient structures. Cannon-fire still boomed, and the crackle of magic could be made out sporadically, but the main sounds were the cries of the dying and the guttural chants of the victors.

'You never replied to my letter,' said Vlad.

Helborg felt light-headed and nauseous. Days of no sleep and constant toil had finally caught up with him, and simply to be in the presence of a vampire lord would have crushed the spirits of a lesser man. As he gazed up at von Carstein's spectral face, he saw something like eternity reflected back at him. The dark orbs of the creature's eyes barely flickered. In an instant, Helborg recognised the gulf in years between them – it was like staring down a god, one who had trodden the paths between the worlds and who had returned to usher in the destruction of them all.

At least the pain had faded. In the vampire's presence, the legacy of the daemon's claws seemed to lose its potency.

'What was there to reply to?' asked Helborg, trying to muster at least a show of belligerence.

'That you recognised the wisdom of my offer,' said Vlad, as smoothly as if he cared little one way or the other. 'I have gone to some trouble to assemble the army you see before you. It will march on my command.'

Helborg smiled cynically. 'And your price?'

'You know it. I wish to be Elector of Sylvania. I wish to preside over my people in peace. I wish to look you in the eye as...' He returned a colder smile. '...an equal.'

Helborg could still hear the sounds of battle. They were impossible to blot out, like constant reminders of everything he had done wrong.

'That power lies with the Emperor,' he said.

'He is here?'

'You know he is not.'

Vlad raised an eyebrow. 'You credit me with too much foresight. Harkon has been disciplined for what he did – I had no part of it. As to Karl Franz's survival or otherwise, a veil remains over it. Even my Master does not know his fate.'

Helborg wished he had something to lean on, to prop up his failing strength, but dared not show the slightest shred of weakness. Everything began to blur, like some nightmare that he had been plunged into. Contempt filled him, both for himself and for the creature he spoke to. That he had been reduced to negotiating with such a horror was humiliation enough, and he sensed there was more to come.

'Why *ask*, von Carstein?' Helborg asked, bitterly. 'You have your armies.'

For a moment, fleetingly, Vlad looked genuinely hurt. 'You always saw us as merely adversaries. You never stopped to ask what might be accomplished, were certain truths acknowledged.' He shrugged. 'The northern gate is the only one you still control. Allow me to enter it, and it will be enough. You will have *invited* me. That is important. I can aid you, but you must say the words.'

Helborg blurted out a sour, disbelieving laugh. 'You... *prey* on us! You drag the dead from their graves and make them march beneath your banners. If Karl Franz were here–'

'Which he is not, Reiksmarshal, and more's the pity, because his wisdom is greater than yours.' The vampire drew a little closer, and Helborg smelled the dry aroma from his armour. 'You are a fighter, Kurt. Your soul is not made for governing. Already you have erred – the storm that tears your city from within could have been prevented. Do not let this thick neck lead you into more error.' His dust-pale face creased in what might have passed for kindness, though it exposed wickedly long fangs. 'Your time is up. I bring you power beyond your wildest hopes. Give me the word, and I will deliver your city.'

Helborg found he could not rip his gaze away from the vampire's. There was no insulating himself from the sounds of destruction, though, nor the acrid smell of burning that drifted across the whole landscape.

Part of him burned to reach for his sword, just as he had planned. If he were quick enough, a single strike might suffice – the runefang had slain mightier creatures that this.

For some reason, he found himself thinking of Schwarzhelm. The gruff old warrior would never have got this close – the very prospect of *talking* to such a foul creature would have enraged him. Huss would have been the same. Helborg felt their eyes on him then, the great and the exalted of the Empire he venerated, judging him, accusing him.

But they were not there. They did not have to endure the screams, nor witness the slow destruction of all he had lived to preserve. He was alone and exhausted, and defeated.

There was nothing else. There were no other roads to take, no other allies to call on.

He looked into the darkness of the vampire's eyes, and felt the footsteps of damnation catch up at last.

'Then you will have what you demand,' Helborg said, the words dragged out from his lips and tainted with loathing. 'Save my city.'

The effect was immediate. All across the city, from the burning tenements to the moss-strangled walls of the Imperial Palace, the slime-covered soils started to shift. Just as at Wurtbad, at Kemperbad, and at every other staging-post along the great rivers, Vlad's command of the Wind of Shyish was total. Whatever lingering power of faith that had existed over Altdorf had long been shattered by the Leechlord's spells, and so the very fabric of Chaos came to the vampire's aid.

The first to lift themselves were those slain in the night's fighting. Cadavers rose from the mud, shaking off the wounds that had ended them and lurching instinctively towards the unwary servants of the plague-god. Huge piles of the dead had been dragged together before the two occupied gates, all of which suddenly began to twitch and stir.

The newly-killed were soon joined by those who had been in the cold earth for far longer. Forgotten graveyards trembled and shifted, their soils broken by dozens of clawed hands. With a sigh of ghostly half-breath, a new army arose amid the terror of the plague-rain, unaffected by fear and undaunted by the driving torrents of pus. They locked blank eyes onto the daemons, and marched towards them. All but the weakest of the aethyr-born were able to dispatch them easily, but the numbers soon rose, clogging the already claustrophobic streets with gangs of silent, eerily calm fighters.

Altdorf had been settled since the time of Sigmar, and had roots going back to the very dawn of human civilisation. With every passing moment, older warriors emerged from the slurry underfoot, tunnelling up from deep catacombs beneath lost chapels and warrior-temples. Armour that had not been seen for generations was exposed again to the uncertain light, and long-lost sigils of fallen houses were illuminated by the ravening flames.

Last of all, dredged up from the river itself, came the first inhabitants of the old Reik homesteads, the tribesmen who had marched with Sigmar himself as he forged his empire in blood. They crawled out of the stinking muds of the viscous waters, clutching onto the chains that still hung across the great wharfs. They emerged into the open, grim-faced, shaggy with stiff beards and long hair, their arms marked with bronze rings and their weapons beaten from iron. Unlike the later generations that had been raised, these looked as hale and strong as they had in life, save for the dull lack of awareness in their faces. They did not gaze in amazement at the enormous structures around them, despite their last living view of the city as a tiny fortress of wooden walls and stockades. All they had retained from their former existence was a primordial hatred of the enemies of mankind, and they raised their blades against the daemons without a moment's hesitation. The blades that had once been borne alongside the living god retained more potency against the daemonic than any others, and soon the fighting was joined all along the riverbanks. Implacable undead took on the foul denizens of the Other Realm in bloodless, bitter combat.

The ranks of living corpses were quickly joined by Vlad's host, which marched through the North Gate in triumph, dipping their sable banners under the portcullis and heading straight into the depths of the inner city. The surviving mortal defenders fell back to allow them passage, staring in horror at the ranks of vampires, ghouls and crypt horrors as they loped through walls that had defied them for a hundred lifetimes of men. For some, the sight was too much, and their will broke at last. They cast aside their weapons and fell to the ground, weeping with despair.

For others, though, the sight of such unnatural allies came as cause for sudden hope. Though the sight of the living dead may have turned their stomachs, witnessing them taking on the vast hordes of corrupted savages was enough to prove their worth. Those defenders remained at their posts, carving out a defence of the North Gate, hanging grimly on to the one slice of territory they had been able to keep unsullied.

Of Helborg himself, though, there was no sign. Leaving the command of the North Gate, the Reiksmarshal headed towards the river, his face a picture of harrowed resolve. Nor did Vlad von Carstein stay with the bulk of his host for long. Like the shades he commanded, the vampire melted into the shadows, leaving the prosecution of the battle to Mundvard and his other lieutenants. The bulk of the undead fanned out into Altdorf's vast hinterland of criss-crossing alleys and thoroughfares, and soon the entire city was gripped by the murderous conflict of perverse life against preternatural death.

Margrit was unaware of all of this as it happened. With the last of the sacred waters sprinkled about the perimeter of the temple, she had taken up arms at last, determined to fight for as long as her strength allowed her. Mumbling litanies over and over, she had joined the remnants of Gerhard's temple guard in the courtyard inside the gates. No more than three-dozen guards remained, the rest having succumbed at last to the contagions that now ran rampant even in the infirmaries. Fewer than a hundred sisters were still able to stand with them unaided, and they clustered close behind Margrit, each bearing whatever weapons had been to hand.

Before them, the inner wall's gates shivered as the creature beyond them hammered on the wood. The defenders inched back across the courtyard, assembling on the stairs leading up to the garden colonnade.

'Courage,' urged Margrit, despite the fear that rose up in her gorge and nearly throttled her.

They all felt fear. They were all trembling. The difference lay in how they dealt with that.

'Can it cross the threshold?' asked Elia, her hands visibly shaking.

Margrit did not know. The line of sacred water snaked across the courtyard in front of them, barely a hand's width wide. It looked so completely insubstantial – a child could have skipped across it without ever noticing it.

And yet, the temple endured while everything around had been reduced to smouldering, slime-boiling rubble. She had held her faith for her whole life, and the precepts had never failed her. The great and the good of the Empire had always looked down on the Sisters of Shallya, seeing them as matronly mystics and little more. And yet the proud Colleges of Magic were now shattered haunts of the daemonic, and the mighty Engineering School was a smoking crater.

'The threshold will endure,' Margrit said, trying to sound like she meant it.

The doors shuddered again, and a gurgling roar echoed out. The creature was becoming frustrated, and its maddened fury was spilling over into raw mania. The stones of the outer wall were rocked, sending trails of dust spiralling down to the earth. Another blow came in, almost snapping the main brace across the doors.

More blows came in, faster and heavier. A crack ran down the oak, splitting it into a lattice of splinters. A clawed fist punched clean through, breaking the heavy beams at last and rocking the iron hinges.

A sister screamed. Margrit turned on her. 'No retreat!' she shouted. 'We stand *here!* We are the blessed ones, the chosen of the Earth Goddess! No creature of the Outer Dark may–'

Her words were obscured by a huge *crack* as the gates gave way at last. With a throaty bellow of triumph, the greater daemon smashed its way through the remains, hurling aside the severed residue and sending the ragged-ended spars spinning.

Margrit shrunk back, her defiance dying in her throat. The creature was *enormous* – far bigger than it had seemed when she had first caught sight of it from the walls. Surely nothing could stop it – no power of magic, no power of faith. She looked up at it as the monster swaggered and hauled itself through the gap, and its enormous shadow fell over her.

Some of her sisters vomited, overcome by the incredible stench. Temple guards dropped their blades, staring slack-jawed at the vision of hell approaching. The behemoth rolled towards them, shedding slime down its flanks as the foul rain washed it into the mire beneath.

It took all her courage, but Margrit managed a single step forward, her blade clutched in two shaking hands. She glared up at the creature of Chaos, planting her feet firmly.

'Go back!' she cried. 'Take one more step, and, by the goddess, it will be your last!'

The daemon looked down at her, and laughed. Huge yellow eyes rolled with mirth, and drool the length of a man's arm spilled from its gaping maw. Moving deliberately, with an exaggerated, mocking studiousness, it lifted a cloven hoof and placed it, heavily, over the line of sacred water.

The liquid steamed and hissed as it was defiled, and Margrit smelled rotten flesh burning. For a moment, she dared to hope that the slender barrier would be enough.

Then the daemon chortled again, and hauled itself closer, dragging its flab through the smeared puddles of water.

Margrit stood her ground, her heart thumping, her last hope gone. Sliding like oil on water, the putrid shadow of the daemon fell across her once more.

━◄ CHAPTER TWENTY-ONE ►━

Ghurk galloped onward, smashing his way up the long causeway to the Palace. Resistance was crumbling now.

Atop his habitual perch, Otto urged his outsize sibling harder, cracking the heel of his scythe across Ghurk's scaly neck.

'No time!' he blurted, feeling a mix of exhilaration and consternation. 'No time at all! Smash and break! Crush and stamp!'

The battle for the West Gate had been a frustratingly slow business, with the defenders lingering at their posts far longer than they had any right to. The cannons had caused havoc with his best troops until Ethrac had finally got close enough to burst their barrels with a few choice spells. Even then, the mortals had stupidly and annoyingly remained in place for much too long. They were led by a redoubtable captain wearing white and black who had roused them to almost insane levels of bravado. Otto had been forced to kill that one himself, leaping from Ghurk's back and going at him with his scythe. They had traded blows on the summit of the gates with green lightning crackling around them. The human had fought well, wielding his broadsword two-handed with both speed and power.

It had done him little good in the end. Otto may have looked bloated in comparison, but his muscles were infused with the raging power of the Urfather. He did not even need Ghurk to come to his aid this time, and his scythe ripped through the knight's stomach, slicing through the breastplate as if being dipped into water.

Once that warrior was thrown down, the defenders' resolve melted, and the resistance began to crack. The gates were broken and the biggest and best of Otto's serried host had flowed into the walls of the city. Just as at Marienburg, the glorious blossoming of the Urfather's pestilential delights followed them in. The place was ripe for it – half-consumed by spores and moss-growths already, it was fertile ground for Ethrac's conjurings.

Otto clambered back onto Ghurk's shoulders, and the onslaught continued. Columns of chanting Norscans surged up the twisting streets, torching the overhanging houses as they went. Bands of marauders broke from the main charge and rampaged through the whole district, greeted with joy by the gangs of petty daemons squatting and slavering on the eaves.

The remaining defenders were driven back, slain in swathes every time they attempted to mount a resistance. Reserves were called up, and were swept away. Lines of artillery, placed in the courtyards on the approach to the Palace, were briefly effective but soon overwhelmed.

It would have been faster if the damned horsemen had not appeared and dragged half his army away into a desperate battle outside the walls. Ghurk had wanted to turn back and take them on himself, and only Ethrac threatening to shrink his stomach to the size of a walnut had persuaded him to keep going. Combat could rage for as long they liked on the plain west of the walls, and it would still not suffice to keep them from their true goal. They would approach the inner city with diminished numbers, it was true, but they still had enough to accomplish their divine task.

Now it approached. The Palace itself reared up into the flame-streaked murk, already covered in a creeping jacket of twisting fibres. Its vast gates were cracked and thrown down, its mighty domes gaping like smashed eggshells, its immense towers burning. Daemons leapt and scampered across its long, rangy battlements, pursuing the few living defenders with commendably spiteful zeal. Lightning snapped and twisted across its shattered vistas, licking like whips along the ragged profile.

'There it lies, o my brother!' shouted Otto, standing up on Ghurk's heaving shoulders. 'You see it? There it lies!'

Even Ethrac was grinning then. He stood too, leaning on his staff. The Imperial Palace – the very heart of the mortals' realm – lay broken before them. No invading army had ever come this far. This was the throne of the boy-god, the very heart of his foul and decadent kingdom, and they were on the cusp of it. They had slain and slain and slain until the mud-mires of the streets were the colours of spoiled wine, and this was the reward.

Otto looked up at the colossal edifice, and began to laugh. The laughter split his lips, burbling like a torrent from his mouth. His ribs ached, his shoulders shook. There was nothing left – they had *done* it.

Ghurk cantered happily up the long straight road towards the Palace, crashing into the statues of old heroes that lined the processional. Behind him came the tribesmen of the wilds, driven into a frenzy by the savage joy of sacking the home of their ancestral enemies.

Otto was the first to spot the newcomers. In defiance of all reason, more defenders were clustering around the Palace's outer walls. As if plucked from the air, they were lining what remained of the parapets and waiting for the onslaught. At first, he could not believe it – thinking it a trick of the flickering half-light.

Then, slowly, he realised the truth.

'The dead,' he muttered.

By then, Ethrac had sensed it, too. 'I knew it!' the sorcerer snapped. 'Did I not warn you?'

Otto glowered at him. More skeletons and living cadavers were taking up position across the Palace approaches, blocking the head of the processional in ever greater numbers. Unlike the mortals they replaced, they showed nothing but implacable dedication, standing silently before the oncoming horde, their pale faces empty and their eyes unblinking.

'Do they fight us for the carcass of this Empire?' blurted Otto, furiously. 'Is that it? We must lay low *two* armies this day?'

Ethrac spat messily onto his brother's hide and started shaking his staff. 'They have joined against us, o my brother. They are united in weakness.' The sorcerer smiled grimly. 'But two rotten planks do not make a life-raft. They will *both* be swept away.'

At that, he brandished the staff two-handed, and the bells clanged wildly. More forks of aethyr-tempest slammed down, breaking up the cobbles and sending the stones flying. The Leechlord's vortex accelerated further, hurling great slaps of mucus into the waiting ranks of undead. The vines and grave-moss that had shot up from every mortar-joint writhed out like snakes.

Ghurk bellowed, pawing the ground like a giant bull. The Norscans at his feet roared in hatred, furious that an easy prize had been snatched away at the last moment.

'We broke the mortals!' cried Otto, his face purple with rage. 'Now we break the immortals!'

And with that, the horrific vanguard of the plague-god surged up the processional, beating for the Palace gates like a sluice of boiled blood flung down an abattoir's drain. With a final roar, the host of the Glottkin charged against the gathering might of the undead, and unholy battle was joined at last in the grounds of Sigmar's Palace.

The scale of the catastrophe had been apparent for miles. As Deathclaw had neared the Reik valley, the column of fire and storm-wind had loomed ever vaster, climbing like a mountain into the skies. It was twisting in a vast, glacial rotation, as if an immense vice were being applied to the city below, gradually squeezing the life out of it like a wine-press eking out the blood of the grapes.

Neither Martak nor Karl Franz said anything for a long time. There were no words to describe the sheer size of it. The heavens themselves were being ripped open, and the fury of the Other Realm poured down onto the land below. Nothing, surely, could stand against that degree of power. Whatever spells had been recited to unleash such devastation must have been beyond any that had been spoken before.

The world was indeed changed. Martak could sense it in his blood – the Laws that governed his art were twisting, buckled under enormous pressure. They had whispered this past year that the bonds of Shyish had been loosened, thinning the boundaries between life and death, but now it seemed that all the Eight Winds were running amok.

'This cannot be halted, lord!' Martak blurted out at last, unable to contain his frustration at what they were doing. He felt insignificant – a mere speck against an infinite sky, hurtling headlong into a maelstrom of terrifying size and power.

The Emperor did not reply. As the scale of the plague-storm had become steadily apparent, he had retreated into himself, driving Deathclaw hard. The griffon still bore the wounds it had taken at Heffengen, and was clearly losing strength, but Karl Franz gave the beast no respite.

Below them, the forest was scored with the paths of mighty armies. Whole swathes had been trampled down, betraying the routes the enemy had taken to beat down Altdorf's gates. The river itself was a thick, olive-green sliver of mud, its energy stripped from it. Even up high, the stench was incredible – an overpowering melange of death, sickness and mortal fear.

'You said you dreamed of this?' shouted Karl Franz at last.

Martak nodded grimly. Everything was as he had foreseen – the flames running riot through the lower portions of the city, the terrible slaughter all around the walls, the burgeoning vegetation rearing up against the Palace walls and breaking them open. As they neared, he could see pitched battles spreading out across the entire valley. To the west and east, mounted horsemen were fighting a desperate rearguard defence against a sea of Chaos infantry. At the North Gate, Empire troops were grimly holding onto a narrow stretch of territory against a tide of war-maddened beastmen. Inside the walls, the fighting was more confused, and appeared to be a messy three-way tussle between corrupted Chaos warriors, the hemmed-in remnants of Empire soldiery, and a host of undead, who had taken whole chunks of the poor quarter and were advancing, street by street, across the city.

The entire world, it seemed, had come to Altdorf – Sigmar's city had sucked them in, from Bretonnia, from Sylvania, from the Wastes of the north and the depths of the forest. All had come to feast on the Empire's harrowed corpse.

'I dreamed of more than this,' Martak cried back. 'You know of what I speak.'

Karl Franz maintained the pace, forcing Deathclaw lower. The city swept closer, spread out below them in all its ravaged glory. 'And yet you tell me the Law of Death is weakened.'

'It is,' replied Martak, struggling to make his own wilful steed follow the Emperor closely. 'But what of it? I am no necromancer – we cannot raise the slain.'

Karl Franz looked up then, a strange expression on his face. Martak had never seen a look quite like it – there was no fear, not even anger, just a kind of resignation.

'Surely even you see it now,' said the Emperor, gesturing towards the heavens.

Martak followed his gaze. Above them, still shrouded by the turning gyre of the heavens, a new light was now visible. Shorn of the competing glow of Morrslieb, the twin-tailed star could be made out, riding high above the drifting filth of the world below. Martak watched it burn, captivated by its strange, otherworldly light.

It was not a comforting light. There was nothing homely or warming about it – Sigmar's star had ever been a harbinger of great trials, and of the changing of ways, and of the passing of one age into another. The flames rippled along behind it, hard to focus on yet impossible to ignore.

Martak felt his heart miss its beat. All citizens of the Empire had been raised on tales of the comet. Men made its sign against their breast before going into battle; mothers made the gesture over the cots of the newborn, warding them against the terrors of the night. It was *their* sign, the mark of humanity, lodged amid a world of war and madness that had hated them for all eternity.

'What does it mean?' Martak asked.

Karl Franz flew on. The city was approaching quickly now. Below them, the gaping great dome of the Palace drew into focus. Vast forces were converging on it now, fighting against one another for the prize. Deathclaw began to plummet.

'That death is not to be feared,' said the Emperor, his voice trailing off as he descended.

Martak hovered above him for a moment longer, unwilling to commit to the dive. Everything below him reeked of corruption and insanity. Screams still mingled with the howl of the plague-wind, and the burning pyre of Altdorf loomed ahead like a festering scar on the hide of a gods-forsaken world.

'What does *that* mean?' he muttered, holding position, unable to share the blithe conviction displayed by his master. 'What has he seen?'

He could still get out. He had delivered the Emperor to the city, just as he had promised, and that was where his duty ended. Even if Altdorf were to be scrubbed from the earth, there might still be places to hide, refuges in the mountains where a man like him could scratch some kind of a living.

He laughed at himself harshly. They really had appointed a terrible Supreme Patriarch.

'I broke you out of that cage,' he said to his griffon, grimacing wryly. 'Time I took you back.'

He gave the command, and the griffon cawed wildly, before furling its wings and following the Emperor down into the inferno below.

Just as the daemon reached out for Margrit, something moving incredibly fast shot out of the skies, streaking like lightning from the storm. She had the vague impression of wings, blurred with speed, and the cry of a human voice speaking a language she did not understand. She scrambled backward, out of the path of the clutching claws, and saw what looked like a massive eagle diving straight at the daemon's face.

But it was not an eagle – it was a beast out of legends, a *hippogryph*, part-horse, part bird, with griffon-like claws and a long, lashing tail. Its rider thrust his long lance straight into the daemon's heart, and its hide broke open with a hideous rip.

The daemon screamed, and clutched at the lance. The rider's momentum carried him onward, and the steel tip drove in deeper, causing black blood to fountain along its length.

The daemon ripped the lance out, hurling both rider and steed clear. With a crash of armour, the hippogryph slammed into the courtyard wall, cracking the stone. The daemon reeled, the skin of its vast chest hanging open in strips. Blood continued to gush freely, pouring like an inky cataract down its sloping stomach and fizzing where it spread across the ground.

Possessed by a sudden impulse to come to the rider's aid, Margrit rushed forward, whirling the blunt blade in her hand. She stabbed it into the daemon's hoof. It took all her strength just to pierce the thick layers of hide encrusting the cloven foot, and she heaved down on the hilt to drive the rusting sword home.

To such an immense creature, the blow must have been little more than a scratch, but it brought fresh bellows nonetheless. The daemon leaned forward, bending double to clutch at her. Margrit staggered out of its reach again, feeling raw fear bubble up inside her. Her attack now seemed more an act of incredible rashness than bravery. Up close, the incapacitating stench was even worse than before, and she nearly retched as the claws reached out for her.

She felt the first talons scrape down her back, dragging at her sweat-stained robes, and prepared for death.

At least I bloodied it, she thought vindictively as she was hauled back.

But then the grip released, and she was dumped to the stone again. Twisting around, she saw the reason – the hippogryph rider had charged back into the fray, his lance gone but now bearing a broadsword.

Even amid all the terror and all the filth, Margrit was struck by his sheer beauty. His blond hair seemed to shimmer like gold, and his armour, though streaked with blood, still glittered with a high sheen. He charged straight at the daemon, spitting words of challenge that sounded like some strange music, working his blade in blistering arcs and hacking into its loose flesh. He moved so *fast*, shrugging off wounds and taking the fight straight to the creature that loomed over him in an almost comical mismatch of sizes. He had to leap into the air even to land a blow, driving his sword once more into the daemon's ribs and twisting the blade as gravity wrenched it out again.

The daemon, howling in rage and frustration, swept its sword at him in a massive, earth-breaking lunge. The knight, incredibly, met the strike with his shield, though the *clang* of metal-on-metal thrust him back six paces and nearly crushed him back against the wall.

Margrit shuffled further out of reach, on her knees, frantically searching for another weapon – something she could use to aid the knight. More cries of battle rang out from elsewhere in the courtyard, and she had the vague, blurred impression of other daemons racing through the broken gates, joining in combat with the rest of the sisters and their guards.

The greater daemon, though, consumed all her attention. It traded huge blows with the knight. Each one, by rights, ought to have broken him, but he just kept on fighting, hammering back with wild strokes, making up in speed and guile what he lacked in stature. He seemed to dance around the daemon's lumbering frame, giving it no time to crush him under its massive fists. The lance-wound in the daemon's chest still pumped blood, visibly draining it as the fight went on.

The monster howled with fury, and launched a backhanded swipe straight at the knight's chest. He managed to get his shield in the way, but the force of the impact slammed him to his knees. The daemon, sensing a kill, raised its other fist high and prepared to slam it down.

With a savage scream, the hippogryph hurtled across the courtyard, flying straight into the daemon's face and lashing out with its claws. The two creatures grappled with one another, gouging and tearing, and the daemon was once more rocked back onto its bloated haunches.

Eventually the daemon managed to scythe its heavy blade around, catching the hippogryph on its wing-shoulder and sending it tumbling back against the courtyard floor. Its wings broken and its chest leaking blood, the beast hit the stone with a wet snap, crumpled to the ground, and moved no more.

But it had given the knight time to recover. He rose again, blade in hand, and cast his battered shield to one side.

As Margrit looked on, both rapt and horrified by the spectacle, her roving hands finally closed on something. She looked down to see an earthenware pot, of the kind used by the sisters to carry the sacred water up from the wells. By some strange chance it was half-full, somehow overlooked when the rest had been poured around the perimeter. She grabbed it and dragged herself to her feet again.

'Master knight!' she cried, then threw it to him.

He caught the pot in his shield hand, more by instinct than anything else. He had no time to guess what it was, nor to protest, for the horribly wounded daemon bore down on him, reaching out to throttle him where he stood.

The knight lashed out with his blade, severing the hooked fingers as they closed, then raced forward, grabbing on to the daemon's slabbed stomach and climbing up its ravaged chest.

The daemon tried to rip the knight away, but was hampered by its own clumsy blade. The knight hurled the pot at the ragged wound-edge, where it smashed open, dousing the bloody flesh-pulp with sacred water.

Huge gouts of steam immediately erupted, engulfing both combatants. The daemon's screams were deafening now, and it clawed at itself in agony, opening up the flesh-rent further and exposing a huge, black heart within.

The knight took up his sword two-handed, holding it point-down above his head, bracing against the sway and twist of the daemon's writhing. With a cry of vindication, he plunged it straight down, bursting the creature's heart open in an explosion of boiling ichor.

The daemon thrashed and bucked, its entire body convulsing in a rippling wave of fat and torn muscle. Its horned head swung from side to side, narrowly missing goring the knight, who clung on somehow, twisting the sword in deeper, ramming it in up to the hilt and pressing it home.

With a horrific shudder, the daemon's struggles gradually gave out. Aethyr-lightning burst into life across its body, snapping and tearing at the fabric of reality. It bellowed again, a sound of pure spite, but now its frame was unravelling fast, dissipating back into the realm from whence it had been summoned.

Still the knight clung on, never letting go of his sword. A huge *bang* resounded across the courtyard, shattering stone and making the earth ripple like water. Margrit was thrown onto her back, and she hit the ground hard. There was a rush of wind, hot as flame, and a long, agonised shriek.

The wind blew out, tearing itself into oblivion almost as soon as it had arrived. Margrit looked up, feeling blood in her mouth. The courtyard was half-demolished, with the bodies of men, women and daemons lying prone in the rubble. A huge slime-crusted crater had opened up where the daemon had been. In the centre of it stood the knight, his shoulders bowed, keeping his feet with difficulty, his armour coated in gobbets of thick black slime.

He limped over to her, pushing his visor up, a weary smile on his drawn face. He bowed low, displaying more courtesy in that one gesture than any Empire soldier had ever given her across a lifetime of service, and addressed her in broken, heavily accented Reikspiel.

'My good lady,' he gasped, breathing heavily, 'you have the thanks of a king. By all that is holy, that was *well done*.'

◀ CHAPTER TWENTY-TWO ▶

Helborg ran through the burning streets, fighting when he had to, hugging the shadows and sprinting hard when he did not. Only Zintler and nine of his most trusted Reiksguard had come with him; the rest had been left to hold the precarious line to the north.

Altdorf was now more populated than it had been for generations. A bizarre mix of Empire citizens, state troops, northmen, daemons and undead warriors fought one another in a bitter and fractured melee, breaking down into a thousand little battles over every scrap of unclaimed terrain. The arrival of von Carstein's army had thrown everything into confusion, locking the previously unstoppable march of the Chaos armies into a grinding stalemate. Across the devastated townscape, the various factions lost, gained and held ground, all under the continuing howl of the plague-storm.

In truth, the petty defeats and conquests now mattered little to Helborg. The city was lost, either to the still-massive hosts of the Ruinous Powers, or to the similarly gigantic force of raised slain that marched against them. Each enemy was as horrifying as the other. The daemons retained their unearthly powers, able to leap and shimmer through reality before bringing their spell-wound weapons to bear, while the dead had terrible strengths of their own. Helborg had seen the wight-kings tear into battle wearing the armour of ages and carrying blades forged at the very birth of the Empire. Ghosts and crypt horrors threw themselves into the fray, each capable of causing terrible damage before being dragged down. They were met by tallymen and plaguebearers, just as dire in combat and with the same lack of fear and preternatural devotion to their cause.

The result was that the mortals were being pushed to one side. Exhausted by weeks of plague, fatigued by the long siege preparations, shocked by the ferocity of the initial assault, the surviving Empire troops clung on to what little ground they could, increasingly only spectators before the real battles between the Fallen and the dead.

That was not enough for Helborg. He had not suffered so long to see his

city torn apart by rival invaders. Vlad could protest as much as he liked –
there was no honour in the scions of Sylvania, and as soon as the battle
was done the vampire lord would revert to type. Even amid all that had
taken place, there were still things that had to be accomplished.

He had to get to the Palace. That had not yet fallen in its entirety, despite
the forces that fought their way towards it, street by street, kill by single kill.

So the Reiksguard ran hard. Helborg's face streamed with blood, and the
pain spurred him on. He fought with an angry, vicious fury now, forgetting
any pretensions at strategy or finesse and giving in to the raw violence that
had threatened to overwhelm him for so long.

As they raced across the Griffon Bridge, its wide span crawling with
whole clusters of desperate duels, he kicked and hacked his way through
the throngs. The *Klingerach* lashed out, taking the head clean off a leering
plaguebearer, before he spun on his heel and smashed the hilt into the face
of an oncoming marauder. Then he was running again, his brother-knights
hard on his heels.

Ahead of them, the Palace reared up into the storm, now covered in a
thick layer of corrupted growths, its outline obscured and its lines tainted.
White-edged flames licked across its broken back, fuelled and perverted
by the poisons now freely coursing through the vegetation. Laughter still
resounded in the storm-wind – the laughter of an amused, sadistic god
that cared little how the battle fared so long as misery and misfortune continued to spread thickly.

'My lord!' cried Zintler, panting hard. 'The skies!'

Helborg looked up sharply, loath to be distracted from the chase. When
he did so, however, his heart leapt.

A star burned brightly in the morning sky, only partly obscured by the
roiling clouds. Its light was austere and hard to look at – a shifting flicker
of pale flame. Behind it trailed two lines of fire, snapping and twisting like
streamers.

He halted, suddenly held rapt by the vision.

The twin-tailed star.

'What does it mean?' asked Zintler.

Helborg laughed. 'I have no idea. But it is *here*.'

As he stared at it, it seemed to him that two tiny specks of darkness
fell from the skies, racing out of the light of the star one after the other,
plummeting like peregrines on the hunt-dive.

He blinked, trying to clear his sweat-blurred vision, and they were gone.
For a moment, it had looked like two mighty eagles had dropped from
the heavens, falling fast towards the open carcass of the Imperial Palace.

'We have to get there,' he said, snapping back into focus. The bridge
terminated less than fifty yards ahead, after which the land rose sharply,
crowned with the mansions and counting-houses of the nobility. Most were
aflame, or slumped into rubble, or blazed with unnatural light, and what

little remained was now contested by the two ancient enemies of mankind who now struggled for mastery.

It would be hellish. They would have to fight their way through a mile of steep, switchbacked roads before reaching the processional leading towards the gates. That was where the concentration of Chaos warriors was greatest, and where even the undead had toiled to make progress. They would be lucky to make it halfway, and unless the twin-tailed star looked kindly on them, they might not even get that far.

Helborg found himself grinning with a kind of fey madness. Everything he cherished was already gone. All that remained was the last, desperate sprint towards the heart of it all, to where he had always been destined to meet his end. The comet showed the way, lighting up the path with its flickering, gold-edged light.

The End Times, he thought to himself grimly as he broke into a run once more. *So this is what they look like.*

Leoncoeur did not have time to speak to the priestess for long – the court-yard was still crawling with plaguebearers. Many had been banished by the shock wave of the greater daemon's departure, but others lingered, re-knitting their aethyr-spun bodies together and advancing once more towards the huddled group of guardsmen and priestesses.

He could barely stand. The fight against the creature of Chaos had drained him to the core, and even with the timely aid of the blessed water he had scarcely prevailed. He backed away from the daemons' advance, gathering his strength for renewed fighting.

The priestess came with him, unarmed now but unwilling to leave his side.

'What is your name, lord?' she asked, her eyes never leaving the hordes of daemons creeping through the ruined outer wall.

'What does that matter now, sister?' Leoncoeur replied. 'We are all fighters.'

She looked satisfied by that. 'I was hoping for an Emperor,' she said dryly. 'Perhaps a king will do.'

Then, barging aside the lesser creatures of Chaos, the obese and horrific scythe-bearer clambered over the wreckage of the gates and fixed them both with a gaze of pure loathing. Though dwarfed by the slain greater daemon, this new creature was scarce less foul, and he stank just as badly. His jowls wobbled as he raised an accusing finger.

'*You*,' the monster drawled through bloody lips. 'You *killed* it.'

'As I will you,' warned Leoncoeur, remaining inside the line of the water. 'You have seen it already – come no closer.'

From outside the walls, sounds of battle had broken out again. Leon-coeur could hear the unearthly cries of the plaguebearers as they took on an unseen enemy. Perhaps some of the pegasus riders still fought on, though he guessed there were few of them left now. He caught the faint whiff of something sepulchral on the air, vying with the stench of decay, and wondered what it meant.

'You *killed* it!' screamed the Leechlord, advancing across the line of sacred water as if it were not there. Though it had proved a barrier against the least of the Chaos warriors, it did nothing to halt those most steeped in the twisting powers of the aethyr. 'Such *beauty*, gone from the world!'

Leoncoeur pushed the priestess behind him, shielding her with his body. The tumult of combat from beyond the walls grew louder. With a sudden realisation, Leoncoeur knew the reason for the creature's fury – the tide had turned. Against all hope, his army of fleshy horrors was being driven back, though by whom or what he could not yet see.

He allowed himself a smile of dark contentment. He had done what he had come for. The temple was secure, and a chink of light would endure amid the darkness. Whatever happened now, the journey had not been in vain.

'Your spells unravel themselves,' Leoncoeur taunted, edging warily closer. 'You will not take this place now, and it turns your mind to see it.'

That proved the final straw. The Leechlord lumbered towards him, raving and spitting, his flabby arms cartwheeling. Leoncoeur raised his sword, and their weapons clashed – steel against iron. They traded blows in a furious whirl. Leoncoeur shattered the creature's scythe with a single swipe, then pressed the attack by driving his blade deep into his overspilled stomach. Entrails flopped out, hanging like strings from the burst skin-sac.

Somehow, that did not stop him. The Leechlord swayed back into the attack, pulling a bone-saw from his belt and slashing wildly. Every blow that landed felt like a warhammer-strike – heavy and deadening. Leoncoeur could feel his arms ache. The long ride, followed by the battle at the gates, then the grinding duel against the greater daemon – the toll was too heavy.

'For the Lady!' he cried, redoubling the blows from his blood-smeared broadsword. He managed to drive another thrust deep into the creature's midriff, further opening the wound and showering the flagstones with speckled gore.

But the Leechlord was immune to pain, and his raddled body could absorb the most horrific levels of punishment. Unlike the daemon, he was a creation of flesh and blood, and would not be banished back to the aethyr. He opened his vast maw and vomited straight at Leoncoeur's chest.

The deluge was horrific, splattering into his eyes and making him gag. He staggered away, blinded by the foul matter. Unable to defend himself, he felt the sharp cut of the bone-saw as it punched into his throat.

He jerked away, flailing wildly with his sword, but he could already feel the hot cascade down his chest. The cut was mortal, and black stars spun before his eyes.

He crashed to the ground, fighting hard to stay conscious. The Leechlord towered over him triumphantly, his whole body sagging open from the wounds he had taken, but with the vicious light of victory in his porcine eyes.

Leoncoeur's blurred gaze wandered over to where the priestess stood, watching in horror, unable to intervene with no weapon to hand.

But she had done enough. The gift of water had proved sufficient, and the irony only then occurred to him.

Look for me in pure waters.

'She has blessed you indeed,' he murmured, just as the Leechlord brought the saw down and cut deep into his chest.

Leoncoeur's back arced in agony. He felt his ribs sever and his muscles part. Fighting back against the pain, he stared straight into the face of his killer, and cracked a grin.

That enraged the Leechlord further, but before he could twist the saw in deeper, he suddenly went rigid. A look of panic flashed across his features, and his arms thrust out, shivering. He tried to turn, but his body was rapidly turning into something else – hard, bark-like matter that burst out from under his pustulent hide.

'What... is...' he stammered, but then his tongue solidified and his whole body shuddered into rigidity.

His awareness slipping away, Leoncoeur just had enough time to see the cause. A tall warrior wearing crimson armour stepped from the shadow of the Leechlord, a bloody stake in his hand and a smoking ring on his pale finger. The two of them looked at one another, and the crimson-armoured lord inclined an ice-white, long-maned head.

With his last sight, Leoncoeur saw the remainder of the daemons being driven from the courtyard, pursued by grey-skinned warriors in archaic armour. With the Leechlord's downfall, there was nothing to bind them together – a new force had arrived, one with the power and the will to take them on.

Leoncoeur's head lolled. When it hit the stone, it felt almost like the feather bolsters of his old cot in Couronne's castle. An overwhelming feeling of numbness shot up his limbs, stifling the pain.

The priestess was at his side then, cradling him. He managed to shoot her a final smile.

'My lady,' he whispered.

So it was that, courteous to the last, Louen Leoncoeur died in the precincts of the Temple of Shallya, ringed by the living and the dead.

The Glottkin tore up to the Palace gates, surging like the unleashed force of nature they had always been. Undead warriors tried to block their path, forming a cordon before the open doorway, but they were swept away like chaff. Ghurk picked up several with one sweep of his fist. Disgusted that he could not eat them, he hurled their bony bodies away.

The cavernous interior of the Palace beckoned. Once it would have stood proudly, a masterpiece of baroque excess, soaring into the skies and ringed by graven images of gods and heroes. Now, mere hours after their arrival, the entire complex ran wild with an overabundance of reeking foliage. Mosses, vines and weeds sprouted from every crevice, prising apart the stone and bringing down pillars and buttresses. The entire structure now listed uneasily on its slime-glossed foundations, and entire wings had collapsed under the weight of the mucus-deluge and the burgeoning plague-growths.

Otto beat Ghurk's hide harder, forcing him to gallop into the heart of the great sprawl of ruination. The undead were everywhere now, spilling from balconies and clawing up from the sewers underfoot. Festus's plague-rain was already beginning to lessen, and the assault teetered on a knife-edge. Seizing the Palace was now imperative – the scryers had all foretold that the end would come there, and that *he*, Otto Glott, paramount servant of the Plaguefather, would be the one to land the killing blow. It would take place at the very centre, the oldest and the grandest edifice of humanity on earth, and no sudden apparitions nor ghosts from the blasted wilds could be allowed to halt that now. They had destroyed the undead at Heffen-gen, they had destroyed them at Marienburg, and now they would destroy them at Altdorf.

'Onward, on, o my brother!' Otto commanded, thrashing Ghurk madly with his scythe-butt.

Ghurk chortled happily, and crashed through a whole string of vine-strewn courtyards, lashing out with his tentacle-arm and crunching apart any skeletons unwary enough to oppose him.

Ethrac was busy too, hurling blast after blast of aethyr-lightning from his staff. Revenants were blown into slivers of spinning bone, their armour shattered and their swords crushed into spiralling shards. He had seen the twin-tailed star again, and this time the omen seemed to trouble him. He uttered no cries of victory, but mumbled an endless series of cantrips and summonings, ringing them all in a lattice of writhing witch-light.

The hosts of Chaos that had accompanied them on the long charge into the Palace grounds now fanned out, taking the fight to the scions of Syl-vania. Every corridor, every passageway and bridge-span was clogged with struggling warriors, locked in a pitiless struggle for mastery. The storm raced above them, lashing the combatants in the plague-rain and drenching the few remaining open spaces. Everywhere else, the foul garden bloomed, spreading its poisons into the very depths of the city vaults.

'I saw them come down,' muttered Ethrac, hurling more green-laced fire from his staff-tip.

'Who?' asked Otto, preoccupied with directing Ghurk towards the centres of resistance.

'The fallen king. I saw him, under the light of the comet. He will be there.'

Otto let a grin slide across his sore-thick lips. 'We knew he would. That is the sacrifice, the one to usher in the end.'

'Cut him deep, o my brother,' said Ethrac, letting rip with a blast of aethyr-energy that blazed across the rain-thick air and exploded in virulent swirls against a formation of wights. 'Cut him so deep that the world beneath him is severed. Nothing else matters.'

The Glott siblings broke into a wide muster-yard just under the shadow of the Palace's colossal main dome. It was less than two hundred yards towards the smashed doorway inside, beyond which they could already see the marble and gold interior glinting.

Before them, though, was arranged the last defence. No living soldiers still guarded the inner Palace, but they were no longer needed. A whole army of zombies waited for them, clambering over one another in a press of squirming limbs. They seemed to be swarming out of the ground itself, piled up in a heap of wriggling, necrotic flesh that looked more like a single organism than a mob of hundreds.

Ghurk barrelled onwards, undeterred. Ethrac began to shriek new chants, and Otto built up momentum with his scythe. The Army of Corruption charged along beside them, pouring into the muster-yard.

With a high-pitched scream, the glut of zombies burst outward, cascading like a lanced boil. The tangled web of undead stumbled and staggered towards them, as thick as the slime-rain, a whole forest of grasping fingers and rusting blades. The two armies slammed into one another, and the muster-yard was immediately filled with the scrabbling, sickening sounds of dry flesh tearing and plague-riddled sinews ripping.

Ghurk waded into the melee, lashing out with his tentacle-arm and scooping up dozens of zombies. Ethrac blasted more of them, infesting their dead hides with virulent parasites that punched out from within, crippling them and leaving them writhing on the stone.

Nothing stopped them completely, though – they came on with inexorable purpose, groaning and reaching, ignoring blows that would have ended a mortal warrior. Zombies latched on to Ghurk's legs and began to climb. Many were kicked away, but others quickly took their place. Soon Ghurk was wading waist-deep in a morass of undead, and still they came on, clambering over one another to get at the creatures riding on his back.

Ethrac began to spit out his frustration, burning the undead with balefire, torching whole bands of them as they reached out to pull up higher. Otto reached down, swinging his long scythe to dislodge those who had dragged themselves into range. A tumbling rain of severed limbs clattered down to the seething mass of bodies below, eliciting not a sound from their stricken owners.

But that was not the worst – the zombie plague was just a foretaste. With an ear-splitting scream, the vampire the triplets had fought – and defeated – at Marienburg flew down from the high parapet of the looming dome, his arms stretched wide and lined with tattered batwings. Other fell creatures came in his wake – a vast winged horror with a skeletal ribcage and bony claws – a *terrorgheist* – egged on by three shrieking ladies in bone-white lace. Clouds of corpse-gas billowed out as they swooped in, reacting with the plague-growths and hissing like snakes.

Ghurk instantly lunged for the winged creature, whipping his tentacle-arm up to haul it down from the skies. He connected, wrapping his arm around the beast's spiny neck, but had underestimated its strength. The terrorgheist remained aloft, and began to drag Ghurk across the ground, pulling him further into the writhing knots of zombies.

The first of the undead clambered onto Ghurk's back, and soon Otto and Ethrac were both fighting them off. They became separated from their own warriors, pulled by the terrorgheist deeper into the scrabbling pall of flesh-eaters.

'*Wither* them!' cried Otto, hacking his scythe down with frantic abandon.

Ethrac obliged, turning a whole gang of zombies into crackling torches of emerald flame, but it was not nearly enough. The terrorgheist continued to haul Ghurk along, forcing the compressed crowds of zombies up to chest-level.

Otto looked up, seeing the vampire lord preparing a spell of his own. Dark shadows began to crystallise around him, sucked out of the air and transfused into the Wind of Death.

'The vampire!' Otto shrieked, too far away to prevent it. 'He is the master! Snap his neck! Blind his eyes! Crack his bones!'

Ethrac, riding Ghurk's lurching back with difficulty, immediately saw the truth of it. The sorcerer lashed out with his staff, making the bells clang wildly. He spat out words of power, and the vampire's spell immediately inverted, turning on its owner in a vortex of ragged shadow. The vampire, taken by surprise, cried out in alarm, suddenly feeling the cold touch of his own magicks, but Ethrac was now in control, and the Chaos sorcerer shook his staff again with real venom.

Mundvard the Cruel's body exploded, flying outward in a welter of tattered strips. His skeleton hung together for an instant, then clattered down to the muster-yard's surface. As soon as the bones hit, they were crushed into the stone by the hundreds of criss-crossing boots. Once the vampire's grip was broken, the terrorgheist immediately lost its momentum, and the pressure on Ghurk abated.

Ghurk hauled back hard with his tentacle, digging his hooves in and tugging. The terrorgheist's bony neck broke, and the creature gasped out a glut of corpse-gas from its gaping jaws. Its sinewy wings flapped pathetically, and it thudded to the ground. With the creature's momentum broken, the mob of zombies collapsed around Ghurk, scattering in twisted piles of confusion at his feet.

'There is no *time* for this!' hissed Otto, using his scythe to clear the last of the clinging zombies from Ghurk's hide. 'Clear them out!'

Ghurk obeyed, bounding after the remaining enemy, swinging both arms like jackhammers.

The three women in lace leapt down from their vantage then, spitting curses. Ethrac was too busy breaking the remainder of the zombies to respond, so Otto hauled his scythe back, swung it around three times, then let go. The blade flew towards the leader of the trio, rotating in a blur of speed. Before she could evade the missile, it sliced clean across her neck, decapitating her in a single strike and spraying blood in broad spatters against the walls of the yard.

'Return!' cried Otto, reaching out with his right claw.

The scythe immediately swung around again, still spinning, and dropped back into his waiting palm.

That broke the spirit of the remaining undead horde. Bereft of the guiding will of their vampiric masters, the zombies lost all cohesion, and were soon mopped up by the oncoming tribesmen. The two remaining ladies fled back into the Palace depths, wailing like infants. Ghurk rampaged through the remaining throng, treading the last survivors into the stone underfoot. He crashed over the carcass of the terrorgheist and repeatedly stamped on it, powdering the bones and trampling the meagre scraps of sinew that still clung to them.

'Is this really the best they can do?' muttered Otto, still busy with his scythe.

'We killed the master,' said Ethrac, hurling more plague-slime about him with great heaves. 'Why do *any* still stand? The dead return to death when the master is killed.'

Otto shrugged. The Palace now lay before them, its doors gaping open and its riches clustered within, and lust was already overtaking his fury. 'Who knows? Perhaps there is another to be found.'

Ethrac kept up the barrage of raw sorcery, exploding zombies at a terrific rate. The broken dome of the Palace loomed up massively, a cyclopean structure even in its ruin. Flames still guttered around it, fuelled by the unleashed lethal energies, and the storm-pattern of clouds formed an immense cupola over the whole scene.

The devastation was now total. Every building in the city had been demolished or dragged into ruins. The death-toll was incalculable, and would never be recovered from. In a sense, it mattered not what happened now – they had done what no warlord of the north had ever done. They had broken Sigmar's city, wreathing it in fell sorcery and drenching it in the blood of the slain.

But there was still the final blow to be struck. The human Emperor still lived, and had come back to his den in time for the denouement. Such had always been predicted, and the Plaguefather had never guided them awry.

'He is *in* there,' said Ethrac, barely noticing as his troops slaughtered and smashed the last remnants of the defence. 'I can *smell* him.'

Otto grinned back at him, his face sticky with blood.

'Then we go inside,' he said triumphantly. 'And bring this dance to its end.'

Margrit looked up at the vampire, not knowing whether to thank him or curse him. His fell warriors had cleared the courtyard of daemons and were now pursuing the remaining Chaos forces out of the square beyond. The surviving humans emerged from whatever places they had managed to barricade themselves behind, mistrust etched on their faces.

Vlad von Carstein was still gazing at the body of Leoncoeur. There was a sadness on the vampire's face.

For all that, the creature's aura still made Margrit shudder. For her whole life, she had been taught to fear and hate the grave-stealers. If any force of the world was truly anathema to hers, it was the bringers of everlasting death.

'And what of us, lord?' she asked, staring up at him defiantly. 'Now you have your victory, what is your purpose?'

Vlad turned to her, as if seeing her for the first time. Margrit could not help noticing that his gaze flickered instinctively down to her throat.

'If there were time, lady, I might show you all manner of wonders,' he said. 'You can see for yourself, though, that none remains.'

He looked up, past the temple dome and towards the Palace hilltop. His eyes narrowed, as if he were focusing on things far away.

'This is your temple again, for a time,' he said, coldly. 'Bury your dead and look to your walls. If all goes well, I *will* be back.'

Then his whole body seemed to shimmer like a shadow in sunlight. The ring on his finger briefly flared with crimson light, and his gaunt frame dissolved into a flock of squealing bats. They fluttered skywards, spiralling into the rain-lashed skies.

Margrit watched the bats go, slumped against the stone of the courtyard with the dead knight leaning against her. The noises of combat were falling away as the undead drove the daemons back from the temple's environs and into the maze of the burning poor quarter.

She looked up. The plague-rain was beginning to lessen, as was the tearing wind. Though the slimy droplets still cascaded, their force was already beginning to fade.

'But what is left?' she murmured to herself, looking around her destroyed temple, at the pools of blood on the stone, at the corroded and gaping rooftops beyond her little kingdom. 'What is there to be salvaged now?'

No answers came. She smoothed the bloodied hair from the knight's brow, and closed his eyes. It would have been nice to have known his name.

⚔ CHAPTER TWENTY-THREE ⚔

Deathclaw landed on the marble floor, its claws skittering on the polished surface. Karl Franz dismounted just as Martak's beast landed on the far side of the chamber.

The place had once been a chapel to Sigmar the Uniter. In its prime, a hundred priests a day would perform rites of absolution and petition, processing up the long aisles with burning torches in hand. The high altar was draped in gold and surrounded by the spoils of war – trophies from a hundred realms of the earth, the bleached and polished skulls of green-skins, the wargear of the northmen's many tribes.

Now all was in disarray. The chapel's arched roof had collapsed under the weight of pulsating mosses, and loops of pus-glistening tendrils hung from the ragged edges. The chequerboard floor had been driven up, exposing masses of writhing maggots beneath. The altar itself was broken, cracked in two by a creaking thorn-stump, and blowflies swarmed and buzzed over every exposed surface.

Karl Franz pulled the reins from around Deathclaw's neck and cast them aside. The very action of laying eyes on the devastation was enough to make him feel nauseous, but there was no time to linger over the desecration. From beyond the listing doorway at the rear of the long central aisle, he could already hear the echoes of fighting. The Palace was rife with it, from the high towers to the deepest dungeons. Even from the air he had seen how complete the defeat was – a huge army of Chaos tribesmen and mutated beasts had cut its way deep into the heart of the complex, resisted only by a motley mix of Palace guards and warriors of Sylvania's cursed moors.

It was just as it had been in Heffengen – the dead fighting with the living. How such allies came to be within the sanctity of the Palace grounds, though, was a question for another time.

'Now what?' asked Martak, dismounting clumsily and skidding on the polished floor.

'The Chamber of the Hammer,' replied Karl Franz, striding out towards the doors with Deathclaw in tow.

Martak took a little more time to persuade his steed to follow suit, and had to haul on its halter to bring it along. 'What of the Menagerie, lord?' he asked. 'The dragon! Can you not rouse the dragon?'

Karl Franz kept walking. He could have done that. He could have opened all the cages and let the beasts loose, but it would not accomplish anything now. There was only one course open to him, one he barely understood, one that could only bring him pain.

'Time is short, wizard,' he said, reaching the doors and peering out through their wreckage. A long corridor stretched away, empty of enemies for the moment and ankle-thick with fungus spores. 'You will have to trust me.'

Martak hurried to catch up. '*Trust* you? You have told me nothing! You saw the armies, you know how close they are.' He fixed the Emperor with a look of pure exasperation. 'What will this *serve?*'

Karl Franz looked back at him with some sympathy. There were no easy answers, and it was not as if his own intentions filled him with any certainty. All he had now were feelings, stirred by the sight of the comet and prompted by vague premonitions and old whisperings.

It could all be futile – everything, every step he had taken since the disaster at the Auric Bastion. But, he reflected, was that not the essence of *faith?* To trust in the promptings of the soul in the face of all evidence to the contrary?

He would have to dig deeper, to drag some surety from somewhere. In the meantime, there was little he could do to assuage the wizard's doubts.

'If you wish to rouse the beasts, then I will not prevent you,' said Karl Franz. 'You have delivered me to this place, and for that alone I remain in your debt. But I will not join you – the time is drawing closer, and I must be under the sign of Ghal Maraz when the test comes.'

He forced a smile. The wizard would have to follow his own path now.

'You may join me or leave me – such is your fate – but do not try to prevent me.' He started walking again, and Deathclaw followed close behind, ducking under the lintel of the chapel doors. 'This is the end of all things, and when all is gone – all magic, all strength, all hope – then only faith remains.'

The spell guttered out, and Vlad reconstituted deep in the heart of the Imperial Palace.

For a moment, it was all he could do not to stare. He had dreamed of being in this place for so long – more than the lifetime of any mortal. The yearning had stretched through the aeons, as bitter and unfulfilled as the love he had once borne for her. For Isabella. He had often imagined how it would be, to tread the halls as a victor, drinking in the splendour of aeons. Long ago, so long that even he struggled to retain the memory, he had imagined himself on the throne itself, presiding over a whispering court of black-clad servants, the candles burning low in their holders and the music of Old Sylvania echoing in the shadowed vaults.

To have accomplished those long hopes should have made him glad. In the event, all he felt was a kind of confusion. Nagash had given him what he needed to get here at last, but it turned out that all that remained was a ruin of foliage-smothered stonework and gaping, eyeless halls. It would never be rebuilt, not now. He had accomplished his goal, only to find that he was a master of ashes.

'My lord,' came a familiar voice.

Vlad turned to see Herrscher and a band of wight-warriors in the armour of the Palace. They must have been raised recently, for their greaves and breastplates were still mottled with soil. Further back stood silent ranks of the undead, interspersed with ragged-looking groups of zombies.

'Where are the rest?' asked Vlad.

'Mundvard and the ladies rode out to halt the plague-host before it reached the Palace,' said Herrscher. 'They did not come back.'

Vlad nodded. Perhaps he should have expected it – the Ruinous Powers had always been too strong for his servants to take on.

'Then their commanders will be within the walls now,' said Vlad.

'They have taken the southern entrance,' said Herrscher. 'They are heading for the centre, and we are in their path. If we leave now–'

'Leave?'

Herrscher looked confused. 'We cannot stay here, lord,' he protested. 'Your army is spread throughout the city, but they have broken into the Palace in force. They cannot be stopped, not by us, not without summoning reinforcements.'

Vlad smiled tolerantly. Herrscher looked genuinely perturbed at the prospect of harm coming to him, which was as good a sign as any that his transformation was complete.

'You are right, witch hunter,' said Vlad. 'The longer this goes on, the worse things will go for us. To bring this beast low, we must sever it at the head.' He smiled thinly. 'The savages of the north lead their armies from the front. If we wish to find the authors of this plague, look to the vanguard.'

Herrscher looked doubtful. 'We are so few,' he muttered.

'Ah, but you have *me* with you now.' Vlad glanced up and down the corridor, trying to get his bearings. 'I wonder, do any of your old kind still live, or do we have this place to ourselves?'

As if in answer, there was a huge, resounding bang from the corridor running away to the south, like a massive door had been flung back on its hinges. Following that came the sound of a low, slurring panting. The floor shook, trembling with the impact of heavy footfalls.

Herrscher drew his blade, as did the wights, and they fell into a defensive ring around their master.

Vlad unsheathed his own sword with a flourish, finding himself looking forward to what was to come. The footfalls grew louder as the beast smashed its way towards them.

'So the hunt is unnecessary – they have come to us.' Vlad raised his sword to his face, noting the lack of reflection in the steel. 'Now look and learn, witch hunter – this is how a mortarch skins his prey.'

With some regret, both Otto and Ethrac had to dismount from Ghurk as he barrelled on into the Palace interior. Their huge steed now scraped the roof of the corridors, bringing down chandeliers and ceiling-panels as he lumbered ever closer to the goal.

Otto and Ethrac ran alongside him now, both panting hard from the exertion. Ghurk himself seemed as infinitely strong as ever, his bulging muscles still rippling under his mottled hide. The vanguard of their suppurating horde came on behind, wheezing through closed-face helms and carrying their axes two-handed before their bodies.

As they came, they destroyed. Paintings were torn from their frames and ripped to pieces, statues were cast down and shattered. Ghurk's hooves tore up the marble flooring, and his flailing fists dragged whole sections of wall panels along with him. They were like a hurricane streaking into the heart of the enemy's abode, breaking it down, brick by brick, into a heap of mouldering refuse.

As they rounded a narrow corner, Otto was the first to catch sight of fresh enemies. A thrill ran through him, and he picked up the pace. 'Shatter them!' he cried, his voice cracking with enthusiasm. '*Smash* them!'

Just as at the Palace gates, the warriors lined up against them were no mortals, but more of the undead that had dogged their passage ever since the breaking of the walls. Otto began to feel genuine anger – they just *could not* be eradicated. They were like a... *plague*.

Ghurk bounded ahead, and Ethrac matched pace, his staff already shimmering with gathering witch-light. The undead wights rushed down the wide passageway to meet them, racing into battle with their unearthly silence. Soon the corridor was filled with the echoing *clang* of blades clashing. Zombies and skeletons went up against marauders and tribesmen in a mirror of the desperate combat still scored across the entire cityscape.

There was only one opponent worthy of Otto's attention, though – a crimson-armoured vampire lord bearing a longsword and wearing a long sable cloak. That one towered over even the mightiest of his servants, and swept arrogantly into battle with the poise of a true warrior-artisan.

Otto swung his scythe, clattering it into the vampire's oncoming blade even as Ghurk and Ethrac blundered onwards, reaping a swathe through the undead ranks beyond.

'You are the master, then,' Otto remarked, parrying a counter-blow before trying to skewer the vampire with his blade's point. 'Do you have a name?'

'My name is known from Kislev to Tilea,' replied the vampire distastefully.

'Vlad von Carstein, Elector Count of Sylvania. You, though, are unknown to me.'

Otto laughed, whirling the scythe faster. 'We are the Glottkin. We come to bury the Empire in its own filth. Why not let us?'

Vlad sneered, trying to find a way through Otto's whirling defence. The vampire carried himself with an almost unconscious arrogance – the bearing of a creature born to rule, and one who knew how to use a sword. 'You would cover the whole world in your stink. That will not be allowed to happen.'

'It cannot be stopped now. You surely know that.'

Vlad hammered his blade into the attack. 'Nothing is certain. Not even death – I should know.'

Otto laughed out loud, enjoying the artistry of the combat. Ghurk would never have understood it, nor Ethrac, but their gifts had always been different. 'You are rather good, vampire,' he observed.

'And you... fight with a scythe,' replied Vlad, contemptuously.

As if to demonstrate the weapon's uselessness, the vampire suddenly changed the angle of his sword-swipe, catching the hook of the blade and pulling it out of Otto's hands. Otto lunged to reclaim it, but it fell, clanking, to the floor. The vampire trod on the blade, advancing on his prey with a dark satisfaction in his unblinking eyes.

Otto let fly with a punch, hoping to rock the vampire, but Vlad was far too quick – he caught Otto's clenched fist in his own gauntlet, and twisted the wrist back on itself. Caught prone, Otto was forced round, his spine twisted.

Before he could do anything else, the vampire's blade punched up through his ribcage, sliding through his encrusted skin with a slick hiss. Vlad lifted him bodily from the floor, held rigid by the length of steel protruding from his torso. The pain was excruciating.

'And so it ends, creature of the Outer Dark,' said Vlad, bringing his sword-tip up to his lips. As was his wont with the defeated, he licked along the sword's edge, drinking deep of the blood that ran freely along the cutting edge.

As soon as he had gulped it down, though, he released his grip. His hands flew to his throat, and his eyes bulged.

Otto laughed, freeing himself of the blade and sauntering over to his scythe to retrieve it. The pain was already passing, thanks to the gifts of the Urfather. 'Drink my blood, eh?' he asked. 'Now, I wonder, have you the stomach for it?'

By now Vlad was retching. He staggered against the wall of the corridor, his cheeks red, bile trickling down his chin. A look of horror flashed across his tortured face as he realised what he had imbibed. 'You... are...' he gasped.

'*Very* unpalatable,' said Otto, reaching for his blade. 'My lord, I fear your appetites have undone you.'

Vlad gazed back at him, all the arrogance bled from his face. He vomited, hurling up a torrent of stinking black ichor. In his eyes was the full realisation of what he had done. He was poisoned to the core. He had taken in not blood but raw pollution, the very essence of plague, and now it was eating him from the inside. Once that finished him, all the souls raised by his arts would collapse back into their state of true death – every wight, zombie, skeleton and ghoul would shiver away, their reanimated corpses disintegrating back into the essence of dust.

Otto raised the scythe, appreciating the imagery of the reaper ending the necromancer. 'That was enjoyable, vampire,' he said, taking aim. 'Almost a shame it has to end.'

With a snarl, the shivering Vlad crossed his shaking arms over his chest, still retching uncontrollably. There was a flash of dark matter, and his body disintegrated into a cloud of fluttering bats.

Otto swiped, but his scythe passed harmlessly through the flock, scraping against the floor in a shower of sparks. He laughed again, admiring the vampire's art. He really had been a worthy opponent. The bats lurched and flapped down the corridor, heading for the outside and too flighty to catch.

With Vlad gone, the rest of his forces melted away. Otto turned to see the skeletons collapsing and the wights slumping to the floor. Ghurk paused in his rampage, his fists stuffed with bones, his mighty head swaying back and forth in confusion as his enemies clattered into tiny heaps around him.

The last to remain on his feet was an oddly mortal-looking warrior in a long coat and with a pair of pistols strapped to his waist. He stared at the spot where Vlad had been, his face a mix of loathing and regret. For a moment, he appeared to fight the inevitable, as if, having been reacquainted with unlife he was now loath to leave it.

But the end had to come. The man's jaw fell open with a sigh, his eyes rolled up into their sockets, and he collapsed to the floor. Once he was down, his body withered quickly, reverting to its true state in seconds.

Otto looked up at Ethrac, and grinned. The vampire's wound had already closed over, sealed with a line of glistening bile. There were advantages to being constituted of such glorious poisons.

'Then we are almost done, o my brother,' Otto remarked, brandishing his scythe.

Ethrac nodded. 'One by one, we devour them all. Now for the final meal.'

◀ CHAPTER TWENTY-FOUR ▶

Karl Franz and Martak entered the Chamber of Ghal Maraz. It had been abandoned long ago as the battle for the Palace was lost, and now stood as silent and as corroded as every other hall in the colossal complex.

The walls were weeping now, dripping with thick white layers of pus that fell in clots from the domed ceiling. The supporting pillars were covered in a hide of matted plant-matter, all of it shedding virulent pods that glowed and pulsed in the semi-dark. The great cupola over the circular space was half-ruined, with ivy tresses suspended like nooses from the broken stone-work. Rain still spattered down through the gap, adding to the slick of mucus that swam across the chamber floor.

The two men both hurried to the high altar, the only structure to have remained relatively unscathed. The two empty chain-lengths still swayed from their bearings, hanging over the heavy iron table below.

Martak had no idea why they were there. The Imperial Palace had hundreds of chambers, many of them grander and more ornate that this one. If they had to select a place to die, why opt for the ancient resting place of the warhammer, a weapon that was now lost in the north and borne, if at all, by the boy-champion?

Karl Franz drew his runefang and backed up towards the altar's edge. Deathclaw remained protectively by his side, growling all the while from its huge barrel chest. Martak took up position at the other end of the iron structure, his own griffon remaining close by and snarling with customary spite.

'I do not–' he began, but then the words died in his mouth. Whether they were being tracked, or whether fate had simply decreed that the end would come then, the doors at the far end of the chamber slammed open, ripped from their hinges and flung aside like matchwood.

Three grotesque creatures burst inside, each one a distorted corruption of a man. The first was a slack-fleshed warrior bearing a scythe in two claw-like hands. His green skin, criss-crossed with bleeding sores and warty growths, glinted dully under the reflected glare of the pus-cascades.

The second was a similarly wizened creature clad in dirty patched robes and brandishing a staff nearly as gnarled as Martak's own.

The third was a true giant, barely able to shove itself through the huge double doors. Once inside the chamber he stood erect, one tentacled arm slack at his side, the other clenched into a hammer-like fist. His greasy, stupid face was deformed into a loathsome grin, and long trails of blood ran down from his mouth like warpaint.

Behind them, jostling for position, came more Chaos warriors, some in the furred garb of the far north, some bearing the mutated marks of more recent conversion. Their three leaders all bled horrific amounts of power from their addled frames. They were living embodiments of corruption, as vile and virulent as the Rot itself.

Karl Franz, unfazed, stepped forward, his blade raised towards them as if in grim tribute.

'I will not repeat this warning,' he said, and his calm voice echoed around the chamber. 'Leave this place now, or your souls will be bound to it forever. The spirit of almighty Sigmar runs deep here, and His sign shines above us. You do not know your danger.'

There was something about the deep authority in that voice, the measured expression, which gave even the three creatures of madness pause. They held back, and the huge one looked uncertainly at his companions.

The sorcerer was the first to laugh, though, breaking the moment. The warrior with the scythe joined in quickly.

'You did not need to be here, Emperor,' said the scythe-bearer, bowing floridly before him. 'We could have destroyed your city well enough on our own, but your death makes the exercise just a little more rewarding.'

The sorcerer bowed in turn, a mocking smile playing across his scarred face. 'We are the Glottkin, your excellency, once as mortal and as sickly as you, now filled with the magnificence of the Urfather. Know our names, before we slay you. I am Ethrac, this is my brother Otto, and this, the greatest of us all, is the mighty Ghurk.'

Ghurk emitted a wheezing *hhur* as his name was recited, then crackled the knuckles of his one true hand.

Martak clutched his staff a little tighter, allowing the Wind of Ghur to flow along its length. The chamber was electric with tension, just waiting for the false war of words to conclude – nothing would be settled now by rhetoric.

Karl Franz's face remained stony. His self-control was complete. Even in the heart of his annihilated kingdom, his visage never so much as flickered.

'I do not need to know your names,' he said, letting a shade of contempt dance around the edge of his speech. 'You will die just as all your breed will die – beyond the light of redemption, forever condemned to howl your misery to the void.'

Otto glanced over at Ethrac, amused, and shrugged. 'Then there is nothing to say to him, o my brother,' he remarked.

Ethrac nodded. 'It seems not, o my brother.'

They both turned back to face the altar, and the three of them burst into movement.

Otto was quickest, sprinting over to Karl Franz with his scythe whirring around his head. Ethrac was next, his staff alight with black energy, all aimed at Martak. Ghurk lumbered along in the rear, backed up by the charge of the northmen.

Deathclaw pounced in response, using a single thrust of its huge wings to power straight into Ghurk's oncoming charge. The griffon latched onto the huge monster, lashing out with its claws and tearing with its open beak. The two of them fell into a brutal exchange of blows, rocking and swaying as they ripped into one another.

Ethrac launched a barrage of plague-magic straight at Martak, aiming to deluge him in a wave of thick, viscous choke-slime. Martak countered with a blast from his own staff, puncturing the wave of effluent and sending it splattering back to its sender. Ethrac lashed his staff around, rousing the vines and creepers hanging from the chamber vaults into barbed flails. Martak cut them down as they emerged, summoning spectral blades that cartwheeled through the air.

Martak's own griffon took on the bulk of the tribesmen, bounding amongst them, goring and stabbing, leaving Otto and the Emperor to their combat undisturbed. The chamber rang with the sound and fury of combat, the runefang glittering as it was swung against the rusted scythe-blade.

'I saw you come back,' said Otto, letting a little admiration creep into his parched voice. 'Why did you do that? You know you cannot beat us.'

Karl Franz said nothing, but launched into a disciplined flurry with his blade, matching the blistering sweeps of the scythe.

Martak, kept busy with his own magical duel, only caught fragmentary glimpses of the combat, but he could hear the taunting words of the Glotts well enough. The mucus-rain continued to fall, tumbling down from the gaping roof and bouncing messily on the torn-up marble.

By then Ghurk was getting the better of Deathclaw. The griffon savaged its opponent, but the vast creature of Chaos was immune to pain and virtually indestructible. With a sickening snap, the griffon's wings were broken again. Deathclaw screamed, and was hurled aside, skidding into the chamber walls.

Martak backed away from Ethrac, fighting off fresh flurries of dark magic. The sorcerer was far more potent than he was, able to pull the very stuff of Chaos from the aethyr and direct it straight at him. With growing horror, Martak saw the first pustules rise on his forearms, and felt his staff begin to twist out of shape. His essence was being corrupted, turned against him and driven into the insane growths that had blighted the Empire from Marienburg to Ostermark.

Karl Franz fought on undeterred, matching Otto's blows with careful precision. He carried himself with all the elegance of an expertly-trained sword-master, adopting the proper posture and giving himself room to counter every blade movement. Otto, by contrast, came at him in a whirl of wild strokes, trying to unnerve him by flinging the scythe out wide before hauling it back in close. In a strange way, they were oddly matched, rocking to and fro before the altar, hacking and blocking under the shadow of the swinging chains.

Martak fell back further, bludgeoned by the superior magic of Ethrac. The pustules on his skin burst open, drenching him in foul-smelling liquids. He unleashed a flock of shadow-crows, which flew into Ethrac's face and pecked at his eyes, but the sorcerer whispered a single word, bursting their bellies and causing them to flop, lifeless, onto the chamber floor. More globules of burning slime were flung at Martak, and he barely parried them, feeling their acidic bite as they splashed across his face.

With a sick feeling in the pit of his stomach, Martak knew he was overmatched. Nothing he summoned troubled the sorcerer, and he could barely keep the counter-blasts from goring straight into him. Even as he retreated further, driven away from the altar and towards the chamber's east door, he saw the futility of it all, just as he had warned the Emperor.

There is no glory in dying here, and he wants *to die.*

Martak found himself snarling at the stupidity of it all. Noble gestures were for the aristocracy, for those with knightly blood or jewels spilling from their fingers. There were still other ways, still other weapons. If the Emperor would not give him leave, then he would go himself. The Menagerie was so *close*, and stocked with creatures that would chew through even the greatest of Chaos-spawned horrors.

His griffon, now bleeding heavily from a dozen wounds, suddenly turned and launched itself at Ethrac. The sorcerer, caught off-balance, had to work furiously not to be sliced apart, and for an instant turned away from Martak.

Seeing the chance, the Supreme Patriarch glanced a final time over at Karl Franz, uncertain whether his instincts were right. The Emperor fought on blindly, hugging the shadow of the altar. He was consumed by the duel, and Martak saw the look of utter conviction on his face. Karl Franz would not leave now, and nor could Martak reach him to drag him out.

Martak turned, and fled the chamber. Once outside, he tore down the narrow corridor beyond, his robes flapping about him. Soon he heard the sounds of pursuit as the northmen followed him, and he picked up the pace.

At least I have drawn them away, he though grimly, battling with incipient guilt at his desertion even as he struggled to remember the quickest way down to the cages. *That will buy him a little more time, and I* will *return.*

Otto watched the wizard flee with a smirk on his face. Given the choice, mortals always took the easier path. That was what made them so easy to turn, and so easy to kill. They had no proper comprehension of hard choices, the kind that would lead a tribesman to give up everything in the service of higher powers.

Sacrifice was the key. Learning to submit before the strenuous demands of uncompromising gods was the first step on the road to greatness. As he slammed the scythe towards the human Emperor's face, he began to feel excitement building.

He would be the one to end the dreams of humanity. *He* would be the one who would bring the City of Sigmar down, its every stone cracked and frozen by the abundance of the plague-forest, its every tower squeezed into cloying dust by the strangle-vines and barb-creepers. Soon all that would be left would be the Garden, the infinite expression of the Urfather's genius, swamping all else and extending infinitely towards all the horizons.

Heady with glee, he cracked the scythe down further, now aiming for the Emperor's chest. Karl Franz blocked the blow, but he seemed to be going through the motions now. A strange expression remained on his haggard face – a kind of serenity.

That bothered Otto, and he pressed harder. With a wild swipe, he managed to knock the runefang aside. He pounced, driving a long gouge down the Emperor's arm and eliciting a stark cry of pain.

Karl Franz staggered back against the altar, half-falling to his knees. Otto rose up triumphantly, holding his scythe high.

'And so it ends!' he screamed, and dragged the blade down.

Just before it connected, though, a sword-edge interposed itself, locking with the curved scythe-edge and holding it fast. Otto looked down to see an Empire warrior in the way, his blade held firm and his eyes blazing with fury. He wore elaborate plate armour, and his hawk-like face was half-hidden by a voluminous moustache.

For a second, Otto was transfixed with shock. All the mortals were supposed to be dead or driven far away from the Palace. He turned to see other armoured Empire warriors charge into the chamber and launch themselves at the remaining northmen.

So there were some humans with the spine to fight on.

Otto twisted his mouth into a smirking leer, and yanked the scythe free. The Emperor, bleeding profusely, fell to his knees, his place taken by the newcomer.

'You come here,' snarled the moustached warrior through gritted teeth, drawing himself up to his full height. 'You bring the plague, you bring the fires, you bring the pain.' His scarred face creased into an expression of pure, unadulterated hatred. 'Now *I* bring the reckoning.'

Martak panted as he ran, feeling his battered body protest. They were already on his heels, and he could almost taste their foul breath on his neck.

He careered down the spiralling stairs, hoping that he had remembered the way, trying to *think* and not to panic. He ought to have been able to smell the beasts by now, but the festering mess in the Palace made it hard to tell the stinks apart.

He reached the base of the stairs, almost slipping on the tiles but managing to push on. He shoved through a thick wooden door, and at last heard the sounds he had been hoping to pick up.

The beasts were roused – they were pawing in their pens, driven mad by the spoor of Chaos within the Palace. The griffons would be tearing at their cages, the demigryphs and manticores would be slavering with fury. And down at the very heart of it all, the mightiest of creatures, the one that only Karl Franz had ever been able to tame, would be waiting, its old, cold mind roused to thoughts of murder.

Martak felt something whirr past his ear, and veered sharply to one side. A throwing-axe clanged from the wall ahead of him, missing by a finger's breadth.

He kept going, trying to keep his shoulders lower. A pair of iron gates loomed before him, still locked and looped with chains. It was all he could do to blurt out a spell of opening before he stumbled into them, pushing through and staggering into the darkness beyond.

From all around him, he suddenly heard the snarls and growls of the caged animals. It was uniquely comforting – he had spent his whole life among beasts, and now they surrounded him once more.

He smiled, and kept running. He knew where he was going now, and there was no hope of stopping him. He could already smell the embers, and hear the dry hiss of scales moving over stone.

Almost there.

Karl Franz watched helplessly as Helborg took the fight to Otto Glott. He had been cut deep, and felt his arm hanging uselessly at his side. The Reiksguard knights Helborg had brought with him threw themselves into battle with the sorcerer and the behemoth, roaring the name of Sigmar as they wheeled their blades about.

Karl Franz could only look on. It was staggeringly brave. He had last seen Helborg on the eve of Heffengen, and could only imagine what trials he had faced in the meantime. He looked a shadow of his earlier, ebullient self – his face was lean, disfigured by long gouges and etched with fatigue. It looked like he could barely walk, let alone fight, but somehow he worked his blade with all the old arrogant flair, driving Otto back with every blurred arc of steel, giving him no room to respond.

Karl Franz wanted to speak out, then – to tell him that he had got it wrong, and that no force of arms could possibly make a difference now. If the Glotts were slain in this chamber, nothing would change – the armies of Chaos would still run rampant, the city would still be lost, the Reik would still be corrupted. For his whole life, Karl Franz had drilled into his subjects the need to fight on, to never give in, to reach for the blade as a first resort. He could hardly tell them any different now, but as he watched his chosen Reiksguard being hacked to pieces by the dread power of Ethrac and the sheer brute force of Ghurk, it made him want to weep.

Moving stiffly, he shoved himself onto one elbow, panting hard as the pain kicked in. He could not move from the altar. That was the key – the great sacrificial slab that had been placed under the dome for a reason. The light of the comet streamed down through the gap, bathing everything in a candle-yellow sheen. He had learned to accept that only *he* could see the light properly, that even Martak had not been able to perceive it truly, and that to others it was a pale flicker in a scoured sky. To him, it was the light of the sun and the moon combined, a brilliant star amid the sour corruption of the earth. It was calling to him even now, reminding him of the great trial, whispering words of power that only he could hear.

Karl Franz stood up, wincing against the pain. It was as Helborg had told him – he was not a man like any other, one whose soul was bound by mortal limits. He had always been set apart, devoted to a purer calling.

You are the Empire.

Helborg was tiring now. He could not sustain the fury, and Otto was beating him back. Karl Franz looked on grimly, knowing that Helborg *had* to be beaten, but nonetheless barely able to watch it unfold.

The Reiksmarshal launched into a final series of devastating strikes, throwing everything into them. The way he moved the runefang then was magnificent, as good as he had ever been, and against any other foe it would surely have brought the kill he was so desperate for. For an instant, Helborg threw off his long weariness, his disappointments and his inadequacies, and became the perfect swordsman again, a vision of pure speed and power. It was all Otto could do to avoid being smashed aside and hacked to pieces, and for the first time a sheen of sweat burst out across his calloused brow.

Karl Franz could have joined him then. He could have limped over, adding his runefang to his Reiksmarshal's, and perhaps together they could have slain the beast. Instead, he remained bathed in the light of the comet, loathing every moment of inaction but staying true to the duty that compelled him.

When the end came, it was swift. Helborg overreached himself, leaving his defence open. Otto pounced, jabbing the point of the scythe down hard. The wickedly curved edge bit deep, cracking Helborg's breastplate and driving into the flesh beneath. With unnatural strength, Otto dragged Helborg off his feet and hurled him to one side, ripping out his heart as he did so.

Helborg skidded across the marble before crashing into the altar, his chest torn open. With his final breath, he looked up at Karl Franz, and there was still a wild hope in those pain-wracked eyes. He shivered, his arms clutching, his body rigid and his back arched.

'Fight... *on*,' he gasped.

Then he went limp, slumped against the altar's edge, his armour drenched in blood. The last defender of Altdorf died at the heart of his city, gazing up at the empty dome above, his haunted features at last free from the pain that had consumed him for so long.

With Helborg slain, Otto advanced on Karl Franz once more, a wide grin on his face. In the background, the Reiksguard were being cut down, one by one.

'You people do not know when to give in,' said Otto. 'It becomes tiresome.'

Karl Franz watched him approach, preparing himself, knowing how painful the transition would be, dreading it and yet yearning for it to come.

'But surely you can see that this thing is over now,' said Otto, drawing back the scythe. His green eyes glittered with triumph. 'There is nothing more to be done, heir of the boy-god. Listen to the truth: the reign of man is ended.'

He swung the blade, and the tip, still hot from Helborg's blood, sliced into the Emperor's chest.

Karl Franz staggered backward, his breath taken away by the agony of it, struggling to keep his vision. Otto ripped the scythe-blade free, tearing up muscle and sinew and leaving a long bloody trail across the altar's side.

The Emperor slid further down, his body pressed against the altar-top, the runefang falling uselessly from his open palm. Each of the three Glott brothers, their enemies destroyed now, shuffled closer, peering with morbid curiosity as the life ebbed out of their victim.

Karl Franz looked up at them, gasping for air, feeling the blood clog in his throat.

They were not even gloating. They suddenly looked like children, shocked at what they had done, as if only now could they contemplate what it might mean.

That made him want to smile. He gripped the altar's edge, and ceased fighting. Everything went cold, then black, and then became nothing. It was like tipping over the edge of a precipice, then falling fast.

And so it was that, under the shattered dome of the Chamber of Ghal Maraz, Karl Franz, Elector Count of Reikland, Prince of Altdorf, Bearer of the Silver Seal and the holder of the *Drachenzahn* runefang, Emperor of all Sigmar's holy inheritance between the Worlds Edge Mountains and the Great Sea, died.

CHAPTER TWENTY-FIVE

Martak reached the very base of the Menagerie's dungeons, his breath heaving and his lungs burning. The last cage was buried deep, surrounded by huge walls of stone and ringed with iron chains. The air stank of flame and charring, and every surface had been burned as black as coal.

He could hear the footfalls at the top of the stairs. They had almost caught him, right at the end, and he could sense their bloodlust burning like a beacon in the darkness.

He reached the iron lattice, slamming into it and fumbling for the great lock. It was the size of his chest, and took a key the length of his forearm, but that would not be necessary now. Stammering over the words, he spoke the spell of unbinding, and the lock fell apart.

Heavy clangs rang out as iron-shod boots thudded down the steep stairs, and Martak barely pushed his way into the cage before metal gauntlets reached out to haul him back.

He wrenched himself free, skidding over to one side as he scrambled for safety. For a terrible moment, grovelling in the dark, he wondered if he had made some awful mistake, and the vast cage was already empty. If so, all he had done was lead his pursuers into a dead end, one from which there was no escaping.

A second later, though, twin gouts of flame lit up the shadows, and he allowed himself a gasp of relief.

The bursts of fire illuminated a curled, twisted and writhing mass of scaly hide, snaking in loops at the rear of the huge pen. Enormous wings folded up against the arched roof, leathery and as thick as a man's hand. Two great eyes, slit-pupilled like a cat's, blinked in the dark, exposing yellow depths that seemed to go on forever.

Blind to the danger, the warriors of Chaos blundered into the cage after Martak, only realising their error too late.

The Imperial dragon opened its vast jaws, sending a stream of crimson flame roaring into them. The marauders screamed, clawing at their own flesh as the dragon's fire tore through them. Those that could tried to retreat, but the curtains of immolation overtook them all, ripping the armour from their backs and melting it across their blistered skin.

Martak pressed himself flat against the cage's curving inner wall, feeling the furious heat surge across his face. He screwed his eyes shut, barely enduring the ferocious blaze even as it thundered past.

After only a few moments, the torrent guttered out. Martak coughed and gasped, falling to his knees as smoke billowed out from the dragon's jaws. He glanced back to the cage entrance, where dozens of bodies lay gently steaming, as black as burned offerings.

He allowed himself a twisted grin, and shuffled up to the dragon's great iron collar.

'That was well done, dragon,' he said, reaching up for the mighty lock.

The dragon hissed at him, sending a fresh burst of flame-laced hot air blasting into his flushed face. Martak whispered words for the quieting of the animal spirits, drawing on the Wind of Ghur that eddied throughout the whole Menagerie. He had no chance of truly mastering a dragon's mind, but he could do just enough to persuade it that *he* was no threat, and that freedom was a small step away, and that the horrors running amok in the Palace above were the real prey.

He placed his hands over the massive padlock, and exerted his will. The lock clicked open, and the iron chains fell to the ground with a resounding clang. Though still hampered by the confines of the cell, the great creature stretched out, its head rising up to the roof and its wings unfurling around the walls. A grating, iron-hard growl emerged from its chest, and its clawed forelegs pawed at the straw.

'Now, take the fight to *them!*' urged Martak gazing up at the creature's snake-like neck and marvelling at just how huge it was. 'You are free – let me guide you.'

The dragon did not move. Though released from its chains, it remained where it was, curled up in a dungeon at the very base of the vast Palace. Its old, old face seemed lost in thought, its eyes narrowing and its nostrils flared.

Martak began to lose patience. If the Emperor still lived, there would be little time to save him. Every moment saw more of the city destroyed, and more lives lost.

'Come *on!*' he commanded, infusing his voice with as much beast-mastery as he could. 'What are you waiting for?'

As soon as he uttered those words, though, he realised what was happening. The dragon *was* waiting for something. It had no intention at all of leaving its cell, and its huge head remained motionless, slightly inclined, as if listening.

It was only then that Martak felt it himself. He had been so preoccupied with survival, so fixed on his goal of releasing the dragon, that the tremors had passed him by completely, but now, with his hunters slain and the mighty beast standing before him, he wondered how he had missed them.

The ground was vibrating. Not strongly, as if in an earthquake, but with a steady, persistent harmonic. The straws under his feet were trembling, and lines of dust were falling from the brickwork roof. A low hum filled the chamber, reverberating just on the edge of hearing. It sounded like it was coming from everywhere – the stone, the earth, the air itself.

Martak backed away from the dragon. Whatever he sensed was nothing like the sorcery that had infused the city since the beginning of the siege. It felt... *older*, somehow, as if it belonged to Altdorf's very bones. After witnessing the dead raised and the order of nature turned against itself, it should have been impossible to conceive of more potent magic coming to the Reik, but Martak was enough of a mage to recognise true power when he felt it.

'What *is* this?' he murmured, looking up at the roof of the dragon's cage, any thought of trying to use the creature now abandoned. 'What comes now?'

For a moment, nothing changed.

Then the first shafts of light angled down from the open dome, harsh and piercing. The Glottkin looked up, as did their surviving troops in the chamber. More shafts lanced through the gaping breach, shimmering like spun gold. They focussed on the altar, seeming to soak into the iron.

Otto started to back away. Ethrac stared at the growing pool of gold, a gathering unease on his face.

'And what?' Otto demanded. 'What is this?'

Spinning points of gold coalesced over the altar-top, clustering together and glittering like stars. Far above, the clouds broke at last, burned away by the lone star riding the high airs. Across the city, beleaguered defenders suddenly stared up into the heavens, noticing the strange play of light dancing across the shattered townscape. The marauders paused in their plunder, and daemons shrunk back, their laughter halted.

'Just a star!' protested Ethrac, outraged. 'You told me – it was just a star!'

The light kept growing, building up into a column of iridescence that hurt the eyes to look upon. A column of pure gold shot down onto the altar where Karl Franz's body lay like the sacrifice it had been. Shimmering luminescence shot out in all directions, trembling with a blaze of metallic light.

Otto was forced back from the altar, his eyes streaming. Ethrac's staff shattered in his hands, and its bells rolled across the marble.

With a roar like distant thunder, the rain of gold turned into a torrent, cascading down from the comet and smashing against the altar-top. Rays of severe iridescence radiated outward, refracting and spinning, making the columns around them glisten as if newly gilded. The stained-glass windows blew out, sending shards of diamond-like glass flying into the plague-storm beyond.

Bathed now in a pillar of shifting gold, the Emperor's body began to change. The harrowed expression left his face and the lines of care smoothed out. His corpse rose, suspended in an aegis of fire. The chains above the altar thrashed and twisted, buffeted by a new wind.

His eyes opened, and golden brilliance flared from the sockets. He righted himself, now floating directly over the altar, and swept his blinding gaze across the cowering mutants below. He seemed to augment, to grow, becoming far more than a man. The last of his armour fell away, exposing a shifting phantasm of pure coruscation beneath. Shafts of gold danced around him, reflecting from the now-dazzling surfaces of the chamber.

It was hard to make out what manner of being now hung above the black iron. Karl Franz's face could be made out amid the sparkling clouds of light, blurred and fractured, but older faces were there too, coexisting in a merger of souls. A series of Emperors gazed serenely out from the blistering fires, unharmed by them, sustained by them, before the vision shifted once more.

Otto's flesh began to burn, curling away from the bone in crisping flaps. Ethrac and Ghurk followed, their withered muscles scorched by the rays of light surging from the gathering inferno of gold. The being that had once been the Emperor continued to expand, until an argent titan hung in the chamber's heart, blazing like the dawn rising.

A voice echoed around the shimmering space, redolent of the old Emperors, but containing a choir of others with it, all speaking in a harmony of different accents and timbres.

'The Law of Death is broken,' it announced, and the words echoed among the roar of golden flames. 'All worlds are now open.'

The titan's face began to flicker, changing from one to another, now bearded, now smooth, now old, now young. A new visage came to the fore – a ruddy-cheeked youth with a mane of long blond hair, laughing with warrior's eyes. The intensity of the golden aura became truly blinding, spreading out across the entire chamber in shimmering curtains of brilliance.

'We are the Empire,' announced the flickering avatar, its flaming eyes sweeping across the burning vista. 'We have always been the Empire.'

It raised its hands high, and it seemed that a mighty warhammer now hung from the clanking chains. The titan took it up, and the weapon blazed with the same intense light that filled the chamber.

'And now,' it said, portentously, 'let *all things change.*'

A hard *bang* rang out, blowing what remained of the glass out of the windows and making the earth shake. The heart of the golden being exploded, filling the vaults with white-hot illumination. A racing wave of energy surged out from the epicentre, sweeping and ethereal, consuming all before it. The burning bodies of the Glotts were devoured, seared to ash and blown away by the racing storm-front.

A radial wave smashed through the walls of the chapel, rising up in a dome of unleashed power. The hemisphere, swimming with translucence, spread across the entire city, a wall of gold, tearing out from the Palace at its heart and scouring everything it touched. The scorching barrage of flame destroyed every lingering creature of Chaos as it thundered outward, stripping the layers of slime and filth clean from the stone beneath and immolating them into nothingness. The fallen undead were blasted apart, their dry bones turned to powder and thrown into the wind.

Above the city, the last of the plague-storm clouds were torn away, exposing a clear sky above. The comet burned vividly now, linked to the earth by the roaring column of gold. The expanding fire-dome ground its way outward across the entire valley, rising into the heavens and encompassing the fields of war below. At its edge, the corrupted forest burst and burned, and its foul taints were stripped clear of the raw earth.

For a moment longer, the entire Palace shimmered from the golden storm within, its every portal bleeding pure comet-fire. The dome of Sigmar's temple flared in answer, reflecting mesmerising rays across a glittering sky. The Reik, for so long a turgid well of slime, burst into cleansing flame, revealing pure waters boiling under the skin of filth. Aeons of grime were scrubbed from the ancient stone walls, revealing Altdorf as in the days of old – the city of white stone, the home of kings, the birthplace of Emperors.

And then, with a final roar, the dome of light shimmered out. The city below it seemed to shudder, and then fall still.

The dead were gone. The corrupted were consumed. Amid the wreckage and the ruins, the surviving human defenders crept out of whatever cover they had found, shading their eyes against the glare that still lingered on the waters.

The air was cold and clear. For the first time in months, the wind tasted fresh. The spores were gone, the cankers had been stripped away.

With a growing sense of awe, they began to realise what had happened. The enemy was destroyed, burned on the altar of wrath, its limitless powers exposed for the sham and trickery they were. Something new had emerged, something unprecedented.

The Palace still glowed from within. Whatever had been unleashed there still lingered, though none dared approach its burning precincts.

All they could do was stare up at the listing battlements and the broken towers, and guess at what new and terrible god now dwelt amid the graven images of the old.

EPILOGUE

Early winter 2525

As the storm clouds gradually headed north, their heavy aegis broken, the rising sun illuminated a scene of gently steaming devastation.

Everything was gone. The mighty walls had been reduced to rubble, and smoke still curled from the charred remains of the great buildings. The temples, the counting-houses, the merchants' mansions, the beggars' hovels – all had disappeared, withered by the fury of the North, rendered down to whitened dust.

The few that had survived lingered in the ruins only for want of somewhere better to go. The remnants of Helborg's command fanned out from their North Gate fastness, blinking in the suddenly pure light. Bretonnian knights stumbled under the gaping arch of the West Gate, already resigned to the loss of their leader but determined to seek him out. Exhausted townsfolk all across the city fell to their knees, gazing around them in blank amazement.

No victory songs were sung, for every living throat was parched raw. A pall of shock had seeped into the earth. None had the words for what they had seen, and none tried to find any.

Slowly, though, the instincts of survival took over. Men and women began to seek one another out, searching through the rubble for survivors. Under the fractured shadow of the still-huge Palace walls, the few living commanders started to try to impose some sense of order on what remained. Food would have to be found from somewhere, and water drawn, and fires lit, and searches launched. Perhaps Helborg still lived. Perhaps some of the electors still lived.

In the city's poorest quarter, at the very centre of where the daemonstorms had been greatest, it took a long time for Margrit to do anything other than stare up into the cleared heavens, her heart beating heavily. Eventually her senses returned to her, though the world around seemed as blurred as a badly-remembered dream.

Her fellow sisters pulled themselves up from the stone, their faces drained with shock, their hands still trembling. From within the temple, weak voices could already be heard, crying out, pleading to know what had taken place.

She had no idea what to tell them. It took her a long time to get up, first gently shifting the body of the slain king from her lap. When she stood, she felt light-headed. She tried to remember how the old tenements surrounding the temple had appeared in the past. Now the dome of Shallya was the only thing still standing, and beyond it stretched an empty landscape of smouldering rubble.

But Margrit was a practical woman, and there were already tasks at hand. The temple had to be secured. They had to look to the gardens, to try to salvage anything that might help with the wounded, for there were sure to be thousands of them. She started moving again, speaking to the others, who trod amid the detritus just as numbly as her.

'There will be answers,' she told them, not knowing if that were true but needing something to say. 'For now, remember your vows.'

Once they had something to do, to occupy them, things became easier. The hours passed again, filled with the old tasks of care. A group of knights found their way to the temple, and bore away the body of their king in reverence. Margrit watched them go, making no attempt to lay claim to him. The warriors barely noticed her.

They would not have spoken to her, in any case. They were men of war, and so few of them had ever paid any attention to the women in their midst, unless they were bejewelled queens or ethereal goddesses, and Margrit was neither.

By the time Martak found her, the sun was high in the sky, and a warm wind had started blowing from the south. The wizard looked as filthy as ever, though his long beard looked to have been singed half away.

As he picked his way towards her through the wreckage, Margrit crossed her arms, and waited.

'You never got me those soldiers,' she said.

Martak shot her an apologetic look. 'He was a hard man to persuade.'

'Was?'

Martak nodded, and Margrit sighed. She had heard men curse Kurt Helborg to damnation during the days of toil, but the Reiksmarshal had stood beside them at the end, and that was worth something.

'You promised me an Emperor, too,' she said.

The wizard looked bone-weary. With a grunt, he sat down on a broad stone step. Margrit joined him, and together they looked out across the rubble-strewn courtyard. For a while, neither of them spoke.

'I do not know what happened,' said Martak eventually.

'If you do not, then no one will.'

Martak looked at her. All his earlier gruffness had been ripped from him.

His voice was still as earthy as the mulch under the forest floor, but something had changed. He looked... humbled.

'I brought him back,' he said, looking unsure how to feel about that. 'Do not misunderstand me – it was *his* choice. I tried to get him to escape it, but he wouldn't listen.'

Margrit placed a calloused palm on Martak's wringing hands. 'When you told me he would come back, I believed you.'

'I was telling you what you wanted to hear.'

'It doesn't matter.' She summoned a weak smile. 'The *words* mattered.'

Martak looked sceptical, but said nothing. He made no attempt to shift her hand from his, and the two of them stayed where they were. Crouched at the edge of ruin, a ragged, dirt-streaked pedlar from the lowliest of colleges and a portly old woman from the most disregarded of temples.

Not much to be proud of, but they were alive.

'So, what now?' she asked him.

Martak shook his head, a wry expression playing across his wrinkled brow. She could tell what he was thinking. Plans would have to be made. Schwarzhelm might yet live. Valten might still carry Ghal Maraz. There were mysteries to delve into, and at some stage someone would have to go back into the Palace, searching for any remains of the... event. They had all seen the tides of gold, and they had all heard the roar of the storm, and they all knew that it had changed everything, and that a new power had been birthed in Altdorf beneath the comet's glare.

For now, though, it was too soon.

'I do not know, sister,' Martak said, clutching her hand tight.

The two of them sat next to one another after that, looking out onto the aftermath of the apocalypse, sharing silence.

Altdorf was destroyed, shriven to its foundations, and there would be no rebuilding. The old city was gone – its garrisons, its theatres, its chapels, its taverns and its storehouses, swept into nothingness.

The End Times had come, but they had not brought the utter destruction the gods of the North desired.

The old stories had ended, their power gone and their magic decayed. Now new stories would be told, but where they would lead, and who would tell them, even the wisest could not tell.

THE BONE CAGE

Phil Kelly

Sage's Ruin
Hunger Wood

'Get out, quick! It's crushing me!'

The ribs of the colossal corpse cart shuddered, straining to snap closed on the scarecrow of a man who was holding them open. The nature-priest cried out with the effort of separating the spars of the bone cage for a few more precious seconds. Almost horizontal in his straining crouch, the priest's spine and the soles of his feet were bleeding badly.

Roaring, a barrel of a man with unkempt white hair moved in to reinforce the skinny priest, shoving his shoulder into the gap. Though he was unmistakably past his prime, the big man had the strength of a veteran woodsman. Together, the two men held the cage's ribs open. A fellow captive, a swarthy knight in filthy golden plate mail, took his opportunity and pitched sidelong through the bars between them. As he rolled out onto the damp grass and came up with his longsword drawn, a winged horror swooped down to intercept him, shrieking like a hag.

Around the bone cage's walls, dozens of pale arms covered in suppurating sores pushed through, grabbing and snatching at the robed inhabitants that were still alive inside. The prisoners kicked and battered at the lunging white limbs, the sound of breaking bone punctuating the excited yelps of the ghouls straining to get inside.

Many of the men and women inside the cage were still manacled to its bone walls, but several of them had slipped their bonds and were piling out onto the wasteland beneath. High above them, a large stone carriage descended from the swirling thunderheads, held aloft by a blue-green court of ghosts. The reliquary at the palanquin's rear held something so evil it made even the night air shiver in disgust.

Mordecaul Cadavion commended his soul to Morr, braced himself and pitched through the gap in the prison's osseus ribs.

* * *

Three Days Earlier
South-west Templehof
The Vale of Darkness

Mordecaul awoke from his uneasy slumber, wincing as the bone prison hit another rut in the rough Sylvanian road. The cloth of the priest's black robes tugged at the scabbing welts across his back, the legacy of his merciless whippings at Castle Sternieste. As if in sympathy, the gaping wound in his opened wrist gave another dull pulse.

Around him, slumped on a bed of dead bodies, were nine men and women shackled to the enormous rib cage structure that formed the cage at the arcane carriage's rear. At its fore was a complex yoke of bone and sinew that was yanked along the road by six corpses clad in lacquered black plate. They were the remains of knights who had confronted the fiend von Carstein outside Castle Sternieste, resurrected to serve him in death where they opposed him in life. Mordecaul could just about make out von Carstein himself riding through the gloom at the head of the strange procession, an armoured silhouette mounted upon a skeletal stallion.

Mordecaul's fellow prisoners were mired in a morass of disembodied limbs and opened torsos. Their heads nodded in silence as the prison trundled and bumped along the path. Each bore the same ragged wound as the priest, red-black and in many cases burning with infection. Most of their number were leaning their backs against the osseous bars of their prison. Some, like Mordecaul, were snatching infrequent moments of sleep in the hope of regaining some strength.

Yet true rest was all but impossible. The stink of the cadavers lining the bottom of the bone cage was tremendous. Plump flies buzzed and frolicked in slit guts, blood-pooled eye sockets, even in the wounds sustained by the captives themselves during their attempts to break free.

The young priest knew that he was going to die, used for whatever foul purposes Mannfred had in mind and then either abandoned far from Morr's embrace or – worse still – resurrected to serve the vampire in death. When he had first been snatched from the renovations at Vance's temple of Morr, the thought had been terrifying and agonising in equal measure. Now Mordecaul almost welcomed the dire truth of his predicament. It fed his anger – anger he could use as fuel to stay alive, and courage to act when the chance came close.

Mordecaul pulled at his bunched robes, scratching through the cloth at the lesions on his back, trying in vain to find a shred of comfort.

'Don't keep picking at them,' hissed the round-faced matron shackled across from him.

The Shallyan priestess ripped another strip of cloth from the wimple she had tucked in the crook of her arm, winding it into a bandage that still had a semblance of cleanliness. Mordecaul had watched her pure white habit turn filthy brown over the last few days as she worked tirelessly to heal those of their number she could reach. Forgoing sleep altogether, she had prayed and prayed to the goddess of healing and mercy, but to no avail. In the end she'd had to resort to battlefield triage and whatever treatments she could administer.

An elderly Sigmarite priest lay slumped unconscious at her side. Though he wore manacles like the rest of them, he had not been bound to the cage's walls. His bloodied bronze cuirass and heavy belt lay discarded in the muck nearby. The priestess had been right to treat the Sigmarite first, for his wounds were without doubt the most severe. Mordecaul could have sworn he'd seen the man's brain glistening greyish-pink through the jagged wound in his skull. Dark with gore, his bandages uncoiled slowly in the Shallyan priestess's lap.

'If you keep picking at those whip-wounds,' she muttered crossly as she fussed with her patient, 'they'll be infected in no time.'

Mordecaul let his good hand fall back down, his expression sullen.

'What does it matter, sister?' he asked.

She ignored him, tying fresh cloth around her patient's split skull.

'The boy's got a point, Elspeth,' said the bearded brute at the foremost point of the carriage. 'We'll all be food for the ravens before long.'

The big man was an Ulrican priest – Mordecaul recognised the wolf-sigil branded into his forehead. He sat with his back to his fellow captives, watching the horizon for a deliverance that no one truly expected to come.

'Then answer me this, Olf Doggert. Why are we still alive? He's already used our blood for that damned ritual at Sternieste, and somehow drained the faith out of this place. So why hasn't he killed us?'

'He needs us for more of the same, I reckon,' replied Mordecaul, darkly. 'Together we're too valuable to let out of his sight. These von Carsteins will stab each other in the back just to pass the time.'

'Perhaps,' offered Lupio Blaze, grinning weakly, 'perhaps the goddess Myrmidia lets us live, so she can find out how many we can take with us into the grave, no?'

The Tilean knight made half-hearted stabbing motions, though his sword was long lost. The man was still clad in his golden armour, though the plate was caked with filth and the proud reliefs of his goddess were smeared with blood. Mordecaul avoided his gaze. The knight's indestructible bravado was hollow as his tone, a bad joke that had long ago turned sour.

There was a grating shriek from the blackening skies and Mordecaul looked up with a start. Above the grotesque carriage wheeled the Swartz-hafen devils: a pair of bat-winged vargheists, massive in frame, yet sunken and spry like ogres on the point of starvation. Mordecaul hated them, perhaps more than he hated any other breed of gravebeast, and that was a high claim indeed. Priests of Morr considered resurrection the worst of all sins, for the unliving were direct blasphemies against the death god and the eternal peace he represented. Vampires were the worst of their kind, and vargheists arguably the most hideous of them all.

Mordecaul's tutors had taught him that the bloodsucking beasts represented the true form of the vampire, a creature of purest evil with all pretence of civility or humanity stripped away. The two fiends wheeling above them now were von Carstein's pets, obedient to his every whim. They had opened Mordecaul's wrist in the dread tower of Castle Sternieste. They had forced their captive's blood to stream out as part of the apostatic ritual that had robbed the power of faith from Sylvania.

The grating, clicking outbursts of the vargheists played on Mordecaul's nerves; their hisses sounded a little too much like laughter. Yet they were certainly not the worst of the sights he had seen in the weeks since his capture.

The clouds above the vargheists glowed red with a dull but ever-present threat. Mordecaul knew what lurked up there in the darkness: an ironbone palanquin bearing an unholy relic of immense power. He shuddered at the thought, his back aflame at the involuntary motion. He was glad he could not see it now, even if the memory of its dark grandeur waited behind his eyelids for whenever he tried to sleep. Sometimes a great black claw appeared in his mind's eye, limned with green fire and beckoning slowly.

There was a murmur from up ahead and something half-growled by von Carstein. It sounded to Mordecaul like half of a conversation, though not in any tongue he recognised. The priest shot a baleful glare at his captor. Clad in ancient, blade-ridged armour, the vampire's pallid scalp glowed grey-yellow in the gloom under a large crown that shimmered with ghostlight.

Mordecaul looked away, his eyes cast down. He dared not look upon the vampire for long. The last time he had, the fiend had sensed the attention on him and turned to meet his gaze. Mordecaul shuddered at the memory of the evils he had seen in von Carstein's eyes.

'What's he saying up there?' asked Olf Doggert.

'Bad things,' said Blaze, unhelpfully.

'He's talking to the crown, I think,' said Mordecaul.

'The crown?' asked Elspeth, doubtfully.

'Yes. No less than the Crown of Sorcery, if my order has it right,' said the young priest. 'There are etchings in my temple's underground vault. It's an ancient artefact, and it's supposed to be under magical guard beneath the Temple of Sigmar.'

'Supposed to be,' said Blaze. 'But the vampire, he stole it. We came from Altdorf with Grand Theogonist Volkmar to get it back.'

'The Crown of Sorcery...' said Olf, his brow furrowed. 'Like the one worn by that orc, the one they called the Slaughterer?'

'The same,' replied Mordecaul. 'Legends say it has part of the Great Necromancer's power inside it. That he speaks to those who wear it, guiding them from the spirit realm.'

Silence stretched out for a few long moments, each of the captives lost in their own dark thoughts.

Von Carstein's voice filtered back to them again as he muttered a phrase that sounded to Mordecaul more like a Morrite psalm than part of a conversation. Suddenly, the bed of dead limbs and torsos underneath him twitched and convulsed, broken fingers clutching and intestines writhing like snakes. Mordecaul could feel worm-like motions under his legs.

On the other side of the cage, a scarecrow-thin priest Mordecaul believed to be a worshipper of the nature god crawled backwards up the bone spars. His manacles clanked around the raw flesh of his wrists and ankles, but he extricated himself from the twitching limbs of the undead below with admirable dexterity.

Most of the other captives flinched, but rode it out, expressions of distaste etched on their faces. Mordecaul shook his head in frustration and flung a disembodied forearm across the carriage. The limb's twitching fingers caught onto the bone spars and it flopped down into the lap of the maiden sitting cross-legged opposite the priest of Morr.

Mordecaul's throat tightened in acute embarrassment, but the gruesome gift did not awaken her from her trance. The elf maiden was so beautiful that Mordecaul could hardly bear to look at her. Gold-wound tresses framed a tapering face, pale and shapely. Her perfect lips mouthed a silent chant. She had not opened her eyes since she had been shackled with the rest of them inside Castle Sternieste.

Mordecaul was grateful in a way. He must hang on to his anger and hatred, not soften it with feelings of awe and admiration. It was the only thing keeping him alive. Instead he focused on the wound at the elf's wrist, the blood-matted tiara dangling from her hair and the disembodied limb in her lap. It was like looking at a rare and beautiful rose that had been trampled into the dirt.

'For winter's sake, stop staring, boy,' sighed Olf Doggert, looking over his shoulder. 'She's one of them Ulthuan lot, and by the look of the jewels, she's royalty, too. You aren't getting under her skirts, not in a thousand years. And if you so much as touch her, Sindt,' growled the Ulrican priest, 'I'll break these manacles off just to wrap 'em around your head.'

'I've not touched a hair on her delicate little head,' said the rangy acolyte opposite Mordecaul, his tone acid. Sindt had spent the first few days pretending to be asleep with his head slumped and his wrists resting on his knees, but on the third night he had finally introduced himself, grudgingly unveiling his allegiance to the trickster god Ranald. Mordecaul had hated him from the moment he had first spoken. He was the sort of man who would steal Morrpennies from a dead man's eyes.

Sindt looked sidelong at Mordecaul through his curtain of long, black hair. 'The old wolf's right, my little grave-grubber. Whatever the hell that elf thinks she's doing, she don't need the likes of us distracting her.'

Mordecaul narrowed his eyes, but said nothing.

'She's seeking aid,' said the tall Bretonnian woman standing shackled to the bone prison's rear. Her tone was courtly, imperious even. Though she was undoubtedly very beautiful, in Mordecaul's eyes she was nothing compared to the elf princess. 'I recognise the cadence of the chant,' she said. 'She summons the beasts of the wild.'

'I should like to see that,' said the nature-priest, a mad light in his eyes. Everyone in the carriage lifted their head towards him, surprised that the skinny vagabond had finally spoken. Mordecaul was unnerved by the way he hung halfway up the cage's bars with his long fingers and toes locked like talons around the curving spars. More like a beast than a man, he thought. As if the Old World didn't have enough of that sort of thing already.

Uncomfortable under the sudden attention, the tangle-haired hermit hissed like a cat and dropped back down to land on all fours on the corpse-bed.

'So it can speak, then,' said Olf, his bushy white eyebrows raised as he turned back to stare at the horizon.

The bone prison clattered on, rattling along the scree-strewn path. The resurrected knights lashed to its multiple yokes moaned and clanked in their battered plate as they dragged onwards through the sharp stones of the Sylvanian road.

On the horizon to the east, Mordecaul noticed Templehof Crag silhouetted against the unhealthy light of Morrslieb. High above the tainted moon was its wholesome twin, Mannslieb, nothing more than a diffuse smudge in the gloomy skies. In the last few weeks the moon's lantern glow had been all but eradicated by the shroud of night that had so thoroughly claimed Sylvania. For one schooled in omens, it was a very bad sign.

'So we *are* heading north, then, if that's Templehof,' said Olf. 'Pay up.'

Sindt snapped the brittle bone splinter that he was using to probe the lock of his manacles and spat an obscenity in frustration. Elspeth tutted and made the sign of Shallya as Sindt kicked over two of the disembodied heads that he and Olf were using as improvised currency in their morbid gambling games.

Olf tapped the symbol of Ulric that scarred his forehead and grinned, exposing wide brown teeth. 'A wolfer's nose is never wrong.'

'Yeah, great,' said Sindt. 'So we're headed for Hunger Wood. I'm thrilled for us all.'

'Hunger Wood?' asked Mordecaul, sitting bolt upright. He drew in breath through clenched teeth as the weals on his back opened again. 'You're sure about that?'

'Aye, that I am,' said Olf. 'Sure as winter's bite.'

'That means ghouls,' growled the nature-priest on the bars above, baring his uneven yellow teeth.

'Yep,' said Sindt, his tone flat.

'It's worse than just ghouls,' said Mordecaul.

'Something worse than being eaten alive, eh?' said Sindt, rubbing his chin. 'Hmm. Olf, looks like we have a new game. I'll start. How about being ground into sausage and served at a Bretonnian banquet?'

The tall noblewoman, shackled to the ceiling of the prison, shot the trickster-priest such a look that the smug smile melted from his face.

'You don't get it!' spat Mordecaul. Something in his tone captured the attention of everyone in the prison, save the elf maiden, whose tapered eyes remained closed.

'Go on, boy,' said Olf. 'What's got a death-priest so spooked?'

'Hunger Wood,' replied Mordecaul sullenly. 'It... changes people.'

'No, that's not it,' said Sindt slyly. 'He's covering something up. Something to do with our young friend's history, or his order, I'll wager. Am I right?'

Mordecaul said nothing.

'Come on, lad,' said Olf. 'The more we know, the more we cooperate, the better chance we have of getting through this alive. What we're heading towards, is it a specific place? Or perhaps something of value?'

'We're all dead in a day or two anyway,' said Sindt. 'So you may as well tell us.'

The young priest gave a long sigh, looking up at a rare glimpse of sky.

'It's a site,' he said. 'The site of a ruined tower, to be exact. A place where my order has hidden something away from the von Carsteins.'

'So why only go there now?' asked Olf. 'What's taken the vampire this long to claim it?'

'A ritual, of a sort. My order can hide the departed from those who would raise the dead, right? Everyone knows you keep a couple of pennies aside for Morr.'

'Yes,' said Elspeth, making the sign of Shallya. 'When there's nothing more to be done, consecrate them unto the god of the afterlife. That way they cannot rise again.'

'Yes. Well, we hide other things too, sometimes.'

'Go on,' whispered Sindt.

Mordecaul looked nervously past the prison's yoke to the armoured vampire up ahead, but their captor was still muttering to himself, his attention focused on the road ahead.

'In Hunger Wood,' whispered the young priest, 'there's a site where Ghalacryst, an old member of our order, was said to have made a pact with Morr. A pact to keep something he discovered secret, something ancient and evil.'

'Like the thing inside that horrible flying carriage up there?' asked Olf.

'Sort of,' said Mordecaul. 'A grimoire he found in the bowels of Mordheim.'

'Mort-heim!' said the nature-priest, his growl like that of a cornered fox. 'It is cursed.' Sindt shot a look up at him, making a slashing gesture across his neck before motioning for Mordecaul to continue.

'Well, this tome he found,' continued Mordecaul, 'he knew it was of great value to the agents of undeath that were hunting the ruins. They didn't care for money, nor for wyrdstone. Just for the grimoire. So Ghalacryst hid it away from the sight of the living and the dead alike, deep in Hunger Wood. He's still there now, guarding his find, or so they high priests say.'

'Seven hells, boy,' said Olf. 'Enough mystery. What does the vampire want with this thing? And why wait 'til now to retrieve it?'

'Well, we know that our gods aren't... I mean our devotions aren't being rewarded. None of us wants to admit it, but there it is. Look at us. An acolyte of Ranald, shackled to his own bad luck. A priest of Morr, trapped amongst the undead. A priest of Taal, caught like an animal behind bars. A Shallyan, unable to heal the wounded. Do I need to spell it out for you?'

'Er... Maybe a little bit,' said Olf.

'The powers of the faithful have no meaning in Sylvania, not any more!' hissed Mordecaul, his manacles clinking as he threw his hands up in frustration. 'Not since the ritual in Sternieste. That means that the spell of seclusion worked by Ghalacryst isn't working!'

'And that our host has hence learned of this priceless... grimoire,' said Elspeth carefully.

'Yes.'

'And that's where we're going now,' said Olf. 'To pick it up.'

'Yes!'

'And if he's listening to us now,' said Sindt, 'and *didn't* know about your order's dirty little secret before, you've pretty much just told him all about it.'

The tall Bretonnian woman gave a short trill of laughter, a note of desperate madness in the dark.

A sudden cry came from the south, so pure and high that it instantly drew their attention. Mordecaul spun around to see a great eagle swoop low towards them, its wingspan the width of the winding road.

Plummeting out of the clouds behind it came one of the Templehof vargheists, screeching in outrage as it folded its wings for a killing dive. The great eagle banked hard, lashing out at its pursuer with talons the size of a farmer's sickle. It tore the wing-devil's face clean off, leaving only a flayed, screaming skull.

As the eagle dived low the second of the two vargheists shot out of the clouds, slamming its own claws into the creature's shoulders and pulling up hard. Above it, something writhed in the clouds, looking to Mordecaul like a mass of ectoplasmic figures. The skies pulsed red as the Mortis Engine slowly descended. The ragged nature-priest shrieked, crying out for Taal to save him. Mordecaul had to fight hard not to scream himself, screwing his eyes shut to blot out the thing's unholy glory. A black claw beckoned behind his eyelids, mocking him, drawing out his dreadful suspicions and making them real. He shook his head in defiance and looked up once more.

The aerial battle between the eagle and the vargheists was becoming more and more frantic. The eagle was biting and slashing, banking and swooping, but it could not shake both the vargheists at once. Wherever it struck, the greyish flesh would heal over once more, caressed by the bilious energies of the unholy palanquin. Blood pattered down onto the upturned faces of the captives, each of them silently willing the eagle to prevail as the aerial struggle unfolded.

As if directed by one mind, both of the winged devils dived in at once, catching the eagle and holding it fast in mid-air. The floating reliquary came in close, the ruddy pulse of its raw power washing over the tableau.

The eagle seemed to age, shrinking in on itself, flesh and feather mouldering away as it became thinner and thinner. The great bird shrieked, cawed a coarse bark, then fell silent. The vargheists released it from their grip. It fluttered downwards for a moment, fleshless and strange, before dissolving into a scattering of desiccated bone.

A single long feather of white and gold wound its way down through the air towards the captives, passing straight through the topmost spars of the bone prison and settling just out of reach on the mound of disembodied limbs inside.

Mordecaul felt tears pricking his eyes as the elven princess gave a long, mournful keen of pure sorrow.

Hunger Wood
Vale of Darkness

'Ranald take these infernal... Just... Elspeth, push against that... Yes...'

Across from Mordecaul, Sindt gave a toothy hiss of triumph. With the healer Elspeth Farrier's help, the trickster-priest had finally managed to get his manacled foot free from his tightly-strapped longboot. Mordecaul's stomach growled; he was so hungry he considered hooking the boot over with his own foot and chewing its leather for whatever meagre sustenance it could provide. It was a cruel irony that they were passing through Hunger Wood, with its reputation for forbidden feasts. Even the trees looked like old flesh clad in wrinkled skin, the branches like dried and elongated fingers. So much meat to hand, rotten and rancid but surely better than nothing, was right there in the corpse-bed beneath them. All going spare for one with the courage to claim it...

The young priest shivered and pulled his attention back to what his fellow captives were doing. With his leg fully extended, Sindt was wiggling his toes through the holes in his stocking. Once the largest two were sticking out, he lowered his foot delicately towards the feather. He strained and grimaced, but was still a few inches short. Mordecaul watched from under hooded eyes, silently hoping the Ranaldite priest would dislocate something in his febrile attempts to snatch his trophy. Sindt stretched again, his face a rictus of effort.

Lupio Blaze puffed out his cheeks and blew a burst of air at the feather, his moustache quivering on either side of his mouth. At first, nothing happened. Then Elspeth caught on and joined in, both of them huffing and blowing like short-changed halflings.

Finally their combined efforts managed to ruffle the feather a few more inches towards Sindt. The trickster-priest grabbed it between his toes and retracted his leg as if he had been stung, quickly curling crosslegged and hiding the feather from sight completely. The vargheist with the red skull for a face swept by overhead, but did not come close enough to notice.

'You can't summon more eagles with just that,' whispered the nature-priest.

'Shut up and watch, Rube,' replied Sindt.

'I'm not Rube,' said the nature-priest. 'I'm Russet.'

Sindt ignored him, hiding the feather in his armpit so that the hollow tip stuck towards his mouth. He bit down into the quill-end with an expression of utmost concentration, nibbling a little here, spitting out a piece there, all the while giving the impression his head was merely nodding with the motion of the bone prison.

'And...' mouthed Sindt, stretching out the word as he finished his work, 'Ranald's your mother's lover.'

The trickster-thief showed the feather's dented tip against his palm for a second, reminding Mordecaul of an Altdorf street sharp showing a Stirland farmer his chosen card.

'Great,' he muttered. 'Now we can write Karl Franz a few strongly-worded letters.'

'No, death priest,' said Lupio Blaze quietly, shaking his head and holding out an admonishing finger. 'You wait.'

As soon as they passed under a canopy thick enough to hide the moonlight completely, Mordecaul heard a faint 'click' of metal, then another. When the moonlight fell on Sindt once more, he sat exactly as he was before, but for the hint of a smug smile on his face.

'So we have a chance, then,' muttered Elspeth. 'If we can get these manacles off... With Shallya's grace, we still have a chance.'

'Not without weapons, we don't,' snorted Olf gruffly. 'They're vampires, woman. There's no way we can take them. And that... that *thing* in the clouds... What's inside it is worse than even the von Carsteins.'

'Just call it what it is, you fat coward,' sneered Sindt. 'You heard the vampire say it, just like the rest of us. It's the Hand of Nagash.'

The woods fell silent. Even the buzzing of insects and rustling of leaves stopped.

The Sigmarite priest in Elspeth's lap stirred in his unconsciousness, crying out. His voice sounded like it came from a great distance away.

'The Hand...' he mumbled. 'It begins... It will bind...the sands... the triplets... the moon... blood and fire... dead gods...'

'Hush, now,' murmured Sister Elspeth, shooting a fierce glance at Sindt as she laid a hand on the old man's brow. 'Try not to move. Be at peace.'

A cackling scream echoed through the forest. Mordecaul felt sweat break out on his forehead. It had not sounded like it had come from a human throat.

His stomach rumbled again. This time he punched it in frustration, but the gnawing sensation was still there.

As the bone prison bumped its way through the twisting paths of the wood, Mordecaul watched in grudging admiration as Sindt went to work. The trickster-priest slumped in feigned sleep over first Olf, then Russet, the odd clink of metal lost under the trundling clank of the carriage's wheels. Russet's face lit up when he realised his manacles had been undone by Sindt's clever hands, and it took four sets of glaring eyes to convince him not to spring up and attempt escape straight away. Sindt whispered something into the nature-priest's ear, and a slow, guileless smile spread across Russet's battered features.

Sindt wasn't done there. Placing the feather in between his toes once more, he extended his leg to its fullest extent and inserted its nib into the lock on the manacles around Blaze's ankles. The trickster-priest's tongue stuck out of the corner of his mouth as he waggled his toes back and forth. Mordecaul found himself hoping that, this time, the Ranaldine thief would succeed.

He was not disappointed. Though Sindt was sweating and gritting his teeth by the end of it, his efforts were rewarded with a soft click.

'It won't make any difference, you know,' said the Bretonnian lady at the rear of the carriage. 'We're all dead already.'

'Nonsense. We'll see you out of here, alive and well,' said Olf.

'Oh no you won't,' she laughed softly, her voice like knives on silk.

Mordecaul hoped against hope for the dawn, even for a single shaft of sunlight to give them hope.

In his heart, he knew it would never come.

The woods around the path were getting denser by the hour. The only illumination within the prison was the occasional shaft of light from Morrslieb, and a soft lambent glow that surrounded the elf princess. Other than the occasional despairing moan and the old man's occasional mutterings from Elspeth's lap, the company had fallen silent. Some of their number were pale with loss of blood, and Mordecaul could smell that some of their wounds were turning rotten.

The prison's wheel hit a large root, and the whole carriage shuddered. A disembodied leg fell out of the back of the corpse-bed, rolling to a halt in Mordecaul's line of sight. The young priest sat bolt upright as one of the loping shadows that had started to follow them a few miles back darted forward and snatched it up. A pallid scavenger of little flesh and too much skin, it leered at him over its prize before receding into the gloom. Its expression had been drawn and crazed, but there had been something undeniably human behind its gormless, blood-flecked grin.

'Ghouls...' he muttered.

Mordecaul's order had a special hatred for ghouls. Cannibals who fed on the flesh of the dead, the creatures regularly raided those crypts and graveyards that were not consecrated in the name of the death god. The young priest had seen a fair few of the creatures in his time, even killed a handful in them himself in defence of his sacred sites. Yet these ones were even more starved and disgusting than usual. The unnatural darkness that had robbed the life from Sylvania, driving its people to flee the province or die, had also robbed the vampire counts' minions of their sustenance.

Here and there the prison had trundled past scattered patches of rags and rusted armour that had been gnawed to scraps, the last remnants of mercenaries and adventurers who had trodden these paths. The stories told that sometimes, lost and starving, they had found new lives as cannibals instead.

As Mordecaul watched them approach a large bundle near the middle of the track, Sindt's hand shot out from the bone prison. Quick as a snake he grabbed a sword hilt and yanked it from its scabbard, the bone spars of the giant cage shuddering as if in shock at the sudden motion. Sindt tossed the sword towards Lupio Blaze and folded his arms back into his loose crouch in one smooth movement. The Tilean knight caught the sword with commendable dexterity, plunging it into the nearest torso so that only its hilt protruded in the shadow of his knee.

Drawn by the flash of movement, the vargheist that had been injured by the elf princess's eagle swooped along the forest path and alighted on the top of the cage's bars. The enormous creature scrabbled around until its beady eyes stared right down at them through a mask of red bone. Strings of bloody drool pattered into their midst, but not one of the prisoners was foolish enough to meet the thing's gaze. Eventually it flapped away, shriek-clicking to the wing-devil that hung upside down from the canopy up ahead.

'Not a bad snatch,' said Mordecaul, his voice a little shaky.

'Lucky fingers,' said Sindt.

Sage's Ruin
Hunger Wood

The path grew wider as it wound onwards, turning into a broad oak-lined clearing. Morrsleib's wan green light threw twitching shadows from the ancient trees, their cracked branches grasping slowly at the air. Mordecaul craned his neck to look past Olf's bulk at the front of the carriage, and saw a shattered ruin atop a small hill in the distance.

'Morr's blade,' he said under his breath. 'We're here.'

At the head of the procession, Mannfred von Carstein cried out in jubilation, taking the Crown of Sorcery from his head and stowing it on the horn of his saddle. His skeletal horse broke into a gallop, its hoofbeats unnaturally loud in the cloying quiet of the wood.

The tower up ahead was a many-tiered mass of tumbledown walls and shattered minarets. Its mossy stone walls were veined by creeping, pulsing black tendrils that looked nothing to do with natural vegetation. Stone skeletons stood vigil around its walls, robed in the manner of priests and clutching roses and stylised scythes in each hand. As the carriage's armoured zombies pulled it closer, Mordecaul could see the sinewy remnants of a corpse dangling from the ruined tower's upper storeys. A thick noose of torn velvet was tight around its neck.

The vampire thundered in close, dismounting from his steed and disappearing from sight into the depths of the ruined tower. As von Carstein descended the stone steps to the basement a cloud of bats were startled from their nest in the corpse hanging high above, revealing that the body still wore the scruffy black robes of a priest. The cadaver's face was a barren mask of bone, though pennies had been pressed deep into its eye sockets, an offering made in the hope of a proper afterlife.

'Ghalacryst,' moaned Mordecaul. 'So it's true. The tome was buried here.'

'One of them, at least,' said the Bretonnian woman archly. 'He still needs three more, I believe.'

'And how come you know so much about all this, my lady?' asked Olf, staring up from under knotted brows.

'You mistake the lady for her messenger,' said the Bretonnian, her hooded eyes glistening with amused contempt. 'And even then, think again.'

'Sindt, look,' said Blaze. 'A helm.'

Lying amongst the scattered debris at the edge of the clearing was a fleshless skeleton, and sure enough, a dented bronze helmet was next to it. As the prison ground forward, it became obvious to Mordecaul that it would pass close by.

Sindt slumped over, his shoulder close to the bone spars nearest the skeleton. As the helmet came within arm's reach, Sindt shot out a pale arm and grabbed for it.

The jagged bone spars closed with a snap, clipping off the trickster's arm in a spurt of blood.

The prison erupted into bedlam. Sindt gave a deafening scream, clutching the ruined shoulder-stump that geysered blood all over Olf's lap. The giant Ulrican stood up with a roar, shrugging off his opened manacles and barging forward to put his shoulder against the gap in the bars. Russett leapt up to wedge himself bodily in the opening, bracing his shoulders and bare feet on either side of the gap and pushing it as wide as he could. Blaze drew the captured sword from its corpse-sheath, muttering prayers to Myrmidia as he tried to lever open his manacles.

Their vargheist jailors shrieked, their oddly angular heads whipping round. Wings snapped wide as the beasts took flight, a pack of ghouls loping from the forest eaves behind them. Ruddy illumination lit the entire clearing as low thunderheads formed a whirling vortex, the reliquary bearing the Hand of Nagash at its centre. The Mortis Engine's spectral guardians emitted soul-splitting shrieks as they lowered its palanquin towards the prisoners. Mordecaul could feel his skin tauten and his scalp tingle as the vile relic came closer.

'Get through the gap!' shouted Olf, his broad face turning an ugly red with the effort of holding the ribs of the cage apart. Above him, Russet's feet were trickling blood down the jagged edges of the bone spars, the nature-priest giving a thin moan as he fought against the unholy strength of the prison's magic. Mordecaul yanked forward, but he was weak with hunger, his shackles still bound tight. The vargheists were nearly upon them, and the ghouls loped in close, arms outstretched and mouth agape.

'Sigmar Unberogen!' shouted the old Sigmarite priest lying amongst the corpses, rearing up from Elspeth's side to bring his discarded metal cuirass down hard upon Blaze's damaged manacles. The blow sent chain links scattering in all directions. Mordecaul's heart filled with hope as he realised the warrior priest was Volkmar the Grim, Grand Theogonist and head of the Sigmarite cult. But rather than banishing the undead clustering around him, the old priest bared his teeth in an atavistic snarl and slammed his jagged cuirass into the pate of one grasping ghoul after another.

Screeching down from above, the faceless vargheist lunged a taloned arm towards Blaze. Its claw grabbed air as the Tilean dived headlong through the gap in the bone cage. The knight landed well enough, tucking into an awkward sideways roll before coming up fast to impale a leaping ghoul on the point of his stolen sword. Sweeping his arm wide, he flung the cadaverous creature from his blade right into the path of the swooping vargheist. The impact knocked the winged monster from the skies in a flurry of leathery flesh.

'Sindt! Help me!' shouted Mordecaul, waving his manacles at the trickster-priest. Grasping hands pushed through the bone spars to grab at the Morrite priest's robe, yanking him closer to the bars. The young priest tasted the bile of true fear as he imagined filthy teeth sinking into the backs of his legs. Volkmar was too far away to intervene, stamping and shouting on the other side of the cage like a man possessed.

Suddenly Elspeth was there, wrapping the chain of her own manacles around the cannibal-thing's throat and drawing it tight. Half-lying, half-kneeling, the matronly priestess braced her foot against its head. She put her hips into it, and broke the creature's spine with a sharp crack.

Sindt scrabbled over to Mordecaul, a thin whine of pain escaping his lips as his ruined arm bumped and scraped. The trickster-priest's eyes ran with tears as he fumbled the feathertip into the death priest's manacles with his off-hand. Keeping his arms as still as possible, Mordecaul kicked away the questing claws of the ghouls that threatened to disrupt Sindt's work.

Nearby, Volkmar struggled to fend off the faceless vargheist, using his broken cuirass as a shield. Badly dazed, the old man was too slow. The bat-devil swatted him across the cage so hard that he crashed into the bars near Olf.

Even in his dazed state, the old warrior priest still had sense enough to roll left, bodily toppling out of the gap in the prison's ribs to crumple into the blackened grass. The winged monster pushed its sharp-mawed head through the cage's bars, snapping at Elspeth's midsection as she fought to scrabble away.

Sindt gave a yelp of relief as Mordecaul's manacles clicked open. The young priest grabbed the heavy chain loops as they fell away and whipped them out sideways, smashing into the nearby vargheist's ruined face. The beast screeched and flapped backwards, a bat-winged silhouette against the red light of the descending reliquary.

Mordecaul caught a glimpse of the deadly palanquin hovering at the height of the treetops. In front of him Sindt moaned and cowered as his eyes. Incredibly, the blood pulsing from his shoulder stump began to flow up towards the ironbone construction, a dozen other streams of gore following suit. Thin rivulets of crimson from around the clearing reached up towards the obscene device as it was borne down on its escort of ghosts.

His attention riveted on the Mortis Engine, Mordecaul was powerless to resist as a muscular ghoul grabbed onto Sindt's good arm and dragged him through the corpse-bed to the bars. Three more of the leering scavengers reached in to pull the trickster close. The lanky priest screamed in agony as the pale, wrinkled ghouls bit down into his back and gnawed their way to his spine in a welter of spurting blood.

Horrified into action, Mordecaul picked up Sindt's fallen feather-pick and pushed it frantically into the keyhole of the manacles binding his feet. He had to get free, to save the princess from the same fate as Sindt. He felt the feather's nib slip and bend, but it was pliable enough not to break.

Outside the cage, Blaze was fighting hard against the second vargheist. The Tilean darted under its gangling reach to take its throat with the point of his blade, but the creature fought on regardless, slamming the knight's longsword out with a wide backhand blow. It bit down hard onto the Tilean's shoulder, breaking its teeth on his ornate plate armour.

Mordecaul forced himself to concentrate on his manacles as his feet slopped and slid in the corpse-mulch underfoot. Nearby, Elspeth was doing her best to keep the scrabbling ghouls away from the elven princess. She hammered at hands and heads with a skull she had seized from the corpse bed, but there just were too many of them.

One of the ghouls grabbed the elf's robe and pulled hard, only to be blasted apart by a flash of pure and blinding light that took Mordecaul's vision for a second. Some kind of elven enchantment, perhaps, not that really it mattered. A chance was a chance.

Bought a momentary reprieve, the young priest felt the lock on his manacles click open. He cried out in triumph, but his voice was lost under the screeching of fleeing ghouls.

The Morrite priest stumbled blindly across the cage, bumping into Olf and knocking them both out of the cage onto the grass below. He could smell the Ulrican's stale sweat and bad breath. Above him, Russett screamed in frustration as the bone cage's bars snapped back into place, and the nature priest was forced to tumble away in a windmill of bloody limbs to avoid its bite.

As Mordecaul disentangled himself from Olf and scrabbled to his feet, his vision began to clear. The ghouls had fled, scared away by the blinding light. Nearby, Volkmar was staggering over to the vargheist that battled Blaze. He raised his manacles in both hands and used them like a chain whip, beating the winged monstrosity's back over and over with a roar of angry despair.

The beast lashed out hard, its razored claw slashing into Volkmar's guts and straight up into his chest. The old man was hurled backwards, slit from navel to breastbone. Gasping, Mordecaul rushed to help him, ripping off a sleeve of his robes and binding the wound as best he could. From inside the cage the Bretonnian noblewoman called out a phrase, quick and strange, and the Theogonist's wound clotted closed in a shimmer of crimson light.

'Thanks!' blurted Mordecaul.

The caged aristocrat sketched a curtsey, her smile strangely mocking.

Nearby, Olf had flung himself bodily at the wing-devil that Blaze was hacking into with his longsword. The Ulrican grabbed the thrashing creature around the neck in a wrestler's grip.

Mordecaul saw his chance. Picking up a jagged splinter of bone that lay nearby, he lunged forward and buried it deep in the monster's heart. It gave a thin screech of pain and denial, flapping its wings and jerking away. Olf was flung to the ground. The creature staggered, cried out with an almost human sound of despair, and collapsed.

His features set in a grimace, Russet picked up a fallen branch and ran at the faceless vargheist staggering blindly around the side of the carriage. As the nature-priest was about to thrust the point of his improvised stake into the creature's back, a pale hand shot out from the bone cage and caught it with a dry slap.

Hollow laughter echoed across the clearing, a sound that told Mordecaul they had already lost.

'Morgiana, my dear,' said Mannfred, riding up close on the back of his undead steed. He held a giant, flesh-bound grimoire, still covered in a thick layer of dust. 'Why not join the celebrations? You certainly deserve it, having kept my latest investment alive, if not well. The old man still has enough life left for my purposes. And my compliments on having put up with these godly fools for so long in your... how shall I put this...' the vampire savoured his own wit for a moment like a fine wine, '*unladylike* condition.'

Von Carstein made a flicking motion with his hand. The bone cage's spars opened wide with a grinding creak, and the Bretonnian woman's manacles fell open into the corpse-mulch. She deftly dropped down out of its rear and in one smooth movement stepped up to Russet, biting down hard into the nature-priest's neck. Russet screamed and thrashed, but Morgiana held on tight, her eyes wide with dark delight. The nature-priest struggled on for a moment, twitched, and fell still.

The Bretonnian woman took a silk kerchief from her ruined finery and dabbed at the blood trickling from her mouth, smiling at Mordecaul like a predatory cat. The young priest spotted elongated fangs amongst her perfect white teeth. She held a finger to her lips, crimson sparks dancing in her eyes. With a jolt, Mordecaul remembered the stories of a telepathic bond between a vampire and its kin, and realised she had likely been passing their plans to her von Carstein master all along.

There was a clatter of hooves as Mannfred rode in close, his cursed palanquin drifting down towards him. Mordecaul could feel his skin writhe in disgust at the thing's nearness.

A terrible tiredness flowed through him. Nearby, Olf stumbled and fell to the ground, lying with his unfocused eyes staring at the red glare of the unholy reliquary.

'A noble effort, my deluded friends,' said the vampire. 'But not nearly enough.'

The last thing Mordecaul saw before the ruddy light swallowed his consciousness was Mannfred stroking the dusty tome, cradling it in his arms like an infant and chuckling softly to himself.

'Nagash... will rise.'

WITH ICE AND SWORD

Graham McNeill

Late Autumn, 1000 (Gospodarin calendar)

Hope was their undoing; hope and the certainty that their gods had inflicted suffering enough to visit yet more misery upon them. They had lost so much already: their homeland, their loved ones, all their worldly possessions. Surely, they prayed, the gods must now keep them from further loss, must surely balance their grief and hardships with deliverance.

What else but hope could explain the march of weary, frostbitten survivors of Kislev's destruction, trudging silently through this unnatural storm hammering the corpse-sown oblast? Almost two hundred starving, sickly and godforsaken souls, numbed by horror and hollowed by the carnage they had witnessed.

Doomsayers and holy men had always claimed that portents of the world's ending were there for all to see, but whoever *really* believed them? Devotees of the apocalypse tore their hair and whipped themselves bloody as they screamed of oncoming doom, but life in Kislev went on as it always had: dry, wind-soured summers and hard, frozen winters.

As regular as the turning of the seasons, the northern tribes raided Kislev in what *Anspracht of Nuln* had dubbed the Spring Driving, a term only someone who had never lived through such times would dare coin. The leather-tough rotamasters of the high stanitsas would gather their riders to meet the northmen in battle, and Kislev's mothers would weave mourning shrouds for their dead sons.

Such was life in Kislev.

As the sages of the steppe had it: *is of no matter*.

Even the terror of the Year That No One Forgets had been endured, the victories at Urszebya and Mazhorod decisive enough to beat the broken tribes back to their desolate homelands. Now it seemed those slaughters had simply been feints in preparation for the death blow.

With the first thaw, the northmen had come again.

Kurgans, Hung, Skaelings, Vargs, Baersonlings, Aeslings, Graelings, Sarls,

Bjornlings and a hundred other tribes came south under a single wrathful banner.

And the End Times rode with them.

Men, beasts of the dark forest and hideous monsters surged through Kislev in numbers never before seen. They swept south, not to conquer or plunder, but to destroy.

Cursed Praag was engulfed by howling daemons and horrors undreamed as Erengrad fell to midnight reavers in wolfships who burned the western seaport to the ground. And Kislev, impregnable fastness of the Ice Queen herself, was taken by storm in a single night of terrifying bloodshed. Its towering walls were now rubble, thick with screaming forests of impaled men and women whose ruined bodies were attended by red-legged carrion-feasters as black as the smoke of the city's doom.

Those who abandoned Kislev before the war-host reached its walls fled into a land gutted by war and bleeding in its aftermath, where mercy was forsaken and savagery the common currency. Ruined settlements burned on every horizon, their timber palisades cast down, the slitted eyes of beasts-that-walked-as-men gleaming as they feasted in the ashes.

All across Kislev, the fleshless bones of its people were stacked like cord-wood as altars to Dark Gods.

And this was but the opening move in the last war.

The girl had seen perhaps six winters, seven at the most. She knelt in the stunted grass beside the body of a woman with white hair, shaking her and sobbing her name, as if that might be enough to return her to life.

Sofia had seen the woman fall, and paused beside the weeping girl. Her hand hovered over the clasp of the satchel containing her few remaining medical provisions, but it was clear no craft she possessed could return the woman to life.

Swirling mud was already blurring her outline, but no one else in their wretched column of brutalised survivors was bothering to stop. Too many had died to mourn one more. They shuffled onwards through the storm, hunched over and wrapped in thick cloaks against the rain sheeting over the open steppe.

'You have to get up, little one,' said Sofia, too exhausted to say much else. 'You'll be left behind if you don't.'

The girl looked up. Her features were angular with Gospodar blood and her eyes were frost-white, steely with defiance. She looked at the refugees shambling through the steppe grass and shook her head, taking the dead woman's hand.

'She wasn't my mother,' said the girl. 'She was my sister.'

'I'm sorry, but she's gone and you have to let her go.'

The girl shook her head again. 'I don't want the northmen to eat her. That's what they do, isn't it, eat the dead?'

'I don't know,' lied Sofia.

'She wasn't a good sister,' said the girl, her voice hard, but brittle. 'She beat me and called me bad names when... But I'm still sorry she's dead.'

'What's your name?'

'Miska,' said the girl.

'A proud name from ancient times,' said Sofia.

'That's what *mamochka* told me,' said the girl. 'What's yours?'

'Sofia.'

Miska nodded and said, 'You're the healer, aren't you?'

'I was a physician in Kislev, yes,' said Sofia. 'A good one too, but I can't help your sister. Morr has her now. She is at peace and beyond the woes of this world. Even though she called you names, I'm sure she loved you and wouldn't want you to die out here. She got you this far, yes?'

'No,' said Miska, standing and brushing wet strands of flame-red hair from her face. 'I got *her* this far.'

'Then you're stronger than you look,' said Sofia.

Miska's head snapped up and Sofia saw the bleak sky of the oblast reflected in her eyes. She bared her teeth and her nostrils flared like an animal sensing danger.

'We need to go,' said Miska. 'Right now.'

'What is it?' asked Sofia, realising that even after all she'd seen and experienced, she could still feel terror.

A bestial howl echoed through the storm.

Something predatory. Hungry.

Close.

They huddled together, crying and clutching one another in fear as the howling came again. Bovine grunts and bellowing roars echoed back and forth, like a wolf pack on the hunt.

Sofia knew these were no wolves.

She and Miska hurried through the rain to rejoin their group. Instinct made them form a circle. Some dropped to their knees in the mud, praying to Ursun, others to Tor, perhaps hoping for a lightning bolt to strike the beasts from the heavens. She heard the names of a dozen gods she knew, half again as many whose names were unknown to her.

But most people simply clutched one another, praying only to die in the arms of a loved one. A defiant few shouted and railed at the unseen beasts, waving woodcutters' axes and makeshift spears at the hammering rain and the blurred shapes moving within it. Sofia caught glimpses of horns, glints of rusted armour and enormous weapons with notched blades. Heavy hoofbeats and scraping paws circled them. Snuffling snorts and bellows-breath.

'What are they?' asked Miska, clutching tight to Sofia's heavy skirt.

Sofia put a hand around her shoulder, feeling the youngster's terror.

Miska was seasoned beyond her years, but she was still a child... A child doomed to die before her time.

'Don't look at them, little one,' she said, pulling Miska tight to her, pressing the girl's tearful face into the rain-stiffened fabric of her dress. What good would it do her to see the blood and horror to come?

A monster with the snarling face of a bear charged from the black rain. A slashing paw ripped the arm and head from a kneeling man. Fangs snapped shut and bit him in half. Goat-headed horrors bounded in its wake, braying howls like war-shouts. Muddy pools bloomed red. People screamed and scattered like frightened sheep.

Kaspar had spoken of how large groups would be quickly destroyed if their formation was broken. He'd been boasting of the Empire's state troops, warriors who trained every day in the employ of an elector count, but these were terrified men and women who knew nothing of war save how to die.

'Stay together,' she yelled, already knowing it was hopeless. 'We're stronger together!'

Her words fell on deaf ears as brutish shapes, red of tooth and claw, roared from the storm. Nightmarish monsters from children's tales given horrifying, gory life: wild killers with slavering jaws and flesh-tearing claws.

Hideously deformed, yet recognisably human, they hunted in packs. Sofia wept to see a mother and child borne to the ground and savaged with snapping bites. A man and his wife were ripped apart by frenzied beasts with distended lupine skulls and bone-bladed hands. A group of sinewy, red-skinned creatures with chittering cries and spiteful hearts finished the wounded with flint daggers or stout clubs pierced by iron-tipped tusks.

The monsters bellowed as they killed, frenzied predators given free rein on a defenceless herd of prey-meat. More slaughters went unseen, mercifully hidden by the rain. The screams still carried on the wind, agonised and piteous. Sofia sank to her knees, holding Miska pressed tight to her breast as the monsters feasted. The girl sobbed, and Sofia felt her own mother's words rising within her, a lullaby from the northern oblast:

'*Sleep, bayushki bayu.*
  Softly the moon looks to your cradle.
  I will sing you a hero's tale
  and all the songs of joy,
  but you must slumber,
  with your little eyes closed,
  my sweet bayushki bayu.'

Her words faltered as a shadow fell across her, a towering beast with curling horns and a frothed maw of broken teeth. Bow-legged and with an umber pelt of matted fur, its blood-blistered flesh was raw with runic weals and war-scars. She heard the hoof-beats of more monsters closing for the kill. Miska tried to look up, but Sofia kept her hand firm against the girl's hair.

'No, little one,' she sobbed. 'Don't look.'

Sofia met the beast's maddened gaze. She had faced evil in the eyes of men before, and at least this creature wore its monstrous nature on the outside.

'Tor strike you dead!' she yelled as its arm swept down.

Hot blood sprayed her as the sharpened tip of a lance exploded from the monster's chest. Its bellow of pain was deafening as the impact hoisted it into the air. The beast thrashed like a hooked fish before the shaft of the lance snapped. The wounded monster crashed to the ground as a mighty warhorse trampled it into the mud before it could rise.

A knight in burnished plate slid from the horse's back, casting aside the broken lance and drawing a long broad-bladed sword from a saddle-sheath. His armour was dented and the black pelt of an exotic animal hung limp across one shoulder.

A knight of the Empire, one of the Knights Panther.

Something in his bearing struck Sofia as familiar, but she hadn't time to process the thought as the wounded beast struggled to its hind legs. It plucked the broken lance shaft from its chest, but the knight was already upon it.

The sword cut the wet air, slicing down in a brutally efficient arc. The blade buried itself a handspan into the meat of the beast's neck. Blood jetted as the warrior cranked the blade to open the wound. Nor did the knight allow the creature any hope of recovery. He dragged his sword clear and spun on his heel to take a two-handed grip on the weapon. The monstrous creature bellowed as the knight hammered the edge against its exposed throat.

Once again the blade bit deep, and the beast's roaring ended abruptly as its head toppled from its neck in a fountain of blood. The knight kicked the headless carcass in the chest and lifted his sword skyward as it fell.

'Fight me!' he yelled. 'In Sigmar's name, fight me!'

The pack hunters heard him and Sofia heard them abandon their slaughters to turn on the lone knight. He backed away from the dead monster, placing himself in front of Sofia and Miska. Once again Sofia was struck by the familiarity of his movements, the ease of his martial bearing.

The beasts loped towards him, more than a dozen blood-slathered maneaters. A dozen more followed, chests heaving with rabid hunger. The knight's steed, a broad-chested destrier with a sorrel coat lathered in sweat beneath a torn caparison of blue and gold, circled around to his side.

'Are you hurt?' asked the knight in clipped Reikspiel, his voice muffled by the heavy rain and the buckled steel of his helm's visor.

Sofia shook her head. 'No.'

'Good,' said the knight. 'Don't move and it will remain so.'

Seeing they had the advantage, the monsters charged in a mass of blood-matted fur and fury. The knight stepped to meet them with a roar of fury and a wide sweep of his blade. Its edge cut like no other weapon Sofia had seen, but a lifetime tending the wounds of Kislev's sons had taught her just how devastating such blades could be.

The knight's sword hewed the beasts with the ease of a woodsman splitting cordwood. He fought with the fluid economy of a warrior born to bloodshed, seasoned by countless campaigns and a lifetime of war. His horse bellowed and kicked around him, churning the mud bloody as it lashed out with powerful limbs. It circled its master, stoving in ribs and cracking skulls with every blow of its iron-shod hooves.

At least ten beasts were dead already, their entrails heaped in a gory circle at the knight's feet. But even so skilled a warrior could not fight so many alone and live. A hulking beast with a bear's width eventually bore the knight to the ground as it died, and in the fractional pause of his blade, the rest were upon him.

He rolled and pushed himself onto one knee as a wolf-headed beast bit down on his vambrace. The metal bent and the knight stifled a cry of pain. He slammed his gauntlet against the side of its skull until the bone cracked and it fell with a gurgling whimper. Another snapped for his gorget. The knight seized it by the jaw and stabbed his sword's pommel spike into its eye. The beast howled and threw itself away from him.

'Behind you!' screamed Sofia, and the knight spun his sword with a glittering flourish, reversing the blade and ramming it upwards beneath his right armpit. The charging creature was scaled and horned, with more limbs than any natural creature ought to possess. It defied any easy description, but died just the same as it spitted itself on the knight's sword.

He surged to his feet and Sofia saw they were surrounded.

A ring of slavering beasts, thirty at least, and the brief ember of hope in her breast was snuffed out. The smaller beasts lurked behind the biggest creatures, and their grunting, hooting barks were filled with monstrous appetite.

Sofia felt the thunder of hooves pounding the sodden earth.

And a skirling shriek echoed over the steppe in time with a host of whooping yells, the sound as wild and unfettered as any heart in Kislev. Her heart soared, recognising the sound at the same time as the riders charged from the storm.

In they swept on steeds painted with mud and coloured dye, winged lancers riding high with rain-slick cloaks streaming like crimson gonfalon. Braided topknots and drooping moustaches were glorious as they rode the beasts down with *kopia* lances lowered. Feathered wing-racks bent at their backs, shrieking in the wind of their charge.

The circle of monsters broke apart, two dozen skewered in the first crashing impact of pennoned lances through mutant flesh. The rest fled into the storm and the painted riders gave bitter yells as they pursued, slashing their curved *szabla* back to split braying skulls. Winged lancers had once laughed as they killed, but few in Kislev laughed now.

The knight lowered his sword as the lancers rode the last of the beasts down, stabbing the blade into the red mud at his feet. Sofia let out a shuddering breath, and Miska looked up at the lone knight with wonderment.

A giant Gospodar warrior on a towering horse in the black and silver of Tor broke away from the main body of riders to rein in his mount before the knight. He sheathed a heavy straight-bladed sword, an enormous six-foot *pallasz*, across his fur-cloaked shoulders.

Sofia had seen none his equal. Even Pavel Leforto – Olric rest his uncouth soul – had not been proportioned as copiously.

'*Levubiytsa!*' yelled the man, climbing from his horse with surprising grace and planting hands like forge-hammers on the Knight Panther's shoulders. 'I think you try get yourself killed, *yha*? You should wait for rest of us, eh?'

'You are correct, Tey-Muraz rotamaster,' said the knight, and his accent was that of the Empire's greatest city. 'Yes, I should have waited, but look. There she is...'

The knight nodded in Sofia and Miska's direction, and the giant turned to face them. His long moustache was braided with silver cords, and his glowering, wind-burned features opened with understanding.

'So it seem at least one god still listen to prayers, my friend,' he said, smoothing out his long hauberk of riveted iron scales and pulling his fur-lined greatcoat across his enormous girth.

'You are Sofia Valencik?' he asked in her mother tongue.

She nodded. 'Yes, but how could you possibly know that?'

'Because I told him,' said the knight, removing his helm.

Sofia's heart lurched at the sight of his face, thinner than she remembered and framed by hair that was now silver. It was a face she had last seen twisted in grief as he told her how Ambassador Kaspar von Velten had died at Urszebya.

'By the gods,' she said. 'Kurt Bremen. How can you be here?'

'Because I came back for you,' he said.

They left the dead to the steppe, even the fallen riders.

By rights each horse ought to have been loosed into the steppe with its rider enshrouded on its back, free to chase Dazh's fire until there was no more earth to ride.

But the lancers could not sacrifice even a single horse to a steppe burial, and after yelling the names of the dead into the wind and pouring *koumiss* on the ground, the riders turned their mounts westwards.

The fifty-two survivors of the attack were hoisted onto the backs of the lancers' horses and Sofia and Miska rode on the back of Kurt's enormous gelding.

Ten miles through the rain, they entered a fog-shrouded cleft in the earth, a steep-sided gully invisible from more than a few dozen yards away. The temperature plummeted within the dark walls of the canyon, and dripping daggers of ice hung from outflung crags of black rock.

At its base, the canyon floor widened, and Sofia saw scores of hide tents pitched in a rough circle around a grand pavilion of shimmering silver. Sheltered fires burned low in the mouths of caves, the smoke already dissipated by the time it climbed to the steppe. At least a thousand dispossessed warriors squatted around the fires, a dozen rota or more. Most were wounded, and all had the haunted look of men who could not yet believe their land was no more.

Sofia knew that look well. She wore it herself, etched into the lines of her handsome features and the grey in her hair.

They rose from the fires to greet the returning warriors, clapping the necks of their mounts and shouting the names of the dead as they heard them. The newly arrived riders dismounted and led their horses away, loosening their girths and grabbing handfuls of rough gorse to wipe the glossy sweat from their animals' flanks.

A rider's first duty was to his horse, and it was a duty every rider of Kislev took seriously.

The survivors of the beasts' attack were directed to a series of fires, over which cook-pots of black iron bubbled with hot food. Priests and wounded men helped them with wooden bowls and what few blankets could be spared.

Sofia held back a sob that this was what the northmen had done to Kislev – pitiful survivors eking out their last existence in the ruins of their murdered homeland.

Kurt took care to dismount, and helped Sofia and Miska from the back of his horse. At least seventeen hands, it dwarfed the lighter mounts of the Kislevite riders. Its chest was wide, and the twin-tailed comet and hammer brand on its rump told her it had come from the Emperor's own stables.

'I call him Pavel,' said Kurt, seeing her admiration for the gelding. 'A stubborn beast, but loyal, and I'd wager he could match any steed of Bretonnia for speed. And he fights harder than any mount I've known.'

'He'd have liked that,' said Sofia, thinking back to the last time she'd seen Pavel Leforto and the harsh words between them. Pavel had been a crude and obnoxious drunkard, a man too passionately in love with his vices to be entirely trustworthy, but he had a heart as big as an ocean, and not a day passed that Sofia didn't miss him.

Like Kaspar, Pavel had fallen to the blade of a Kurgan war leader named Aelfric Cyenwulf at the great battle fought in the shadow of Ursun's Teeth. Kurt Bremen had slain Cyenwulf and the Ice Queen's powerful magic had destroyed the Kurgan army. The people of Kislev celebrated the great victory, believing the armies of the north would not come south for years after such a bloody rebuttal.

How wrong they had been.

Kurt led Sofia and Miska to a low-burning fire where a slender young man sat cross-legged with his head hung low over his chest. He snored softly, swaying in his sleep with an open book in his lap and a quill still held in his fingers.

'Master Tsarev, look who I found,' said Kurt, with a gentle shake of the young man's shoulder.

'Ryurik?' said Sofia, dropping to her knees and wrapping her arms around him. He awoke with a start and his bleary, exhausted eyes couldn't at first comprehend that what they were seeing was true.

'Sofia? Gods alive, is it really you?' he said, looking up at Kurt. 'Morskoi's tears, Kurt, you found her!'

Ryurik Tsarev had travelled to the city of Kislev from Erengrad in the wake of the Year That No One Forgets with dreams of becoming great a recounter of history. He sought veterans of Mazhorord and Urszebya, of Praag and Voltsara, Chernozavtra and Bolgasgrad. He had hoped to craft a great work to rival that of Friederich 'Old' Weirde of Altdorf, Gottimer, Ocveld the Elder or even the great Anspracht of Nuln himself.

Ryurik arrived at a time when all men wanted to do was forget war, to escape the bloodshed they had endured and the terrors they yet suffered. No one would talk to him, and the little money he had saved from his time as keeper of shipping manifests in Erengrad soon dried up.

Sofia had met Ryurik within the forsaken walls of the Lubjanko, a grim edifice built by Tzar Alexis to care for those wounded in the Great War Against Chaos. The building had long since fallen from that noble purpose, becoming instead a nightmarish gaol where the wretched, the mad and the crippled went to die.

Ruryik had ventured within the Lubjanko's grim walls a few times, hoping to secure testimony from a man who claimed to have seen Surtha Lenk die. It had been a ruse, and the man overpowered the young writer, leaving him chained to a wall before walking away with new clothes and a stolen identity.

The Lubjanko's uncaring warders ignored Ruryik's protestations of his true identity and sealed him in with the madmen. Four months later, upon being called to the Lubjanko to care for a birthing lunatic, Sofia had come upon the young scribe, imploring her to heed his words. Sofia was well used to the cunning of the Lubjanko's denizens, but something in the earnest nature of the lad's desperation rang true.

She swiftly discovered the truth of Ryurik's tale and had him released to her care. As he convalesced, she learned of his ambitions to write, and put him to work in cataloguing her healing methods, the ingredients and mixes of her poultices and instructional procedures for physicians.

Ryurik would not compose a historical work, but an authoritative medical text, and soon became an indispensable asset to Sofia and her practising of medicine within the city.

'How did you get here, Ryurik?' asked Sofia, incredulous. 'And you, Kurt? I never expected to see either of you again.'

Kurt removed his sword belt and propped the weapon against the walls of the cave. Ryurik rose and began unbuckling the straps and hooks holding the knight's armour in place.

'I came to Kislev to find you,' said Kurt. 'When we received word of the Starovoiora pulk's defeat, I rode from Middenheim and came north to Kislev.'

'You crossed the Auric Bastion? Why?' asked Sofia as Miska knelt beside the fire to warm her hands. The flames danced in her grey eyes.

'Because Kaspar would have wanted me to,' said Kurt, nodding towards the smooth blue stone wrapped in a web of silver wire that hung on a thin chain around her neck.

Sofia's hand closed on the pendant as a wave of memory all but overwhelmed her. She'd given it to Kaspar and asked him to keep it next to his heart in the coming battle. Kurt had later returned it to her, together with Kaspar's final words.

'I understand, but how did you find me?'

'I arrived at Kislev's gates just before the Zar's hordes invaded the city,' explained Kurt, shrugging off his mail shirt and undoing the corded ties of his undershirt. 'I found your home, together with Master Tsarev here, who told me you'd travelled into the western oblast to return home. For the price of a retelling of Urszebya and my campaigns in Araby, I was able to secure his services as a guide to the Valencik Stanitsa.'

'It's gone, Mistress Sofia,' said Ryurik. 'We reached it a week ago, but the northmen had already burned it and killed everyone within.'

'I know,' she said, sitting down by the fire and letting the exhaustion and fear of the last weeks pour out of her. 'I mean, I didn't *know*, we hadn't reached it yet, but I knew. How could it be otherwise?'

Kurt knelt beside her and put a hand on her shoulder.

'I'm sorry, Sofia,' he said.

'Kislev is no more, is it, Kurt?' asked Sofia.

Kurt nodded, his face etched with pain. He didn't truly understand Kislev, not like its people did, but he had come to love the land of the steppe and had shed blood in its defence.

'And the Empire?' said Sofia. 'It rallies? The Emperor's armies will defeat the northmen, won't they?'

'I don't know,' said Kurt. 'I really don't know.'

The herd's bigger beasts called him *No-Horn-Turnskin* as an insult, but when the Chaos moon had shone upon the herdstone, it had told him his true name that night in a dream: *Khar-zagor*. Which in the squealing brays of the ungors meant *Beast-cunning*.

It was a name aptly-earned as he lay on his pale-furred belly overlooking the hidden valley and the armoured men filling it. More riders than he had ever seen, even when he had hunted as a young man and watched the rotas ride madly from the log walls of his stanitsa. He saw many tents, many horses and many weapons. An army. Nothing to trouble the warhosts of the gods or the even the beast herds, but an army nonetheless. Perhaps the last army left in Kislev.

Kislev.

That was what men called this land, what *he* had once called it, but a charnel house was unworthy of a name. The cities of shaped stone and felled timber were aflame, its people meat for the herdfeasts.

Driven from his home by his family when he could no longer disguise his developing pelt and budding horns, Khar-zagor had found a place in the great herd of the Lightning Crags: distant peaks where monsters from the beginning of the world were said to slumber until the time of its ending was at hand.

The mountains had toppled as the earth cracked open and scaled titans, more powerful than dragons and taller than giants, climbed from lava-spewing crevasses. A hurricane of dark winds had blown in from the Northern Wastes to herald their rebirth and the gods' decree that the world was at an end.

Khar-zagor would watch it burn.

The tribal host of chosen warriors marched south under the bale-banner of the gods' last and greatest champion, leaving the beasts to pick the earth's carcass clean.

Khar-zagor's intimate knowledge of the huntsmen's secret paths made him invaluable as a scout and tracker, and he had led the Outcast's ravager packs to every last group of scrawny survivors. This was the sixth such group Khar-zagor had tracked, and Ungrol Four-horn had assured him of the gods' blessing for the meat he found for the herds.

He'd caught the riders' scent moments before they charged with their wing-banners screaming and their glittering lances dipped. He'd fled into the storm and left the gors to die. What good could he have done with his looted recurve bow and serrated gutting knife?

Lying motionless in the mud, he'd heard the riders speak of their war-leader, the mighty she-champion the Outcast forever sought, and when they had left, Khar-zagor dug himself from concealment. He'd gorged himself on the glut of warm meat before following their overladen horses through the oblast to this hidden place, leaving a spoor trail of urine even a wine-sodden centigor could follow.

The smoke from below carried the smell of roasting meat, and the desire to feast was almost overwhelming, but he fought down the hunger in his belly. The Outcast was always railing against his fate and seeking a way to return to his former glory, and what better way was there to earn the eye of the gods than to slay the enemy's war-leader?

The beastherd outnumbered this army many times over, and Ungrol Four-horn would be sure to offer Khar-zagor first cut of the meat. His mouth filled with hot saliva at the thought of flesh clawed from the bone.

He stiffened as he caught an unknown scent.

Another beast.

One whose noble heart pounded with ancient blood.

An old and awesomely powerful predator.

Prey-fear surged in Khar-zagor's limbs, and he scrambled from the edge of the hidden gully, fleeing back to his herd in terror.

Sofia hurried through the campsite, her meagre bag of medical supplies clutched tight to her chest. Kurt walked with her, as did Ryurik, already scrawling in his book.

'Perhaps you will get to pen that historical epic after all,' said Sofia.

Ryurik smiled weakly. 'Let's just hope there's someone left to read it.'

Boyarin Wrodzik looked back in annoyance, but said nothing as he led them through the campsite towards the shimmering tent of silver at its heart. His lancer's coat and finely cut tunic of emerald silk had once been richly ornamented, but had long since succumbed to the ravages of the steppe. One of the legendary Gryphon Legion, Wrodzik had spent years fighting for various elector counts in the Empire until the threat of Aelfric Cyenwulf had drawn him back to Kislev. In the wake of the Year That No One Forgets, Wrodzik renounced his duty to Emmanuelle of Nuln and swore to remain at the Tzarina's side.

He had arrived at Kurt's fire only a moment before, barking that he and his healer woman must come with him. Now.

A krug of weary kossars surrounded the tent at the camp's centre, each man swathed in furs and bearing a recurved bow of horn at his back. Their axes were enormous hewing weapons, too heavy for most men to even lift, never mind swing in battle for hours at a time. Many bore hastily bandaged wounds that ought to have seen them carted off to a field hospital, but the grim set of their moustachioed faces told Sofia they would sooner cut their own throats than forsake this duty.

A shimmer of hoarfrost clung to the silken fabric of the tent, like morning mist at the last instant of its dissolution. The kossars nodded to Wrodzik and pulled back the thickly-furred opening of the tent. Sofia shivered as frigid air sighed from within, together with the sharp tang of fruit on the verge of going bad.

Inside, a diverse group awaited: armoured boyarin, steely-eyed kossars, black-cheeked strelsi, bow-legged lancers and bare-chested warriors with curved daggers sheathed in folds of flesh cut in their flat bellies. Nor were women excluded, for Kislev was, above all others, a land where prowess had the final say in deciding whose counsel was worth heeding. At least three of those closest to the centre of the tent were armed hearth-maidens.

They all looked up as Wrodzik led Sofia, Kurt and Ryurik within, and she felt the weight of their last hopes settle upon her. Hope for what, she didn't yet know, but she intuitively understood that much now depended on her. Like the kossars encircling the tent, these warriors were blooded and drained by utter defeat.

'Why am I here?' she asked, as Wrodzik gestured for her to approach.

'You are a healer, yes?'

Sofia nodded.

'So heal.'

'Heal who?' said Sofia. 'You *all* need a healer's hand.'

'Me,' said a feminine and regal voice from the centre of the warriors' circle. 'They want you to heal me.'

Sofia moved closer as the warriors parted and her lips opened in shock when she saw the speaker: a woman with cut-glass features of aloof majesty and alabaster skin threaded with branching black veins. Hair the colour of a waning moon spilled over her shoulders like drifts of melting snow.

'Tzarina Katarin!' said Ryurik, almost dropping his book.

The Ice Queen of Kislev sat on a simple camp chair, holding a glittering sword of unbreakable ice before her. The tip of its sapphire blade was driven into the earth, and she rested her hands across its silver hilt. Sofia imagined the Tzarina's grip on the sword was the only thing keeping her upright.

The Ice Queen's sky-blue dress was torn, but remained a fantastical enchantment wrought from ice and velvet, silk and frost. Hung with glittering mother-of-pearl and woven from winter itself, it suggested fleeting vulnerability and eternal strength at the same time.

'Oh, my queen,' said Sofia, tears spilling down her cheeks. 'What have they done to you?'

The herd laired in a fire-gutted human settlement that had died in a long night of howling madness and feasting. Smoke still curled from the blackened timbers of the ataman's hall as Khar-zagor scrambled up the inner slope of its defensive ditch and over the splintered timbers of its outer palisade.

Khar-zagor kept his gaze on the dark earth.

He did not like to look up.

The sky of Kislev was too vast and too empty. He craved canopies of dark, clawing branches, the rustle of wind-struck leaves and the darkness of wild, overgrown places. Out here on the oblast, the sky merged with the wide horizon, where distant steppe fires razed the wild grasses and the land withered beneath the hooves of the gods' children.

Leather-winged harpies circled overhead, hungry to scavenge the bones piled before the new herdstone. Ungrol Four-horn's hunt-beasts squealed as they perched on tumbled ruins and loosed crooked shafts into the cold air. The scavenger beasts were too high to be troubled by their poorly aimed shafts, but the harpies screeched in frustration at the taunts of the beasts below. Khar-zagor ignored them, skirting the many snorting, heaving piles of bull-horned gors made sluggish with this latest feast of flesh.

The bigger beasts gathered at the centre of the stanitsa, around a carved menhir the one-eyed giant had ripped from the cliffs over Urszebya. Cairns of skulls and the bones of men, women and children sucked dry of marrow and licked clean of meat surrounded it. Ancient human script had been cut into the towering, fang-like megalith, but smeared faeces and daubed runes of power obscured most of it.

Curled around the menhir's base was a monstrous figure the herd knew as Bale-eye. Three times the height of even the largest minotaur, its rune-scarred flesh was a mottled patchwork of ever-shifting hues and runic brands. The insane giant's single, sorcerous eye was shut and its horns gouged troughs in the earth as ropes of drool formed acrid puddles around its bovine head.

Khar-zagor had found Ungrol Four-horn defecating in the bowl of a shrine to the household spirits within the remains of a stone-walled grain store. Fire had destroyed its roof timbers, and the smell of roasted harvest grains mixed with beast excrement was a heady mix of territoriality and hate.

'Where meat? Where ravager pack?' demanded Ungrol Four-horn with one of its two shaggy, horn-crowned heads. The second head drooled over his shoulder, chewing the mangy hair like rotten cud.

'Meat gone. Pack dead,' answered Khar-zagor.

Four-horn cocked his head to the side, the splintered horns bound to his distended skulls gouging the matted fur of its twin. The second head bleated in anger, but the speaking head paid it no mind.

'Dead? How dead?'

'Humans. Fast riders with screaming wings kill pack with horse spears.'

Four-horn quickly grasped the seriousness of his words. Both heads nodded, and Khar-zagor saw that the strapped horns seemed less bound to him than grown into his flesh.

'Come,' said Ungrol Four-horn, loping in the direction of the ataman's hall. 'We tell Outcast of fast riders. You know their scent?'

Khar-zagor nodded, keeping behind Four-horn. 'Followed it. Found human lair. Found she-champion that leads them.'

Ungrol Four-horn gave a bray of bitter laughter.

'Outcast be pleased if you right.'

'Khar-zagor never wrong. Was her.'

The ungor bobbed its heads up and down. 'Better be not wrong. Outcast kill you if you wrong.'

Khar-zagor shrugged as words tumbled from his throat, words he had last spoken as a man.

'Is of no matter,' he said.

Together they ventured into the ruins of the ataman's hall, where a single warrior armoured in brazen plates of darkest cobalt knelt before an altar wrought in bone and rock. A short cloak of raven feathers hung from one spiked shoulder guard; stiffened skin flayed from the backs of mothers yet to birth draped the other. A pallasz taller than either of the ungors was slung across the warrior's back.

Khar-zagor spat a mouthful of bloody phlegm. Just being near the blade made him sick, as though it was killing him just by looking at it.

'Why do you disturb my devotions to Tchar?' asked the Outcast, rising to his feet and turning to face the cringing ungors. His bulk was enormous, the equal of Magok the Stone Horn, and the burning eyes beneath his raven-winged helm were a hard, empty blue.

Ungrol Four-horn's heads bowed so low they scraped the scorched floor of the hall. He licked traces of curdled fat from the flagstones.

'Ravager pack dead,' he grunted. 'Human riders with wings and with spears kill them.'

'Lancers? This far west?' said the warrior. 'That seems unlikely. We killed the last of the lancers at Praag.'

'Khar-zagor say so and Khar-zagor never wrong.'

The warrior turned his pitiless gaze on Khar-zagor. 'You truly saw winged lancers?'

Khar-zagor nodded, his mouth dry and his belly aflame with fear. The gods were watching through the Outcast's eyes, and though the human wallowed in disgrace with the beasts, his dominance could not be challenged.

'Does it speak?' asked the Outcast.

Ungrol Four-horn butted him with his nearest head, and Khar-zagor squealed in pain as the sharpened iron tip of the horn sliced open his arm.

'Tell what told me,' ordered Four-horn.

'Saw she-champion too,' said Khar-zagor.

'The Ice Queen?' snapped the Outcast. 'You saw her? She lives? You are sure of this?'

'Khar-zagor never wrong,' he said.

'How far from here?'

'Half a day run for beasts,' said Khar-zagor.

The Outcast threw back his head and laughed, his clawed gauntlets bunching to fists. 'Tchar sends me a mighty gift! Sound the horns and rouse your beasts to war, I'll have the cold bitch's head on a horn by nightfall!'

The warrior's excitement made Khar-zagor bold.

'Why you so need to make she-champion dead?' he asked.

'Because many years ago, I killed her father,' said the warrior once known as Hetzar Feydaj. 'And while the last of the Tzar's line yet lives, his white daemon will never rest until it kills *me*.'

Morrslieb hung low on the horizon, its outline crisp in the cold, cloudless night. Katarin felt its malign influence deep in her bones, like an

GRAHAM McNEILL

oncoming sickness no amount of sweet tisane could keep at bay. She stood alone at the opening of the gully, letting the soft emptiness of the night enfold her.

She heard the muffled curses of her kossar guards as they hacked at the wall of ice she'd raised behind her. Nightfall had brought a craving for solitude, not the company of armed men. Queen or not, Wrodzik, Tey-Muraz and Urska Pysanka would berate her for such wilful behaviour.

She closed her eyes and listened to the wind howl over the steppe, a mournful sound freighted with all the pain and fear benighting her realm.

'So many dead,' whispered Katarin, turning her gaze southwards. 'So many yet to die.'

Katarin's thoughts turned to the last remnants of her people below, clinging to life in the face of utter extinction. She wished she had hope that those who'd fled south at the first signs of the tribal warhosts still lived. Perhaps they had crossed the enchanted barrier the Empire's wizards had wrought. Perhaps a tiny enclave of Kislev's people yet lived beyond its borders, but she doubted it.

The Emperor's soldiers would allow nothing to enter their lands. Karl Franz was a man unafraid of hard decisions, and if the choice was to risk the Empire or let Kislev's people die, then it was no choice at all.

Katarin wanted to feel anger toward the Emperor. Kislev's sons had fought and died for centuries to keep the northern reaches of the Empire safe, but had geography reversed their roles, she knew she would do the same.

Like a gangrenous limb cut away to save the body, her realm had been forsaken. This fog-bound gully might very well be the last scrap of land that could rightfully be called Kislev.

Tears spilled down her cheeks.

'Kislev is land, and land is Kislev,' she whispered.

Until now, she'd thought that was what made her strong.

Her land was no more. Fell powers corrupted the steppe and its cities were corpse-choked abattoirs ruled by daemons.

Katarin thought of her childhood around the enormous hearth-fire in the Bokha Palace, where her father and his boyarin had spun fiery tales of Kislev's legendary *bogatyr*. These brave warriors from ancient times were said to slumber in forgotten tombs until the land needed them once more.

She had been thrilled to tales of Magda Raizin, Dobrynya of the Axe, Kudeyar the Cursed, Vadim the Bold, Babette the Bloody and a hundred others. In every story, the hero would rise to fight alongside their people in the last great battle, finally laying to rest the evil that threatened the world.

The killing fields of Starovoiora, Praag and Kalyazin, of Erengrad and Kislev, were bloody testament to the conspicuousness of the absence of those heroes now.

When legends of the past failed to rise, her people had turned to the gods for deliverance. They prayed for Ursun to bestride the world and rend the northmen with his mighty claws, for Tor to cleave the heavens with his axe and rain down lightning, for Dhaz to send forth his eternal fires.

But the gods were not listening.

'Where are you, Ursun?' she cried, sinking to her knees in despair. 'And Sigmar, where are you? I saw your comet, the twin-tailed herald of your return, so where are you, damn you? Why do you all forsake us?'

Katarin rose to her feet, looking to the uncaring stars with the purest hate at their indifference. What did they care that her land was lost and her people dead? Would they weep at her passing? In a thousand years, would anyone even remember there had once been a land called Kislev, where a proud and noble people had lived and loved, fought and died?

She wondered what it might be like to just walk away, to lose herself in the darkness and let the night take her. Death would take her people one way or another, whether she stood with them or not.

'Is of no matter,' she said, taking a single faltering step, then another.

'Why are you out here on your own?' asked a small voice.

Katarin spun and drew Fearfrost, reaching inside for what little magic remained to her, but stilled the ice as she saw only a young girl with hair the colour of embers.

'I could ask you the same thing,' said Katarin, lowering her glimmering blade and looking over the girl's shoulder to the wall of ice blocking the gully. 'How did you get here?'

The girl shrugged, as if that was answer enough.

'You came in with Mistress Valencik. You are her daughter?'

The girl said, 'My name is Miska.'

'The first khan-queen.'

Miska smiled. 'That's what my *mamochka* said, but you didn't answer my question.'

'What question?'

'Why you're out here on your own.'

No easy answer presented itself.

'I find the quiet of the darkness comforting,' said Katarin, all too aware of how ridiculous that sounded. Darkness in the Old World was a time to fear more than any other.

'So do I,' said Miska, coming forward and taking her hand.

Tears pricked Katarin's eyes at the comfort she took in the innocent compassion of a child and the realisation of how close she had come to abandoning all she held dear.

'It's like all the sadness and pain in the world isn't there, as if it never happened,' continued Miska. 'But it did happen, and when the sun rises it's going to be worse than it was yesterday.'

'I know,' said Katarin as a wave of guilt surged hot in her chest. 'And it's all my fault. I was entrusted with Kislev's protection and I failed.'

'I think you only fail if you don't try,' said Miska. 'Whether we live or die is of no matter.'

Katarin knelt beside Miska and ran a hand through her wild hair. The girl was clearly of Gospodar ancestry, and her eyes matched her own. She wore a silver chain with a blue stone wrapped in silver wire around her neck. Katarin saw something of herself in Miska's steely determination.

'That's a pretty pendant,' said Katarin, lifting the stone and rubbing her thumb across its smooth surface.

'Mistress Valencik wanted me to have it,' said Miska.

Katarin sensed something unsaid in the girl's answer.

'Then you are very lucky indeed,' said Katarin. 'This is an elven *cynath* jewel. I wonder how Sofia came to own it.'

'I don't know.' Miska smiled, and its warmth was a ray of sunlight after a storm, a breath of life when hope failed.

Katarin took a deep breath, letting the frozen chill that lay at the heart of Kislev fill her lungs and spread through her flesh.

'I think you and I should go back,' she said.

'Will your warriors be angry you came up here alone?' asked Miska, nodding towards the wall of ice being steadily demolished by kossar axes.

'I expect so,' said Katarin, 'but they love me and they will forgive me.'

Morning brought an end to the unseasonal rains and the sun dried the earth hard, making it ideal terrain for the Kislevite horses. Though nothing else had changed, this fact alone lifted the spirits of the Tzarina's riders.

Sofia was exhausted. After doing what little she could to restore the Ice Queen, she and Ryurik had spent the night passing through the camp. She tended injured warriors until her supplies ran out while he recorded the words of those who would not live to see the dawn.

Miska was asleep by the smouldering remains of the fire by the time they returned, but she stirred as Kurt threw his heavy saddle onto the gelding's back.

'Gather your things,' said Kurt, bending to tighten the girth before hanging his scabbard from the horn. 'We are leaving.'

'Where are we going?' asked Ryurik.

'West,' said Kurt. 'To Erengrad.'

Once again Sofia and Miska rode with Kurt on Pavel's enormous back. Sunlight lifted the human spirit like little else, and she heard faint hopes that Dhaz now favoured them.

They rode in the lancer krug surrounding the Tzarina, who had decreed – for reasons known only to herself – that Miska was now an honorary hearth-maiden. This pleased the young girl immensely, and her proud smile illuminated all who saw it.

The Tzarina's frost-sheened horse had died in battle before the walls of Kislev, and she now rode a roan mare that was slowly becoming dappled grey. Sofia had no doubt it would be purest white by the time they reached the coast.

Just over a thousand men, women and children followed the course of the Lynsk as it flowed westwards. Fell stormclouds pursued them as they rode into the sunset for five days. The hope that sunlight had brought turned slowly to shadow as each dawn brought more vistas of utter devastation, a land brutalised beyond endurance: burned villages where carrion birds circled in flocks thicker than any had seen, roads lined by corpses impaled on barbed lances.

Howling steppe wolves picked at the bodies of those who had fled the destruction of their homes, bold where once they would have feared the dwelling places of men.

Worst of all were the many hideous flesh-totems the northmen had left in their wake, idols to Dark Gods wrought from corpses threaded into the wiry branches of black trees that grew where no tree should grow. Lifeless limbs writhed with piteous motion and fleshless skulls muttered dark curses on any who came near. Hung with brazen icons of the northmen's gods, the blood-nourished trees squirmed in the earth and men's hearts despaired at the sight of these grotesque obelisks.

Ryurik spent the journey filling his book with soldiers' memories and the deeds of their forefathers. A wealth of oral tradition unknown to anyone beyond Kislev's borders was laid down in his book of living history.

'They understand it's the only way anyone will ever know of them,' said Miska one night when Ryurik marvelled at the newfound willingness of the warriors to speak to him.

The dawn of the sixth day brought ocean scent from the Sea of Claws and gave Sofia hope they might reach Erengrad without attack. As the light faded on another day's ride, they made camp in the rising haunches of Kislev's coastal marches, finding shelter in a soaring ice-canyon of a great waterfall.

Hateful winds surged from the Northern Wastes, but the Tzarina's warriors kept them at bay in a krug around a towering bonfire that burned with a wild and exuberant light.

Sofia sat next to Kurt, with Miska dozing across her lap. Beside her, Ryurik scribbled noteworthy turns of phrase and deeds in his book, a book that was rapidly filling with all manner of colourful tales of Kislev's last days.

Across the fire, the Tzarina listened to the boyarin swap easy banter, good-natured insults and ludicrously exaggerated boasts with an indulgent smile.

'I should not put much stock in *these* tales, Master Tsarev,' said the Tzarina. 'Perhaps one word in ten will be truth.'

'Still better than most history books,' roared Wrodzik.

'You can read?' demanded Tey-Muraz. 'Next you'll be telling me your horse can play the tambor.'

'I read about as well as you ride,' admitted Wrodzik.

'Then you are a scholar worthy of Athanasius himself.'

'Who?' asked Wrodzik, and the krug laughed as the koumiss passed around the fire.

The laughter faded and Tey-Muraz asked, 'Norvard by noon?'

Heads nodded around the fire.

'Norvard?' said Kurt, leaning towards Sofia. 'I thought we were heading to Erengrad?'

'Norvard is the Ungol name for Erengrad, before Tzarina Shoika and her Gospodars captured it and renamed it.'

'Midmorning if the ground stays dry and there's good grass left on the hills,' said Urska Pysanka, one of the hearth-maidens Sofia had met in the Tzarina's tent.

Urska had not been born a warrior, but when Kyazak raiders had attacked the Kalviskis stanitsa five years earlier, she had rallied its widows, mothers and daughters to fight back. When the men returned from the pulks at the onset of winter, they found their women with swords, clad in armour and bearing grisly war-trophies. And when the tribes came south the following year, they stayed away from the Kalviskis stanitsa.

Urska Pysanka still wore a shrivelled pouch around her neck that had once belonged to the Kyazak war-chief.

'Urska Seed-taker has the truth of it,' agreed Boyarin Wrodzik, passing the koumiss onwards. 'That horse of Tey-Muraz needs all the grass it can eat to carry him further. Yha, you should swap mounts with levubiytsa and spare it more misery.'

'Pah!' sneered Tey-Muraz. 'Ride a soft-bellied Empire steed? I'd sooner walk.'

'My horse is glad you think so,' said Kurt.

'Thank your Sigmar we need you in saddle, levubiytsa!' said Urska with a savage elbow to Kurt's ribs. 'That fat horse of yours be in my pot by now if not.'

'Eat a grain-fed horse?' spat Wrodzik, pounding a massive fist against his chest. 'Such fare's taste is too thin. Give me grass-fed meat. More blood in it to make a man strong.'

'Then you must have eaten a whole herd of long-horns,' shouted Tey-Muraz.

Wrodzik leaned over the fire and said, 'Aye, and every time I bed your wife she feeds me another from your herd.'

Tey-Muraz bellowed with laughter and kicked a burning branch from the fire. It landed in a flurry of sparks on Wrodzik's lap, who leapt into the air and hurled it away with windmilling arms. It bounced through a krug around another fire, and a pair of bare-chested warriors leapt to their feet, hurling a string of curses.

'Your mothers know you speak this way?' yelled Wrodzik to the Ungol riders, standing to make an obscene gesture with his groin and both hands.

'I never expected to see this again,' said Sofia.

'See what?' asked Kurt, as the boyarin began a furiously vulgar argument with the neighbouring krug.

'*This*,' said Sofia. 'We've seen so much misery I thought it would be impossible for these men to know mirth again.'

'It's because you're all mad,' said Kurt. 'Why else would you live here?'

'This is our home,' snapped Ryurik, before correcting himself. 'This *was* our home.'

'No, Ryurik, you were right the first time,' said Sofia, and the argument with the other krug ceased instantly as her voice echoed throughout the canyon. 'This *is* our home, and it always will be, no matter what comes to pass. That is what those from other lands will never understand about us. When you live every day in the shadow of death, every moment of life stolen from from its jaws is sweeter than honey. When all you have can be taken away in a heartbeat, every breath is precious, every laugh a gift, every moment of love a miracle.'

'If that is so, then why are you all possessed of insane cheer or consumed by grim fatalism?' said Kurt, putting his hands up to show he intended no insult.

Sofia looked at the boyarin to answer Kurt's question, and it was left to Tey-Muraz to give the only possible reply.

The rotamaster shrugged and said, 'This is Kislev.'

Feydaj rode a night-scaled steed with nuggets of garnet fire for eyes. Its skin rippled like the tar pools of Troll Country and its breath was straight from the Fly Lord's crevice.

He alone rode, for the forest beasts needed no steeds. The horned packs of disgusting, furred flesh ran the steppe with a feverish hunger for mortal meat. As great a host as it had become, it galled Feydaj to be the master of such creatures.

Once he had been hetzar to a warhost whose bloody rampages were known and feared across the wasteland. The utter rout of that host on the banks of the Lynsk at the hands of Tzar Boris the Red had all but ended Feydaj's rise to power.

The Everchosen was wrathfully unforgiving of failure.

But he was not stupid or wasteful.

Dozens of tribes were bloodsworn to the hetzar's sword, and word had reached the Everchosen that Feydaj had cut the Tzar from his monstrous bear at the battle's end. Such things had currency, and to execute Feydaj would have caused more problems than it would have solved.

His life was spared, but he could not entirely escape punishment. The Everchosen threw him to the beasts and Hetzar Feydaj became the Outcast, earning the name *Ghur-Tartail* among the tribesmen.

They traversed a landscape blessed by the touch of the Dark Gods, following the unmistakable trail of the Ice Queen and her riders. The wretched turnskin beast claimed to have seen around a thousand riders. That it had once been human gave the account some credence. Feydaj wouldn't have trusted one born a beast to know such numbers.

Dark clouds rolled overhead like pyre smoke, bearing ash and ice from the Changing Lands. Even if the Everchosen's warriors were defeated, the southlands would never be the same. Sheets of polluted rain turned the steppe to foetid black mud, but it slowed them not at all. The howls and brays of the beasts were roared into the unending storms, and with each moonrise, their ranks were swelled by yet more.

There were packs of bull-headed minotaurs, stamping herds of horn-blowing centigors and monsters so blessed by the changing power of the gods that they could be likened to no beast known by man. Word of the Ice Queen was spreading through the steppe, and drew the beasts like fresh-killed meat. Her frigid sorcery had slain legions of their kind, and they were hungry for her death.

Each night the beastherds gathered to brawl and feast around the craggy menhir borne by the cyclopean Bale-eye. They burned the weakest members of the herd as offerings to the lurid glow of the dark moon. By nightfall of the sixth day, less than two days' march from the coast, Feydaj rode at the head of more than ten thousand beasts.

Nor were such malformed creatures the only servants of the gods to heed their guttural cries. Though Feydaj never saw them, he felt towering presences growing within the dark stormclouds, *things* of immense power that waited for their prey to reveal itself before ripping a path into the earthly realm. He felt them as a fire behind the eyes, a sourness in his belly and unrest within his flesh.

The eyes of the gods had turned this way and they sent their most powerful servants to bear witness. Victory would earn their favour and a return to the forefront of this war.

He did not dare think of the consequences of failure.

The sun had just reached its zenith when Erengrad came into sight. Weeks had passed since reavers had burned the city, yet a pall of shadow still hung over it like a shroud. Despite reaching Kislev's western coast, Sofia felt a cold sliver of dread enter her heart.

The Tzarina's column of riders followed the road towards what had once been the city's eastern gate, but was now a smashed breach in a toppled barbican. High walls of salt-pitted stone curled around the headland and the first scouts to approach the city thought its walls still defended.

Riding closer, they saw only the dead standing sentinel over Erengrad, a legion of corpses impaled on long spears and lifted high to better see their homeland's destruction. Thousands more lay in fly-blown drifts, filling the ditch at the wall's base.

'The city died hard,' said Kurt with a shiver that had little to do with the thunderstorm at their back, blowing in against the wind from the ocean.

'That supposed to make us feel better, levubiytsa?' said Tey-Muraz, his brow thunderous.

Kurt met his unflinching gaze. 'It means they fought to the bitter end, that even when all hope was lost they did not surrender. So, yes, it ought to make you feel better that your countrymen fought with such bravery.'

Tey-Muraz nodded curtly and Sofia saw tears in his eyes.

'You think Elena Yevschenko lives?' asked Wrodzik.

Tey-Muraz wiped his eyes and shook his head. 'She's dead.'

'You know this how?' asked Urska Pysanka.

'Because she was my cousin and she was a fighter,' said Tey-Muraz, waving to the broken city walls. 'Levubiytsa is right, even one-armed, Elena would have fought for her city. And so she will be dead.'

The others nodded at Tey-Muraz's logic.

Sofia held tight to Miska, who dozed with her face pressed to Kurt's back. With the city in sight, a strange mood overtook the riders, as though a long-dreaded fate had finally arrived and found to be less fearful than had been imagined.

The Tzarina was first to enter the city, her mount now entirely frost white and shedding motes of ice with every step. Its eyes were pearlescent, and its mane had grown long with streamers of ice. Urska Pysanka and Wrodzik flanked the queen, with Tey-Muraz and Kurt forming the wings of a 'V' behind her.

The rest of the Tzarina's pulk rode with their lances dipped, silent as they took in the devastation around them.

Sofia thought she had prepared herself for what lay within Erengrad. A lifetime spent healing young men and women ripped apart by war had shown her just what horrors men were capable of wreaking upon one another. She had tended the wounded and the insane in the melded warrens of Praag's twisted streets. She had pulled survivors from the ruins of burning stanitsas in the northern oblast.

But nothing had prepared her for the sack of Erengrad.

The reavers from the sea hadn't just captured the city, they had defiled and tortured it before putting it to the flames. The ruins of the High City were thick with corpses, the flesh of men, women and children used as playthings then left as scraps for black-winged corpse-eaters.

She heard Ryurik vomit from the back of his horse, weeping at the sight of what the northmen had done. The men of Kislev, proud warriors all, fared little better, their faces wet with tears at the sight of their kinsmen's fate.

Everywhere Sofia looked, she saw some new horror, some fresh atrocity to turn the stomach and blacken her heart. The mutilated bodies of men and boys had been nailed to charred roof beams and used as archery targets, and heaps of torn dresses spoke to the terrible fate of Erengrad's women. Sofia sobbed as she saw tiny bones in the ashes of cook-fires, turning Miska's head away when she looked up.

'No, little one,' she said through her tears. 'You don't want to see this.'

'I don't want to,' agreed Miska. 'But I have to. Kislev is my country and these are my people. I want to see what they've done to them.'

Sofia nodded and took her hand from Miska's head. She looked around her, at the hanging bodies, the feasting ravens and the ravaged shell of the city. Once again, Sofia saw the girl's core of strength and marvelled at the ability of the young to endure. She felt Miska's thin body shake, and her grip was like a steel trap.

'They'll pay for this,' she said, and cold tears streamed down her delicate features. 'Won't they?'

'They will, child,' said the Tzarina, reining her horse in beside Kurt's towering mount. 'Count on it.'

'Why would they do this?' said Kurt. 'It makes no sense.'

'War seldom does, sir knight,' answered the Tzarina.

'To my eternal regret, the horrors of war are well known to me, Queen Katarin,' said Kurt, 'but only a fool burns so valuable a prize as a port. The enemy could raise hundreds of ships and send his fleets south to ravage the coasts of the Empire and Bretonnia.'

'The northmen don't make good sailors,' said Wrodzik.

'I know coastal towns in the Empire that would dispute that claim, Master Wrodzik.'

'Yha, they can sail, levubiytsa,' said Tey-Muraz, spitting on the broken remains of a tribal shield, 'but they don't like boats. A northman likes to walk to war.'

'It makes perfect sense when you understand that the northmen do not make war for the same reasons as us,' said the Tzarina. 'They do not fight for survival or gold, for land or their children's futures. They do not march south because some distant lord in his castle owns their lands or to right a host of ancient grievances.'

'Then why do they fight?' asked Miska.

'They fight because they are men possessed of a terrible idea that their gods require it of them,' said the Tzarina, and her eyes glittered with fearful ice. 'What makes them so dangerous is that they truly believe in the things they *say* they believe; that they are the chosen warriors of an ancient power whose sole purpose is to destroy any who oppose it. Such men cannot be reasoned with, for their every belief is enslaved to the idea that the destruction of our world is their sacred duty.'

'How can we hope to defeat such a foe?' asked Ryurik.

'We fight them,' said the Tzarina, drawing her winter-hued blade. 'With ice and sword, we fight.'

* * *

The Tzarina led her riders deeper into Erengrad, following the High City's widest streets. So thorough was the destruction that it became impossible to tell where one building ended and its neighbour began. Stone and timber lay smashed together, and burned scraps of fabric flapped in the ruins like obscene flags.

Onwards they rode, past the pale ruins of once-graceful structures surely too wondrous to have been shaped by any craft of men. Fine-boned skeletons, ethereal even in death, were crucified upon elegant representations of strange, otherworldly gods. Even amid all the horror vying for her tears, the sight of such violated beauty touched Sofia deeply.

'The elven quarter,' said Ryurik, similarly afflicted at such inhumanly exquisite artifice cast down without care. He pointed to a burned hall of golden heartwood, now blackened by smoke and flame. A slow blizzard of silken pages drifted in ashen flakes from its gutted shell.

'I was... friendly with their keeper of books, Nyathria Eshenera, and before the new outer walls were finished, she allowed me to see their collection. It was the most beautiful place I ever saw. She told me some of the books were over three thousand years old, and that one was said to have been written by Bel-Korhadris, the Scholar King himself.' Ryurik shook his head. 'And they burned it all.'

'The elves fought for Norvard too,' said Tey-Muraz, seeing hundreds of snapped shafts and bloodied arrowheads in the street beyond the shattered walls of the compound.

'Man or elf,' said Wrodzik. 'Makes no difference to a northman. They care not whose blood they spill.'

Beyond the carnage of the High City, they rode to where the city opened up and the land dipped sharply towards the ocean.

The remains of Erengrad's Low City filled the bay like driftwood, and the ocean was frothed with fatty runoff from pyres raised on the shore. Sofia's first thought was a memory of a faded tapestry she'd seen in Kislev's Imperial embassy. Kaspar had told her it was the work of van der Plancken and depicted the comet's destruction of Mordheim.

To the south, the temple of Dhaz smouldered, as though its eternal flame might yet still be lit, and across the Lynsk, the Temple of Tor remained untouched atop its solitary peak. Barely visible past Tor's hill, the shattered remains of a glassy tower of ice lay fallen in the ruins.

'Frosthome,' said the Tzarina, icy tears glistening on her pale cheeks.

The harbour was almost entirely gone, but the great dwarf-built bridge linking the city's north and south remained intact. Ram-ships with beaked iron prows had smashed against its immense stone piers, but the craft of the mountain folk was beyond their power to destroy. Half-sunk trading vessels listed in the ruins of the harbour, and scores of broken hulls jutted from the surface. Torn sails held in place by fraying rigging streamed from splintered masts and forlorn flags snapped in the cold winds.

'Sigmar's blood,' cried Kurt. 'Look!'

Amid the wreckage of so many ocean-going vessels, it took Sofia a moment to identify the reason for Kurt's oath.

An Imperial mercantile galleon, its decks bustling with activity, was moored to the bridge. It flew a flag of vivid scarlet and blue, emblazoned with a griffon rampant bearing a golden hammer.

The flag of Altdorf.

A line of smoking flint-lock handguns lowered as the pulk's vanguard approached the high barricade built around the end of the bridge. Constructed from the abundance of wreckage strewn around the Low City, the barricade was like something thrown up in the midst of a riot.

A tall, wolf-lean man in gaudy doublet and hose climbed into an embrasure formed between a portion of smashed decking and a series of lashed walkways. A tricorn hat with an ostrich feather was pulled down tight over his ears and he carried a meticulously crafted three-barrelled wheel-lock pistol. Kurt noticed each hammer striker was a miniature Ghal-maraz.

'Halt!' cried the man in sharply accented Reikspiel. 'Come no closer or we will shoot.'

'You shoot us, Empire man?' shouted Tey-Muraz. 'You blind?'

'Walk that horse any further and you'll find out just how good our eyes are.'

Tey-Muraz turned to Kurt, a perplexed look on his open face.

'What is the matter with him? Why does he point gun at me?'

'A ragged troop of winged lancers probably don't look much different from marauding northmen,' said Kurt.

The boyars took offence at this, but before they could do anything too rash, too *Kislevite*, Kurt jabbed his spur's into Pavel's flank. A dozen powder-dusted muzzles followed him as he picked a path through the debris towards the barricade.

He was acutely aware of how easily those lead balls could punch through his breastplate. Such weapons were transforming war, and the days of armoured knights on the charge were numbered. Even were half these weapons to misfire, more than enough remained to shred him.

'I am Kurt Bremen of the Knights Panther,' he shouted up to the man with the elaborate pistol. 'To whom am I speaking?'

The man peered at him, eyeing him suspiciously before saying, 'Ulrecht Zwitzer, captain of the *Trinovante*.'

'Well met, Captain Zwitzer,' said Kurt. 'I never thought to see a vessel of the Empire this far north again.'

'You say you're Knights Panther?' said Zwitzer. 'How do I know you didn't just peel that armour from a dead knight?'

Kurt's temper frayed at the man's tone, but he held it in check. Given Erengrad's devastation and the unlikelihood of meeting a Knight Panther, Zwitzer's suspicion was forgiveable.

'That pistol,' said Kurt. 'Was it by any chance fashioned by Master Viedler on the Koenigplatz? The Grand Master of my order commissioned a twin-barrelled version from the irascible old gunsmith. And since we were to fight in the service of Graf Boris of Middenheim, he ordered one hammer to be wrought as a hammer, the other as a leaping wolf.'

'Aye,' said Zwitzer. 'It's Master Viedler's work, sure enough. And if you've met the old rogue, then you'll know how what became of his little finger, yes?'

Kurt grinned. 'He told people it was bitten off by a rat and later turned up in one of Godrun the Pieman's savouries.'

'Aye, that's what he told folk,' agreed Zwitzer, 'but what *really* happened to it?'

'His wife shot it off with one of his own pistols after she caught him dipping his ramrod into the Widow Braufeltz,' said Kurt, remembering the Altdorf Town Crier gleefully printing the sordid details of the affair.

Zwitzer laughed and lowered the hammers of his pistol.

'Lower your weapons, lads,' said Zwitzer. 'This one's Altdorf born and bred.'

Kurt let out a relieved breath as the handguns were withdrawn and Zwitzer put up his pistol. He cocked his ostrich-feathered hat and said, 'So what in Sigmar's name brings a Knight Panther to Erengrad when all with any sense are already in the south?'

'I could ask you the same question,' replied Kurt.

'I asked first,' said Zwitzer. 'And I have handgunners.'

Kurt twisted in the saddle as the winged lancers walked their horses to the side and the Ice Queen rode her snow-white steed into view. Sofia walked beside her and Miska sat in the saddle before the Tzarina.

Zwitzer's face fell open in a picture of comic surprise.

'Ghal-maraz strike me sideways,' said Zwitzer. 'It's you. I didn't dare hope it could be true...'

The captain climbed over the barricade and scrambled down the slope of smashed timber. He removed his hat and tucked it under his arm before marching briskly towards the Ice Queen.

'Your majesty,' said Zwitzer, bowing deeply and sweeping his feathered hat in an elaborate flourish.

The Tzarina dismounted and looked up at the *Trinovante*.

'Captain Zwitzer,' she said. 'You are a most welcome sight, and please do not think me ungrateful when I ask what exactly brought you to Kislev? To Erengrad?'

'You did, my lady,' said Zwitzer.

'*I* did?'

'I saw you in my dreams,' said Zwitzer with the heartfelt wonder of a man who wakes to see his nighttime flights of fantasy are not delusions at all, but reality.

'You dreamed of me?' said the Ice Queen.

'Every night for two months,' said Zwitzer. 'I saw your face and heard your voice calling me here. Thought I was going mad. To even consider coming north when every other captain worth his salt was sailing as far south as he dared. I had to pay every scurvy knave on the *Trinovante* every coin I had just to get them to come with me.'

Before the Tzarina could respond, the rain that had dogged their course for days finally broke. It fell suddenly and hard from onrushing thunderclouds bloated with titanic shadows. One minute the day was dry and still, the next a hammering black rain beat the wharf's stones and churned the ocean.

A chorus of ululating warhorns brayed from the city walls, drawing every gaze upwards. Moments later the horns were answered by howls of bloodlust torn from the rabid maws of ten thousand beasts as they poured into the High City.

'Men of Kislev!' yelled the Tzarina. 'To arms!'

A dozen lancers vaulted from their mounts, bending their backs to helping the *Trinovante*'s crew demolish the barricade and clear a path to the ship. Wreckage was shoved into the sea as frightened men and women ran to its gangway.

Sofia and Ryurik pulled a protesting Miska between them as sailors sawed through the sodden ropes securing the galleon to the bridge's rune-carved mooring rings. Sofia had no idea how much time was necessary to ready a ship this big to sail, but prayed to all the gods to grant them enough.

'Let me go!' cried Miska, squirming and fighting them every step of the way. 'I need to go to her!'

'No, little one,' said Sofia. 'We need to get aboard!'

'Please!' begged the girl, her eyes brimming with tears. 'Please, you don't understand...'

Sofia looked over her shoulder, and the breath caught in her chest at the host swarming from the city above: an unending horde of flesh-hungry beasts and monsters.

'Faster,' she said. 'Go faster.'

No sooner had she spoken than Ryurik slipped on the rain-slick stone and lost his grip on Miska. Small as the youngster was, her struggles dragged Sofia down too. Nimble as an oblast fox, the girl was up and running a heartbeat later.

'Miska!' cried Sofia. 'Gods, no!'

The girl sprinted back towards the assembling lancers. Few people tried stop her, too afraid for their own lives to care if this youngster wanted to choose her own ending.

Sofia picked herself up and ran after her.

'Sofia!' cried Ryurik, turning to come after her.

She didn't answer him and ran after Miska, losing sight of the girl in the rain as a barging krug of winged lancers rode past. The warriors thrust their lances to the sky and yelled words of praise to Tor and Dhaz and Ursun.

'Miska!' she cried, turning in a circle. 'Gods, please! Miska! Please, come back to me. We have to go!'

A vast horse reared up before her, a sorrel gelding bearing an armoured warrior upon its back.

'Sofia? What are you doing?' demanded Kurt. 'You need to get on the *Trinovante*.'

'I can't find Miska,' she said. 'She ran away.'

'What? Why?'

'I don't know!' snapped Sofia. 'Miska!'

Then she saw the girl, thin arms wrapped around the Tzarina's neck as she wept into her shoulder. Sofia's heart broke to see such sorrow, feeling a splinter lodge in her own heart as she realised what the Ice Queen must be telling Miska.

Tzarina Katarin looked up and met Sofia's gaze, and her eyes were filled with icy tears. Sofia forged a path towards the Ice Queen, who tilted Miska's head back and lifted a blue pendant hung around her neck.

Sofia recognised the silver chain and wire-wrapped stone. How could she not? It was hers. Why was Miska wearing it? The Tzarina kissed the blue stone and smiled, whispering in the young girl's ear.

'My queen,' began Sofia. 'I...'

'Katarin,' said the Tzarina, gently prising the sobbing girl from her neck. 'No more titles.'

She passed Miska to Sofia, who held her tight as Wrodzik, Tey Muraz and Urska Pysanka rode up. Their faces were more alive and their eyes wilder than Sofia had yet seen them.

The Ice Queen nodded and mounted her frost-white steed.

She looked to Sofia and her grief at this parting was almost too much to bear. 'Promise me you will keep that little one safe.'

'I will,' sobbed Sofia as the queen nodded and turned her horse. Tey-Muraz yelled an ancient Ungol war-shout before circling Sofia with his teeth bared and topknot unbound.

He hammered a fist against his chest and said, 'Be sure Master Tsarev tells a grand tale of our ending.'

Sofia nodded, her throat too choked to speak.

'Yha!' shouted Tey-Muraz and the lancers followed the icy beacon of the Tzarina's glittering sword. Their wild whoops, glorious laughter and shrieking wing banners dared the wind and rain to drown them out.

Kislev's last warriors rode across the river towards the rocky peak bearing Tor's temple at its summit.

What better place was there to meet the gods?

* * *

'Where in Sigmar's name are they going?' cried Kurt, watching the Tzarina's warriors ride over the bridge. 'The ship is leaving and we need to be on it.'

Sofia held Miska tight and swallowed her tears as she ran towards the *Trinovante*. She didn't look back, didn't trust herself to speak.

'Sofia, what's going on?' asked Kurt, easily catching up to her on his horse. 'The *Trinovante* is leaving! The Tzarina needs to get aboard.'

'She's not going to the Empire,' said Sofia, between sobs.

'What? Where else is there to go?'

'She's not *going* anywhere,' said Sofia, finally reaching the gangway. Captain Zwitzer and Ryurik were waiting at the gunwale, urging them to board. Lines of handgunners stood on the foredeck and the crack of their black powder weapons made Sofia flinch. Miska sobbed and held tighter at the gunfire.

'She's staying?' said Kurt. 'Why?'

'Because she must,' said Sofia.

'I don't understand.'

'And you never will, Empire man!' snapped Sofia, unwilling to even look at him.

'Kurt, Sofia!' cried Ryurik. 'Quickly! Get aboard!'

The gangway stretched out before her, but she couldn't place her foot on it. To flee Erengrad would be admitting her homeland was gone, that all she loved of Kislev was dead.

'I can't do it,' said Sofia.

Miska lifted her head from Sofia's shoulder, her face now that of a frightened child with the palest grey eyes.

'You promised you'd keep me safe,' she said and Sofia's resolve hardened in the face that simple truth.

'You're right, little one,' she said. 'I did. And I will.'

Sofia climbed the gangway, each step feeling like a betrayal, until she reached the *Trinovante*'s deck. Ryurik's arms enfolded her as Kurt followed her aboard, leading Pavel by the reins.

Zwitzer's men kicked the gangway into the sea and the ship's sails boomed as the ropes holding them to the bridge were cut. The ship lurched from the wharf as packs of frenzied beasts hurled themselves into the ocean in a futile attempt to catch the departing vessel.

Kurt strode to the opposite side of the ship, looking up towards Tor's high temple. Sofia saw him struggle with grief and the horror of what was to come.

'They are all going to die,' he said, watching the tide of beasts surround the peak upon which the Tzarina's warriors prepared for one last, glorious charge. 'And for what? There was never a fight here to win!'

'Because she'll die if she leaves,' said Sofia.

'Die? There isn't a wound on her.'

Sofia shook her head.

'Your Emperor is elected,' she said. 'He is a man, chosen by other men. That is not Kislev's way. Here, the *land* chooses who will rule. The land has chosen her and so she must stay.'

'That makes no sense. Kislev is gone.'

'She knows that,' said Sofia. 'And yet she stays.'

'But the Empire endures,' said Kurt. 'Imagine the boost to morale had the Ice Queen stepped onto the Altdorf docks! Think of the hope such news might have brought. And with her power allied to the Supreme Patriarch's, the Auric Bastion would have endured for a thousand years.'

'All you say is true,' said Sofia, knowing Kurt would never understand what abandoning Kislev would have done to its queen. 'But it does not change anything.'

Kurt's head sank to his chest. 'Then all hope is gone.'

'No,' said Miska, holding fast to a wire-wrapped pendant of glittering frost-blue. 'Not all hope.'

Katarin watched the *Trinovante* clear the wreckage choking the harbour, and let out a mist of breath that froze the rain. That at least some of her people would live beyond her own death was a comfort.

Tey-Muraz drank from a skin of *koumiss*, watching the thousands of grunting beasts massing at the base of the hill. Beneath the walnut of his skin, the Ungol horseman was ashen at the sight of so many beasts.

Katarin felt the monsters' hate and returned it tenfold.

She looked down at her fingers, the skin pale to the point of translucency. The magic was still within her, but Kislev was all but dead. And as the land died, so she weakened.

She saw Tey-Muraz looking at her and said, 'I think I might need some of that.'

Tey-Muraz grinned, exposing yellowed teeth, and tossed the skin to her. She drank a mouthful, letting the milky spirit core a burning line down her gullet.

'From my own herd,' said Tey-Muraz proudly.

'You have any more?' asked Wrodzik as Katarin passed it to Urska Pysanka. 'I don't want to my face death sober.'

'That's the last one,' said Tey-Muraz sadly. 'The last one there will ever be in the world.'

Wrodzik spat a mouthful of brackish rainwater.

'Ach, is of no matter.'

Urska Pysanka said, 'Yha, you never faced life sober, so why be any different with death?'

'What son of Kislev ever fought sober?' demanded Wrodzik, draining the last of the *koumiss* and dropping the skin to the waterlogged earth.

'None of mine,' said Tey-Muraz, his voice choked with emotion. 'All six were lost at Starovoiora. They died bravely and drunk as Tileans.'

'Two of my sons fell at Mazhorod,' said Urska, her jaw set tight. 'Another at Chernozavtra.'

'No daughters?' asked Katarin.

'Just one,' said Urska, and a tear rolled down her cheek, quickly lost in the rain. 'Praag took her while I nursed her in swaddling clothes.'

'Erzbeta never bore me sons,' said Wrodzik. 'It saddened us, but our daughters filled my life with joy. They married well and bore me many grandchildren.'

'Do they yet live?' asked Katarin.

Wrodzik shrugged. 'I do not know. Their stanitsas were overrun in the Year That No One Forgets. I know what the northmen do to the women they capture, and though all the gods curse me, I hope Morr took them swiftly.'

They nodded in agreement and Katarin felt her love for these brave warriors fill her. Not one of the thousand riders upon this hill had even thought of boarding the Empire ship. Such was their devotion that the thought never occurred to them.

Against impossible odds, they remained at her side.

She could imagine no greater love.

'Tey-Muraz. Wrodzik. Urska. You are my *bogatyr*, my faithful knights,' said Katarin, feeling the frozen chill of Kislev's magic swell within her body. 'And when men speak of this battle in all the centuries to come, you will be its greatest heroes, Kislev's mightiest warriors who will return when the land's needs is greatest.'

They wept at her words, honoured and humbled to be so beloved. The icy soul of Kislev surged in her veins as she stood tall in the saddle and called out to her warriors.

'You all know I bore no heirs,' said Katarin, her voice carrying to every man and woman who stood with her at Tor's high temple. 'But I have all my sons and daughters here with me today. On this rain-soaked hill, we are all one people, one land. Today we fight for Kislev! Today we fight for her lost sons and daughters, for her proud mothers and fathers!'

The warriors cheered, thrusting swords and lances to the benighted sky, yelling their defiance to the beasts below.

Katarin thought of the oft-repeated sentiment, words that had been spoken since the first khan-queen of the Gospodars had crossed the mountains.

Kislev is land, and land is Kislev.

Only now did she realise how wrong that was.

'Kislev is *people*, and people are Kislev.'

Tey-Muraz repeated the mantra. Wrodzik joined him, then Urska Pysanka. They bellowed it until the rotas took up their shout, and Erengrad echoed to the sound of this new war-cry.

'Kislev is people, and people are Kislev!'

Jagged bolts of lightning exploded above the stricken tower, forking from the clouds to strike the ruined city. More followed in bursts of zig-zagging purple that sent roaring flames curling into the ever-darkening sky.

'Maybe Tor favours us?' said Tey-muraz.

Deafening thunder boomed like the mockery of insane gods and the day was plunged into darkness. Fractures of void-black night tore the sky with the sound of ripping cloth, and the earth shook to the impact of bloody hammers on brazen anvils.

Things moved within the darkness: titanic, impossible things with wet meat bodies. They cloaked themselves in shadow, but Katarin's seer-sight saw bloody crimson armour, eyes that watched worlds end and deadly weapons forged from purest rage. The grave-reek of rancid flesh and burning fur filled the air, like the remains of a plague pyre left too long in the sun.

'The Lords of Ruin,' she whispered.

Katarin bent double as searing agony exploded within her belly, as though invisible hands were ripping at her womb.

'My queen!' cried Urska.

Katarin pulled herself upright and let out a hissing breath straight from winter's white heart. The magic of her homeland filled her more than it ever had, a cold so intense it turned the ground beneath her steed to solid ice.

The beasts roared as a single rider on a dark horse moved to the head of this host of beasts and daemons. He carried a rippling banner, its sigil that of a clawed hand tearing down an icy crown, the banner of her father's killer.

'Feydaj,' said Wrodzik, his hands balling to fists. A towering brute of a creature with ruddy skin and a single, unblinking eye lumbered into sight alongside the hetzar. An enormous menhir was lashed to its back, a tapered stone encrusted with ancient sigils.

'Ursun's teeth!' the Ice Queen said.

'Yha, it's a big bastard, right so,' agreed Wrodzik.

'No. That stone it's carrying,' said Katarin. 'It is one of the stones from Urszebya.'

The roaring of beasts grew louder at the sight of the hetzar and the giant beast. They bellowed their blood-challenge, baring their chests, stamping their hooves and thrusting their horns.

And that challenge was answered.

A thunderous roar echoed from the summit of Tor's hill.

It came from within the abandoned tower.

Lancers wheeled their terrified mounts away from its arched entrance as something enormously ancient and powerful lumbered from within. Its shoulders rolled with vast muscles, its thick fur pale as winter's first ice. Its body was enormous, easily the biggest creature anyone gathered on the hill had ever seen, with fangs like tusks and claws like ebon daggers.

'It can't be...' said Wrodzik.

The enormous white bear stood on its hind legs and roared again. The monsters below quailed before its raw power.

Katarin's heart leapt to see her father's bear once again.

'Urskin,' she said.

They charged from Tor's hill, a thousand warriors with lances lowered and wing banners shrieking. They rode into history, following their radiant queen and the great white bear of her father.

The ground shook to the hoofbeats of their painted steeds as the soul of Kislev rose up alongside its people.

The dark winds blowing from the north were snuffed out.

The rains turned to snow.

And a blizzard of unimaginable ferocity swept over the walls of Erengrad. The High City froze solid as the Ice Queen's magic gave the winter spirits of the steppe piercing form and fury. Sleeting blades of razor-edged hail tore through the forest beasts as Kislev's doomed lancers smashed into their midst.

A rolling crash of swords and splintering lances burst upon the followers of the Dark Gods as the Ice Queen and Urskin cut a path through the snowstorm towards Hetzar Feydaj.

The blizzard engulfed Erengrad and the swirling darkness.

It rages still.

MARIENBURG'S STAND

STAND

David Guymer

Late Winter, 2525
Midnight

I

Sea of Claws

The stars glittered coldly in the clear black sky. The face of Mannslieb shone like a coin, its silver glow sparkling across the cresting waves of the otherwise inky Manannspoort Sea. The three-mast galleon, *Meesterhand*, tacked east to west, plotting a zig-zagging course against the north wind and deeper into the Sea of Claws. The wind sighed through the rigging and the loose raiment of the duty watch, bringing an unobtrusive ripple from the ensign of Marienburg that fluttered from the sterncastle.

It carried a faint, rotten, smell.

The navigator wrinkled his nose, compared the stars to his charts with a silent prayer to Manann for clear skies and in a lowered voice called their course and bearing to the helm. The merchantman came slowly about, bow riding high as it nosed into the wind towards a port tack. Dark and quiet as a Nordlander spy in Marienburg's South Dock, the vessel shushed ever northward. Even before the razing of Erengrad and the destruction of the Bretonnian navy at L'Anguille, these had been treacherous waters, haunted by Norscan raiders and dark elf pirates. Even with Marienburg plagued by the spectre of war, only the most reckless or desperately indebted fools would risk leaving harbour at all.

Next time, Captain Needa van Gaal would think twice before wagering the *Meesterhand* on such a cold run of the dice.

'Get me lanterns prow and starboard,' said Captain van Gaal, an urgent whisper that aped the chill night wind. He leaned over the gangrail from the high sterncastle and peered into the susurant, silver-black sea. The captain pointed north, to a raft of deeper black floating amongst the moonlit glitter, and then emitted a triumphant bark. 'Wreckage! Helm, hard to starboard, bring us about.'

Van Gaal hurried down the pitching steps to the main deck as the twelve-gun merchantman heaved to.

The high elves' mighty Marienburg fleet had left harbour in the early hours of the previous evening and, while the proud princes of the sea were as disdainful of their enemies as they were of their fleet's human hosts, van Gaal was not nearly so choosy about the spoils he was willing to pick through. Just one Norse longship laden with furs and silver would pay off his debt to that serpent van der Zee.

'Helmsman, station keeping,' van Gaal shouted back to the shadowy mass of the sterncastle as the ship pulled through the loose island of flotsam with a series of soft, distant *bangs*. 'Ready lines. And give me that light, damn it.'

There was a stab of illumination as a boatswain nervously unshuttered his storm lantern. The waves shadowed under the gunwales turned from black to a deep nightshade. Light glinted from hooks as they were lowered. Van Gaal gripped the gangrail anxiously as the debris was drawn up. His brow knotted in confusion. Norscan craft were generally of pitched black oak or pine, but the torn piece of planking hanging from his ship's hook and twirling slowly before his eyes was as white and smooth as a pearl.

But that... couldn't be right.

'Shut off the light,' he murmured, the ship sinking back into blackness just as the wind dipped. A dying ripple ran across the sails.

The horizon was dark, too dark. Van Gaal could not avert the prickling certainty that thousands of unseen sails had just passed between his rig and the wind.

When the wind returned it bore a putrid reek of rancid flesh and decay, as if the ocean itself had become diseased.

'Hard astern, full sails,' van Gaal choked, voice muffled by the sleeve held to his mouth and broken by dry heaves.

The elves had been defeated.

The very idea stunned him into mute inaction as the first bloated, creaking shadow appeared beneath the ocean of stars, and he felt in that moment that he understood how it was to have one's ship teeter above a whirlpool.

All he could do was gape.

They were heading south. To Marienburg.

And there were so many.

Dawn

I
Paleisbuurt

The shrill sea-whistles of the captains-at-arms called through the mist that hung over the city-port's docks, mingling with the cries of the gulls and terns that circled the fog above Marienburg's government district. Caspar

Vosberger rose from his table in the members' lounge of the exclusive Rijk-side gentleman's club and paced towards the window. The Rijkside was deserted at this hour. Portraits of merchant grandees and a proud ivory bust of Emperor Dieter IV – toasted on Secession Day – looked down from the oak-panelled walls as he slipped back the curtains and peered into the bay spread below.

A sore finger of red light was just pushing at the misted horizon. The private warships of the merchant elite swayed at anchor in the dim light, shadowed by the high stone bridge that joined the east and west halves of the city via the heavily fortified Hightower Isle. As the Rijk widened down-river, the view grew poorer. The vague, and at turns troubling, forms of ships plied the mist. The white spires of the Elf Quarter rose like the necks of cranes from the Cursed Marsh. On the poorer side of the water, the city's main dockland, the South Dock, churned with indistinct activity. Caspar kept his gaze there for a second, the expensive glass cloistering him from the chill, reducing the foul odour to a tang in the nostrils and muffling the whistles that cried out from the docks.

It was easy to convince himself that it really was just the birds.

'It is just an exercise,' said the only other man in the room. He was reclined in a green leather smoking chair and swirled a twenty-five year old Estalian white in a crystal glass shaped like a scallop's shell. The dawn light glittered redly across the rubies, garnets and spinels of his beringed fingers. Engel van der Zee held no rank or title that Caspar knew of – and being himself descended from the old Westerland nobility, he made it his pride to know – but Marienburg was a city like no other. Land and lineage counted for less than it should when the business that mattered was conducted through the intermediary of shadow. It allowed ghouls like van der Zee to grow rich. The man took a measured sniff of his wine. 'General Segher assures me that this was all planned in advance.' With a faint grimace of distaste, he set down the glass. 'Leave thoughts of war to those it concerns. You should be more worried about that smell driving down the value of this place.'

Marienburg was renowned in ports the world over for its pungency, and had been for centuries. Caspar no longer even smelled it. This was different.

'Most of my members are putting their money into fast ships or arms for their men.' Caspar only half-turned from the window. Lights flashed in silence between the skeletal shards that drifted through the mists over the Rijk. 'And you wake me before the gulls to make an offer on my establishment?'

'This will blow over,' said van der Zee, a dismissive wave towards the window. 'Gold will still be gold and the future will be there waiting for us. But–' A silken shrug of damasked shoulders. '–if it is men or ships you prefer then I am sure my employer can reimburse you accordingly. You *do* know who it is that I work for.'

'Do you?' asked Caspar, answering the man's statement with a question. There were wealthy and influential men amongst the Rijkside's regular patrons who thought the omniscient crime lord, that local myth called the Master of Shadows, was nothing but a conspiracist's fancy dreamt up in the ale dens and meat markets of the South Dock. Caspar scanned his guest's quietly arrogant face.

He suspected those men had been well compensated for their 'beliefs'.

Caspar looked over the portraits and tapestries that adorned the walls. There was history here. The Vosbergers had been custodians of the most well connected institution in Marienburg since the days of the van der Maacht line when Westerland had still been a province of Nordland. He turned again to the window and shivered. The whistles had grown shrill, and the shouts of men reached out from the dockyard slums to touch the glass. It rattled softly in its frame.

Perhaps van der Zee was right. His family still held estates in the old country.

It was time to get out while he still could.

II

Suidstrasse

Captain Alvaro Cazarro blew his whistle until his cheeks were red and his temples ached. The Verezzo Twenty-Four Ninety-Five had just been engaged in a mock defence of the South Road Fishmarket Score crossroads against the combined force of the Drakwald Greyskins and a band of Erengrad kossars. As a result his men were scattered all over the intersection. Behind the sloping roofs of shops and tall riverside mansions, the masts and crow's nests of ships in dock yawed to and fro. Urgent cries were filtering down through the mist. In the distance, cannons boomed like thunder.

Was this part of the exercise?

Soldiers in a confusion of colours clattered through the gelid mist that clung to the buildings as they sought to pick out their own captains and banners. Company honour ensured that there were plenty of genuine wounded amongst their number.

Cazarro drew the whistle from his mouth and almost gagged on the miasmic air that laced the morning mist. It was offensive even by the standards of Fishmarket Score, as if every fish in the Rijk had died and rotted over the course of the night. Strange black motes like drifting spores washed through the sky on the wind.

His company – with plumed helms lank and sodden, breastplates and brass mouldings prickling with condensation – coughed on the foetid mist and straightened their pikes to form a block roughly eight-by-six, while Cazarro cast about for somebody who knew what he was doing. All he saw were mercenary companies like his own. He met the gaze of his counterpart

Herman Giesling, the broad-shouldered and wolf-pelted sergeant of the Greyskins, who answered his questioning look with blank eyes and a shrug.

Genuine Marienburger officers were rarer than ithilmar dust.

'To the docks!' yelled a bookish-looking youth in a gold-trimmed cloak and sleeveless doublet. He bore the coin and sceptre of Marienburg's merchant council and was trying to push his way through the burly, heavily armoured sergeants surrounding him.

At last, thought Cazarro, pushing his way through the crowding soldiers to join the scrum of officers that already had the unfortunate herald pinned down under a barrage of questions.

'Is it an attack?'

'From where?'

'How many?'

Breathless and angry, the young herald answered as curtly as he could. 'A Norscan fleet pushes into the Rijk. Warriors have landed already on the northernmost docks. And in the Temple District.'

Cazarro looked north to where the great temple of Manann, lord of the oceans and patron of the sea-faring city-state, loomed somewhere within the fog. Over the shouts and whistles, he thought he could hear the temple's bells tolling the alarm. He coughed, and then smeared blood from his palm onto his red cloak. 'How did they breach the Vloedmuur sea wall? It has stood for a thousand years.'

More questions and a few jeers greeted that.

'The docks, all of you!' the herald spat. 'On the word of Lady von Untervald, there's a gelder in the pocket of every man when the Norscans are driven back into the sea.'

The men cheered, loosening enough for the herald to force his way through, heading northward along Suidstrasse.

'You'll find nothing in the Norse Quarter,' Cazarro shouted after him.

The east-sider courtling clearly had no clue where he was going. That entire district had been put to the torch by a mob just weeks earlier, reputedly in retaliation for a raid by their countrymen on a flotilla of fishermen and their escort off the coast of Bretonnia. The Twenty-Four Ninety-Five were billeted near the docks, however, and Cazarro knew that there had been no fishing since the raising of the Auric Bastion had moved the war from Kislev onto the Sea of Claws. He was also travelled enough to know an instigated riot when he saw one and to suspect motives, darker than mere jingoism, behind the edict that the dead be denied Morr's blessing and left in their hovels to rot.

Perhaps it also took an outsider to recognise the smell emanating from the quarter as the very same that native Marienburgers laughingly put down to bad goods or an unlucky wind blowing in from the Cursed Marshes.

'I have my instructions,' said the herald, flourishing an envelope bearing the wax seal of von Untervald. 'And you have yours.'

Cazarro cleared his throat, bringing up black-flecked sputum. Whatever this black dust was, it was a devil on the throat. The Lady von Untervald was said to be the widow of a late member of the merchant council – although no one could say exactly which one – and she was certainly good for her promised coin.

Since their founding year, the Twenty-Four Ninety-Five had been putting the merchant princes' coin towards an expedition back to their homeland. There were sailors locked in dock who claimed that Verezzo herself was besieged. Others claimed that all of Tilea and Estalia had fallen into the dark earth, and that rat-men now ruled amongst the ruins and turned their ravenous eyes north. Cazarro did not believe that. He *would* get his men home.

Cazarro emitted a rasping cough and pointed down Fishmarket Score towards the docks.

'You heard the man.'

III
Rijksmond

The great sea wall of Marienburg was called the Vloedmuur, a dwarf-built miracle of engineering that encircled the gaping mouth of the Rijk. The waves crashed against the buttressing monoliths of muscular mer-folk and the structure bristled with enough cannon to sink an armada. Built for the elves during the golden age of the dwarfs, it had withstood tide and trial since time immemorial – and now it crumbled into the Manannspoort Sea.

A tangle of mouldering vegetation crushed the life out of those fortifications that still stood and through the breach came the Norscans, hundreds of warships cleaving the seething waters under a cloud of black spores. The virulent munitions that had brought low the sea wall had left their sails rotten and black, but by some daemoncraft they still managed to catch the wind. Snarling figureheads depicting sea dragons and kraken rose and fell in sprays of brine as the longships rode the bow-waves of the colossal capital hulks that led the armada down the mouth of the Rijk.

They were huge teetering hulks with no earthly duty to remain afloat. Barnacles crusted their bloated hulls up to the load lines like iron cladding while vast mould-blackened sails tugged the foetid plague hulks towards the South Dock.

The largest of them, the flag of the invading fleet, was a lurching behemoth cloaked in green algal webbing and hanging spores, surrounded by an escort of longships. Its high deck bristled with catapults and ballistae, and a coterie of champions gathered around a warlord whose own sorcerous mana bathed the hulk's bridge in a sickly green light. An ensign bearing the image of a pustulent and semi-decayed wolf wafted from the sterncastle while the same design flew from the topgallant and snarled in rotten wood from the figurehead.

A string of rocky islands peppered the delta, forcing what had previously been an unstoppable mass of warships to break up, while the brine-lashed bastions that had been erected upon them poured scathing volleys of Helblaster-fire and gouts of dwarf flame into the incoming fleet. Boats were blown asunder, shredded bodies staining the Rijk red between rafts of burning debris. Shoreside batteries poured ballista- and cannon-fire into the maelstrom. Loose cannonballs sent great geysers of seawater spuming over the hard-rowing Norscans.

The *Greenwolf*'s hull was riddled with iron bolts, its barnacle cladding splintered where cannonballs had scored direct hits, but it came on, unstoppable as a tidal surge.

More than half of the Marienburger navy were still in anchorage – those few sloops and schooners under weigh hurriedly ordering themselves into a bow-to-stern formation across the South Dock, presenting a wall of broadsides to the incoming armada. The defenders' ships were outnumbered dozens to one, but their position was strong – the landside batteries were reaping a terrible harvest and the Norscans would be fighting against the wind as well as the Marienburgers' broadsides in order to bring their own weapons to bear. The fleet took further heart from the indomitable presence at the centre of their formation of the *Zegepraal*, a seventy-four-gun dreadnought that in its sixty years as the flagship of Marienburg had yet to know defeat.

The *Greenwolf* sailed into a fusillade of such ferocity that the *Zegepraal* was pushed several yards out of formation. Angry black smoke drove back the mist and stung the smell of rot with honest saltpetre. Heavy iron rounds punched through the hulk's prow in explosions of calcified crust and mildewed wood. Chain shot scythed through its rigging, the warriors crowding its deck screaming as masts splintered and fell. Quickly, *Zegepraal*'s well-drilled gunners reloaded while the smaller ships in the line of battle opened up with their own belching salvos.

But somehow, still, the *Greenwolf* endured.

The crew of the *Zegepraal* watched aghast as a mutant creature larger than a fisherman's cottage loaded a heavy black urn into a catapult fixed into a forward firing position on the *Greenwolf*'s bridge. The creature's muscle-bound frame was the green of rancid flesh and split by boils and buboes. Entrails hung from its hanging belly. One huge arm tapered to a bone-spike tip; the other ended at the wrist in a mouth rimmed by rows of teeth and suckered tentacles. Flies buzzed around its horns as it transferred its virulent payload to the catapult.

The life rafts from the Vloedmuur had borne a handful of survivors, and their tale had spread like a pox.

Plague!

The men of the *Zegepraal* cried out in unison as, with naught but its own strength, the brute hauled back the catapult arm and loosed.

* * *

Midmorning

I

Oudgeldwijk

'This,' said Count Mundvard firmly, arms crossed over his broad chest as he looked down over the canals and half-timber townhouses of the Old Money Quarter to the string of melees raging along both banks of the Rijk. 'This is not happening.'

'Believe it,' came a woman's voice from the darkness of the audience chamber behind him. Her voice was clipped and haughty, toeing the line between empathy and outright spite. 'Can you not hear the temple's bells cry it out?'

The count's sunken face wrinkled still further with distaste. The clangour of steel and raised voices carried across the city on rot-scented winds. He had invested too much in this city – time and wealth, blood and soul. As he watched, an explosion bloomed amongst the warehouses on the Suid-dock. He knew it well. He knew it all too well. He continued to look on as the blast settled. The north wind blew debris and the strange black moss of the Norscans deeper into his city. Buildings older than he was fell to rot and decay wherever it landed, blades blunting with rust and men choking on spores in the street. This was no mere Norscan raid. It was a full-fledged incursion. The aethyr reeked of plague magic, of a champion of decay.

Disorder. How he despised it.

He turned from the window, dismissing the chaotic scenes from his mind.

The audience chamber of his townhouse was dark due to the blackened glass that filled its windows, crafting the orderly illusion of perpetual twi-light. The luxurious carpet was redolent with the spice of roasted Arabayan coffee. An ornate granite fireplace stood against one wall, but it was for appearances only and was unlit. Books in matching blood-red bindings were neatly ranked along the walls. Silk throws from Ind lay over armchairs made by Estalian masters. Daylit landscapes of lost Sylvania wallowed grimly in the dark. With a ruffle of moon-white feathers, a long-tailed bird dived from one of the bookshelves and swooped towards the mantel-piece above the hearth. It was a parakeet from the subterranean jungles of southern Naggaroth, rare and prized for a harmonious song that it would perform only by night. In the penumbral murk of the chamber, it trilled contentedly.

Alicia von Untervald watched it settle out of the corner of her eye like a cat. She was garbed in a gown of black lace ornamented with mother-of-pearl that was almost identical in hue and lustre to her flesh. Her eyes were as white as a blind woman's and her fingers ended in long, delicate claws. The tilt of her jaw was regal, the curl of her lip proud. To a gentleman of a certain era she was passably attractive, but after four hundred years Mundvard found her increasingly loathsome on the eye.

And yet he loved her as he loved this despicable city – both were his beyond all doubt, and yet while a single burgher or errant thought remained beyond his control there could be no satisfaction. What fool could take pleasure from so partial a conquest?

'You have been building a trap of this city for the past four centuries,' she said, voice becoming suddenly as bitter as that coffee odour. 'Is there no small pleasure in seeing all that patience come to fruition, watching the jaws of that trap close at last around mortal necks? Will it not be all the sweeter for watching the arrogance crushed from these invaders at the very cusp of their triumph?'

'No,' said Mundvard quietly. 'It is not ready.'

'You would push pawns around your board for eternity!' Alicia hissed. 'It is time we stepped out of the shadows, *master*. Our Sylvanian kindred rise again. Lady van Mariense whispers to me that Vlad himself fights this same scourge in the north.' Her claws closed over her hips and she pushed out her chest with a repugnant pout. 'Now there is a man.'

'Insolence,' said Mundvard, raising a hand ready to strike her and baring his fangs as Alicia presented an alabaster palm and slipped back. She ran her claws along the spines of Mundvard's books. He snarled at the disturbance to the carefully cultivated pattern of dust. 'Do you think I dote here, senile and blind? Was it mere chance that sent a ship and captain indebted to me following the elf fleet into the Sea of Claws? There was no guarantee that the elves would soon return to bring word of their triumph or defeat. Van Gaal however would be back as soon as he had looted enough wealth to repay the debt on his ship – if he survived.'

'I assume he did not.'

'And how blessed with good fortune we must be that the *Zegepraal* was on patrol this morn rather than at anchorage as was scheduled. What luck our stars shine upon us that the strength of Marienburg was already roused for exercises on the South Dock.'

Alicia shook her head. 'It was in your power to do more than that, dear heart.'

'And risk exposing myself? I told you, it is too soon.'

'Marienburg is on the brink,' Alicia spat, twisting around in a snap of lace to face him.

'You exaggerate. The city I have built is better prepared than that which defeated Mannfred all those years ago. It will prevail, and we will continue. And I will succeed where our master faltered.'

'It will not,' said Alicia, fingers nestling over one red-bound volume amongst the hundreds and tilting it towards her. Count Mundvard's cold flesh tightened as his consort slid it from the shelf, slipped off its leather exterior, and unmasked something far older and viler than anything the

ignorant folk of Marienburg would believe lay within the bounds of even
their sordid city.

The Black Tome of Vlad von Carstein.

'How did you...?' Mundvard ground his jaw shut. Knowledge was power
and ignorance weakness. 'It is too soon.'

'Liliet van Mariense and her pale sisters are already in the dock. The
beast stirs under the Rijk.' Alicia held out the tome. 'It is time, and if you
will not act then I will.'

II
Suiddock

With a spine-splintering crash of wood, scores of Norscan longships
ploughed into the docks, disgorging rabid berserkers and huge armour-clad
champions onto the shore. Men dropped even as they ran, bodies marked
not by arrow or spear but by blistering black abscesses on their throats.
A block of Marienburger regulars fought on amongst the rushing shapes,
striking out with halberds while their captain whistled furiously and their
horn-blower sounded the order to rally and reform.

Marienburg stood, but without the mercenary auxiliaries and high elf
naval power on which she had come to depend she stood alone, and one
by one her soldiers fell.

'Plague!' Cazarro cried, tearing off his helmet in a bid to clear the cotton
wool fug from his head and keeping shoulder-to-shoulder with his fellow
Verezzians to either side as the company withdrew. They did so with flaw-
less disciple: pikes low, shields front. Ordinarily, Cazarro would have been
proud. A mercenary could fight for many things – wealth, the honour of
his regiment and the reputation of his homeland.

But no man could fight a disease.

They fell into an alley. A warehouse loomed to the right and a ship-
wright to their left. The cramped air smelled of guts and sawdust. Cazarro
had hoped that discipline and the narrow front would confer an advantage on their retreat, but if anything it was the reverse. Man-for-man, they
had nothing to contend with the might and fury of what came after them.

A Chaos warrior in bulky armour scarred by boils and verdigris hoisted
a weeping axe and led a score of howling warriors in a charge. Cazarro
parried a sword thrust as the Verezzian to his left was cleft in two by a
downward slash of the barbarian's axe. The man to his right met a Norscan's
blade with a *clang*, then coughed blood and black spores as he fell in the
grip of some seizure. Another man took his place before he too was split
open from hip to hip by a deathstroke of that infernal warrior's axe. Men
were being carved open left and right. Even those to the rear were not
spared, coughing and spluttering as they fell to be trodden on by those
that followed. The horror was as inescapable as the stink.

'Retreat. Run. Back to the road.'

Alvaro Cazarro cast down his sword and helm and ran.

III
Oudgeldwijk

Bats congregated above the townhouse roof. Some power compelled them, and more of them came flapping over the rooftops from all quarters of the city until their seething, squealing mass blocked out the sun and Count Mundvard threw back the doors and strode out. The riot of screams rose up in full force to assail him and he checked his stride with a grunt. The air was thick with blood, so much so that he could almost open his mouth and drink of it. It had been decades – centuries – since he had last killed with his own hands, but the sight of the Rijk running red was enough to threaten even his measured self discipline. He shook off the urge to flex his claws, walking slowly to the edge as he bore witness to the anarchy that had been unleashed upon his realm.

Alicia had been right. Curse her, she had been right.

The enemy's shipping was so numerous that they choked the wide mouth of the Rijk with sails and a warrior so inclined could run deck-to-deck from the lighthouse-temple of Manann in the west, to the gothic sea-fort of Rijker's Island to the north, and then on the slender spires of the Elven Quarter to the east. The mass of sails pushed further towards Hightower Bridge and the city's heart. The river's fortifications had been reduced to rubble, and of the *Zegepraal* and the Marienburger navy even his keen eyes could discern no sign amidst the haze of flies and spores.

Two thirds of his city had already been lost and tens of thousands had been slaughtered. Outnumbered, on the run, and under the scourge of this unnatural contagion, it was clear that the living were no longer in a position to defend their city.

'So the defence of order must fall at last upon the undying.'

'Did I not say, dear heart?' said Alicia.

Offering nothing further, Count Mundvard held out an open hand, feeling an alien sensation coil like a constricting serpent through his breast as Alicia set the Black Tome in his palm.

Count Mundvard took a hard sniff of the air, disregarding now the charnel reek and focusing instead on the currents of magic that blew against and through the wind. The putrid laughter of daemons echoed through the aethyr – tiny things, mindless, too small even for a vampire's eyes to perceive, but delighting like children in the plague they spread. Such a deadly disease could only have been the work of a master of spellcraft.

No matter.

With a word of power Mundvard blasted the clasps that held the Black Tome's force sealed within and with a snarl peeled back the first page. The book held the accumulated knowledge of necromancy that Vlad, first and greatest of the Sylvanian counts, had accrued over his long life. In safe-guarding the precious volume from Vlad's warring get after his death – and then masking its existence from his successors – Mundvard had gleaned enough to approach, and even surpass, his former mentor in mastery.

'Recite with me, Alicia,' he said, planting one white-bone digit onto the page and beginning his recitation of the ancient Nehekharan script. A second voice twinned itself with his. Alicia von Untervald was a compe-tent sorcerer only, but the addition of her power to his drove a beacon in the aethyr and set it aflame. Count Mundvard spread his hands wide to encompass *his* city and laughed as power unbound flowed from the page, through him, and out into the vastness.

And slowly, in the city's dark and foetid places, things better left buried began to stir.

IV
Paleisbuurt

The screams of children, women and men rang through the marble arches and faux-Tilean palazzos of Marienburg's centre of governance. Caspar Vosberger fought against the tide of humanity, his mind running to the stables he kept near the city's south gate even as he was dragged under and pulled along with the flood. There were rich and poor men, as well as lords and their maids.

Their blood was equal now.

The clatter of arms echoed through the ornate stonework as the elite palace guards fought with the Norscans swarming up from the harbour. Screams came from every direction. Fires cast vast, daemonic shadows against the tall stone buildings. Black spores hung on the rot-scented air. People dropped like flies.

A scream started somewhere up ahead and found its way into Caspar's mouth as Hightower Bridge emerged from the fog. One corner of the indo-mitable keep had crumbled into the Rijk under the onslaught of a thrashing mass of sickly black vegetation and a battle raged in the breach. With every minute that passed, more longships grounded themselves on the rocks that held the bridge's struts and threw up grapnels and ladders.

Caspar's mind whirled. His world was coming apart around him.

There was another scream, this one strikingly immediate, and Caspar watched as a young maid in a cotton shawl was cleaved in two by a Norscan's axe. The warrior charged through the blood spray and more followed, streaming onto the main concourse and into the crowd with an outpouring of bloodthirsty laughter.

Heart hammering against his breast, Caspar fled into a side street with about a dozen others. It was lined with shops with fresh white walls – since

Marienburg was forever being rebuilt – that hit Caspar with the sharp odour of wet paint and lime. Caspar sobbed for breath as he hurtled up the gradual climb. He wasn't accustomed to the exertion, but the screams from behind were coming closer.

Sigmar, he thought, praying to the unfamiliar warrior god of the Empire, *spare me.*

An older man in front of Caspar stumbled on a barrow filled with pots of lime and ladders that had been abandoned in the path after the attack and he pushed the man aside. He was breathless and weak and in the brief second that their limbs were tangled, Caspar tripped and, with a panicked gasp, spun sideways into a shopfront wall. The fresh plastering where he hit cracked and expelled a rotten meat stench that closed Caspar's throat as if a corpse had physically reached out from the wall to choke him.

A body had been interred here, Caspar realised. Judging from the smell, more than one. He looked past the panicked mob to the row of freshly whitewashed walls and swallowed.

A lot more.

A pair of arms punched through the wall either side of Caspar's head and he dropped into a ball under a rain of plaster, squealing as a poorly coordinated hand with grey flesh hanging off its bone tore out the remaining wall from within.

Sigmar spare me, he repeated. *Sigmar spare me.*

V

Noorsstad

The Norscan stumbled from the tinder ruins of the old Norse Quarter. He wore a bullhide shirt with metal plates sewn in and a cloak with a fur trim that was clotted with gangrenous slime. His beard was coming away in clumps and the face beneath undulated with the passage of maggots. What hair remained was brittle and crisp, and his skin was puckered as if from exposure to intense heat.

Markus Goorman, herald of the merchant privy council, watched dumb-struck as the corpse reached out with coal-black fingers and roughly took the envelope that he had forgotten he was still holding. Black flakes fell from the Norscan's fingers as he clumsily broke the seal. One split eyeball and one socket that crawled with larvae examined the contents, then the zombie emitted a mournful sigh and drew an axe from his belt.

Mutely, Markus watched as more scorched bodies shambled from the mist.

There were hundreds of them, thousands, and with a collective moan that chilled Markus to his mortal soul, the army of the dead marched on the South Dock to wrest their city from the living.

* * *

VI
Oudgeldwijk

Count Mundvard closed the Black Tome between shaking hands and stared across the rooftops of Marienburg's old and wealthy. Flames tracked the paths of the canals, screams rising in their wake like smoke. As he watched, a canalboat caught alight, only to be crushed to kindling a moment later by the collapse of a wine shop. It had been owned by an Estalian family that Mundvard, seeing in that line a potential merchant councillor one day, had nurtured for almost fifty years.

The whole structure sank into the water in a column of sparks. Mundvard ground his teeth. Not since the defeat of Mannfred von Carstein at this city's walls had he felt anger.

This, however. This was fury.

He turned to Alicia, marble-hard and cold, unmoved by the terror of the bats that flapped around his face.

'Fetch my armour.'

Noon

I
Suidstrasse

From false doorways and forgotten cellars throughout the old city, Marienburg's dead rose to oppose the Norscan invaders. Skirmishes raged across nearly every street. In Hightower Keep, thousands of skeleton warriors in clinking mail rose from a mass grave to those lost in the Bretonnian occupation of 1597 in order to sally forth and drive the astounded Norscans back to their boats. It was on Suidstrasse however that the main southward push of the Chaos forces met the army of undead in pitched battle.

Before the Bretonnian civil war and the closure of the sea lanes, goods from every corner of the globe had poured in through the South Dock on their way to the markets of Altdorf. The wealth of the world had paved it, if only figuratively, with gold, and tall, brightly painted mansions and offices had risen along its way. Count Mundvard had watched it grow as an expansion of the docks as the city had risen in prominence under his stewardship as a sovereign state – a powerhouse in world trade.

He no longer recognised it.

The proud buildings were riven with varicose lines of black mould, and the highway that only yesterday had been filled with wagoners and bawdy seamen now heaved with warriors. Ranks of Norscans – more disciplined than their berserker reputation gave them credit for – pushed against a resolute cordon of skeletal warriors and zombies. The battle line bulged in the centre. There the strongest and bravest bellowed their war cries in the hope of attracting the blessings of the pestilential champions of decay that fought beside them. In the crush of combat, surrounded by screams and the rattle of bone, it was impossible to distinguish those heavily armoured warriors from the worm-eaten cadavers they waded through.

How could so many lives, so many ambitions and plans, be overturned in such a short time? Chaos, it seemed, was the sunlight in which the night's dreams were burned away.

Well this, thought Count Mundvard, observing with crossed arms amidst a coterie of acolytes and retainers, *is where this anarchy stops*. It was an odd feeling to be in armour after so many years and the winged scarlet plate was freckled with rust. He felt immediate, connected to the moment in a way that, for all his influence, he now realised that he had not been in a long time.

With a stab of anger he bolstered the battle line with freshly fallen warriors, delighting in the barbarians' horrified cries as their own dead rose against them. A pulse of will quickened stiff muscles and hardened bone and Mundvard watched with bared fangs as the Norscan push came to a standstill. He was tireless and the dead unlimited – a stalemate would end only one way.

The certain outcome left his blood still hot, his fury strangely unfulfilled. He knew he should have limited his intervention to the reinforcement of his lines, let the inevitable play out, but for once in his long and circumspect unlife the voice of reason found itself appealing to a dead heart.

There was no victory to be had here. Too much had already been destroyed, catspaws he had cultivated over generations slaughtered, and with the clarity of prescience he saw the future: a city shattered and leaderless, an Empire on its border that had waited seventy years to bring its wayward province to heel. He saw witch hunts, reckoners of the Imperial treasury in every counting house, the all-powerful merchant companies brought firmly under the yoke of the house of Wilhelm. He could win a crushing victory here and still be set back another five hundred years.

Mundvard extended a hand towards the battle line and turned his palm up. Anger burgeoned into power, black eddies swirling around his arm. Then he clenched his fist with a snarl and the road split in two with a calamitous *crack* that broke the Norscan ranks and sent them reeling backwards. Mundvard voiced a command and the buildings shuddered, the fissure emitting an existential scream before ejecting a legion of rabid, inhuman spirits that tore into the terrified Norscans from below.

'Too much,' moaned Alicia von Untervald. While Mundvard worked his magicks to bolster their forces, the rest of his coterie were engaged in countering the enemy's sorcerers. His consort's face was drawn with the effort, fingers twitching like divining rods attuned to the flows of the aethyr, and she had until now been bewitchingly silent. 'You will draw attention.'

Good, thought Mundvard as the stones underfoot began to rattle and the water to churn.

He pushed his hands towards the river, then tucked them into his chest and strained as if to raise a great weight. The crimson waters frothed white and the Norscans' longships began to groan. He hoped the Chaos warlord would come for him. Mundvard wanted to see the look on the plague-dog's face as he tore its head from its neck with his bare hands and drank.

The vampire bared his fangs as dark energy flashed before his pallid eyes. He had only just started.

They would learn why even Mannfred von Carstein had once seen fit to dub him *Mundvard the Cruel*.

II
Suiddock

Every sailor had his own tale of the South Dock beast, a winged horror – by some accounts, at least – that was rumoured to roost amidst the sunken wrecks at the bottom of the Rijk and to feast upon those who defied the Master of Shadows.

They were good and grisly tales. And every word was true.

The terrorgheist burst from the river in a foaming pillar of water and splintered longships, flinging out skeletal bat-wings and issuing a scream that hit the docks like the wave of an explosion. Norscans and Chaos warriors alike spasmed and bled from their eyes as their minds were blown apart. Ships bowed away from the monster as the power of its voice filled their sails.

Then the monster beat its wings, air hissing through the bare bones of its jaw as it glided to where the great hulk, *Greenwolf*, had been run aground. The decking groaned as the monster flapped onto the prow and proceeded to demolish the ship with a furious combination of teeth and claws. Hurling a length of mainmast from its jaws, the terrorgheist issued a frustrated shriek at finding only dead prey and bunched rotten muscles to launch itself into the air once more.

The violent imperative to hunt down the Chaos warlord and rend him limb from limb filled its small, dead mind. It sniffed the air, recovered the trail, and soared towards the scent of battle.

III
Suidstrasse

The large warehouse window shattered under the sudden onslaught of sound and burst inwards, showering Alvaro Cazarro and the surviving Verezzians with broken glass. The men screamed, covering their ears as the flying terror beat its wings and made the roof over their head tremble.

'Out!' the captain yelled, glass tinkling from his shoulders. He pulled himself from the ground and threw himself through the gaping window just as the ceiling gave way, dropping a tonne of diseased spores onto the storage chamber beneath.

He came up in the alley outside in a coughing fit. Cazarro almost choked on the stink of death and disease. It was as if the air itself had been infected and was slowly dying. The sky seemed to writhe in torment, and the mercenary captain noticed that the noonday sun had been swallowed by a cloud of bats. Their frenetic flapping left the darkness foetid and warm.

The warehouse collapsed slowly from the inside, coughing out a cloud of dust. Cazarro retreated to the other side of the alley as a column of shambling troops in the garb of Erengrad kossars marched silently through the hanging dust. He glanced up as two men in tarnished breastplates brushed glass and mould from their doublets and coughed. Only two – all that remained of the Twenty-Four Ninety-Five. Even the banner of Verezzo had been lost in the rout from the docks. Their eyes were bloodshot, with pupils that seemed far too wide. Their cheeks were pox-marked, their skin laced with black veins. He laid a hand upon his own face, and brushed numb and blistered flesh.

The doomed reality of their situation finally settled. They were not going home. 'What do we do?' shouted one of the two between heaving coughs.

'Fight,' Cazarro coughed. 'For the Lion of Verezzo and the honour of Tilea.' Cazarro drew his cinquedea from its scabbard and thrust the short stabbing sword into the air. He tried to deliver a war cry, but ended up spluttering into the back of his elbow as he staggered from the alley and into the madness of Suidstrasse.

It was like falling into the ocean. The bluffs of tall buildings rose high through the haze of dust and flapping shadows, flanking a turbulent cauldron of death and life. The three men fought with the strength of drowning men, as if, knowing in their hearts that they were the last men of Tilea, they sought vengeance for their own deaths in advance. One went down to an axe across the throat, another was doubled over by a spiked mace that ruined his belly. Cazarro rammed his cinquedea through the Y-shaped split of a Norscan's barbute helm and emitted a scream that crackled from his lungs. Through a break in the maelstrom, he saw Sergeant Goesling and the Drakwald Greyskins. They were dead. Everyone was dead. Except for those who wanted to kill him. With a cry of despair, Cazarro buried his fist-wide blade into a Norscan's armpit.

A terrible roar shook the street to its guts and a great cry went up from the Norscans. The dead fought on, unperturbed, but Cazarro looked up to see a hideous mutant beast bull through the Norscan ranks towards the battle line.

'*Glöt!*' the warriors roared, shaking weapons and standards in the air as the beast stormed nearer. '*Glöt! Glöt!*'

Cazarro felt its footfalls through the paving slabs and as the beast finally reached the front rank he realised that this *Glöt* was not one creature but three. Between the monster's shoulders rode a hideously obese warrior with a rusted scythe and, sheltered behind his corpulent bulk and cracked armour, a three-armed hunchback whose quivering flesh was surrounded by a halo of flies. This final figure held his crooked frame on its perch with the aid of a staff and wore fluttering green robes, woven with runes seeping with disease and gum that seemed to shut the eye that dared to try and read them.

The Glöttkin hit the undead rank like a steam tank, bones flying asunder as the skeletal warriors were smashed high and wide.

Cazarro was still watching when he felt a blow like a punch to the ribs. He looked down to find a Norscan spear spitting his chest. The warrior twisted the haft. He heard rather than felt his own ribs split and he finally produced a gasp, pulled to his knees as the blade was yanked from his diseased flesh. His eyesight glimmered out as the strength left him, but there was a prickling at the edge of consciousness, something of shadow and terror just waiting for the last spark of life to fade. To the very last Alvaro Cazarro fought the darkness, his mind living just long enough to shiver from the unlife that suffused his dying muscles. The last of the Verezzians, he staggered to his feet to plunge his cinquedea into his killer's heart and moaned.

Like Marienburg, Cazarro was dead, but his suffering had only just begun.

IV
Suidstrasse

'Sewer rats and festering gulls, come!'

Count Mundvard brought his hands together as his entourage retreated like whipped dogs before the onrushing mutant. Let them. He would take retribution with his own hands. Power laced through his fingers and from hand to hand, tracing a shell within that manifested a grinning black skull. The apparition screamed, shattering its magical caul, and then rocketed forwards, leaving a tail of ectoplasm in its wake. The robed hunchback on the mutant's back pointed his staff at the missile and the skull disintegrated back into the aethyr with a wail.

Mundvard snarled. Here then was the plague-sorcerer at last. A congealed stream of gibberish ran from the mage's lipless gums and a sickly green aura seeped from the pinnacle of his staff. Mundvard glared at Alicia, but his consort was too busy getting out of the way to work a counterspell. With an intricate sequence of gestures and phrases, Mundvard drove back the light with such vehemence that the staff was almost knocked from the plague-sorcerer's hands.

'I fear neither disease nor decay,' Mundvard roared as the big mutant slowed its charge, blinking in idiot confusion at its master's hiss of pain. The huge creature flexed its muscles and drooled. The corpulent champion moved protectively in front of the sorcerer and brought up his scythe. With a chuckle, Mundvard turned his gaze to a growing point of blackness in the sky behind the champion's back. 'There is nothing in your god's power to move one such as I.'

The sorcerer placed a steadying hand on the hanging meat of the warrior's shoulder and turned. As he did so, the terrorgheist dropped out of the sky further up the street, flung wide its wings just before hitting the road and ripping forward with bony claws spread through the Norscans in its path. With a hiss, the sorcerer clutched his staff, that gangrenous glow returning before Mundvard haughtily dispelled it with a wave. He turned to watch his mighty thrall-beast tear through the Norscan ranks. Soon. Soon. Even the mutant giant was a runt by comparison. Too late, Mundvard noticed the sorcerer's third hand, hidden behind the tumourous mass of boils and rolling eyeballs that hunched the sorcerer's back and frantically tracing a separate web of arcane symbols.

Count Mundvard bellowed in outrage – that he, the Master of Shadows, should be deceived by such sleight-of-hand – and spat out a counterspell, but it was too late. A nova of yellow-brown mould swallowed the terrorgheist whole and the monster shrieked as decomposition long held in abeyance ran riot: in the span of moments flesh liquefied and fell away, bones turning brown and crumbling. A second later all that fell upon the plague-sorcerer and his retainers was powder.

'Even bone must become dust,' spoke the sorcerer in the breathless wheeze of a lanced boil.

Mundvard's eyes whitened with fury. The sorcerer would die last, and in ways that Mundvard had spent centuries conceiving.

'Ghurk,' said the enemy sorcerer, sagging to his haunches and addressing the mutant beast beneath him, who responded with a sonorous belch and a dribble. 'Otto.' A grunt from the fat warrior. 'Get this over with. Then we three brothers can move on, and nuture our own garden of plagues within Altdorf's walls.'

The creature, Ghurk, lumbered forward and lashed out with its hawser-like arm while Otto struck down with his rusted scythe. Mundvard's lip curled as he danced easily from the swollen goliath's blind swipe, then parried the scythe as though it had been swung by a centenarian knight and cut a riposte across Ghurk's neck that sent pus dribbling through the folds of its chest. The stench would have poleaxed an orc, but with neither the need to breathe nor a stomach to upset Mundvard ignored it. Otto struck again and again with strength enough to cut down a barded warhorse, but Mundvard was swift as a viper and cagey as an old fox. He fought as he had always lived – with guile and forethought, and instants of subtle incision deliberated several exchanges in advance. Driven by cold-boiling rage the vampire beat through Otto's guard in a keening blizzard of swordplay, then plunged his blade up to the hilt in Ghurk's belly. The monster grunted in pain.

'*Suffer*,' Mundvard hissed.

A single tear ran down the mutant's one, sad-looking eye and Mundvard twisted the blade deeper before wrenching it from the monster's guts. His cruel laugh became a snarl as a rotten tide of bile and viscera gouted from the wound and slapped him in the face. He spluttered, blinded for just one second before he could twist his head out of the torrent and clear the muck from his eyes. A rusty scythe struck towards his neck. With superhuman speed he twisted, but for the third time in one short day he had seen the danger too late.

Pain as he had forgotten he could still feel exploded in his shoulder. The warrior's scythe cracked the bone, speared his heart, and tore through the wizened organs that filled his gut.

The vampire sank to the ground with an unbreathing gasp, paralysis creeping through his body from his riven heart

Impossible, he thought. *Impossible*. His thoughts fractured under a pain he could not vocalise as the plague champion pulled his weapon free. Before he could fall, the monstrous Ghurk wrapped his tentacle limb around the vampire's chest. Mundvard felt his breastplate buckle and his ribs creak. Desperately, he willed blood to the damaged heart to speed its healing, but he couldn't so much as blink, and the monster dragged him towards a single eye full of hurt and opened its drooling maw.

It had been human once. Before Chaos had quashed its dreams too.

'Suffer,' Ghurk belched.

The huge mutant tightened his grip, then whirled the vampire once overhead and loosed. A foetid wind whipped through Mundvard's long white hair as he flew. On the road beneath him he saw the army five hundred years in the making collapse as his driving will abandoned them. Then there were no more fighters. He was over water, the unsettled surface whispering and calling and glittering mirthfully with firelight.

The Rijk.

Horror filled him. A stake through the heart could take a vampire's strength, the sun could claim his life, but the running water would do neither of those things. It was only torture; an evisceration of his very soul.

Count Mundvard summoned the last of his strength to drive a desperate plea into the wind of Death, but no one heard his scream as the water lapped up and took him.

Dusk

I

Rijkspoort

Marienburg's south-facing walls were tall and thick, as throughout her brief dalliance with sovereignty she had feared her powerful southern neighbour more than she ever had the reavers of the distant north. How provincial that seemed to Caspar Vosberger now as he saw the banners of Carroburg borne along the Altdorf Road from the south gate and kicked his horse into a wild canter towards the gate. The terrified black stallion clattered down the cobbled road. The scent of death filled the poor beast's nostrils and it shied at intervals to evade the corpses strewn over the street. Most of the bodies looked years old – they were rotten, some covered in plaster or brick dust while others were coated with mud as if they had dug their way out of the marsh. They showed no signs of moving now.

Men and women still alive ran to and fro, carrying their possessions in great bundles, but scattered at the passage of the nobleman and his panicked mount.

When the dead had risen, Caspar had prayed to Sigmar for his deliverance and the man-god of the Empire had spared him. He had to warn the Empire general what he was marching into. More even than that! He had to warn Altdorf before it too shared Marienburg's fate.

The horse skidded on the cobbles as Caspar pulled it around in a sharp turn, and then reared at the appearance of a figure in the middle of the road who refused to get out of the way. Caspar cursed and hurriedly shortened his grip on the reins as the horse backed up onto hind legs. The animal was a dispatch horse, not a warhorse, and its instinct remained to avoid an obstacle rather than run it down.

'Out of my way, peasant!'

The man turned drunkenly around and Caspar gasped. He was soaked from his short-trimmed dark hair to his shiny-buckled leather boots. His black damask shirt clung wetly to his narrow frame, torn and stained dark red over the chest and shoulder as if he had been grabbed by a bear. Milky eyes stared blankly through Caspar's forehead and his head lolled over a savage-looking wound in the side of his neck as he came about. It was Engel van der Zee. Or it had been.

Caspar cried out as the dead man lurched forward and grabbed his knee. He slapped the side of Engel's head, then emitted a gargling scream as he was dragged from the saddle.

Moaning over his bruised shoulder, Caspar looked up from the cobbles as a second man slid his foot into the horse's vacated stirrup and swung up into the saddle. His noble face was pale and drawn, his white hair lank against a battered suit of scarlet plate. He took up the reins in hands as bloodless as bone, hunched sideways to shield what looked to be a fatal wound in his shoulder.

'My gratitude for the horse,' spoke the man in a deathbed whisper.

'My lord, I must get away. I must warn our brothers in Altdorf.'

The rider chuckled. River water gurgled from his throat. His expression soured as the Carroburgers' bugles sounded a warning tattoo. Contact with the enemy made. A series of horn blasts followed, ordering units formed and battle lines drawn. The rider turned his horse back towards the south gate to leave Caspar on his back with van der Zee staring limply on.

'Powerful forces gather in Altdorf, infant. These vermin have bested the Master of Shadows once. They will not do so again.'

ABOUT THE AUTHORS

David Guymer's work for Black Library includes the Warhammer Age of Sigmar novels *Kragnos: Avatar of Destruction, Hamilcar: Champion of the Gods* and *The Court of the Blind King,* the novella *Bonereapers,* and several audio dramas including *Realmslayer* and *Realmslayer: Blood of the Old World.* He is also the author of the Gotrek & Felix novels *Slayer, Kinslayer* and *City of the Damned.* For The Horus Heresy he has written the novella *Dreadwing,* and the Primarchs novels *Ferrus Manus: Gorgon of Medusa* and *Lion El'Jonson: Lord of the First.* For Warhammer 40,000 he has written *Angron: The Red Angel, The Eye of Medusa, The Voice of Mars* and the two Beast Arises novels *Echoes of the Long War* and *The Last Son of Dorn.* He is a freelance writer and occasional scientist based in the East Riding, and was a finalist in the 2014 David Gemmell Awards for his novel *Headtaker.*

Phil Kelly is the author of the Warhammer 40,000 novels *Shadowsun: The Patient Hunter, Farsight: Crisis of Faith* and *Farsight: Empire of Lies,* the Space Marine Conquests novel *War of Secrets,* the Space Marine Battles novel *Blades of Damocles* and the novellas *Farsight* and *Blood Oath.* For Warhammer he has written the titles *Sigmar's Blood* and *Dreadfleet.* He has also written *The Woman in the Walls* for the Warhammer Horror portmanteau *The Wicked and the Damned,* and a number of short stories. He works as a background writer for Games Workshop, crafting the worlds of Warhammer Age of Sigmar and Warhammer 40,000. He lives in Nottingham.

Graham McNeill has written many titles for The Horus Heresy, including the Siege of Terra novellas *Sons of the Selenar* and *Fury of Magnus,* the novels *The Crimson King* and *Vengeful Spirit,* and the *New York Times* bestselling *A Thousand Sons* and *The Reflection Crack'd,* the latter of which featured in *The Primarchs* anthology. Graham's Ultramarines series, featuring Captain Uriel Ventris, is now seven novels long, and has close links to his Iron Warriors stories, the novel *Storm of Iron* being a perennial favourite with Black Library fans. He has also written the Forges of Mars trilogy, featuring the Adeptus Mechanicus, and the Warhammer Horror novella *The Colonel's Monograph.* For Warhammer, he has written the Warhammer Chronicles trilogy *The Legend of Sigmar,* the second volume of which won the 2010 David Gemmell Legend Award.

Josh Reynolds' extensive Black Library back catalogue includes the Horus Heresy Primarchs novel *Fulgrim: The Palatine Phoenix,* and three Horus Heresy audio dramas featuring the Blackshields. His Warhammer 40,000 work includes the Space Marine Conquests novel *Apocalypse, Lukas the Trickster* and the Fabius Bile novels. He has written many stories set in the Age of Sigmar, including the novels *Shadespire: The Mirrored City, Soul Wars, Eight Lamentations: Spear of Shadows,* the Hallowed Knights novels *Plague Garden* and *Black Pyramid,* and *Nagash: The Undying King.* He has written the Warhammer Horror novel *Dark Harvest,* and novella *The Beast in the Trenches,* featured in the portmanteau novel *The Wicked and the Damned.* He also penned the Necromunda novel *Kal Jerico: Sinner's Bounty.* He lives and works in Sheffield.

Chris Wraight is the author of the Horus Heresy novels *Warhawk, Scars* and *The Path of Heaven,* the Primarchs novels *Leman Russ: The Great Wolf* and *Jaghatai Khan: Warhawk of Chogoris,* the novellas *Brotherhood of the Storm, Wolf King* and *Valdor: Birth of the Imperium,* and the audio drama *The Sigillite.* For Warhammer 40,000 he has written the Space Wolves books *Blood of Asaheim, Stormcaller* and *The Helwinter Gate,* as well as the Vaults of Terra trilogy, *The Lords of Silence* and many more. Additionally, he has many Warhammer novels to his name, and the Warhammer Crime novel *Bloodlines.* Chris lives and works in Bradford-on-Avon, in south-west England.

YOUR
NEXT READ

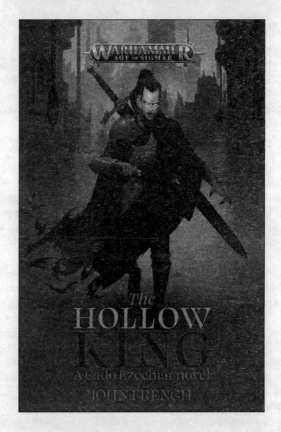

THE HOLLOW KING
by John French

Cado Ezechiar, a cursed Soulblight vampire, seeks salvation for those he failed at the fall of his kingdom. His quest for vengeance leads him to Aventhis, a city caught in a tangled web of war and deceit that Cado must successfully navigate, or lose everything.